THE UNSINKABLE

Walker Bean

AND THE KNIGHTS OF THE WAXING MOON

Written and illustrated by Aaron Renier

Colored by Alec Longstreth

:01

First Second

New York

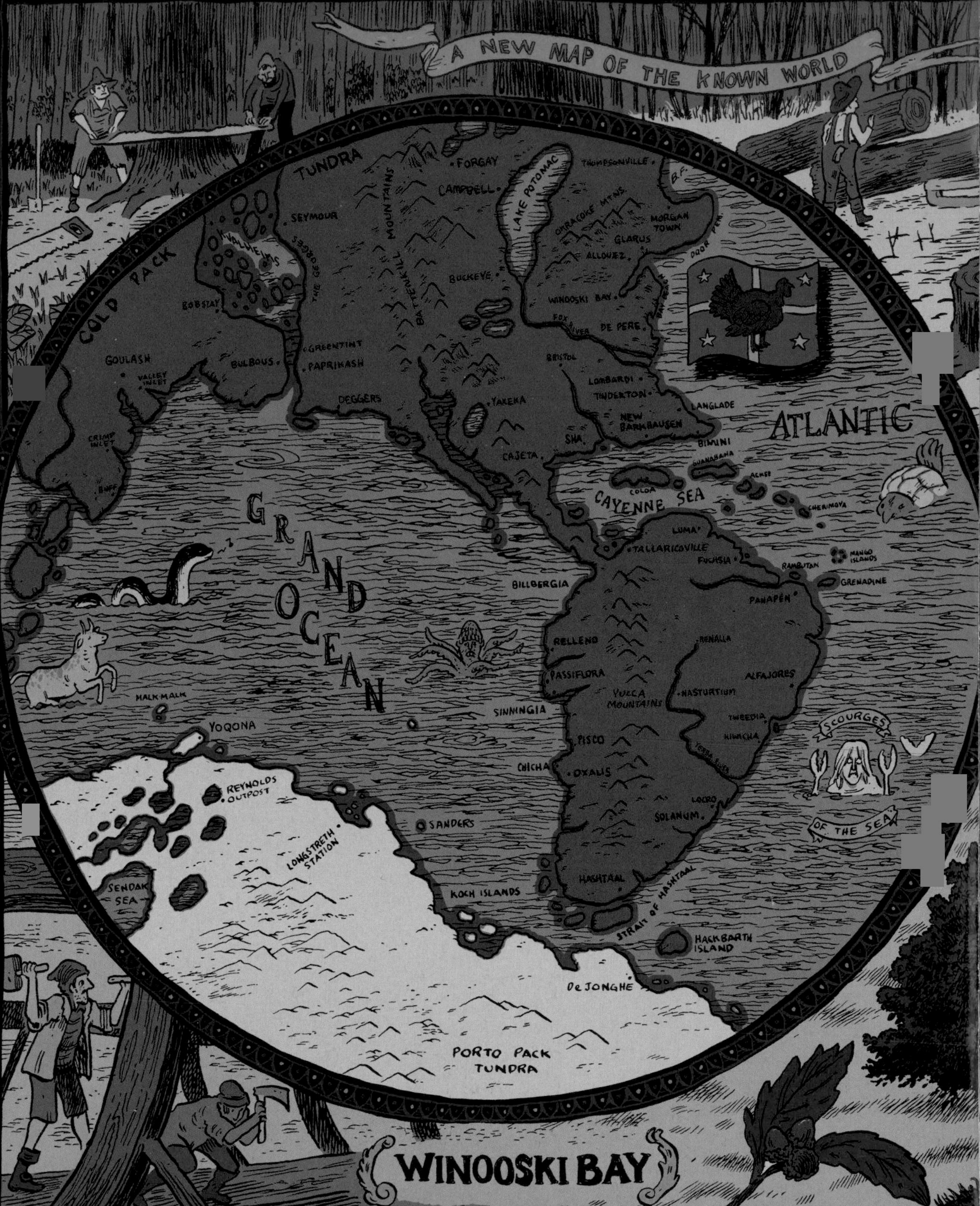
A NEW MAP OF THE KNOWN WORLD
TUNDRA
FORGAY
THOMPSONVILLE
CAMPBELL
LAKE POTOMAC
MOUNTAINS
SEYMOUR
OKRACOKE MTNS.
MORGAN TOWN
GLARUS
ALLOUEZ
DOOR PEN.
THE GEORGES
BATTENKILL
BUCKEYE
COLD PACK
BOBSTAY
WINOOSKI BAY
FOX RIVER
DE PERE
GREENTINT
PAPRIKASH
GOULASH
VALLEY INLET
BULBOUS
BRISTOL
LOMBARDI
TINDERTON
DEGGERS
YAKEKA
LANGLADE
NEW BARKHAUSEN
ATLANTIC
CRIMP INLET
SHA.
CAJETA
BIMINI
GUANABANA
COLOA
CAYENNE SEA
CHERIMOYA
GRAND OCEAN
LUMA
TALLARICOVILLE
FUCHSIA
RAMBUTAN
MANGO ISLANDS
GRENADINE
BILLBERGIA
PANAPEN
RELLENO
RENALLA
PASSIFLORA
ALFAJORES
YUCCA MOUNTAINS
NASTURTIUM
MALKMALK
SINNINGIA
TWEEDIA
YOQONA
PISCO
SCOURGES OF THE SEA
CHICHA
OXALIS
REYNOLDS OUTPOST
LOCRO
SOLANUM
SANDERS
LONGSTRETH STATION
SENDAK SEA
KOCH ISLANDS
HASHTAAL
STRAIT OF HASHTAAL
HACKBARTH ISLAND
DeJONGHE
PORTO PACK TUNDRA
WINOOSKI BAY

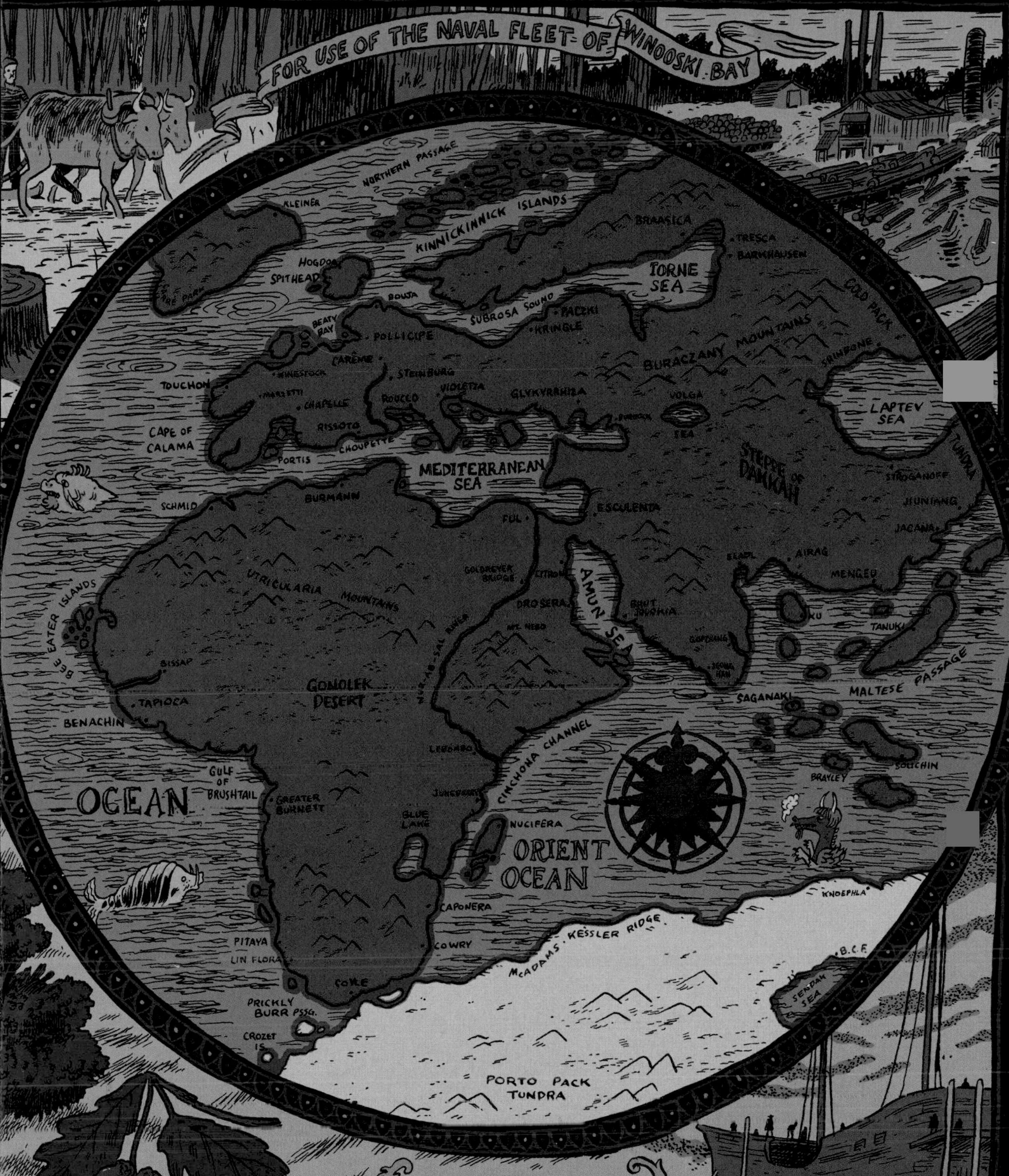

FOR USE OF THE NAVAL FLEET OF WINOOSKI BAY
NORTHERN PASSAGE
KLEINER
KINNICKINNICK ISLANDS
BRASSICA
TRESCA
BARKHAUSEN
HOGDON
SPITHEAD
TORNE SEA
BOUJA
SUBROSA SOUND
PACZKI
KRINGLE
COLD PACK
POLLICIPE
BURACZANY MOUNTAINS
CARÊME
STEINBURG
TOUCHON
VIOLETTA
GLYKYRRHIZA
VOLGA
SEA
LAPTEV SEA
CHAPELLE
ROCCO
RISSOTO
CAPE OF CALAMA
CHOUPETTE
PORTIS
MEDITERRANEAN SEA
STEPPE OF DAKKAH
TUNDRA
STROGANOFF
SCHMID
BURMANN
ESCULENTA
JIUNIANG
JACANA
FUL
AIRAG
MENGED
UTRICULARIA MOUNTAINS
AMUN SEA
DROSERA
TANUKI
BEE EATER ISLANDS
BISSAP
GONOLEK DESERT
MALTESE PASSAGE
SAGANAKI
TAPIOCA
BENACHIN
CINCHONA CHANNEL
GULF OF BRUSHTAIL
OCEAN
GREATER BURNETT
SOLCHIN
BRAYLEY
BLUE LAKE
NUCIFERA
ORIENT OCEAN
KNOEPHLA
CAPONERA
COWRY
KESSLER RIDGE
McADAMS
PITAYA
B.C.F.
CORE
SENDAK SEA
PRICKLY BURR PSSG.
CROZET IS.
PORTO PACK TUNDRA
LUMBER CO.

First Second

Copyright © 2018 by Aaron Renier

Published by First Second
First Second is an imprint of Roaring Brook Press,
a division of Holtzbrinck Publishing Holdings Limited Partnership
175 Fifth Avenue, New York, NY 10010

Library of Congress Control Number: 2017957419

ISBN: 978-1-59643-505-6

Our books may be purchased in bulk for promotional,
educational, or business use.

Please contact your local bookseller or the Macmillan Corporate
and Premium Sales Department at (800) 221-7945 ext. 5442 or by
e-mail at MacmillanSpecialMarkets@macmillan.com.

First edition, 2018

Book design by Aaron Renier and Molly Johanson

Printed in China by RR Donnelley Asia Printing Solutions Ltd.,
Dongguan City, Guangdong Province

10 9 8 7 6 5 4 3 2 1

To MICHAEL, who appears and disappears in crowds.

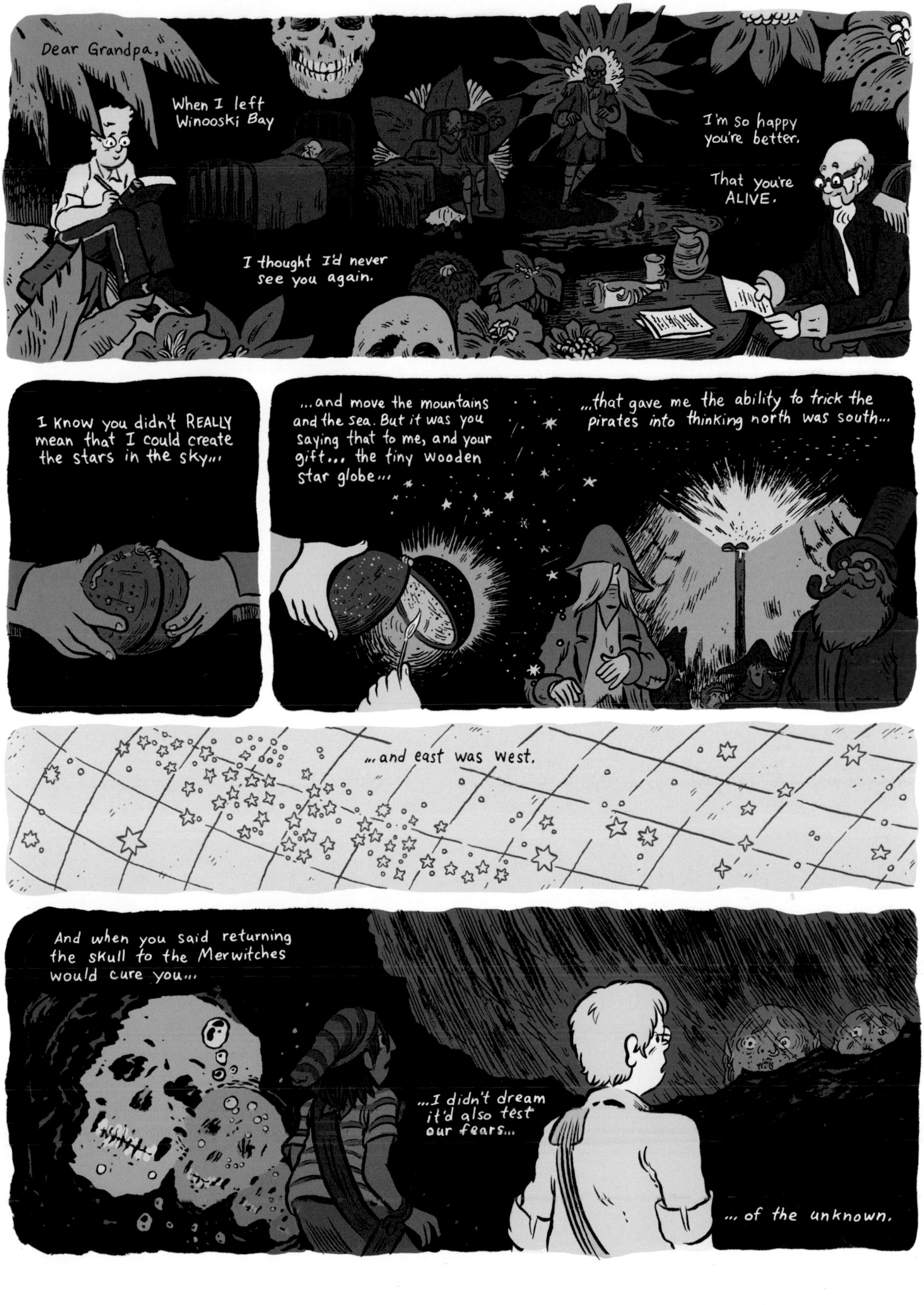
Dear Grandpa,
When I left Winooski Bay
I thought I'd never see you again.
I'm so happy you're better.
That you're ALIVE.
I know you didn't REALLY mean that I could create the stars in the sky...
...and move the mountains and the sea. But it was you saying that to me, and your gift... the tiny wooden star globe...
...that gave me the ability to trick the pirates into thinking north was south...
...and east was west.
And when you said returning the skull to the Merwitches would cure you...
...I didn't dream it'd also test our fears...
... of the unknown.

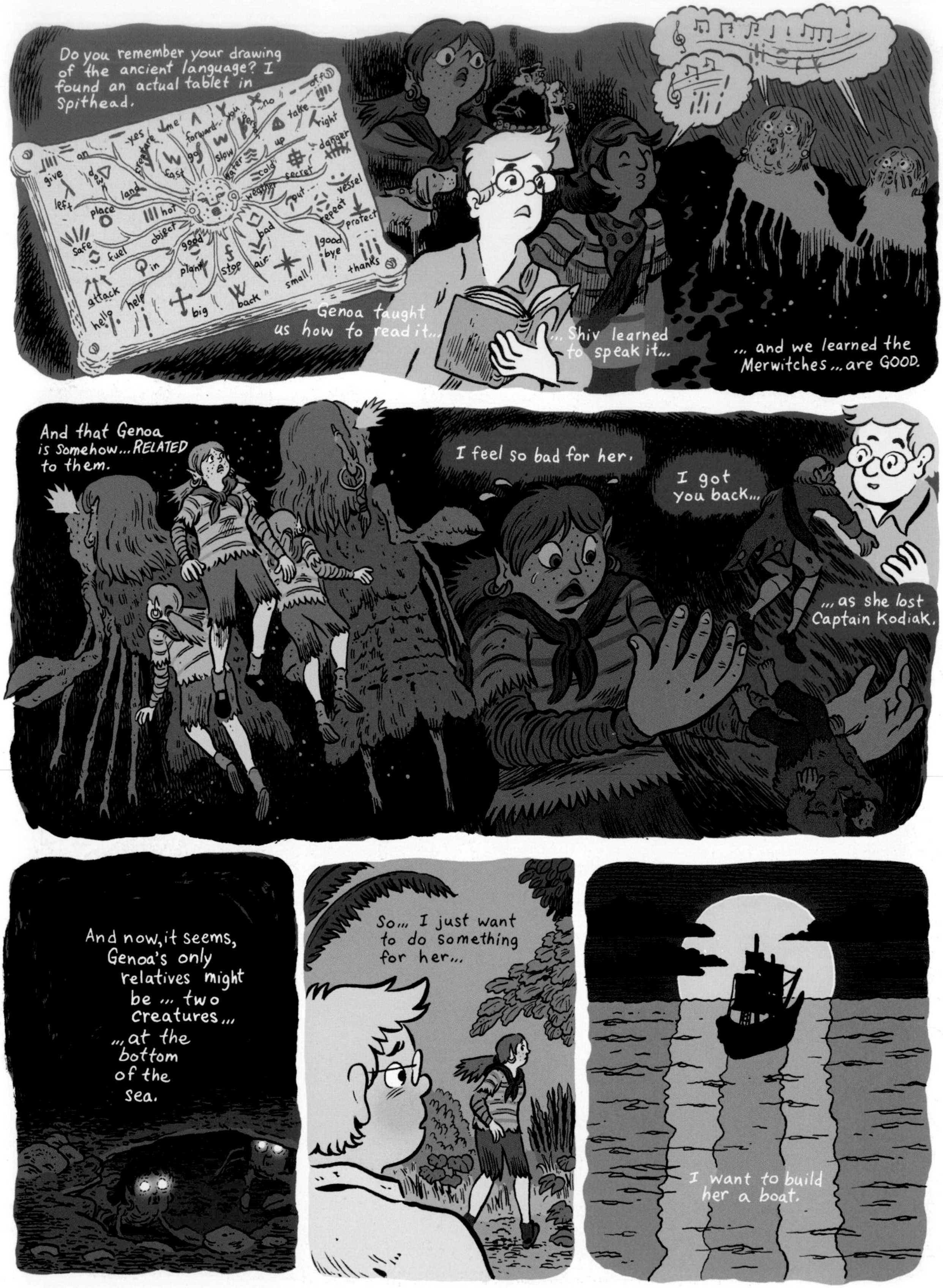
Do you remember your drawing of the ancient language? I found an actual tablet in Spithead.
Genoa taught us how to read it...
... Shiv learned to speak it...
... and we learned the Merwitches ... are GOOD.
And that Genoa is somehow... RELATED to them.
I feel so bad for her.
I got you back...
... as she lost Captain Kodiak.
And now, it seems, Genoa's only relatives might be ... two creatures...
... at the bottom of the sea.
So... I just want to do something for her...
I want to build her a boat.

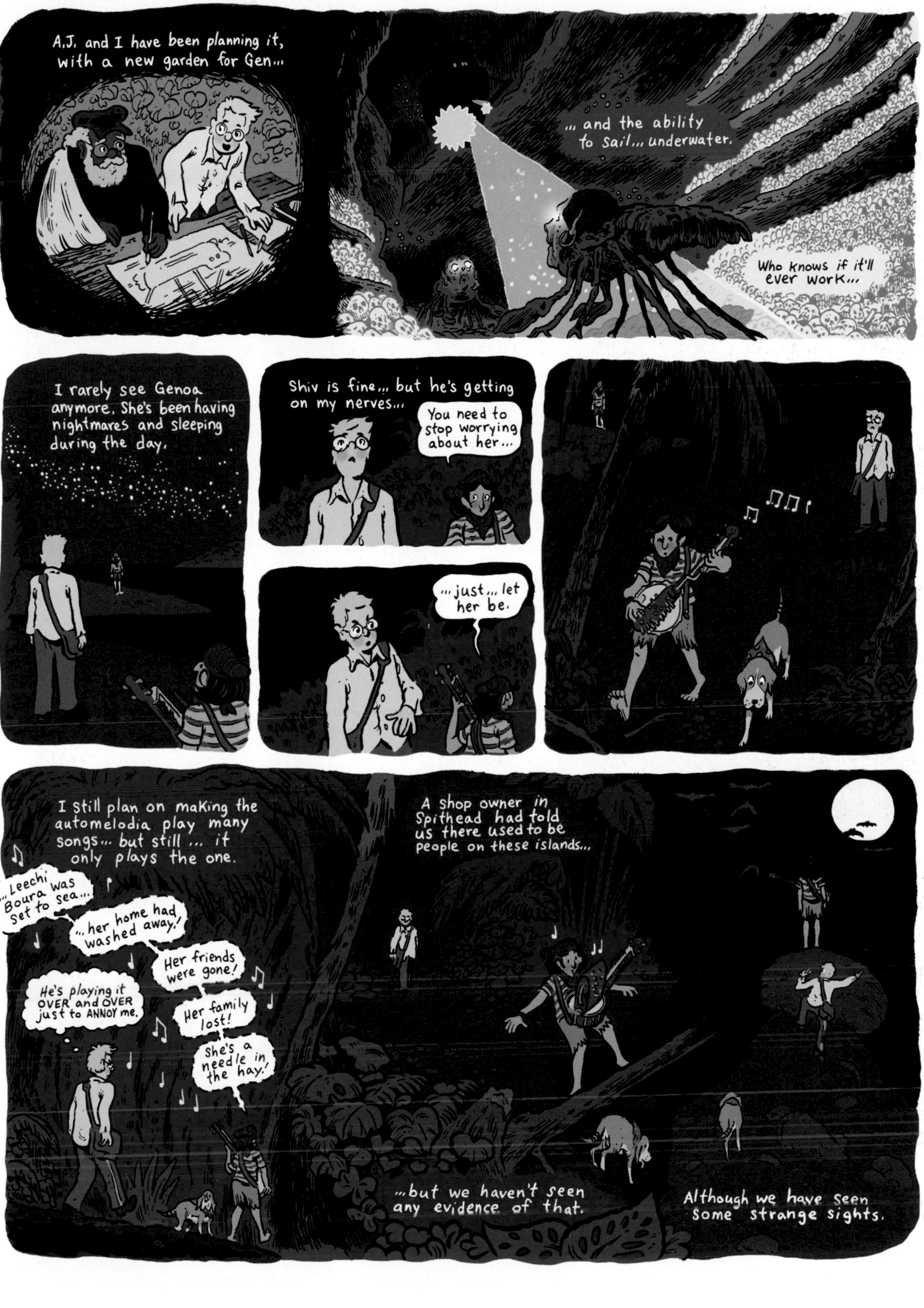

A.J. and I have been planning it, with a new garden for Gen...
... and the ability to sail... underwater.
Who knows if it'll ever work...
I rarely see Genoa anymore. She's been having nightmares and sleeping during the day.
Shiv is fine... but he's getting on my nerves...
You need to stop worrying about her...
...just... let her be.
I still plan on making the automelodia play many songs... but still ... it only plays the one.
...Leechi Boura was set to sea...
...her home had washed away!
Her friends were gone!
He's playing it OVER and OVER just to ANNOY me.
Her family lost!
She's a needle in the hay!
A shop owner in Spithead had told us there used to be people on these islands...
...but we haven't seen any evidence of that.
Although we have seen some strange sights.

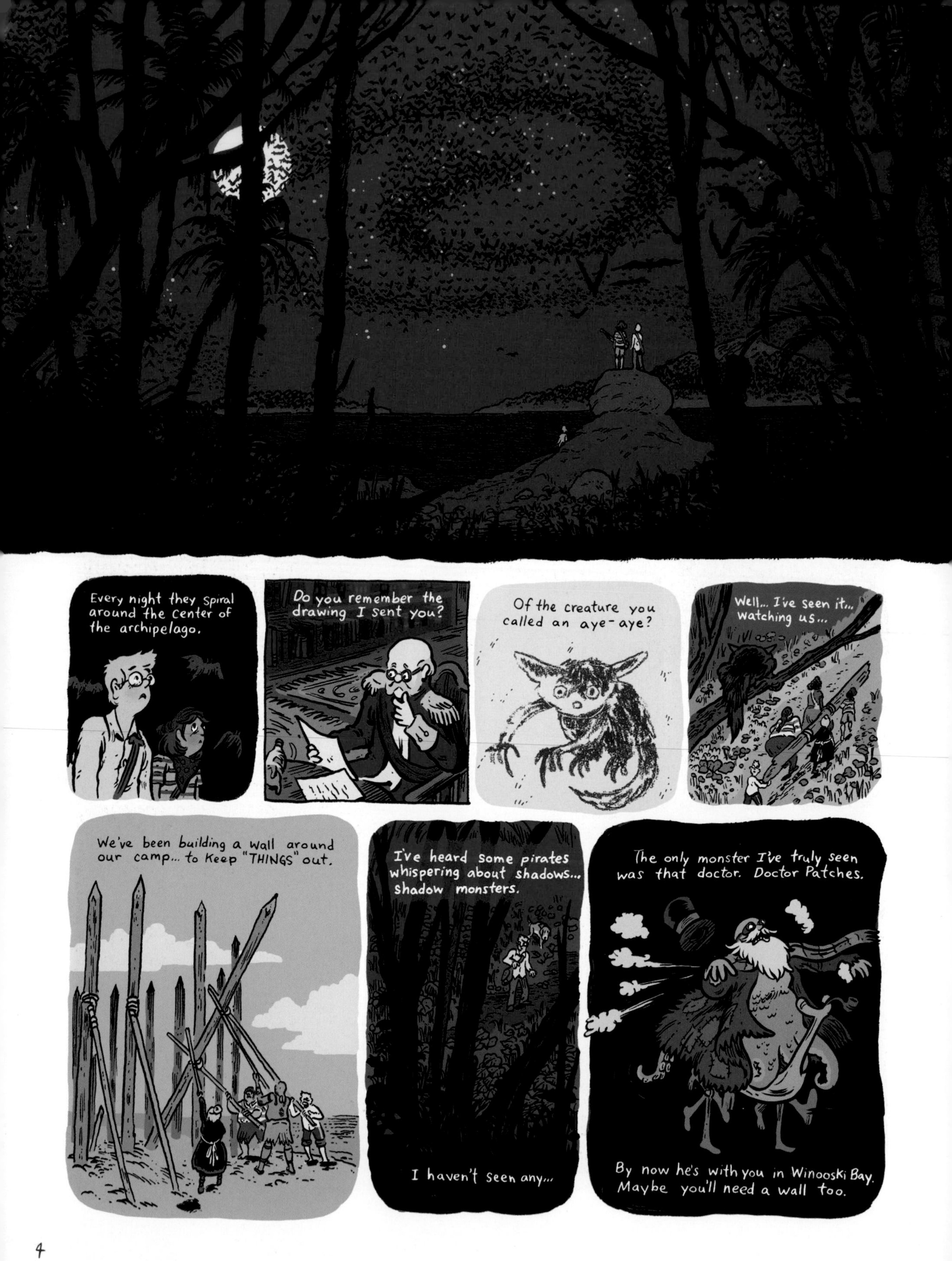
Every night they spiral around the center of the archipelago.
Do you remember the drawing I sent you?
Of the creature you called an aye-aye?
Well... I've seen it... watching us...
We've been building a wall around our camp... to keep "THINGS" out.
I've heard some pirates whispering about shadows... shadow monsters.
I haven't seen any...
The only monster I've truly seen was that doctor. Doctor Patches.
By now he's with you in Winooski Bay. Maybe you'll need a wall too.

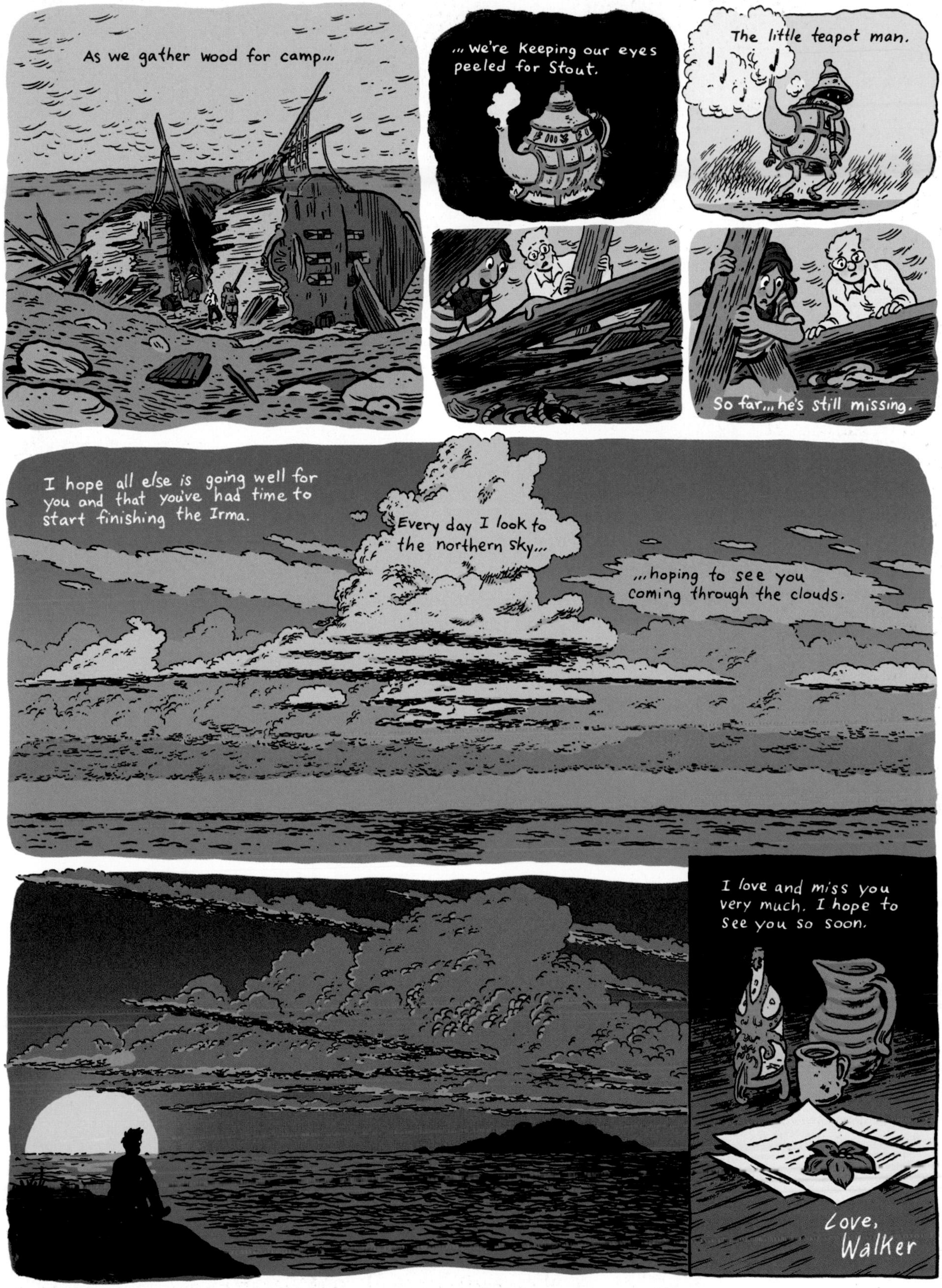

As we gather wood for camp...
...we're keeping our eyes peeled for Stout.
The little teapot man.
So far... he's still missing.
I hope all else is going well for you and that you've had time to start finishing the Irma.
Every day I look to the northern sky...
...hoping to see you coming through the clouds.
I love and miss you very much. I hope to see you so soon.
Love,
Walker

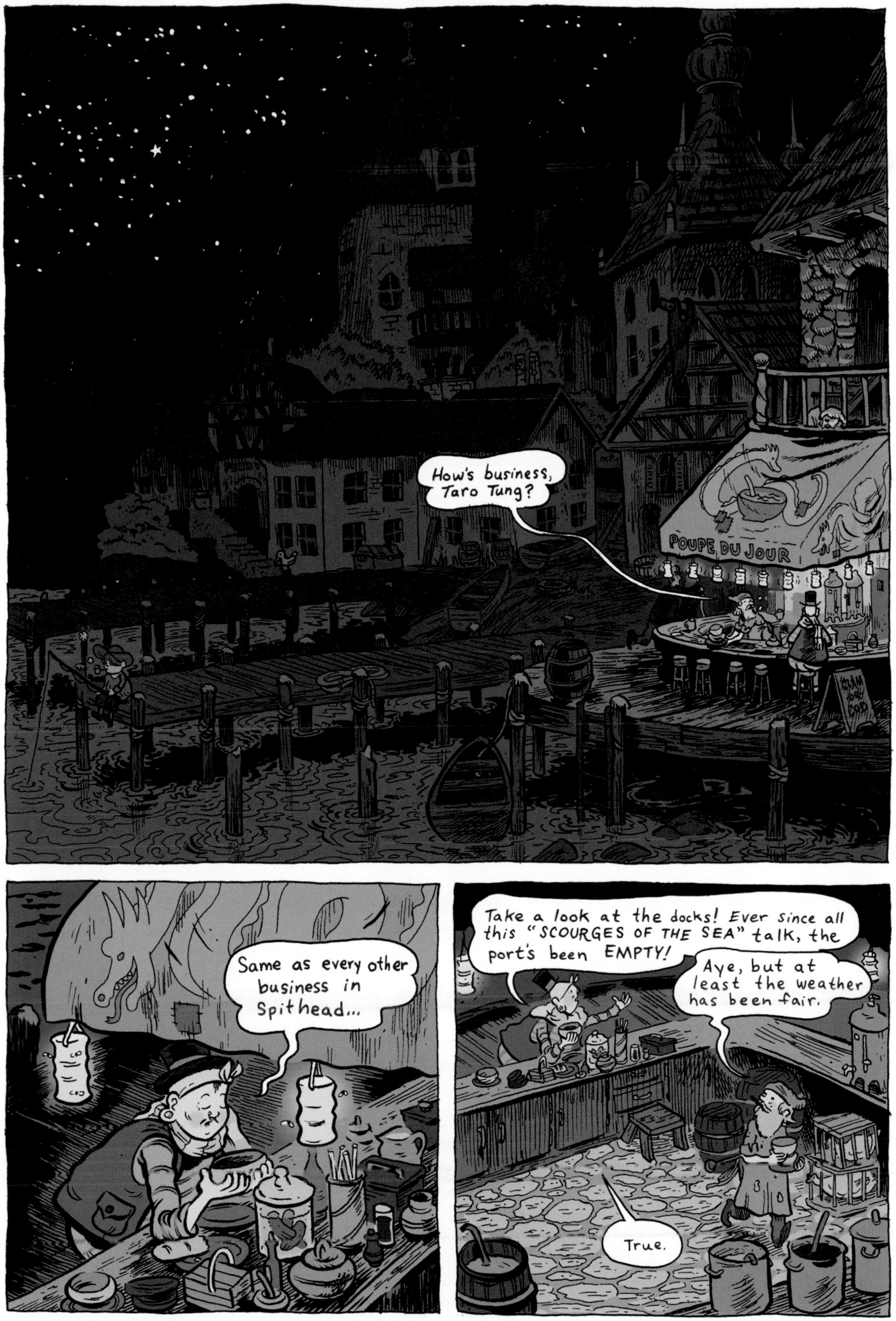
How's business, Taro Tung?
POUPE DU JOUR
Same as every other business in Spithead...
Take a look at the docks! Ever since all this "SCOURGES OF THE SEA" talk, the port's been EMPTY!
Aye, but at least the weather has been fair.
True.

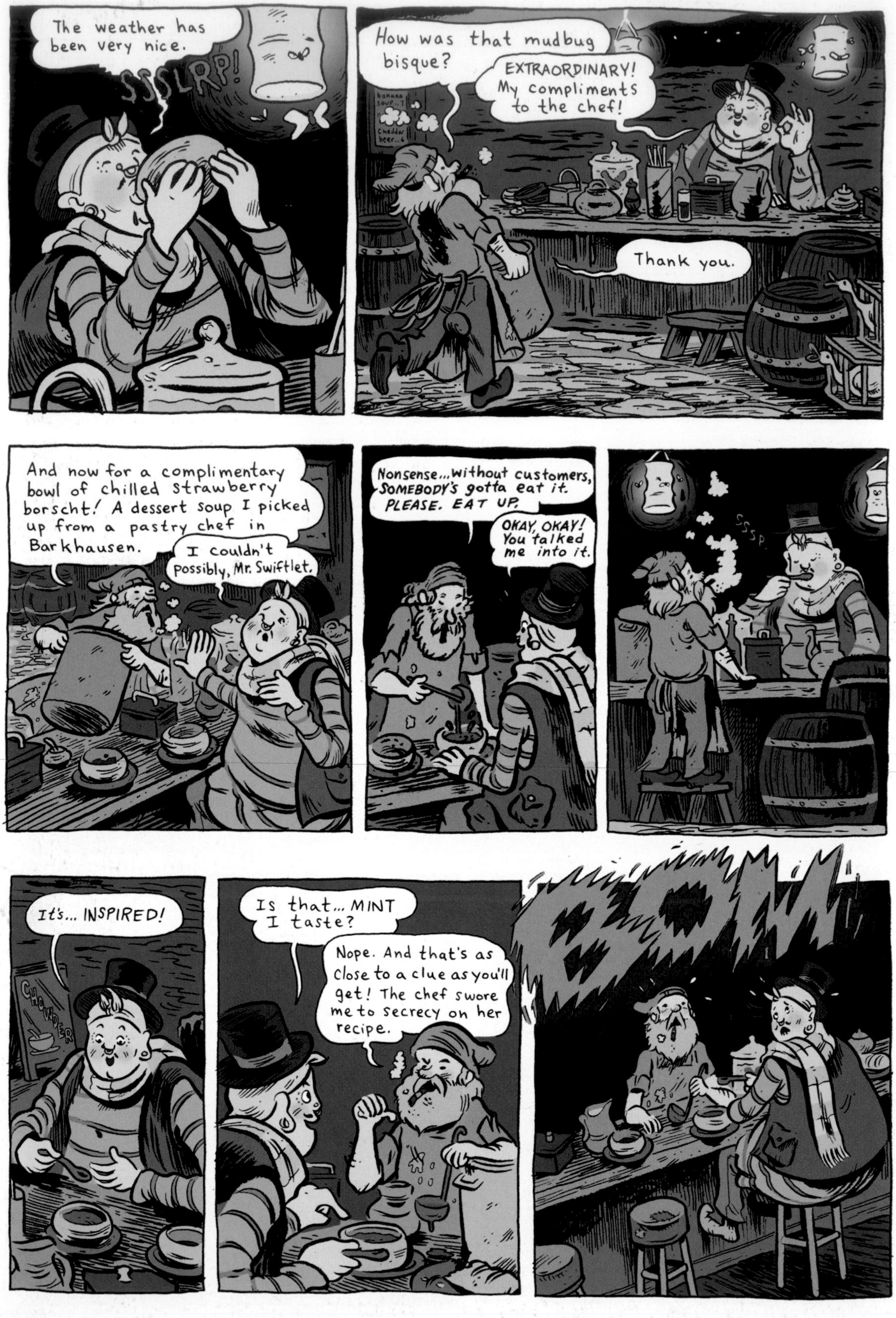

The weather has been very nice.
SSSLRP!
How was that mudbug bisque?
EXTRAORDINARY! My compliments to the chef!
Thank you.
And now for a complimentary bowl of chilled strawberry borscht! A dessert soup I picked up from a pastry chef in Barkhausen.
I couldn't possibly, Mr. Swiftlet.
Nonsense... without customers, SOMEBODY's gotta eat it. PLEASE. EAT UP.
OKAY, OKAY! You talked me into it.
SSSP.
It's... INSPIRED!
Is that... MINT I taste?
Nope. And that's as close to a clue as you'll get! The chef swore me to secrecy on her recipe.
BOOM

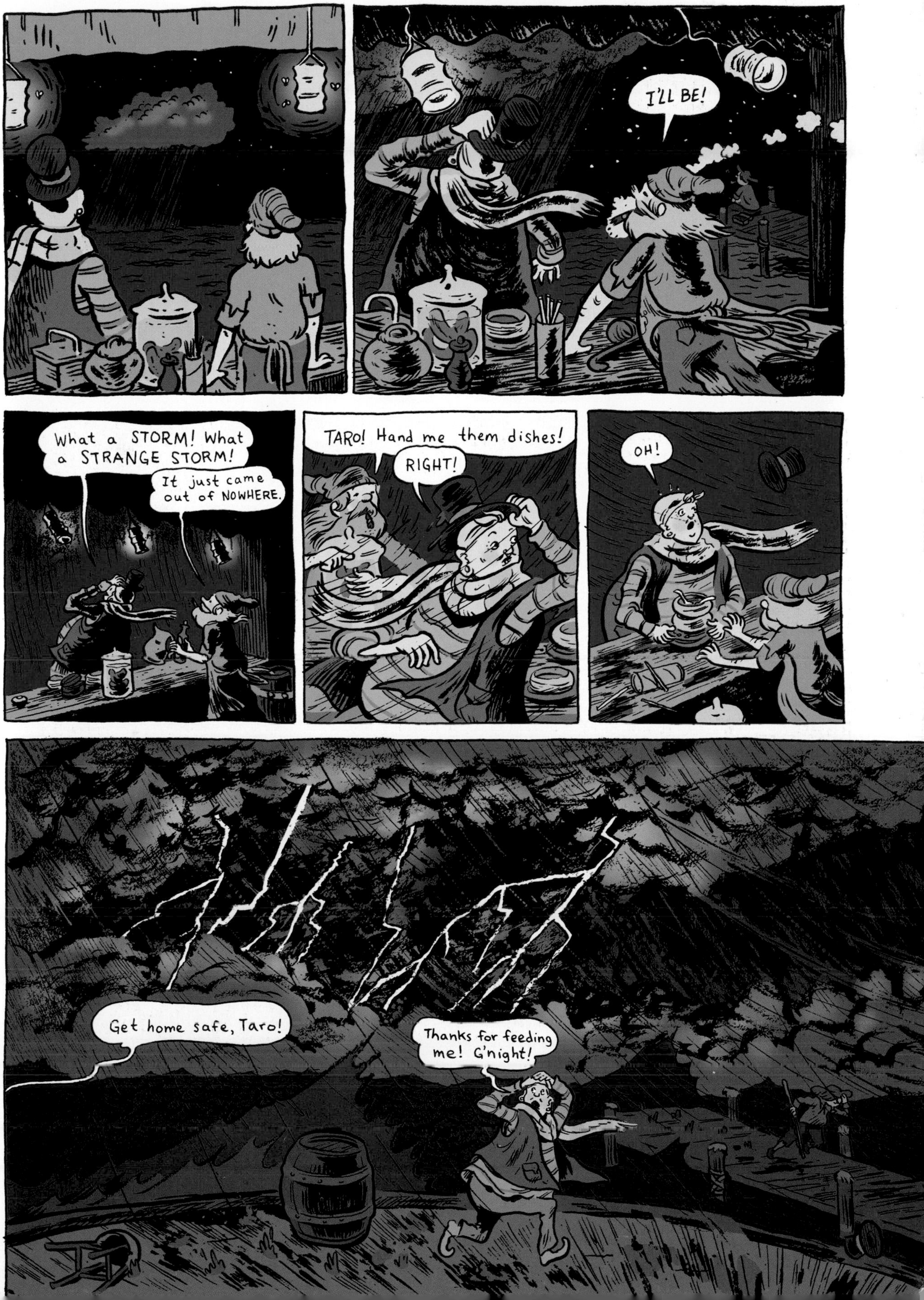
I'LL BE!
What a STORM! What a STRANGE STORM!
It just came out of NOWHERE.
TARO! Hand me them dishes!
RIGHT!
OH!
Get home safe, Taro!
Thanks for feeding me! G'night!

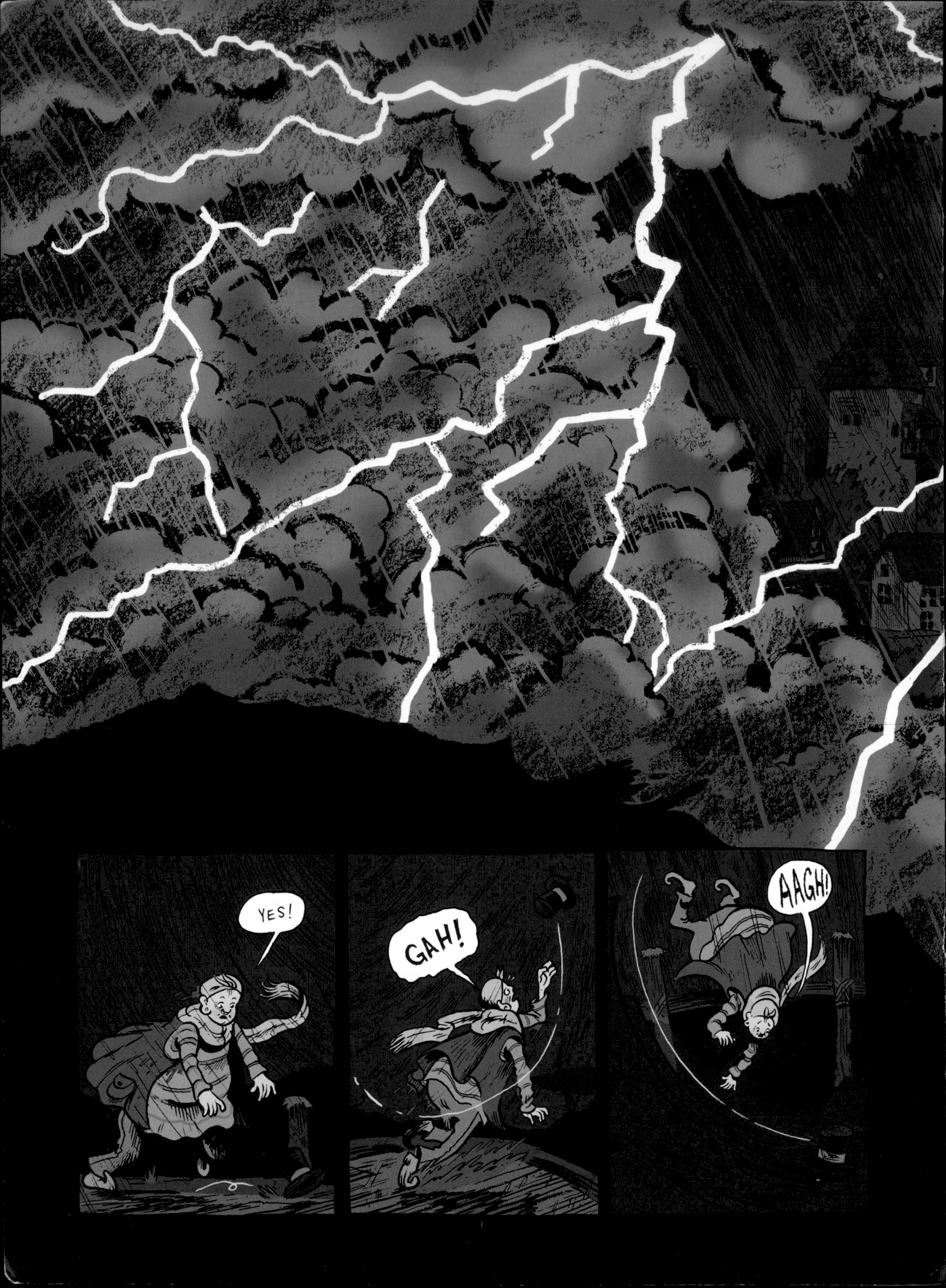
YES!
GAH!
AAGH!

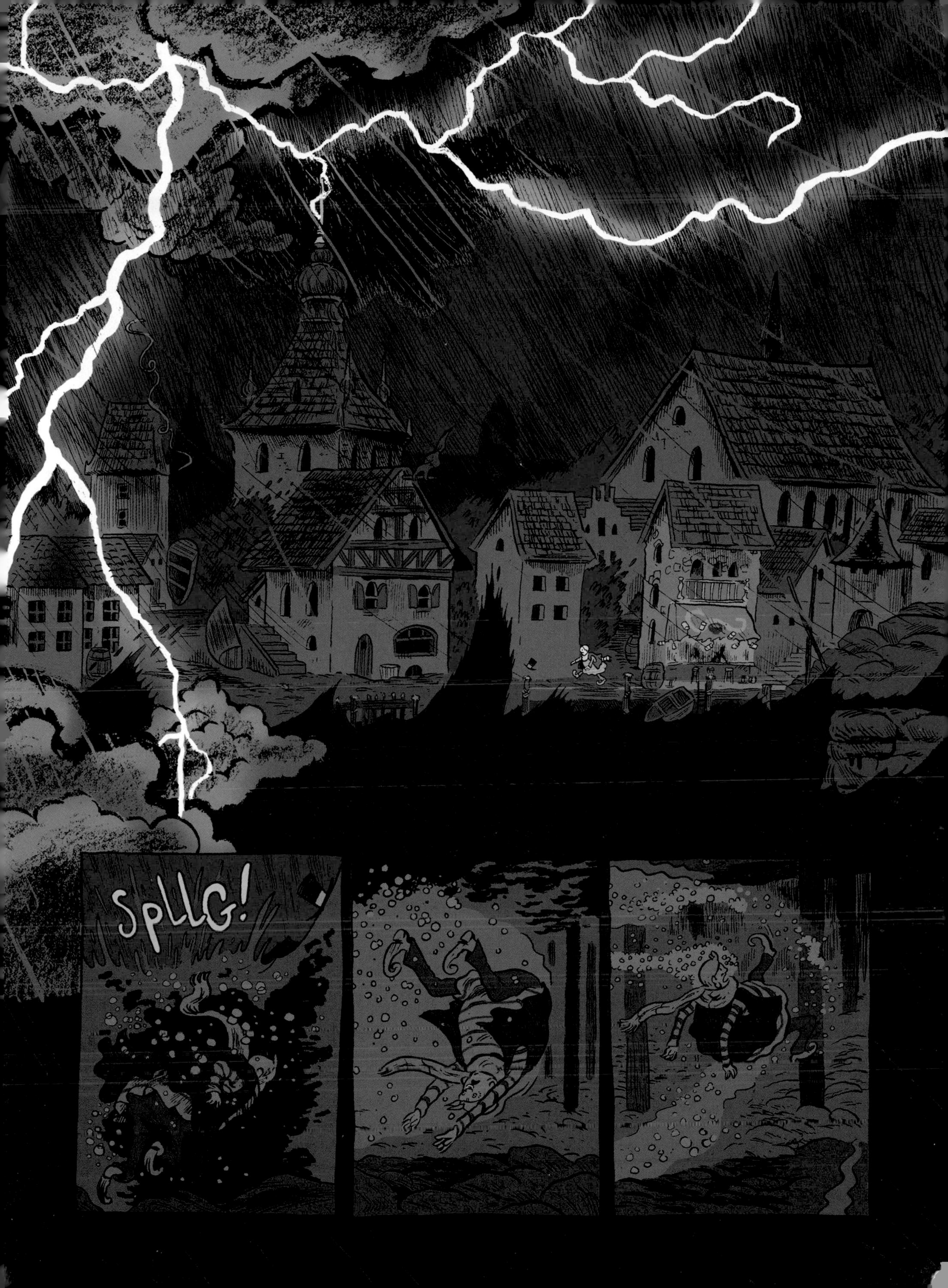
SPLLG!

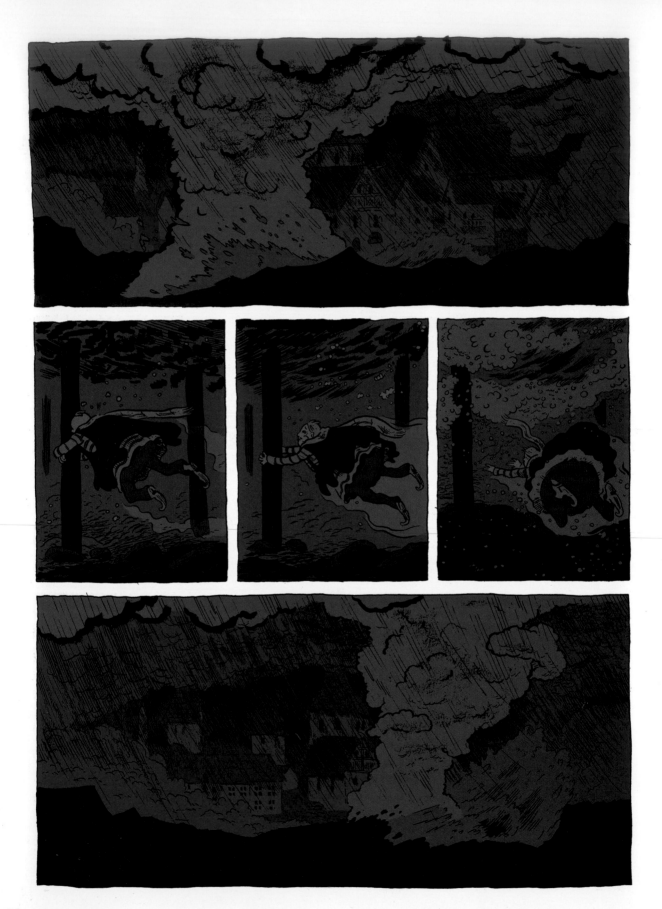

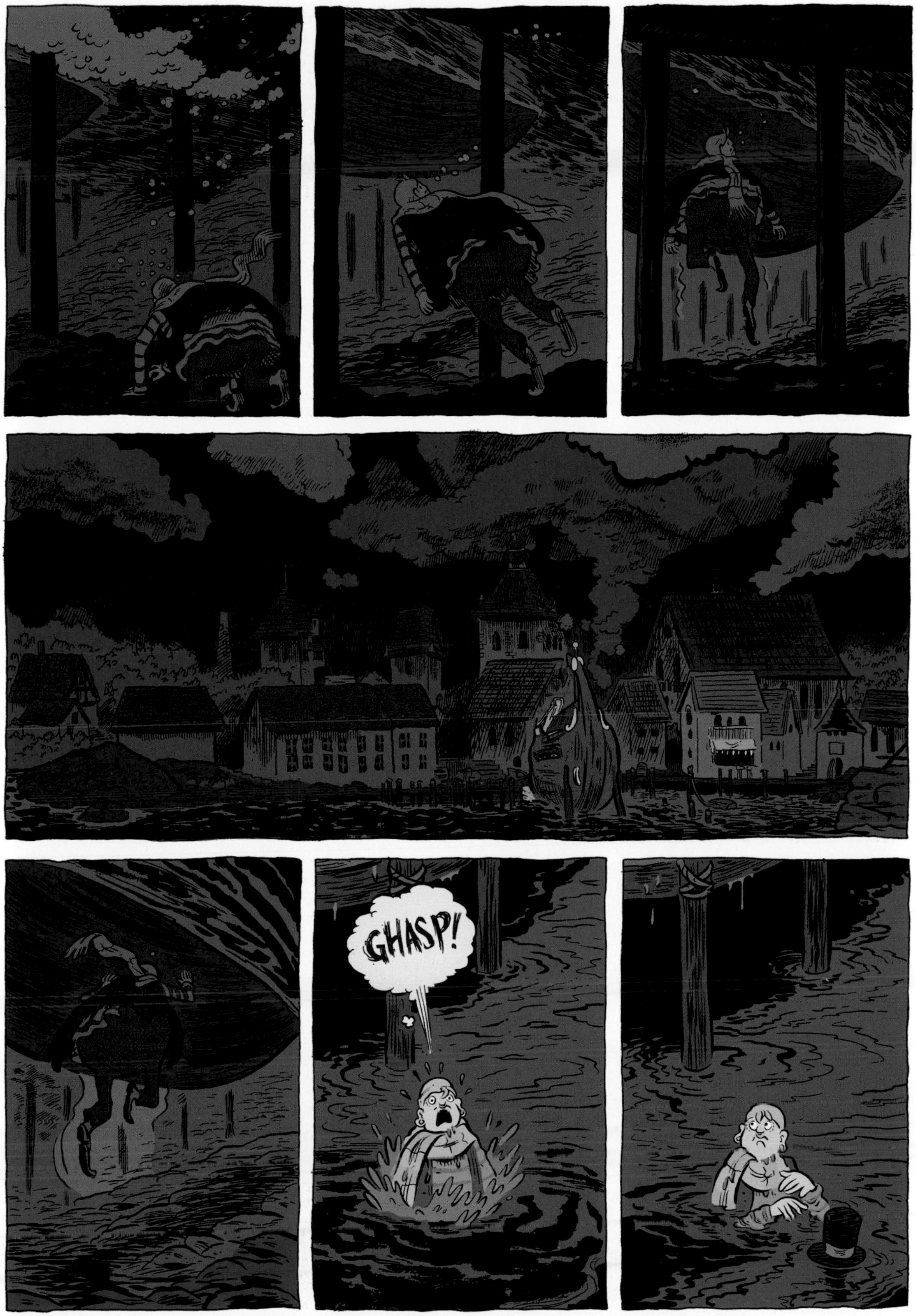
GHASP!

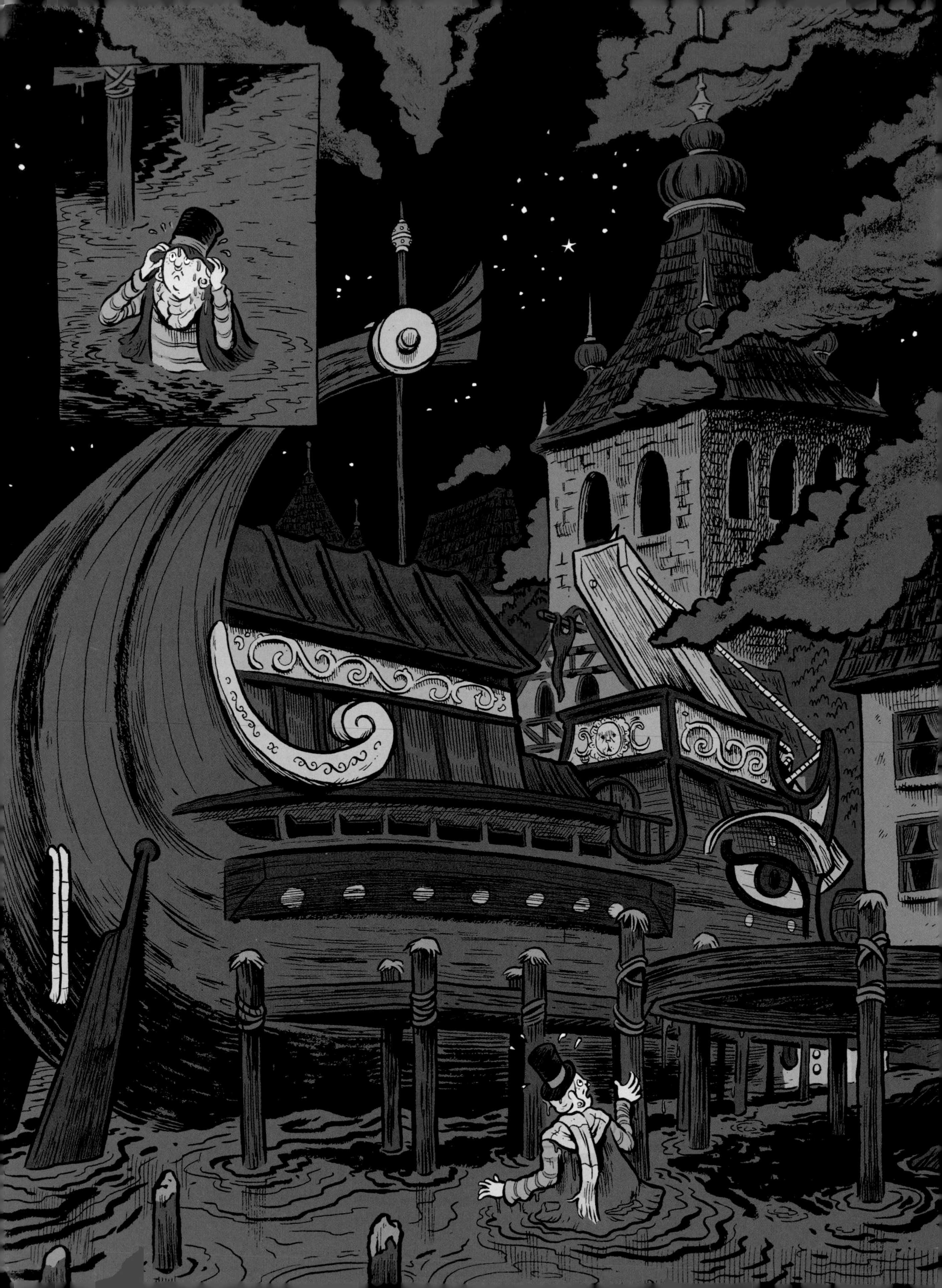

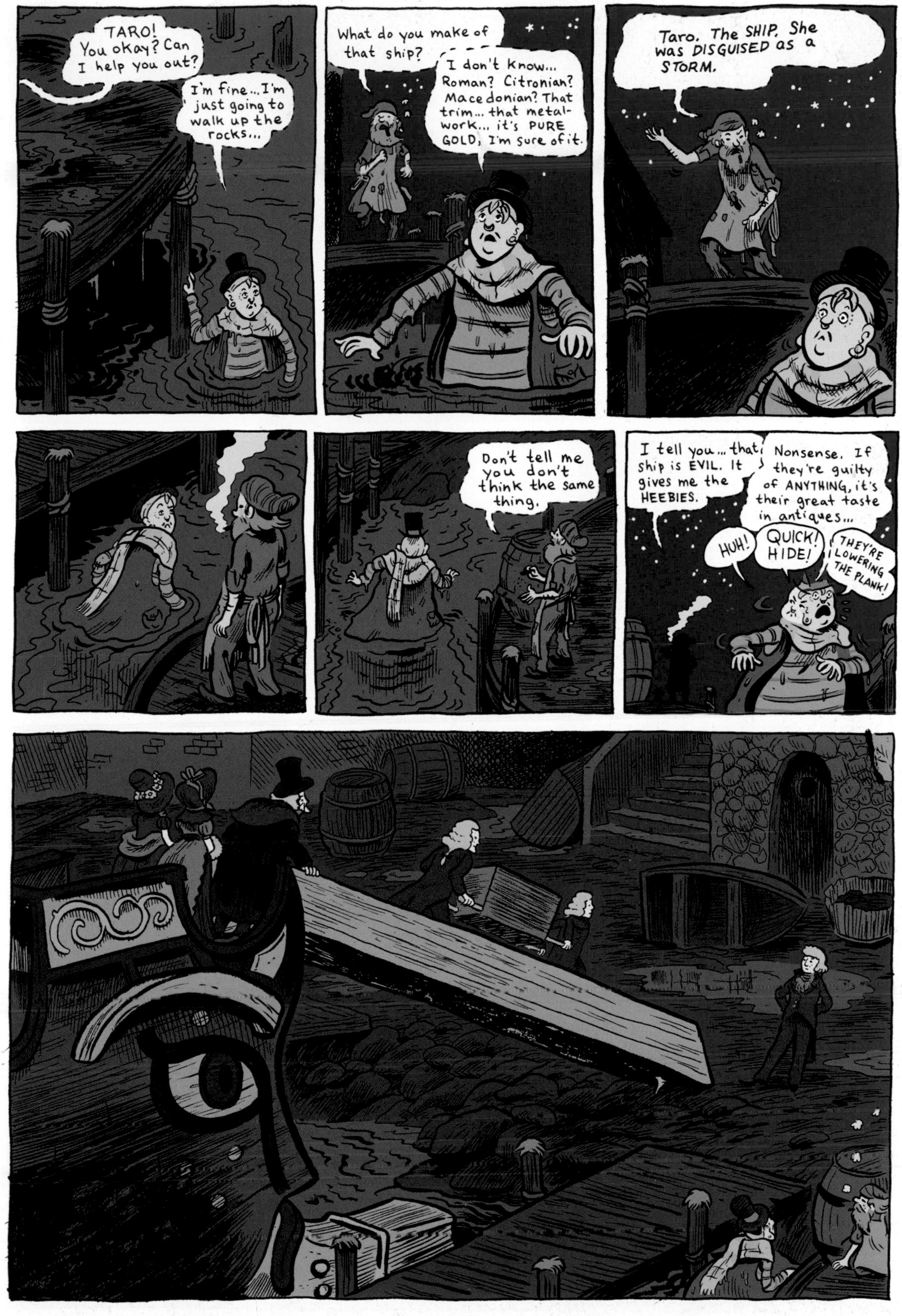
TARO! You okay? Can I help you out?
I'm fine... I'm just going to walk up the rocks...
What do you make of that ship?
I don't know... Roman? Citronian? Macedonian? That trim... that metal-work... it's PURE GOLD, I'm sure of it.
Taro. The SHIP. She was DISGUISED as a STORM.
Don't tell me you don't think the same thing.
I tell you... that ship is EVIL. It gives me the HEEBIES.
Nonsense. If they're guilty of ANYTHING, it's their great taste in antiques...
HUH!
QUICK! HIDE!
THEY'RE LOWERING THE PLANK!

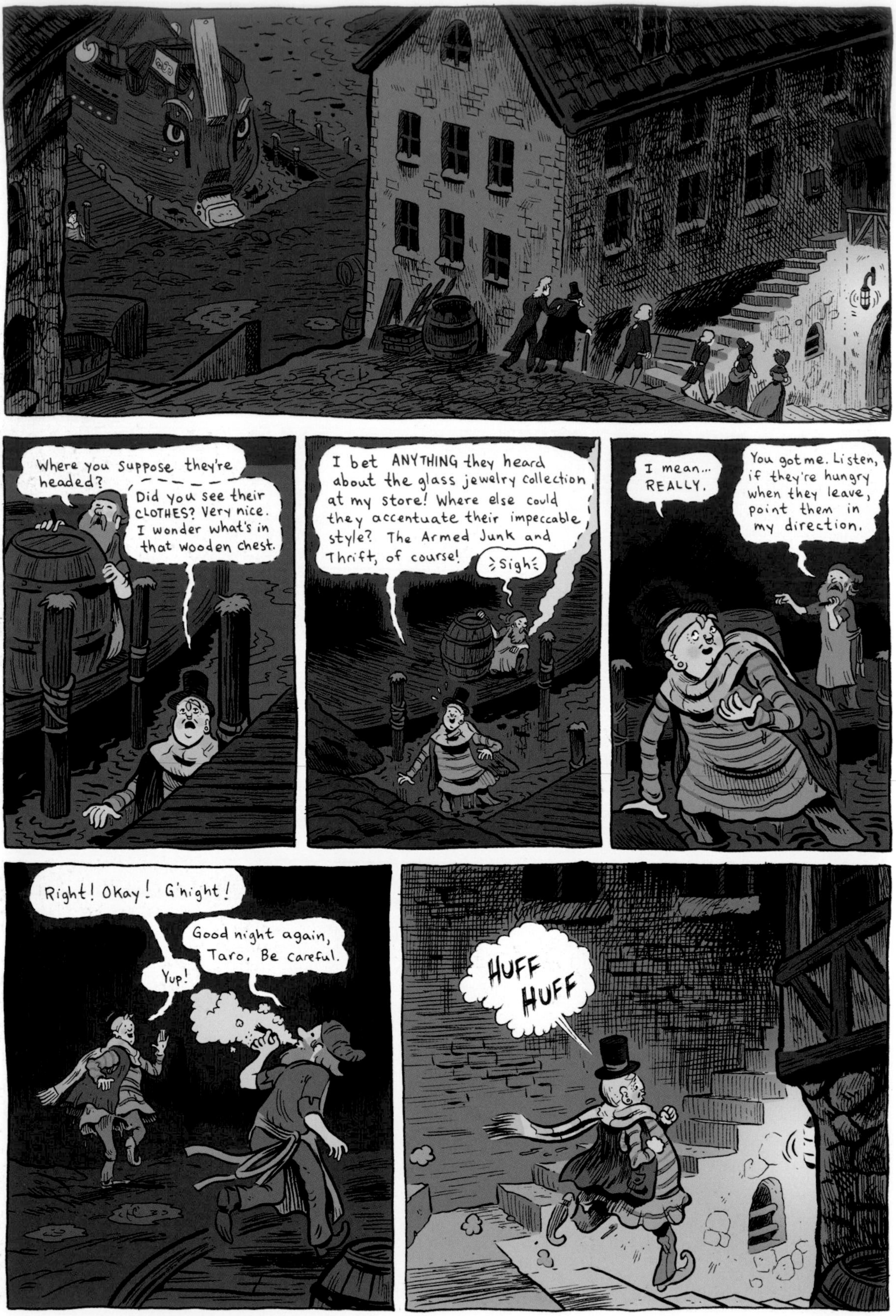
Where you suppose they're headed?
Did you see their CLOTHES? Very nice. I wonder what's in that wooden chest.
I bet ANYTHING they heard about the glass jewelry collection at my store! Where else could they accentuate their impeccable style? The Armed Junk and Thrift, of course!
Sigh
I mean... REALLY.
You got me. Listen, if they're hungry when they leave, point them in my direction.
Right! Okay! G'night!
Good night again, Taro. Be careful.
Yup!
HUFF HUFF

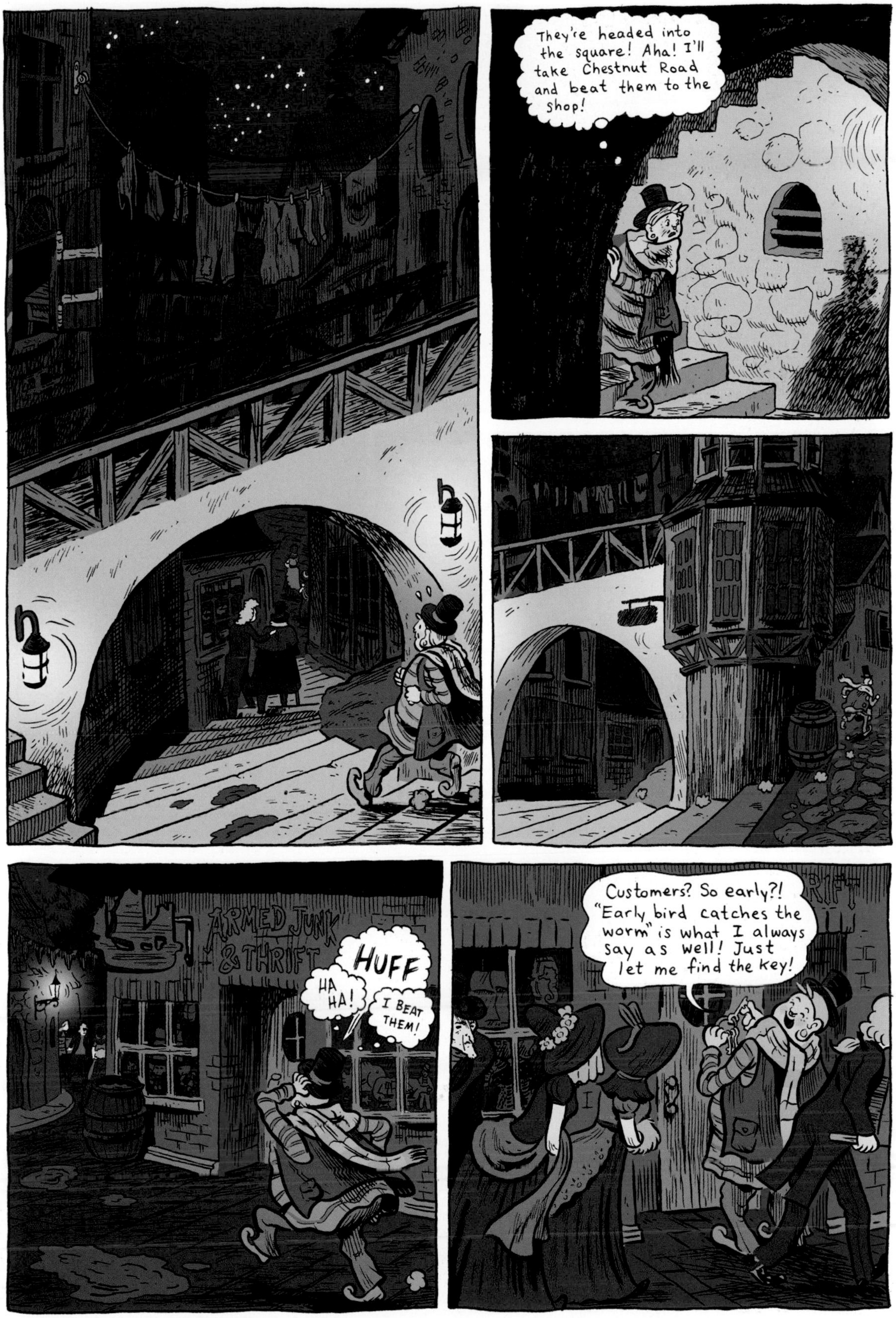
They're headed into the square! Aha! I'll take Chestnut Road and beat them to the shop!
ARMED JUNK & THRIFT
HUFF
HA HA!
I BEAT THEM!
Customers? So early?! "Early bird catches the worm" is what I always say as well! Just let me find the key!

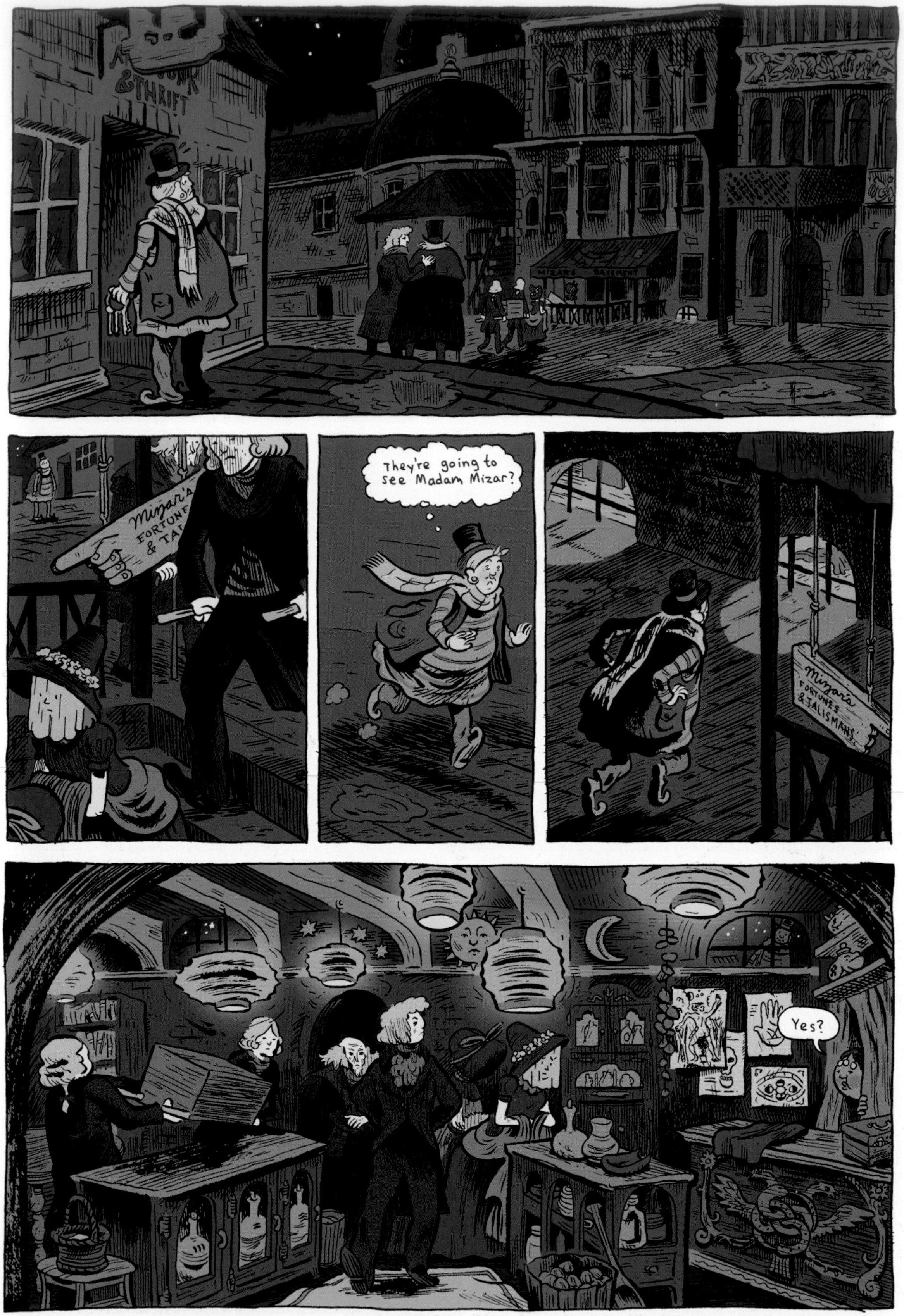
&THRIFT
MIZAR'S BASEMENT
Mizar's
They're going to see Madam Mizar?
Mizar's FORTUNES & TALISMANS
Yes?

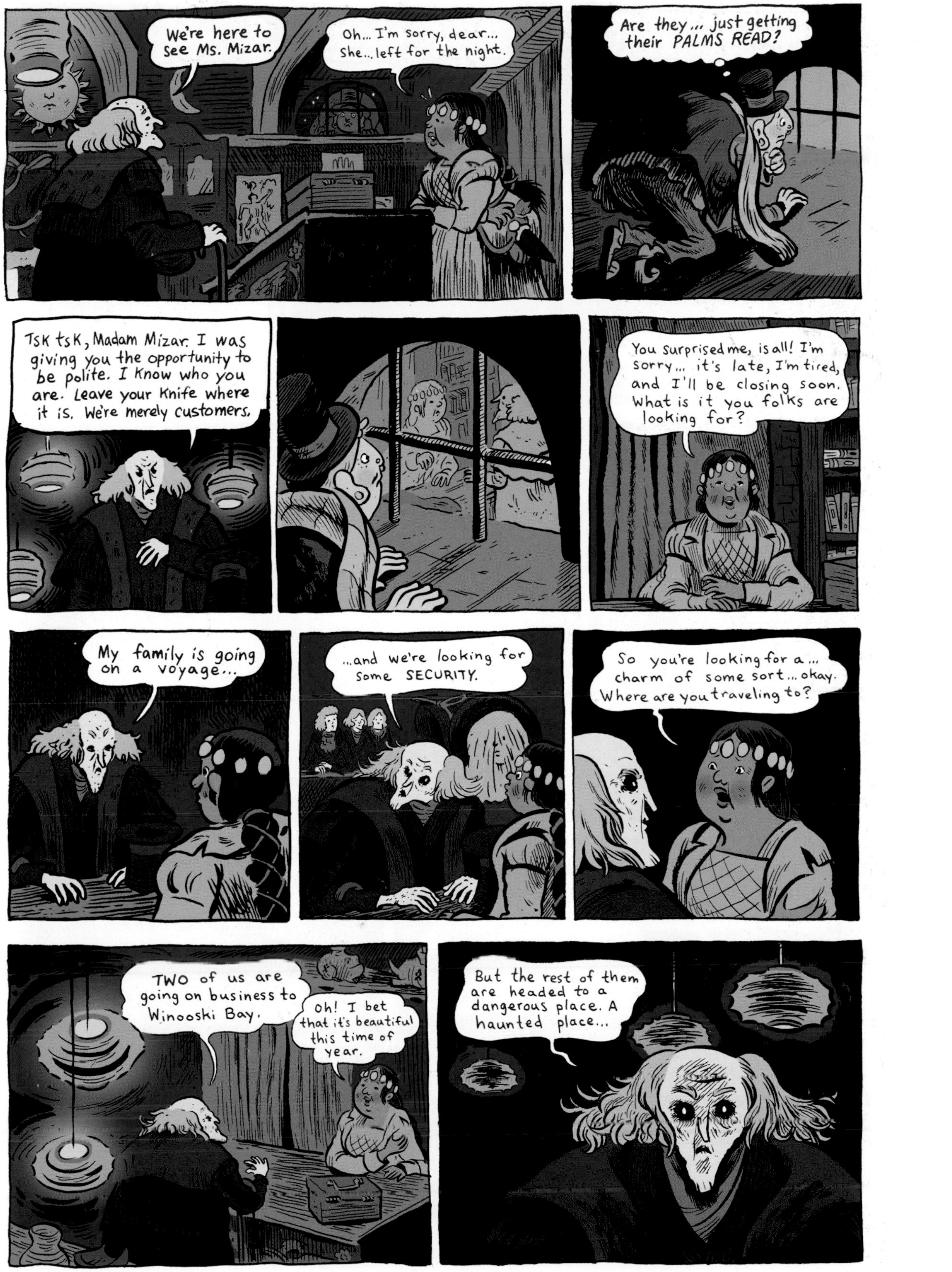
We're here to see Ms. Mizar.
Oh... I'm sorry, dear... She... left for the night.
Are they... just getting their PALMS READ?
TSK tsK, Madam Mizar. I was giving you the opportunity to be polite. I know who you are. Leave your knife where it is. We're merely customers.
You surprised me, is all! I'm sorry... it's late, I'm tired, and I'll be closing soon. What is it you folks are looking for?
My family is going on a voyage...
...and we're looking for some SECURITY.
So you're looking for a... charm of some sort... okay. Where are you traveling to?
TWO of us are going on business to Winooski Bay.
Oh! I bet that it's beautiful this time of year.
But the rest of them are headed to a dangerous place. A haunted place...

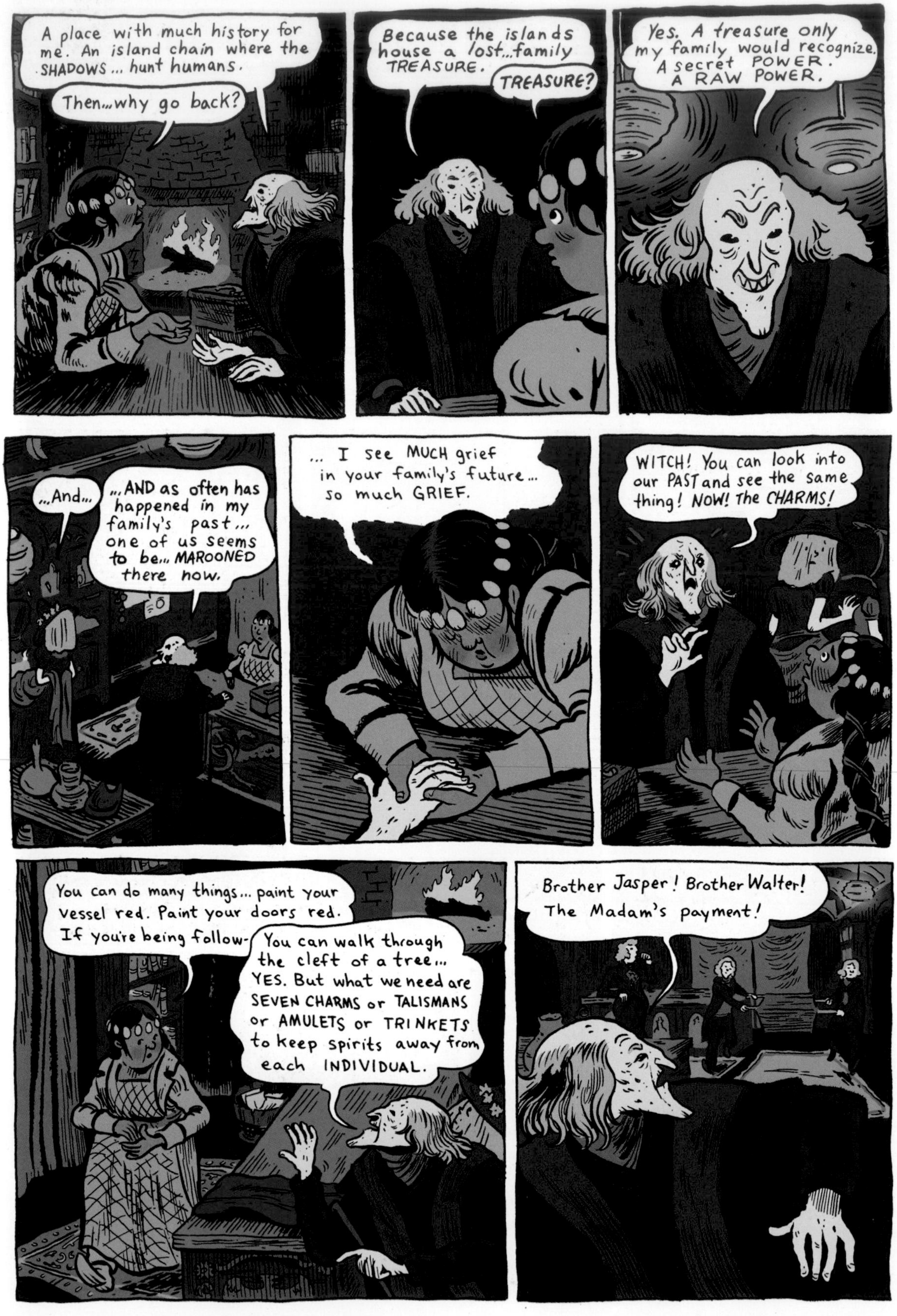
A place with much history for me. An island chain where the SHADOWS... hunt humans.
Then...why go back?
Because the islands house a lost...family TREASURE.
TREASURE?
Yes. A treasure only my family would recognize. A secret POWER. A RAW POWER.
...And...
...AND as often has happened in my family's past... one of us seems to be... MAROONED there now.
... I see MUCH grief in your family's future... so much GRIEF.
WITCH! You can look into our PAST and see the same thing! NOW! The CHARMS!
You can do many things... paint your vessel red. Paint your doors red. If you're being follow-
You can walk through the cleft of a tree... YES. But what we need are SEVEN CHARMS or TALISMANS or AMULETS or TRINKETS to keep spirits away from each INDIVIDUAL.
Brother Jasper! Brother Walter! The Madam's payment!

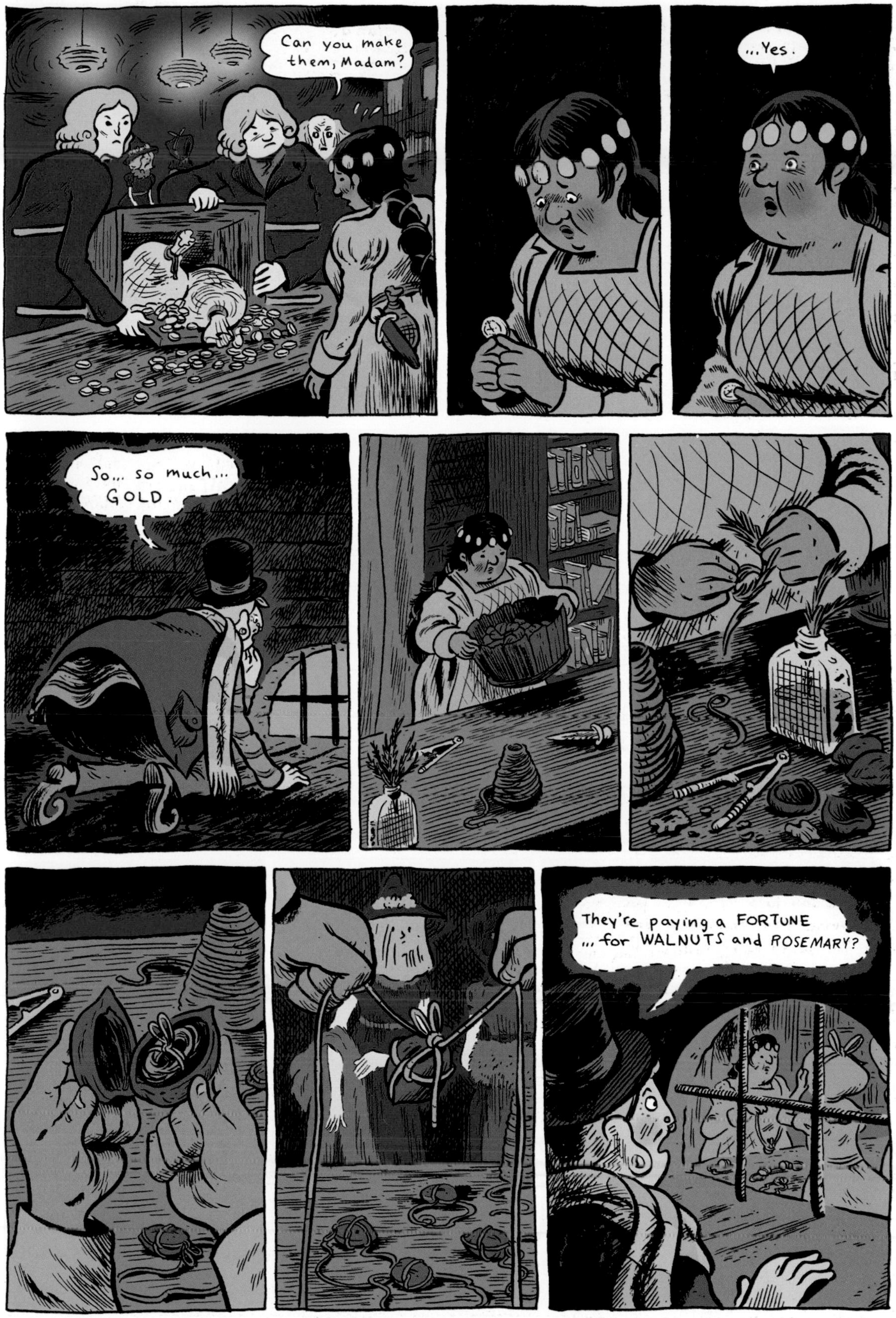
Can you make them, Madam?
...Yes.
So... so much... GOLD.
They're paying a FORTUNE ... for WALNUTS and ROSEMARY?

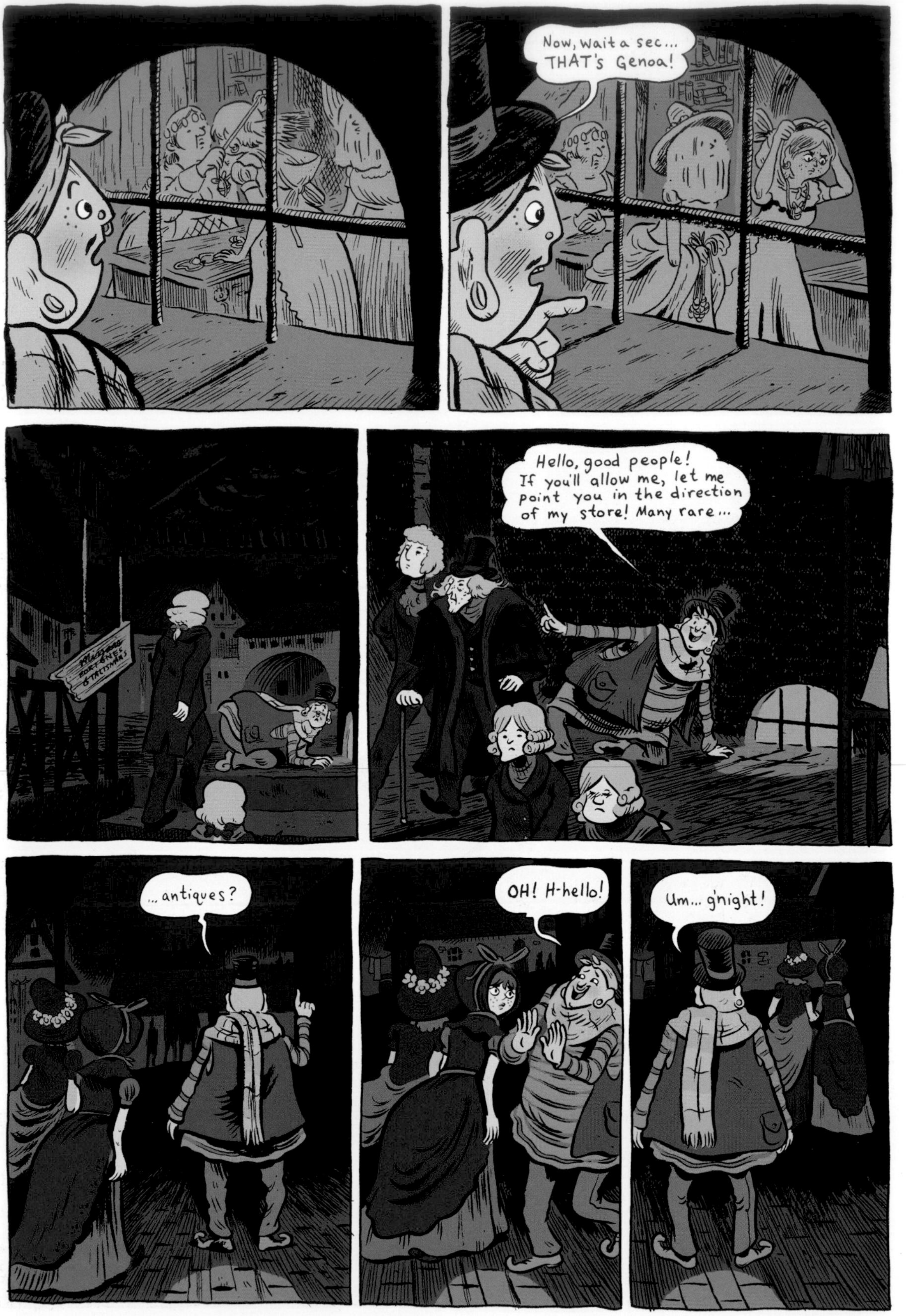
Now, wait a sec...
THAT's Genoa!
Hello, good people!
If you'll allow me, let me point you in the direction of my store! Many rare...
...antiques?
OH! H-hello!
Um... g'night!

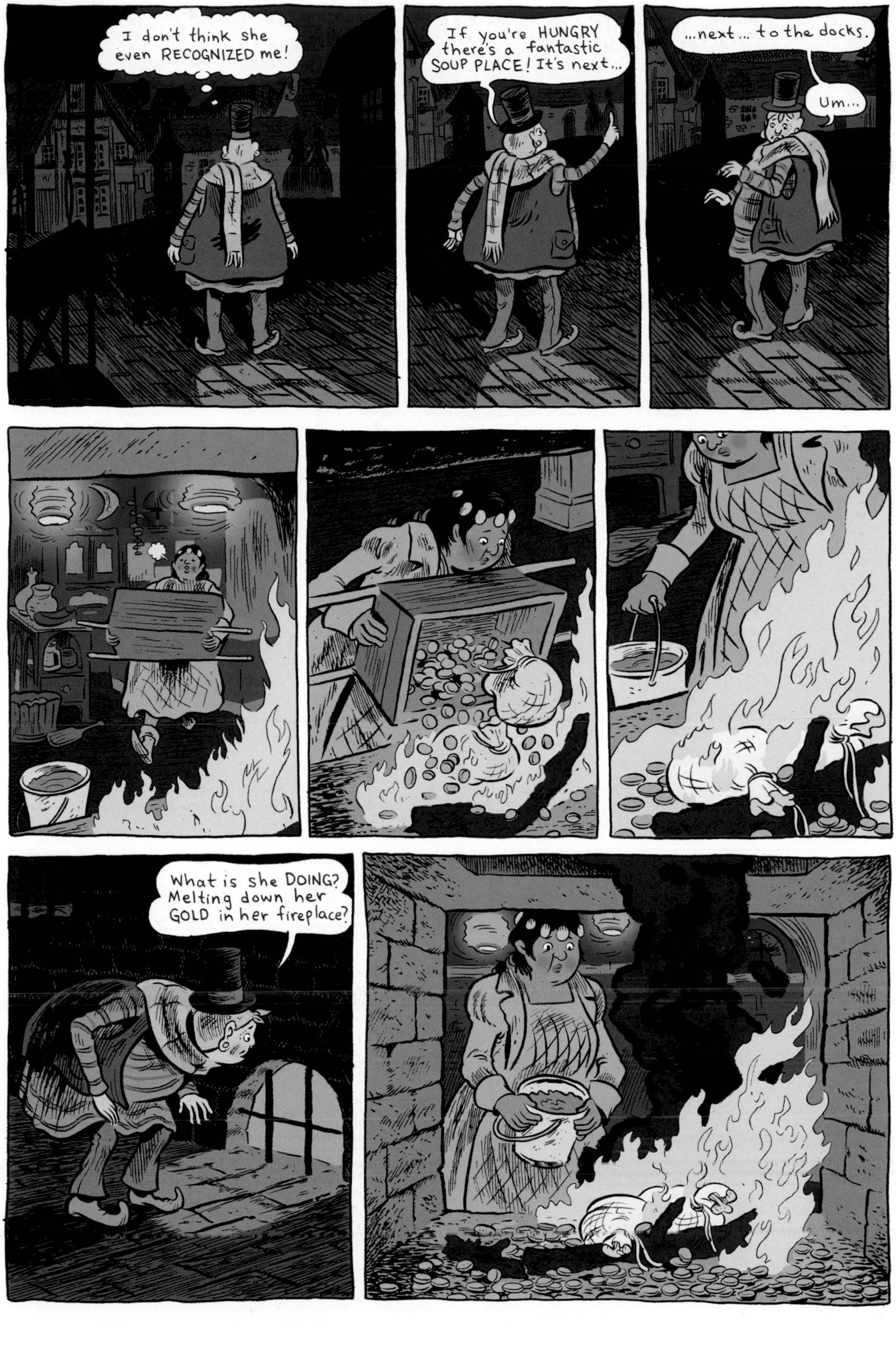
I don't think she even RECOGNIZED me!
If you're HUNGRY there's a fantastic SOUP PLACE! It's next...
...next... to the docks.
Um...
What is she DOING? Melting down her GOLD in her fireplace?

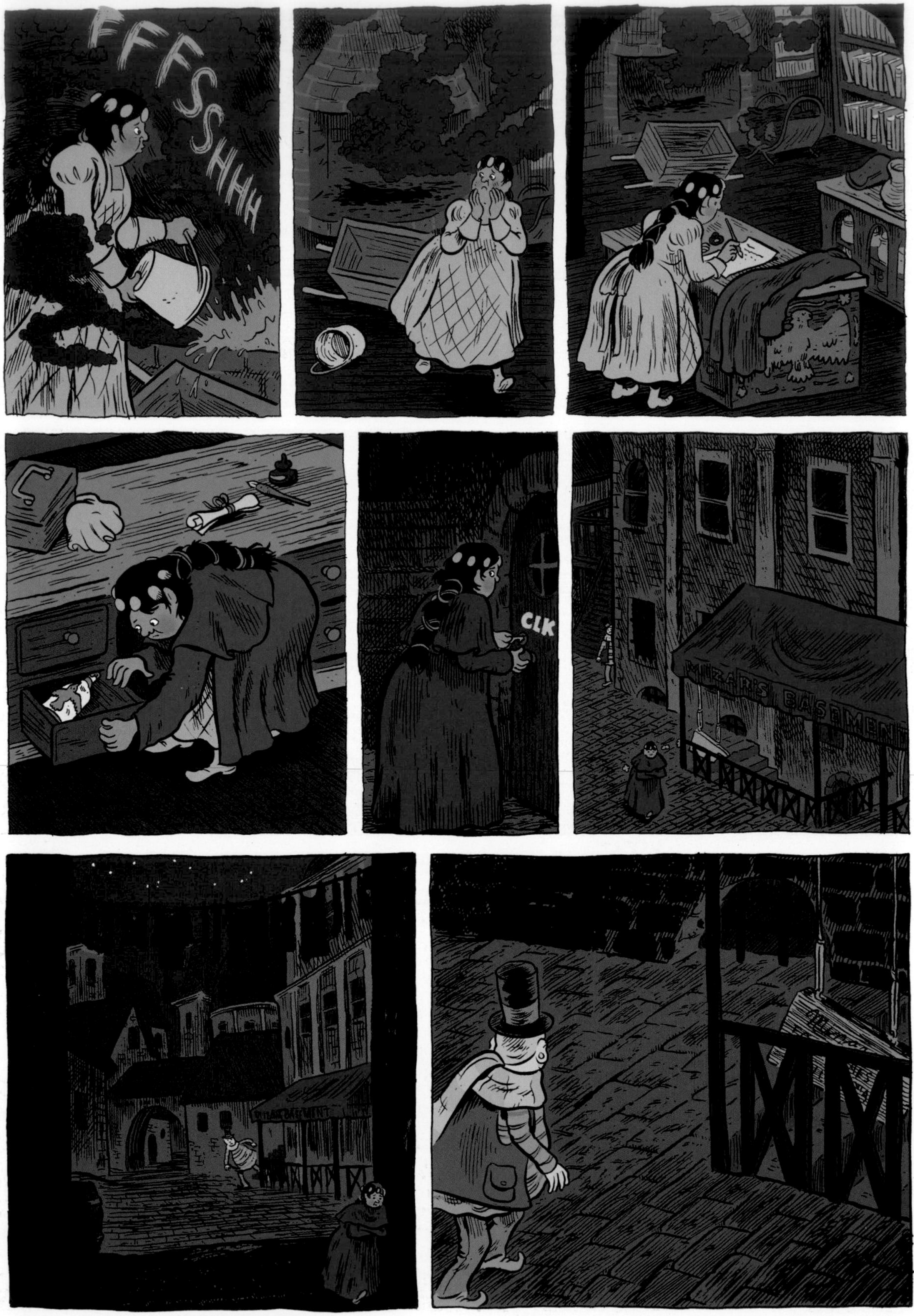
FFFSSHHH
CLK
MIZAR'S

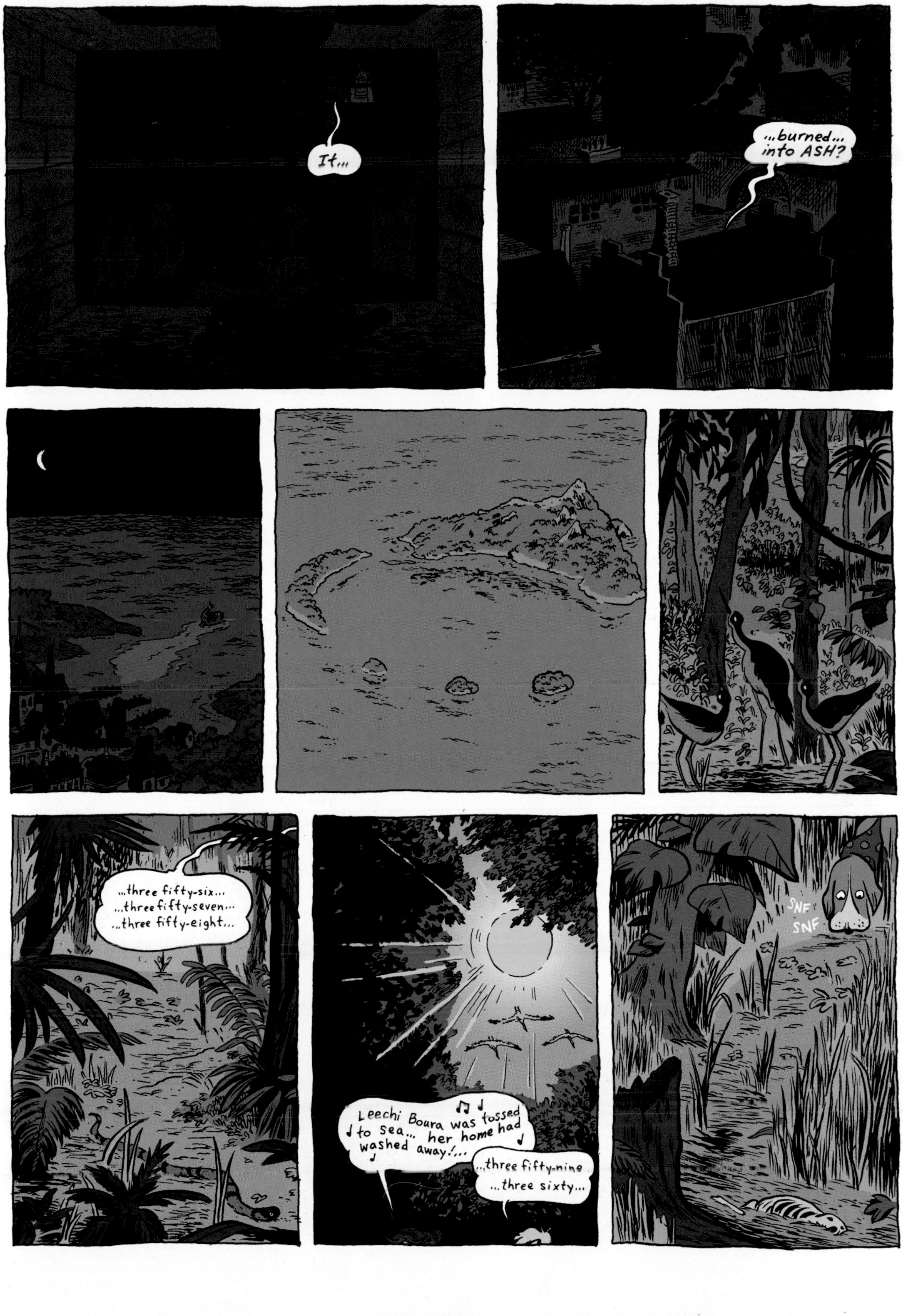
It...
...burned... into ASH?
...three fifty-six... ...three fifty-seven... ...three fifty-eight...
Leechi Boura was tossed to sea... her home had washed away!...
...three fifty-nine ...three sixty...
SNF SNF

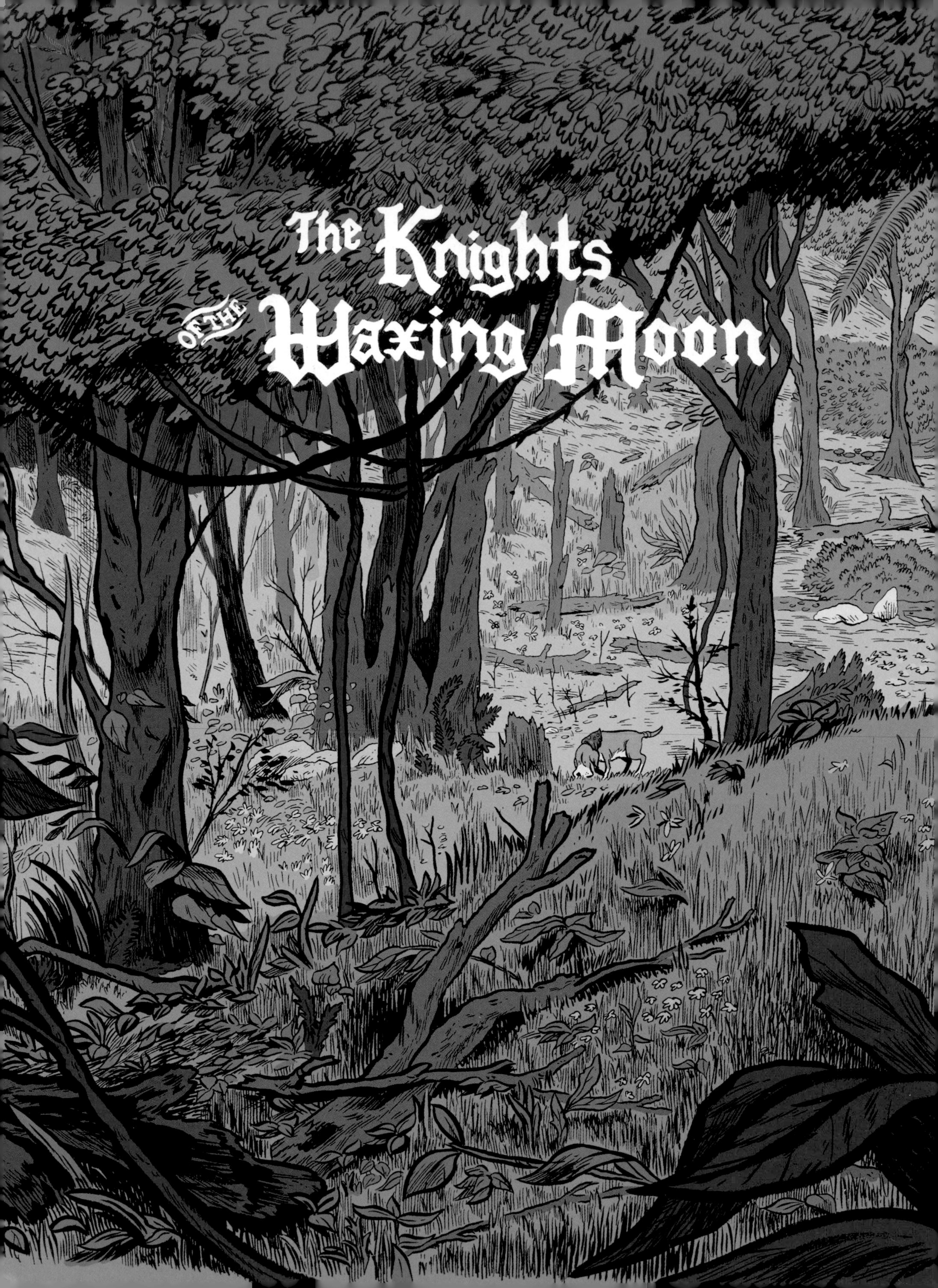
The Knights of the Waxing Moon

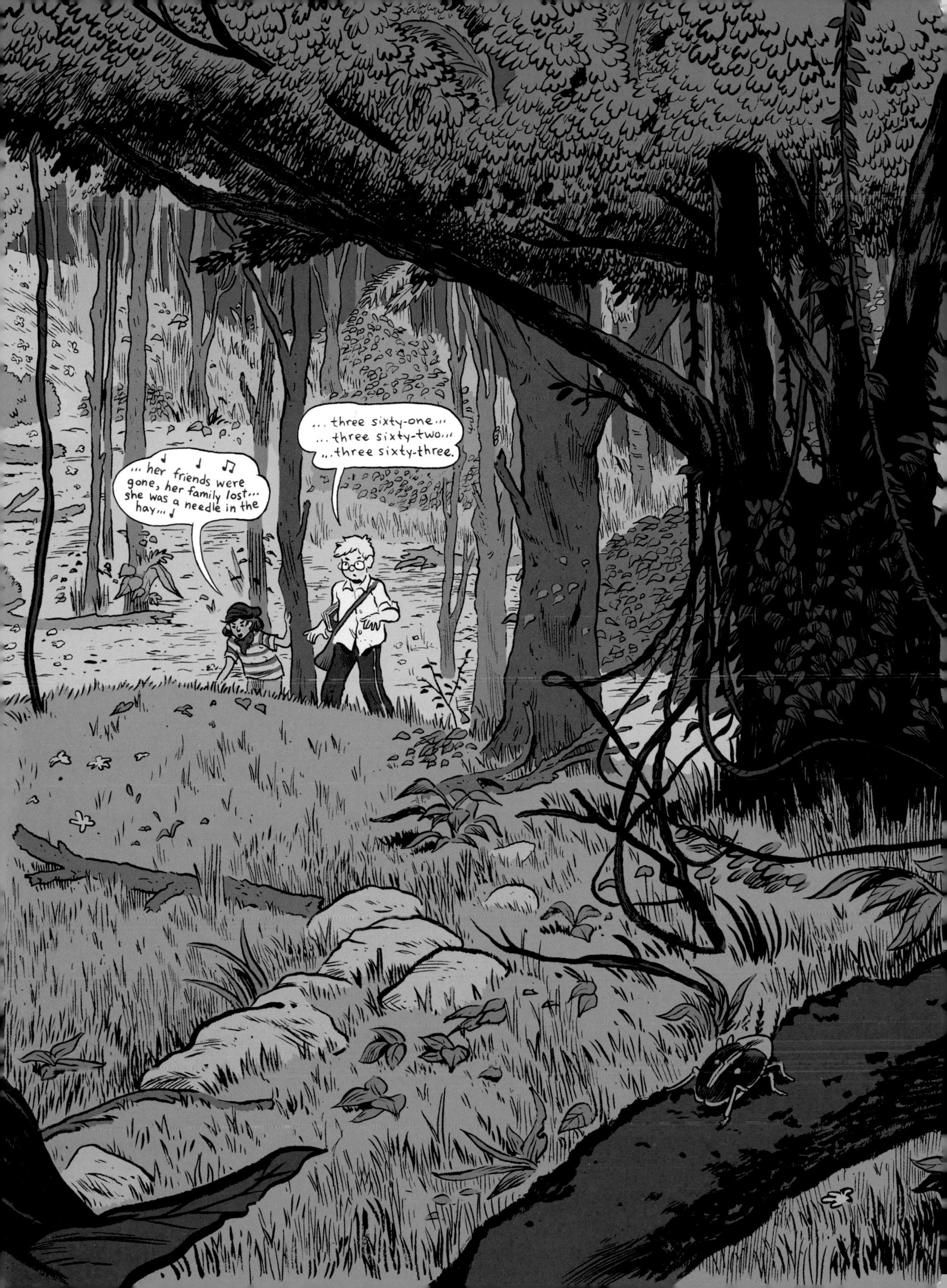
... her friends were gone, her family lost... she was a needle in the hay...
... three sixty-one... ... three sixty-two... ...three sixty-three.

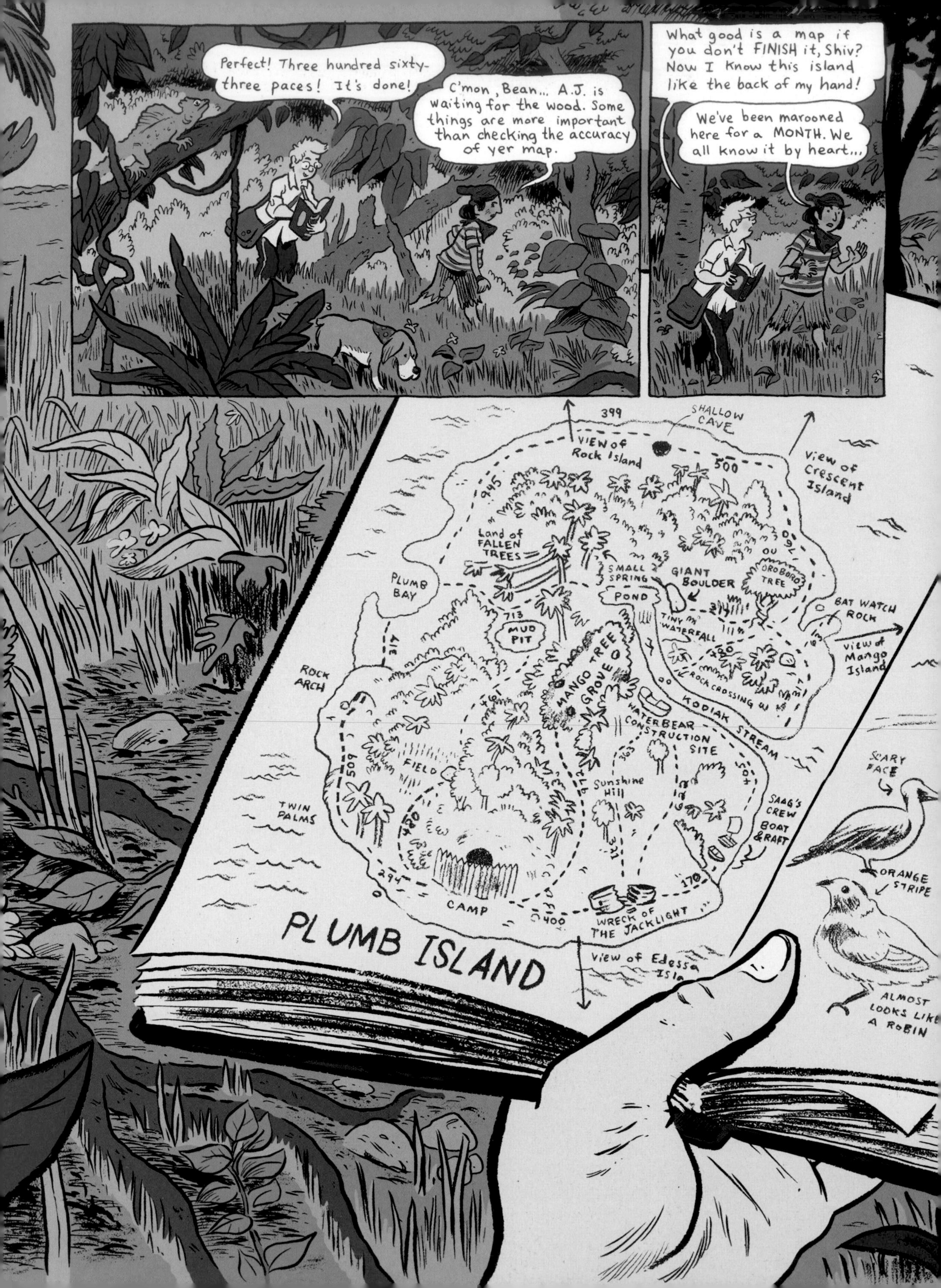
Perfect! Three hundred sixty-three paces! It's done!
C'mon, Bean... A.J. is waiting for the wood. Some things are more important than checking the accuracy of yer map.
What good is a map if you don't FINISH it, Shiv? Now I know this island like the back of my hand!
We've been marooned here for a MONTH. We all know it by heart...
399
SHALLOW CAVE
VIEW of Rock Island
500
View of Crescent Island
945
Land of FALLEN TREES
SMALL SPRING
GIANT BOULDER
OROBORO TREE
PLUMB BAY
POND
713
MUD PIT
TINY WATERFALL
BAT WATCH ROCK
View of Mango Island
MANGO TREE GROVE
ROCK CROSSING
KODIAK STREAM
ROCK ARCH
WATERBEAR CONSTRUCTION SITE
363
509
FIELD
Sunshine Hill
SAAG'S CREW
BOAT &RAFT
TWIN PALMS
420
294
170
CAMP
400
WRECK OF THE JACKLIGHT
PLUMB ISLAND
View of Edessa Isla
SCARY FACE
ORANGE STRIPE
ALMOST LOOKS LIKE A ROBIN

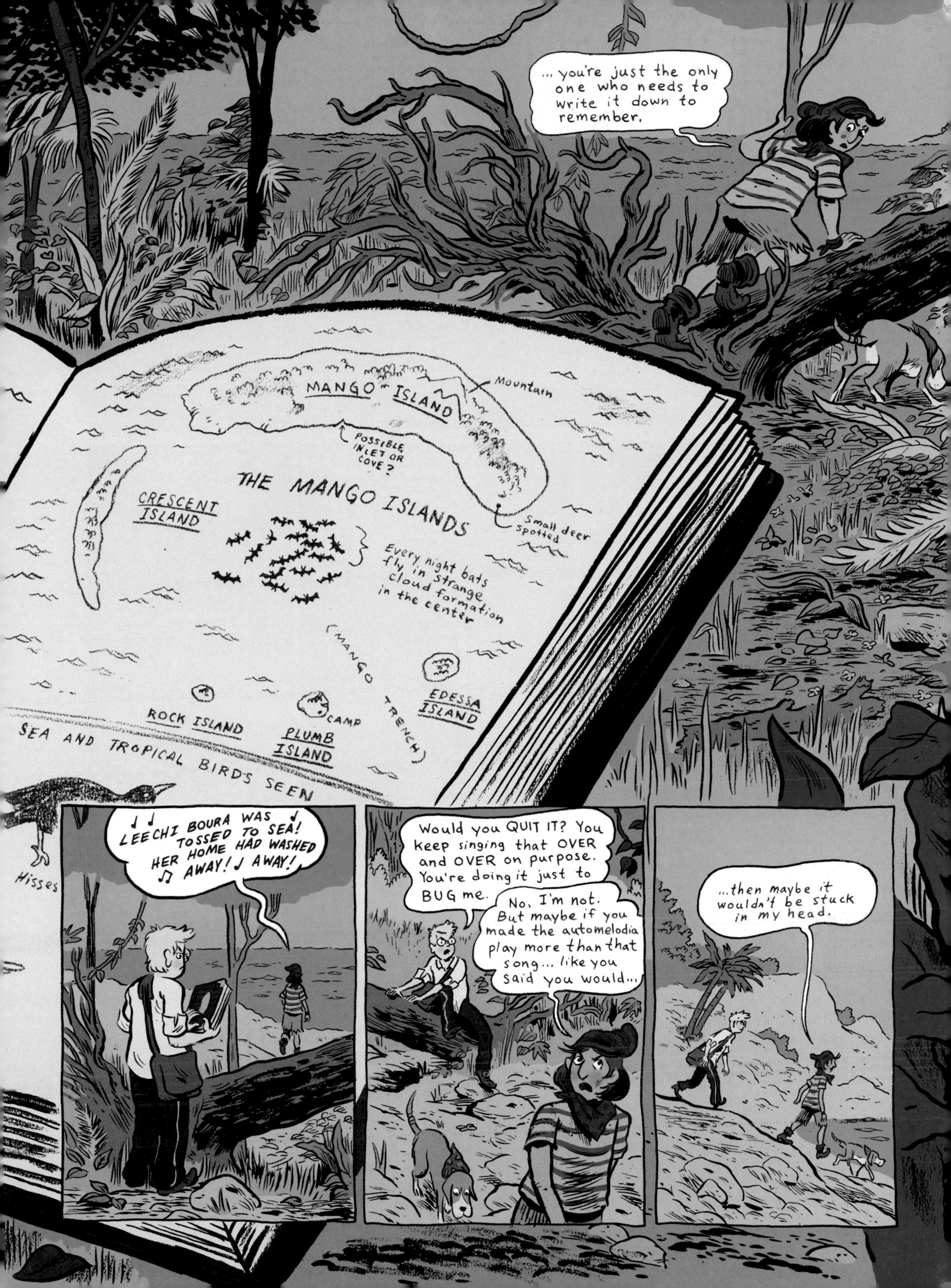
...you're just the only one who needs to write it down to remember.
MANGO ISLAND
Mountain
POSSIBLE INLET OR COVE?
THE MANGO ISLANDS
CRESCENT ISLAND
Small deer spotted
Every night bats fly in strange cloud formation in the center
(MANGO TRENCH)
EDESSA ISLAND
CAMP
ROCK ISLAND
PLUMB ISLAND
SEA AND TROPICAL BIRDS SEEN
Hisses
LEECHI BOURA WAS TOSSED TO SEA! HER HOME HAD WASHED AWAY! AWAY!
Would you QUIT IT? You keep singing that OVER and OVER on purpose. You're doing it just to BUG me.
No, I'm not. But maybe if you made the automelodia play more than that song... like you said you would...
...then maybe it wouldn't be stuck in my head.

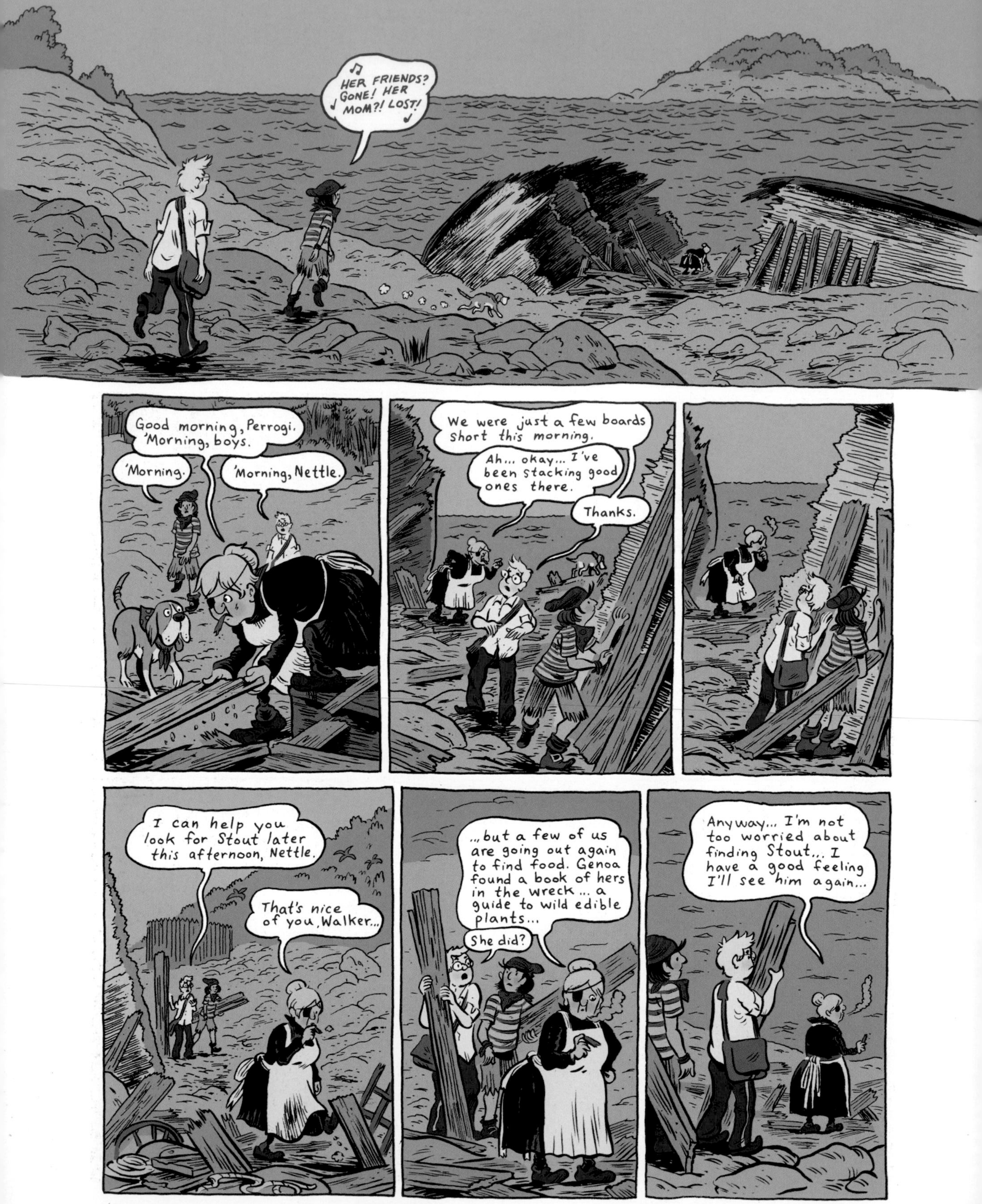
HER FRIENDS? GONE! HER MOM?! LOST!
Good morning, Perrogi. 'Morning, boys.
'Morning.
'Morning, Nettle.
We were just a few boards short this morning.
Ah... okay... I've been stacking good ones there.
Thanks.
I can help you look for Stout later this afternoon, Nettle.
That's nice of you, Walker...
...but a few of us are going out again to find food. Genoa found a book of hers in the wreck... a guide to wild edible plants...
She did?
Anyway... I'm not too worried about finding Stout... I have a good feeling I'll see him again...

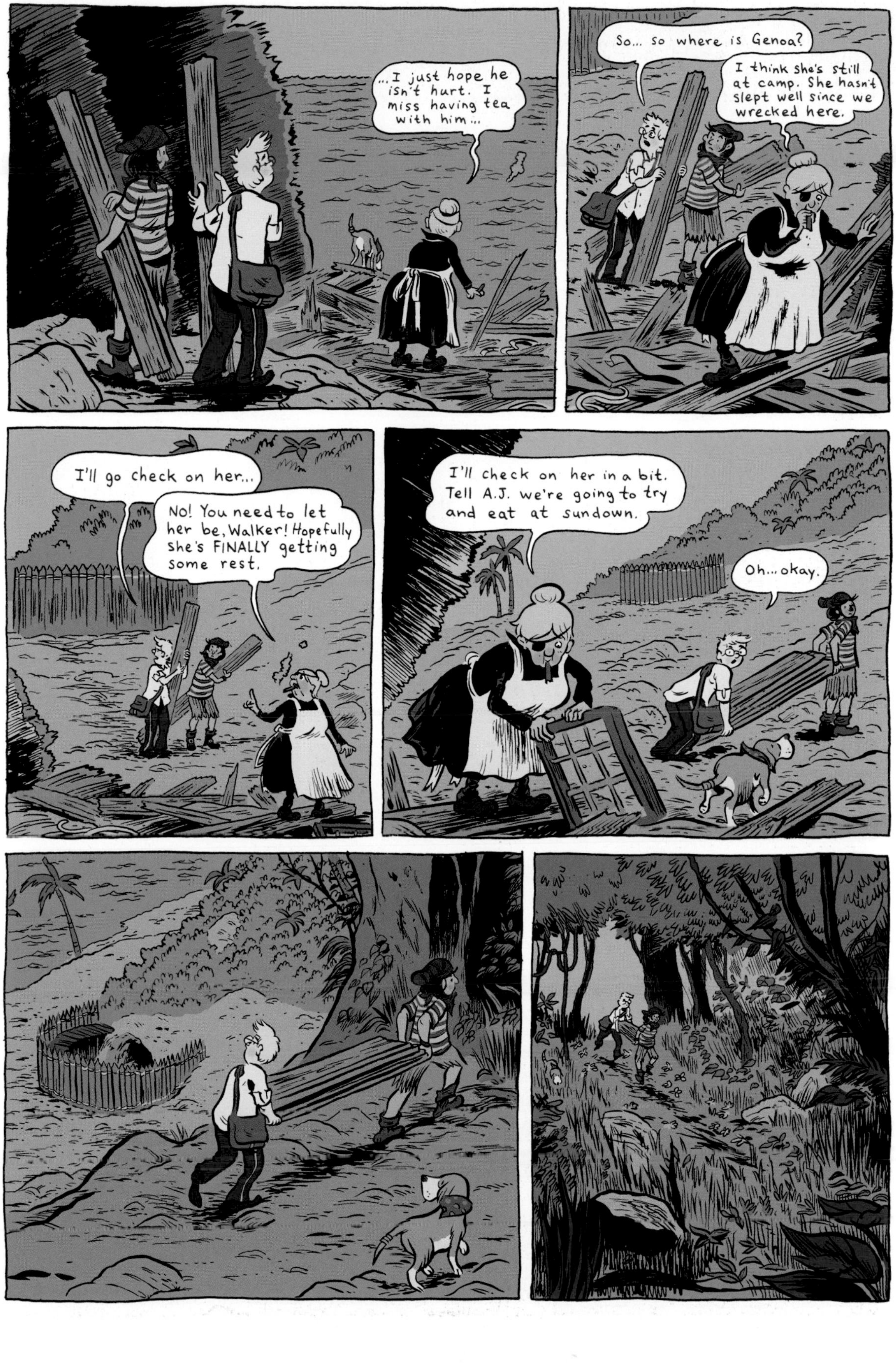
...I just hope he isn't hurt. I miss having tea with him...
So... so where is Genoa?
I think she's still at camp. She hasn't slept well since we wrecked here.
I'll go check on her...
No! You need to let her be, Walker! Hopefully she's FINALLY getting some rest.
I'll check on her in a bit. Tell A.J. we're going to try and eat at sundown.
Oh... okay.

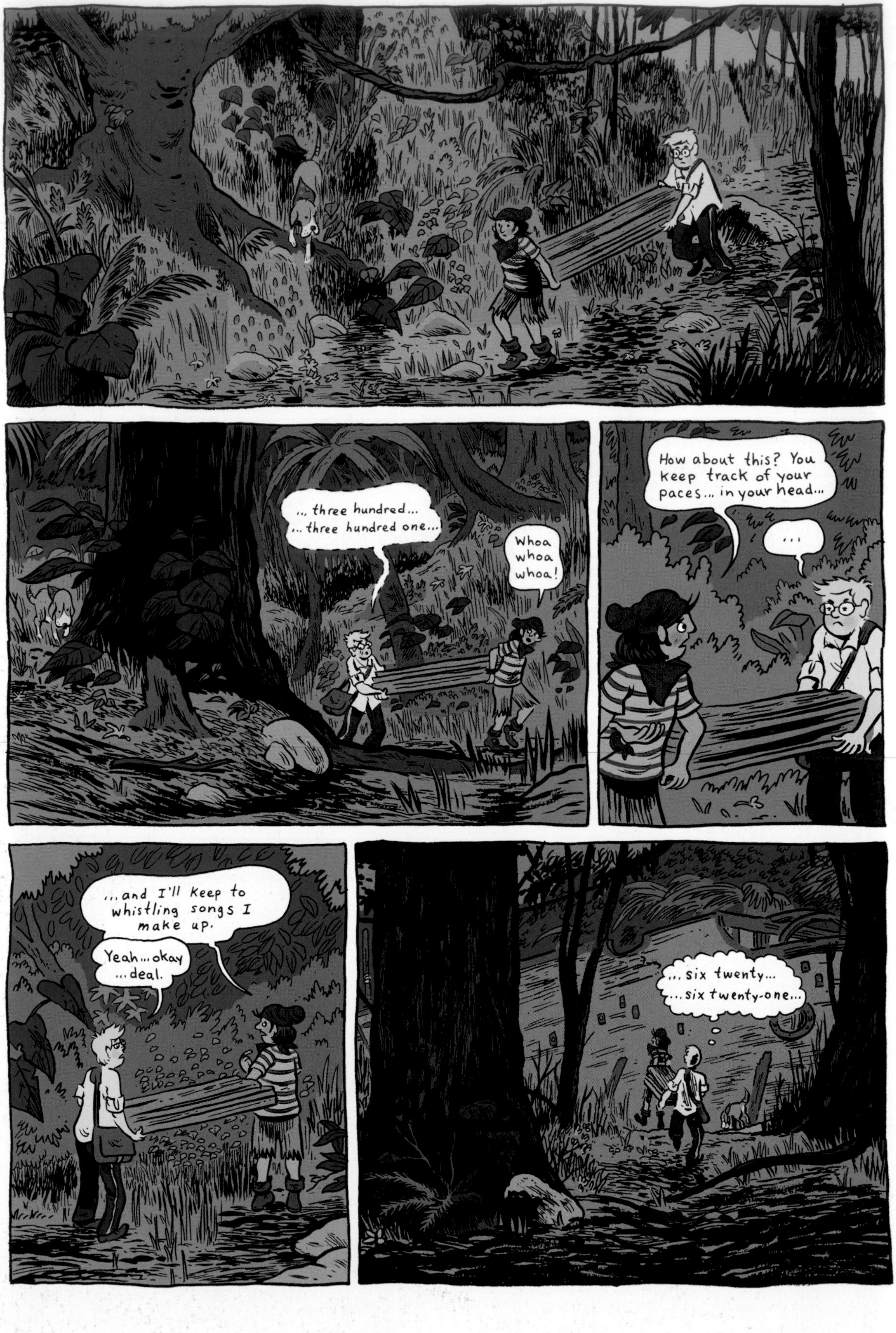

... three hundred...
... three hundred one...
Whoa whoa whoa!
How about this? You keep track of your paces... in your head...
...
...and I'll keep to whistling songs I make up.
Yeah... okay ...deal.
... six twenty...
... six twenty-one...

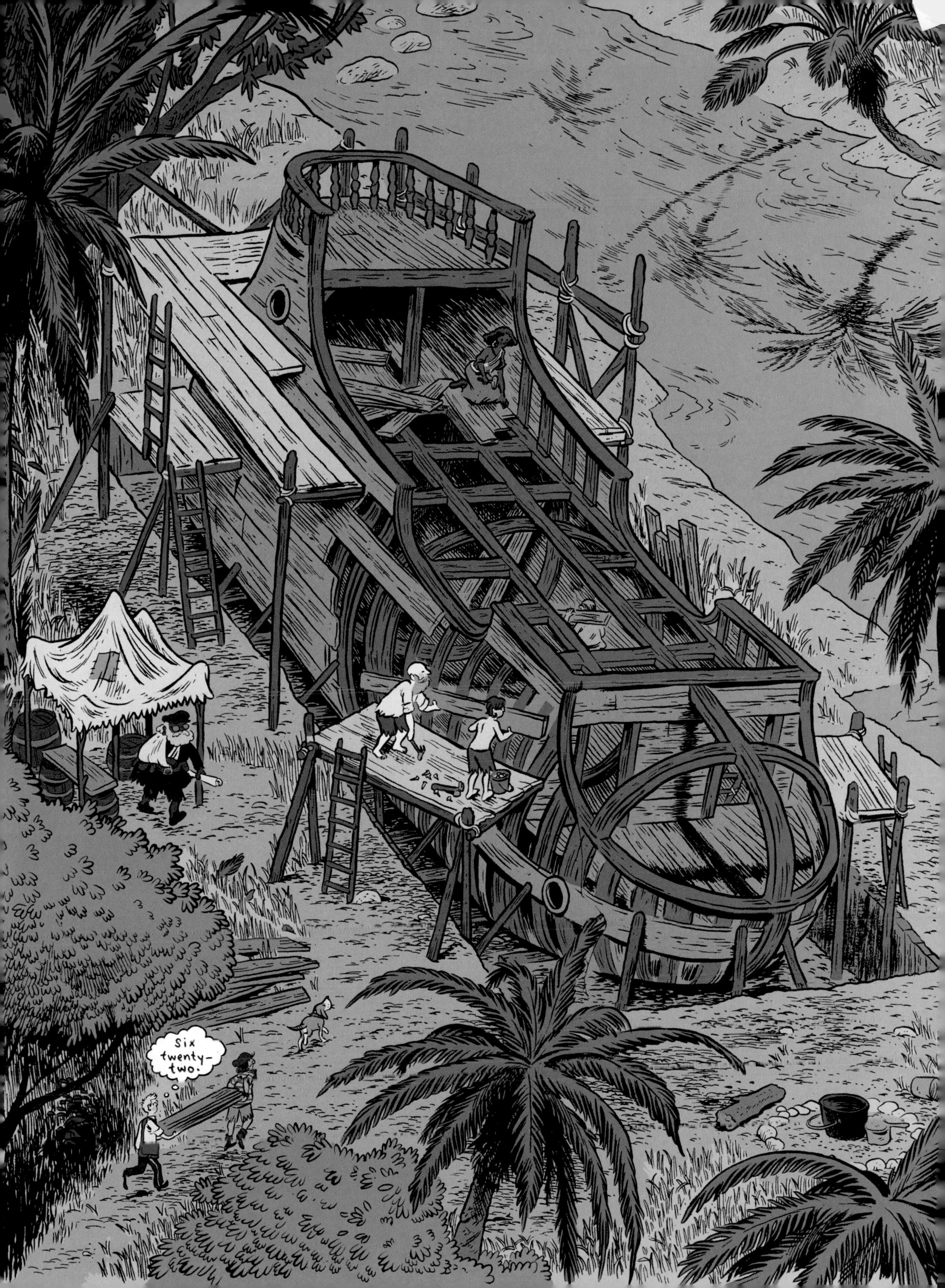
Six twenty-two.

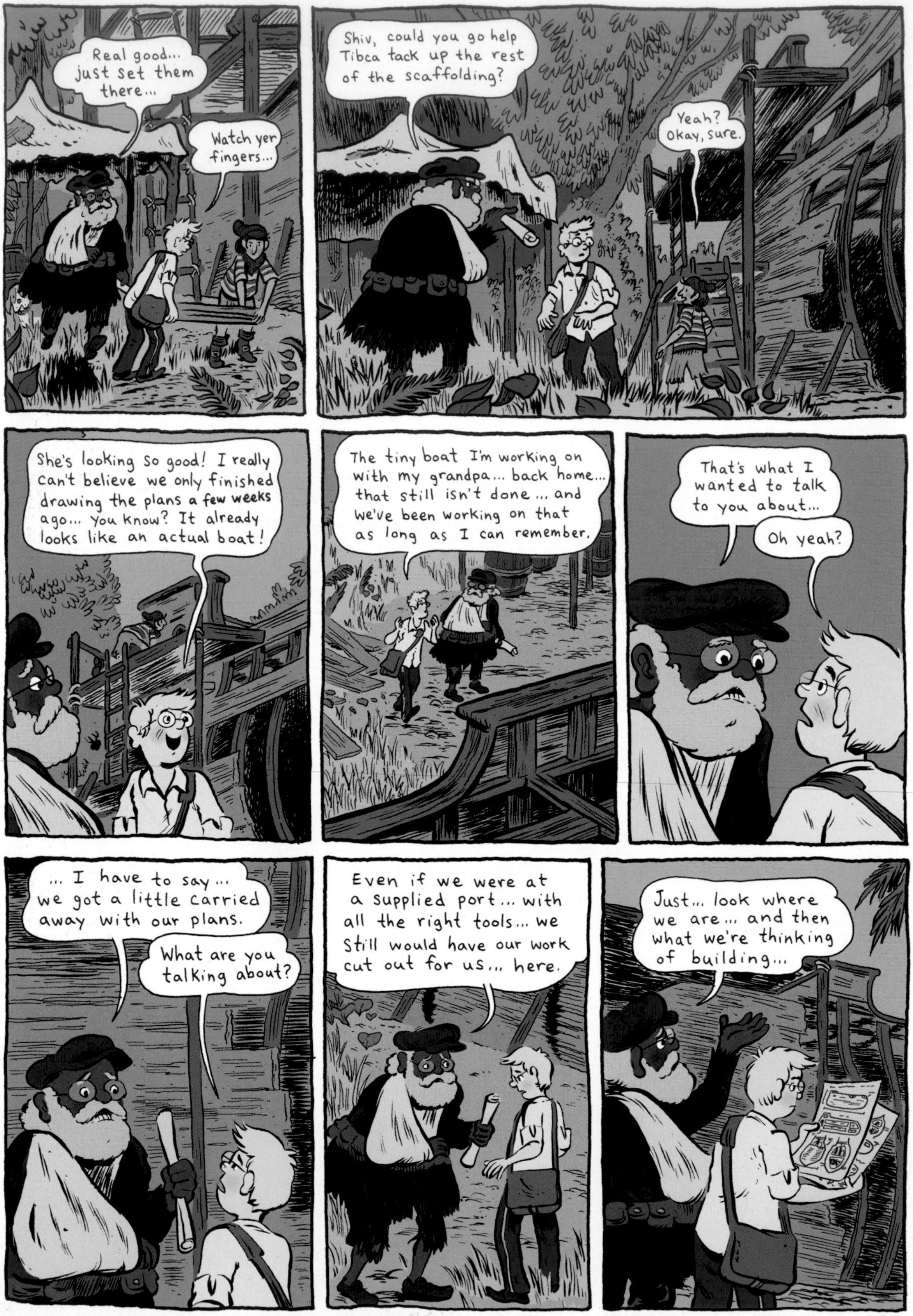
Real good... just set them there...
Watch yer fingers...
Shiv, could you go help Tibca tack up the rest of the scaffolding?
Yeah? Okay, sure.
She's looking so good! I really can't believe we only finished drawing the plans a few weeks ago... You know? It already looks like an actual boat!
The tiny boat I'm working on with my grandpa... back home... that still isn't done... and we've been working on that as long as I can remember.
That's what I wanted to talk to you about...
Oh yeah?
... I have to say... we got a little carried away with our plans.
What are you talking about?
Even if we were at a supplied port... with all the right tools... we still would have our work cut out for us... here.
Just... look where we are... and then what we're thinking of building...

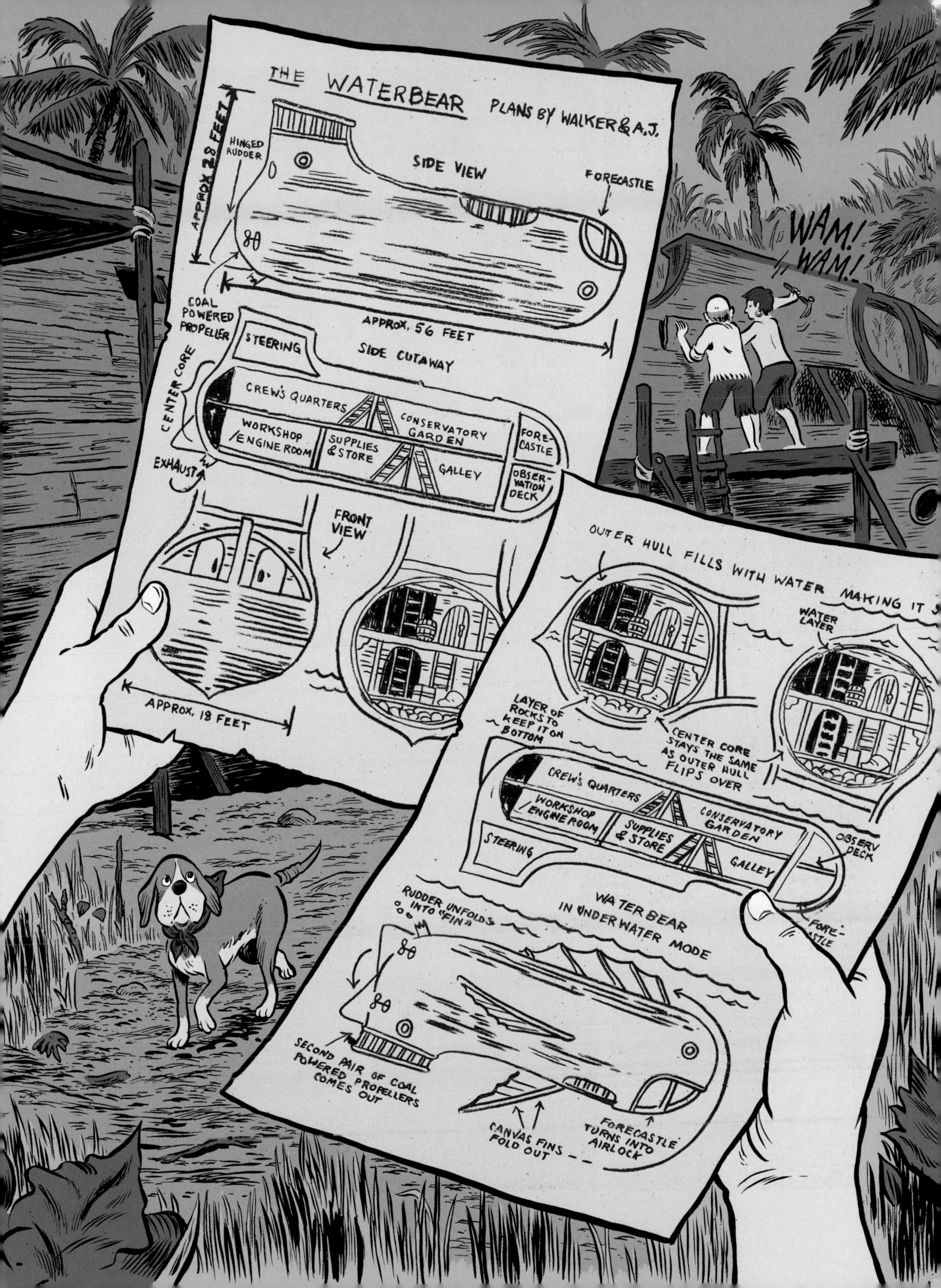
THE WATERBEAR PLANS BY WALKER & A.J.
HINGED RUDDER
APPROX. 28 FEET
SIDE VIEW
FORECASTLE
COAL POWERED PROPELLER
APPROX. 56 FEET
STEERING
SIDE CUTAWAY
CENTER CORE
CREW'S QUARTERS
WORKSHOP /ENGINE ROOM
SUPPLIES & STORE
CONSERVATORY GARDEN
GALLEY
FORE-CASTLE
OBSERVATION DECK
EXHAUST
FRONT VIEW
APPROX. 18 FEET
WAM! WAM!
OUTER HULL FILLS WITH WATER MAKING IT S
WATER LAYER
LAYER OF ROCKS TO KEEP IT ON BOTTOM
CENTER CORE STAYS THE SAME AS OUTER HULL FLIPS OVER
CREW'S QUARTERS
WORKSHOP /ENGINE ROOM
SUPPLIES & STORE
CONSERVATORY GARDEN
STEERING
GALLEY
OBSERV DECK
FORE-CASTLE
WATERBEAR IN UNDERWATER MODE
RUDDER UNFOLDS INTO "FIN"
SECOND PAIR OF COAL POWERED PROPELLERS COMES OUT
CANVAS FINS FOLD OUT
FORECASTLE TURNS INTO AIRLOCK

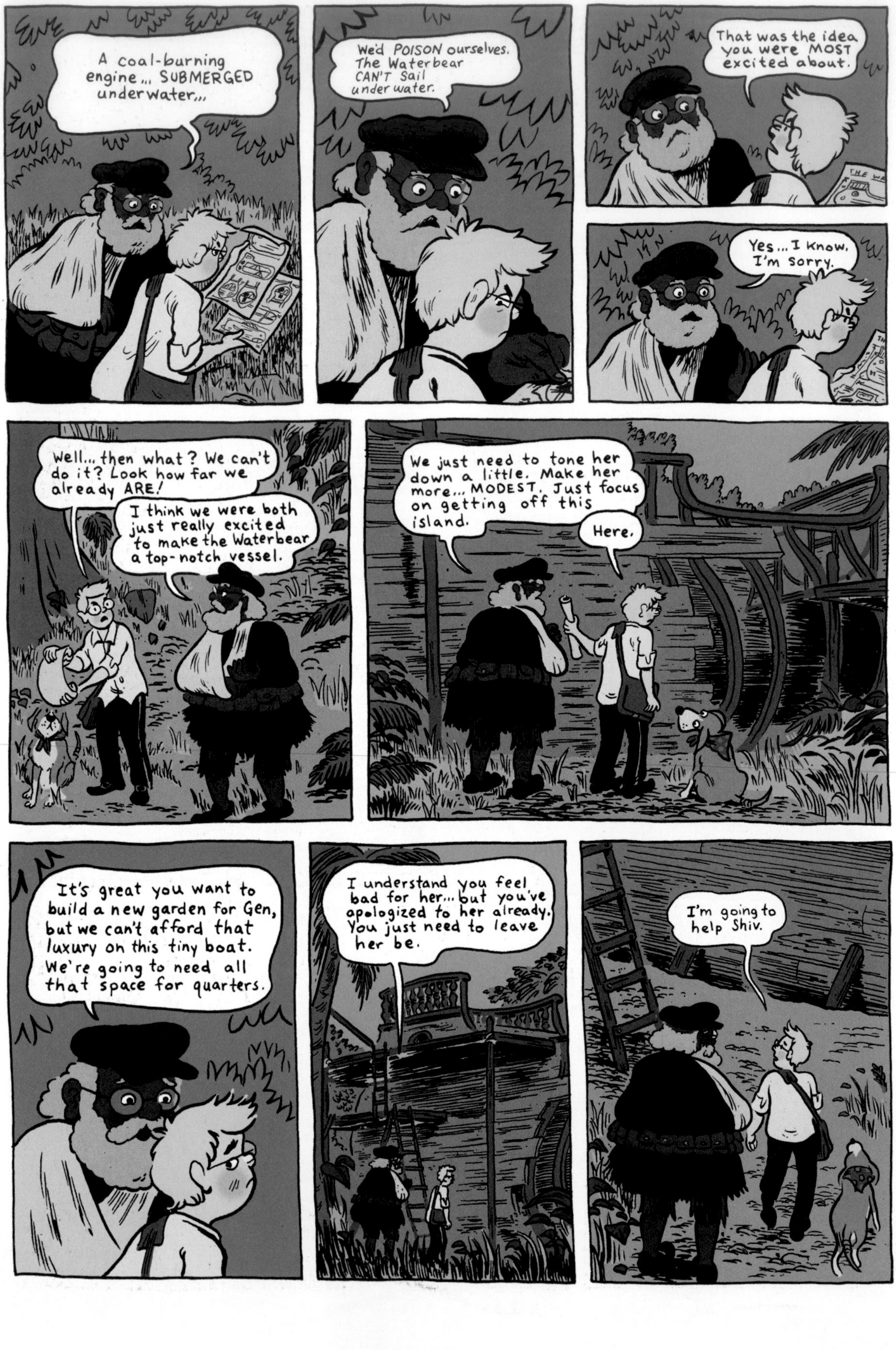

A coal-burning engine... SUBMERGED underwater...
We'd POISON ourselves. The Waterbear CAN'T Sail underwater.
That was the idea you were MOST excited about.
Yes... I know. I'm sorry.
Well... then what? We can't do it? Look how far we already ARE!
I think we were both just really excited to make the Waterbear a top-notch vessel.
We just need to tone her down a little. Make her more... MODEST. Just focus on getting off this island.
Here.
It's great you want to build a new garden for Gen, but we can't afford that luxury on this tiny boat. We're going to need all that space for quarters.
I understand you feel bad for her... but you've apologized to her already. You just need to leave her be.
I'm going to help Shiv.

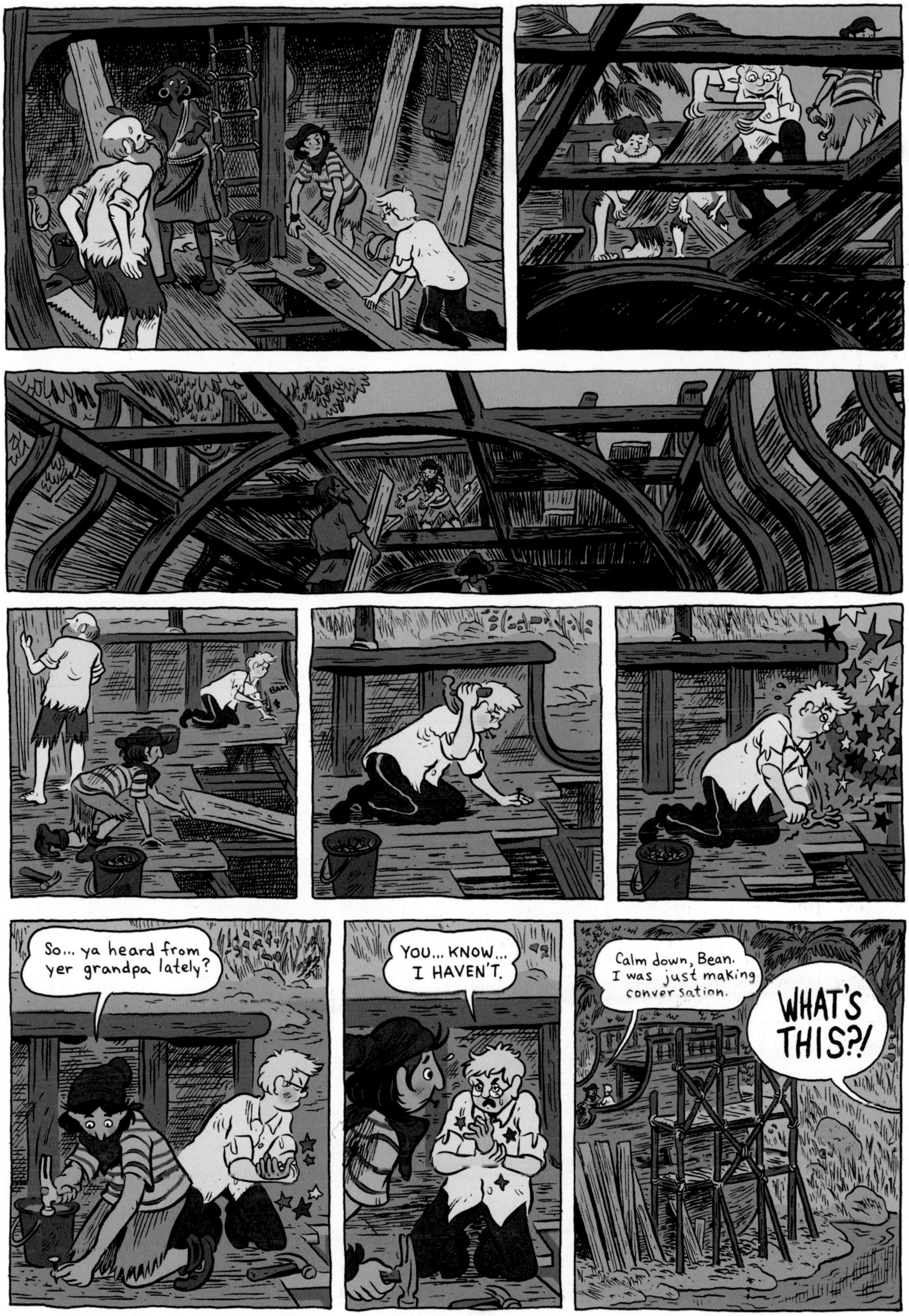
BAM
So... ya heard from yer grandpa lately?
YOU... KNOW... I HAVEN'T.
Calm down, Bean. I was just making conversation.
WHAT'S THIS?!

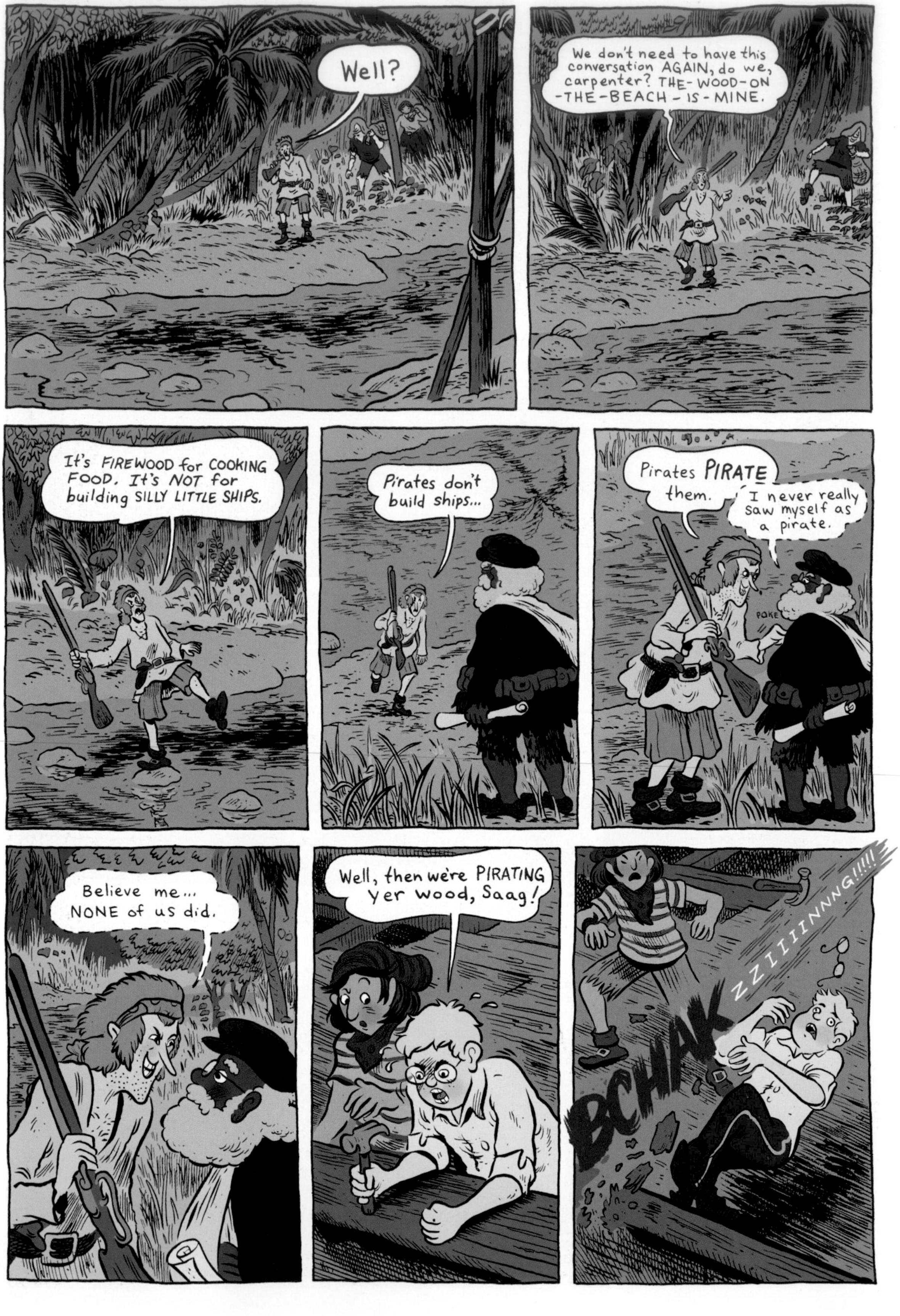
Well?
We don't need to have this conversation AGAIN, do we, carpenter? THE-WOOD-ON-THE-BEACH-IS-MINE.
It's FIREWOOD for COOKING FOOD. It's NOT for building SILLY LITTLE SHIPS.
Pirates don't build ships...
Pirates PIRATE them.
I never really saw myself as a pirate.
POKE
Believe me... NONE of us did.
Well, then we're PIRATING yer wood, Saag!
BCHAK
ZZIIIINNNG!!!!!

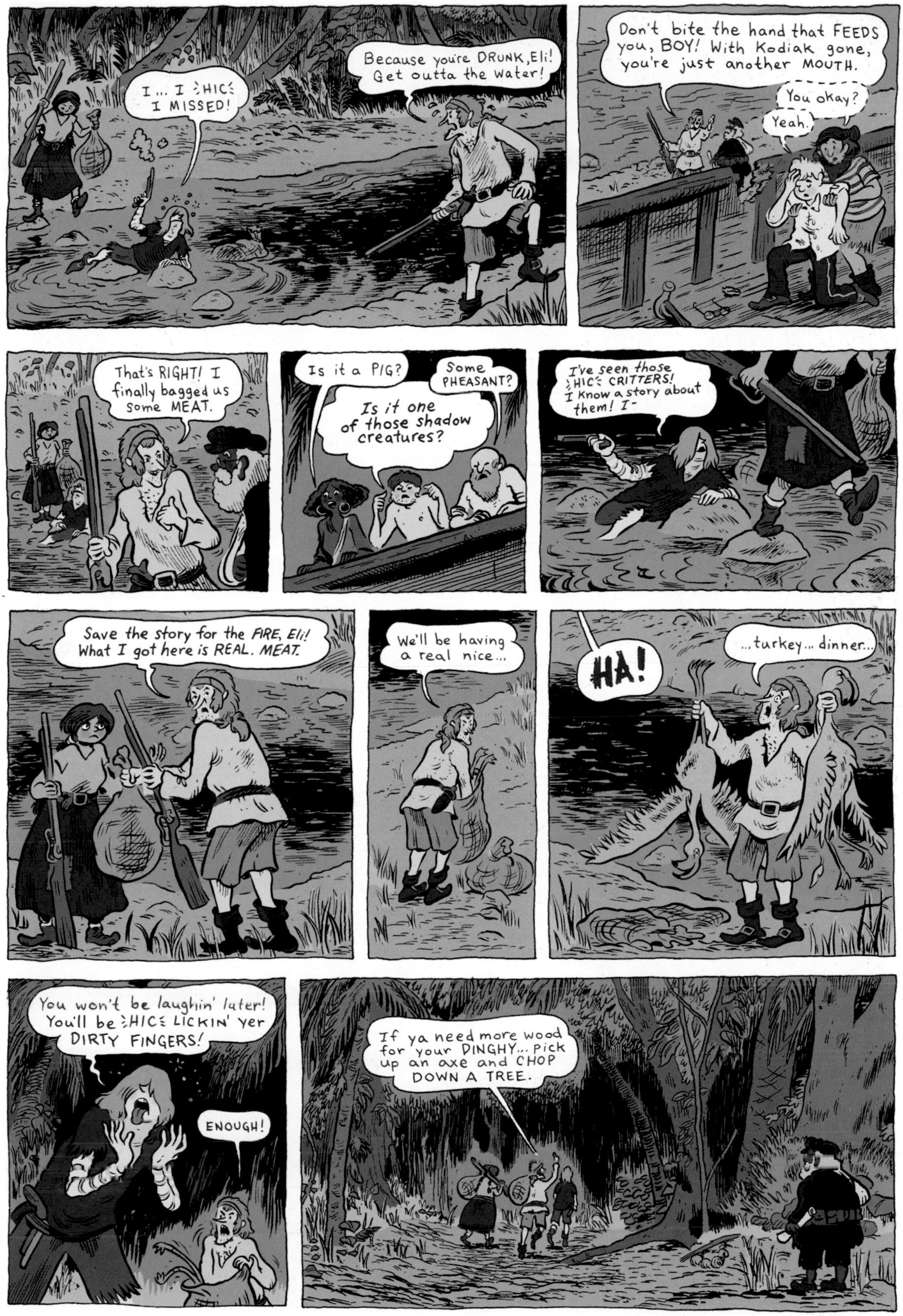
I... I HIC I MISSED!
Because you're DRUNK, Eli! Get outta the water!
Don't bite the hand that FEEDS you, BOY! With Kodiak gone, you're just another MOUTH.
You okay?
Yeah.
That's RIGHT! I finally bagged us some MEAT.
Is it a PIG?
Some PHEASANT?
Is it one of those shadow creatures?
I've seen those HIC CRITTERS! I know a story about them! I-
Save the story for the FIRE, Eli! What I got here is REAL. MEAT.
We'll be having a real nice...
HA!
...turkey... dinner...
You won't be laughin' later! You'll be HIC LICKIN' yer DIRTY FINGERS!
ENOUGH!
If ya need more wood for your DINGHY... pick up an axe and CHOP DOWN A TREE.

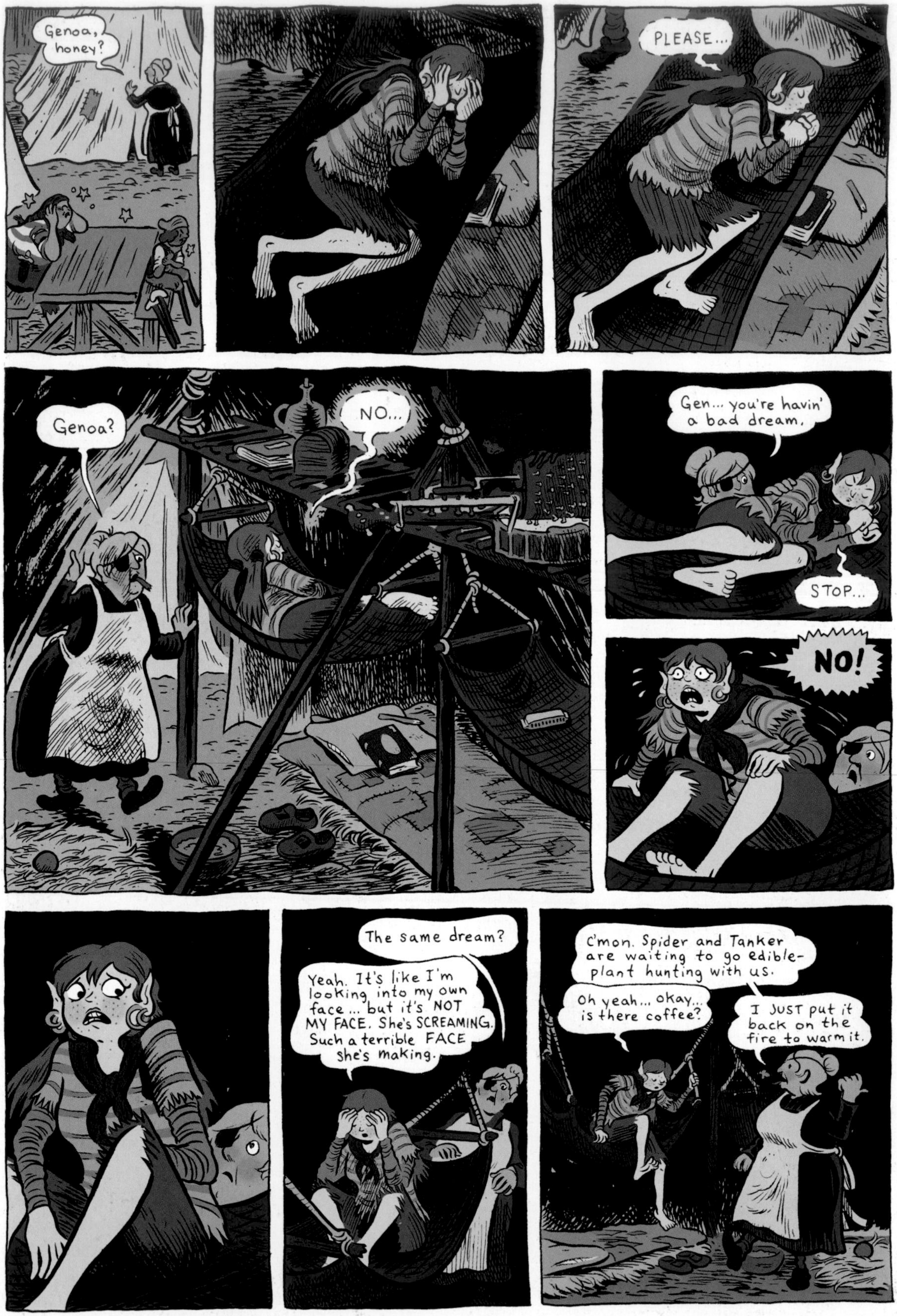
Genoa, honey?
PLEASE...
Genoa?
NO...
Gen... you're havin' a bad dream.
STOP...
NO!
The same dream?
Yeah. It's like I'm looking into my own face... but it's NOT MY FACE. She's SCREAMING. Such a terrible FACE she's making.
C'mon. Spider and Tanker are waiting to go edible-plant hunting with us.
Oh yeah... okay... is there coffee?
I JUST put it back on the fire to warm it.

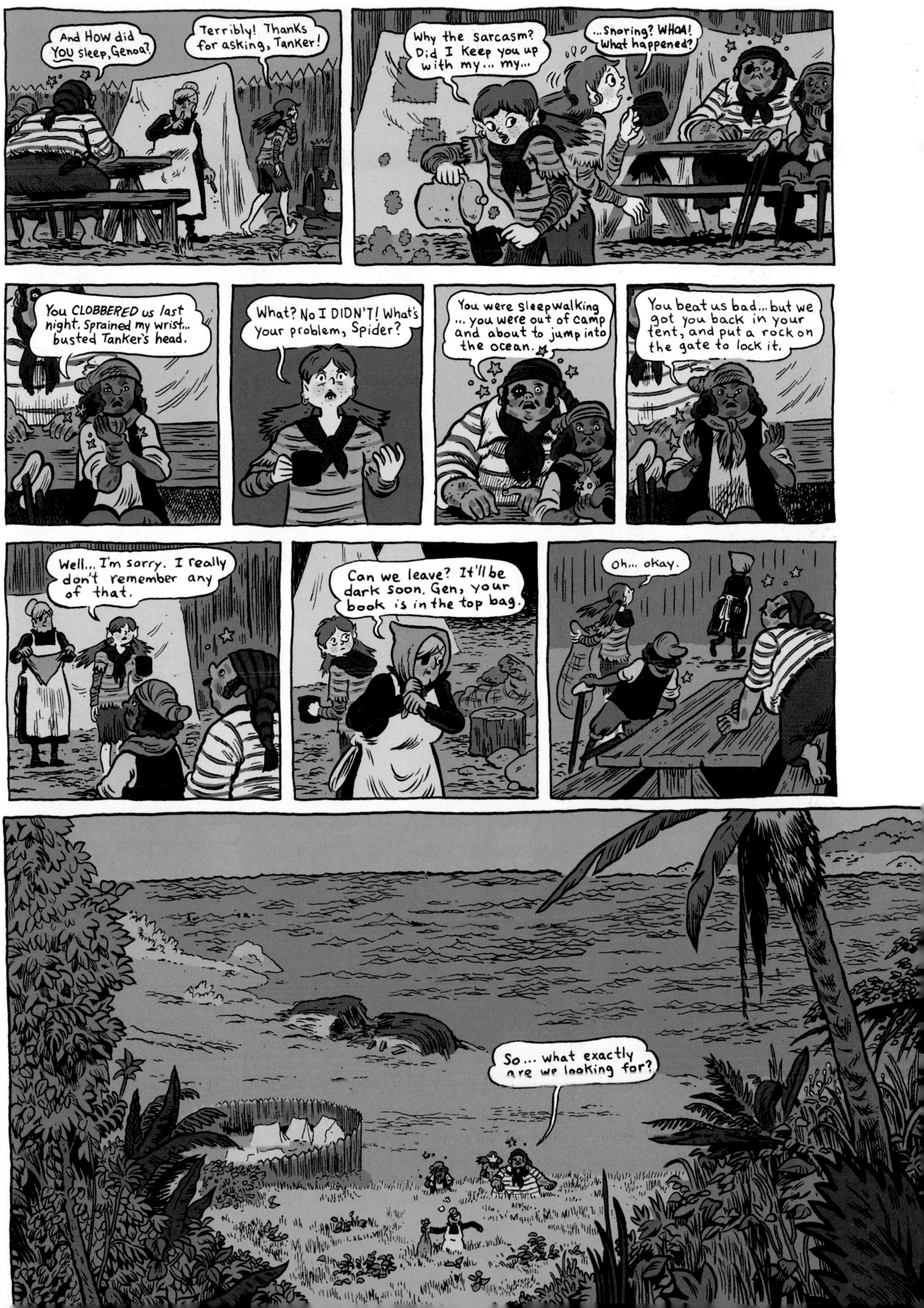
And HOW did YOU sleep, Genoa?
Terribly! Thanks for asking, Tanker!
Why the sarcasm? Did I keep you up with my... my...
...Snoring? WHOA! What happened?
You CLOBBERED us last night. Sprained my wrist... busted Tanker's head.
What? No I DIDN'T! What's your problem, Spider?
You were sleepwalking ... you were out of camp and about to jump into the ocean.
You beat us bad... but we got you back in your tent, and put a rock on the gate to lock it.
Well... I'm sorry. I really don't remember any of that.
Can we leave? It'll be dark soon. Gen, your book is in the top bag.
Oh... okay.
So... what exactly are we looking for?

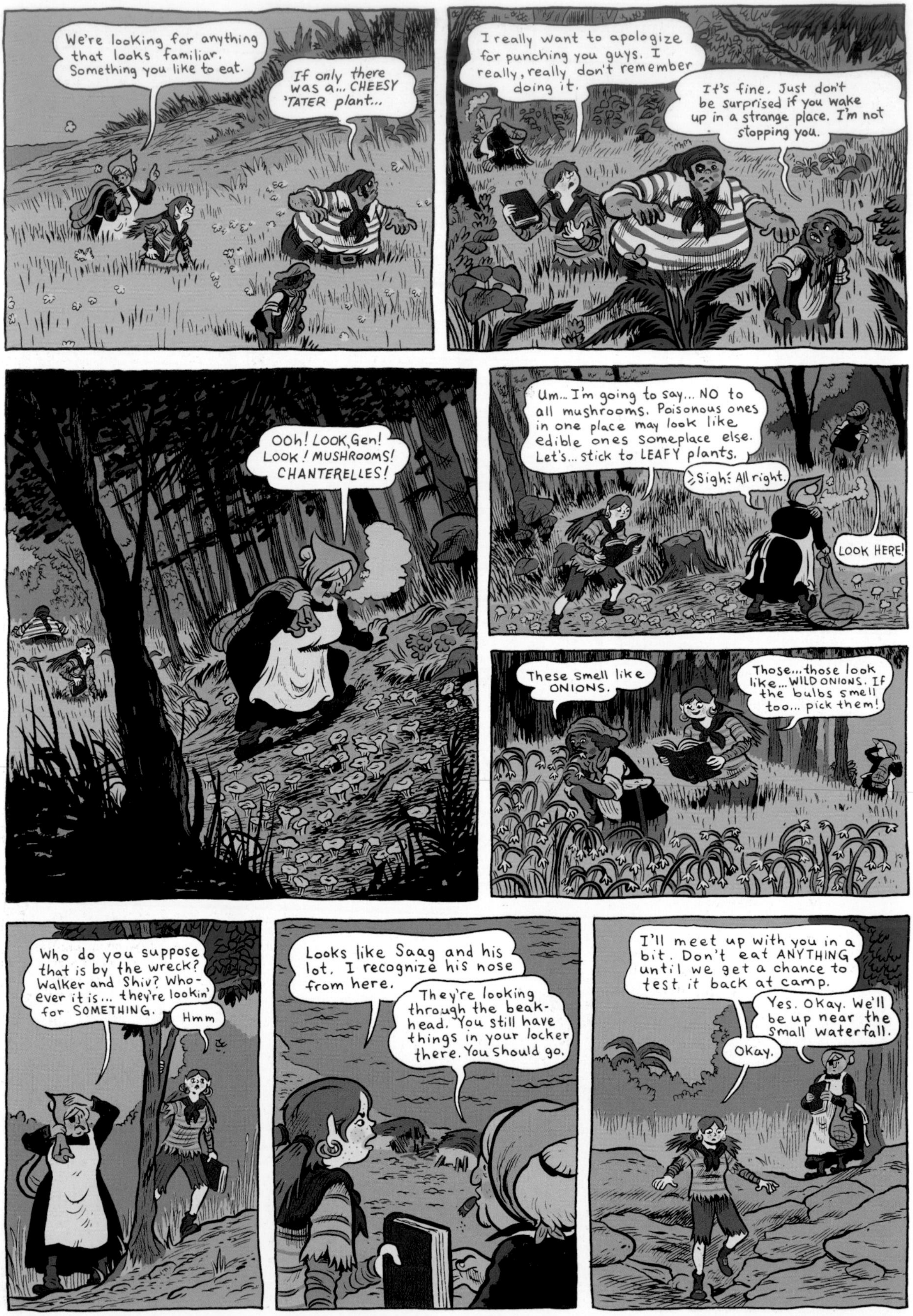
We're looking for anything that looks familiar. Something you like to eat.
If only there was a... CHEESY 'TATER plant...
I really want to apologize for punching you guys. I really, really don't remember doing it.
It's fine. Just don't be surprised if you wake up in a strange place. I'm not stopping you.
OOh! LOOK, Gen! LOOK! MUSHROOMS! CHANTERELLES!
Um... I'm going to say... NO to all mushrooms. Poisonous ones in one place may look like edible ones someplace else. Let's... stick to LEAFY plants.
Sigh: All right.
LOOK HERE!
These smell like ONIONS.
Those... those look like... WILD ONIONS. If the bulbs smell too... pick them!
Who do you suppose that is by the wreck? Walker and Shiv? Who-ever it is... they're lookin' for SOMETHING.
Hmm
Looks like Saag and his lot. I recognize his nose from here.
They're looking through the beak-head. You still have things in your locker there. You should go.
I'll meet up with you in a bit. Don't eat ANYTHING until we get a chance to test it back at camp.
Yes. Okay. We'll be up near the small waterfall.
Okay.

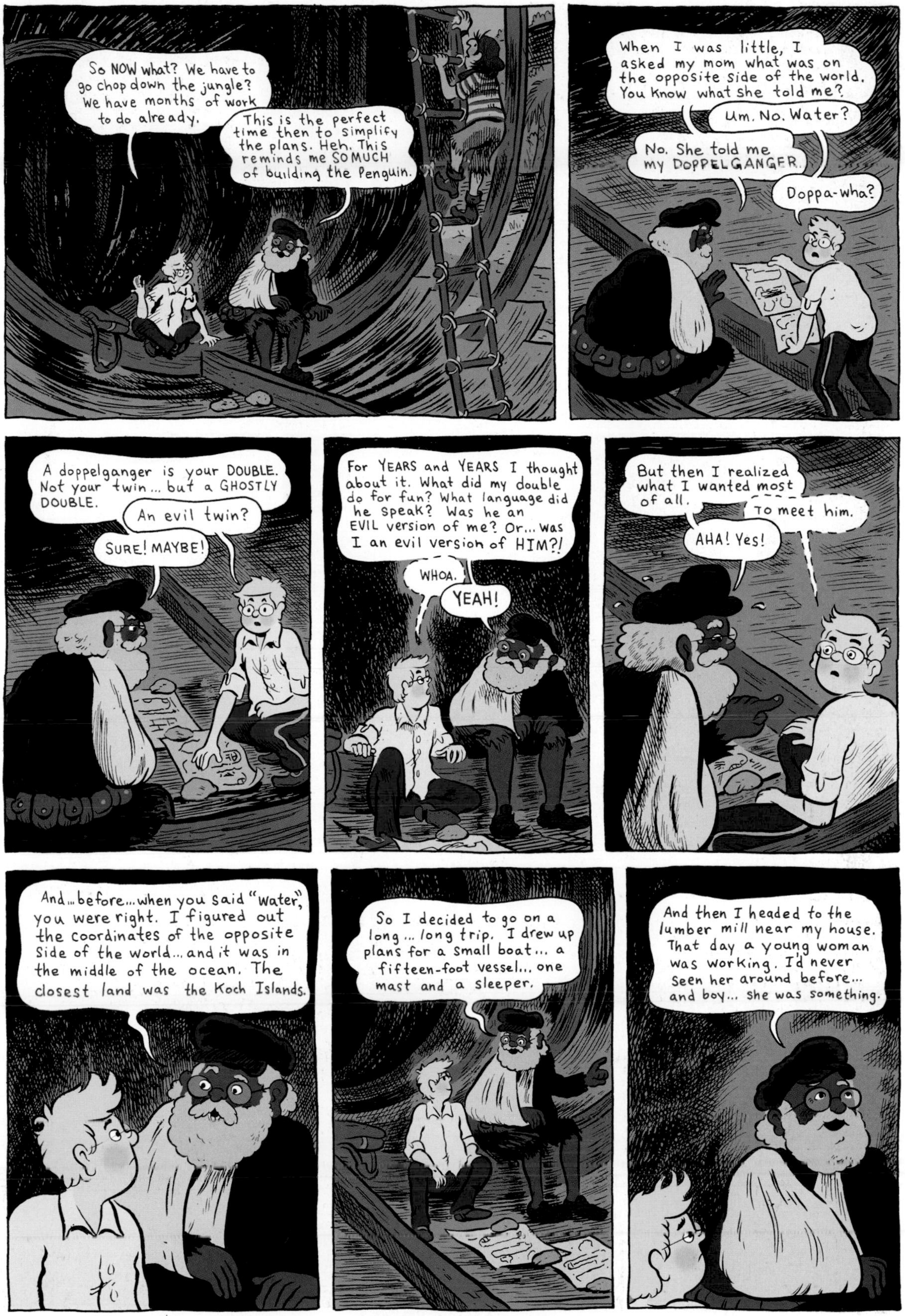
So NOW what? We have to go chop down the jungle? We have months of work to do already.
This is the perfect time then to simplify the plans. Heh. This reminds me SO MUCH of building the Penguin.
When I was little, I asked my mom what was on the opposite side of the world. You know what she told me?
Um. No. Water?
No. She told me my DOPPELGANGER.
Doppa-wha?
A doppelganger is your DOUBLE. Not your twin... but a GHOSTLY DOUBLE.
An evil twin?
SURE! MAYBE!
For YEARS and YEARS I thought about it. What did my double do for fun? What language did he speak? Was he an EVIL version of me? Or... was I an evil version of HIM?!
WHOA.
YEAH!
But then I realized what I wanted most of all.
To meet him.
AHA! Yes!
And... before... when you said "water", you were right. I figured out the coordinates of the opposite side of the world... and it was in the middle of the ocean. The closest land was the Koch Islands.
So I decided to go on a long... long trip. I drew up plans for a small boat... a fifteen-foot vessel... one mast and a sleeper.
And then I headed to the lumber mill near my house. That day a young woman was working. I'd never seen her around before... and boy... she was something.

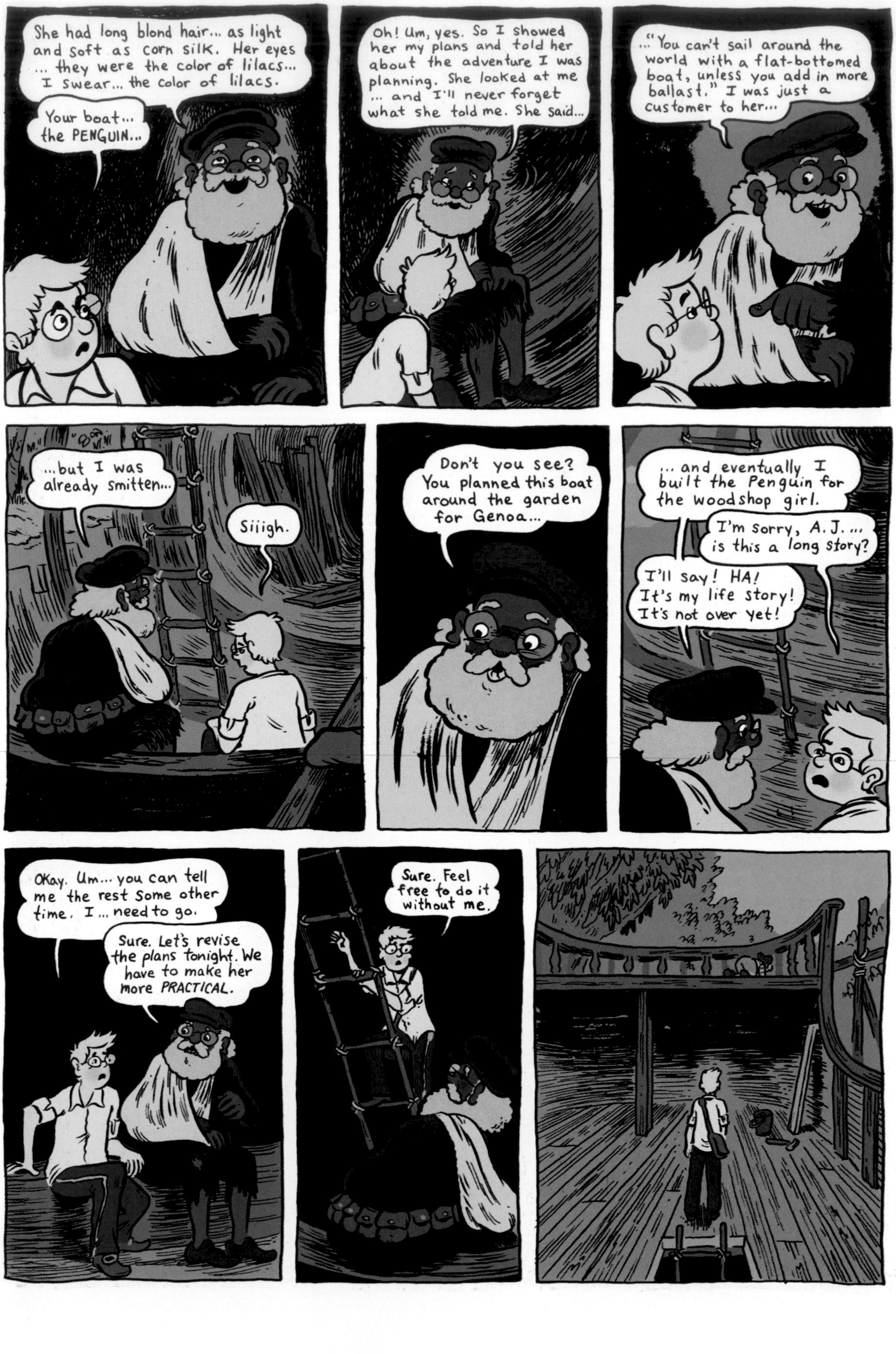
She had long blond hair... as light and soft as corn silk. Her eyes ... they were the color of lilacs... I swear... the color of lilacs.
Your boat... the PENGUIN...
Oh! Um, yes. So I showed her my plans and told her about the adventure I was planning. She looked at me ... and I'll never forget what she told me. She said...
..."You can't sail around the world with a flat-bottomed boat, unless you add in more ballast." I was just a customer to her...
...but I was already smitten...
Siiigh.
Don't you see? You planned this boat around the garden for Genoa...
... and eventually I built the Penguin for the woodshop girl.
I'm sorry, A. J. ... is this a long story?
I'll say! HA! It's my life story! It's not over yet!
Okay. Um... you can tell me the rest some other time. I... need to go.
Sure. Let's revise the plans tonight. We have to make her more PRACTICAL.
Sure. Feel free to do it without me.

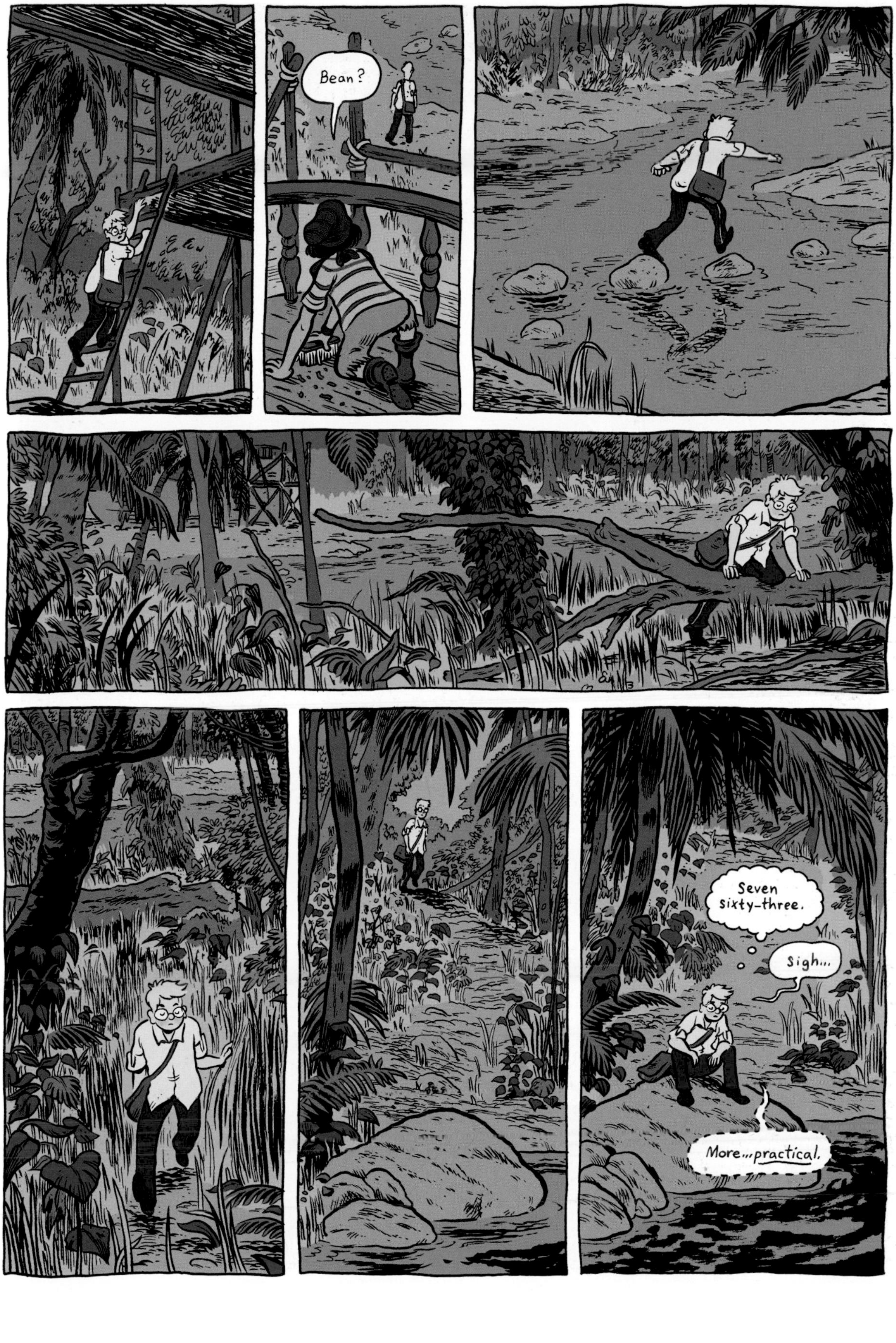
Bean?
Seven sixty-three.
Sigh...
More... practical.

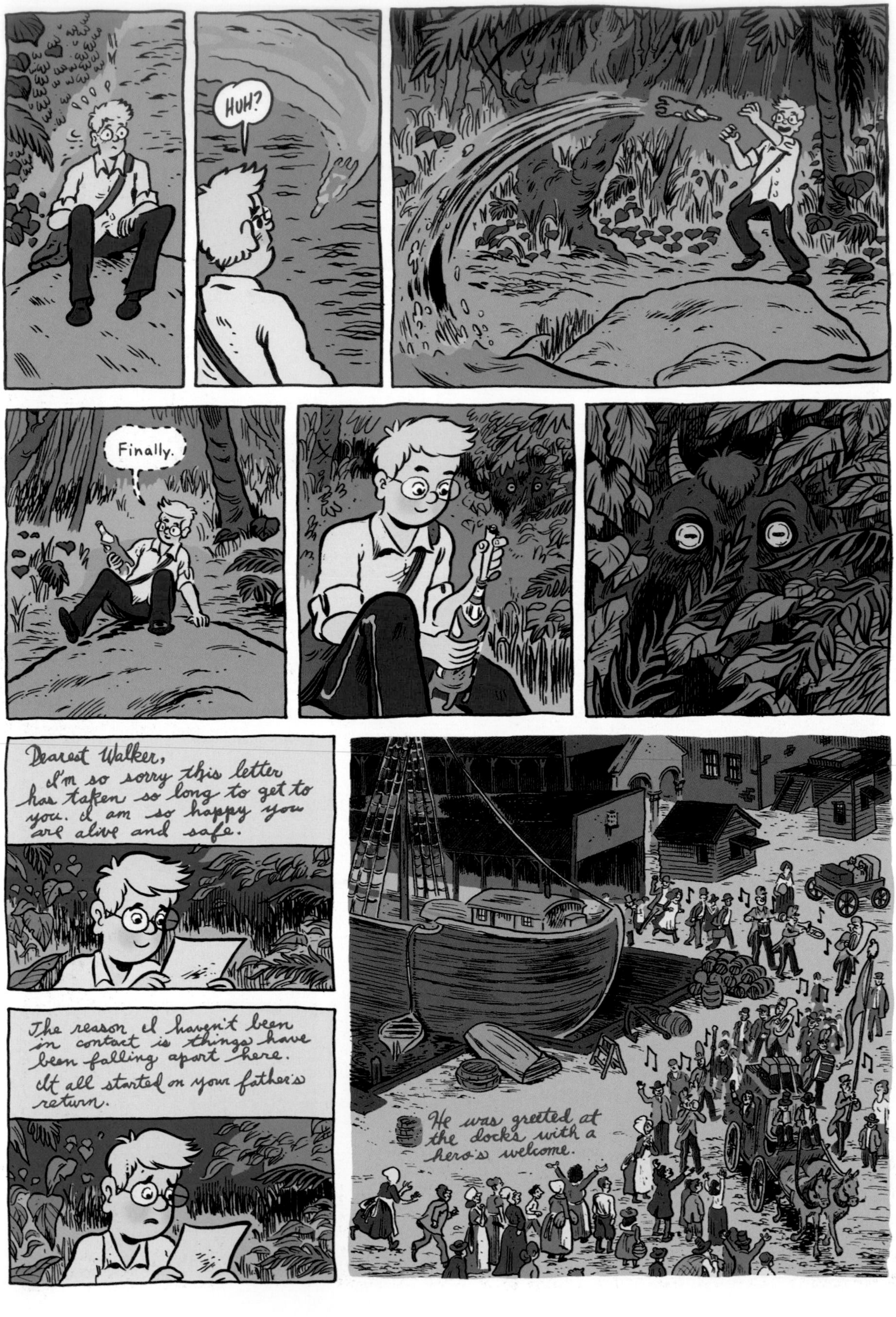
HUH?
Finally.
Dearest Walker,
I'm so sorry this letter has taken so long to get to you. I am so happy you are alive and safe.
The reason I haven't been in contact is things have been falling apart here.
It all started on your father's return.
He was greeted at the docks with a hero's welcome.

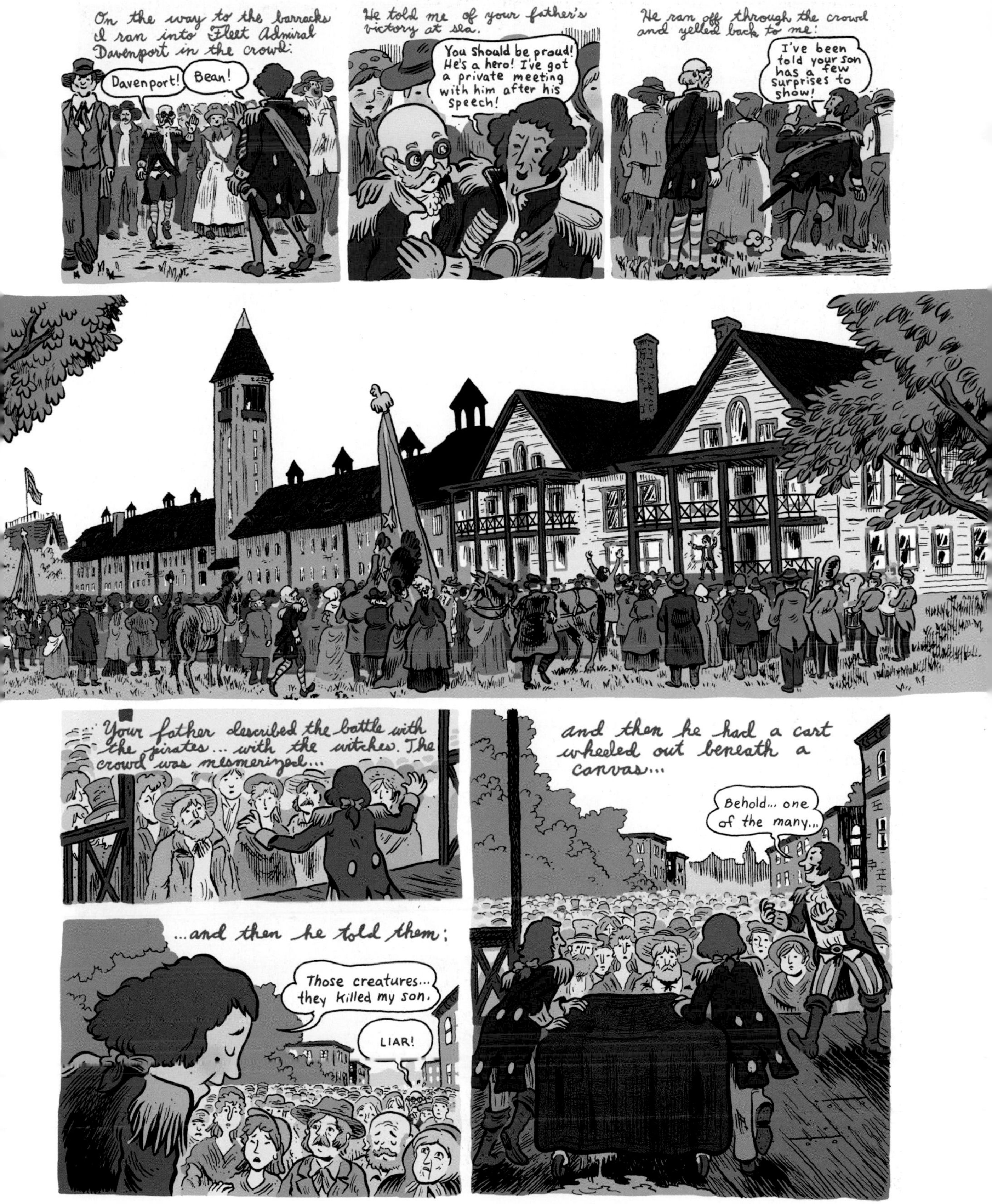
On the way to the barracks I ran into Fleet Admiral Davenport in the crowd:
Davenport!
Bean!
He told me of your father's victory at sea.
You should be proud! He's a hero! I've got a private meeting with him after his speech!
He ran off through the crowd and yelled back to me:
I've been told your son has a few surprises to show!
Your father described the battle with the pirates... with the witches. The crowd was mesmerized...
and then he had a cart wheeled out beneath a canvas...
Behold... one of the many...
...and then he told them:
Those creatures... they killed my son.
LIAR!

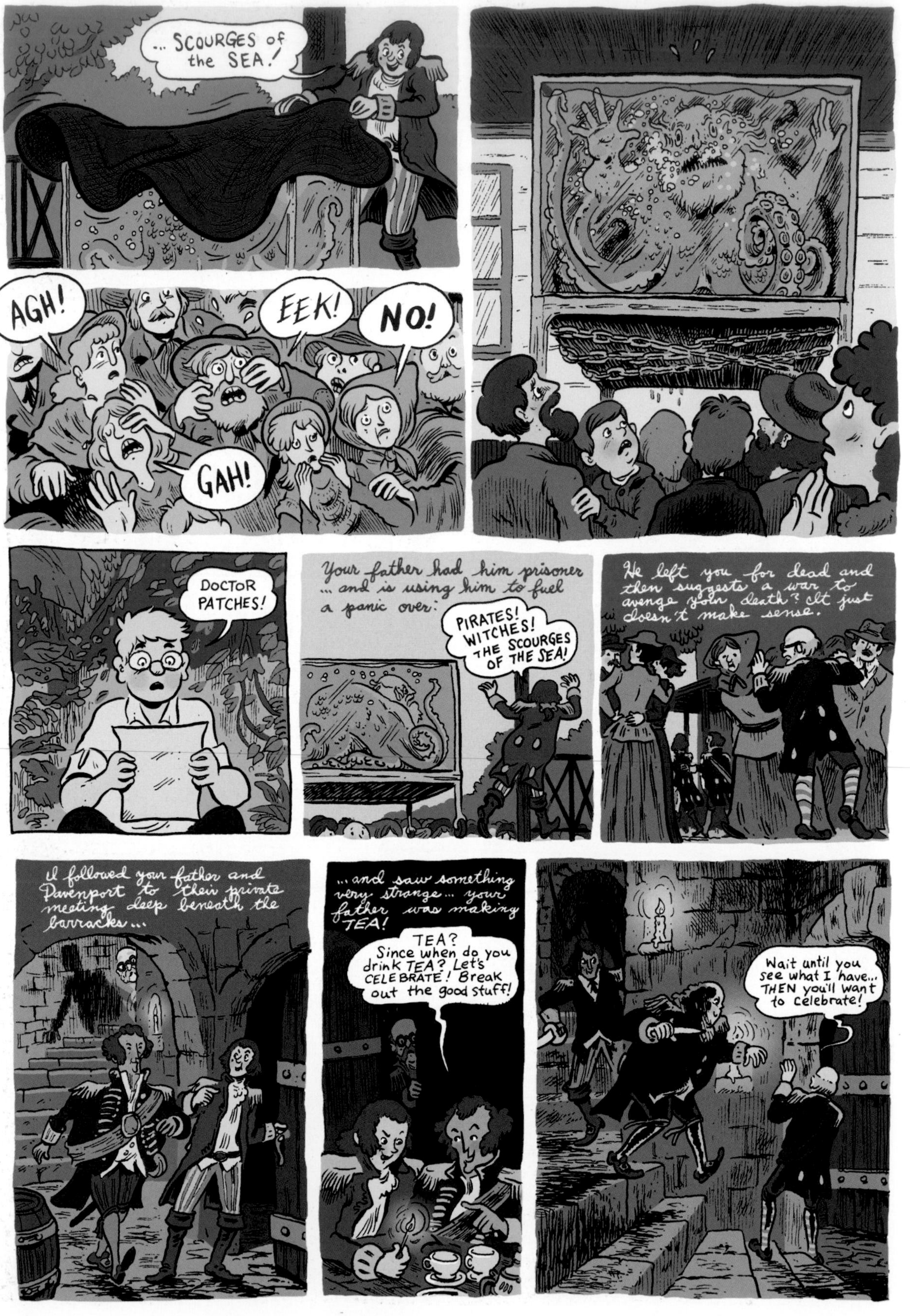
... SCOURGES of the SEA!
AGH!
EEK!
NO!
GAH!
DOCTOR PATCHES!
Your father had him prisoner ... and is using him to fuel a panic over:
PIRATES! WITCHES! THE SCOURGES OF THE SEA!
He left you for dead and then suggests a war to avenge your death? It just doesn't make sense.
I followed your father and Davenport to their private meeting deep beneath the barracks...
...and saw something very strange... your father was making TEA!
TEA? Since when do you drink TEA? Let's CELEBRATE! Break out the good stuff!
Wait until you see what I have... THEN you'll want to celebrate!

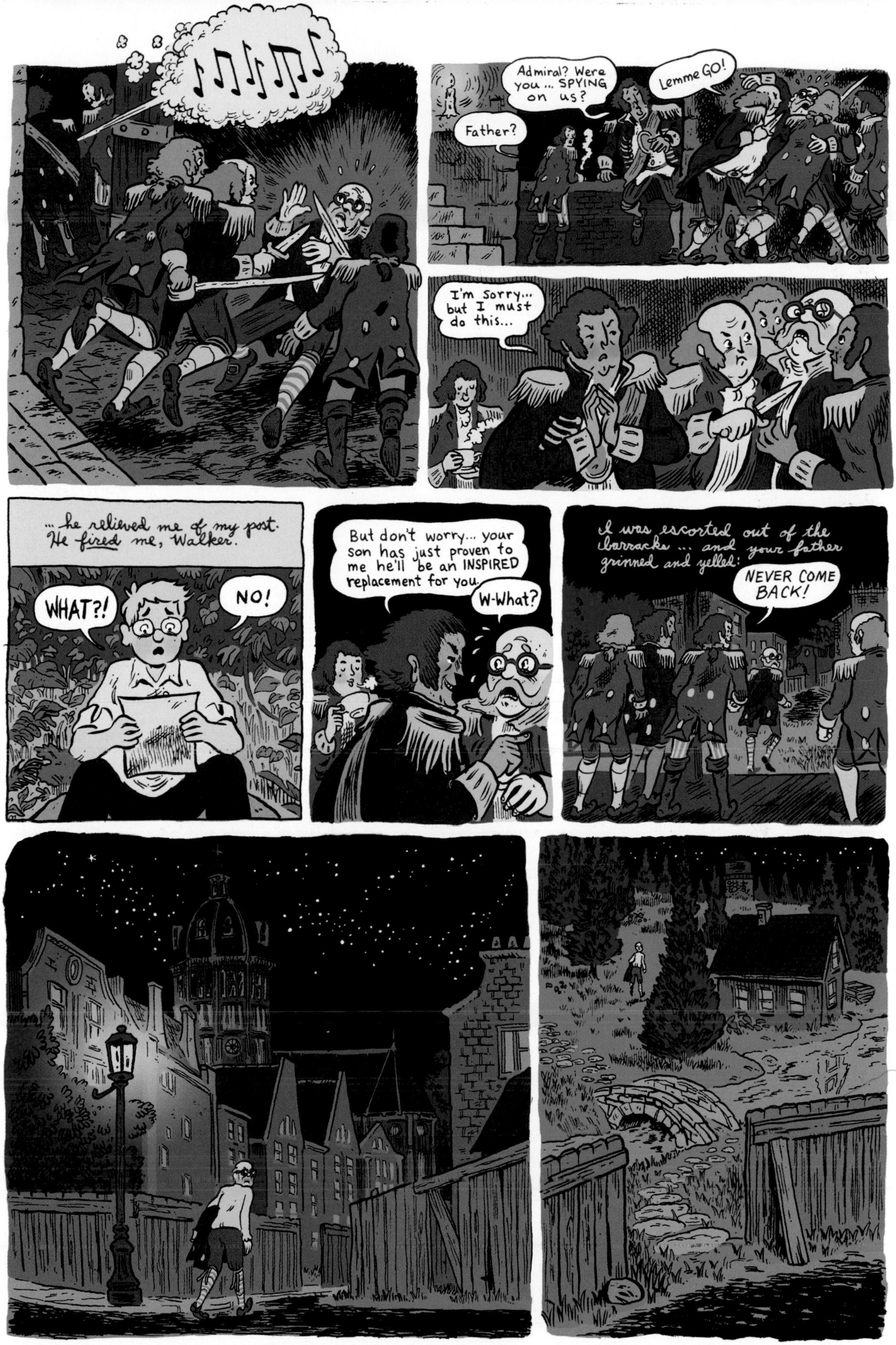
Admiral? Were you ... SPYING on us?
Lemme GO!
Father?
I'm sorry... but I must do this...
... he relieved me of my post. He fired me, Walker.
WHAT?!
NO!
But don't worry... your son has just proven to me he'll be an INSPIRED replacement for you.
W-What?
I was escorted out of the barracks ... and your father grinned and yelled:
NEVER COME BACK!

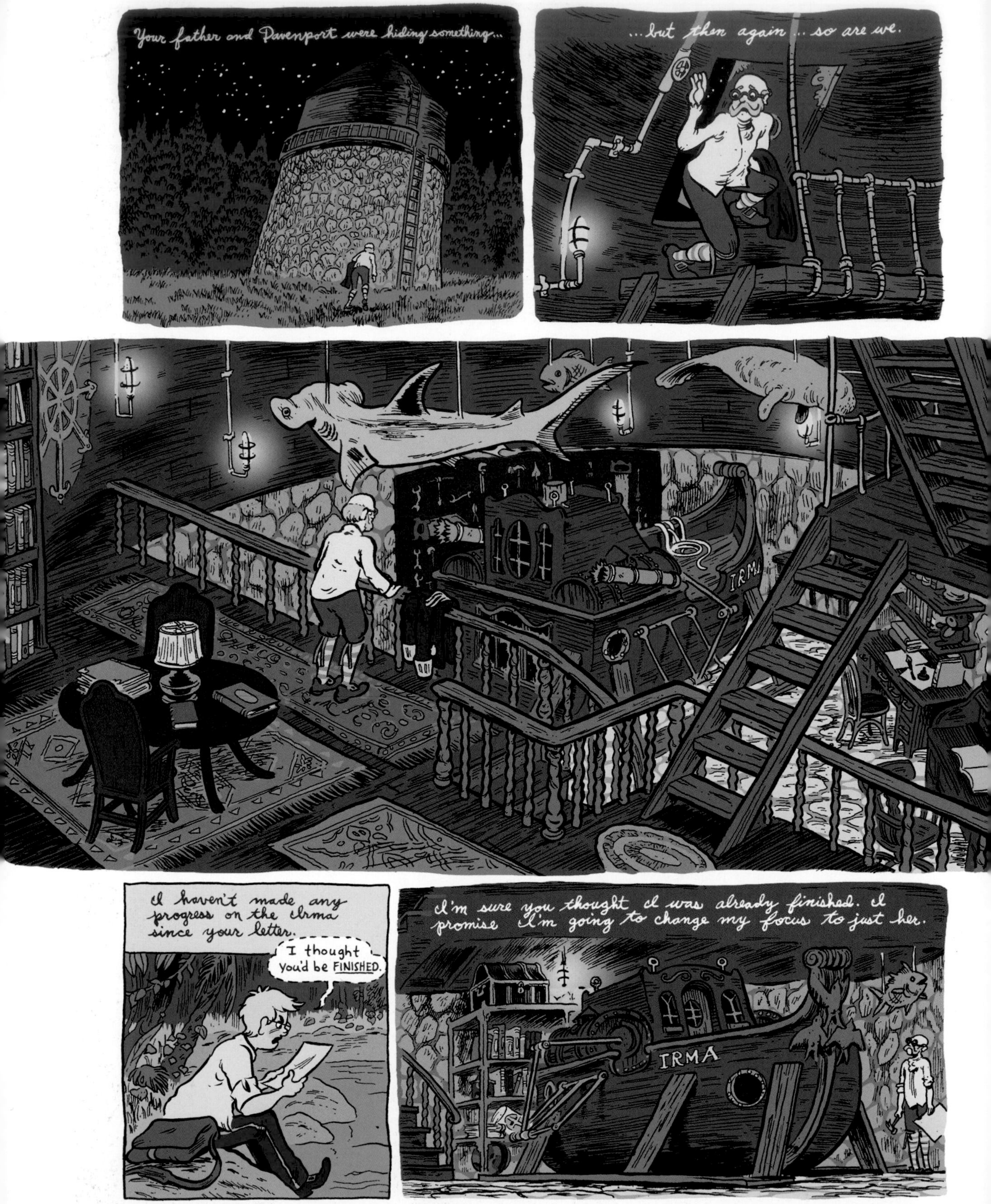
Your father and Davenport were hiding something...
...but then again... so are we.
IRMA
I haven't made any progress on the Irma since your letter.
I thought you'd be FINISHED.
I'm sure you thought I was already finished. I promise I'm going to change my focus to just her.
IRMA

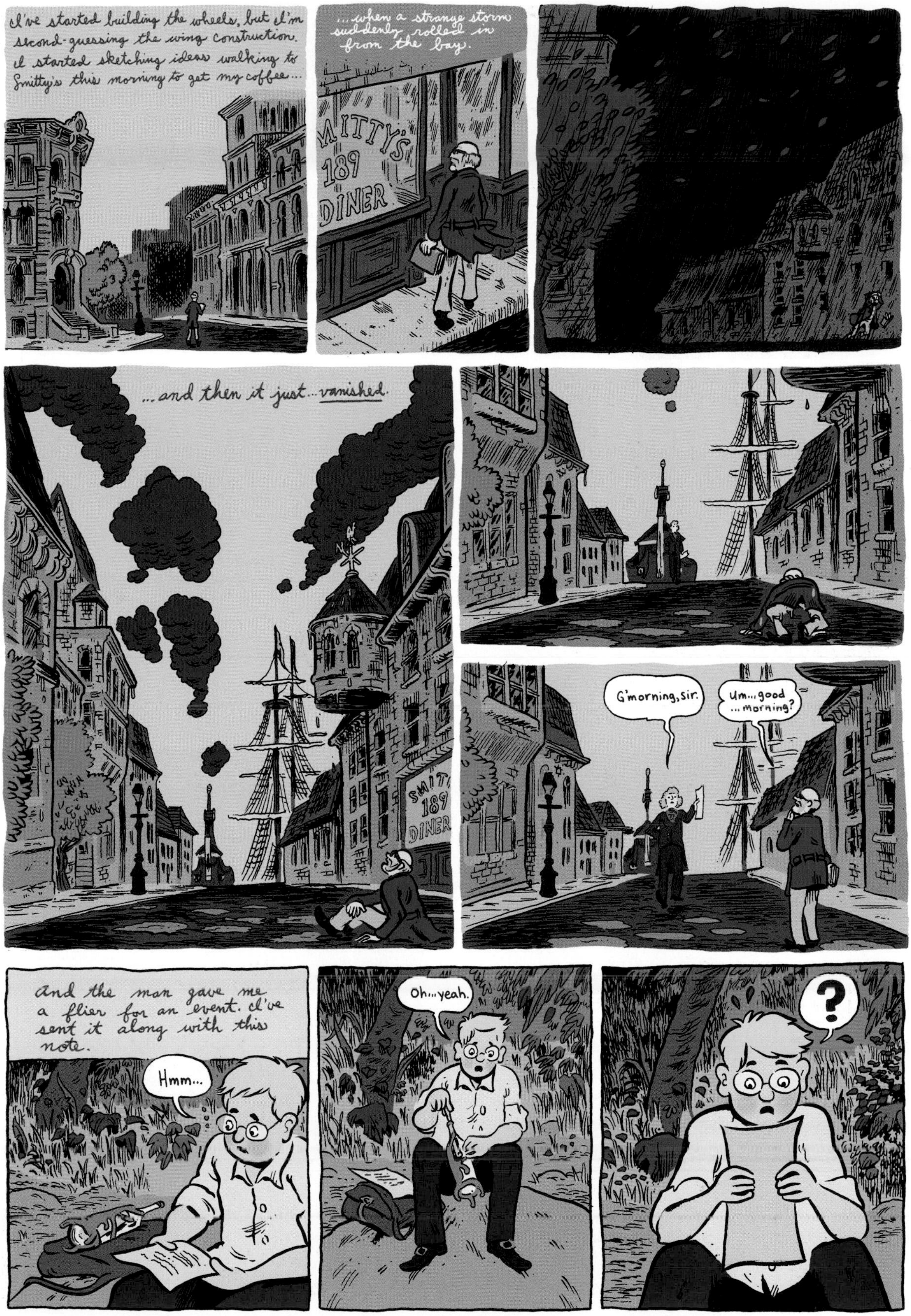
I've started building the wheels, but I'm second-guessing the wing construction. I started sketching ideas walking to Smitty's this morning to get my coffee...
...when a strange storm suddenly rolled in from the bay.
SMITTY'S 189 DINER
...and then it just...vanished.
SMITTY'S 189 DINER
G'morning, sir.
Um...good ...morning?
And the man gave me a flier for an event. I've sent it along with this note.
Hmm...
Oh...yeah.
?

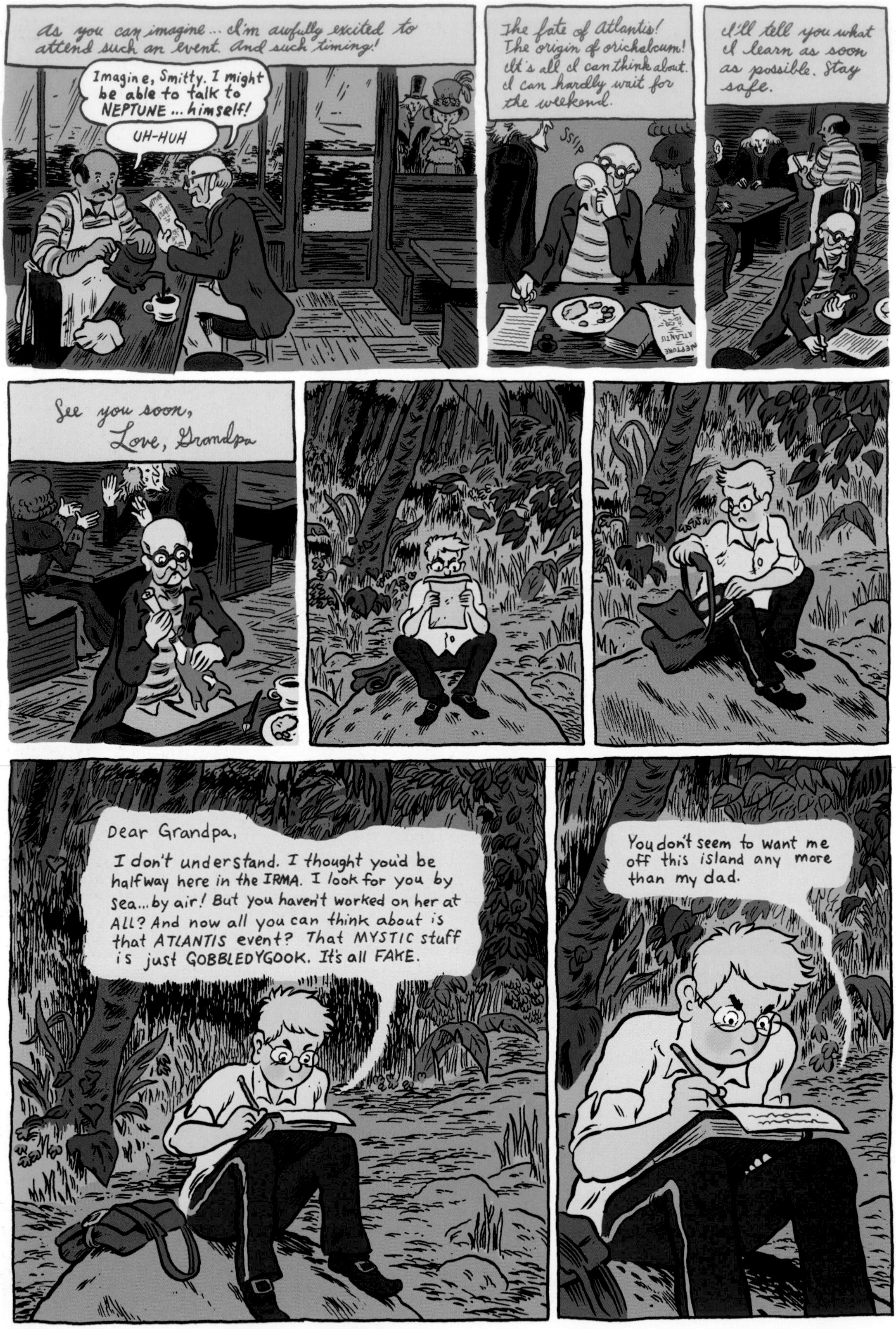
As you can imagine... I'm awfully excited to attend such an event. And such timing!
Imagine, Smitty. I might be able to talk to NEPTUNE... himself!
UH-HUH
The fate of Atlantis! The origin of orichalcum! It's all I can think about. I can hardly wait for the weekend.
SSlip
I'll tell you what I learn as soon as possible. Stay safe.
See you soon,
Love, Grandpa
Dear Grandpa,
I don't understand. I thought you'd be halfway here in the IRMA. I look for you by sea... by air! But you haven't worked on her at ALL? And now all you can think about is that ATLANTIS event? That MYSTIC stuff is just GOBBLEDYGOOK. It's all FAKE.
You don't seem to want me off this island any more than my dad.

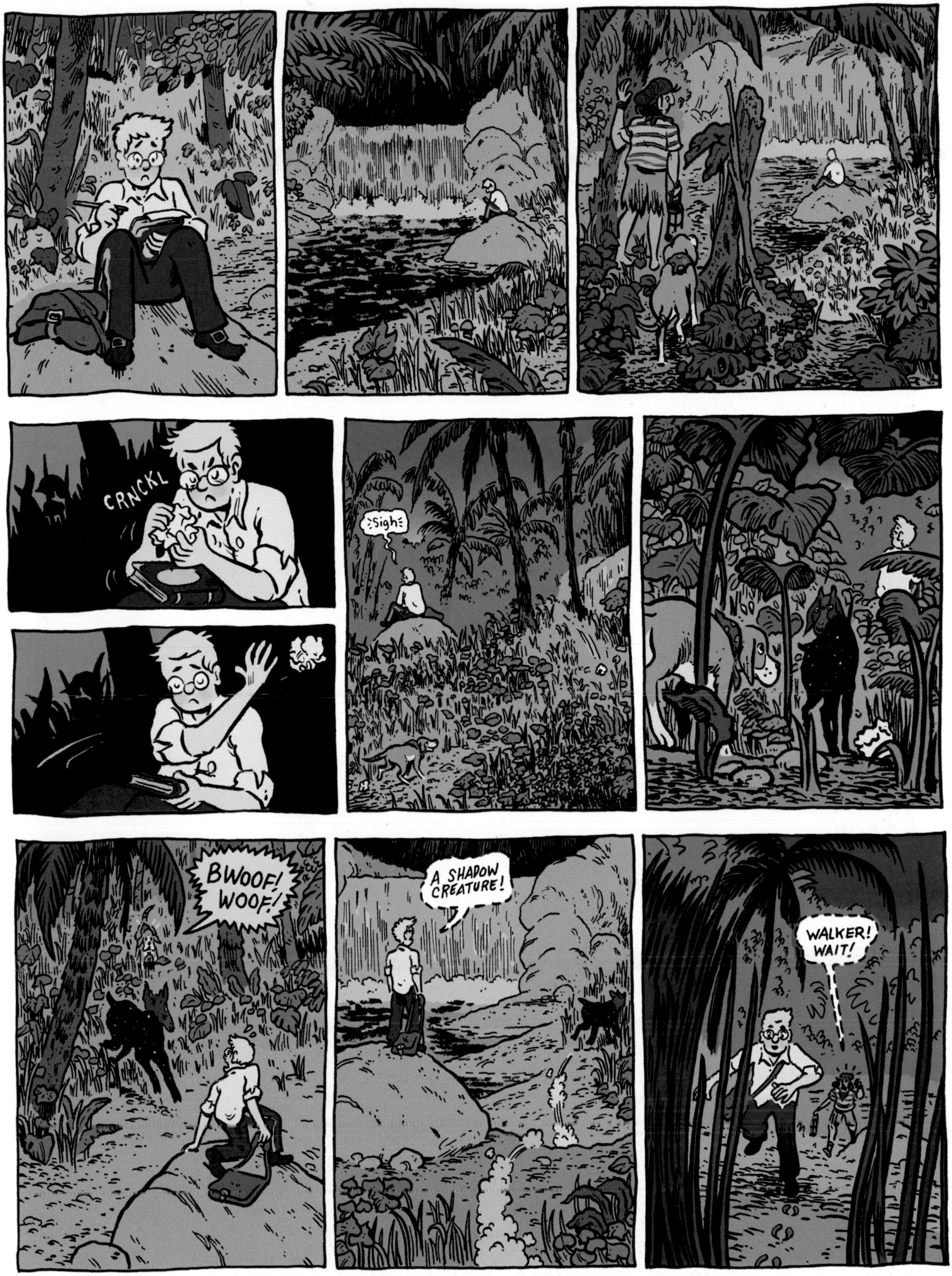
CRNCKL
Sigh
BWOOF! WOOF!
A SHADOW CREATURE!
WALKER! WAIT!

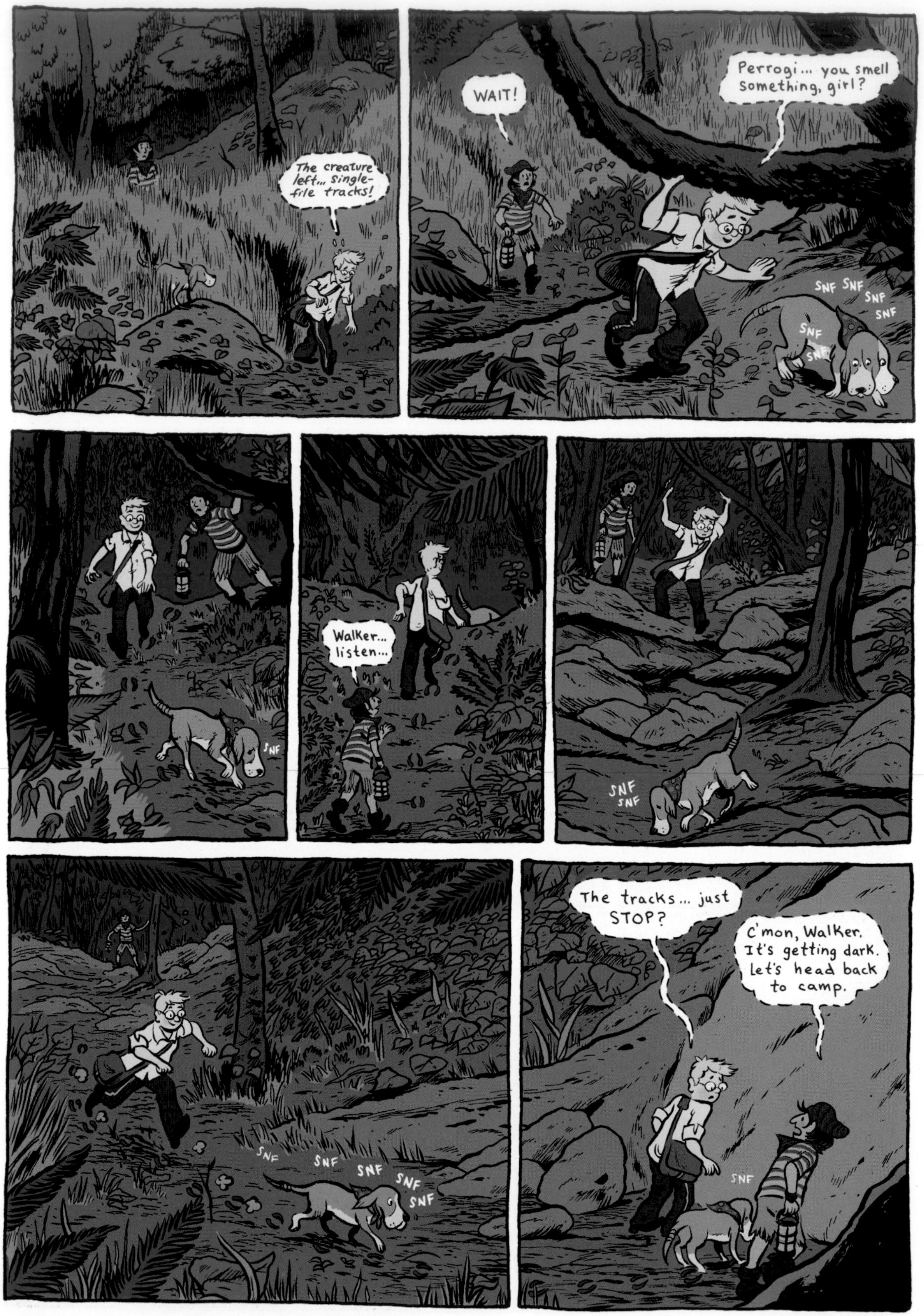
The creature left... single-file tracks!
WAIT!
Perrogi... you smell something, girl?
SNF SNF SNF SNF
SNF SNF
SNF
Walker... listen...
SNF SNF
SNF SNF SNF SNF SNF
The tracks... just STOP?
C'mon, Walker. It's getting dark. Let's head back to camp.
SNF

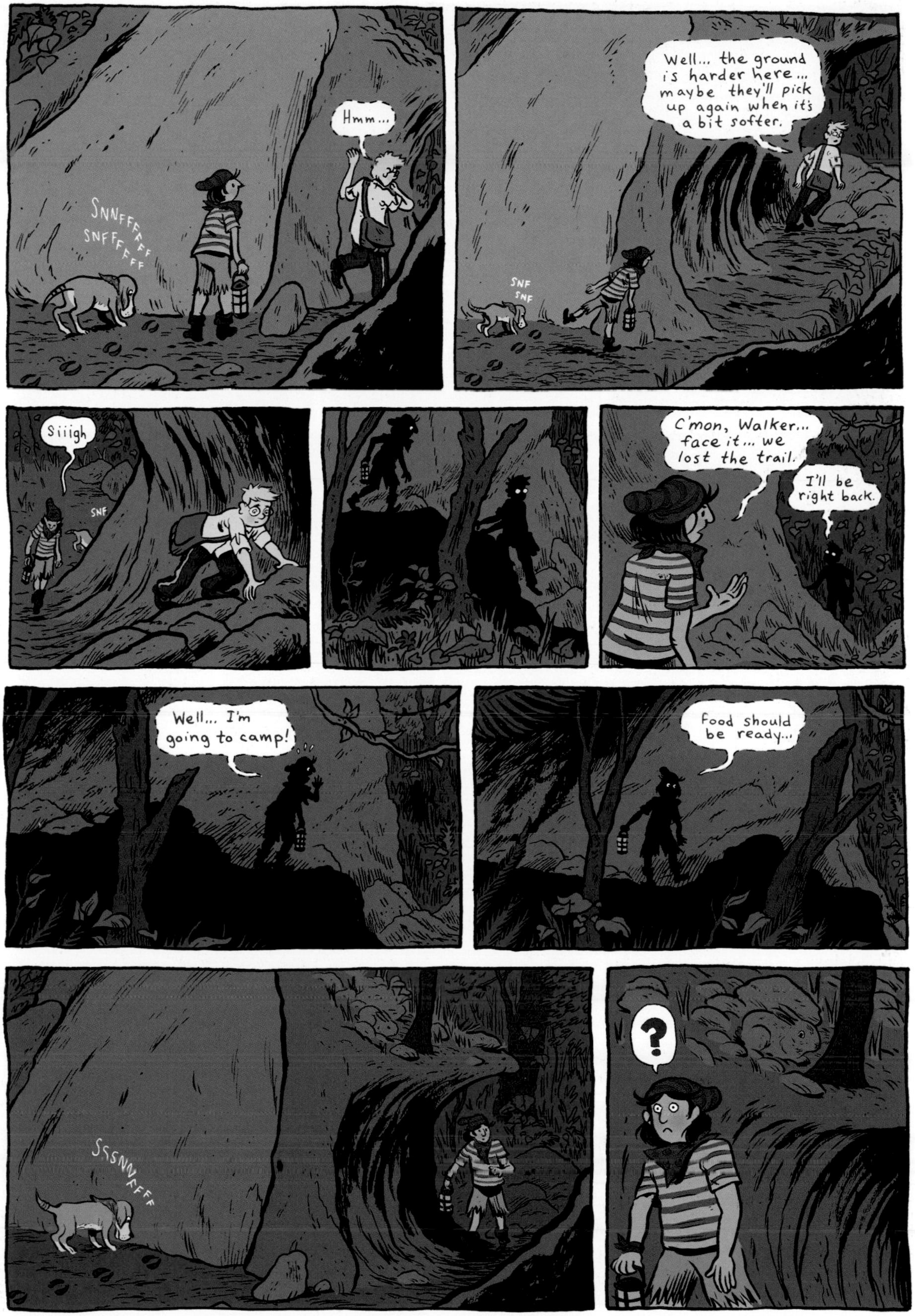
SNFFFFFFF
SNFFFFFFF
Hmm...
Well... the ground is harder here... maybe they'll pick up again when it's a bit softer.
SNF
SNF
Siiigh
SNF
C'mon, Walker... face it... we lost the trail.
I'll be right back.
Well... I'm going to camp!
Food should be ready...
SSSNNFFF
?

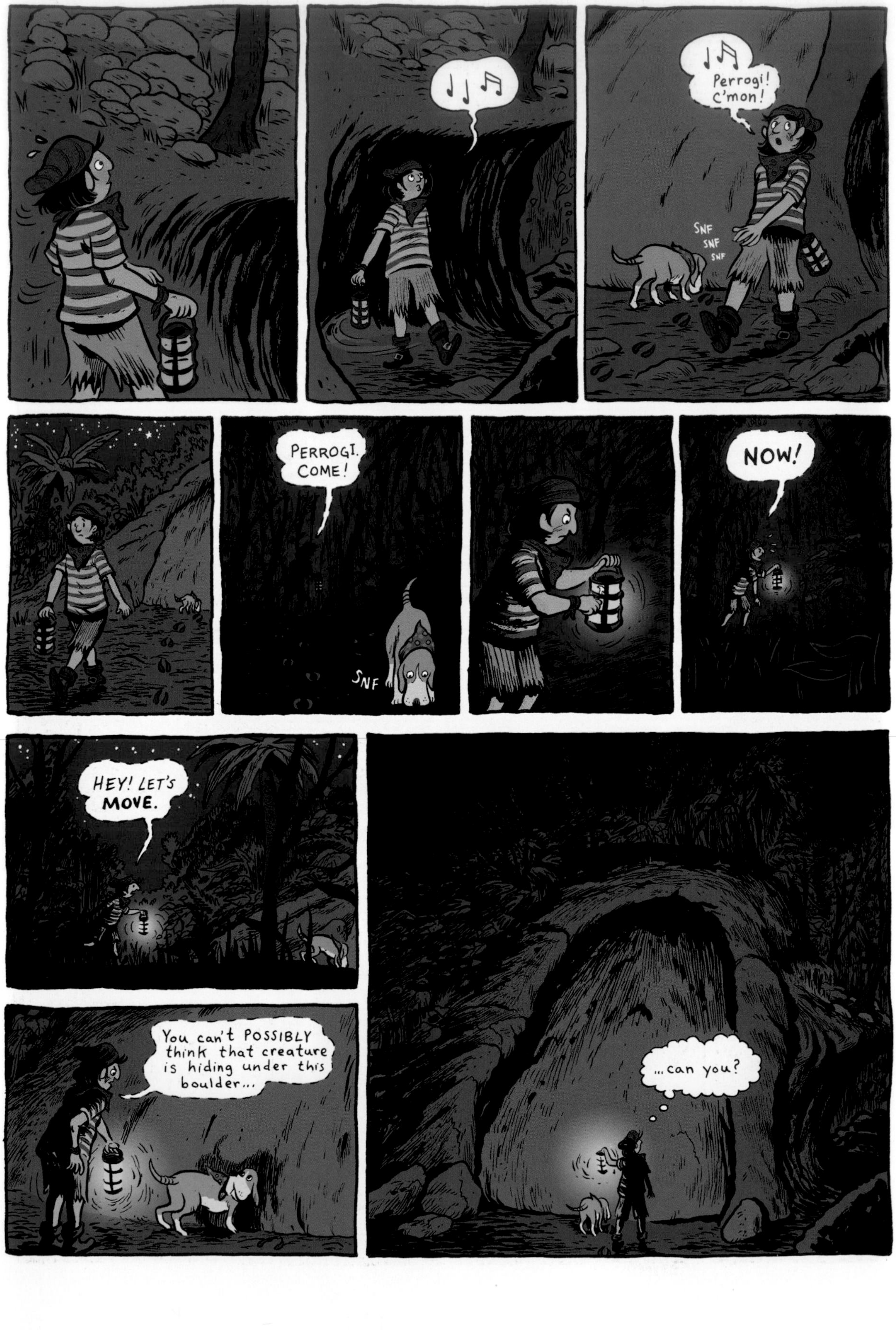
♩♩♫
♩♫ Perrogi! C'mon!
SNF SNF SNF
PERROGI. COME!
SNF
NOW!
HEY! LET'S MOVE.
You can't POSSIBLY think that creature is hiding under this boulder...
...can you?

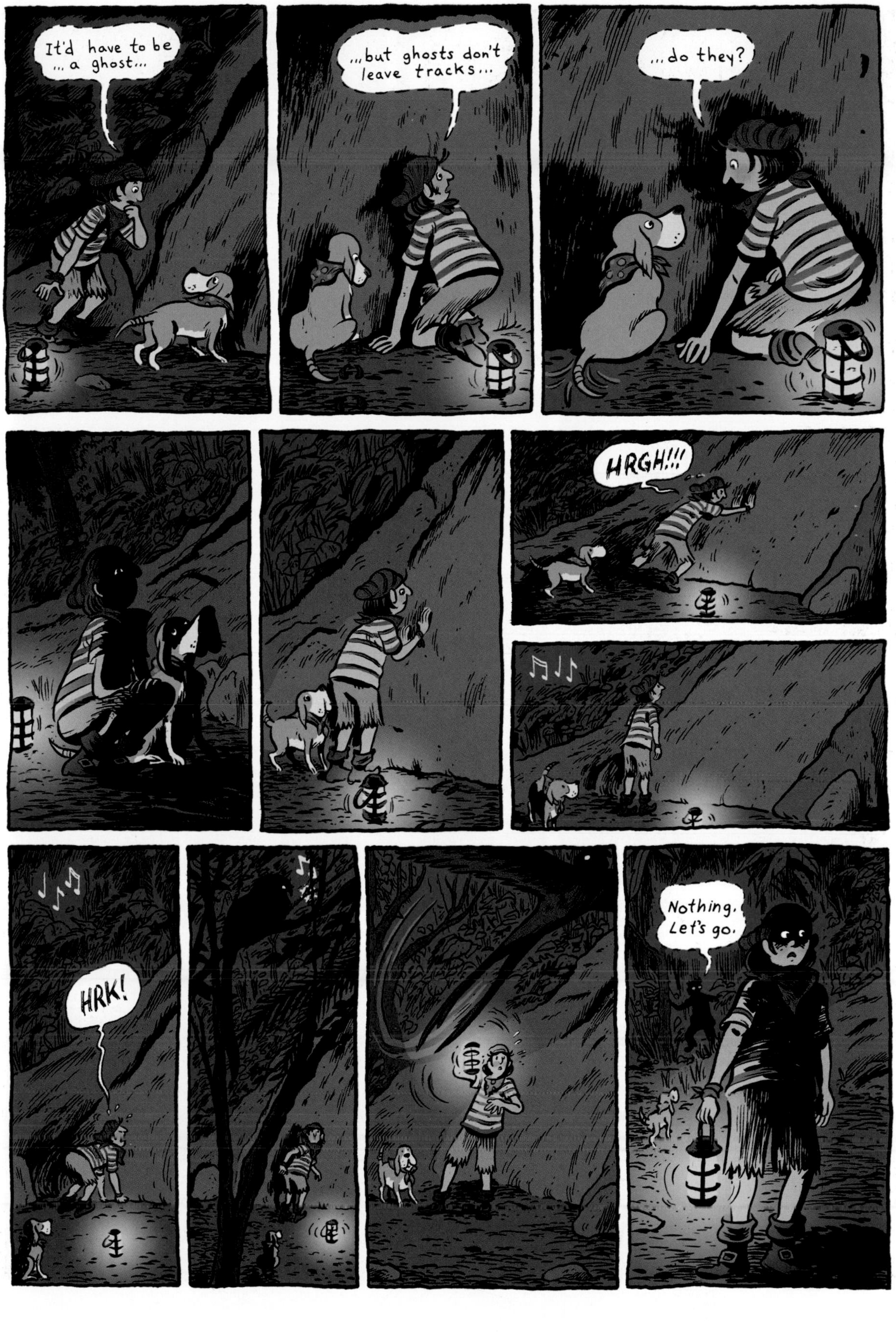
It'd have to be ... a ghost...
...but ghosts don't leave tracks...
...do they?
HRGH!!!
HRK!
Nothing. Let's go.

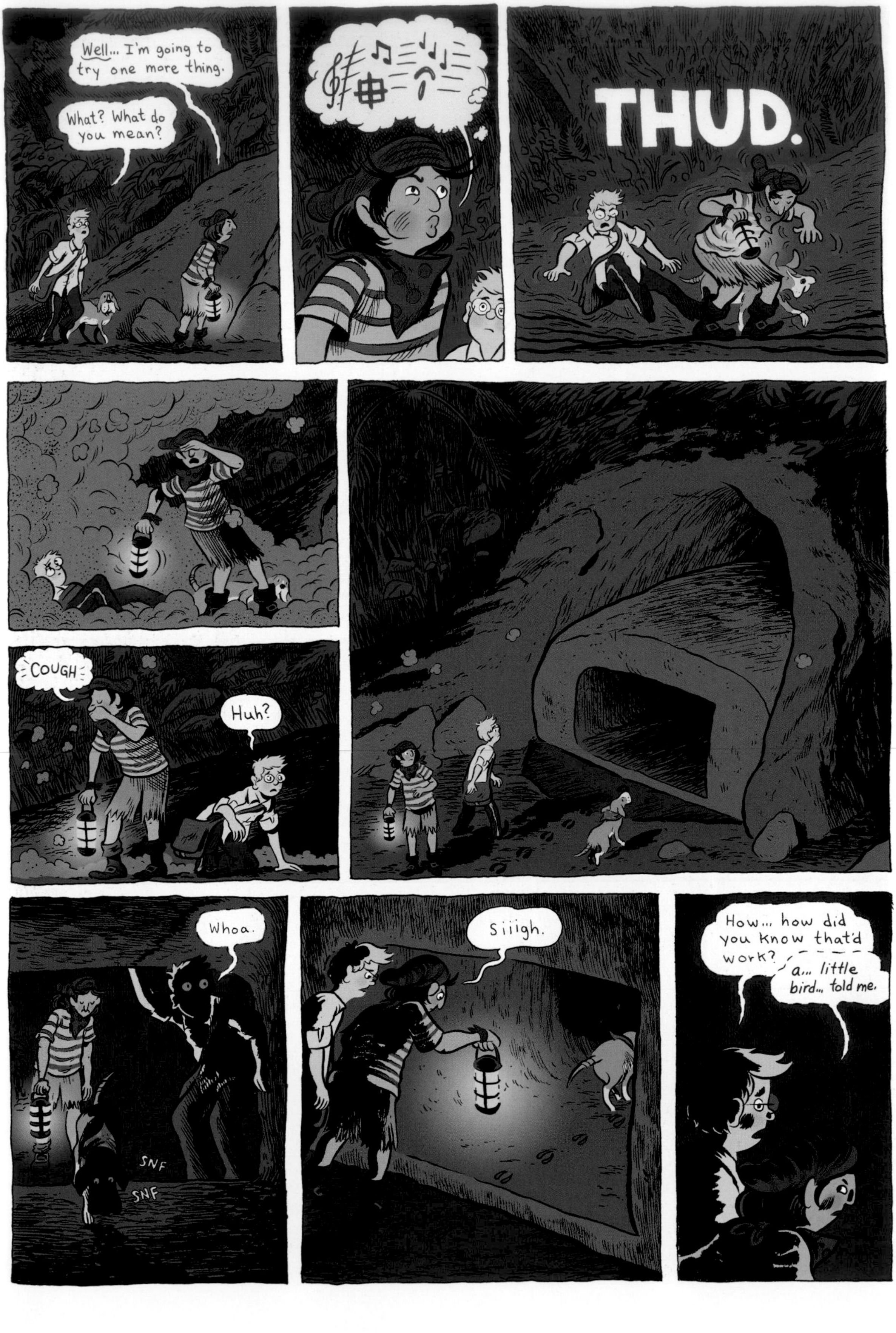

Well... I'm going to try one more thing.
What? What do you mean?
THUD.
COUGH
Huh?
Whoa.
SNF
SNF
Siiigh.
How... how did you know that'd work?
a... little bird... told me.

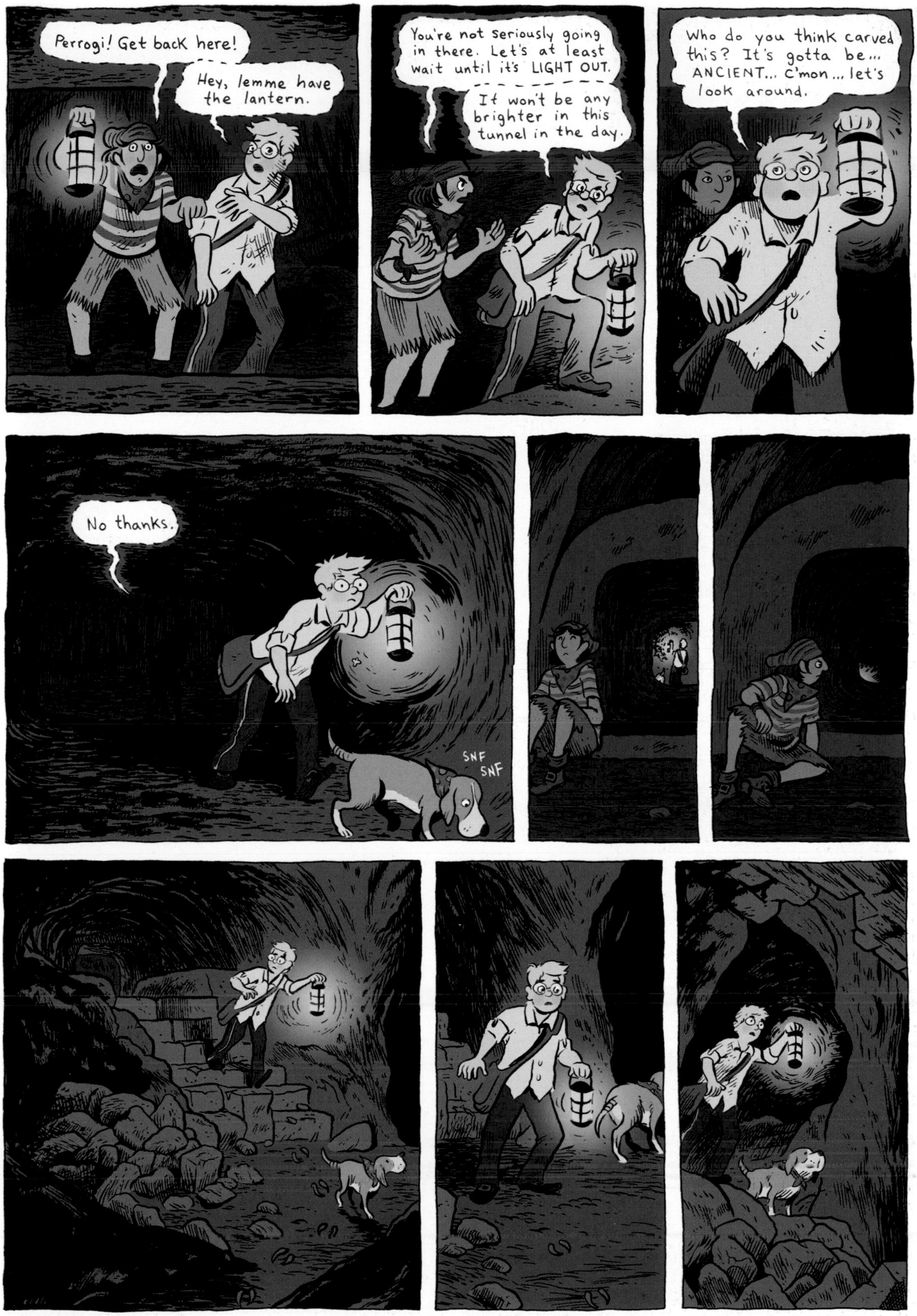

Perrogi! Get back here!
Hey, lemme have the lantern.
You're not seriously going in there. Let's at least wait until it's LIGHT OUT.
It won't be any brighter in this tunnel in the day.
Who do you think carved this? It's gotta be... ANCIENT... C'mon... let's look around.
No thanks.
SNF SNF

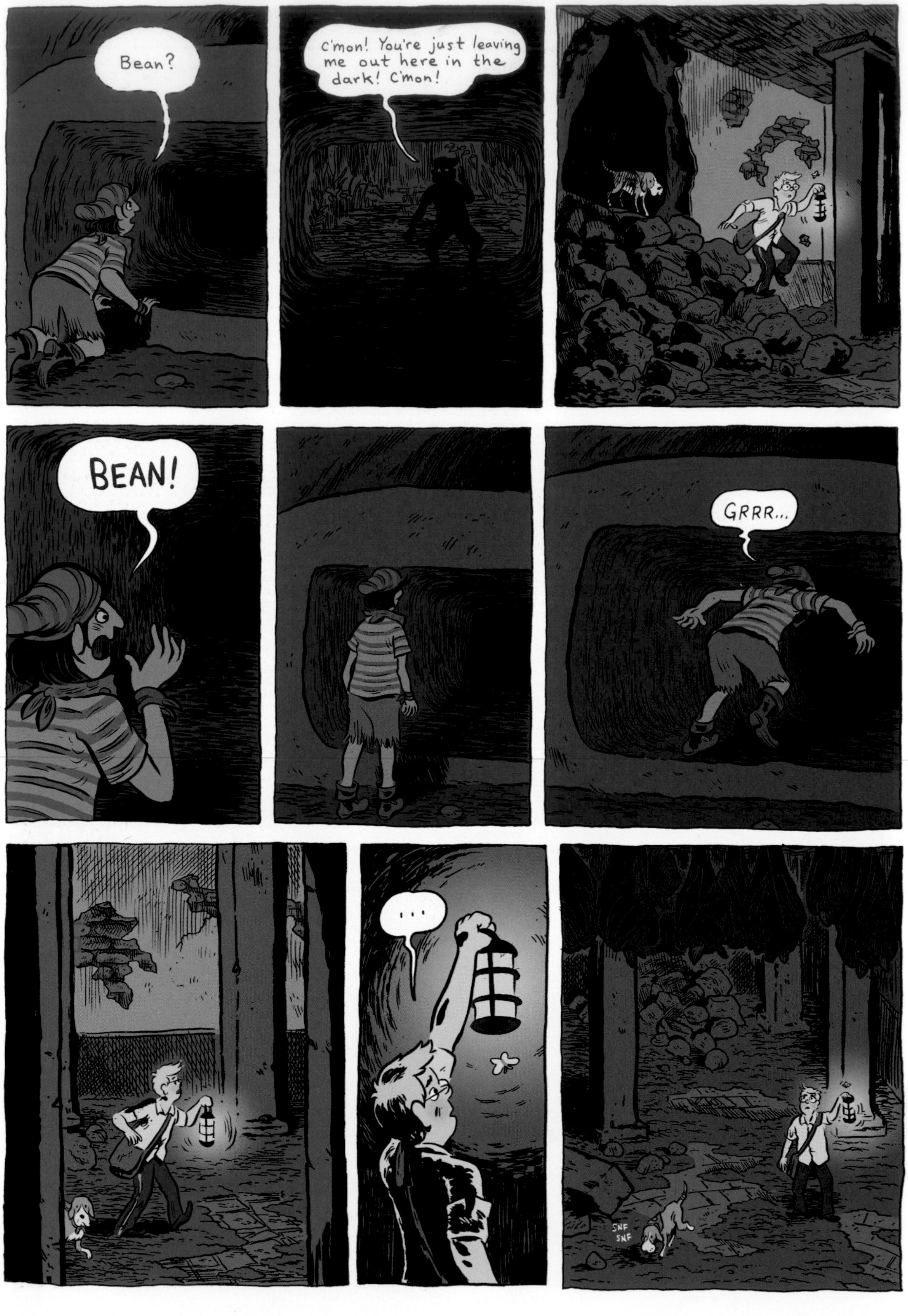
Bean?
C'mon! You're just leaving me out here in the dark! C'mon!
BEAN!
GRRR...
...
SNF SNF

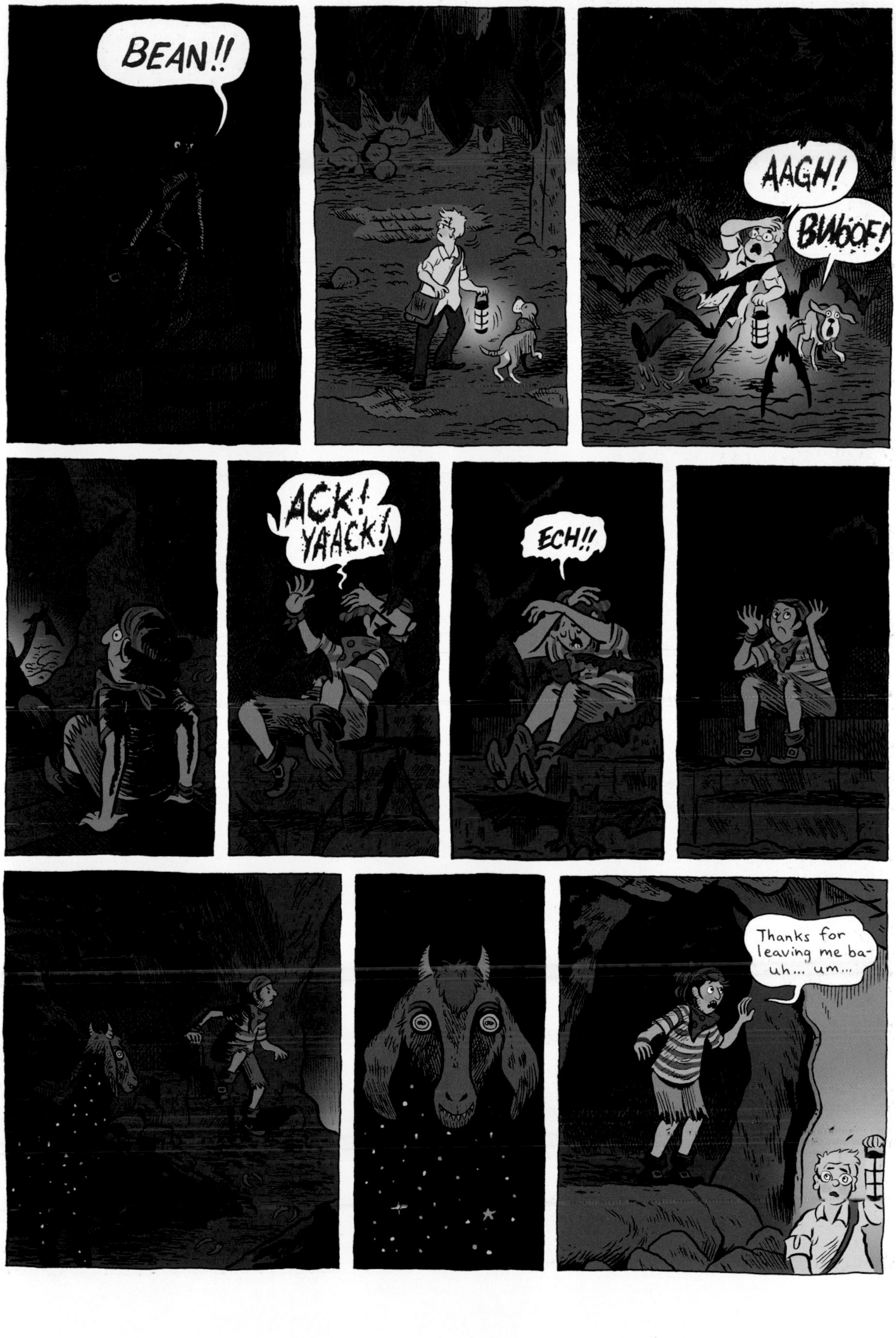
BEAN!!
AAGH!
BWOOF!
ACK! YAACK!
ECH!!
Thanks for leaving me ba- uh... um...

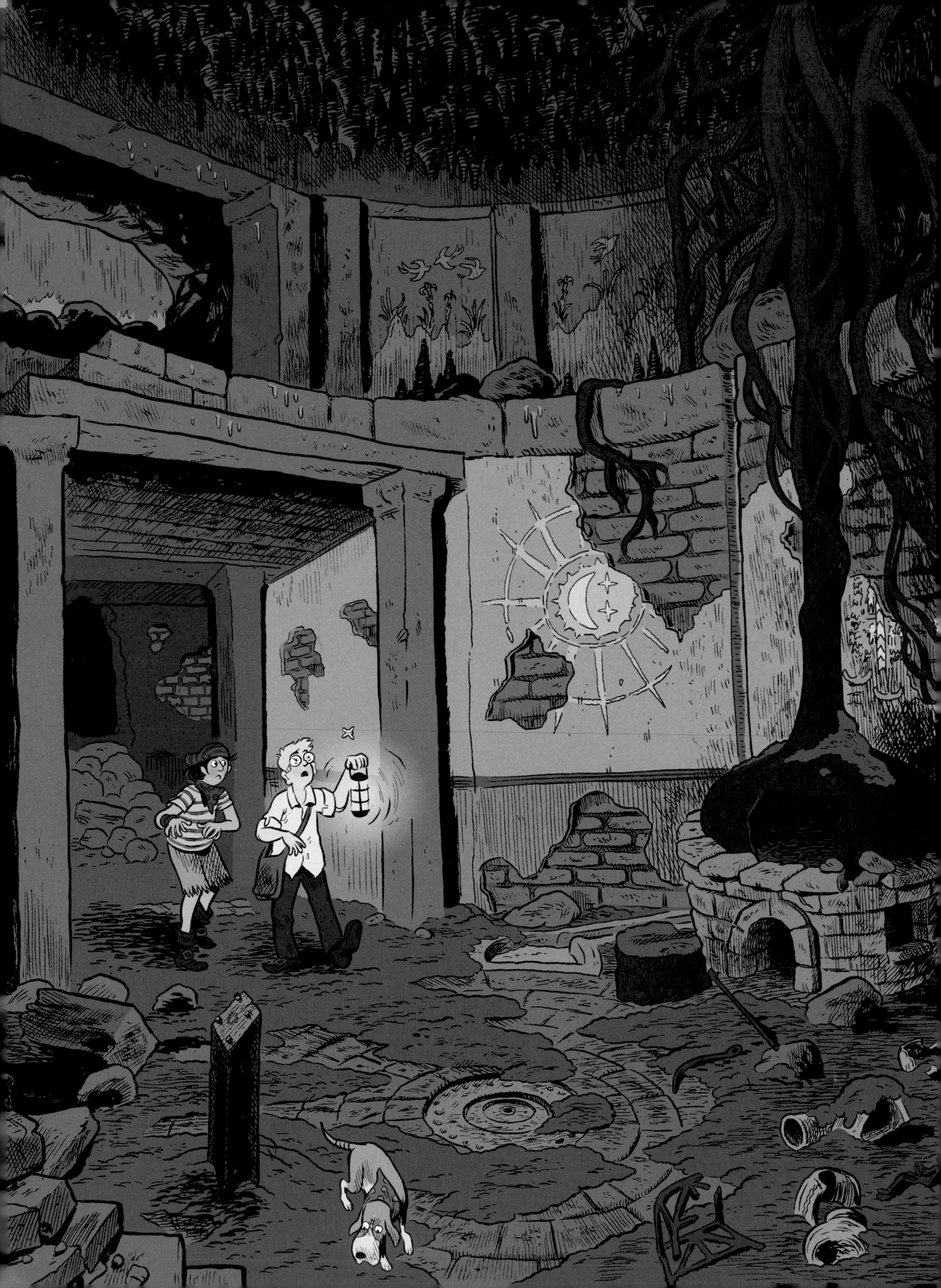

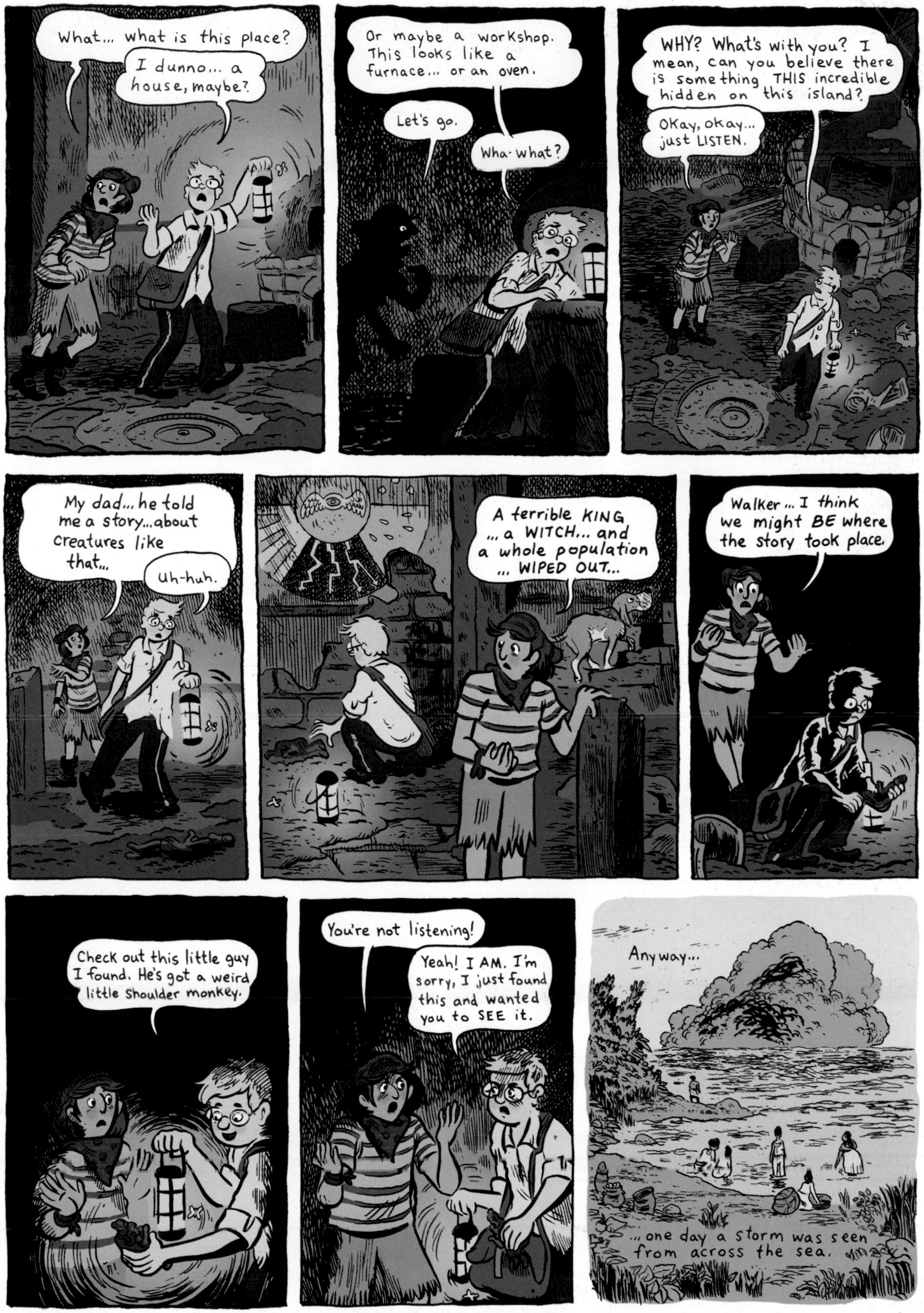

What... what is this place?
I dunno... a house, maybe?
Or maybe a workshop. This looks like a furnace... or an oven.
Let's go.
Wha-what?
WHY? What's with you? I mean, can you believe there is something THIS incredible hidden on this island?
Okay, okay... just LISTEN.
My dad... he told me a story... about creatures like that...
Uh-huh.
A terrible KING ... a WITCH... and a whole population ... WIPED OUT...
Walker... I think we might BE where the story took place.
Check out this little guy I found. He's got a weird little shoulder monkey.
You're not listening!
Yeah! I AM. I'm sorry, I just found this and wanted you to SEE it.
Anyway...
...one day a storm was seen from across the sea.

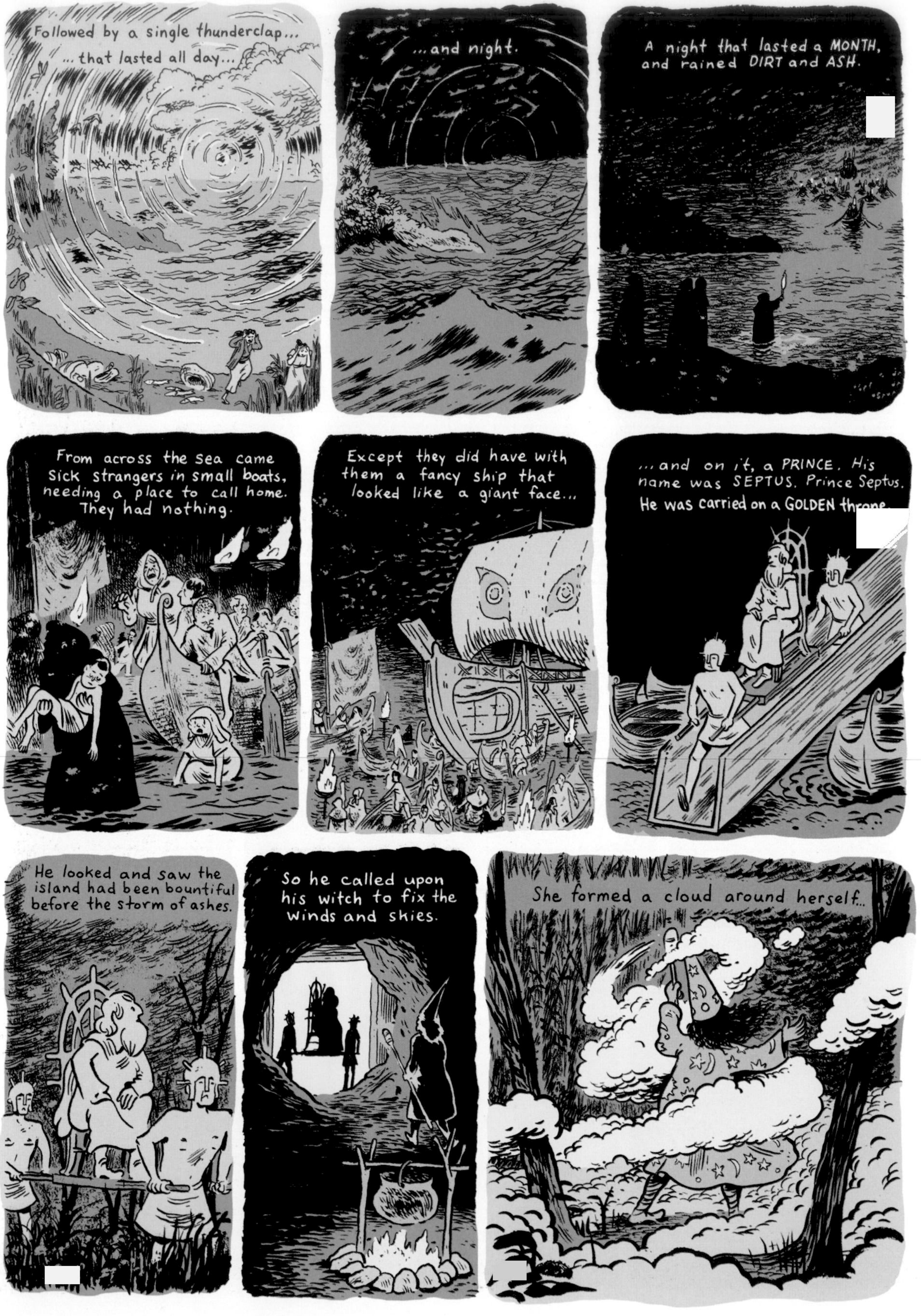
Followed by a single thunderclap...
... that lasted all day...
... and night.
A night that lasted a MONTH, and rained DIRT and ASH.
From across the sea came sick strangers in small boats, needing a place to call home. They had nothing.
Except they did have with them a fancy ship that looked like a giant face...
... and on it, a PRINCE. His name was SEPTUS. Prince Septus.
He was carried on a GOLDEN throne
He looked and saw the island had been bountiful before the storm of ashes.
So he called upon his witch to fix the winds and skies.
She formed a cloud around herself...

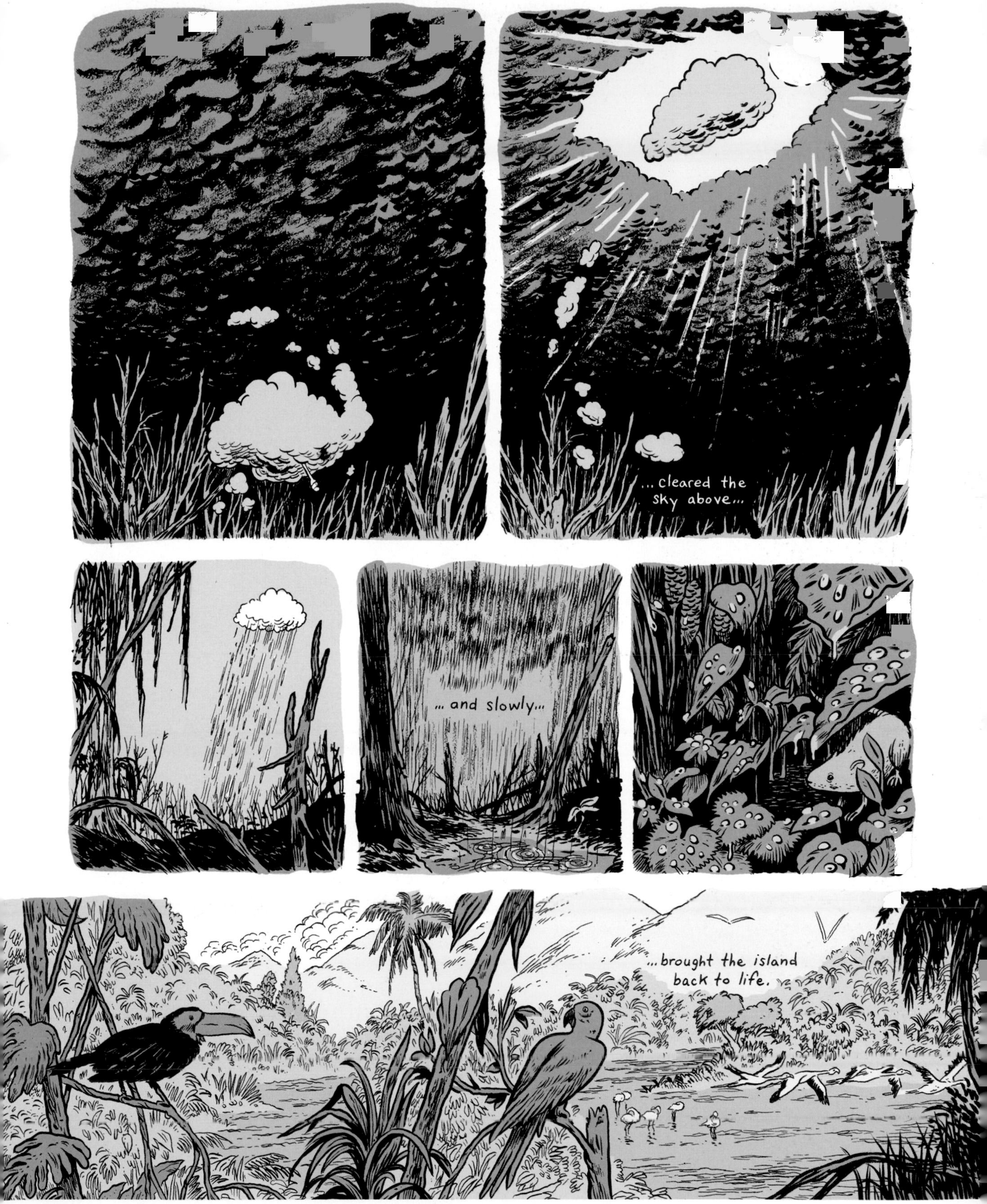
...cleared the sky above...
... and slowly...
...brought the island back to life.

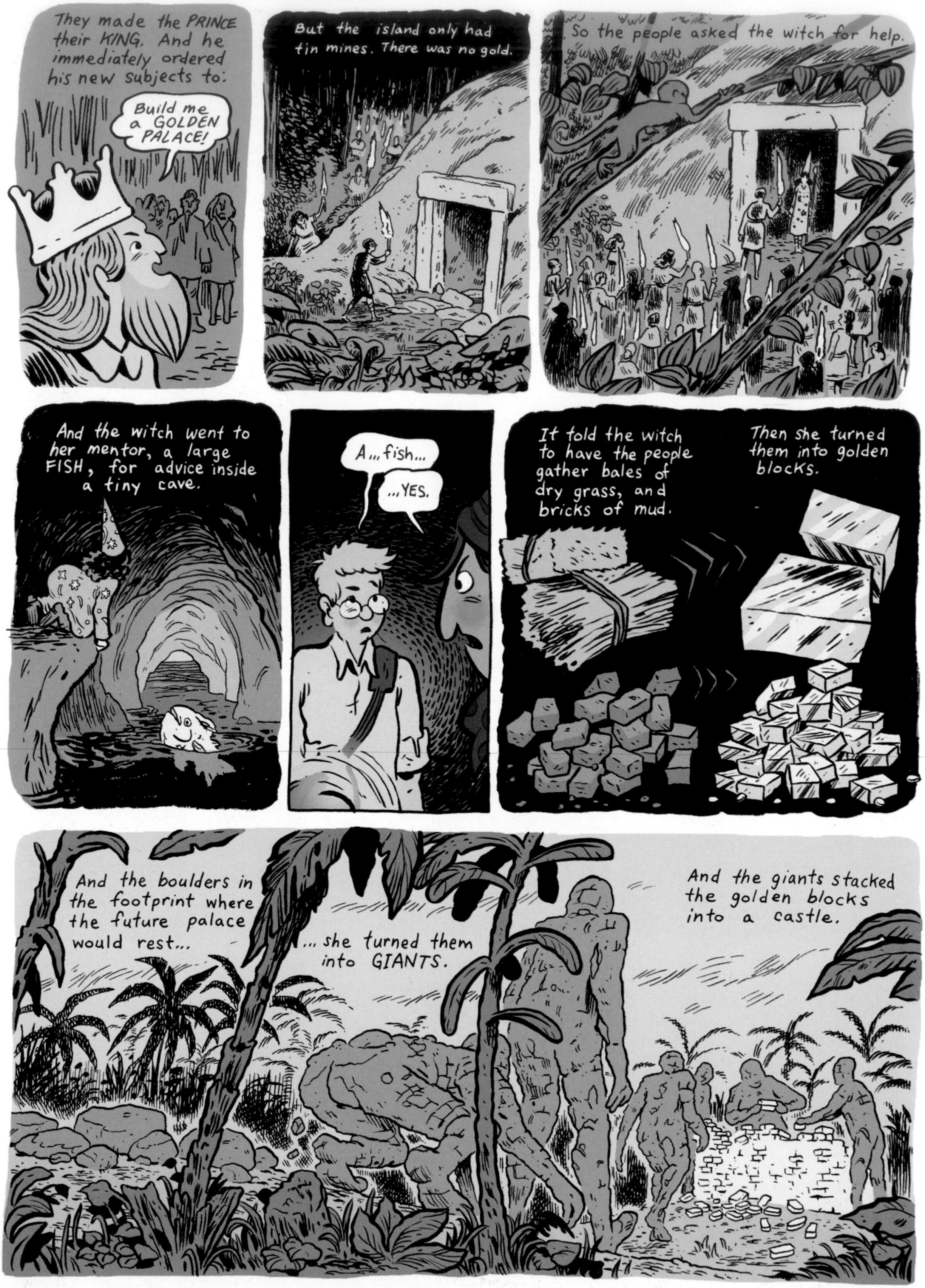

They made the PRINCE their KING. And he immediately ordered his new subjects to:
Build me a GOLDEN PALACE!
But the island only had tin mines. There was no gold.
So the people asked the witch for help.
And the witch went to her mentor, a large FISH, for advice inside a tiny cave.
A... fish...
...YES.
It told the witch to have the people gather bales of dry grass, and bricks of mud.
Then she turned them into golden blocks.
And the boulders in the footprint where the future palace would rest...
... she turned them into GIANTS.
And the giants stacked the golden blocks into a castle.

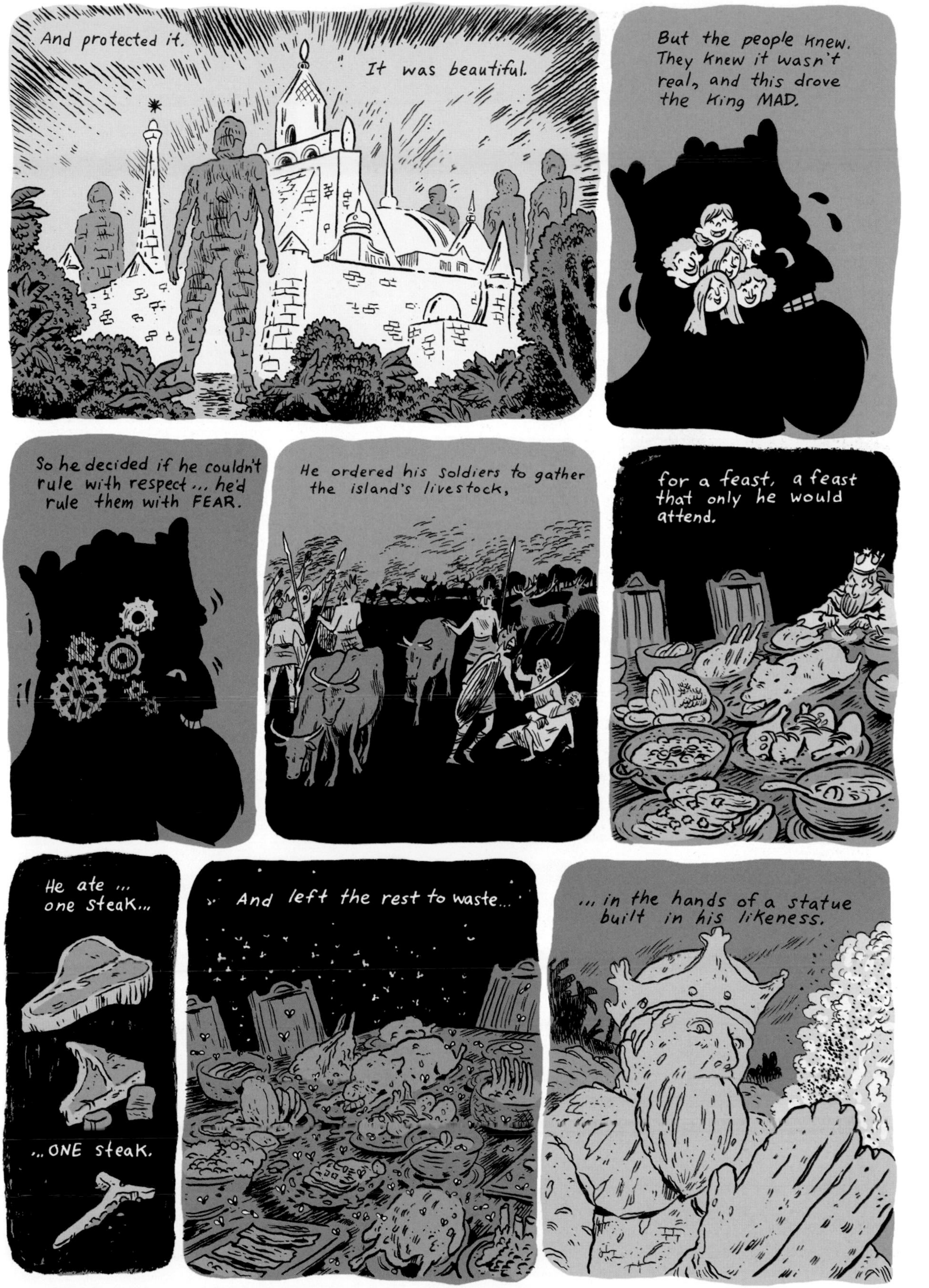
And protected it.
It was beautiful.
But the people knew. They knew it wasn't real, and this drove the King MAD.
So he decided if he couldn't rule with respect ... he'd rule them with FEAR.
He ordered his soldiers to gather the island's livestock,
for a feast, a feast that only he would attend.
He ate ... one steak...
...ONE steak.
And left the rest to waste...
... in the hands of a statue built in his likeness.

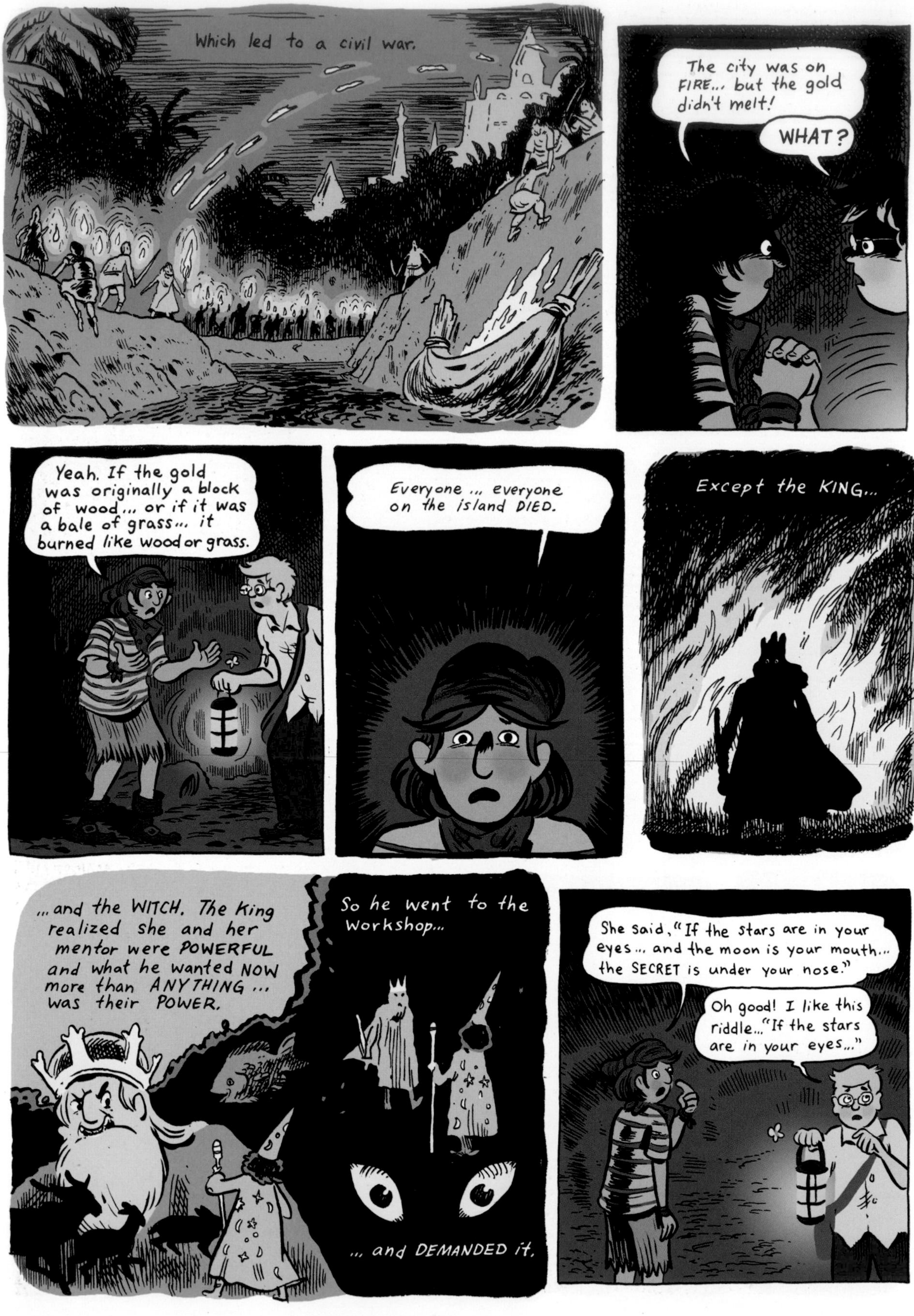
Which led to a civil war.
The city was on FIRE... but the gold didn't melt!
WHAT?
Yeah. If the gold was originally a block of wood... or if it was a bale of grass... it burned like wood or grass.
Everyone ... everyone on the island DIED.
Except the KING...
...and the WITCH. The King realized she and her mentor were POWERFUL and what he wanted NOW more than ANYTHING ... was their POWER.
So he went to the Workshop...
... and DEMANDED it.
She said, "If the stars are in your eyes... and the moon is your mouth... the SECRET is under your nose."
Oh good! I like this riddle..."If the stars are in your eyes..."

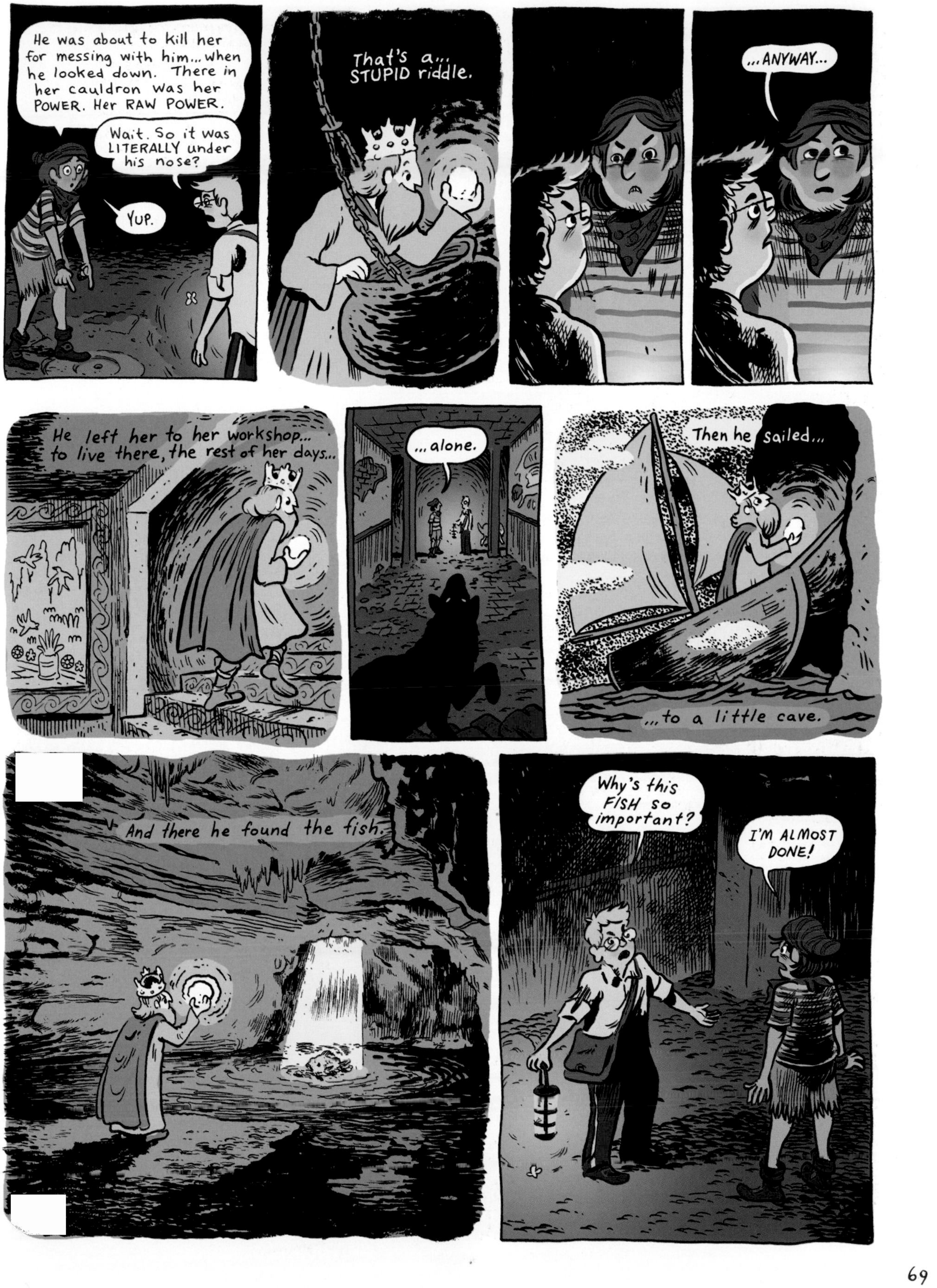

He was about to kill her for messing with him... when he looked down. There in her cauldron was her POWER. Her RAW POWER.
Wait. So it was LITERALLY under his nose?
YUP.
That's a... STUPID riddle.
...ANYWAY...
He left her to her workshop... to live there, the rest of her days...
...alone.
Then he sailed...
...to a little cave.
And there he found the fish.
Why's this FISH so important?
I'M ALMOST DONE!

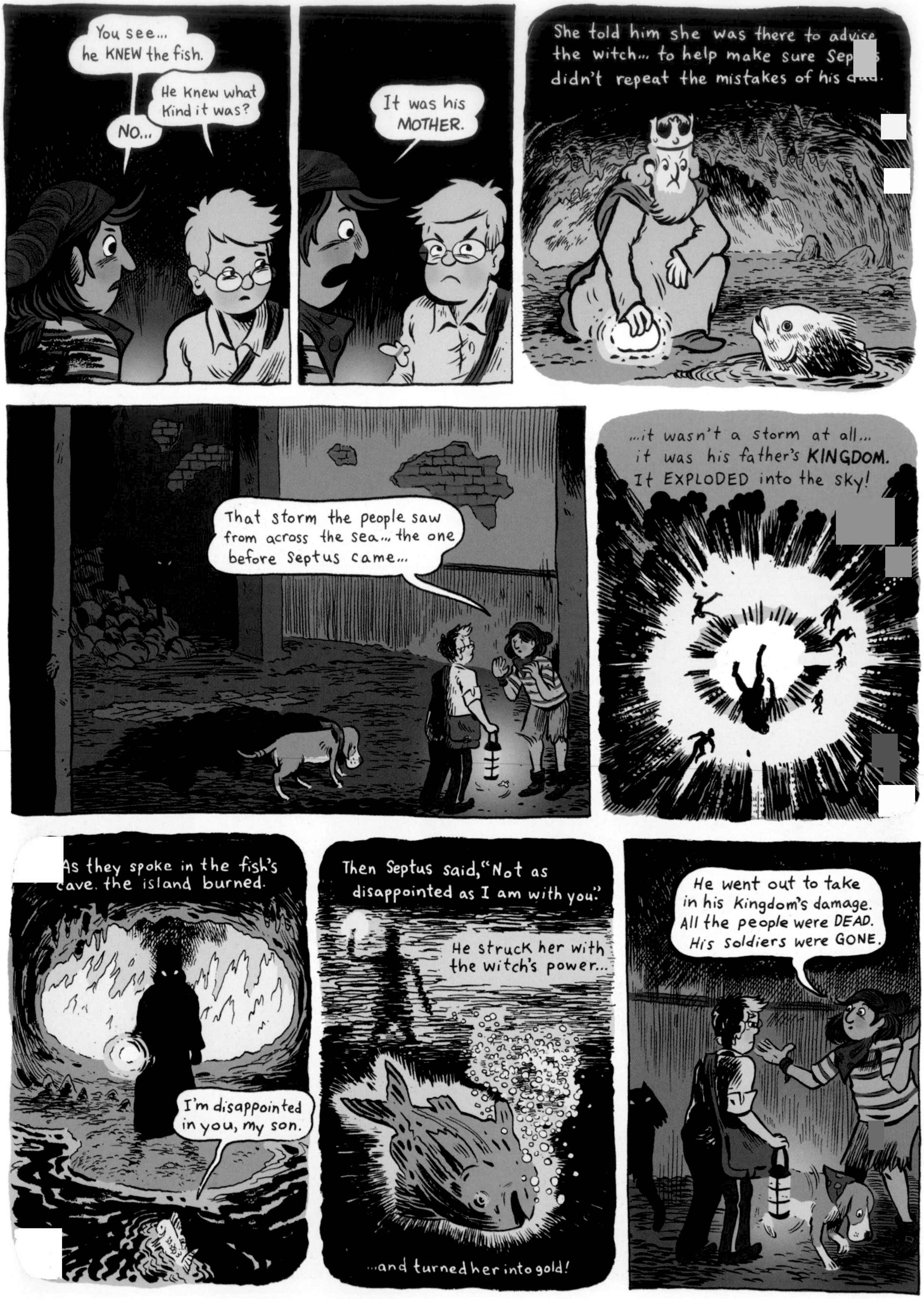
You see... he KNEW the fish.
He knew what kind it was?
NO...
It was his MOTHER.
She told him she was there to advise the witch... to help make sure Sep
didn't repeat the mistakes of his
That storm the people saw from across the sea... the one before Septus came...
...it wasn't a storm at all... it was his father's KINGDOM. It EXPLODED into the sky!
As they spoke in the fish's cave. the island burned.
I'm disappointed in you, my son.
Then Septus said, "Not as disappointed as I am with you."
He struck her with the witch's power...
...and turned her into gold!
He went out to take in his kingdom's damage. All the people were DEAD. His soldiers were GONE.

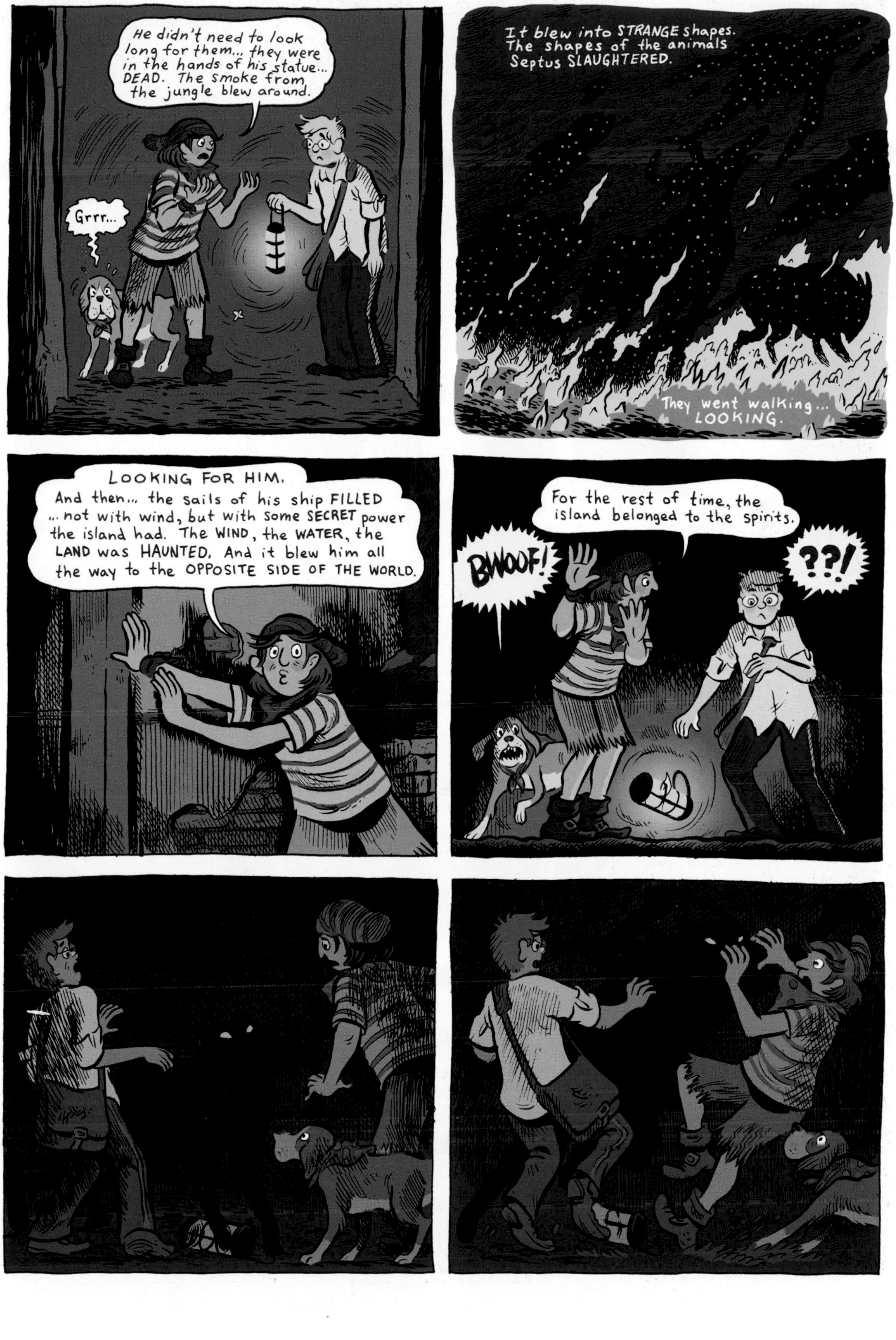
He didn't need to look long for them... they were in the hands of his statue... DEAD. The smoke from the jungle blew around.
Grrr...
It blew into STRANGE shapes. The shapes of the animals Septus SLAUGHTERED.
They went walking... LOOKING.
LOOKING FOR HIM.
And then... the sails of his ship FILLED ... not with wind, but with some SECRET power the island had. The WIND, the WATER, the LAND was HAUNTED. And it blew him all the way to the OPPOSITE SIDE OF THE WORLD.
For the rest of time, the island belonged to the spirits.
BWOOF!
??!

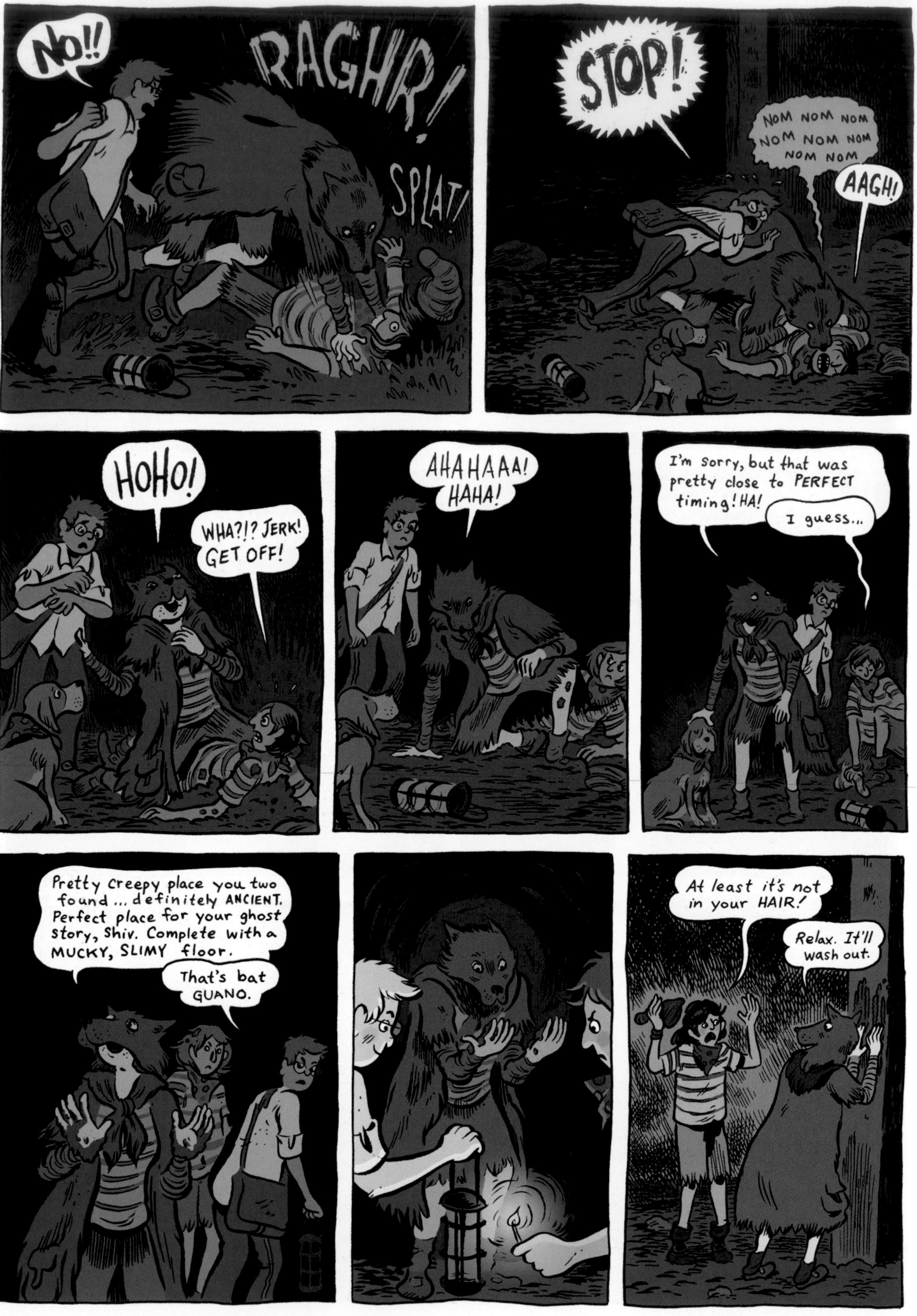
NO!!
RAGHR!
SPLAT!
STOP!
NOM NOM NOM
NOM NOM NOM
NOM NOM
AAGH!
HOHO!
WHA?!? JERK! GET OFF!
AHAHAAA! HAHA!
I'm sorry, but that was pretty close to PERFECT timing! HA!
I guess...
Pretty creepy place you two found... definitely ANCIENT. Perfect place for your ghost story, Shiv. Complete with a MUCKY, SLIMY floor.
That's bat GUANO.
At least it's not in your HAIR!
Relax. It'll wash out.

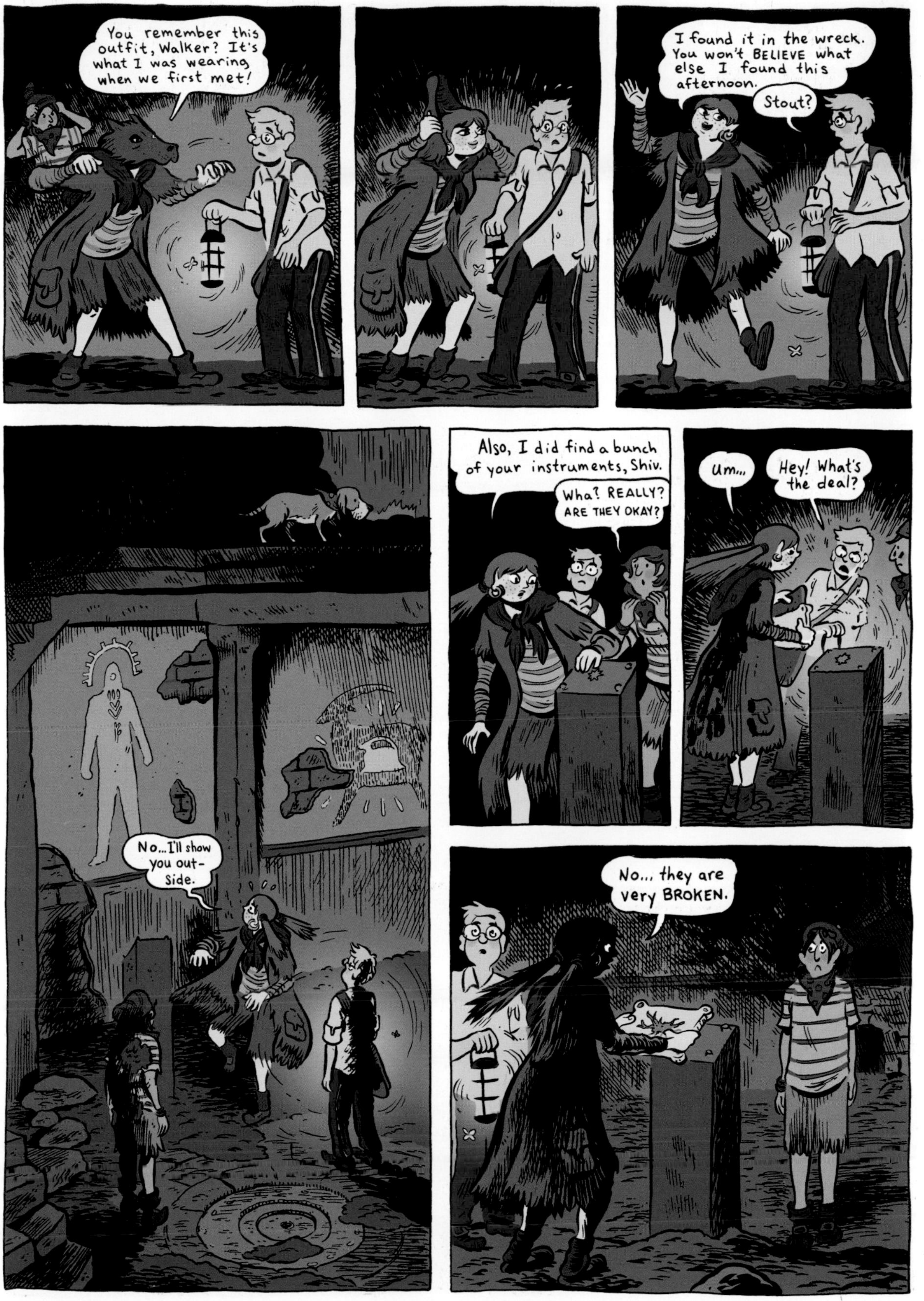

You remember this outfit, Walker? It's what I was wearing when we first met!
I found it in the wreck. You won't BELIEVE what else I found this afternoon.
Stout?
No... I'll show you out-side.
Also, I did find a bunch of your instruments, Shiv.
Wha? REALLY? ARE THEY OKAY?
Um...
Hey! What's the deal?
No... they are very BROKEN.

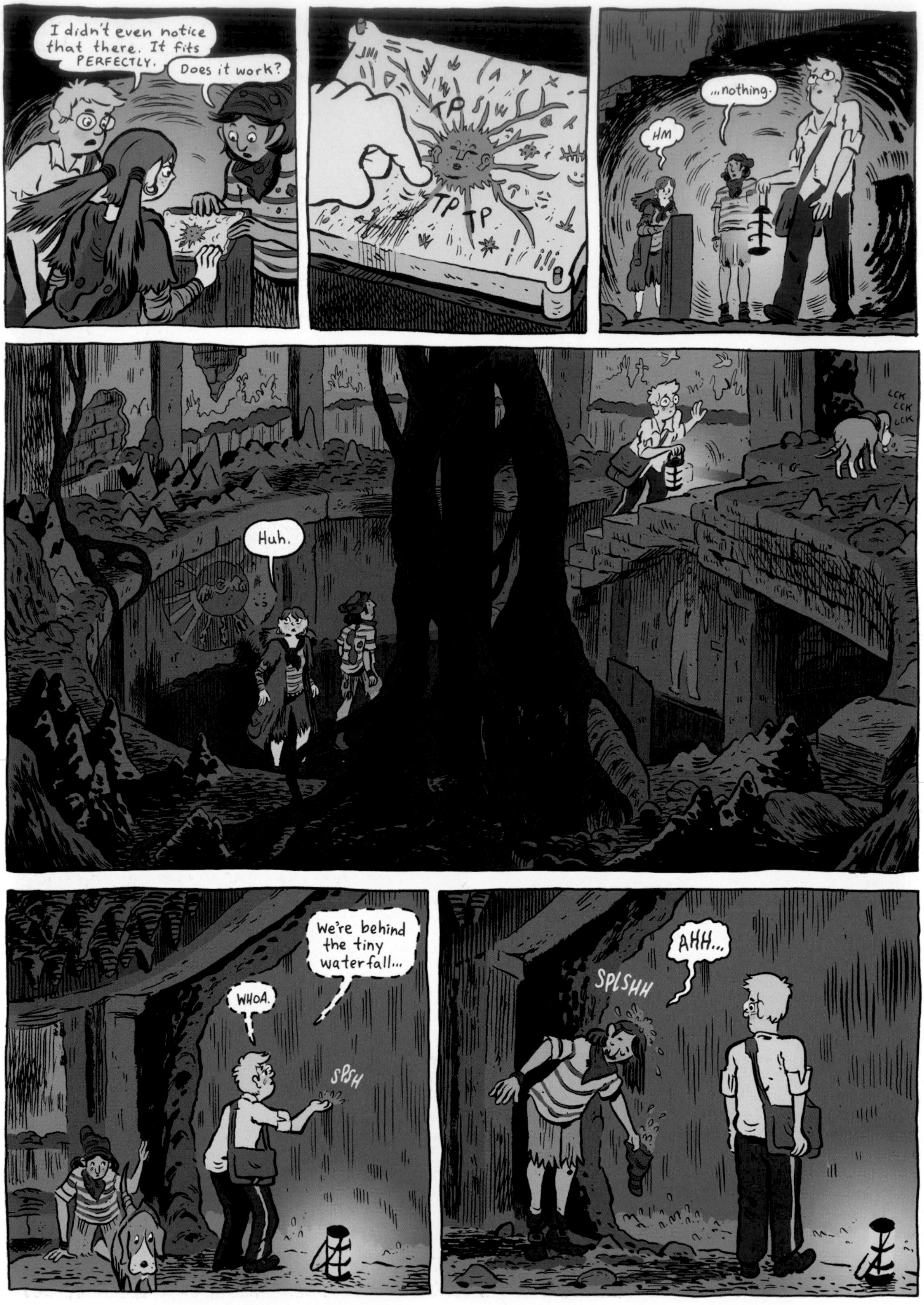
I didn't even notice that there. It fits PERFECTLY.
Does it work?
TP
TP
TP
HM
...nothing.
LCK LCK LCK
Huh.
WHOA.
We're behind the tiny waterfall...
SPSH
SPLSHH
AHH...

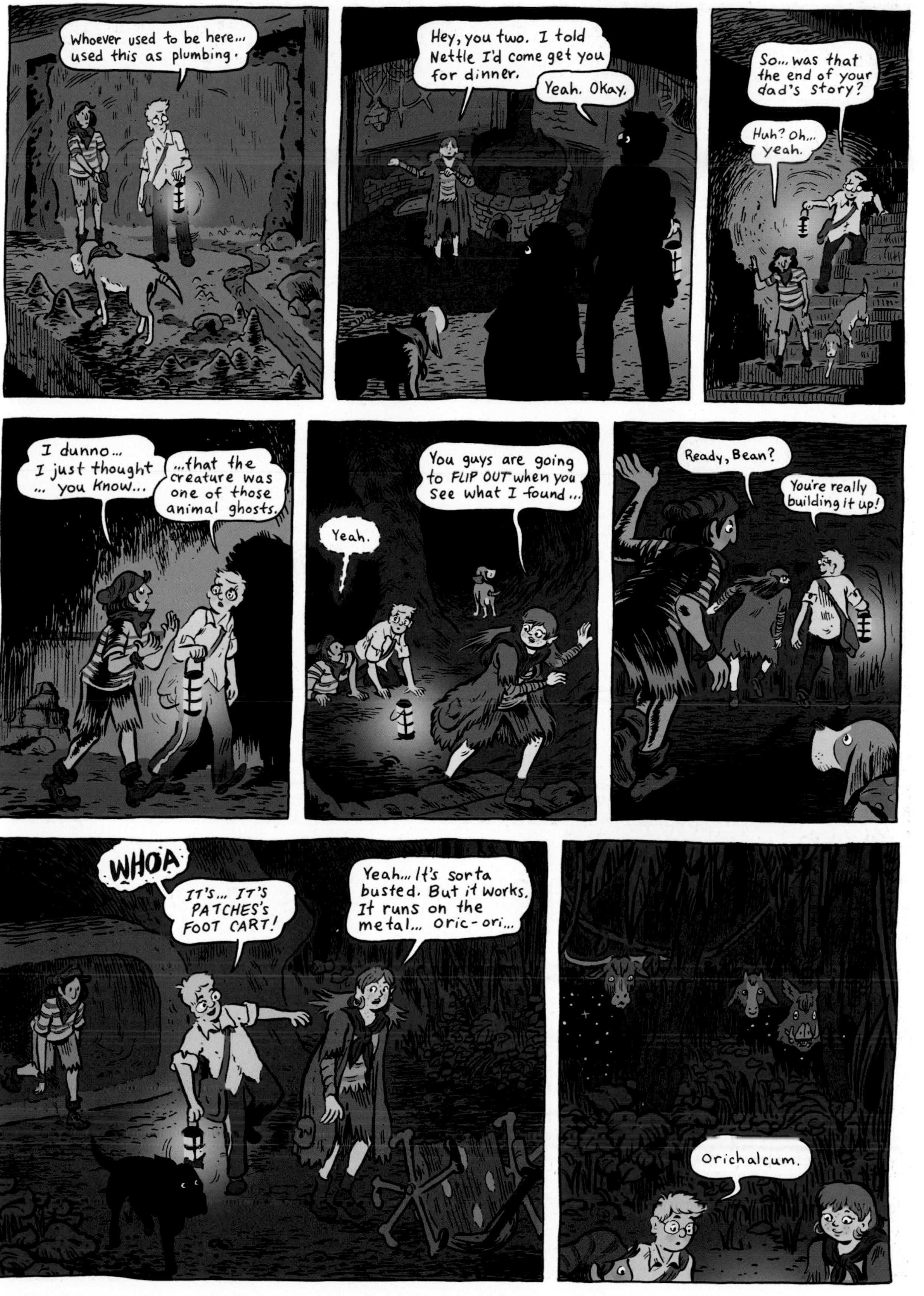

Whoever used to be here... used this as plumbing.
Hey, you two. I told Nettle I'd come get you for dinner.
Yeah. Okay.
So... was that the end of your dad's story?
Huh? Oh... yeah.
I dunno... I just thought ... you know...
...that the creature was one of those animal ghosts.
You guys are going to FLIP OUT when you see what I found...
Yeah.
Ready, Bean?
You're really building it up!
WHOA
IT'S... IT'S PATCHES's FOOT CART!
Yeah... It's sorta busted. But it works. It runs on the metal... oric-ori...
Orichalcum.

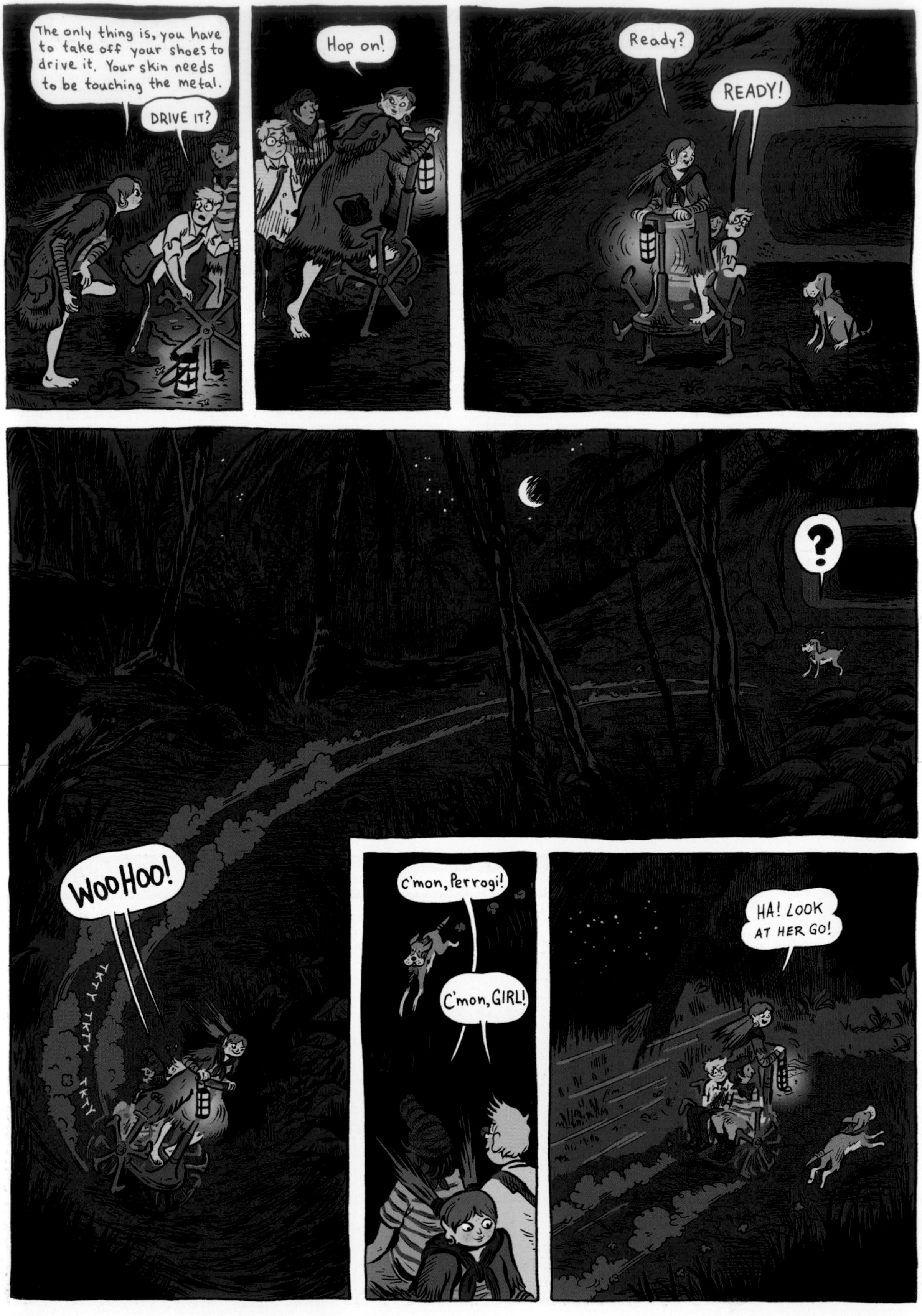
The only thing is, you have to take off your shoes to drive it. Your skin needs to be touching the metal.
DRIVE IT?
Hop on!
Ready?
READY!
?
WOOHOO!
TKTY TKTY
TKTY
C'mon, Perrogi!
C'mon, GIRL!
HA! LOOK AT HER GO!

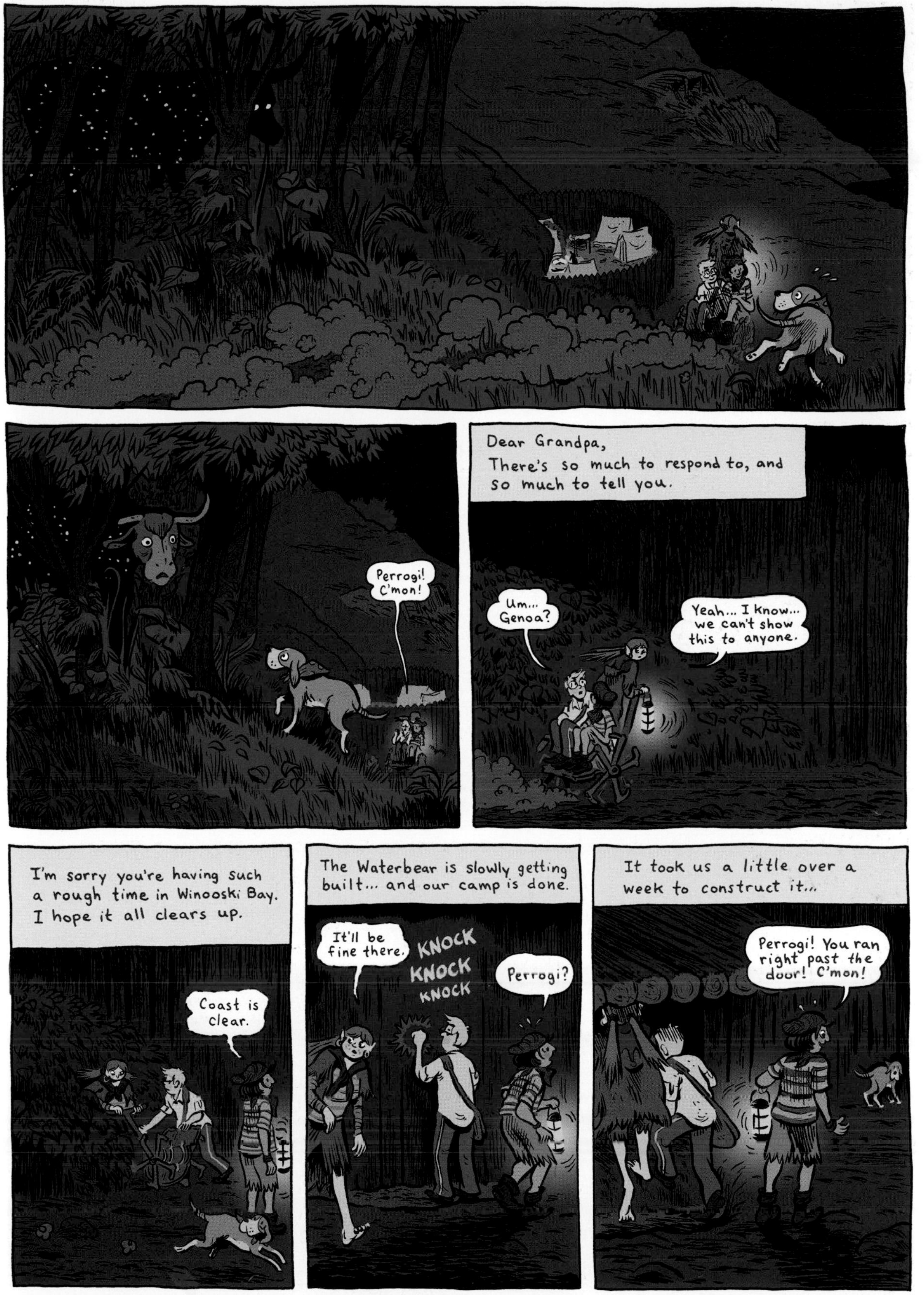
Perrogi! C'mon!
Dear Grandpa,
There's so much to respond to, and so much to tell you.
Um... Genoa?
Yeah... I know... we can't show this to anyone.
I'm sorry you're having such a rough time in Winooski Bay. I hope it all clears up.
Coast is clear.
The Waterbear is slowly getting built... and our camp is done.
It'll be fine there.
KNOCK
KNOCK
KNOCK
Perrogi?
It took us a little over a week to construct it...
Perrogi! You ran right past the door! C'mon!

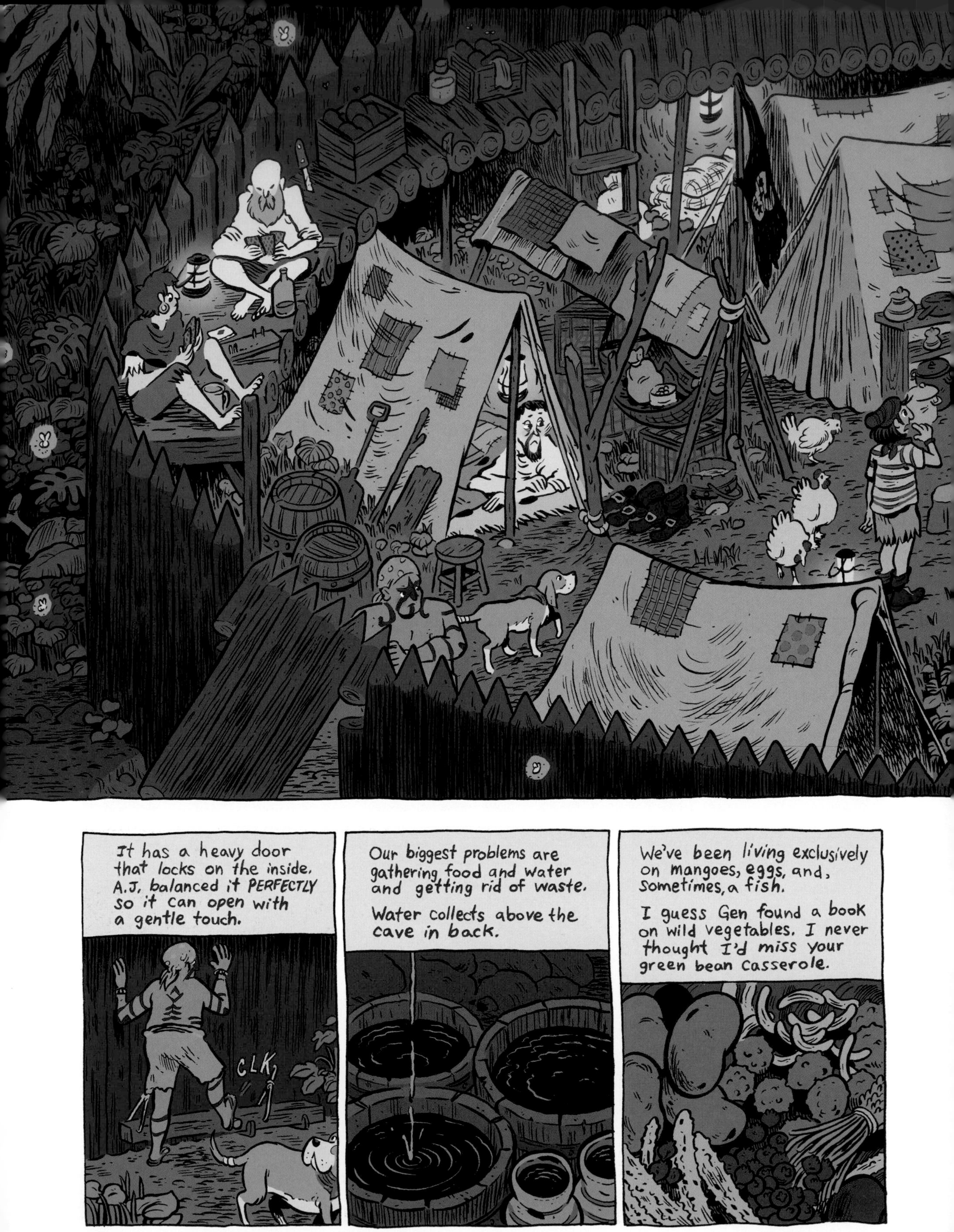
It has a heavy door that locks on the inside. A.J. balanced it PERFECTLY so it can open with a gentle touch.
CLK!
Our biggest problems are gathering food and water and getting rid of waste.
Water collects above the cave in back.
We've been living exclusively on mangoes, eggs, and, sometimes, a fish.
I guess Gen found a book on wild vegetables. I never thought I'd miss your green bean casserole.

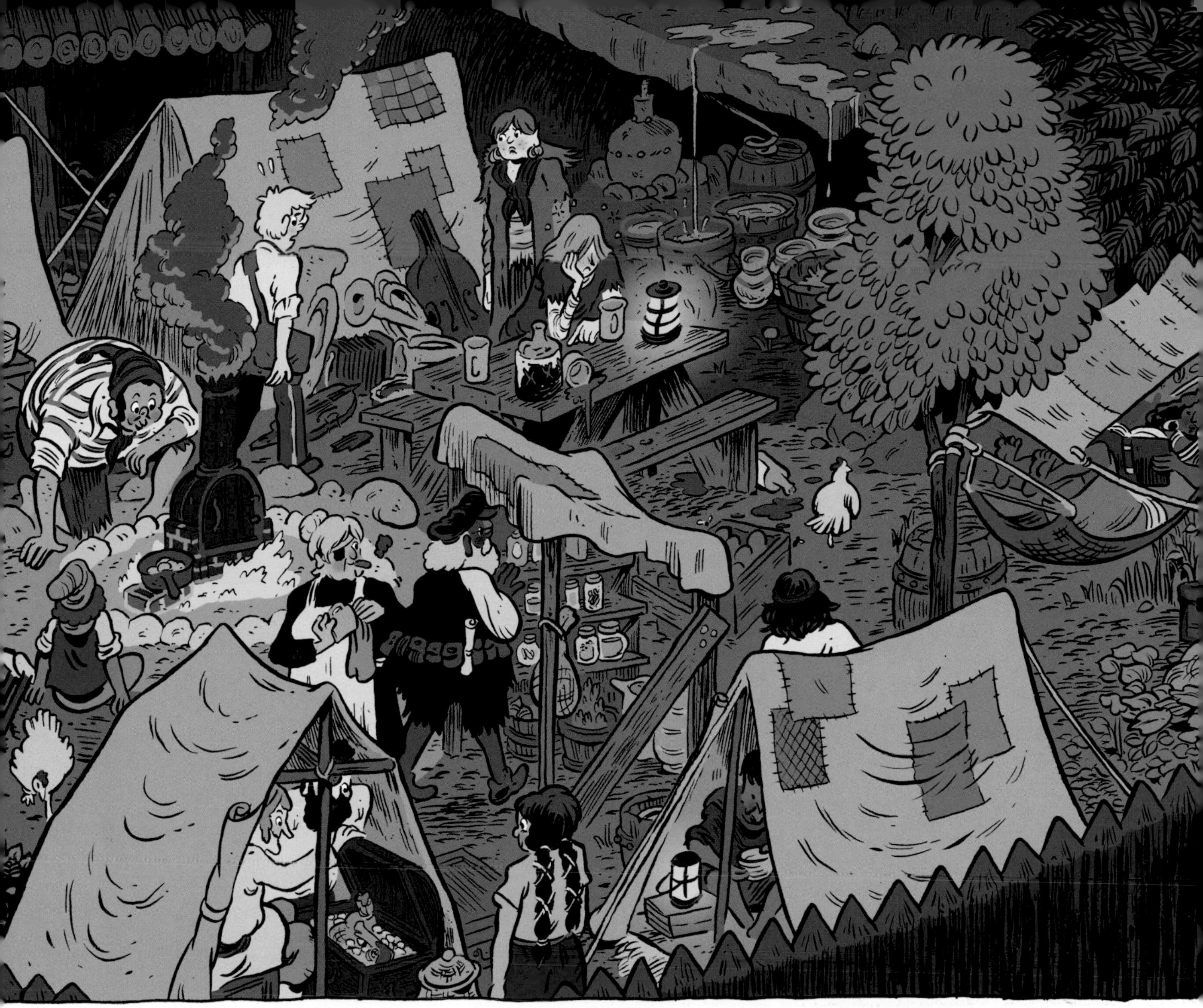

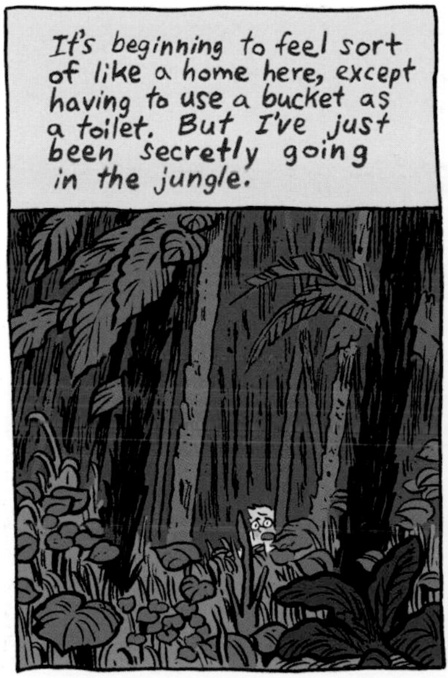
It's beginning to feel sort of like a home here, except having to use a bucket as a toilet. But I've just been secretly going in the jungle.

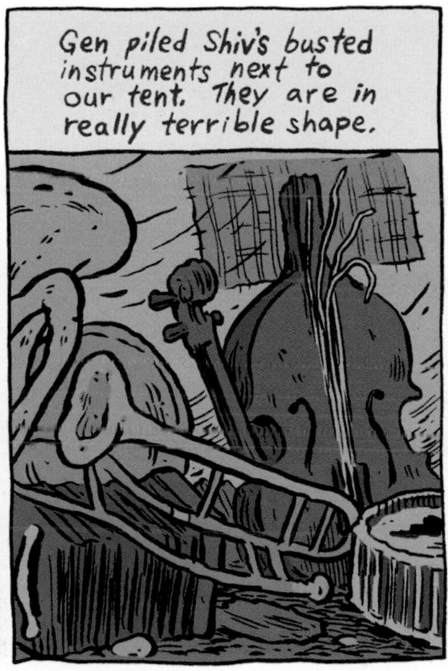
Gen piled Shiv's busted instruments next to our tent. They are in really terrible shape.

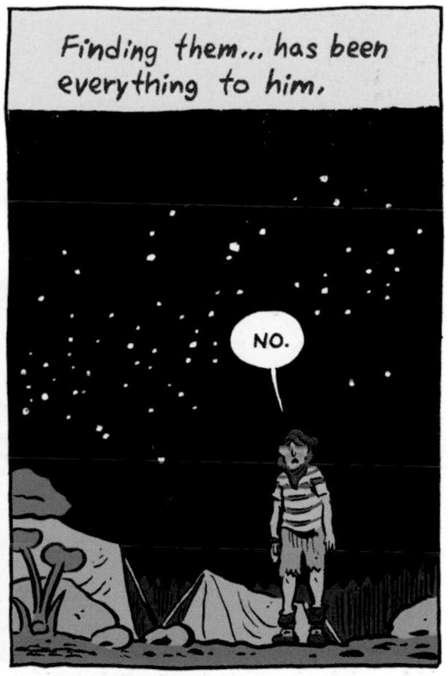
Finding them... has been everything to him.
NO.

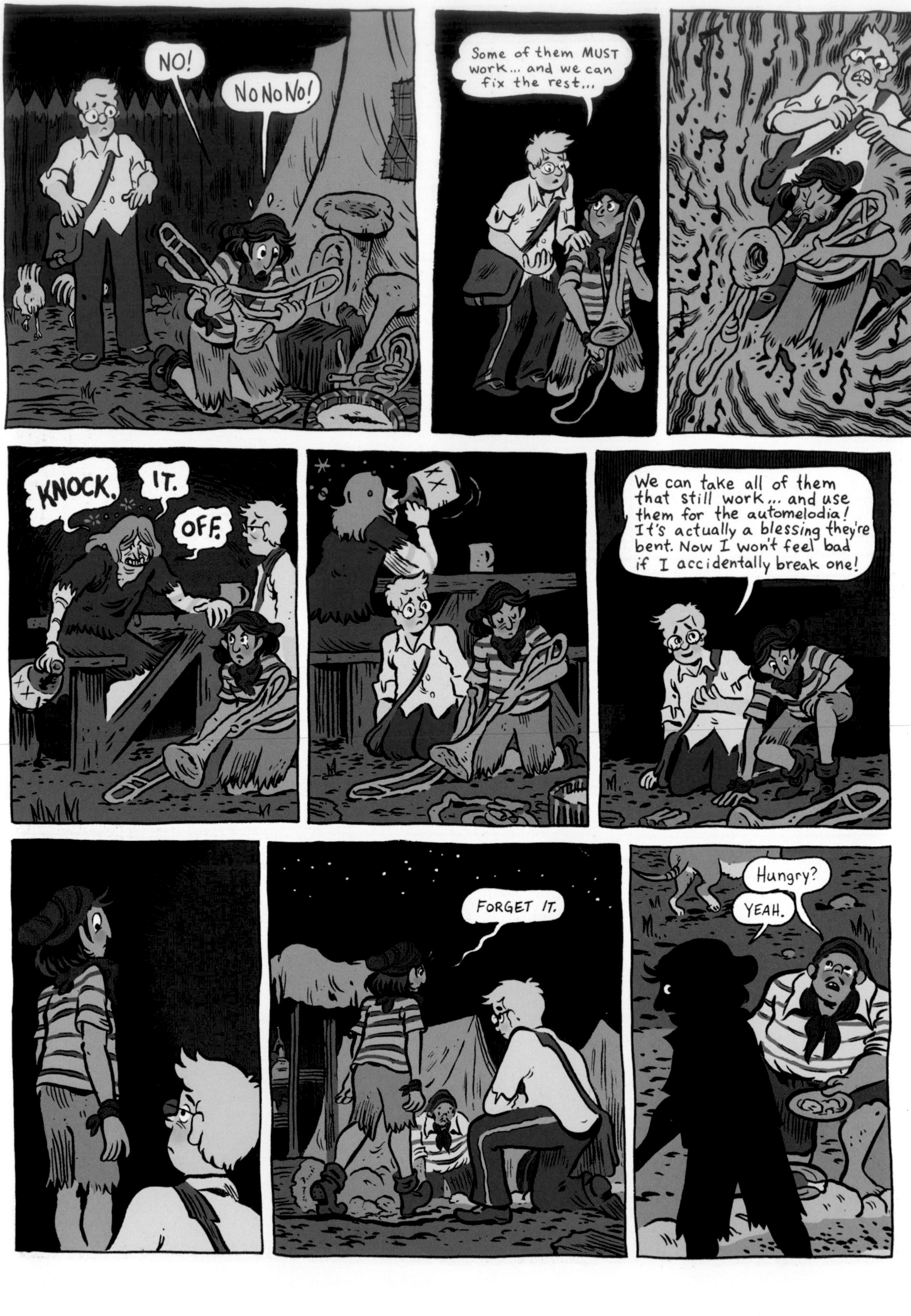
NO!
NoNoNo!
Some of them MUST work... and we can fix the rest...
KNOCK.
IT.
OFF.
We can take all of them that still work... and use them for the automelodia! It's actually a blessing they're bent. Now I won't feel bad if I accidentally break one!
FORGET IT.
Hungry?
YEAH.

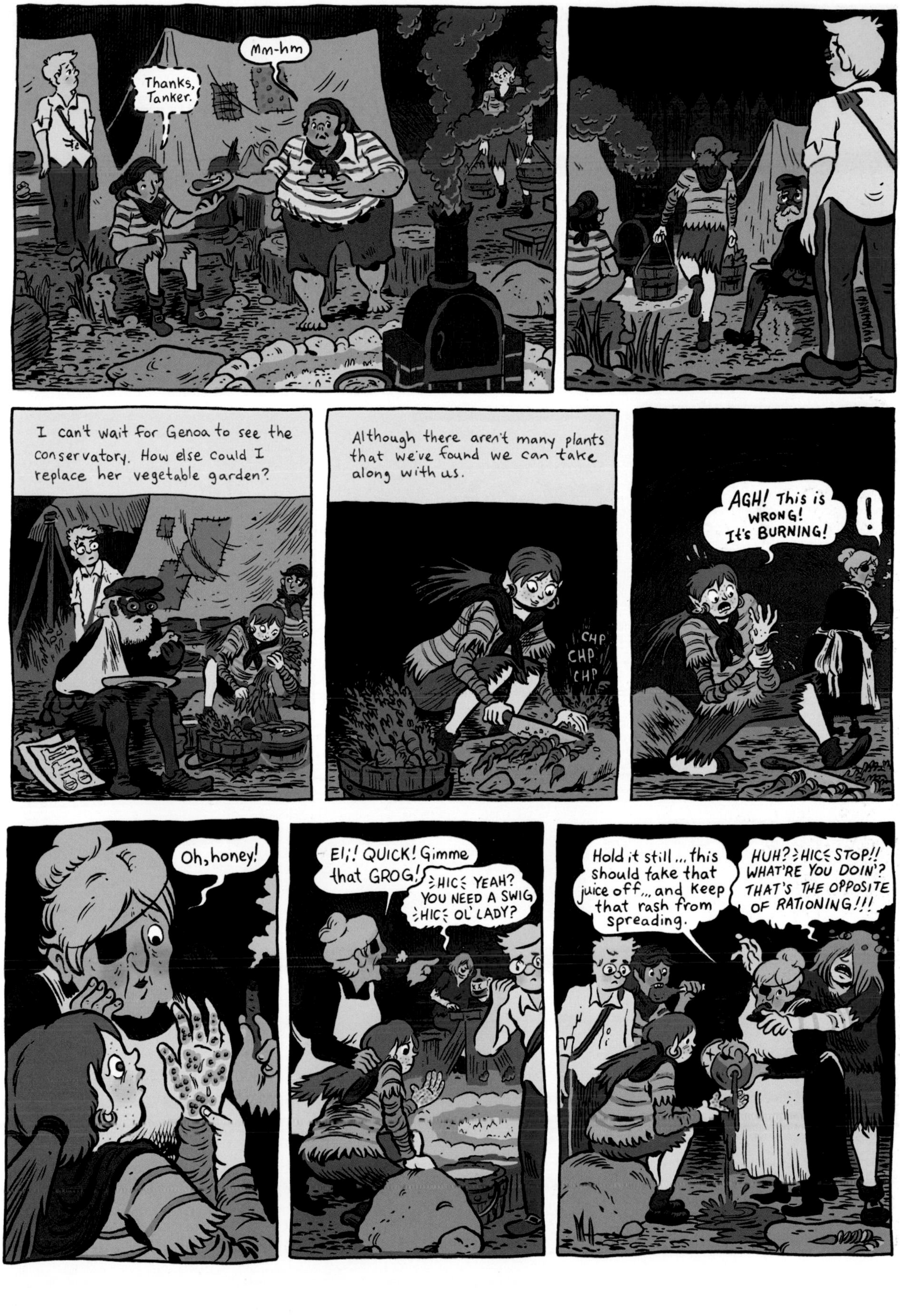
Mm-hm
Thanks, Tanker.
I can't wait for Genoa to see the conservatory. How else could I replace her vegetable garden?
Although there aren't many plants that we've found we can take along with us.
CHP CHP CHP
AGH! This is WRONG! It's BURNING!
!
Oh, honey!
Eli! QUICK! Gimme that GROG!
HIC YEAH? YOU NEED A SWIG HIC OL' LADY?
Hold it still... this should take that juice off... and keep that rash from spreading.
HUH? HIC STOP!! WHAT'RE YOU DOIN'? THAT'S THE OPPOSITE OF RATIONING!!!

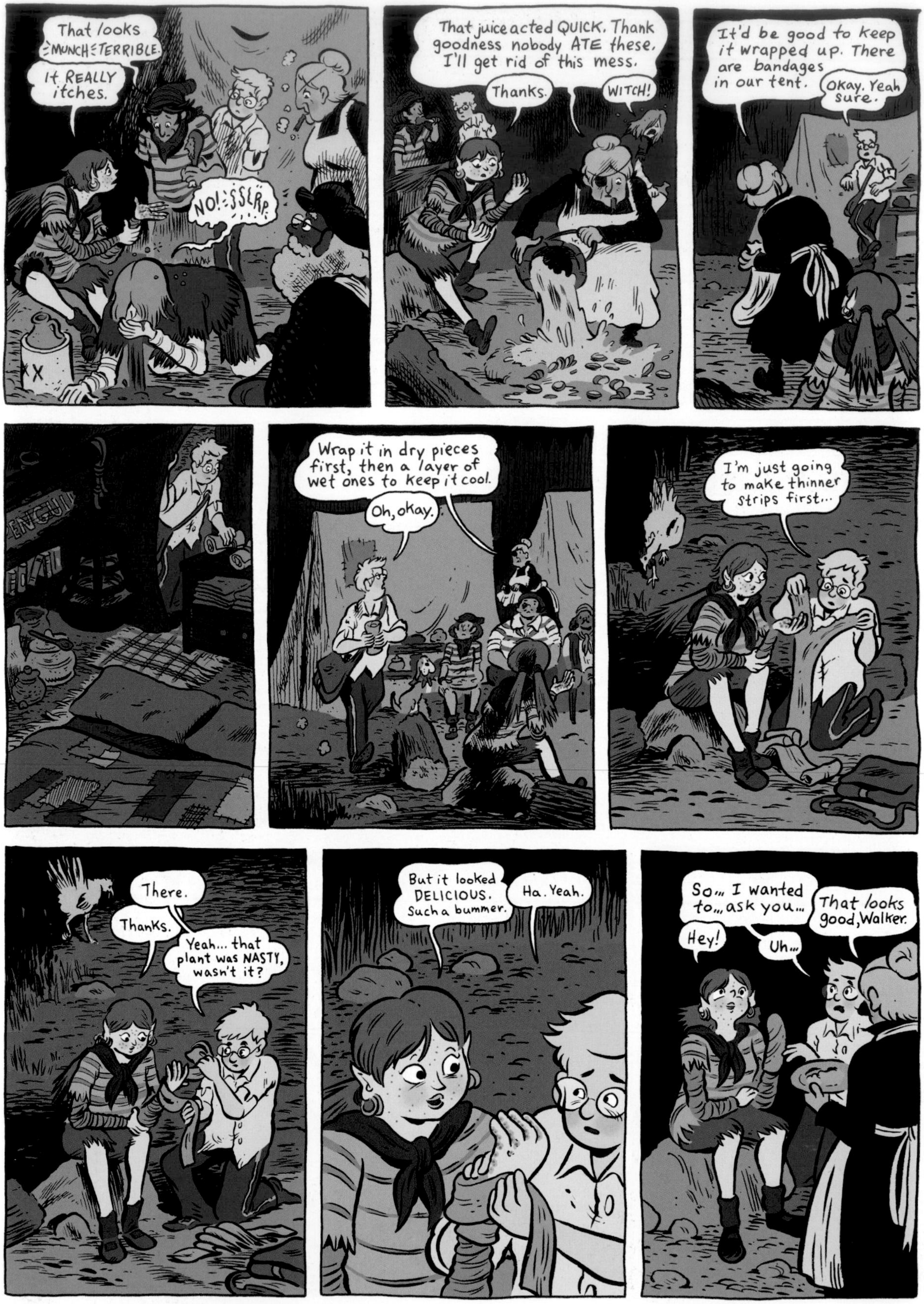
That looks
MUNCH TERRIBLE.
It REALLY itches.
NO! SSLRP.
That juice acted QUICK. Thank goodness nobody ATE these. I'll get rid of this mess.
Thanks.
WITCH!
It'd be good to keep it wrapped up. There are bandages in our tent.
Okay. Yeah sure.
Wrap it in dry pieces first, then a layer of wet ones to keep it cool.
Oh, okay.
I'm just going to make thinner strips first...
There.
Thanks.
Yeah... that plant was NASTY, wasn't it?
But it looked DELICIOUS. Such a bummer.
Ha. Yeah.
So... I wanted to... ask you...
That looks good, Walker.
Hey!
Uh...

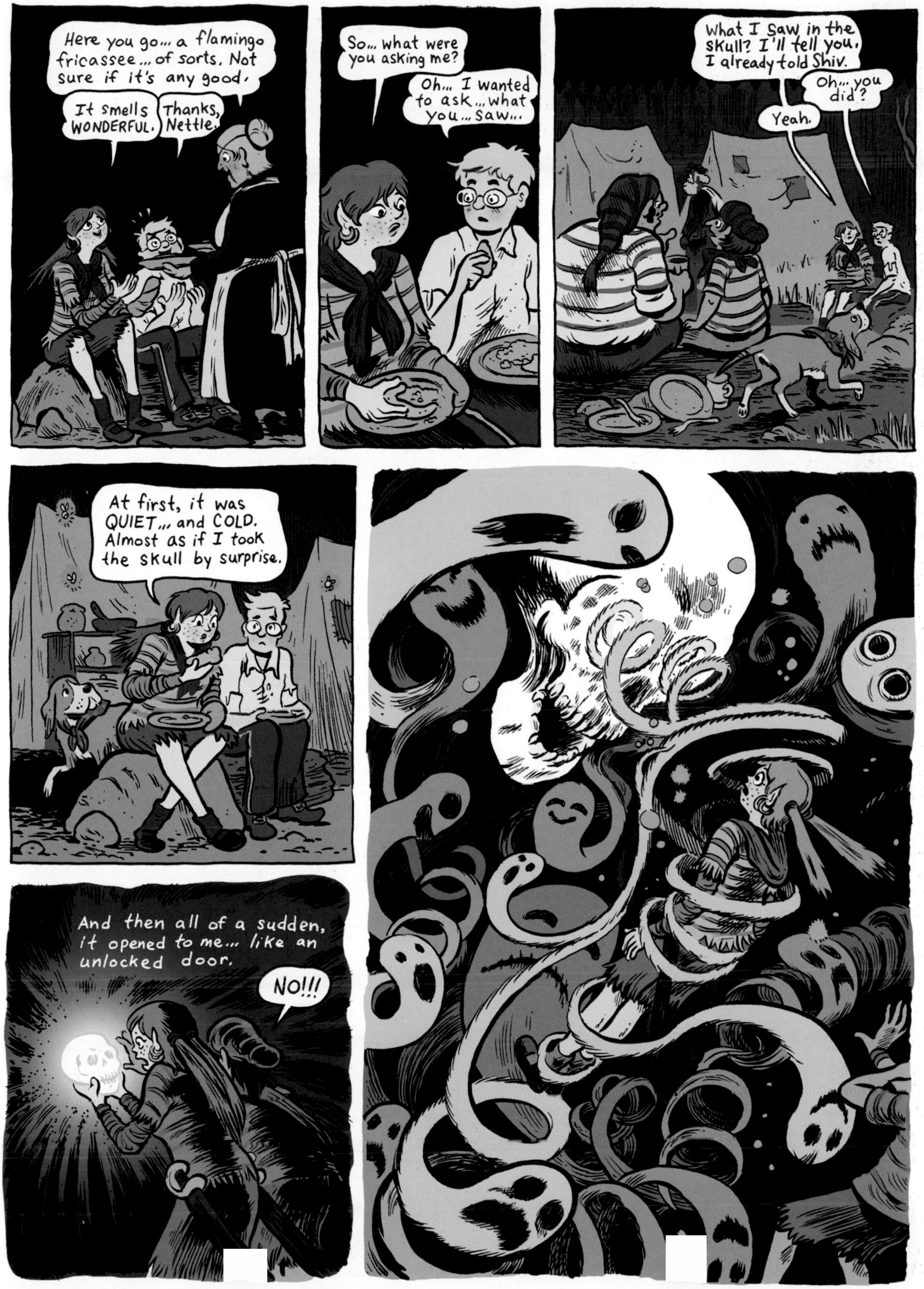
Here you go... a flamingo fricassee... of sorts. Not sure if it's any good.
It smells WONDERFUL.
Thanks, Nettle.
So... what were you asking me?
Oh... I wanted to ask... what you... saw...
What I saw in the skull? I'll tell you. I already told Shiv.
Yeah.
Oh... you did?
At first, it was QUIET... and COLD. Almost as if I took the skull by surprise.
And then all of a sudden, it opened to me... like an unlocked door.
NO!!!

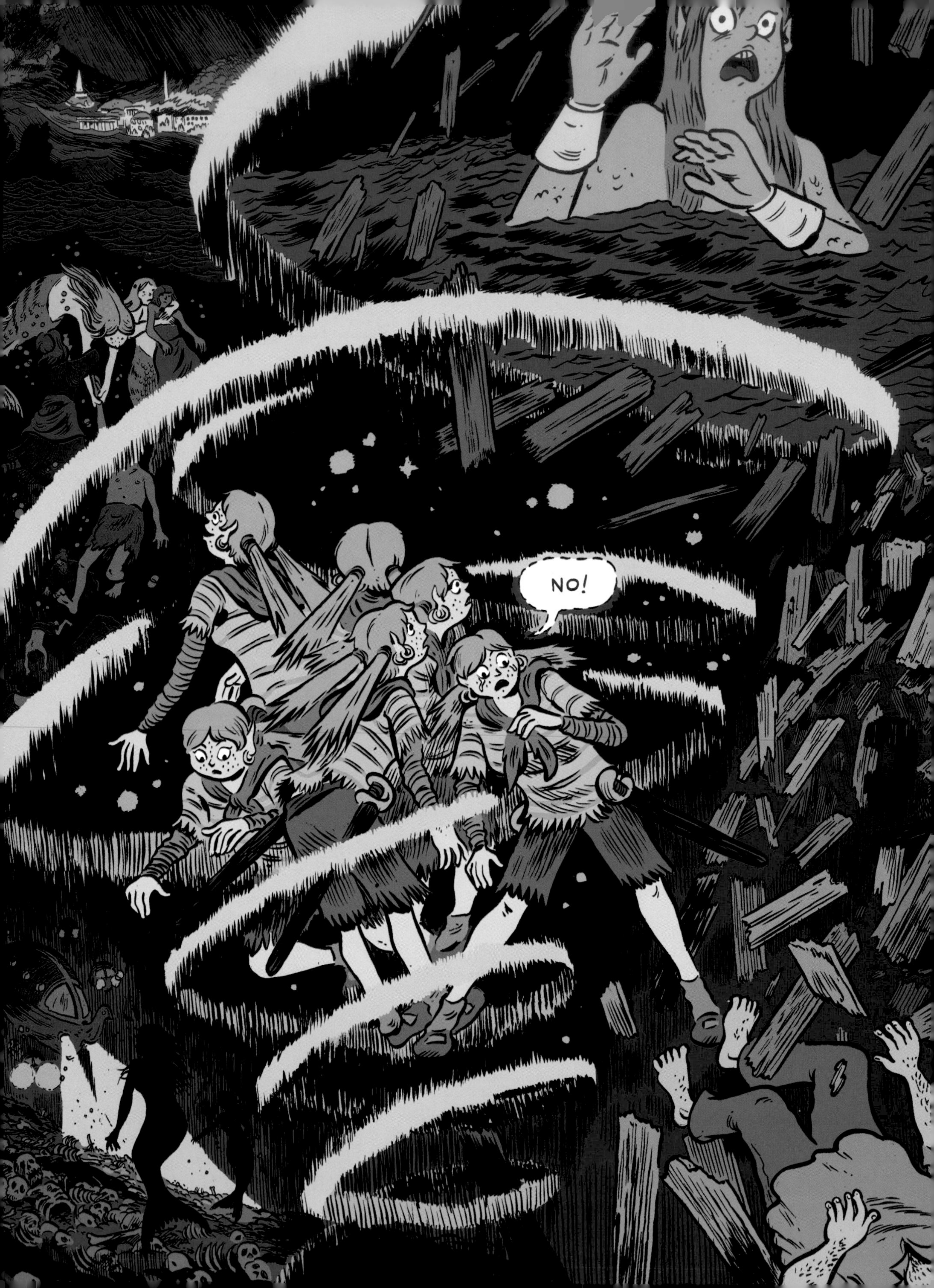
NO!

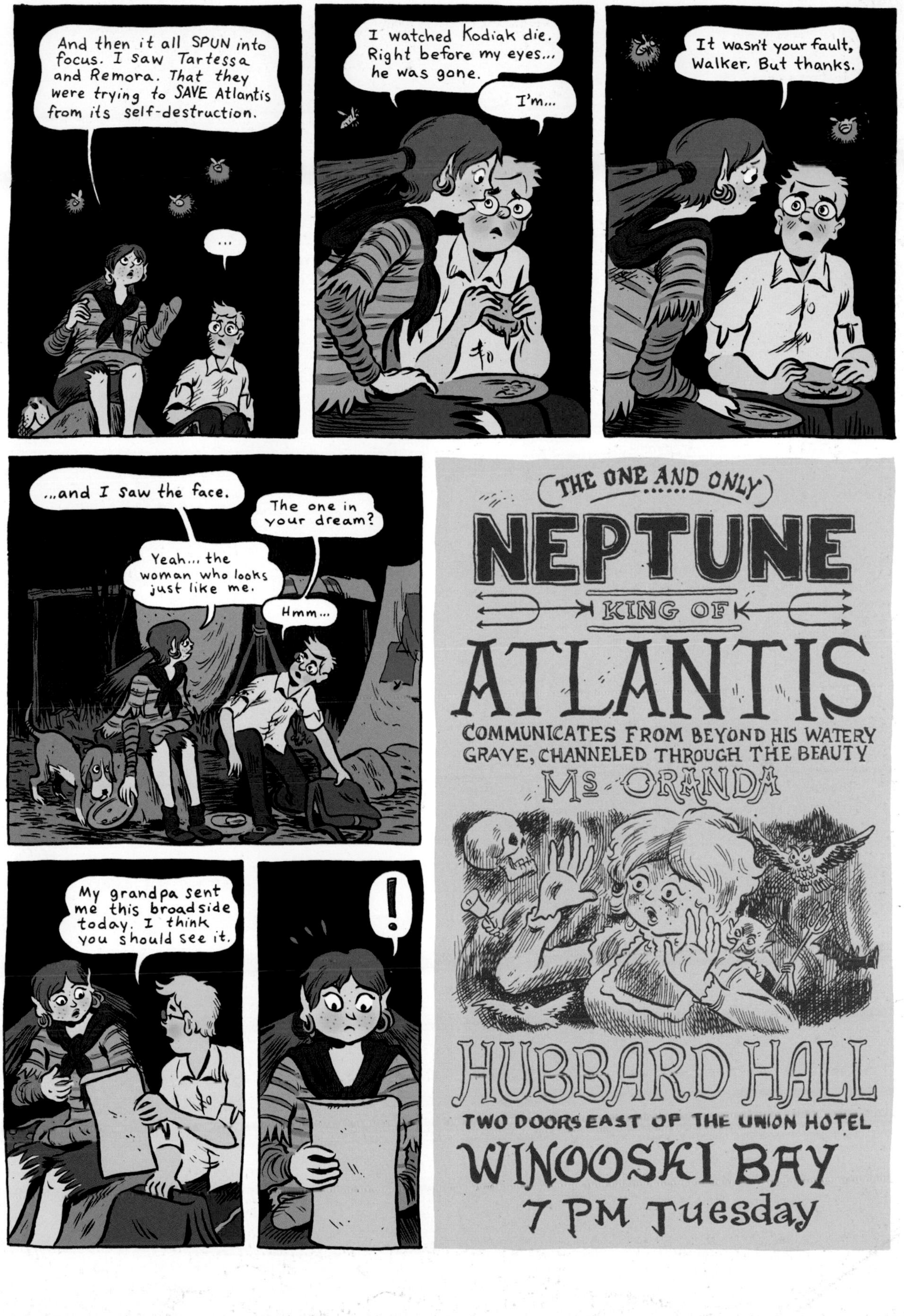

And then it all SPUN into focus. I saw Tartessa and Remora. That they were trying to SAVE Atlantis from its self-destruction.
...
I watched Kodiak die. Right before my eyes... he was gone.
I'm...
It wasn't your fault, Walker. But thanks.
...and I saw the face.
The one in your dream?
Yeah... the woman who looks just like me.
Hmm...
My grandpa sent me this broadside today. I think you should see it.
!
THE ONE AND ONLY
NEPTUNE
KING OF
ATLANTIS
COMMUNICATES FROM BEYOND HIS WATERY GRAVE, CHANNELED THROUGH THE BEAUTY
Ms ORANDA
HUBBARD HALL
TWO DOORS EAST OF THE UNION HOTEL
WINOOSKI BAY
7 PM Tuesday

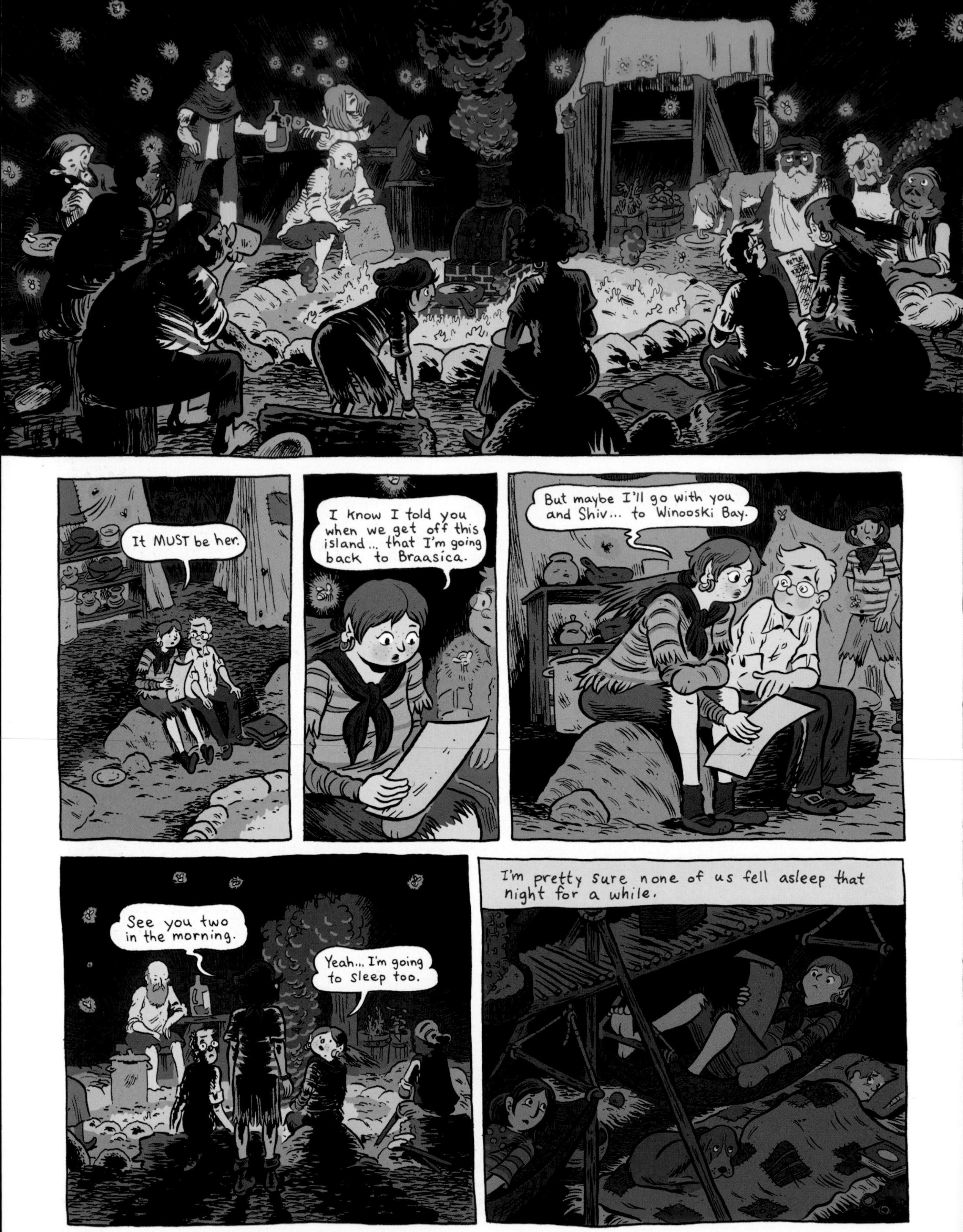
It MUST be her.
I know I told you when we get off this island... that I'm going back to Braasica.
But maybe I'll go with you and Shiv... to Winooski Bay.
See you two in the morning.
Yeah... I'm going to sleep too.
I'm pretty sure none of us fell asleep that night for a while.

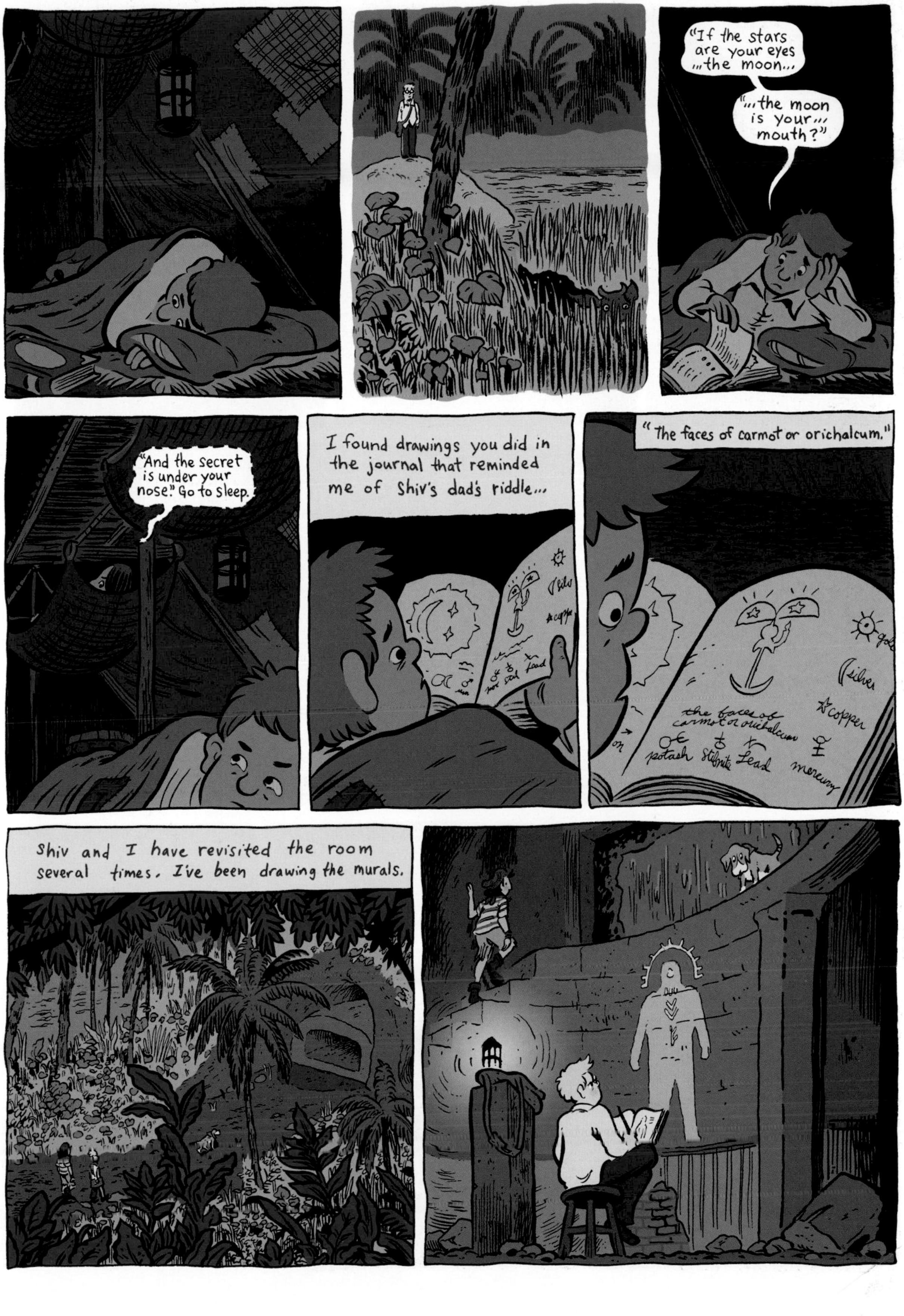
"If the stars are your eyes ...the moon...
"...the moon is your... mouth?"
"And the secret is under your nose." Go to sleep.
I found drawings you did in the journal that reminded me of Shiv's dad's riddle...
"The faces of carmot or orichalcum."
silver
copper
the faces of carmot or orichalcum
potash
Stibnite
Lead
mercury
Shiv and I have revisited the room several times. I've been drawing the murals.

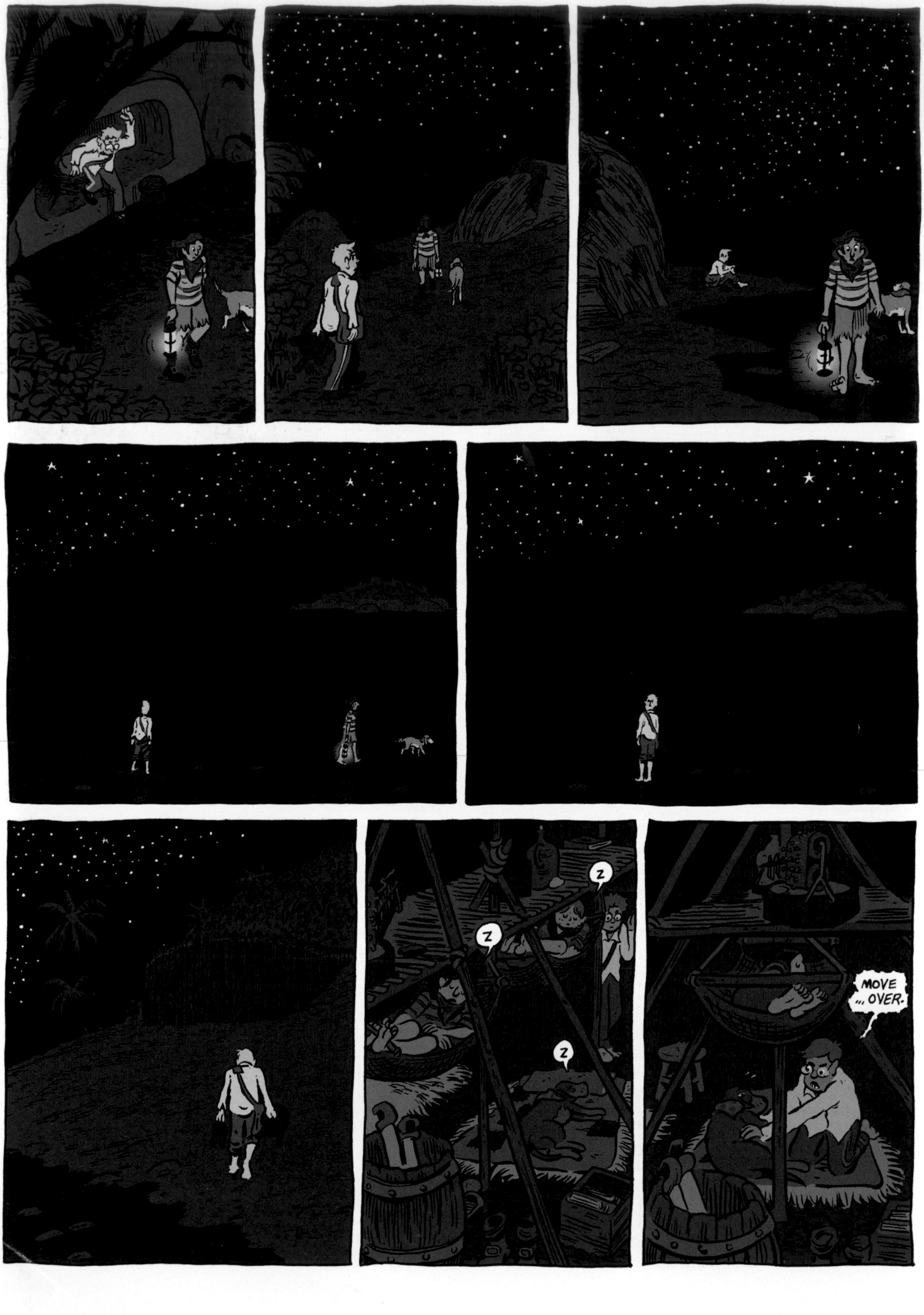
Z
Z
Z
MOVE
... OVER.

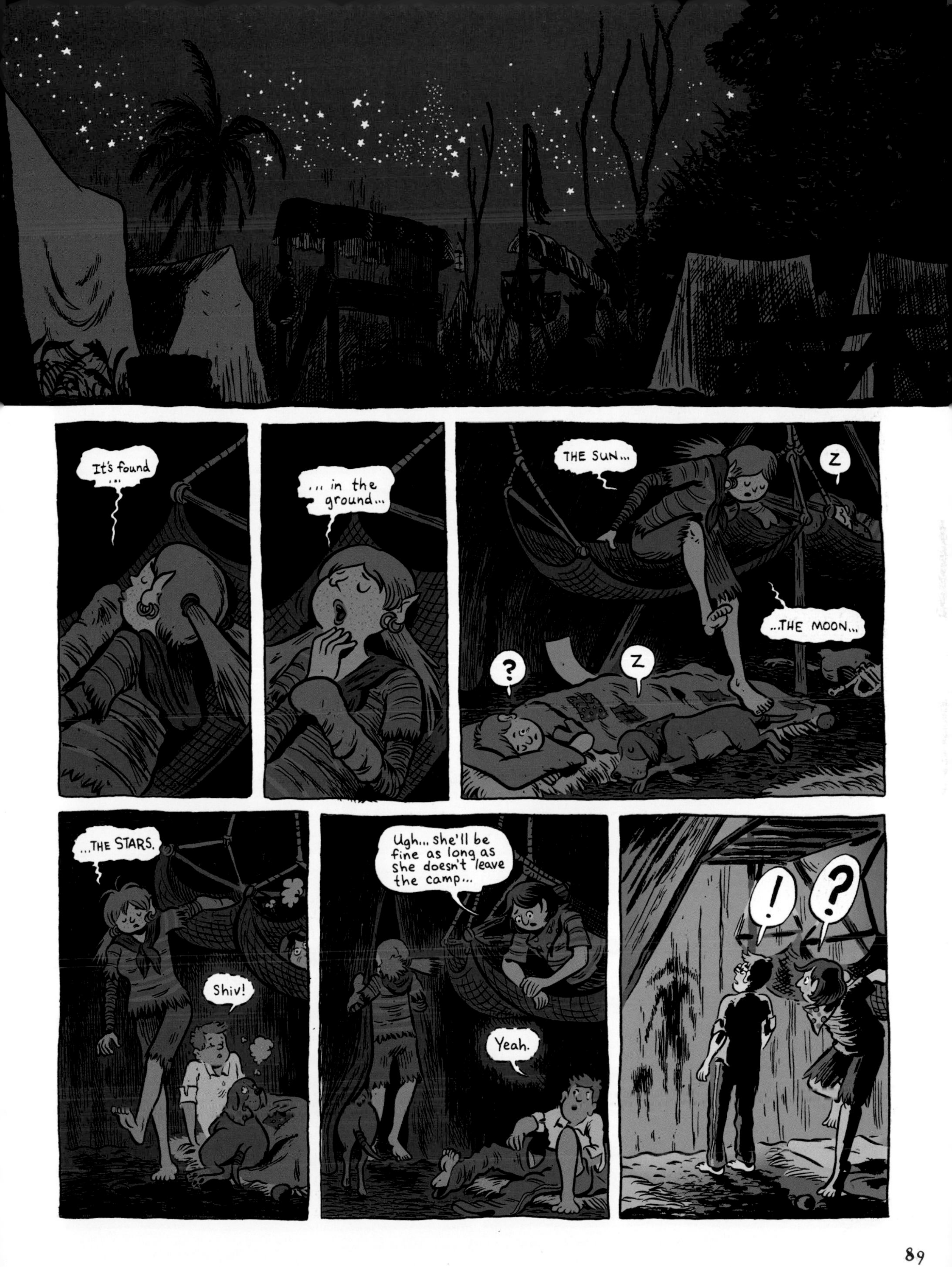
It's found ...
... in the ground...
THE SUN...
Z
...THE MOON...
?
Z
...THE STARS.
Shiv!
Ugh... she'll be fine as long as she doesn't leave the camp...
Yeah.
!
?

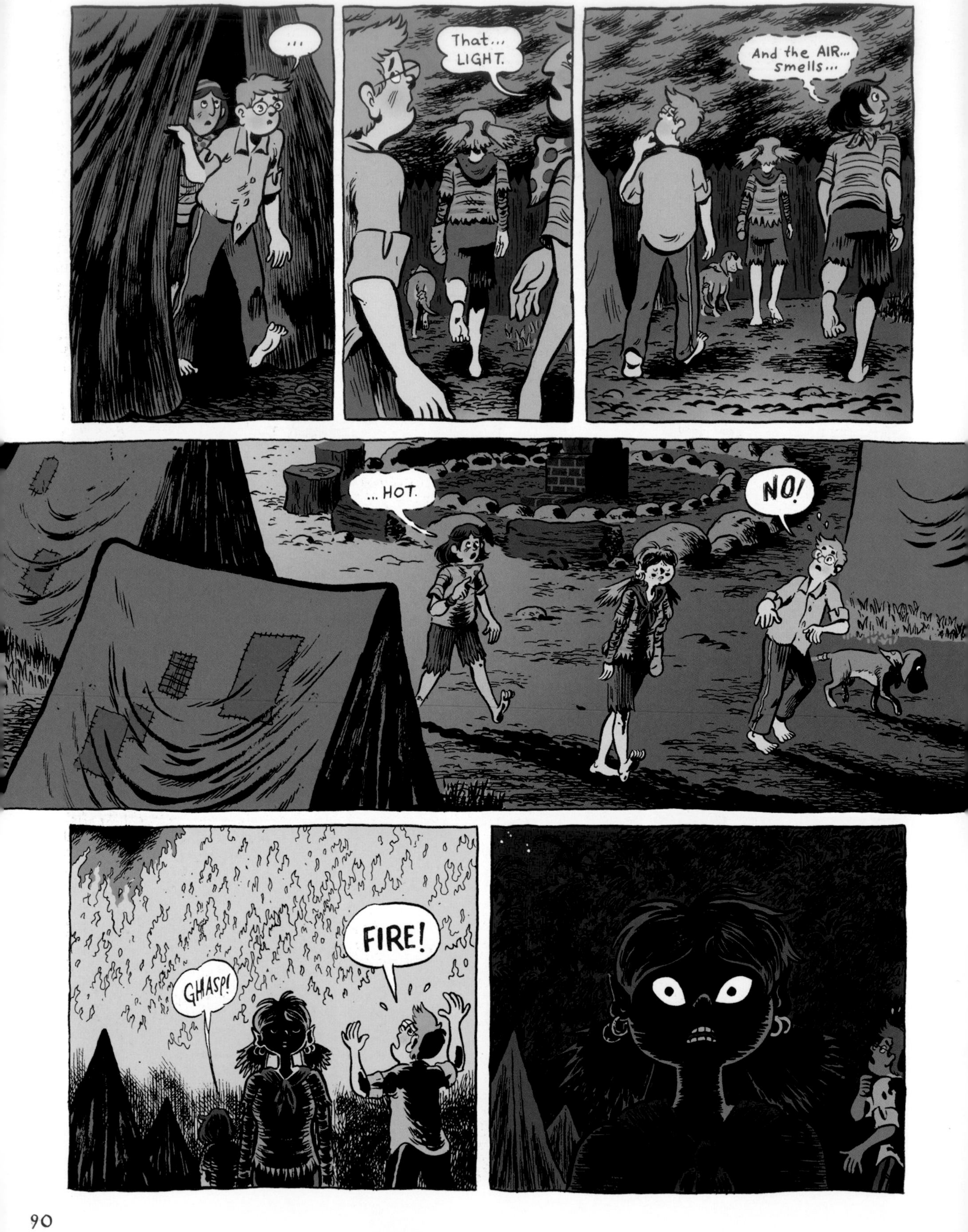
...
That... LIGHT.
And the AIR... smells...
...HOT.
NO!
GHASP!
FIRE!

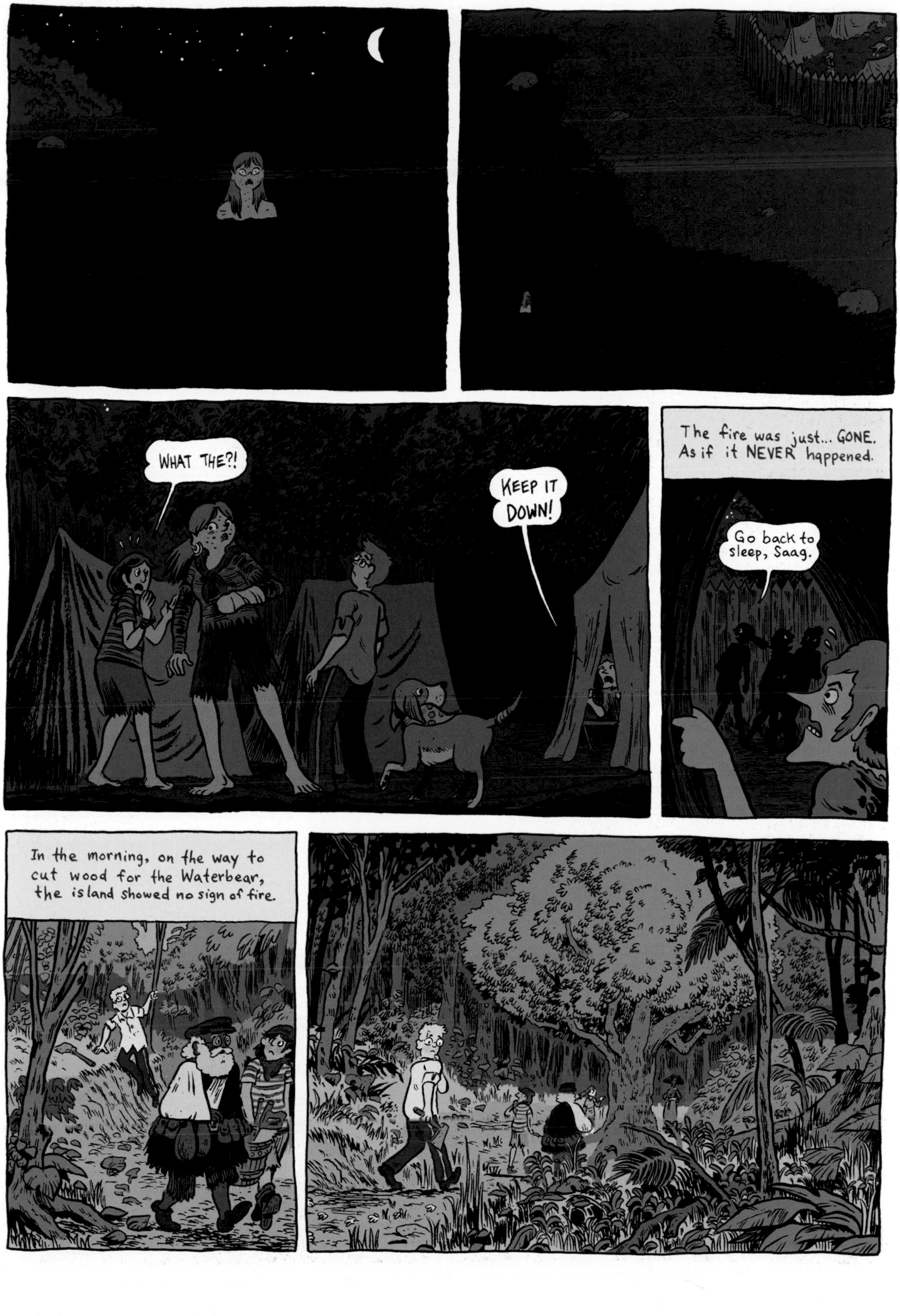
WHAT THE?!
KEEP IT DOWN!
The fire was just... GONE. As if it NEVER happened.
Go back to sleep, Saag.
In the morning, on the way to cut wood for the Waterbear, the island showed no sign of fire.

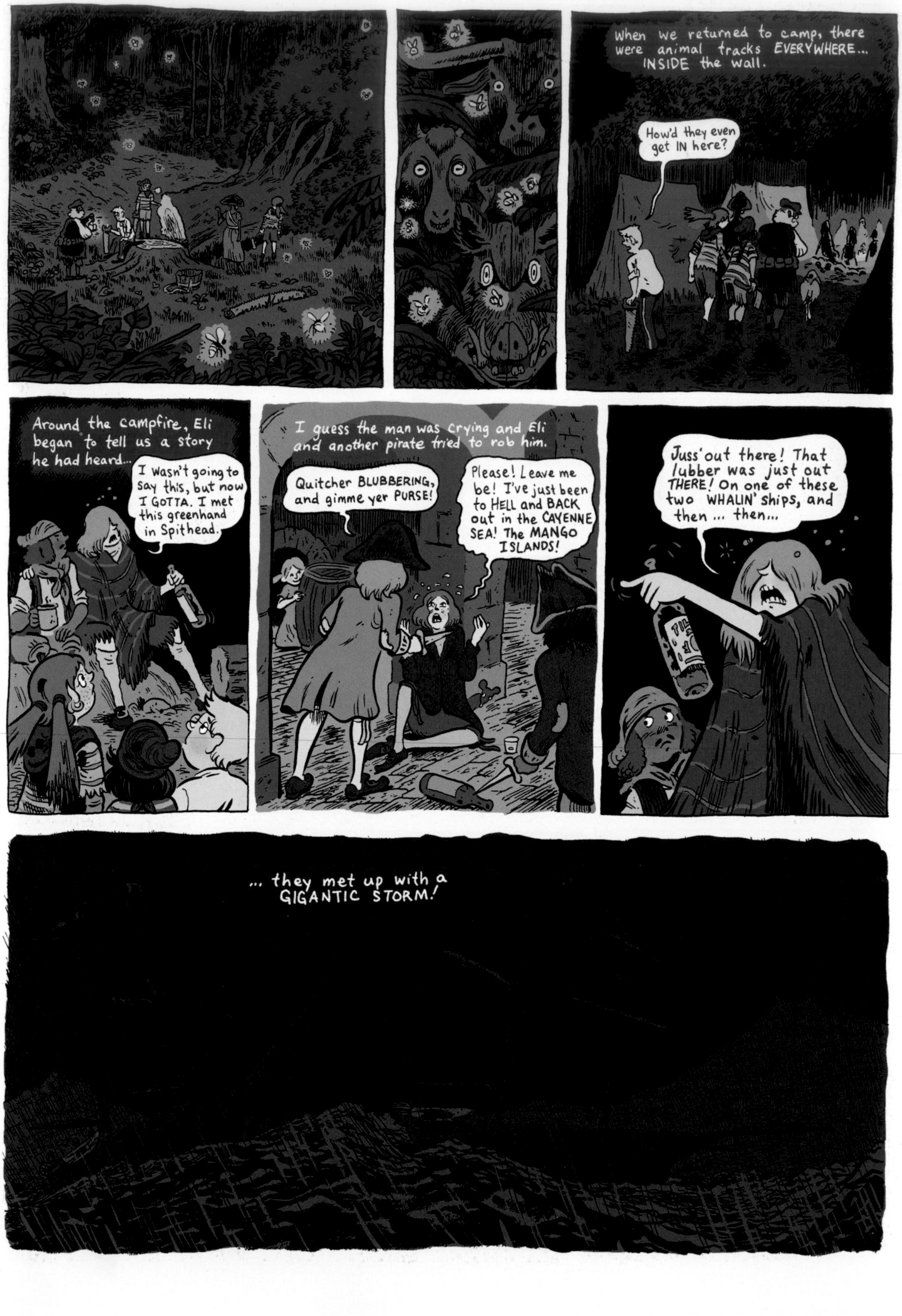
When we returned to camp, there were animal tracks EVERYWHERE... INSIDE the wall.
How'd they even get IN here?
Around the campfire, Eli began to tell us a story he had heard...
I wasn't going to say this, but now I GOTTA. I met this greenhand in Spithead.
I guess the man was crying and Eli and another pirate tried to rob him.
Quitcher BLUBBERING, and gimme yer PURSE!
Please! Leave me be! I've just been to HELL and BACK out in the CAYENNE SEA! The MANGO ISLANDS!
Juss'out there! That lubber was just out THERE! On one of these two WHALIN' ships, and then ... then...
... they met up with a GIGANTIC STORM!

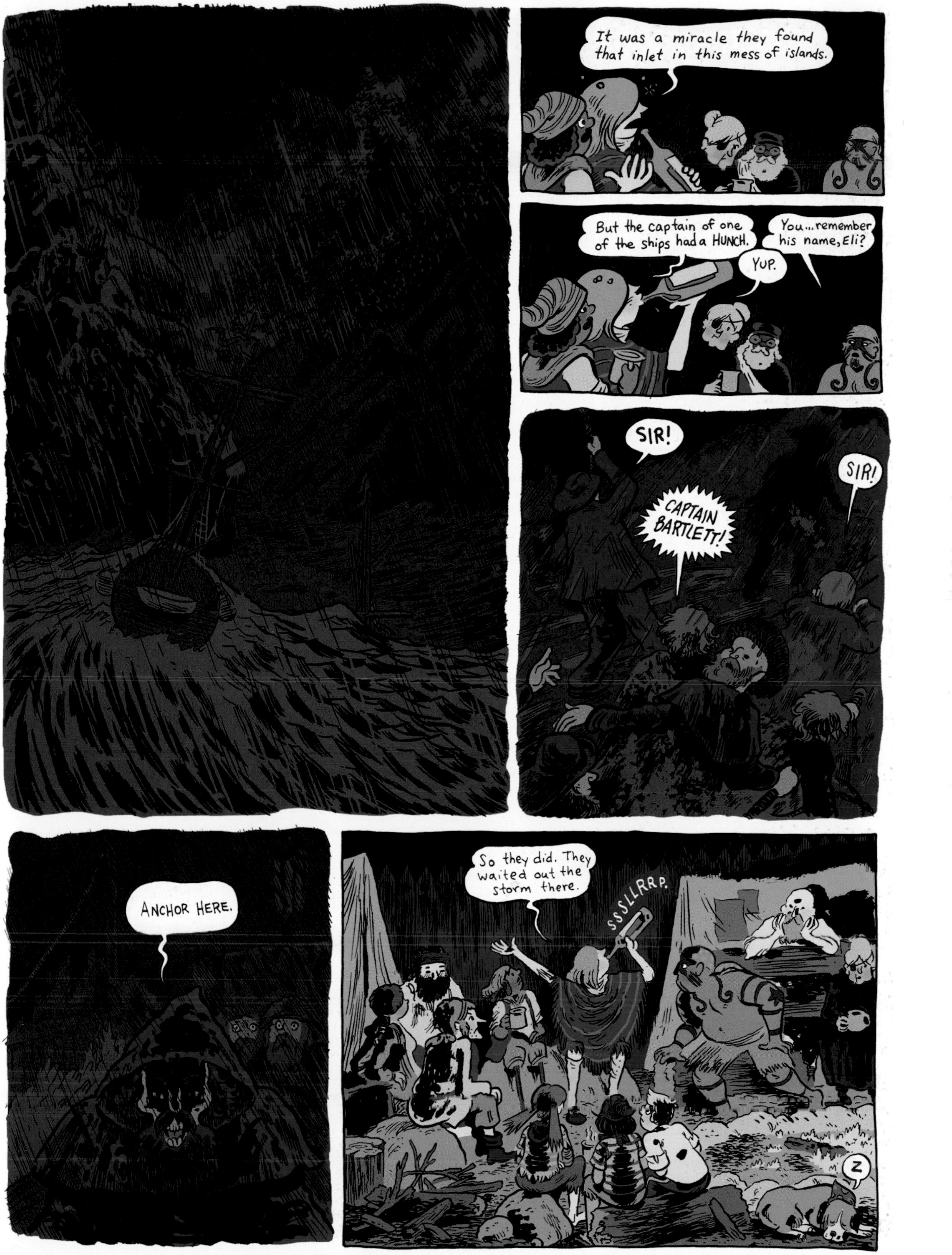

It was a miracle they found that inlet in this mess of islands.
But the captain of one of the ships had a HUNCH.
You... remember his name, Eli?
YUP.
SIR!
CAPTAIN BARTLETT!
SIR!
ANCHOR HERE.
So they did. They waited out the storm there.
SSSLLRRP.
Z

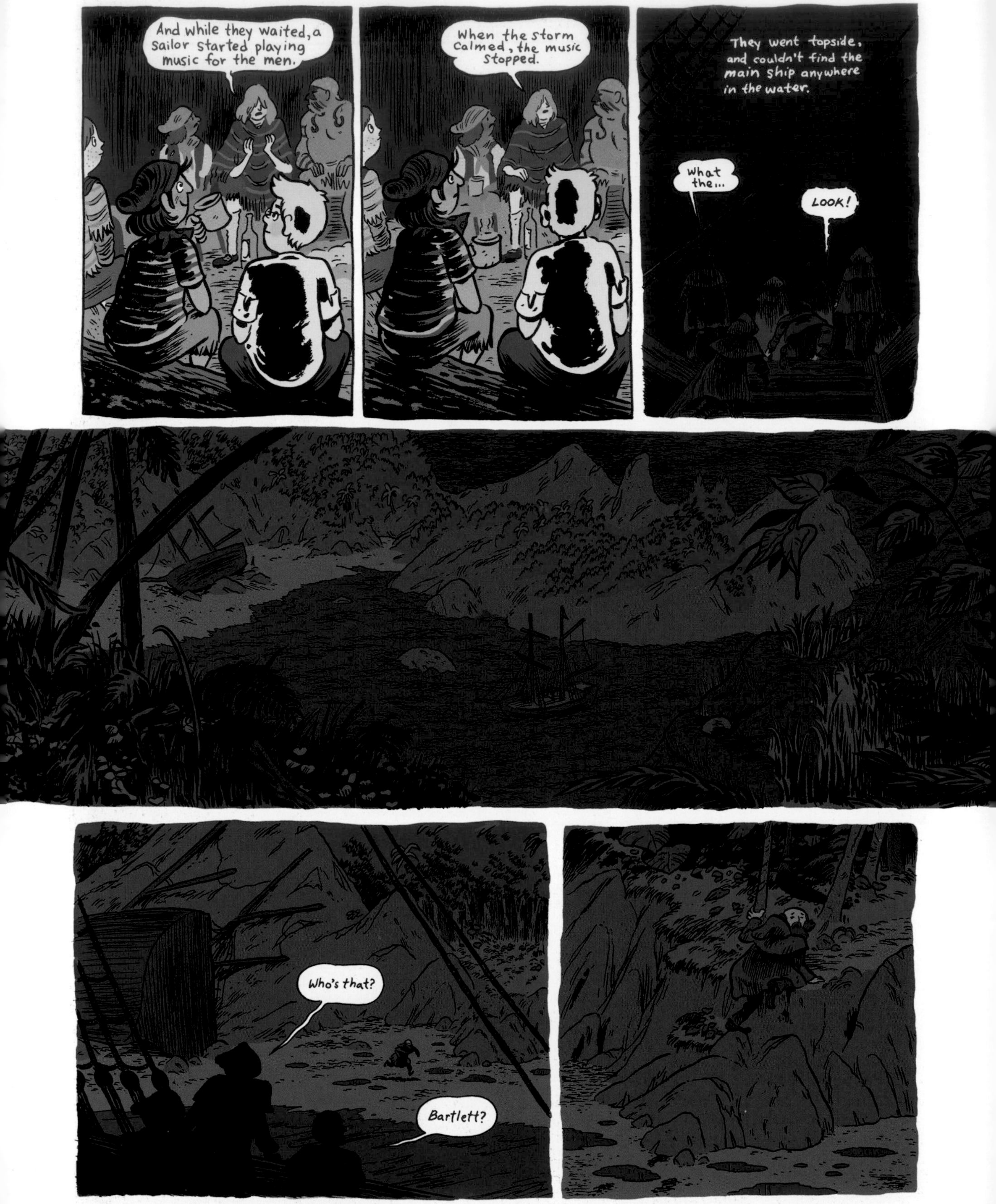
And while they waited, a sailor started playing music for the men.
When the storm calmed, the music stopped.
They went topside, and couldn't find the main ship anywhere in the water.
What the...
LOOK!
Who's that?
Bartlett?

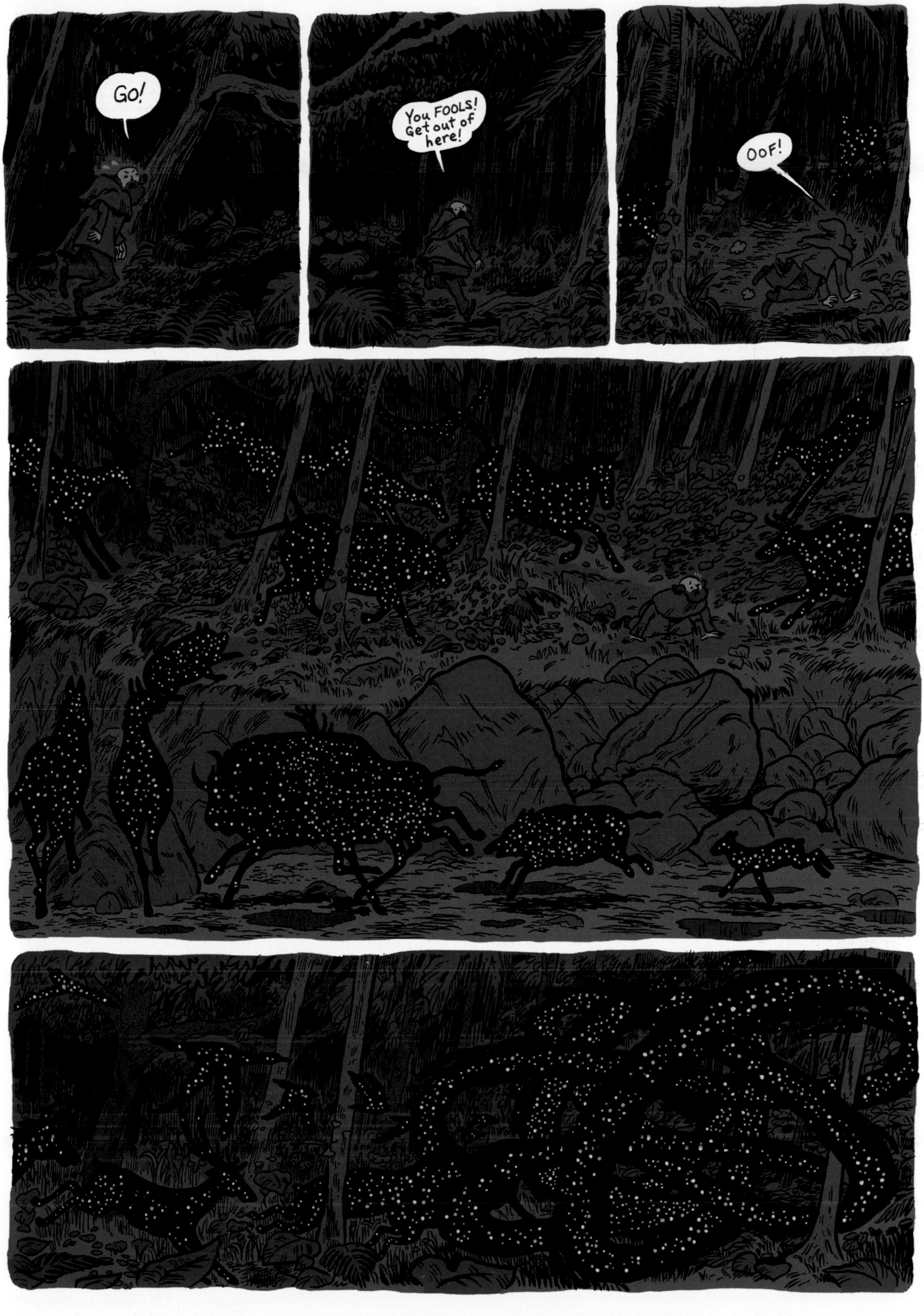
GO!
You FOOLS! Get out of here!
OOF!

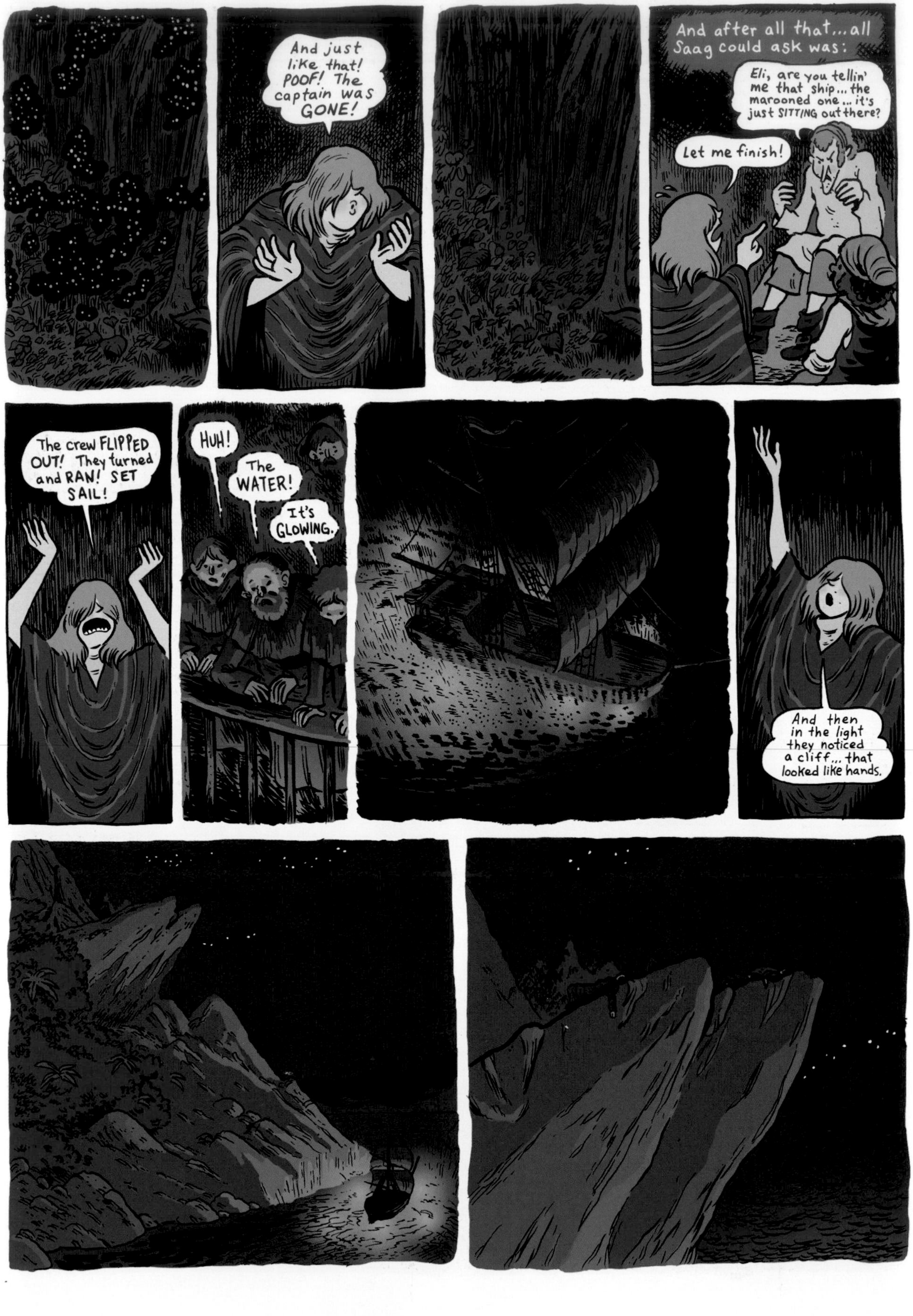
And just like that! POOF! The captain was GONE!
And after all that... all Saag could ask was:
Eli, are you tellin' me that ship... the marooned one... it's just SITTING out there?
Let me finish!
The crew FLIPPED OUT! They turned and RAN! SET SAIL!
HUH!
The WATER!
It's GLOWING.
And then in the light they noticed a cliff... that looked like hands.

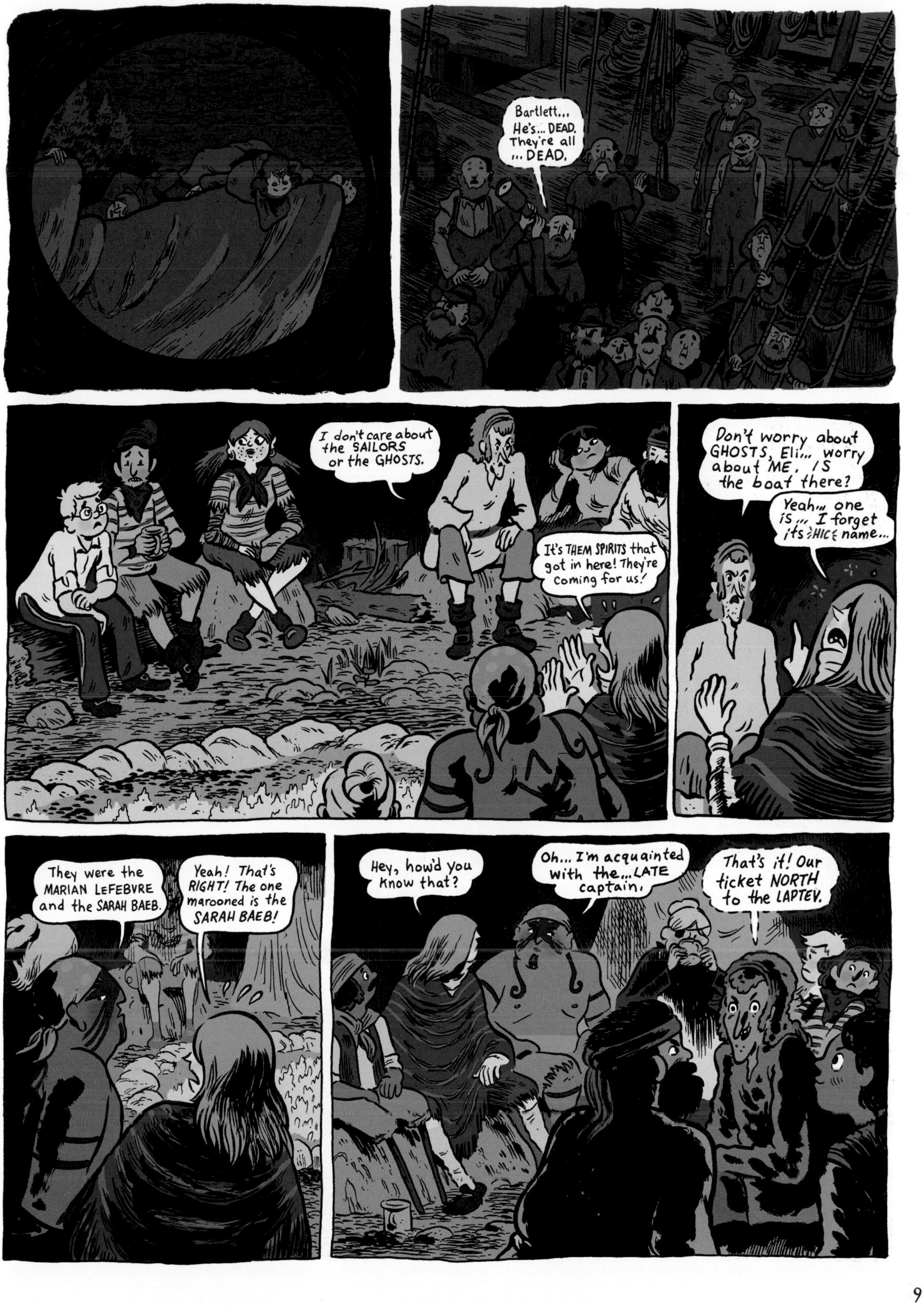

Bartlett... He's... DEAD. They're all ...DEAD.
I don't care about the SAILORS or the GHOSTS.
It's THEM SPIRITS that got in here! They're coming for us!
Don't worry about GHOSTS, Eli... worry about ME, IS the boat there?
Yeah... one is... I forget its HIC name...
They were the MARIAN LEFEBVRE and the SARAH BAEB.
Yeah! That's RIGHT! The one marooned is the SARAH BAEB!
Hey, how'd you know that?
Oh... I'm acquainted with the... LATE captain.
That's it! Our ticket NORTH to the LAPTEV.

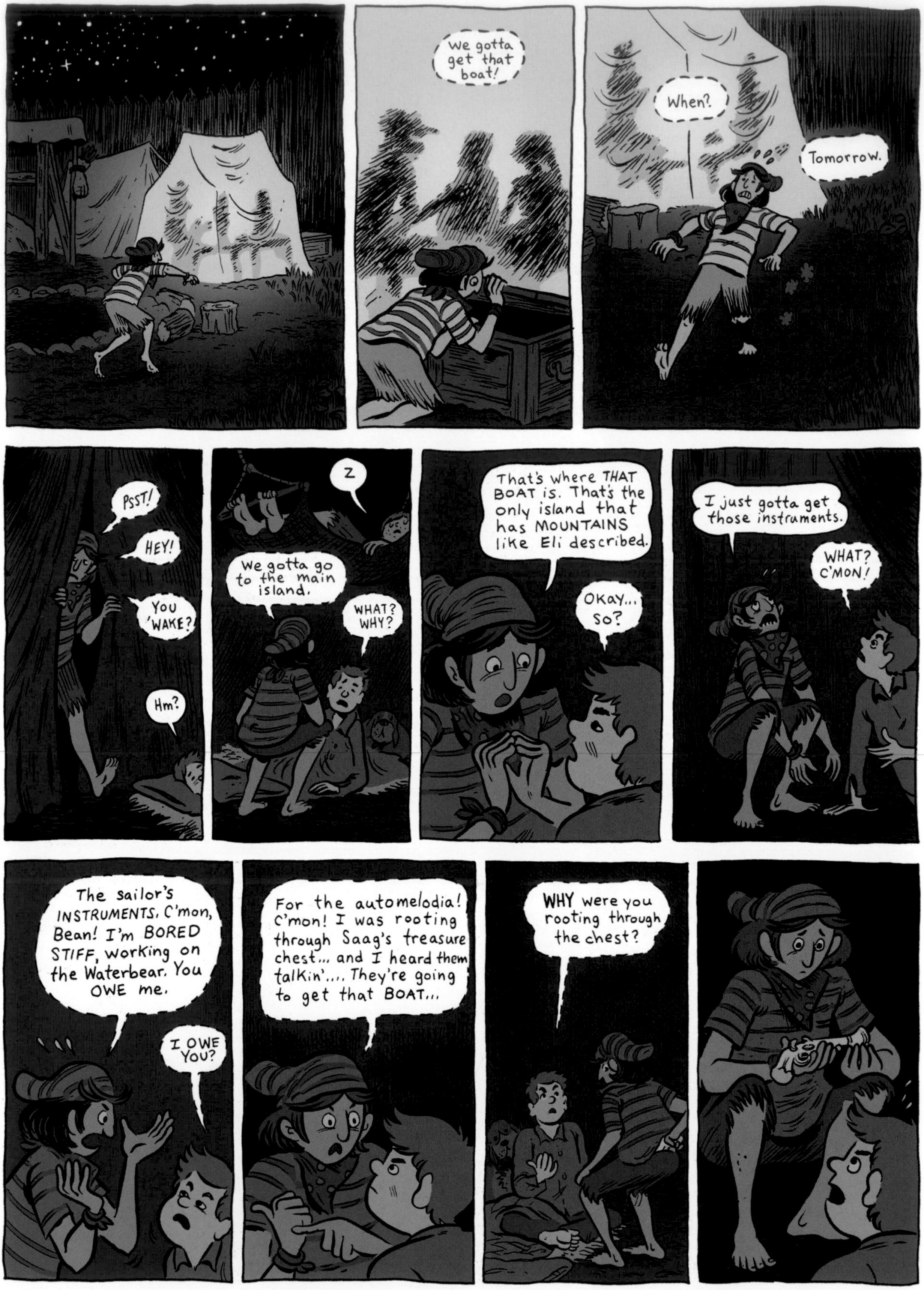
We gotta get that boat!
When?
Tomorrow.
PSST!
HEY!
YOU 'WAKE?
Hm?
Z
We gotta go to the main island.
WHAT? WHY?
That's where THAT BOAT is. That's the only island that has MOUNTAINS like Eli described.
Okay... so?
I just gotta get those instruments.
WHAT? C'MON!
The sailor's INSTRUMENTS. C'mon, Bean! I'm BORED STIFF, working on the Waterbear. You OWE me.
I OWE YOU?
For the automelodia! C'mon! I was rooting through Saag's treasure chest... and I heard them talkin'.... They're going to get that BOAT...
WHY were you rooting through the chest?

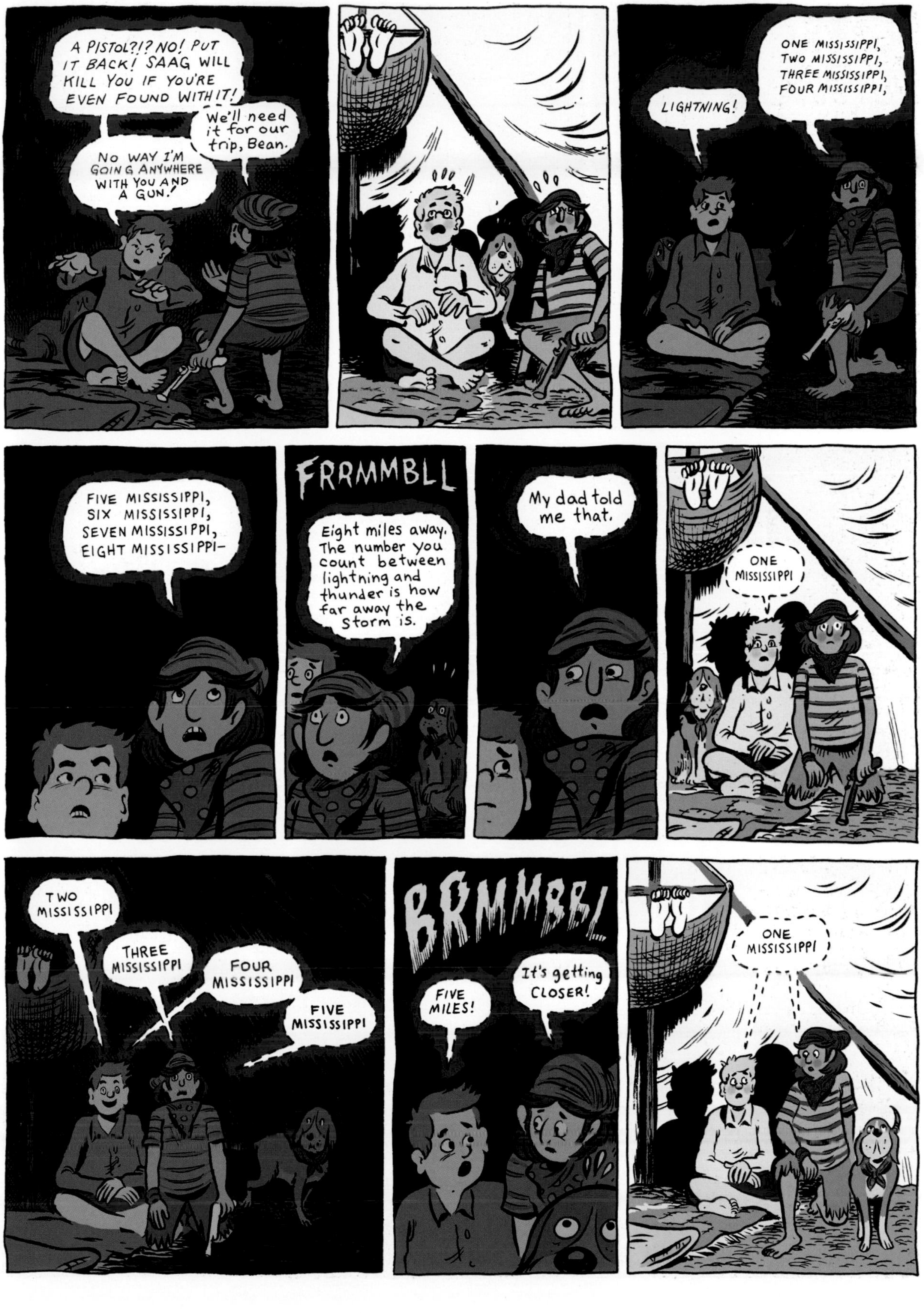
A PISTOL?!? NO! PUT IT BACK! SAAG WILL KILL YOU IF YOU'RE EVEN FOUND WITH IT!
We'll need it for our trip, Bean.
NO WAY I'M GOING ANYWHERE WITH YOU AND A GUN!
LIGHTNING!
ONE MISSISSIPPI, TWO MISSISSIPPI, THREE MISSISSIPPI, FOUR MISSISSIPPI,
FIVE MISSISSIPPI, SIX MISSISSIPPI, SEVEN MISSISSIPPI, EIGHT MISSISSIPPI–
FRRMMBLL
Eight miles away. The number you count between lightning and thunder is how far away the storm is.
My dad told me that.
ONE MISSISSIPPI
TWO MISSISSIPPI
THREE MISSISSIPPI
FOUR MISSISSIPPI
FIVE MISSISSIPPI
BRMMBBL
FIVE MILES!
It's getting CLOSER!
ONE MISSISSIPPI

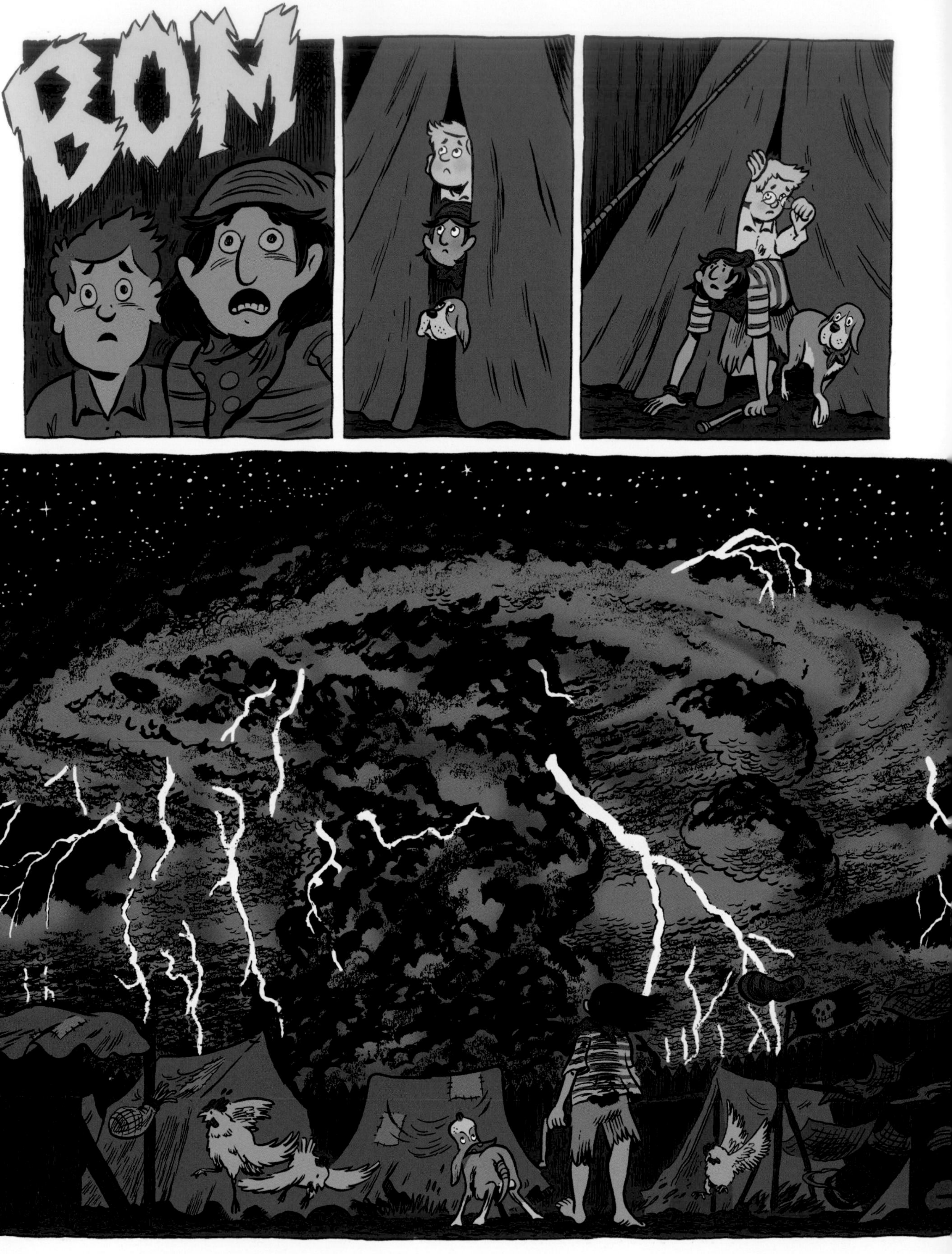
BOM

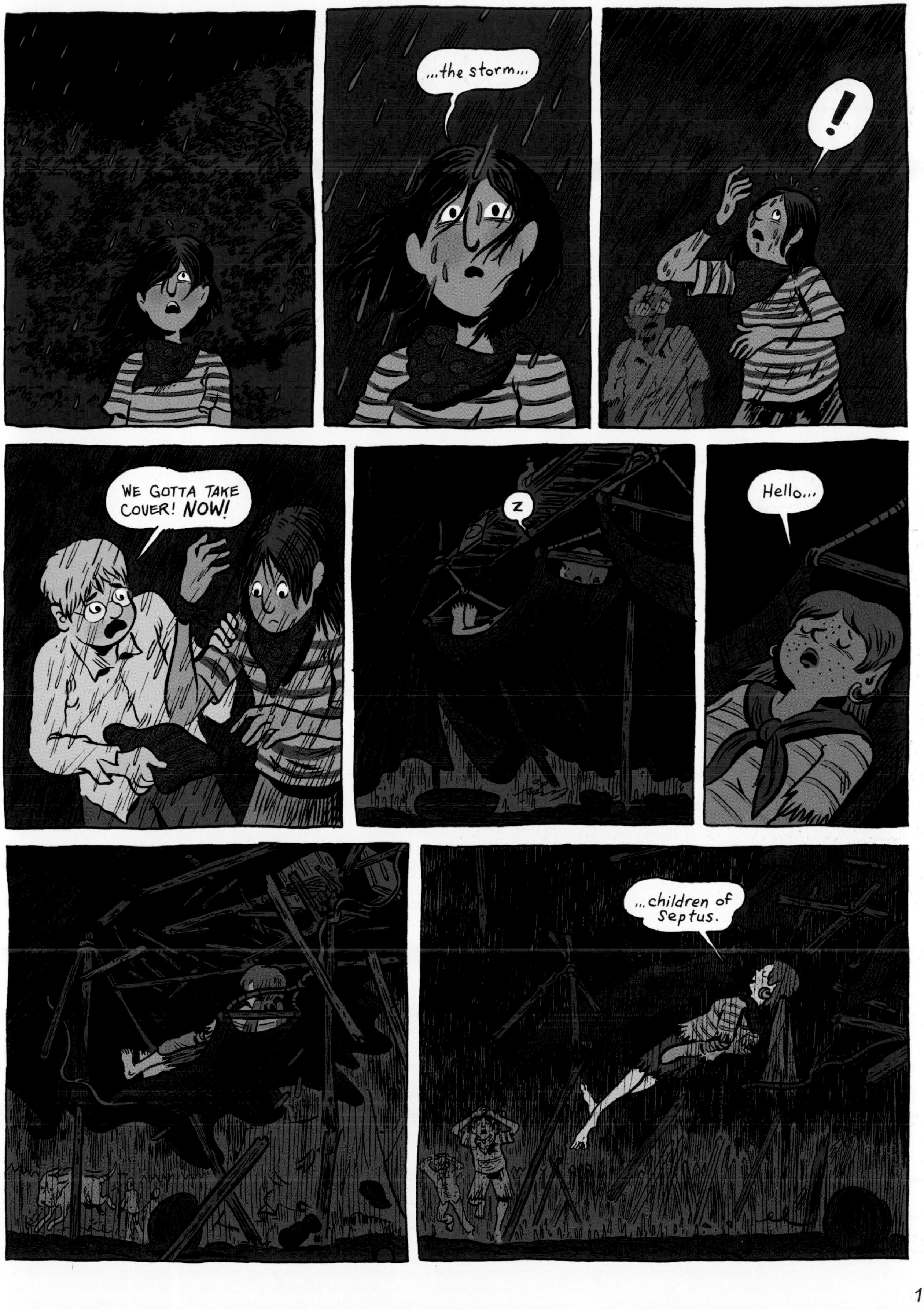
...the storm...
!
WE GOTTA TAKE COVER! NOW!
Z
Hello...
...children of Septus.

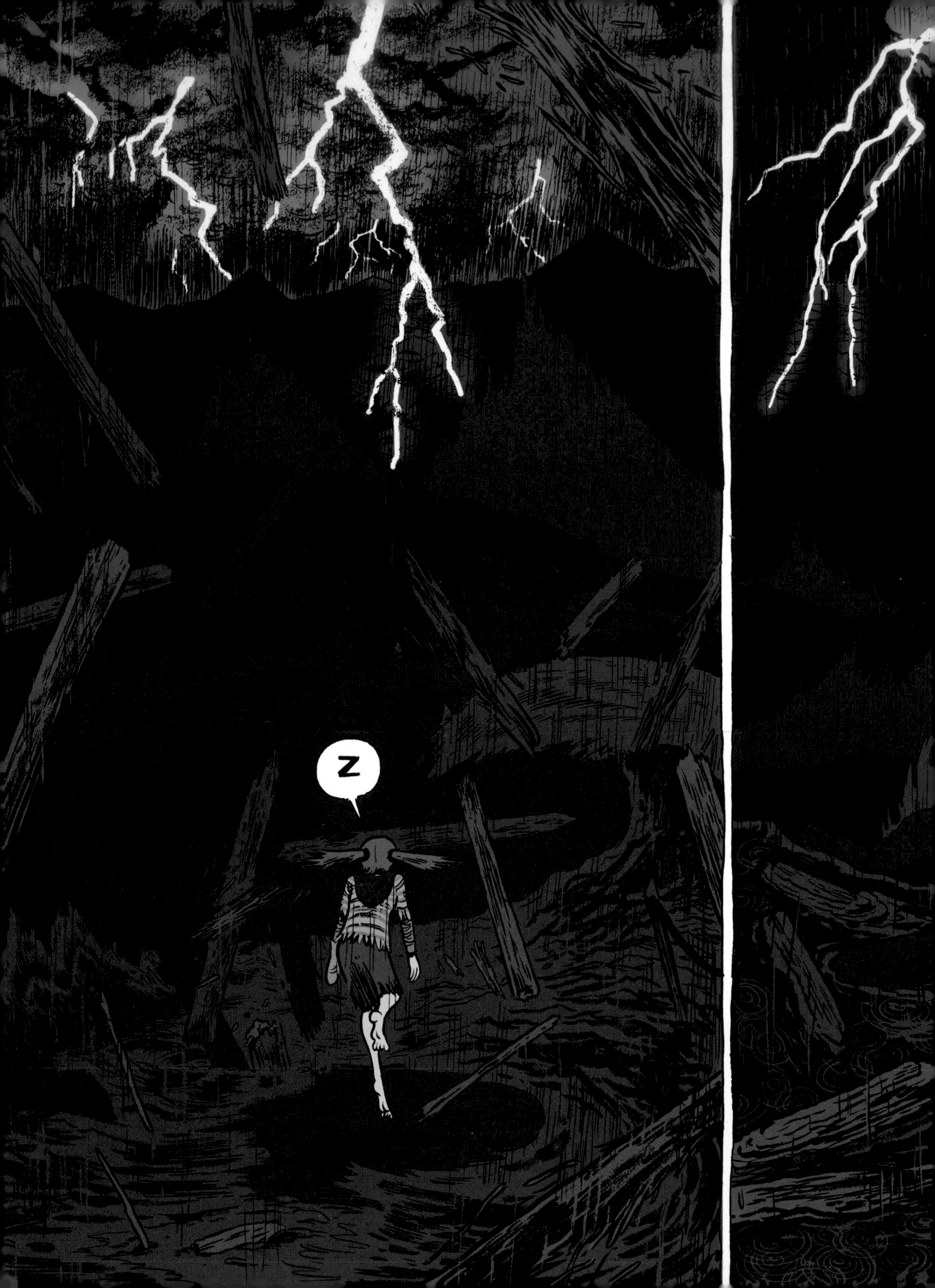
Z

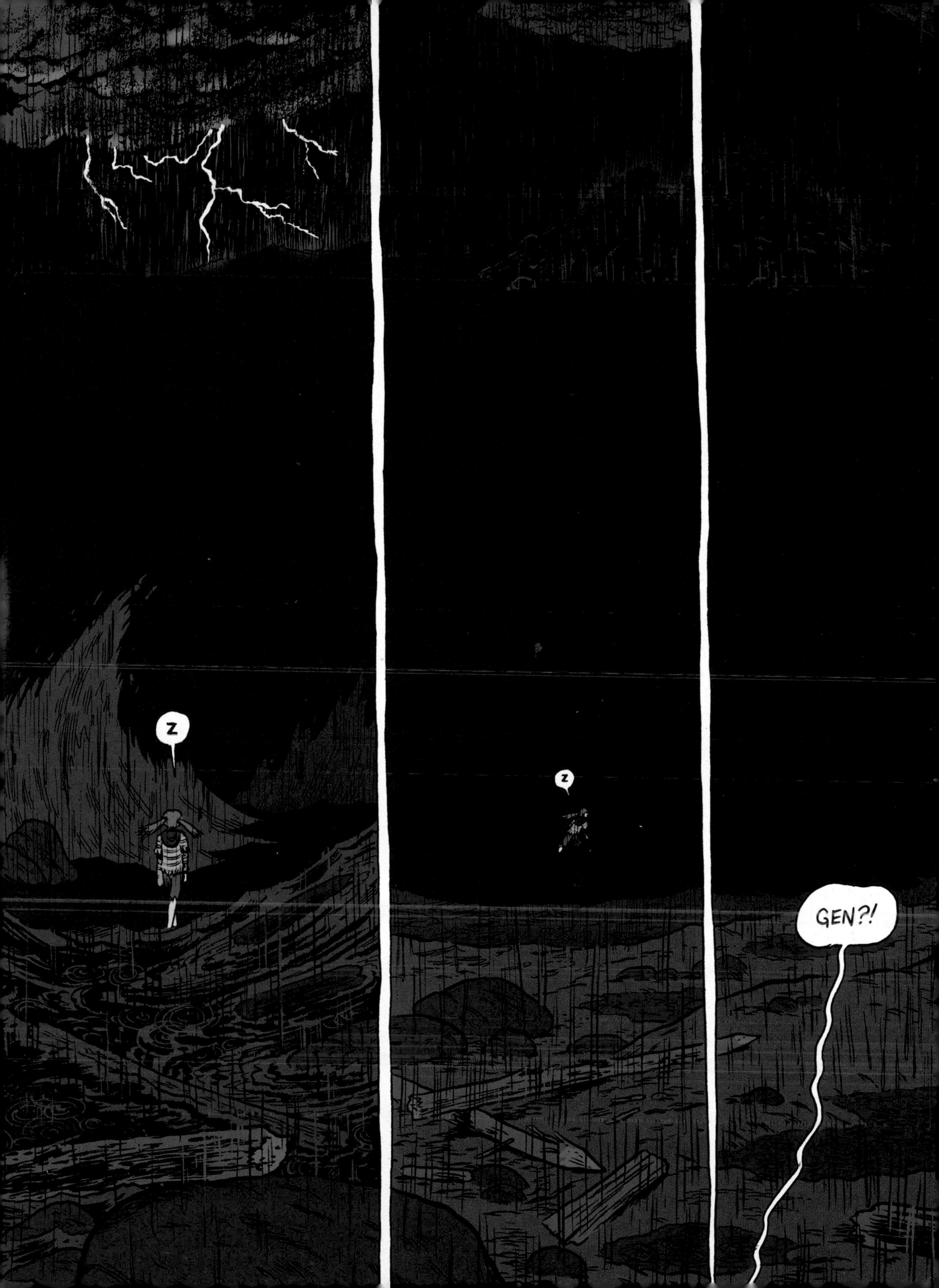
Z
Z
GEN?!

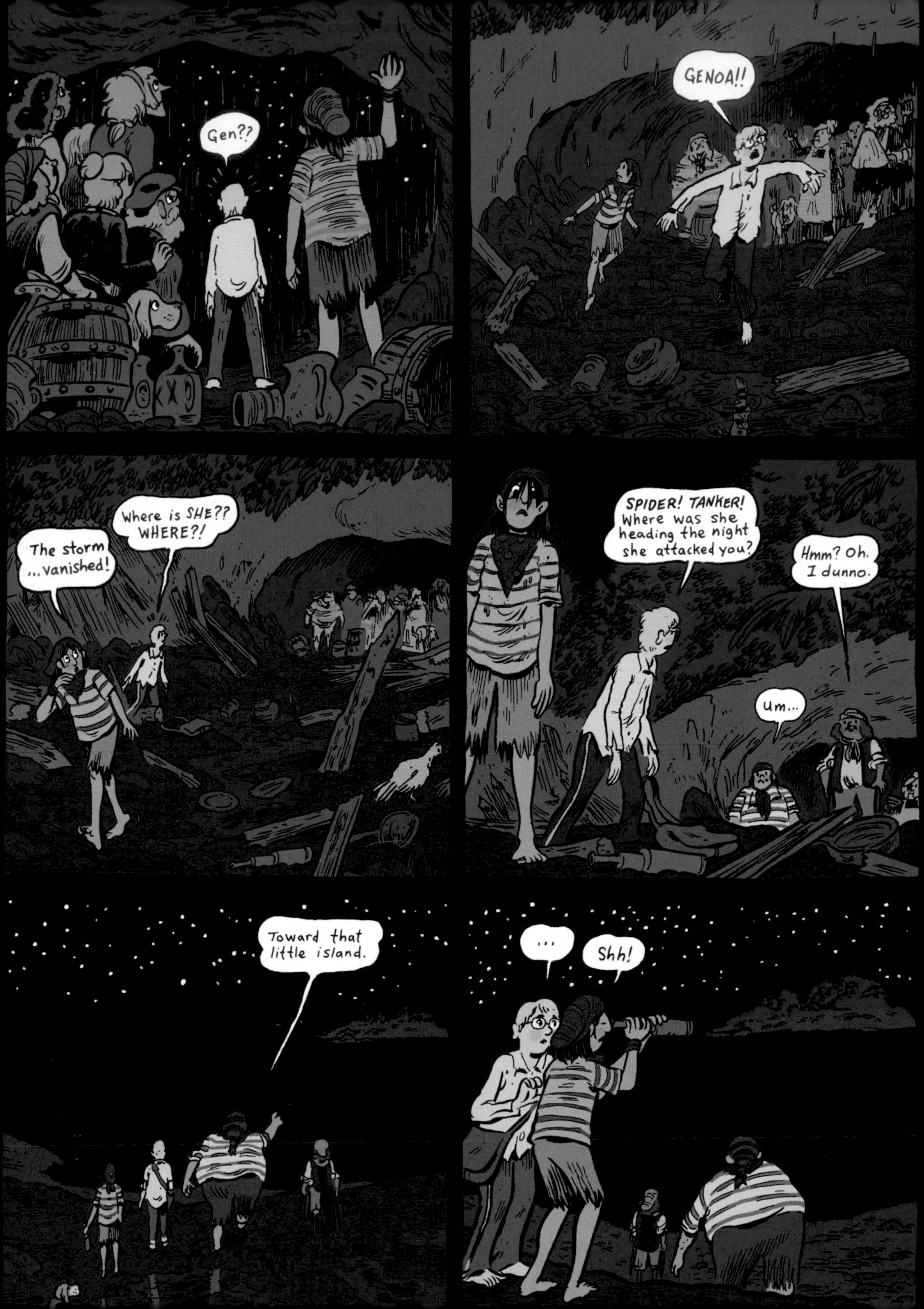
Gen??
GENOA!!
The storm ...vanished!
Where is SHE?? WHERE?!
SPIDER! TANKER! Where was she heading the night she attacked you?
Hmm? Oh. I dunno.
Um...
Toward that little island.
...
Shh!

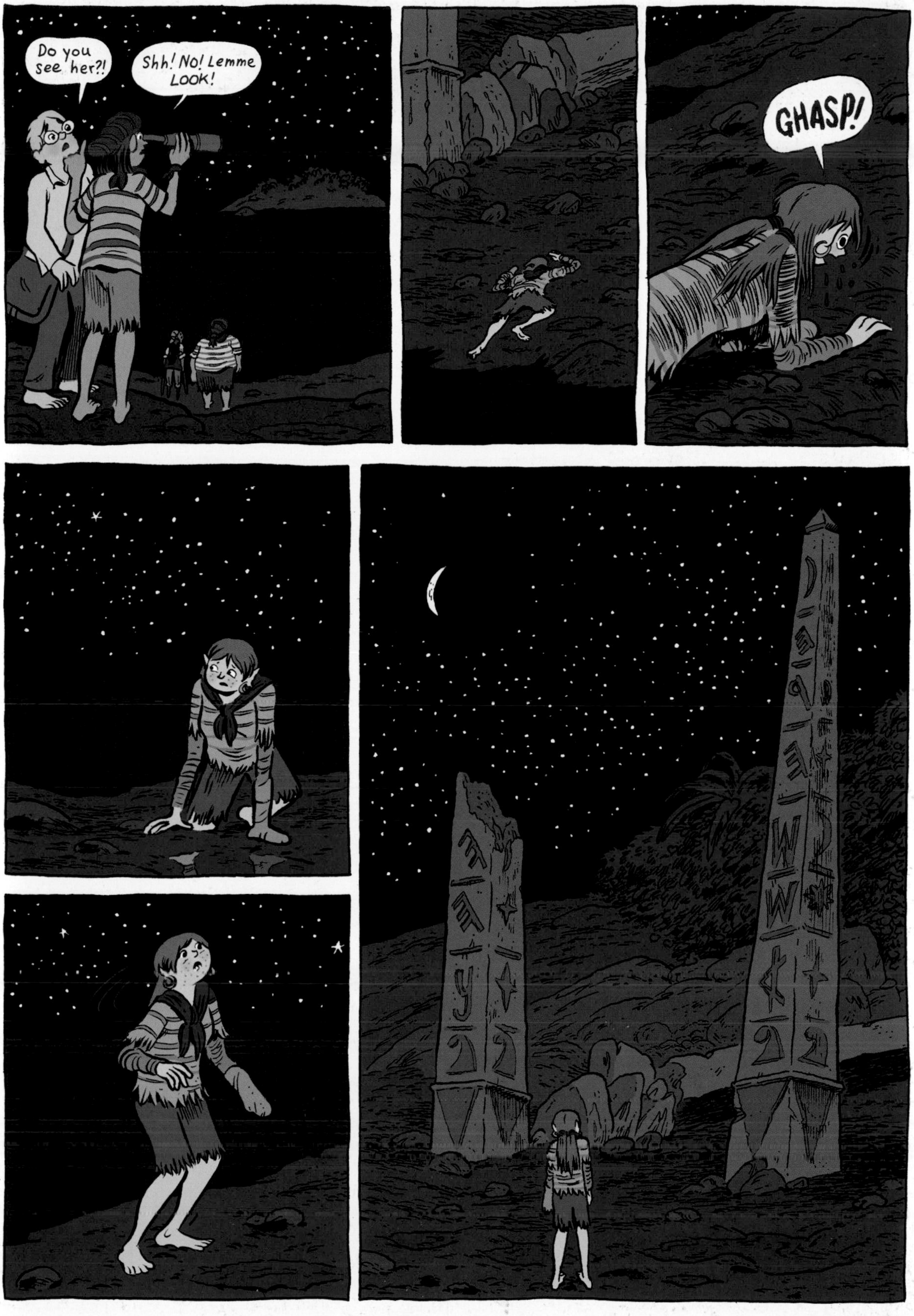
Do you see her?!
Shh! No! Lemme LOOK!
GHASP!

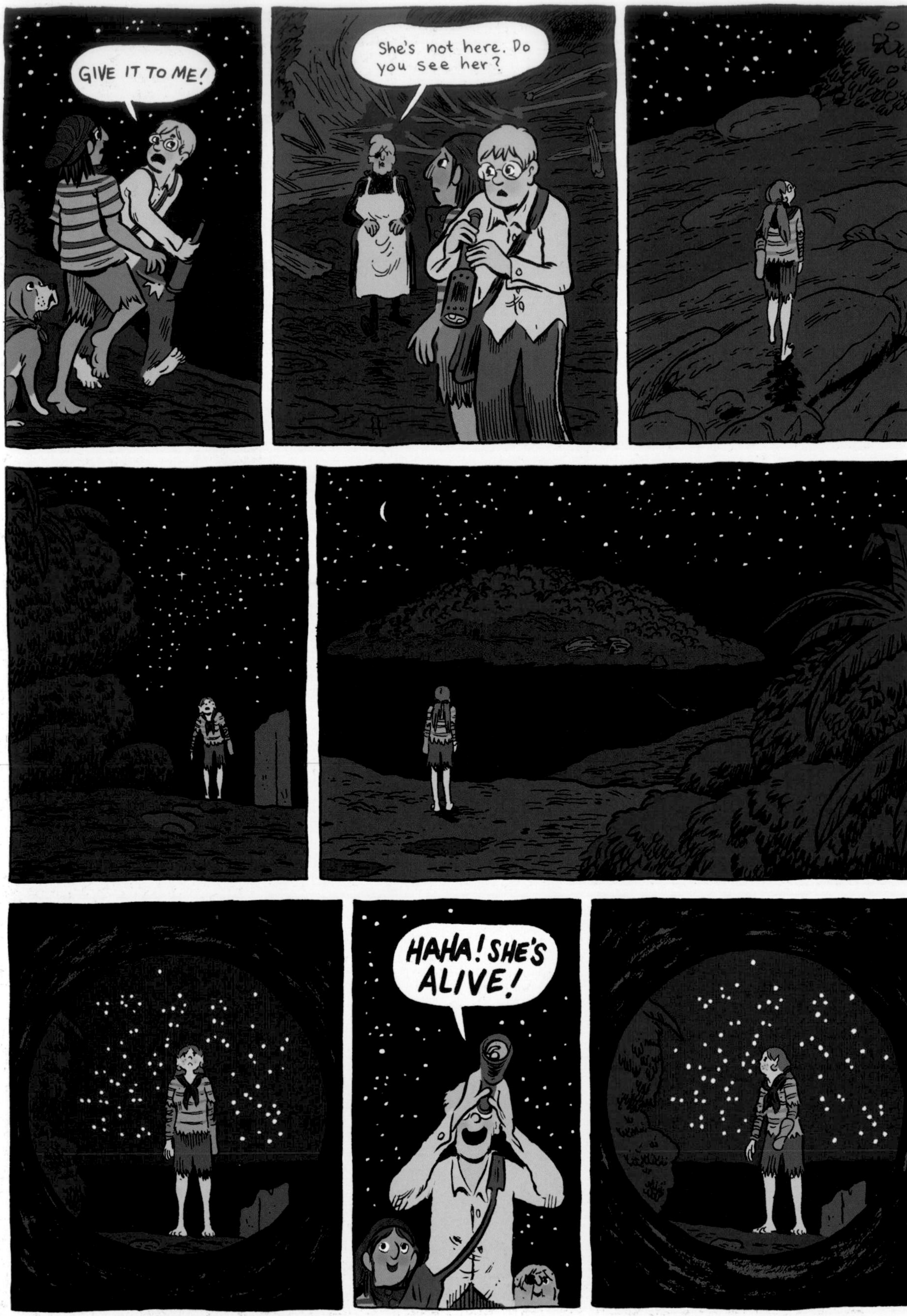
GIVE IT TO ME!
She's not here. Do you see her?
HAHA! SHE'S ALIVE!

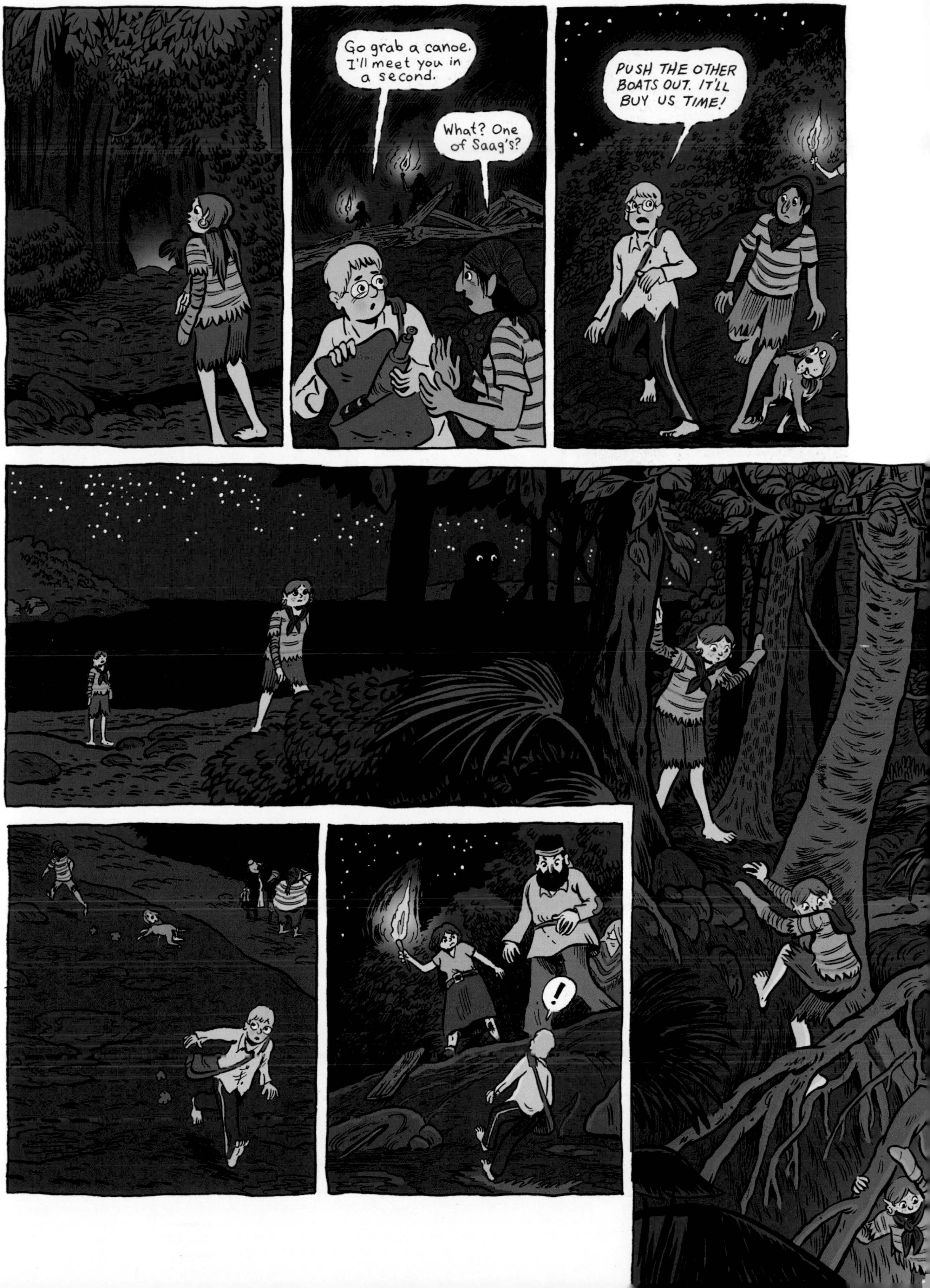
Go grab a canoe. I'll meet you in a second.
What? One of Saag's?
PUSH THE OTHER BOATS OUT. IT'LL BUY US TIME!
!

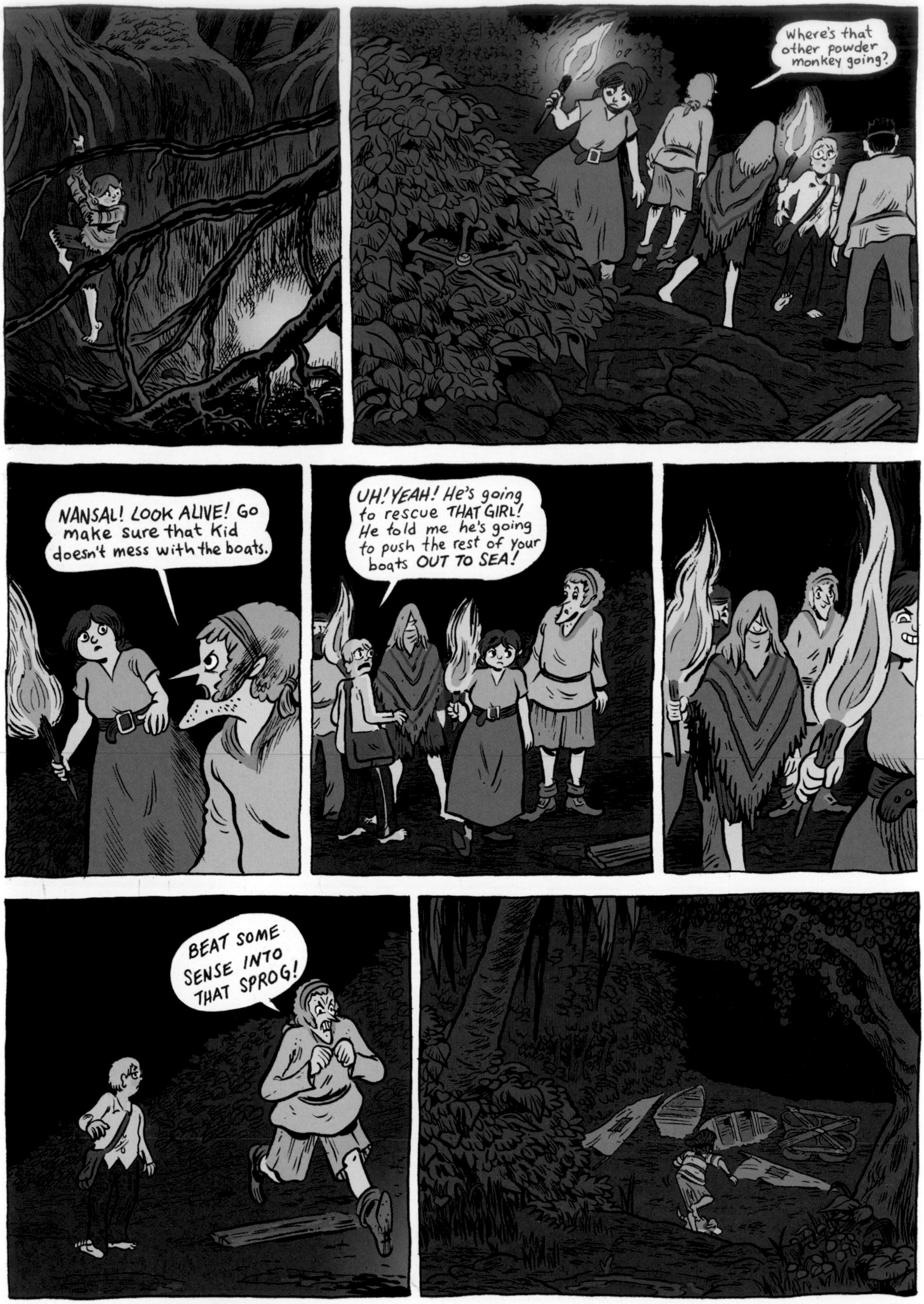
Where's that other powder monkey going?
NANSAL! LOOK ALIVE! Go make sure that Kid doesn't mess with the boats.
UH! YEAH! He's going to rescue THAT GIRL! He told me he's going to push the rest of your boats OUT TO SEA!
BEAT SOME SENSE INTO THAT SPROG!

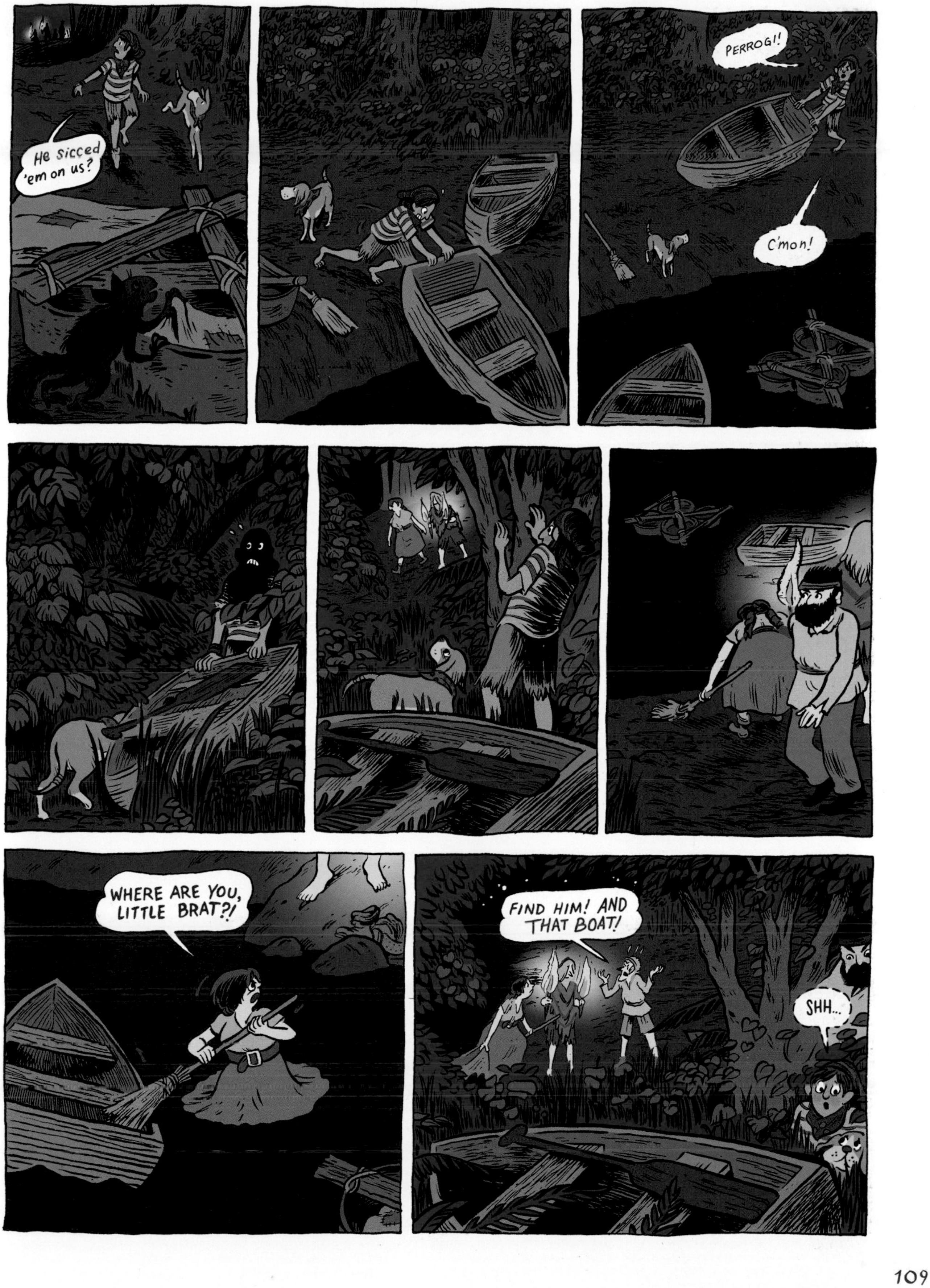
He sicced 'em on us?
PERROG!!
C'mon!
WHERE ARE YOU, LITTLE BRAT?!
FIND HIM! AND THAT BOAT!
SHH...

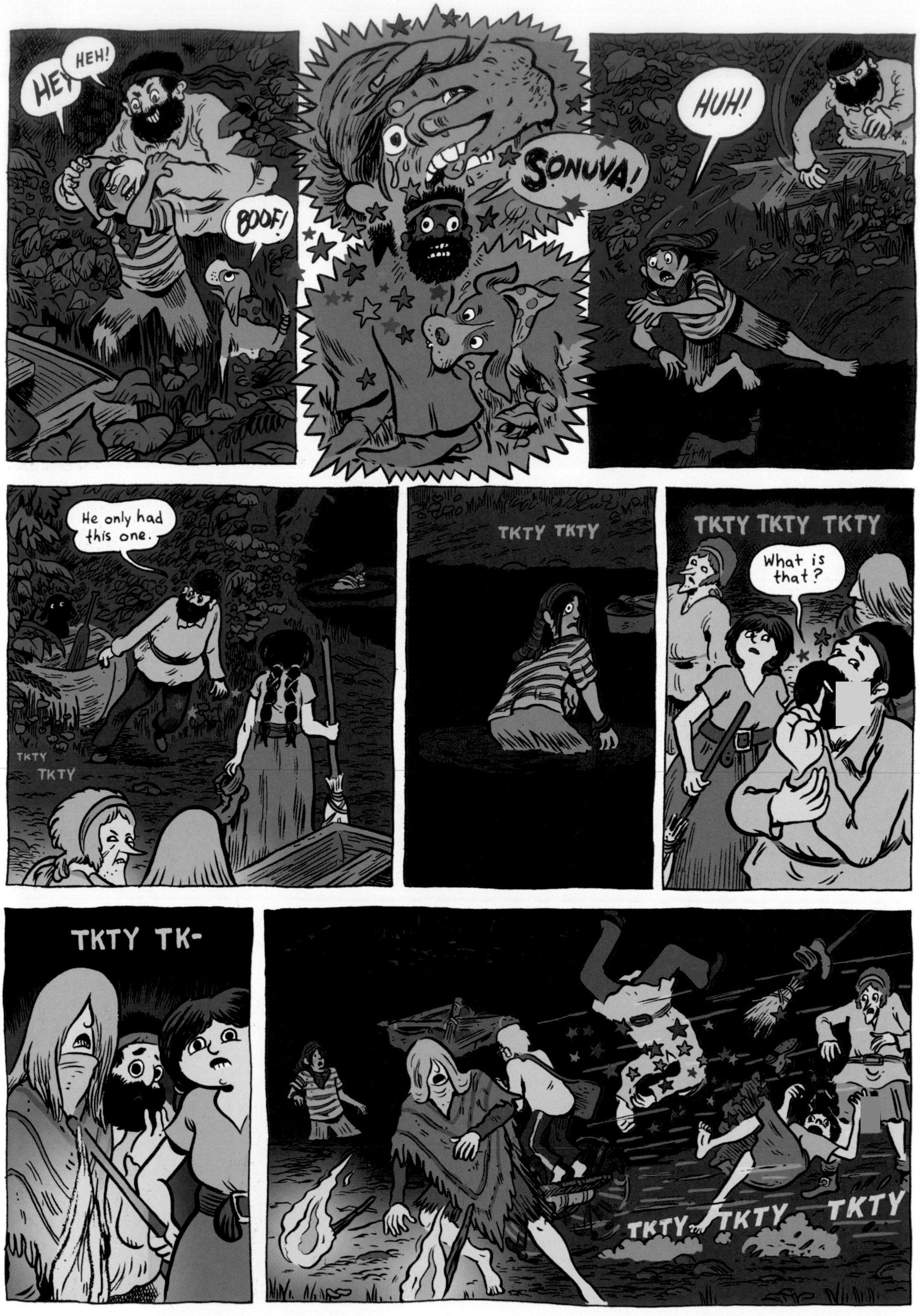
HEY
HEH!
BOOF!
SONUVA!
HUH!
He only had this one.
TKTY TKTY
TKTY TKTY
TKTY TKTY TKTY
What is that?
TKTY TK-
TKTY TKTY TKTY

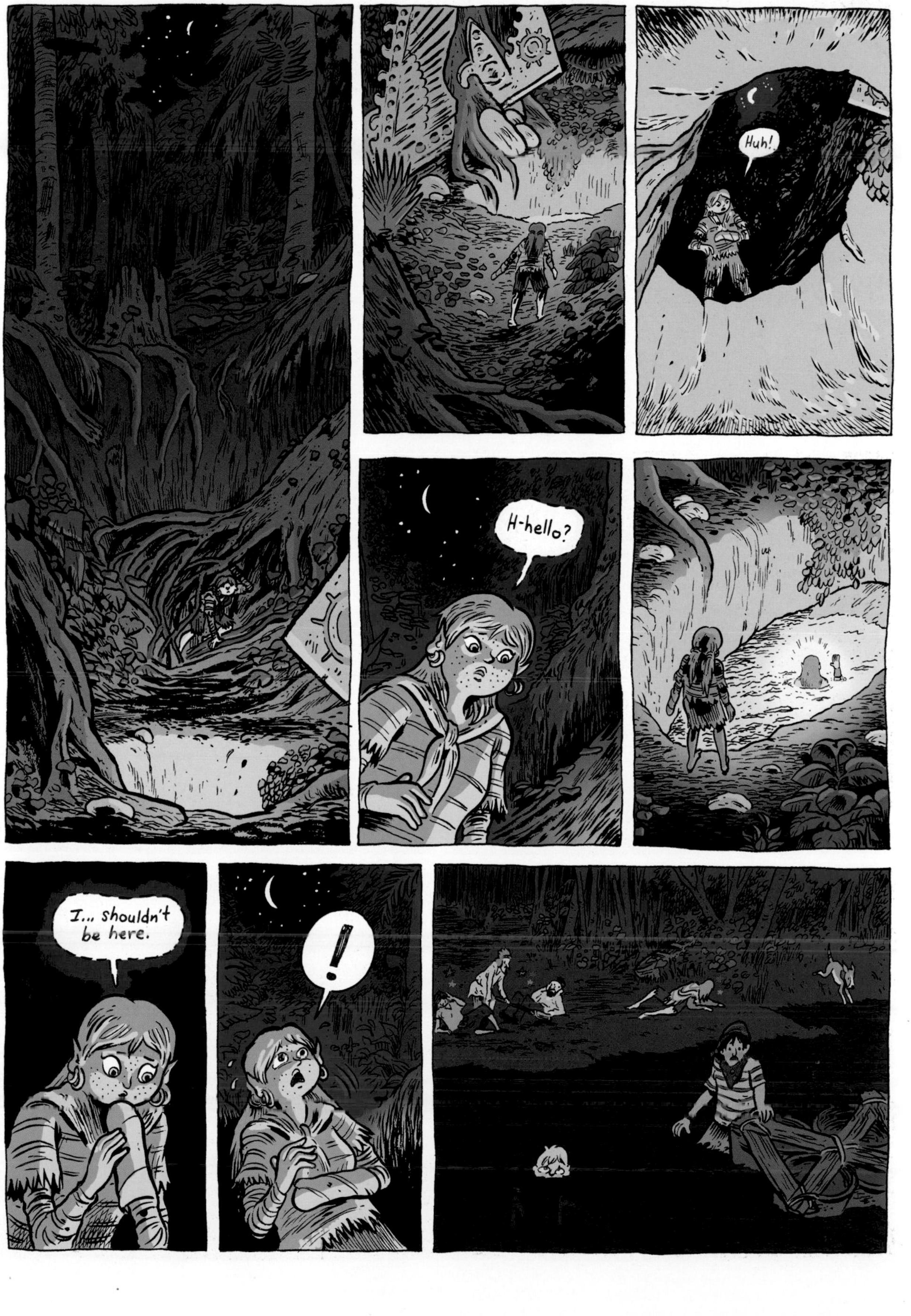
Huh!
H-hello?
I... shouldn't be here.
!

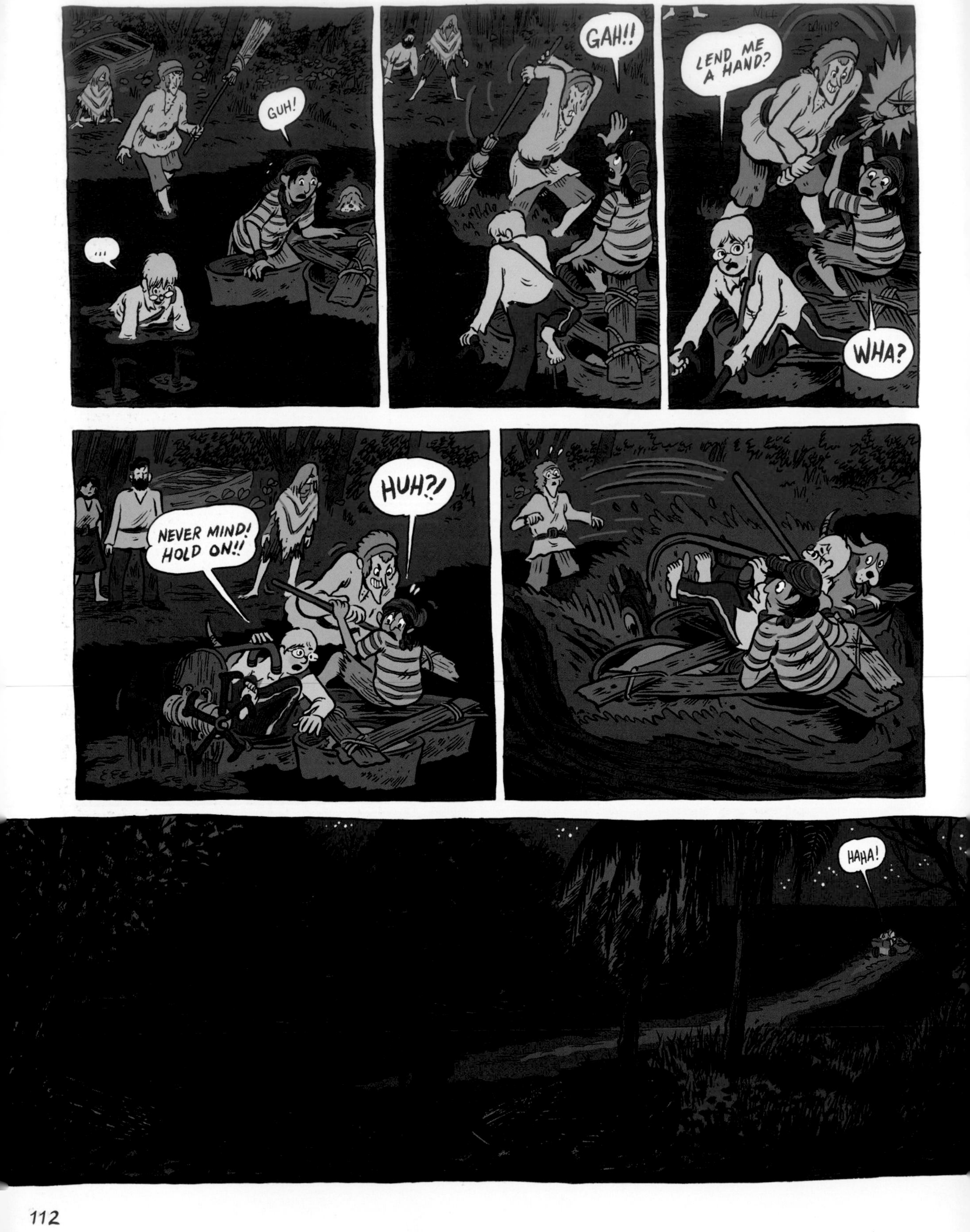
GUH!
...
GAH!!
LEND ME A HAND?
WHA?
NEVER MIND! HOLD ON!!
HUH?!
HAHA!

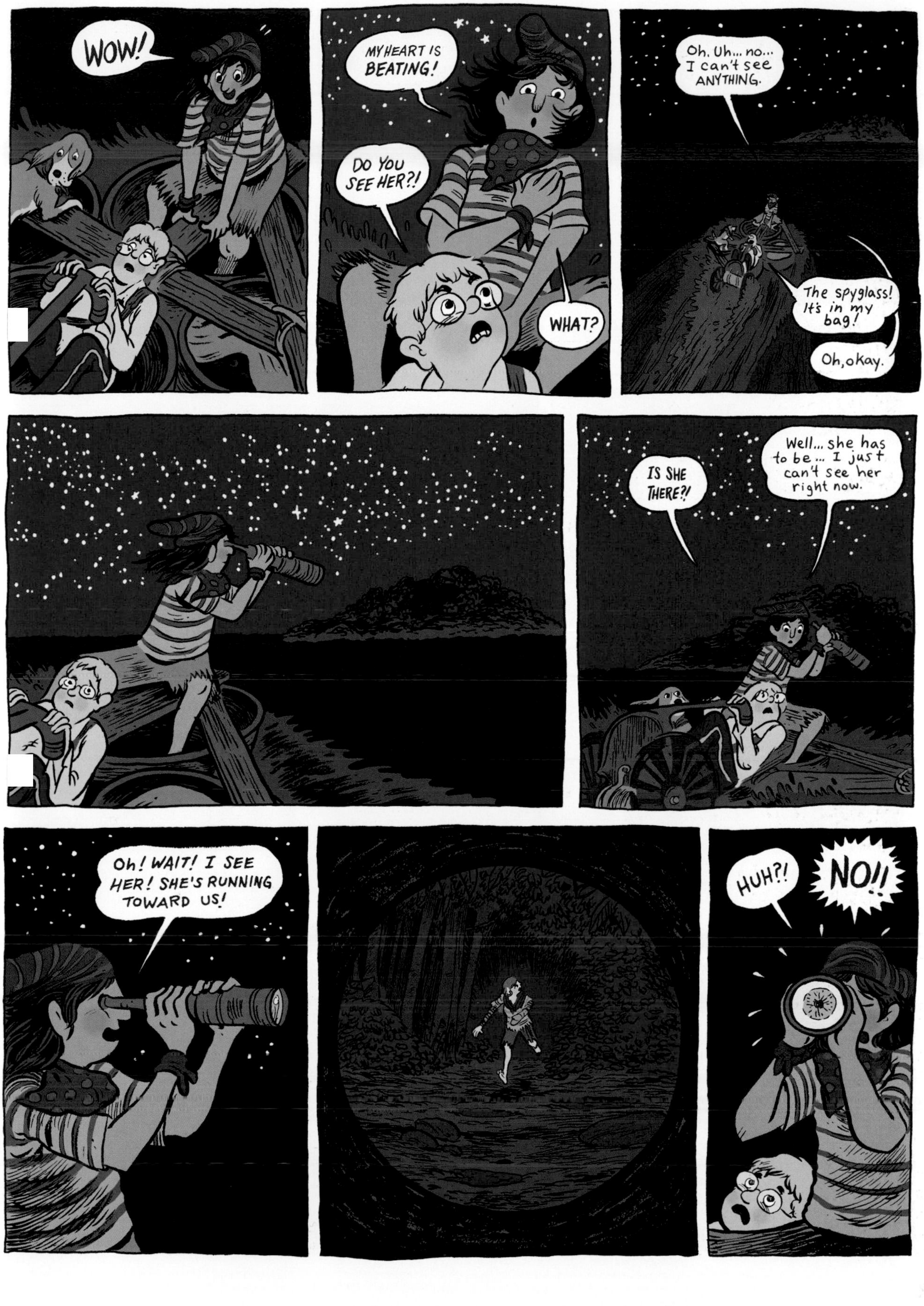
WOW!
MY HEART IS BEATING!
DO YOU SEE HER?!
WHAT?
Oh. Uh... no... I can't see ANYTHING.
The spyglass! It's in my bag!
Oh, okay.
IS SHE THERE?!
Well... she has to be... I just can't see her right now.
Oh! WAIT! I SEE HER! SHE'S RUNNING TOWARD US!
HUH?!
NO!!

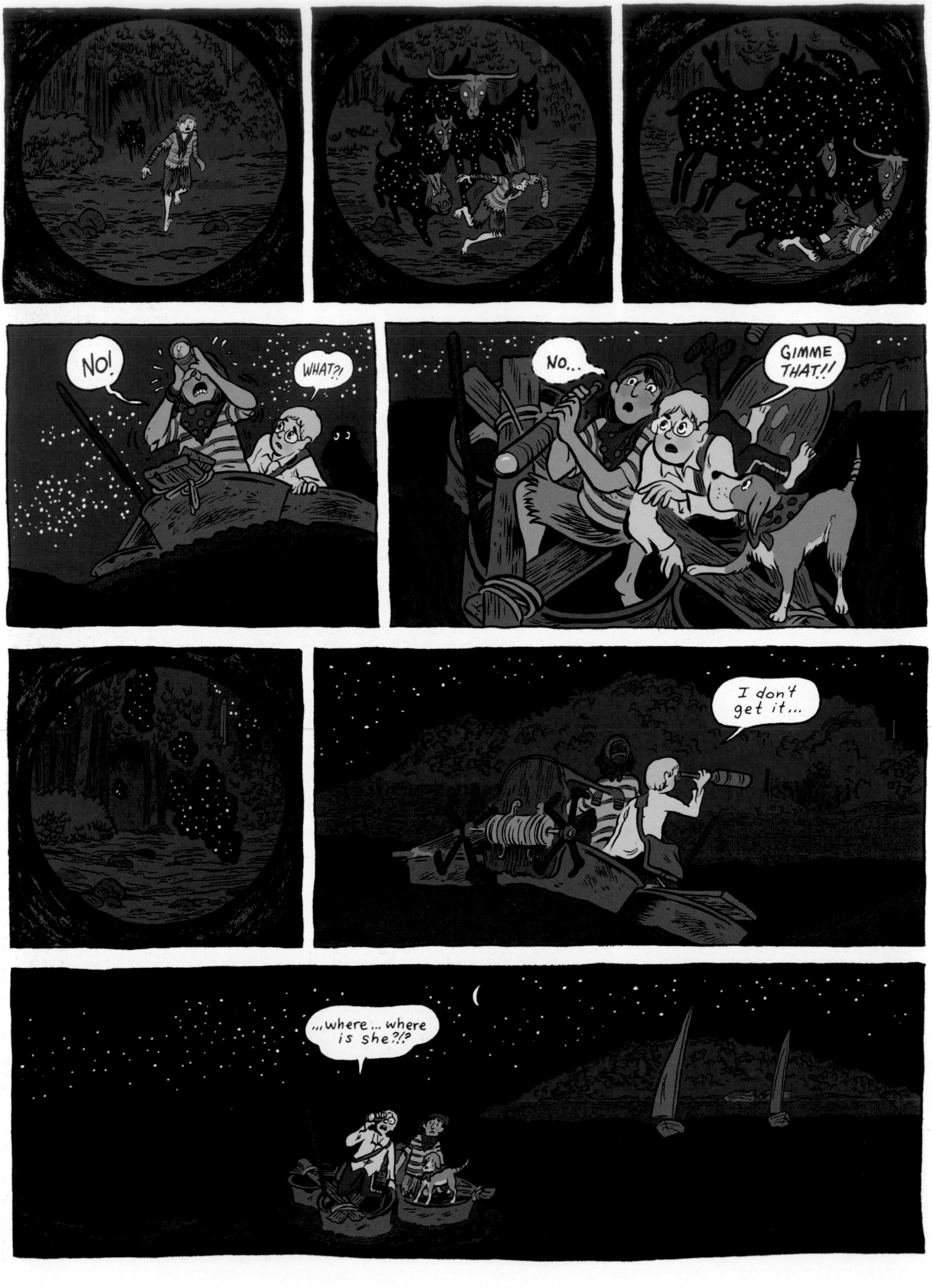
NO!
WHAT?!
NO...
GIMME THAT!!
I don't get it...
...where... where is she?!?

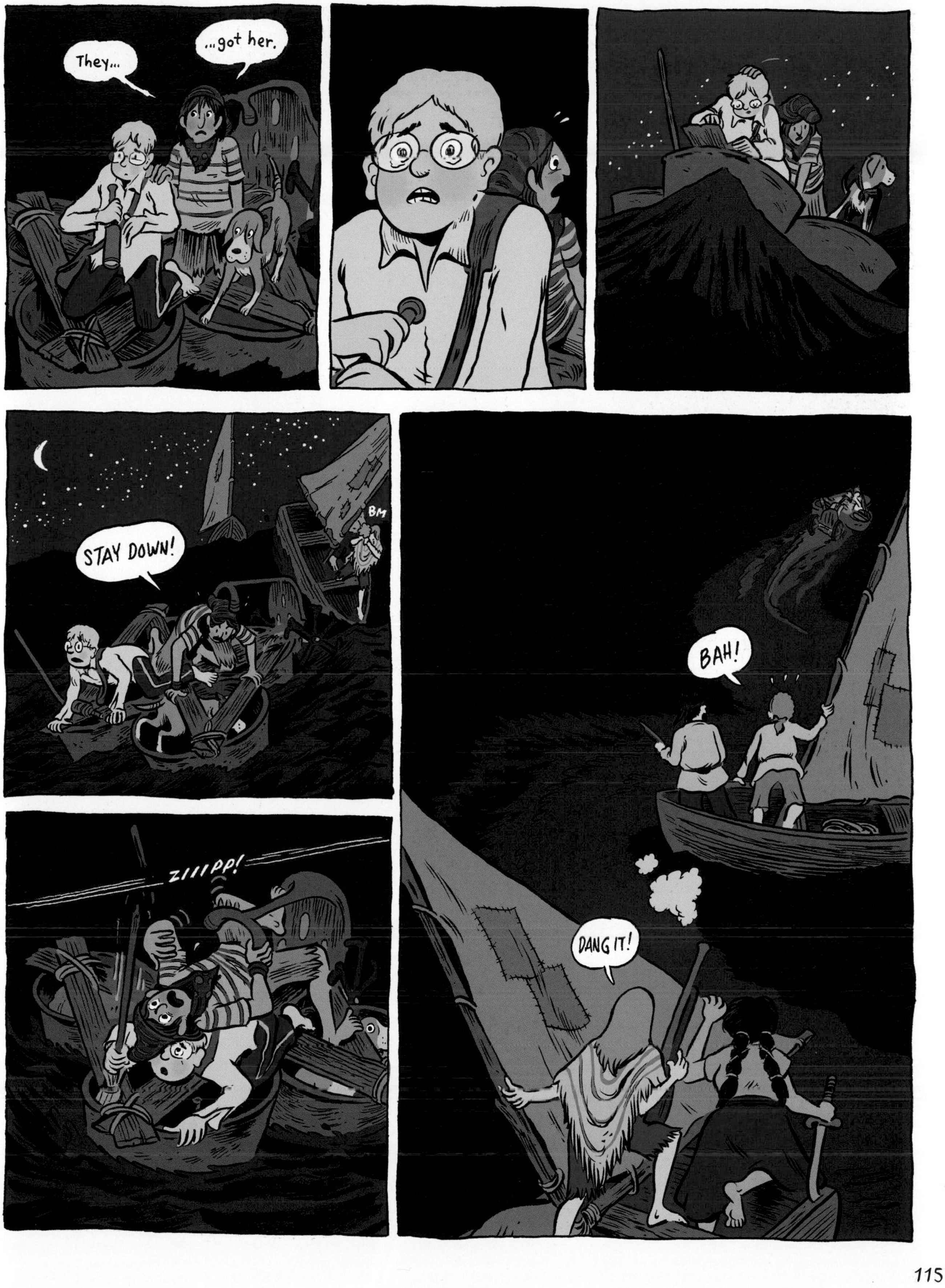
They...
...got her.
STAY DOWN!
BM
ZIIIPP!
BAH!
DANG IT!

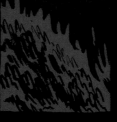

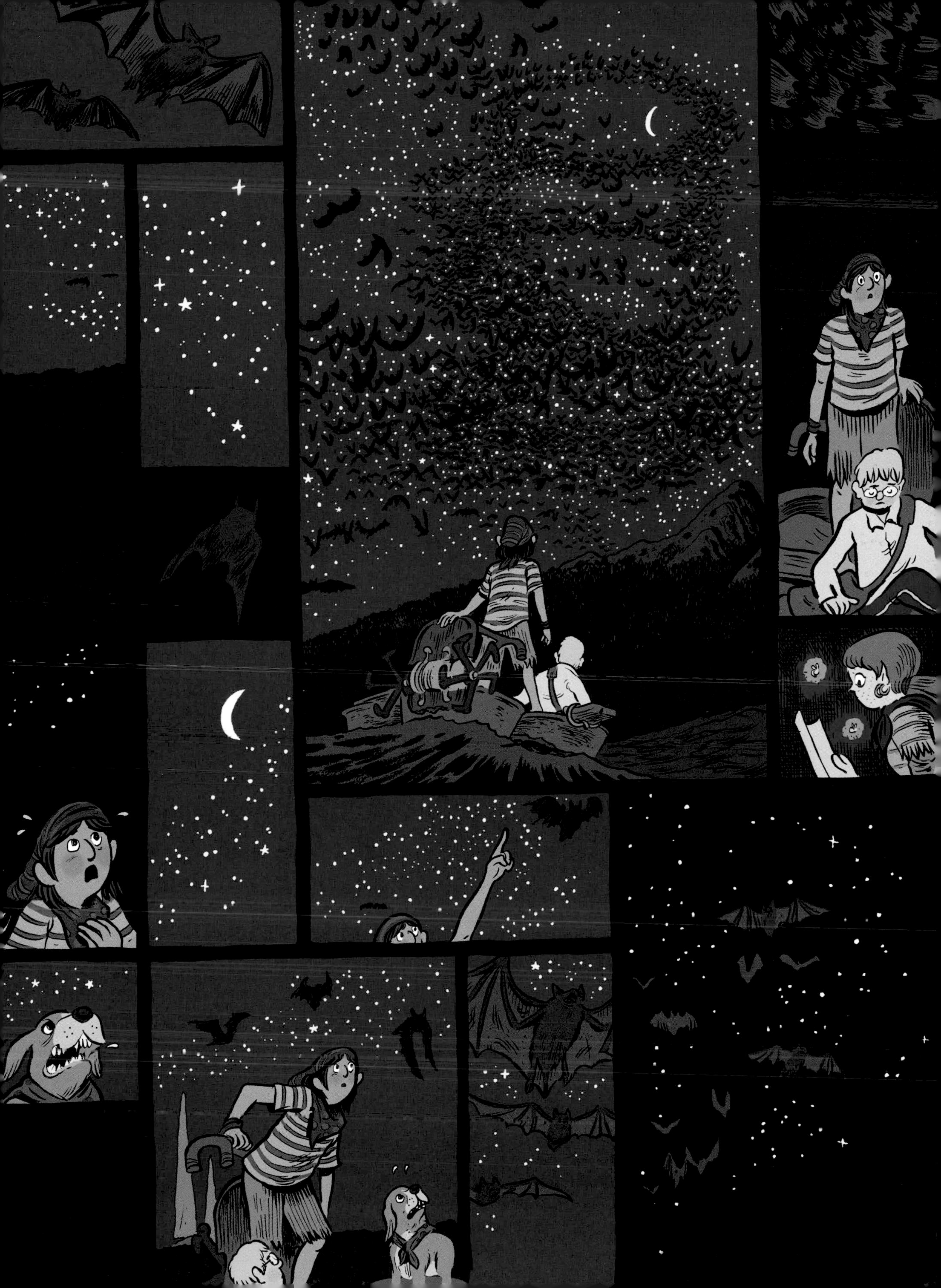

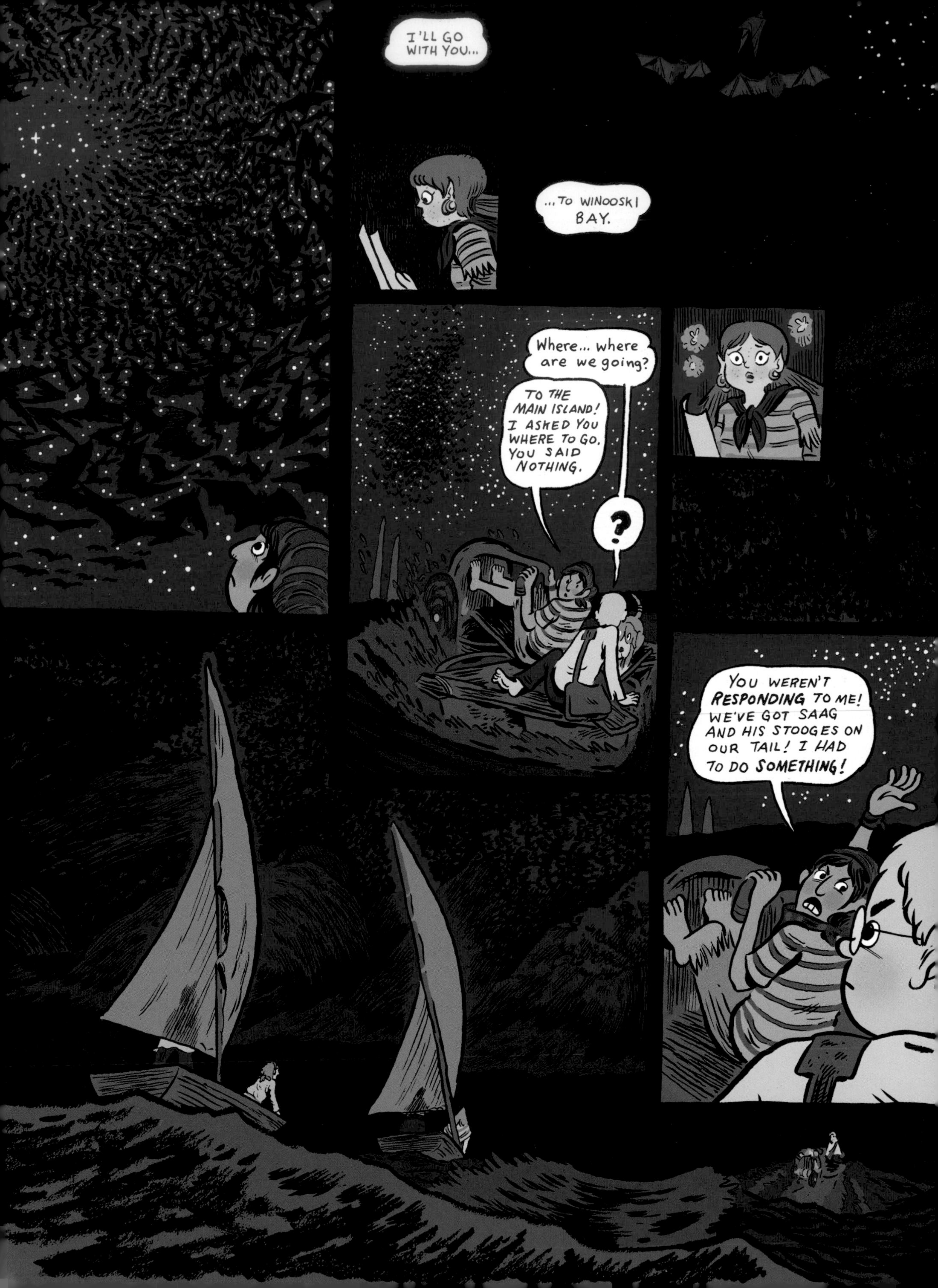
I'LL GO WITH YOU...
...TO WINOOSKI BAY.
Where... where are we going?
TO THE MAIN ISLAND! I ASKED YOU WHERE TO GO. YOU SAID NOTHING.
?
YOU WEREN'T RESPONDING TO ME! WE'VE GOT SAAG AND HIS STOOGES ON OUR TAIL! I HAD TO DO SOMETHING!

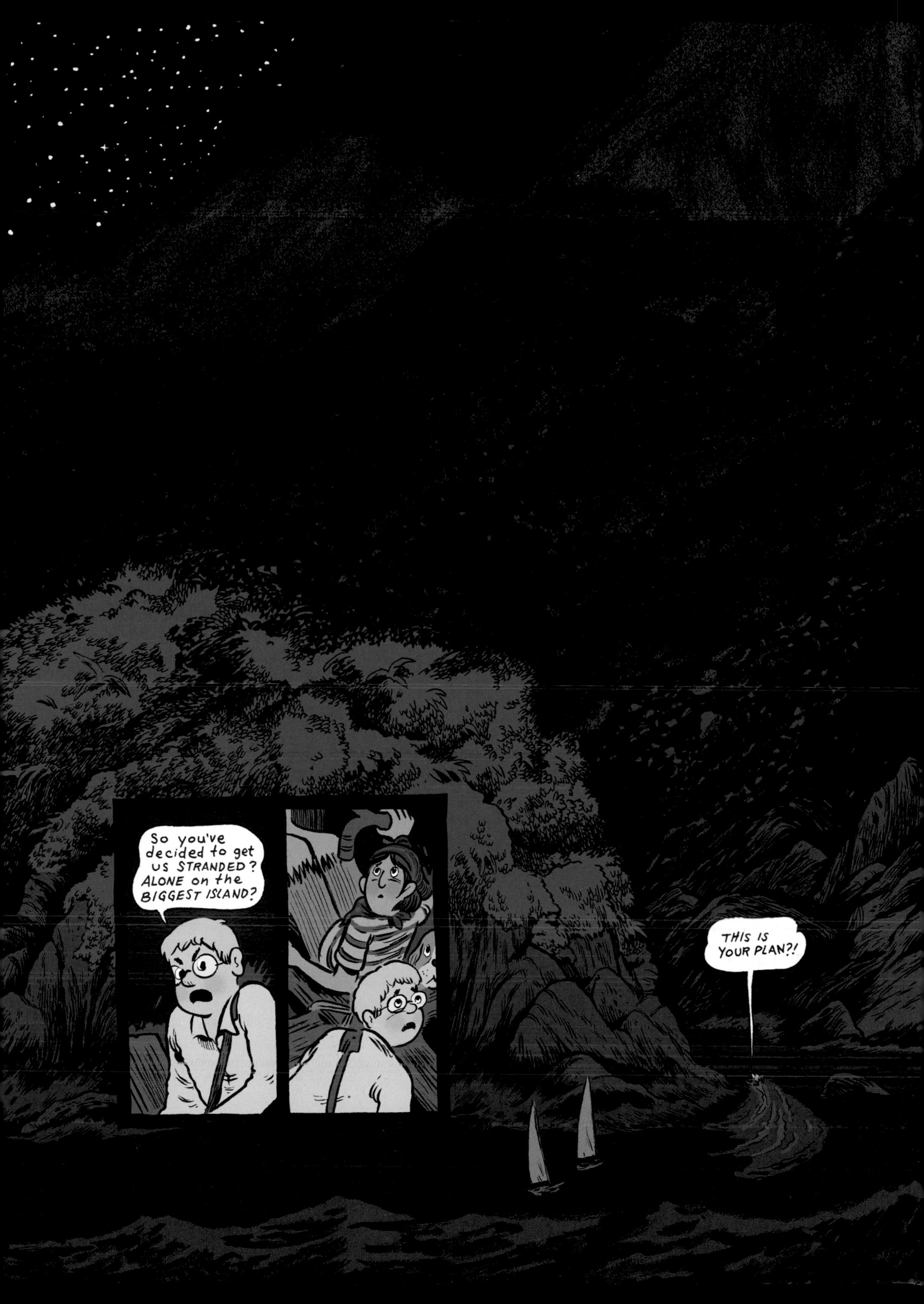
So you've decided to get us STRANDED? ALONE on the BIGGEST ISLAND?
THIS IS YOUR PLAN?!

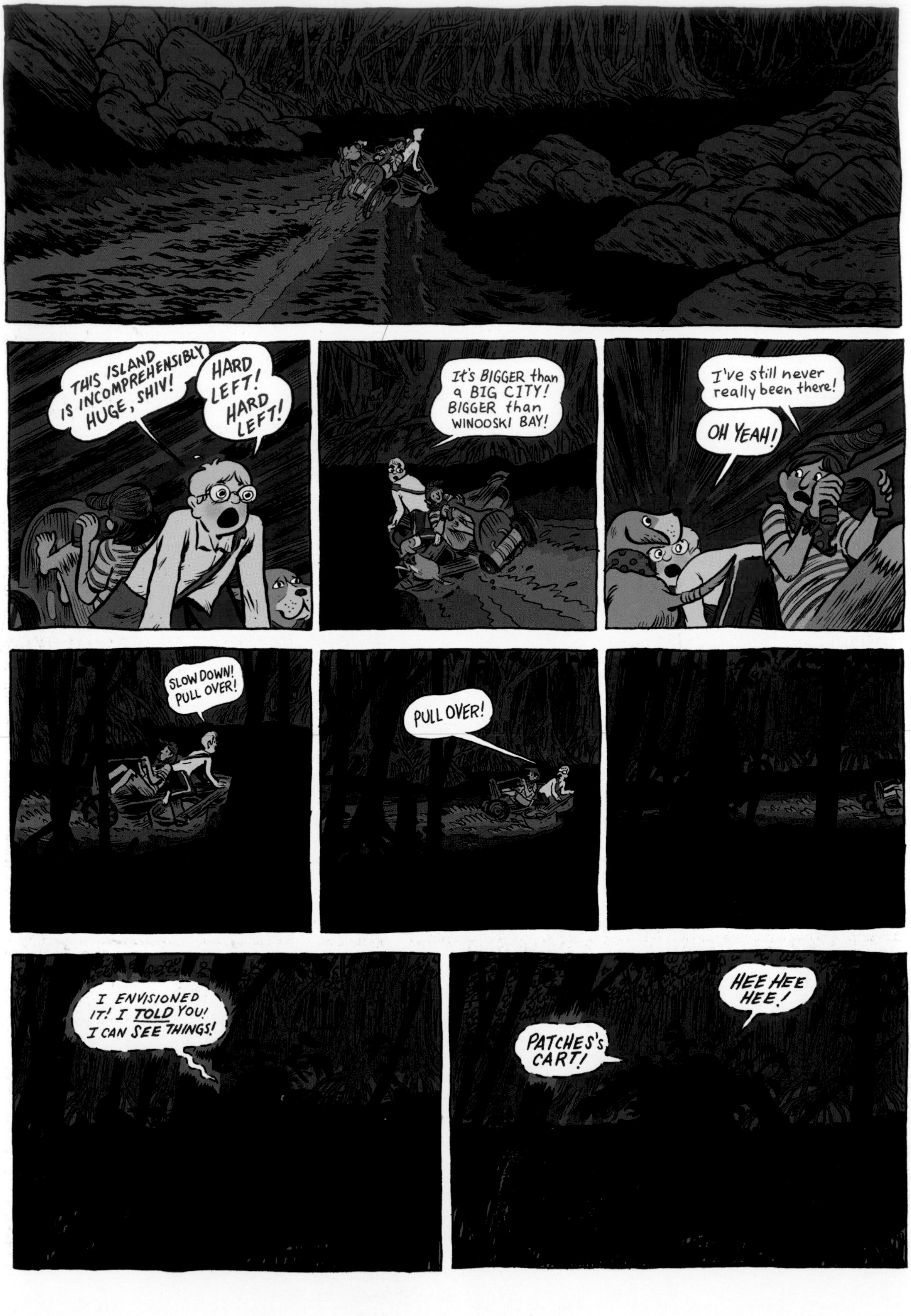
THIS ISLAND IS INCOMPREHENSIBLY HUGE, SHIV!
HARD LEFT! HARD LEFT!
It's BIGGER than a BIG CITY! BIGGER than WINOOSKI BAY!
I've still never really been there!
OH YEAH!
SLOW DOWN! PULL OVER!
PULL OVER!
I ENVISIONED IT! I TOLD YOU! I CAN SEE THINGS!
HEE HEE HEE!
PATCHES's CART!

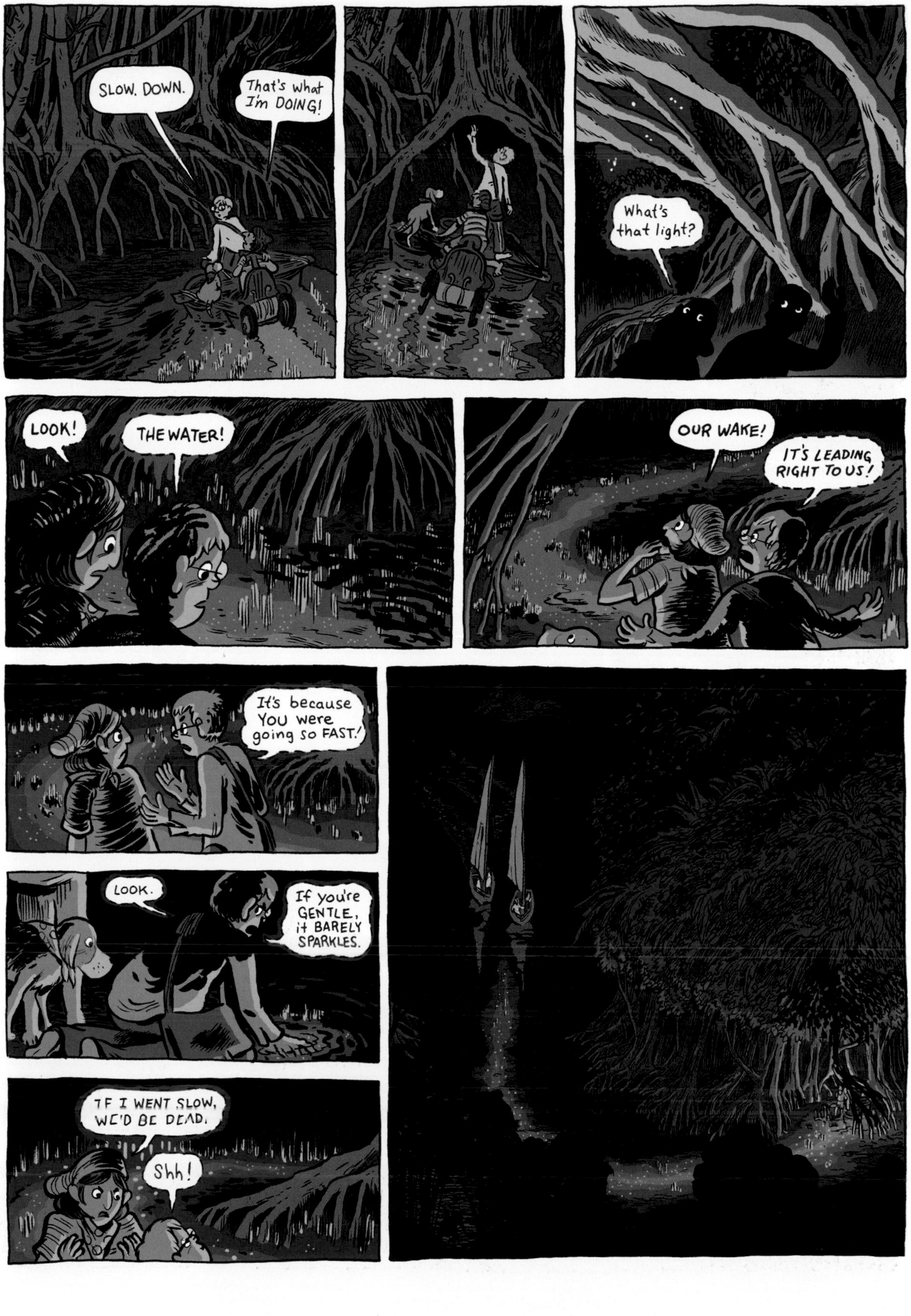
SLOW. DOWN.
That's what I'm DOING!
What's that light?
LOOK!
THE WATER!
OUR WAKE!
IT'S LEADING RIGHT TO US!
It's because YOU were going so FAST!
LOOK.
If you're GENTLE, it BARELY SPARKLES.
IF I WENT SLOW, WE'D BE DEAD.
Shh!

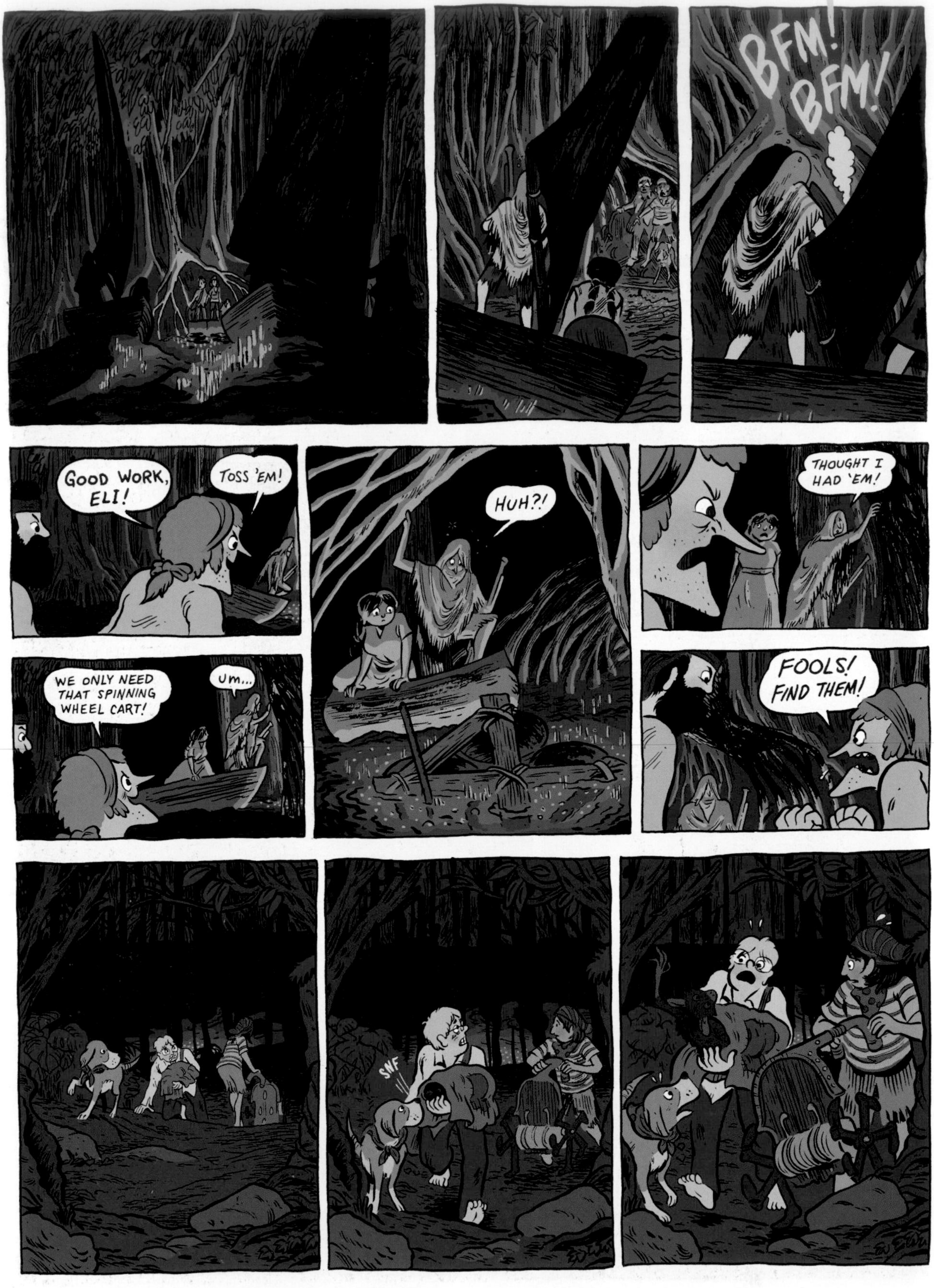
BFM! BFM!
GOOD WORK, ELI!
TOSS 'EM!
HUH?!
THOUGHT I HAD 'EM!
WE ONLY NEED THAT SPINNING WHEEL CART!
UM...
FOOLS! FIND THEM!
SNF

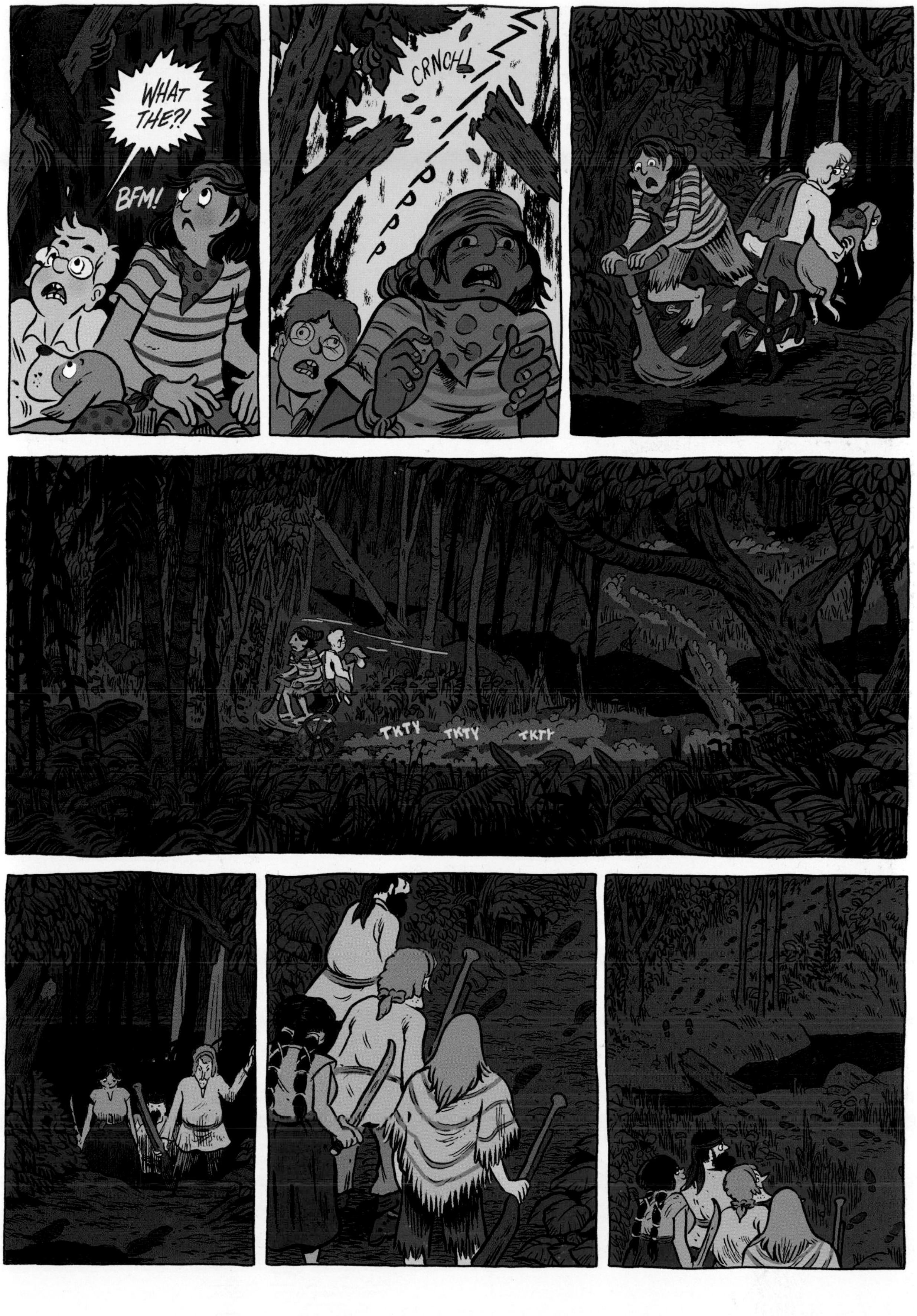

WHAT THE?!
BFM!
CRNCH!
TKTY
TKTY
TKTY

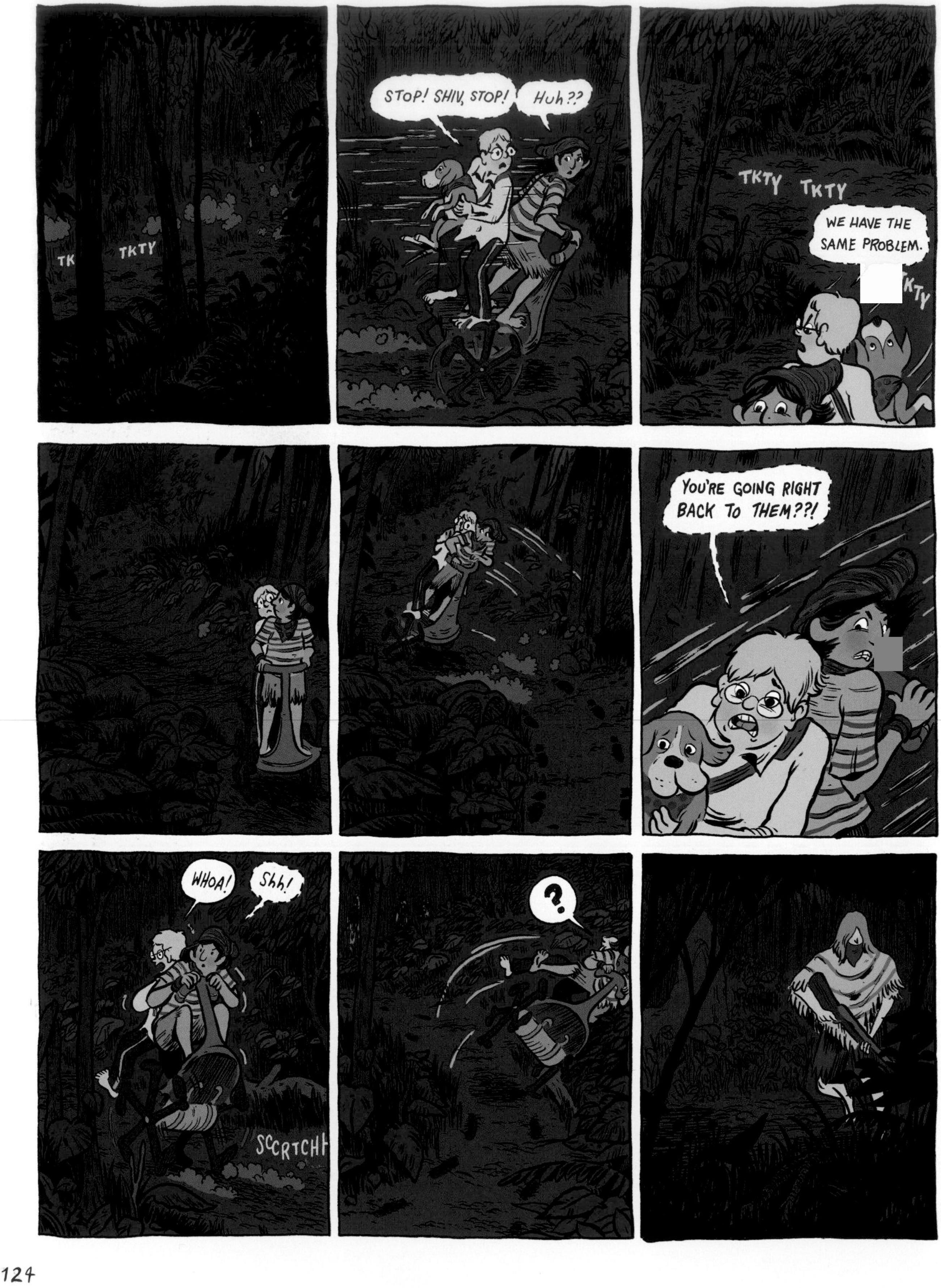
TK
TKTY
STOP! SHIV, STOP!
Huh??
TKTY TKTY
WE HAVE THE SAME PROBLEM.
YOU'RE GOING RIGHT BACK TO THEM??!
WHOA!
Shh!
SCCRTCHH
?

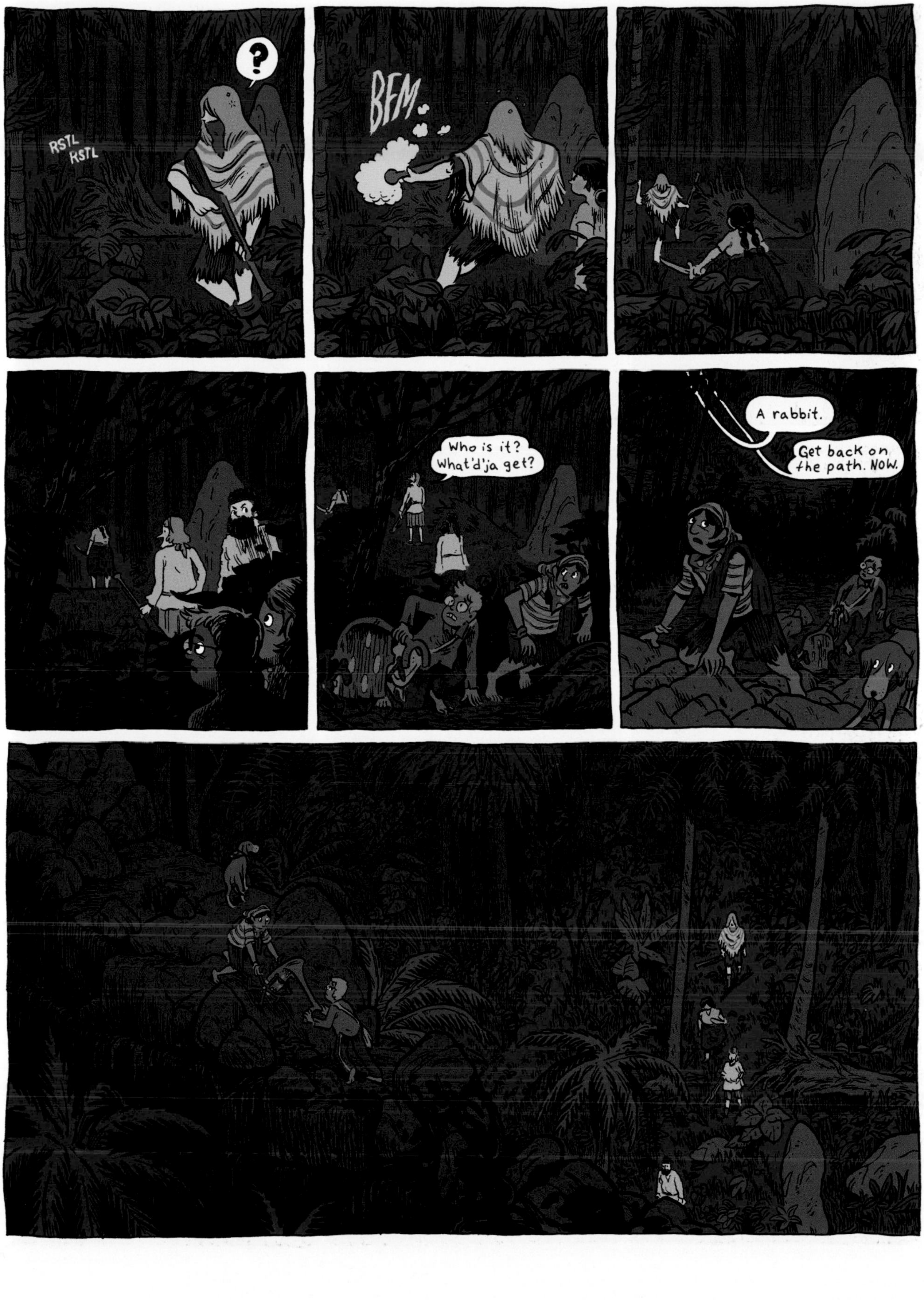
RSTL
RSTL
?
BFM.
Who is it? What'd'ja get?
A rabbit.
Get back on the path. NOW.

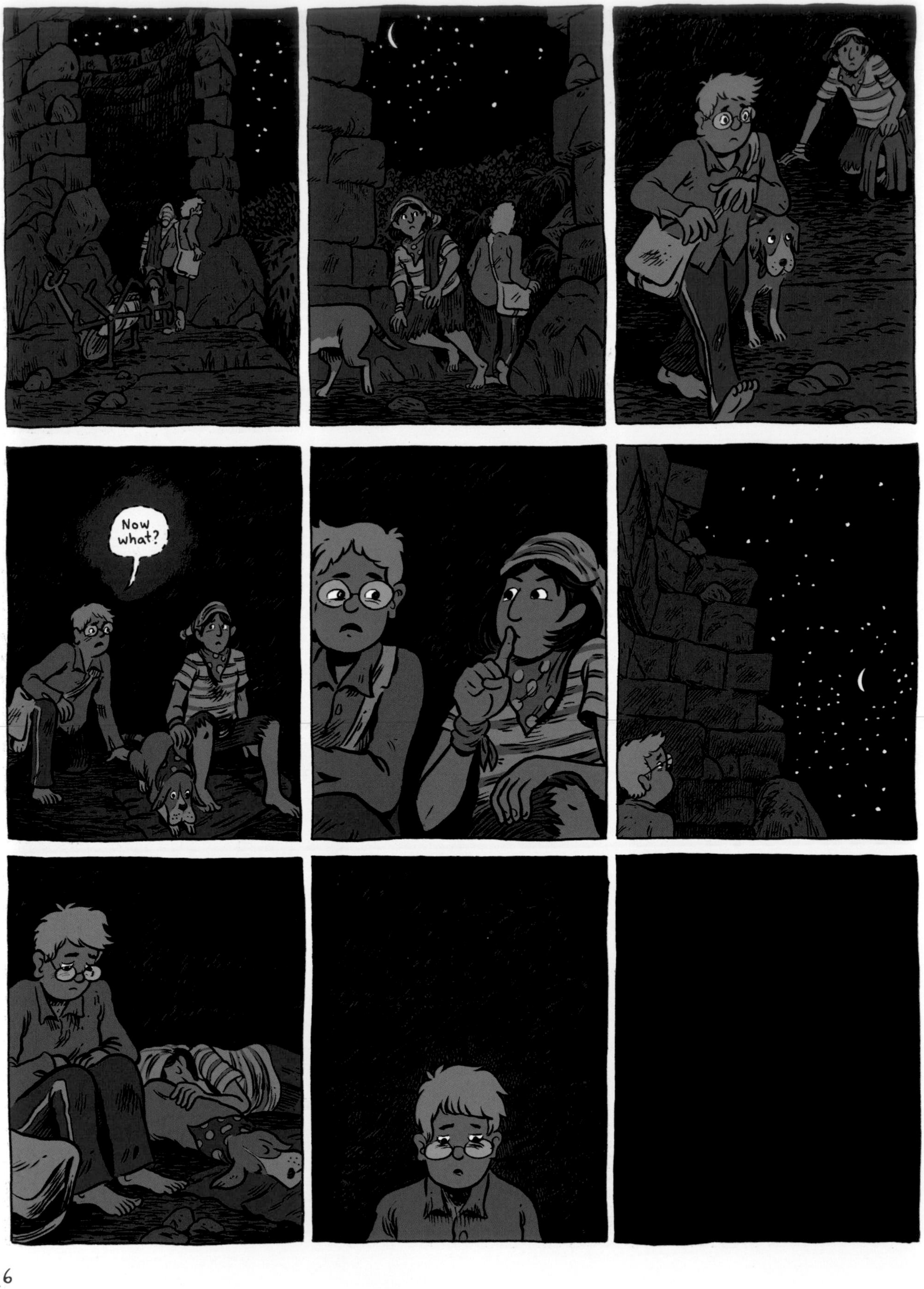
Now what?

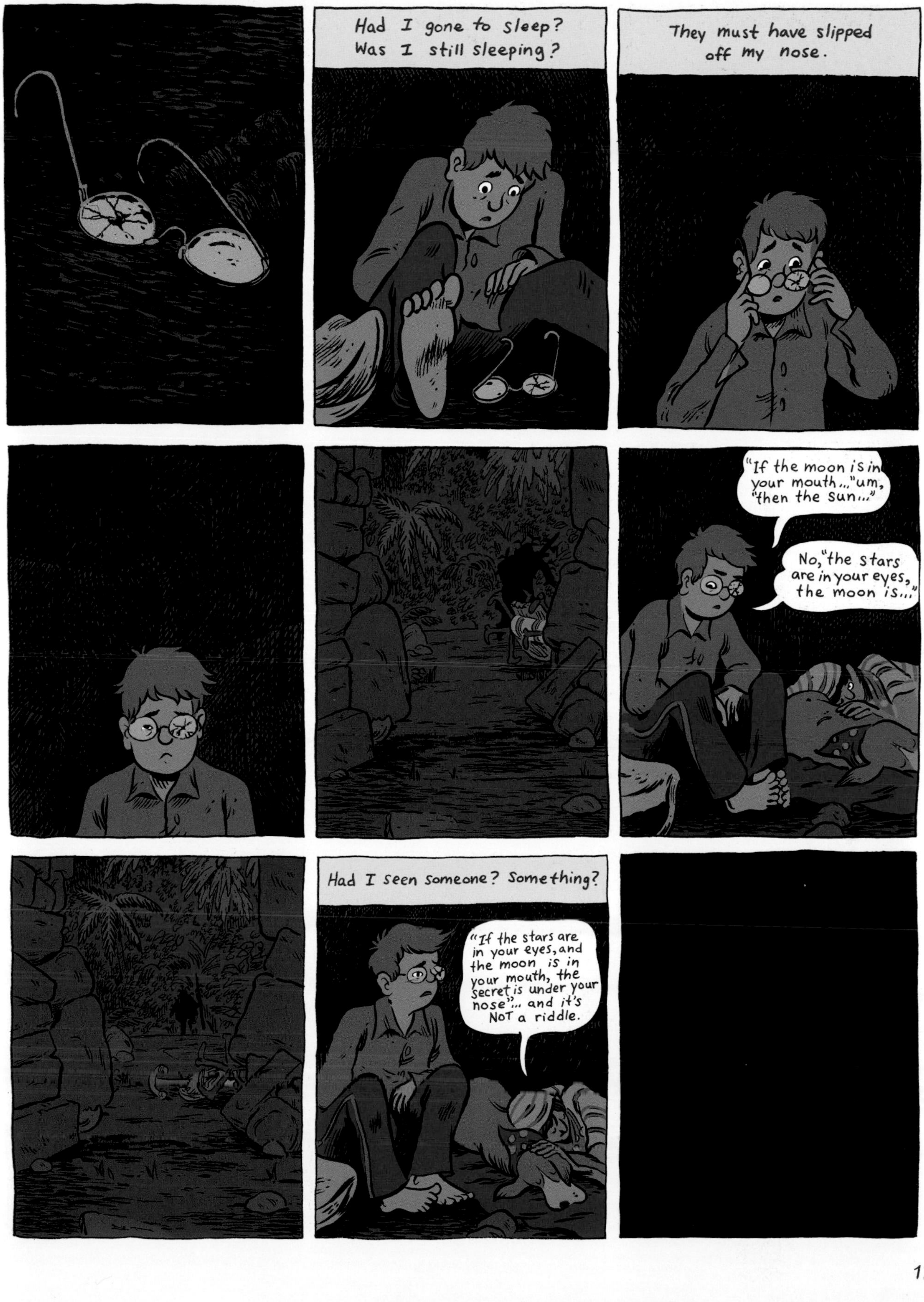
Had I gone to sleep? Was I still sleeping?
They must have slipped off my nose.
"If the moon is in your mouth..." um, "then the sun..."
No, "the stars are in your eyes, the moon is..."
Had I seen someone? Something?
"If the stars are in your eyes, and the moon is in your mouth, the secret is under your nose"... and it's NOT a riddle.

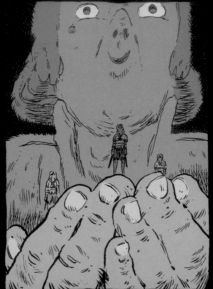

BFF

GHASP!

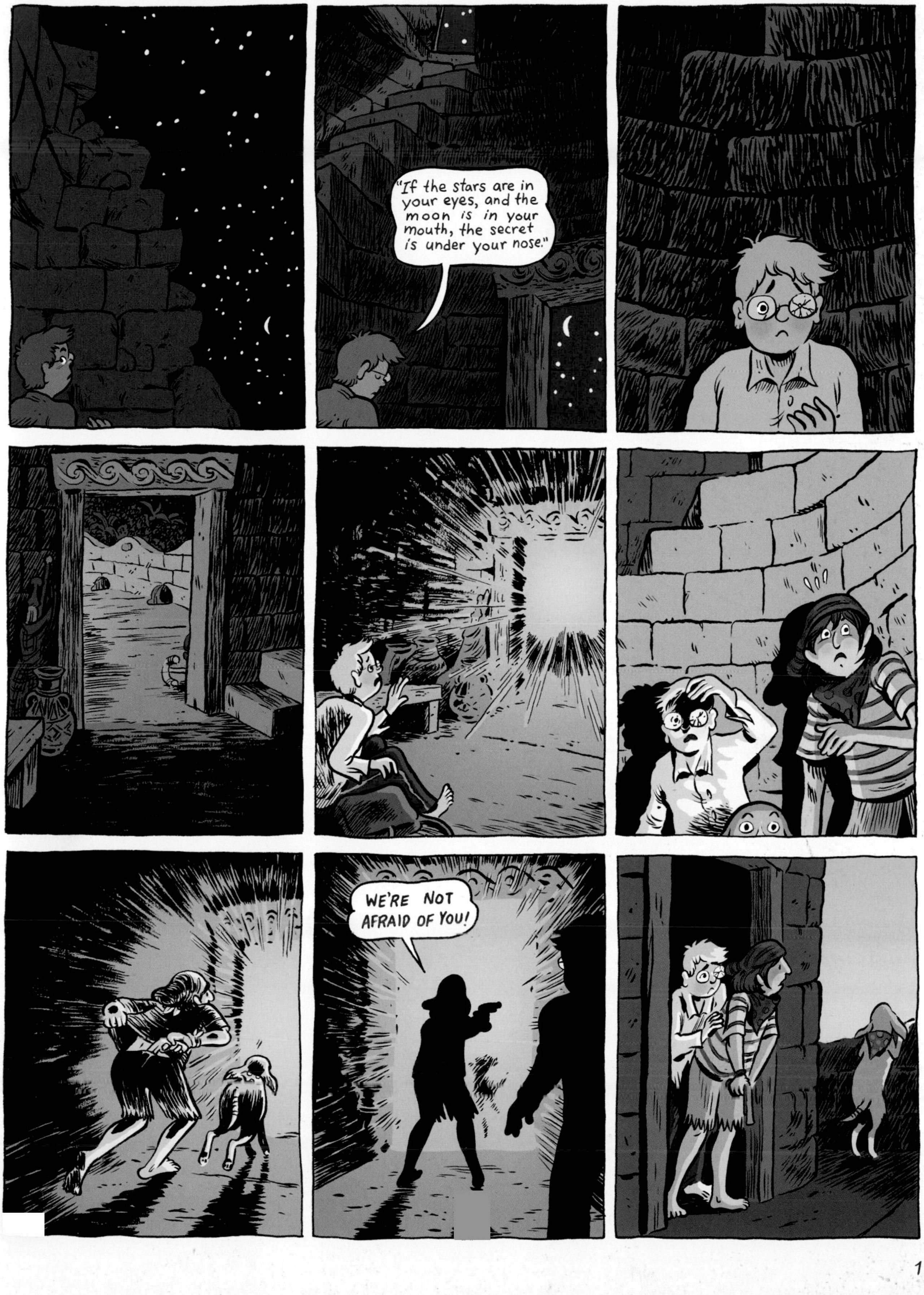
"If the stars are in your eyes, and the moon is in your mouth, the secret is under your nose."
WE'RE NOT AFRAID OF YOU!

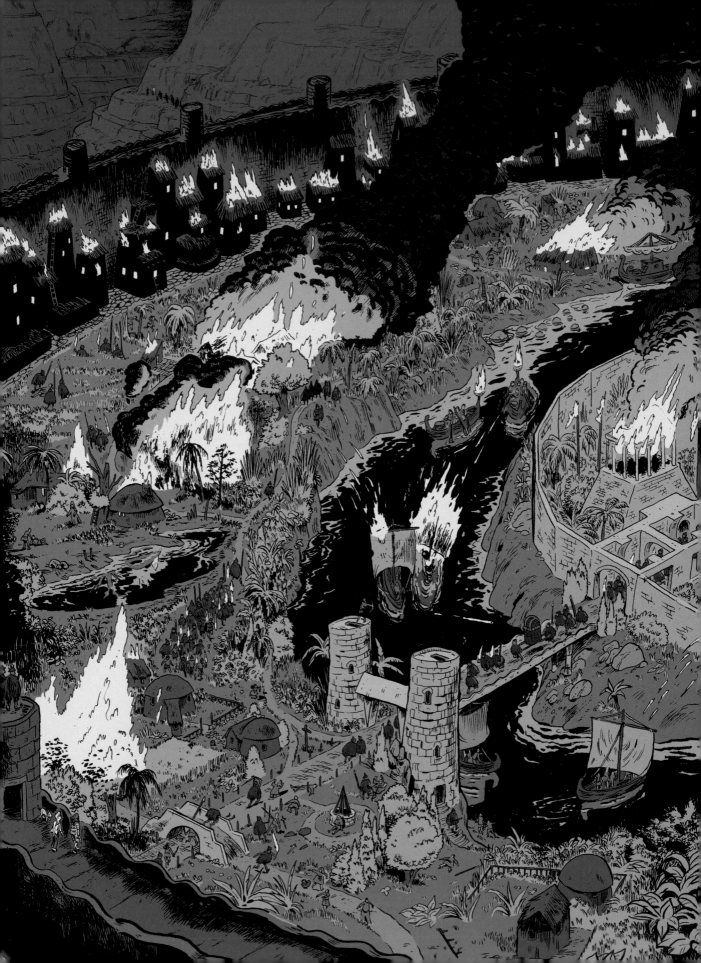

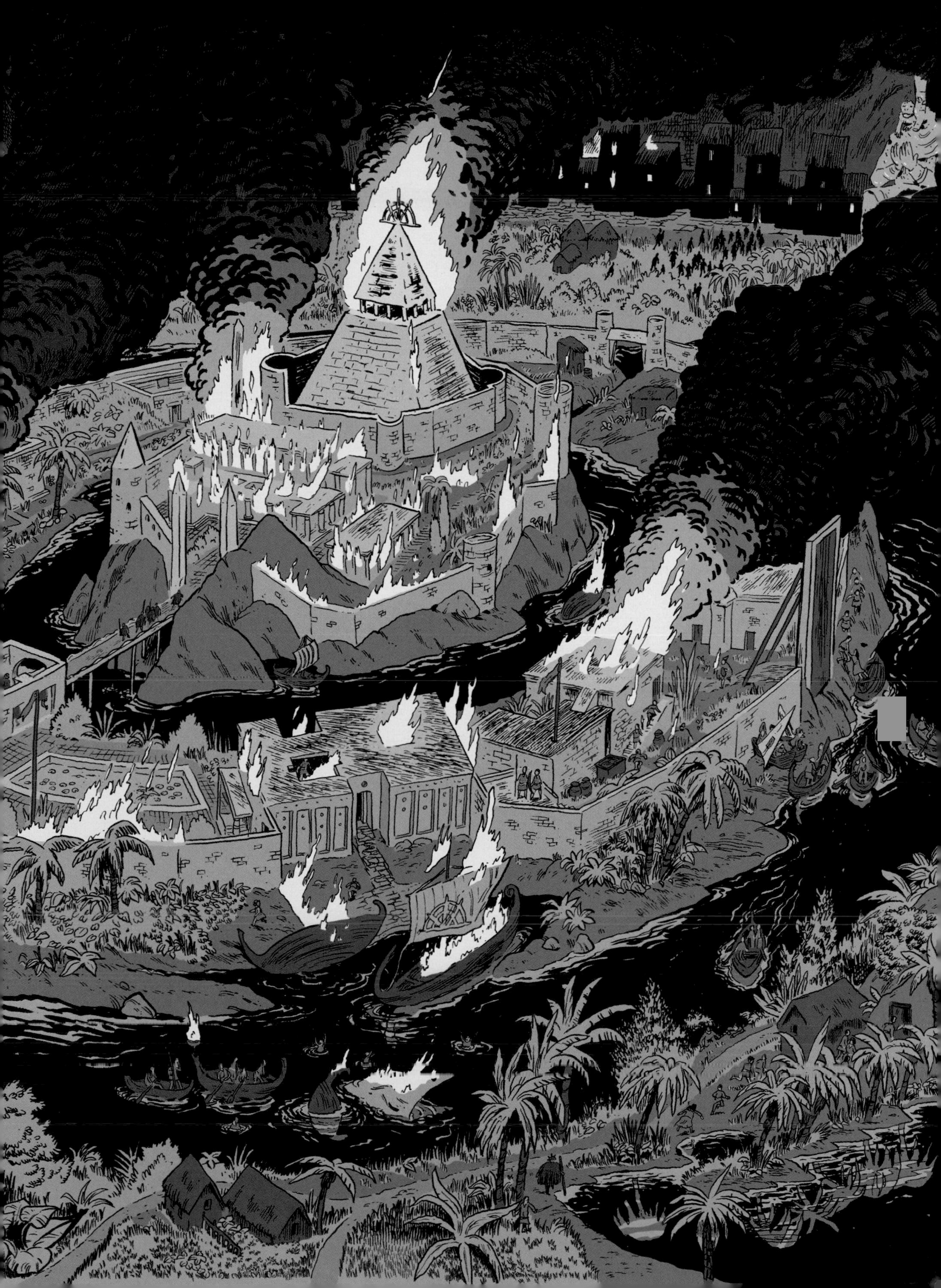

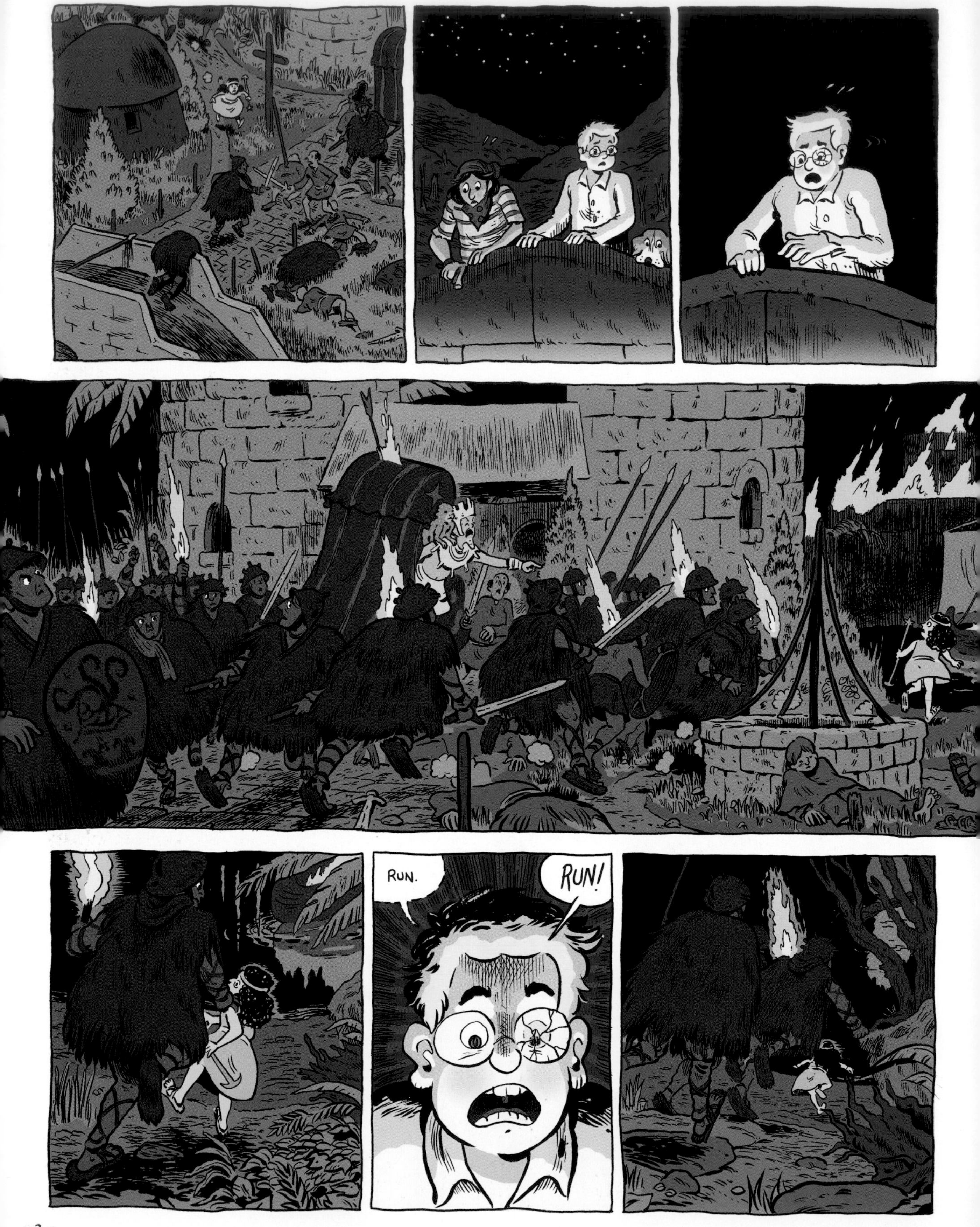
RUN.
RUN!

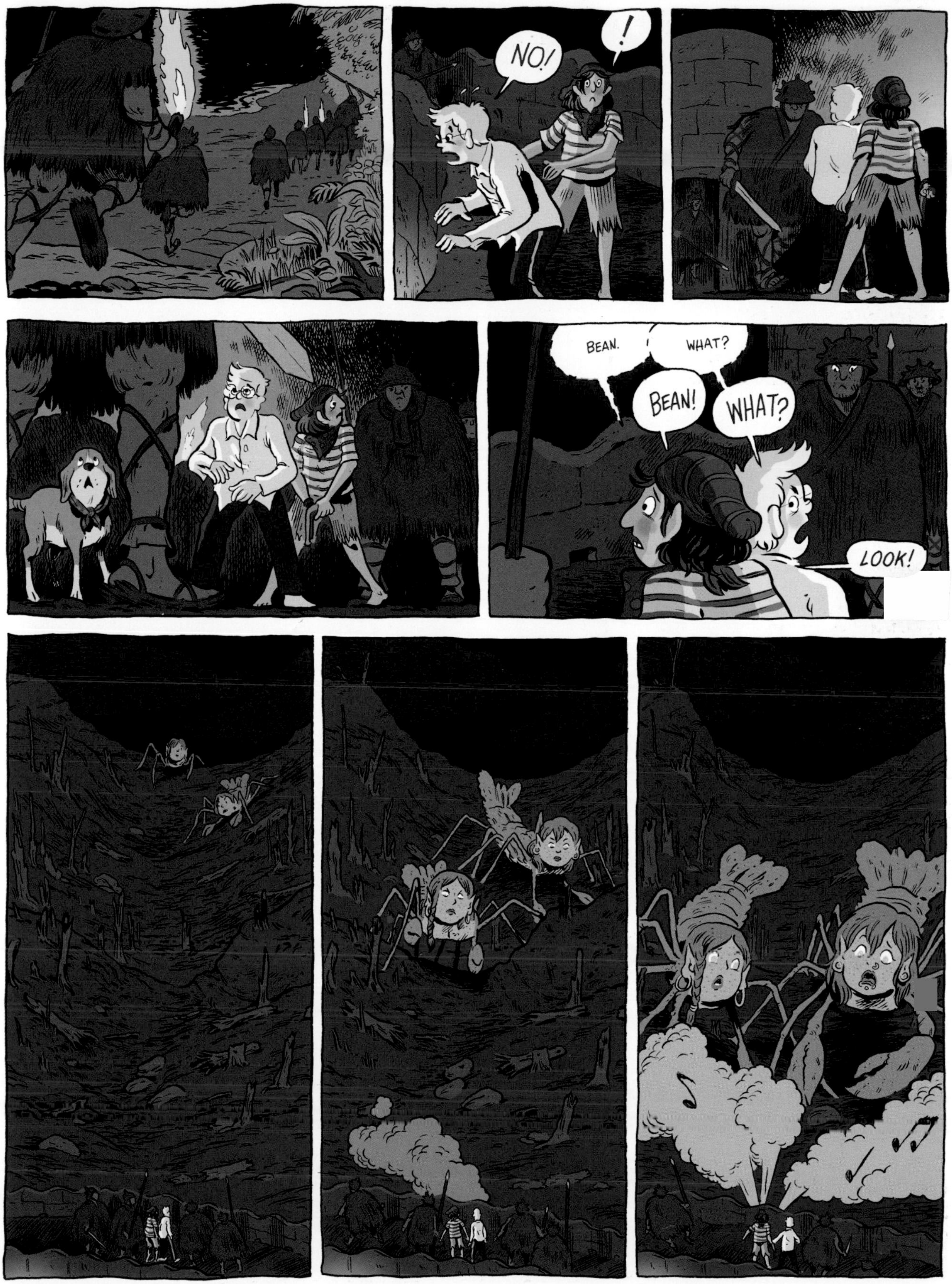
NO!
!
BEAN.
WHAT?
BEAN!
WHAT?
LOOK!

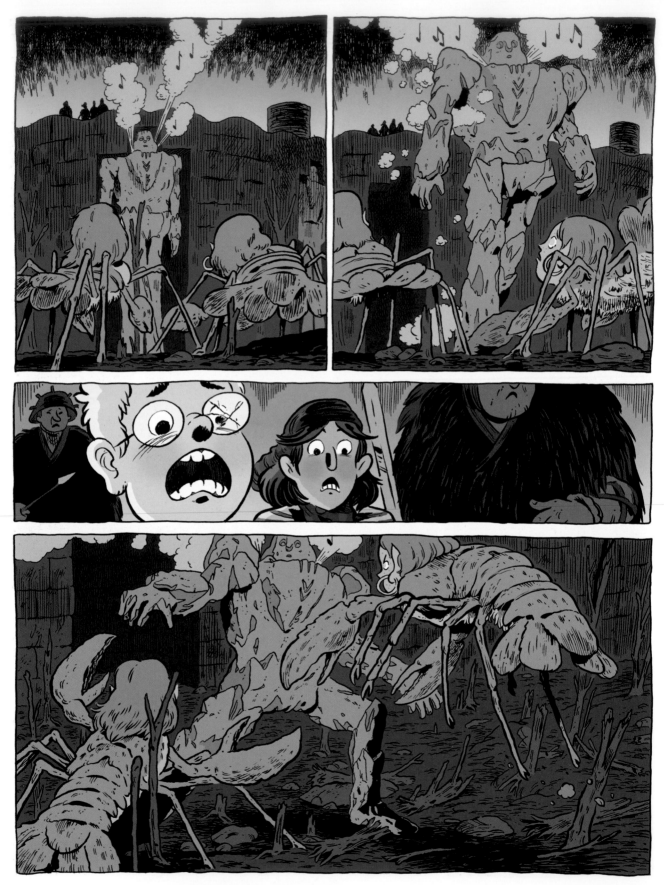

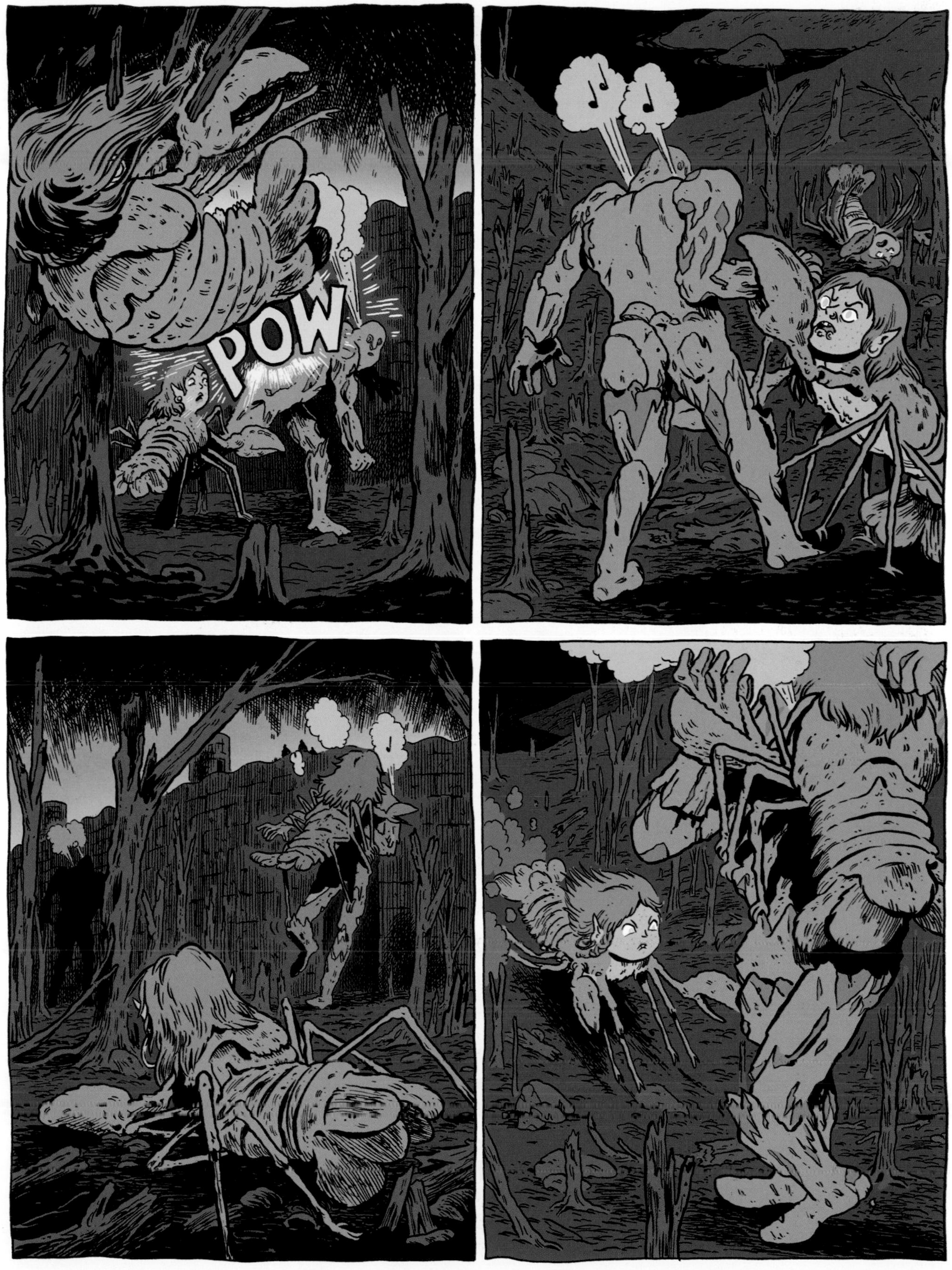
POW

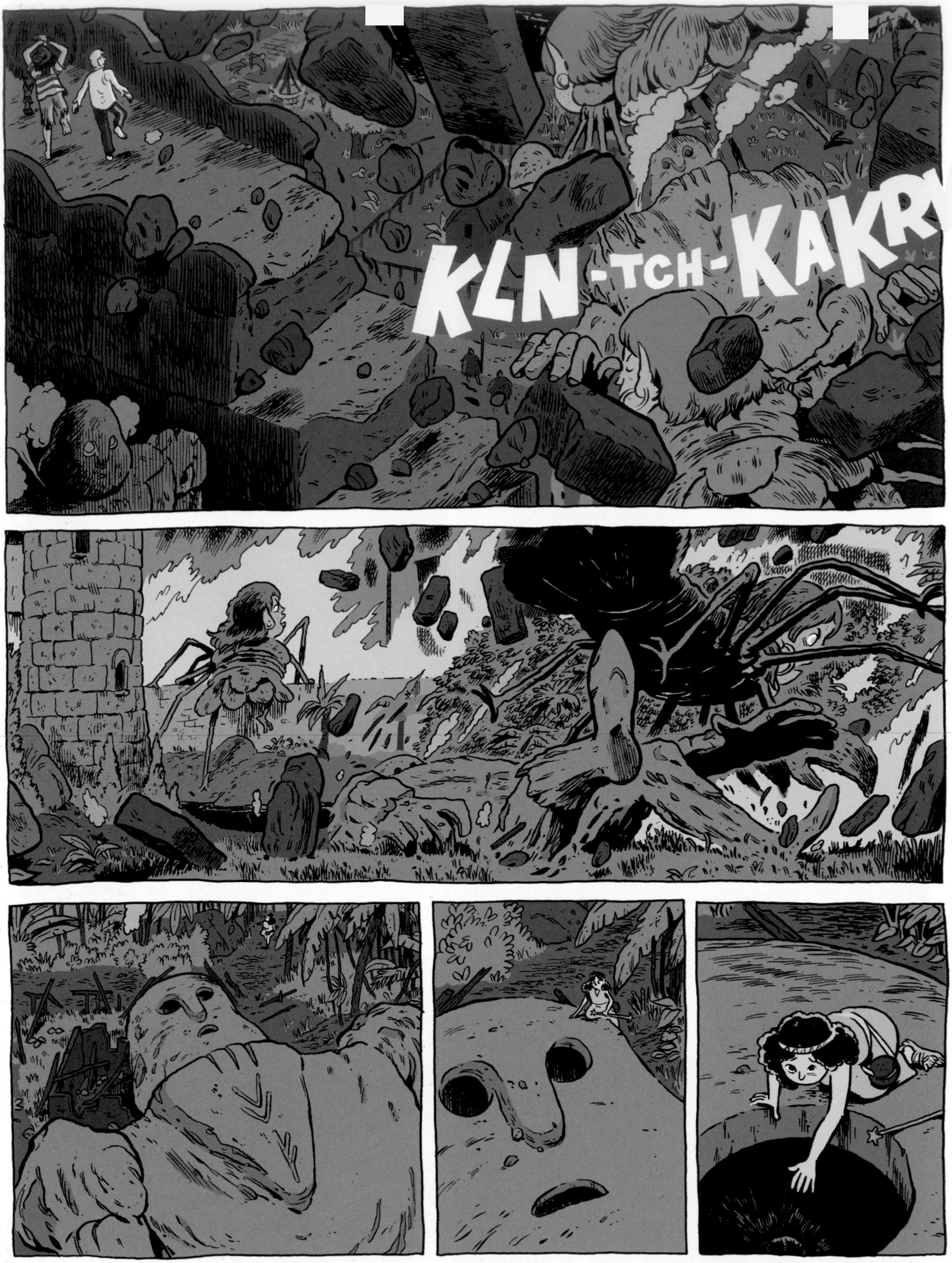
KLN-TCH-KAKR

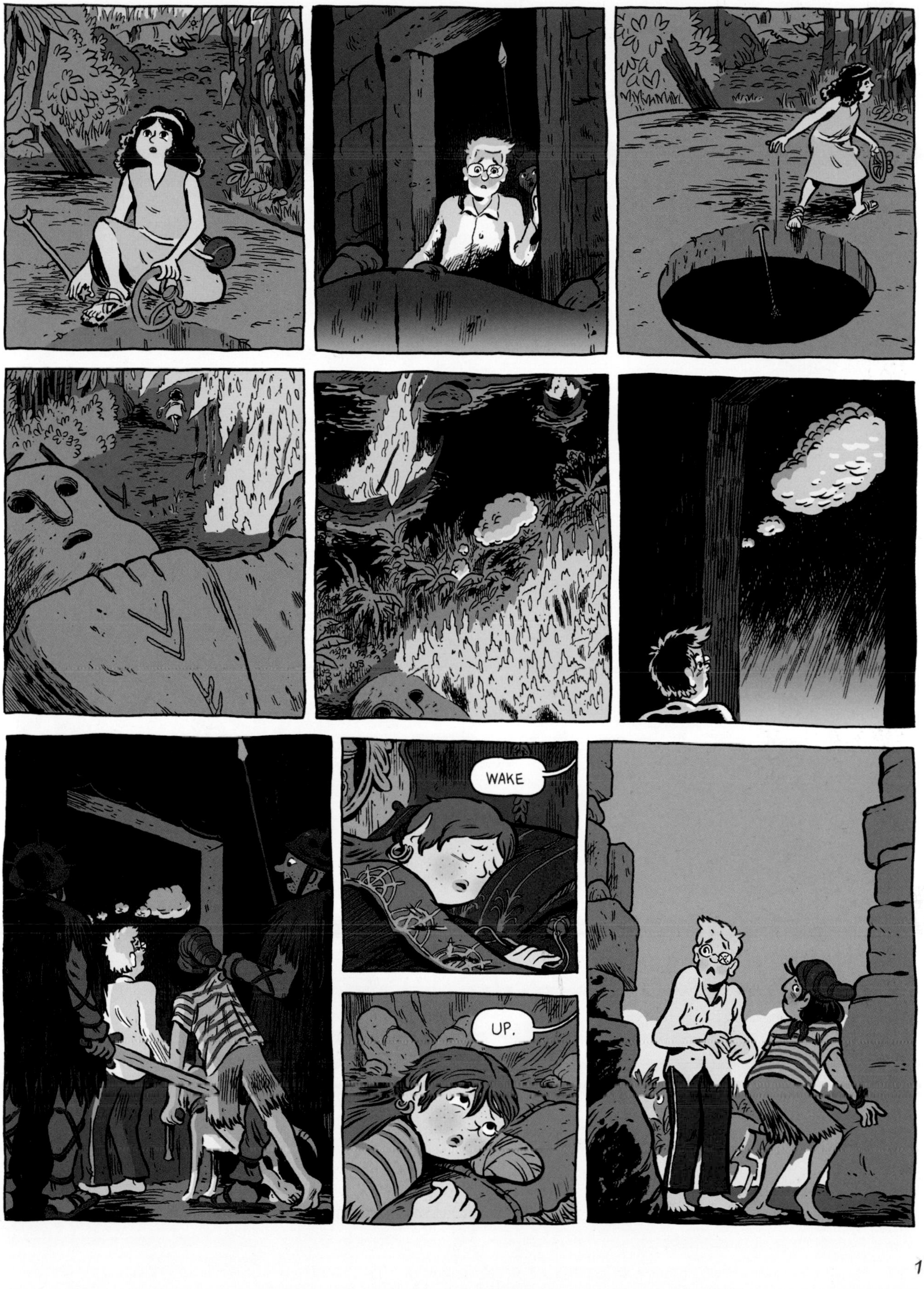
WAKE
UP.

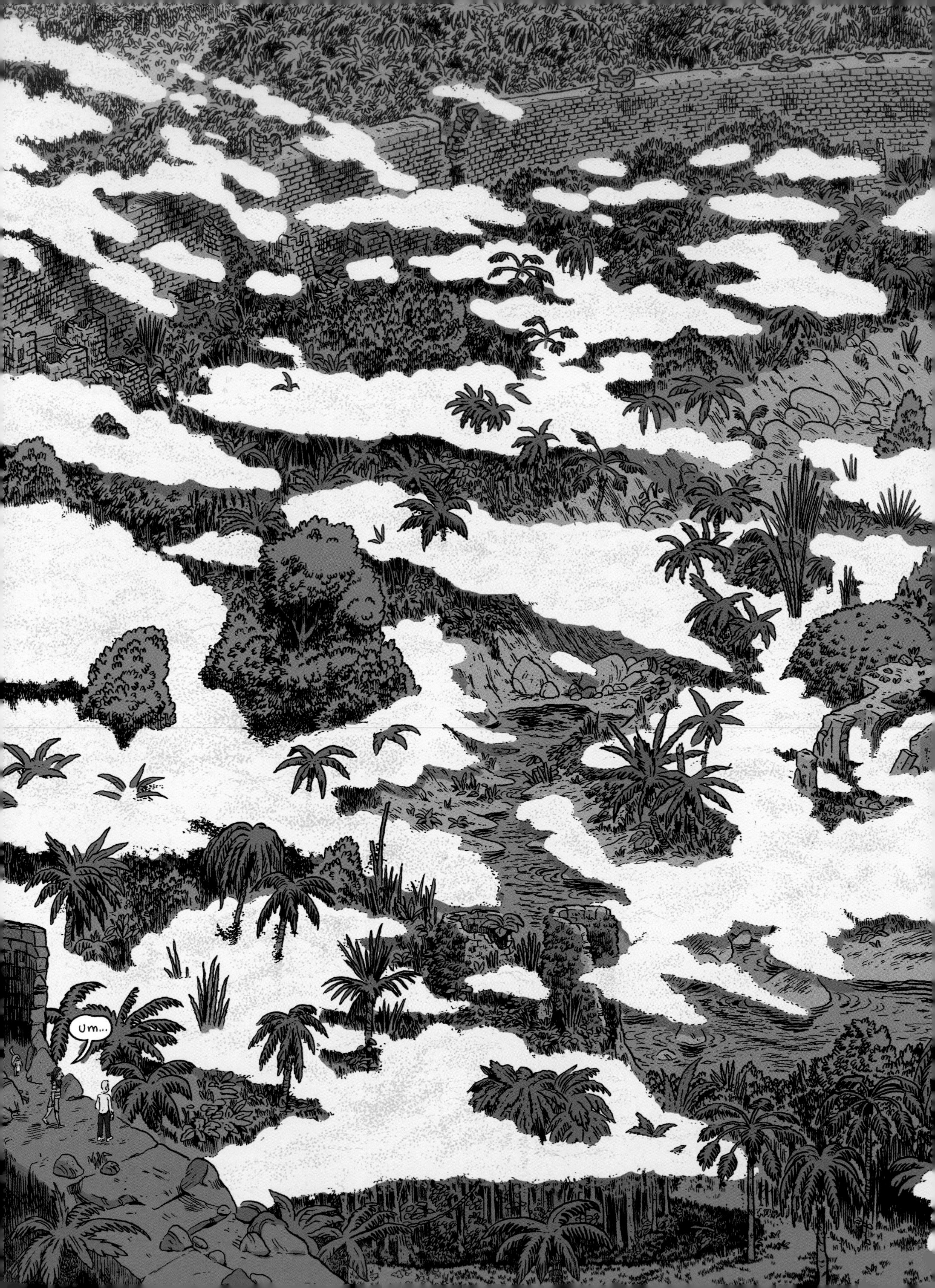
Um...

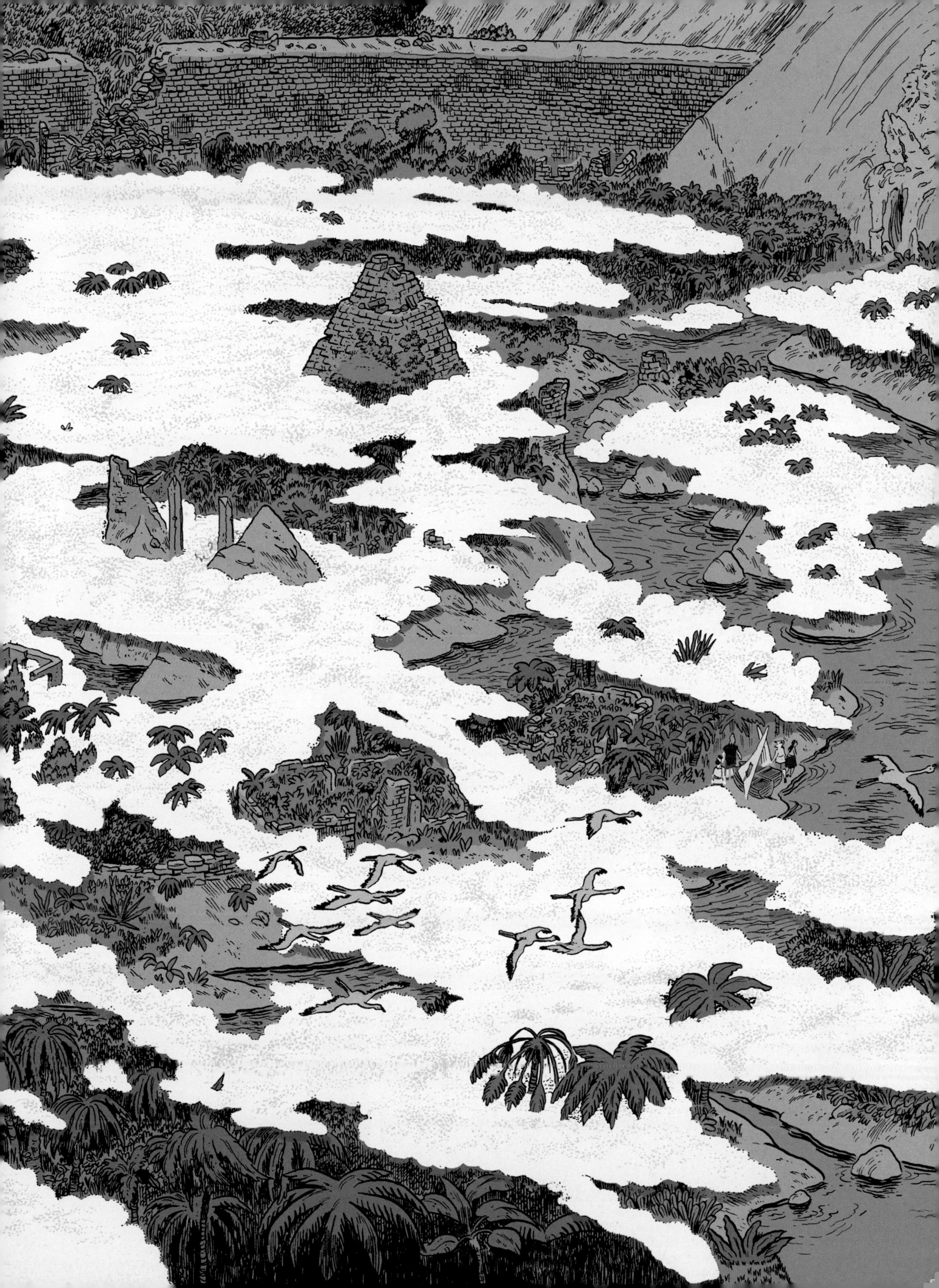

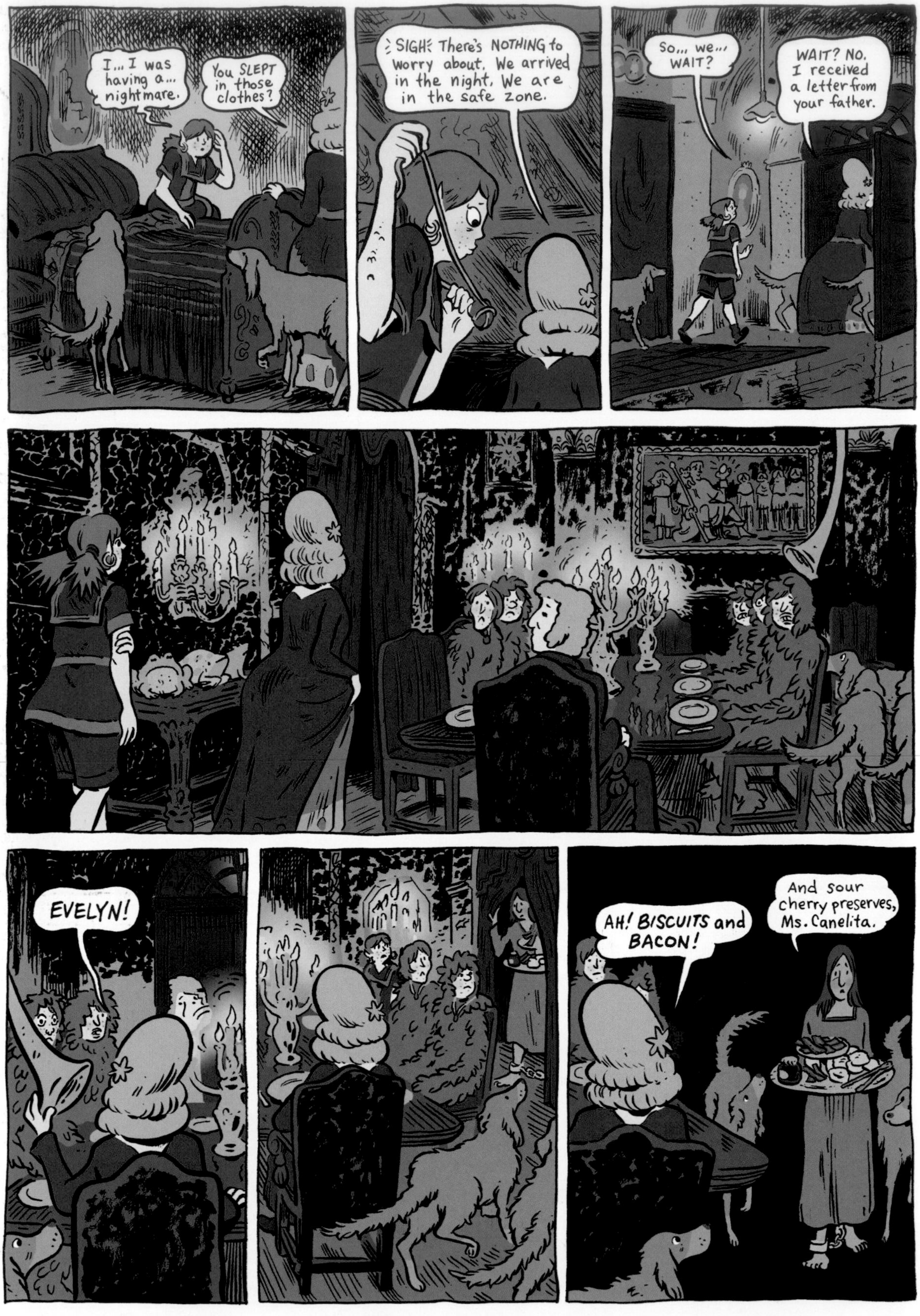
I... I was having a... nightmare.
You SLEPT in those clothes?
⁑SIGH⁑ There's NOTHING to worry about. We arrived in the night. We are in the safe zone.
So... we... WAIT?
WAIT? NO. I received a letter from your father.
EVELYN!
AH! BISCUITS and BACON!
And sour cherry preserves, Ms. Canelita.

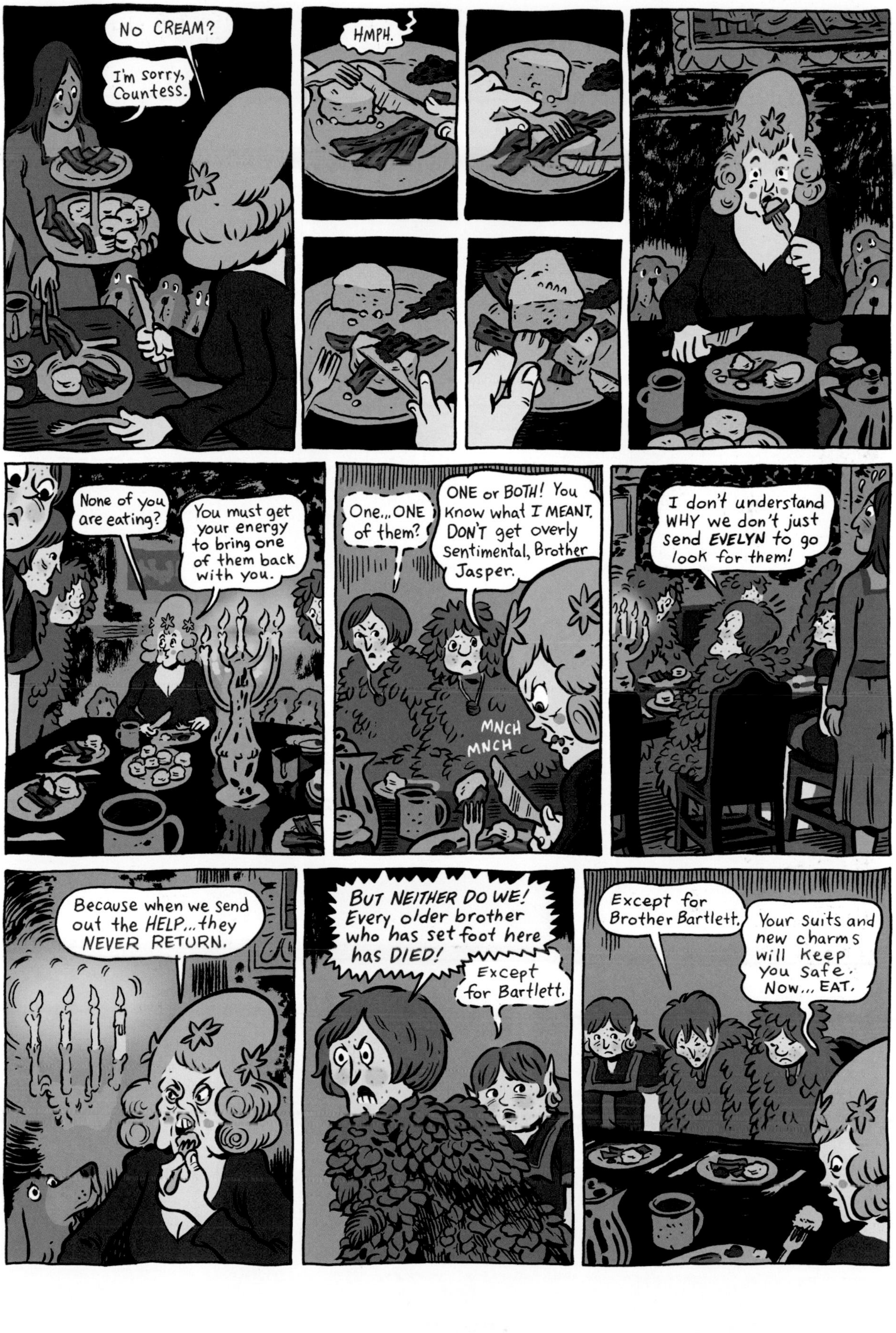
No CREAM?
I'm sorry, Countess.
HMPH.
None of you are eating?
You must get your energy to bring one of them back with you.
One... ONE of them?
ONE or BOTH! You know what I MEANT. DON'T get overly sentimental, Brother Jasper.
MNCH MNCH
I don't understand WHY we don't just send EVELYN to go look for them!
Because when we send out the HELP... they NEVER RETURN.
BUT NEITHER DO WE! Every older brother who has set foot here has DIED!
Except for Bartlett.
Except for Brother Bartlett.
Your suits and new charms will keep you safe. Now... EAT.

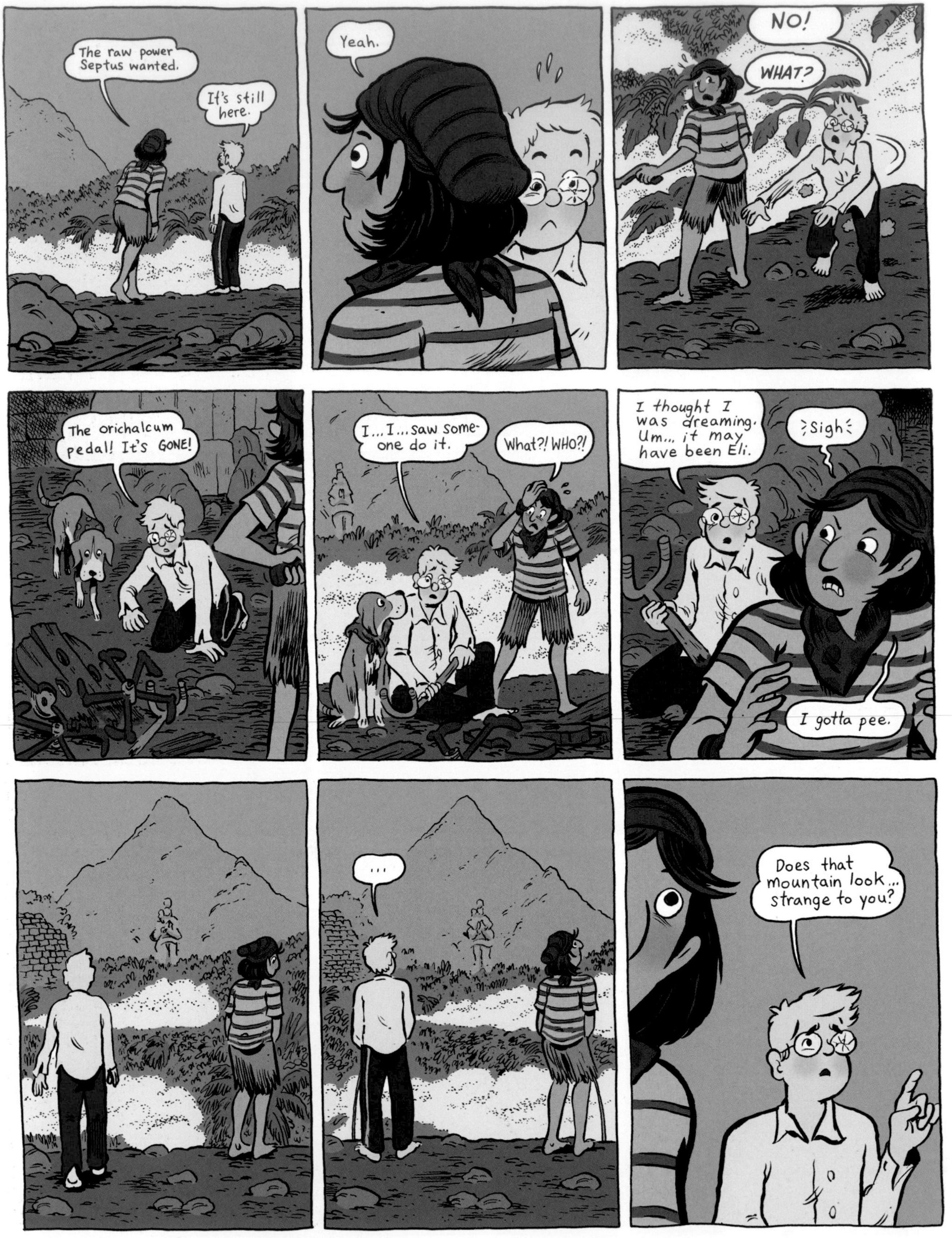
The raw power Septus wanted.
It's still here.
Yeah.
NO!
WHAT?
The orichalcum pedal! It's GONE!
I... I... saw some-one do it.
What?! WHO?!
I thought I was dreaming. Um... it may have been Eli.
Sigh
I gotta pee.
...
Does that mountain look... strange to you?

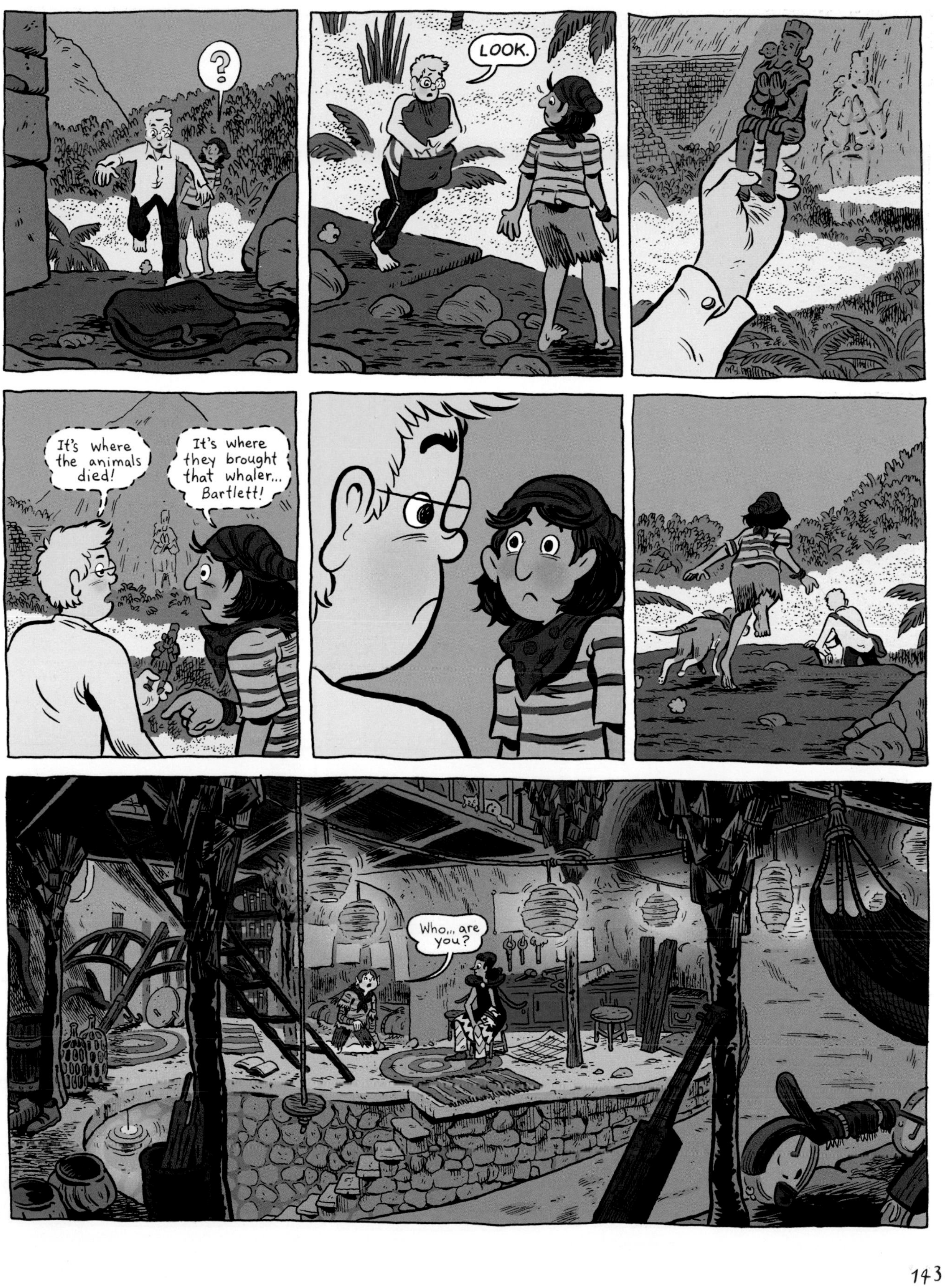
?
LOOK.
It's where the animals died!
It's where they brought that whaler... Bartlett!
Who... are you?

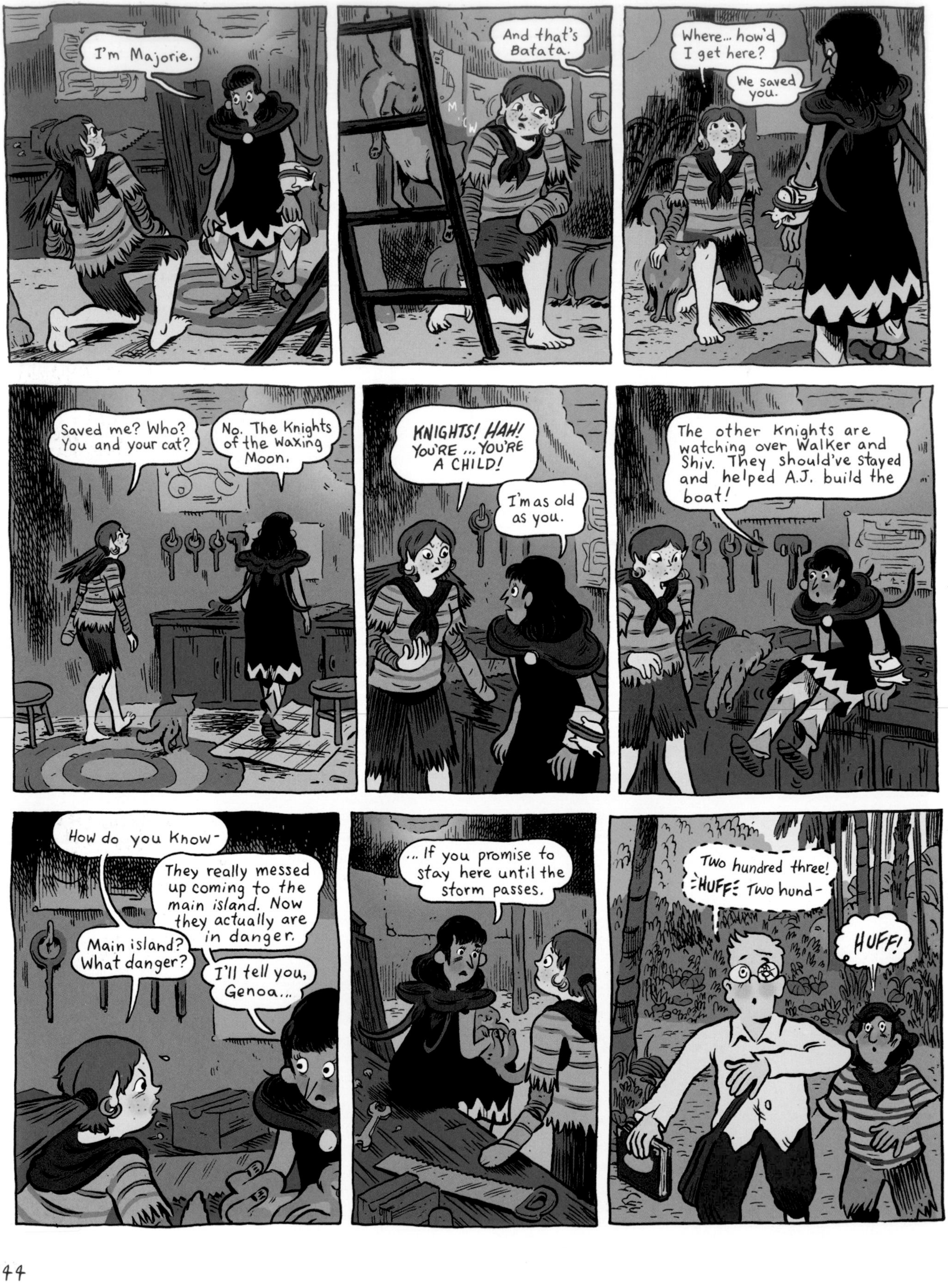
I'm Majorie.
And that's Batata.
M
'OW
Where... how'd I get here?
We saved you.
Saved me? Who? You and your cat?
No. The Knights of the Waxing Moon.
KNIGHTS! HAH! YOU'RE ... YOU'RE A CHILD!
I'm as old as you.
The other Knights are watching over Walker and Shiv. They should've stayed and helped A.J. build the boat!
How do you know-
They really messed up coming to the main island. Now they actually are in danger.
Main island? What danger?
I'll tell you, Genoa...
... If you promise to stay here until the storm passes.
Two hundred three! HUFF Two hund-
HUFF!

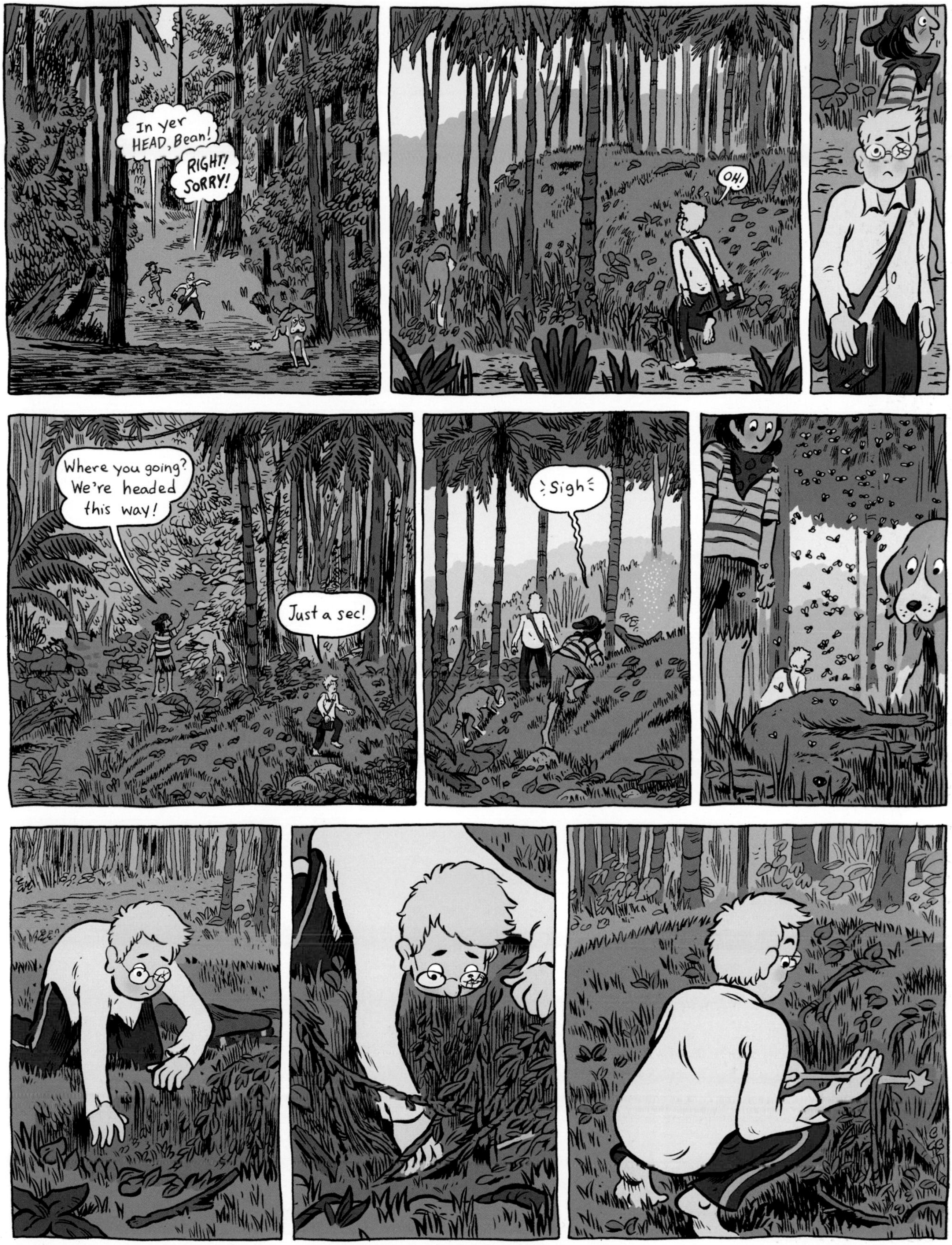

In yer HEAD, Bean!
RIGHT! SORRY!
OH!
Where you going? We're headed this way!
Just a sec!
Sigh

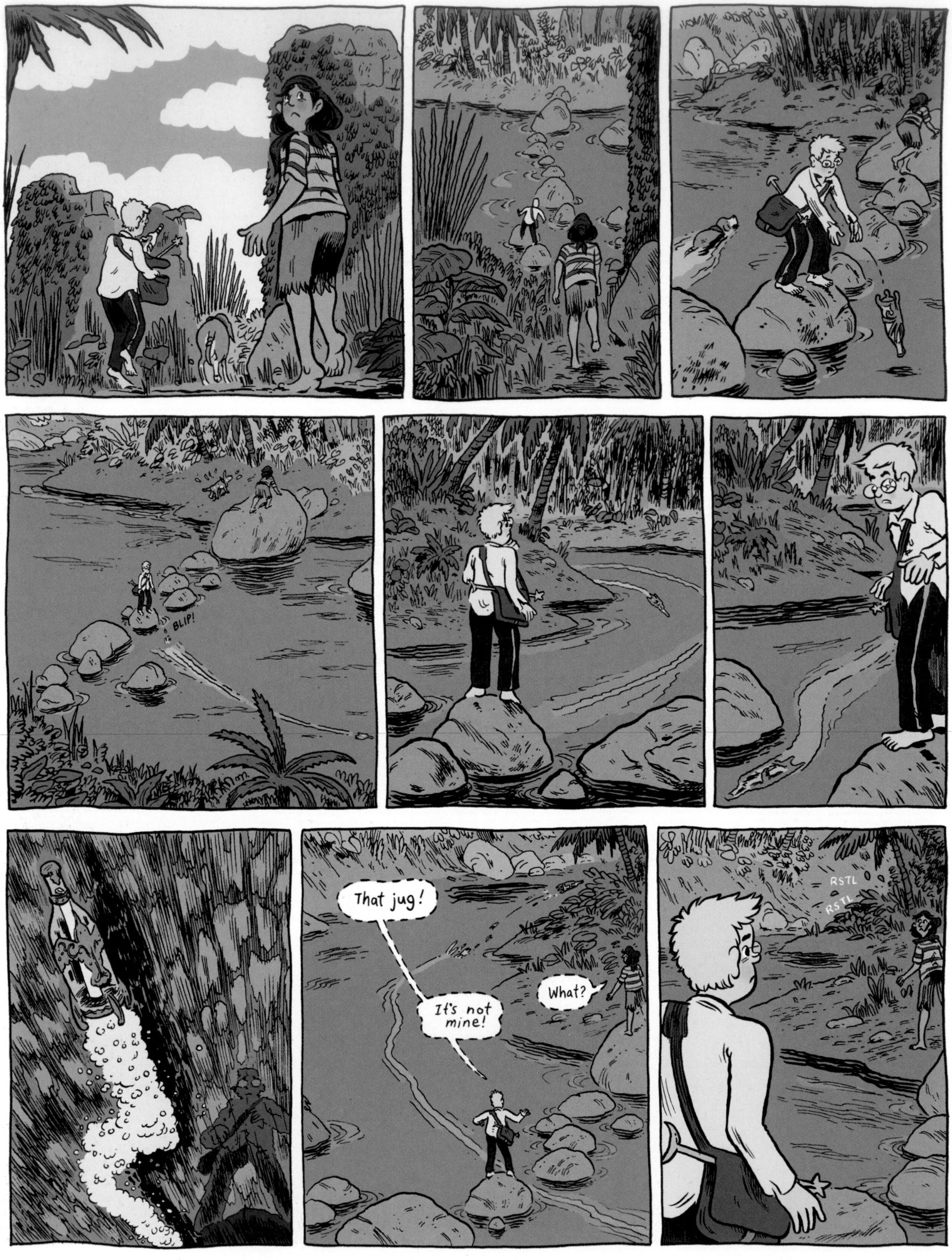
BLIP!
That jug!
It's not mine!
What?
RSTL
RSTL

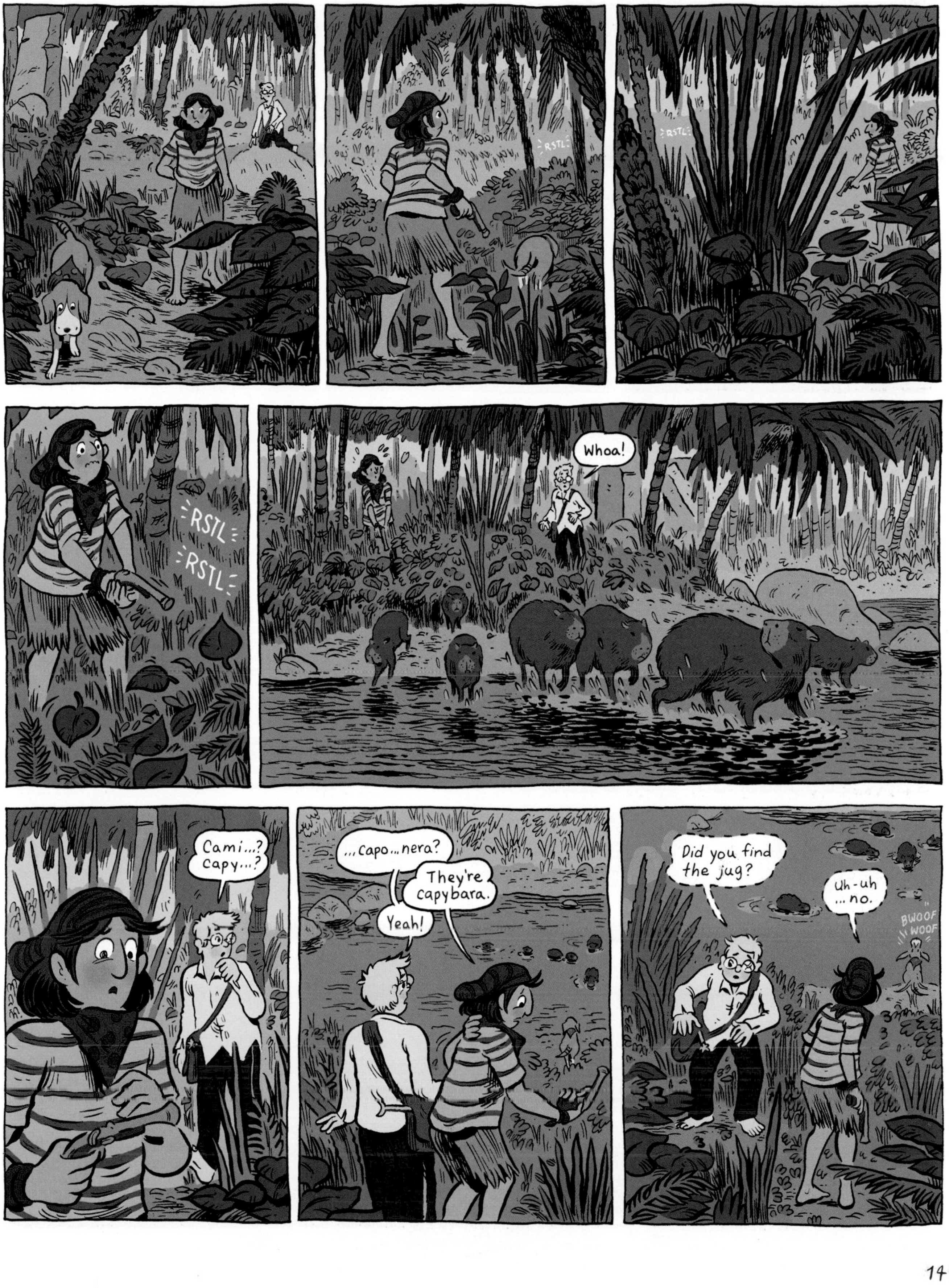
RSTL
RSTL
RSTL
RSTL
Whoa!
Cami...? Capy...?
...capo...nera?
They're capybara.
Yeah!
Did you find the jug?
Uh-uh ...no.
BWOOF WOOF

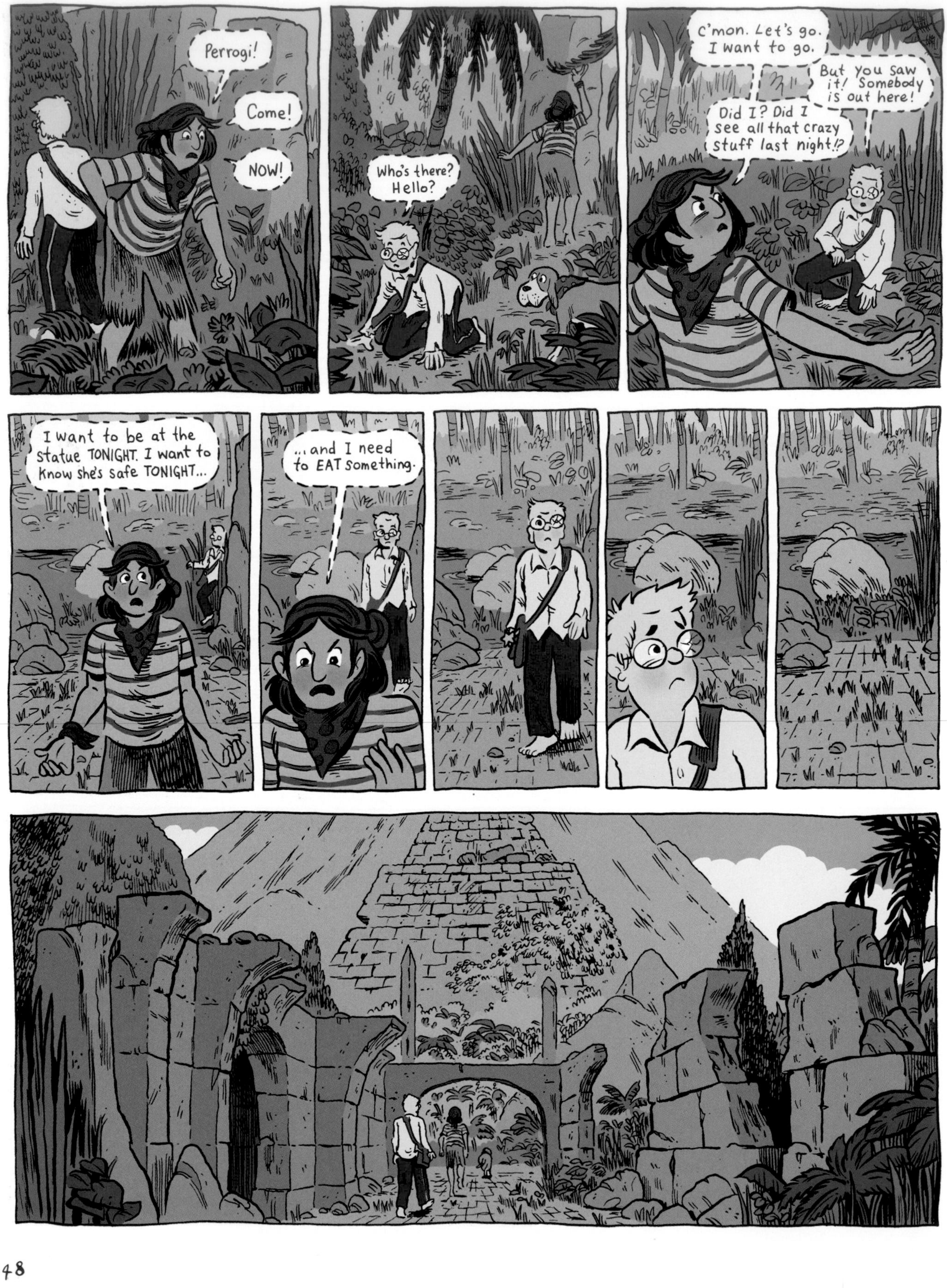
Perrogi!
Come!
NOW!
Who's there? Hello?
C'mon. Let's go. I want to go.
But you saw it! Somebody is out here!
Did I? Did I see all that crazy stuff last night!?
I want to be at the statue TONIGHT. I want to know she's safe TONIGHT...
...and I need to EAT something.

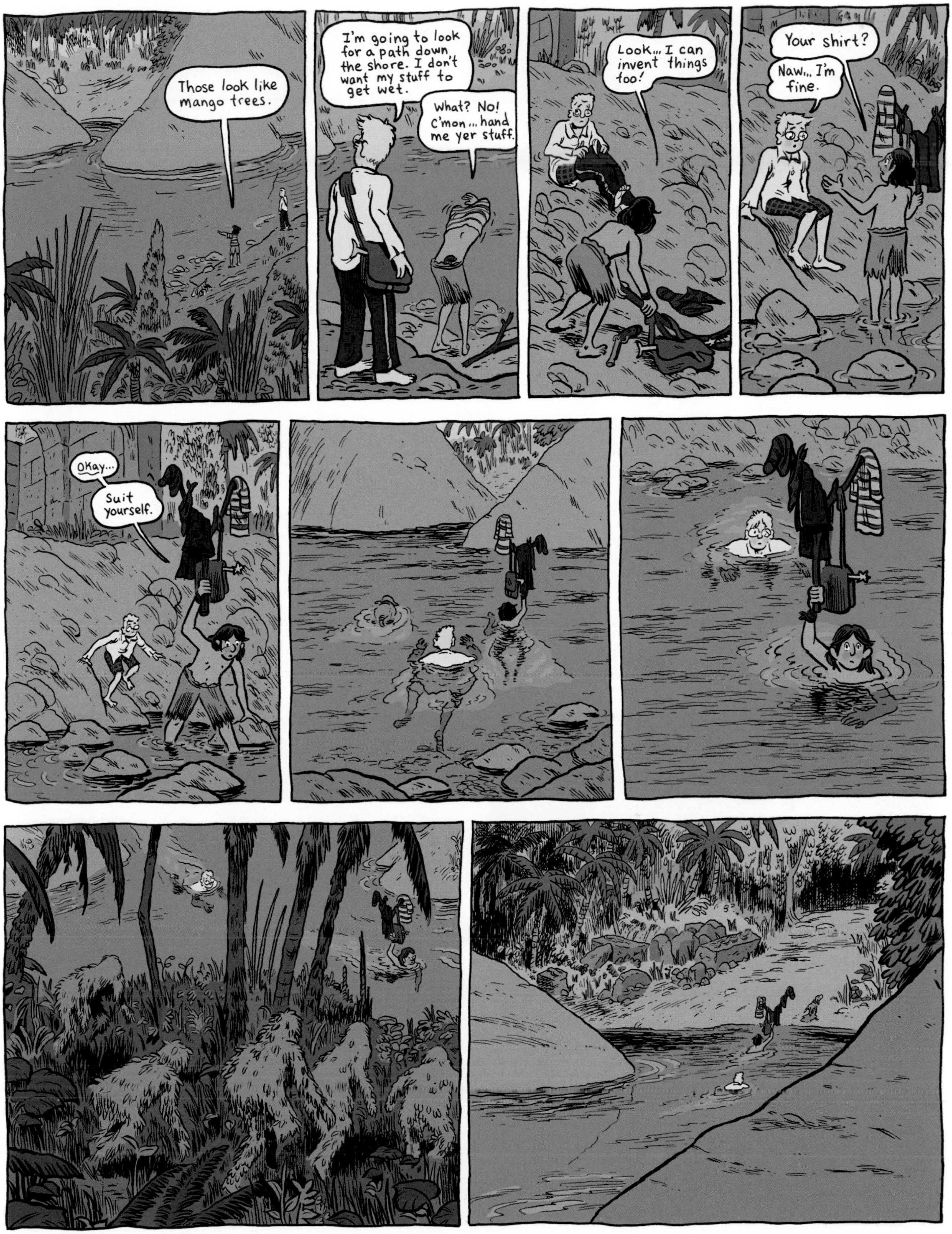
Those look like mango trees.
I'm going to look for a path down the shore. I don't want my stuff to get wet.
What? No! C'mon... hand me yer stuff.
Look... I can invent things too!
Your shirt?
Naw... I'm fine.
Okay...
Suit yourself.

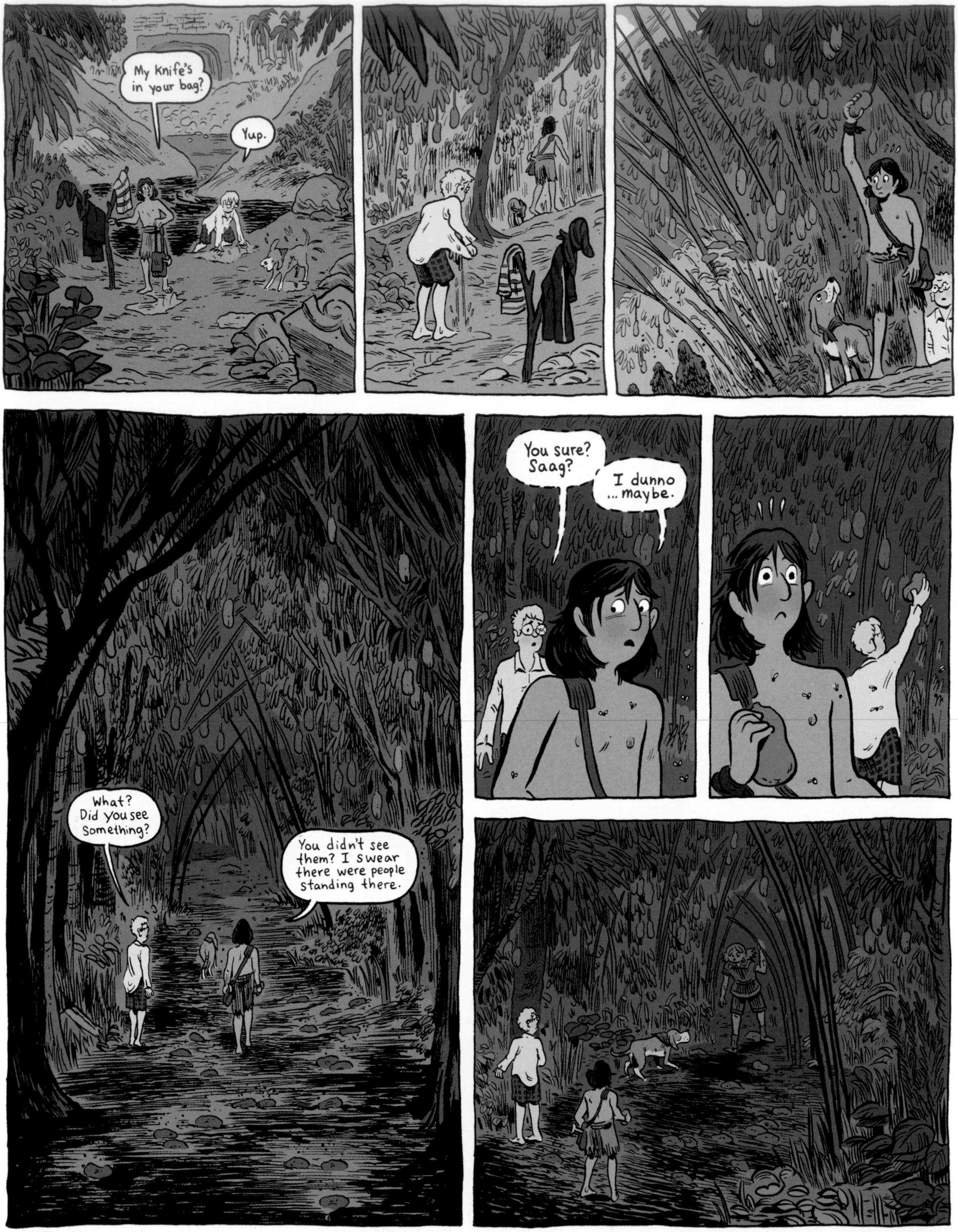

My knife's in your bag?
Yup.
You sure? Saag?
I dunno ...maybe.
What? Did you see something?
You didn't see them? I swear there were people standing there.

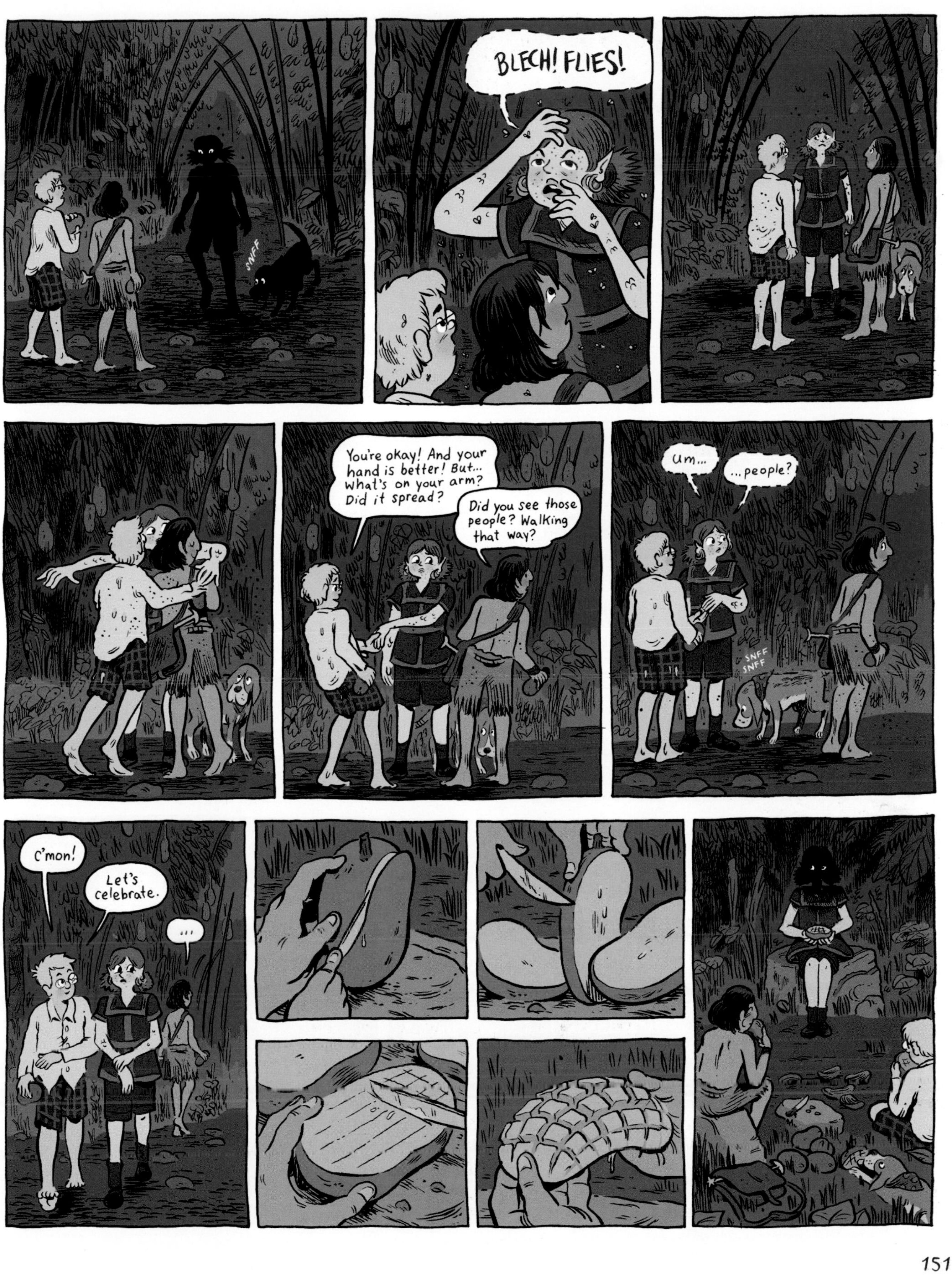
SNFF
BLECH! FLIES!
You're okay! And your hand is better! But... What's on your arm? Did it spread?
Did you see those people? Walking that way?
Um...
...people?
SNFF SNFF
C'mon!
Let's celebrate.
...

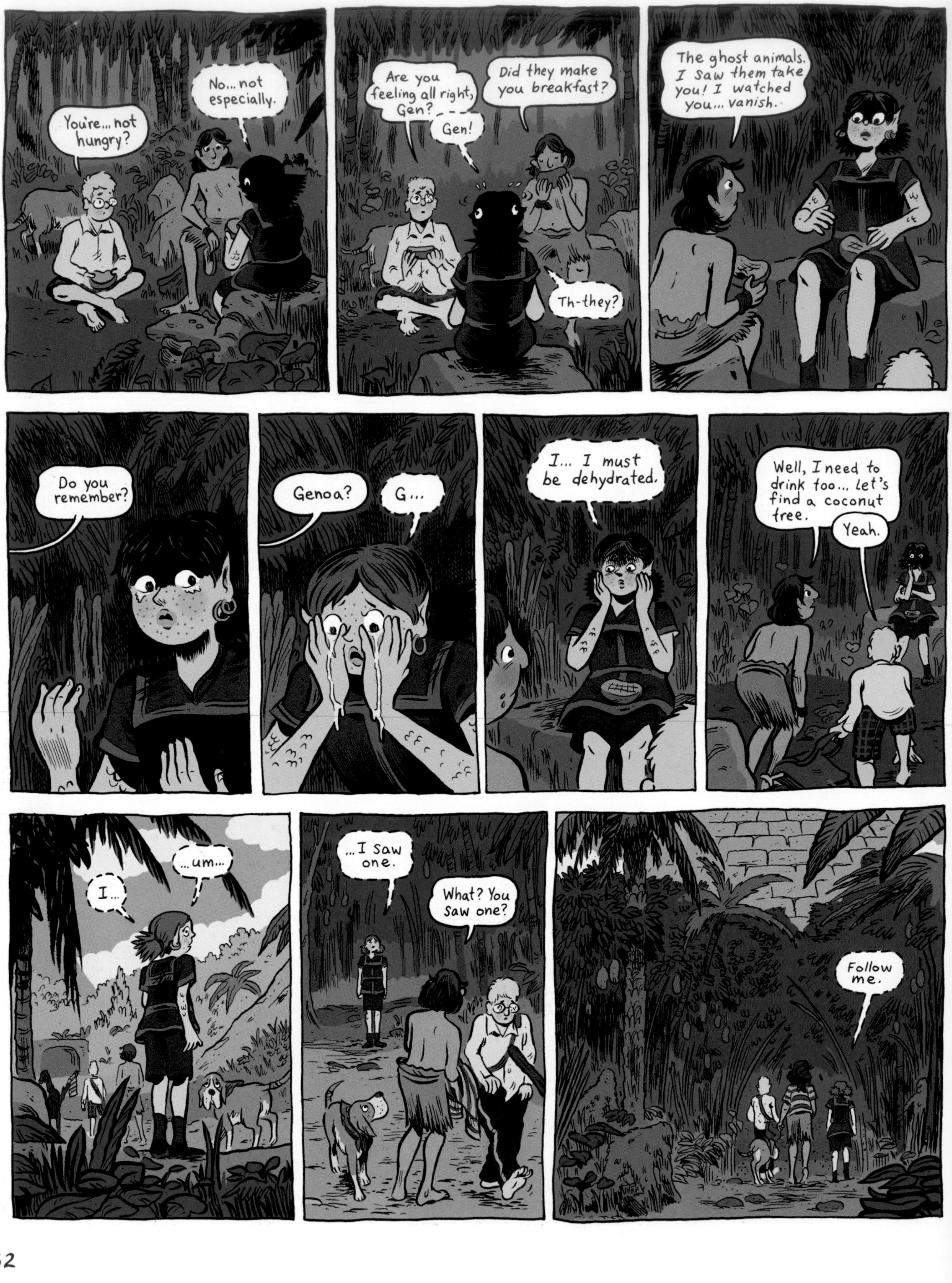
You're... not hungry?
No... not especially.
Are you feeling all right, Gen?
Did they make you breakfast?
Gen!
Th-they?
The ghost animals. I saw them take you! I watched you... vanish.
Do you remember?
Genoa?
G...
I... I must be dehydrated.
Well, I need to drink too... let's find a coconut tree.
Yeah.
I...
...um...
...I saw one.
What? You saw one?
Follow me.

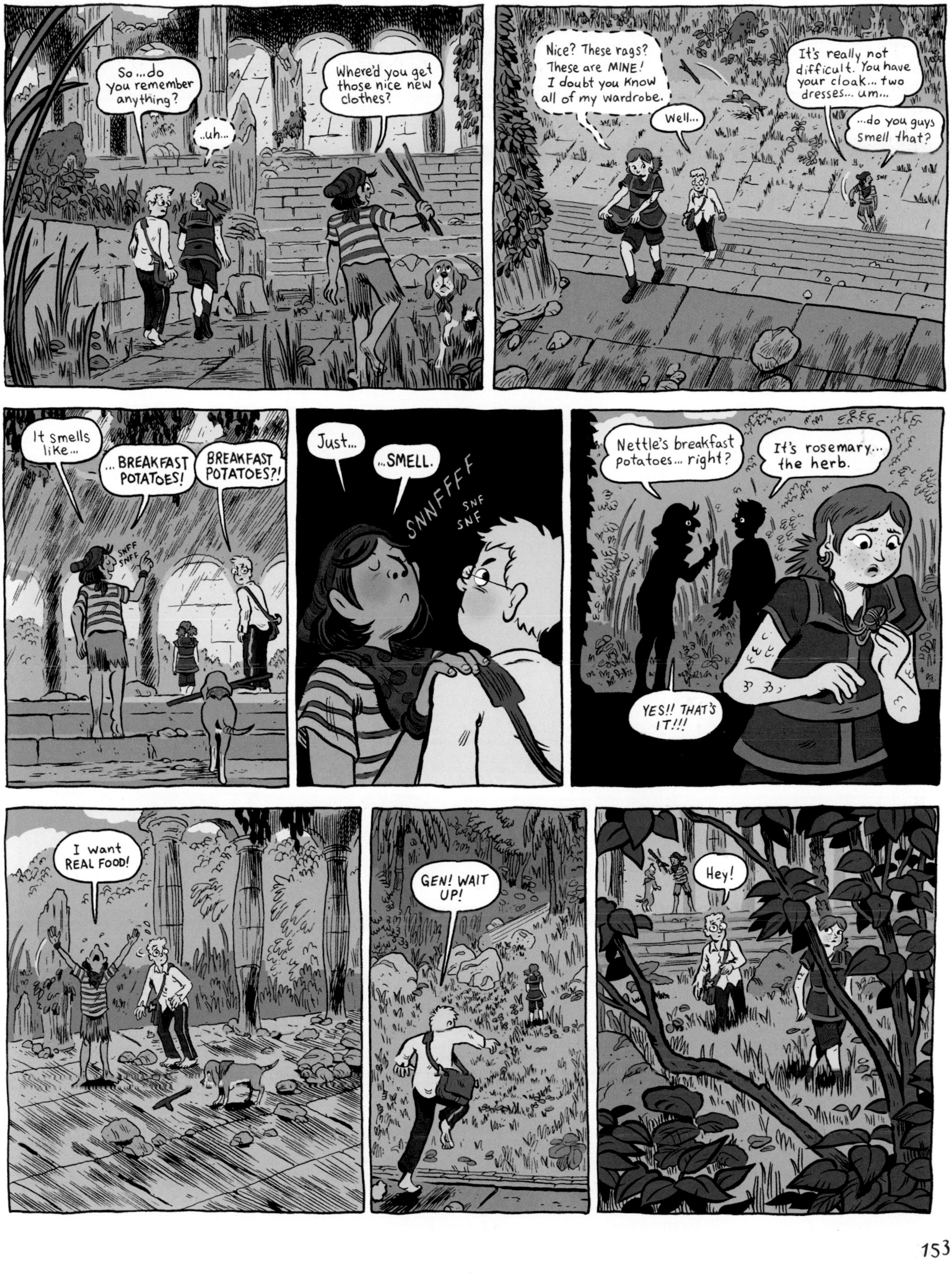

So...do you remember anything?
..uh...
Where'd you get those nice new clothes?
Nice? These rags? These are MINE! I doubt you know all of my wardrobe.
Well...
It's really not difficult. You have your cloak... two dresses... um...
...do you guys smell that?
SNF
It smells like...
...BREAKFAST POTATOES!
BREAKFAST POTATOES?!
SNFF SNFF
Just...
...SMELL.
SNNFFFF
SNF SNF
Nettle's breakfast potatoes... right?
It's rosemary... the herb.
YES!! THAT'S IT!!!
I want REAL FOOD!
GEN! WAIT UP!
Hey!

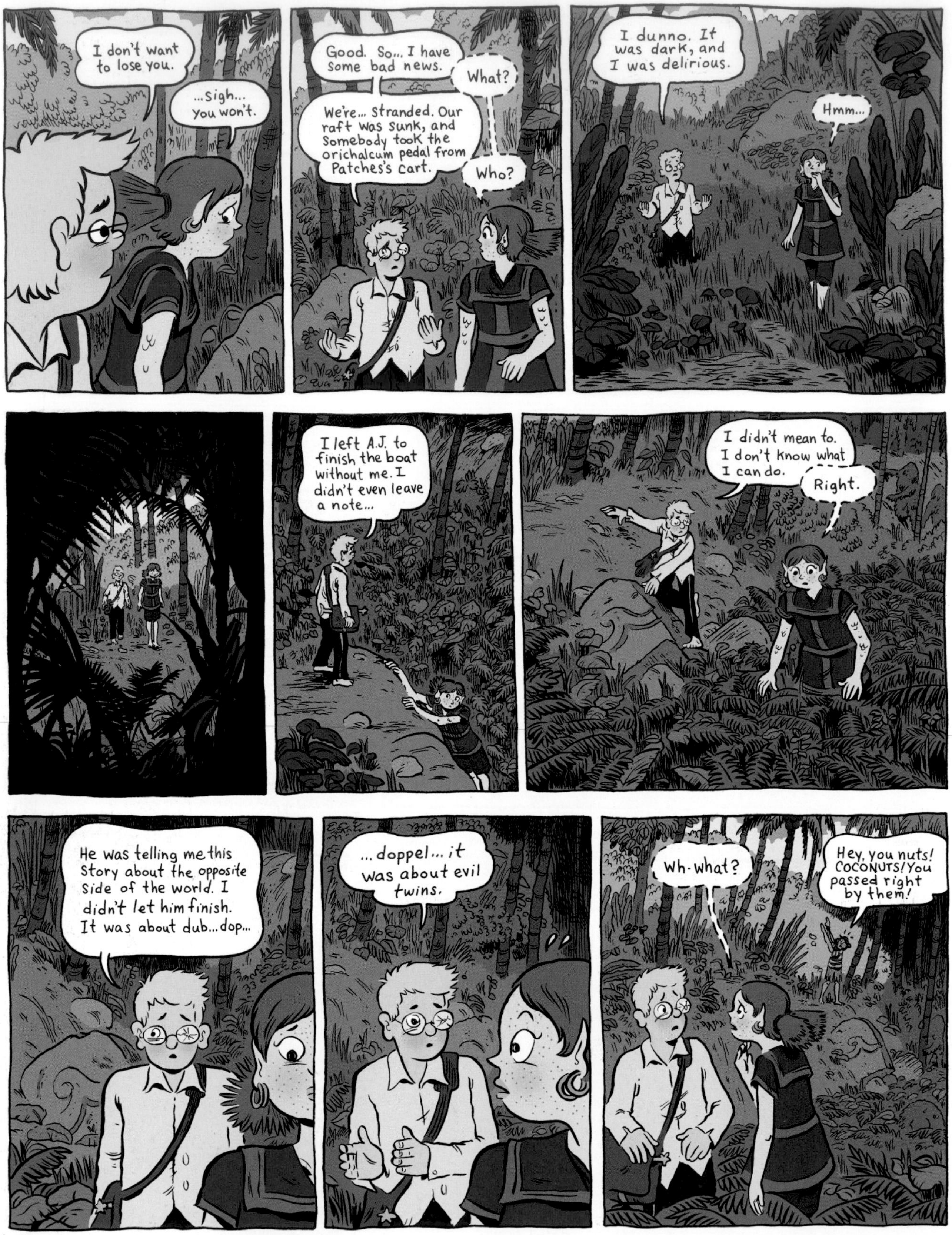
I don't want to lose you.
...sigh... you won't.
Good. So... I have some bad news.
What?
We're... stranded. Our raft was sunk, and somebody took the orichalcum pedal from Patches's cart.
Who?
I dunno. It was dark, and I was delirious.
Hmm...
I left A.J. to finish the boat without me. I didn't even leave a note...
I didn't mean to. I don't know what I can do.
Right.
He was telling me this story about the opposite side of the world. I didn't let him finish. It was about dub...dop...
...doppel... it was about evil twins.
Wh-what?
Hey, you nuts! COCONUTS! You passed right by them!

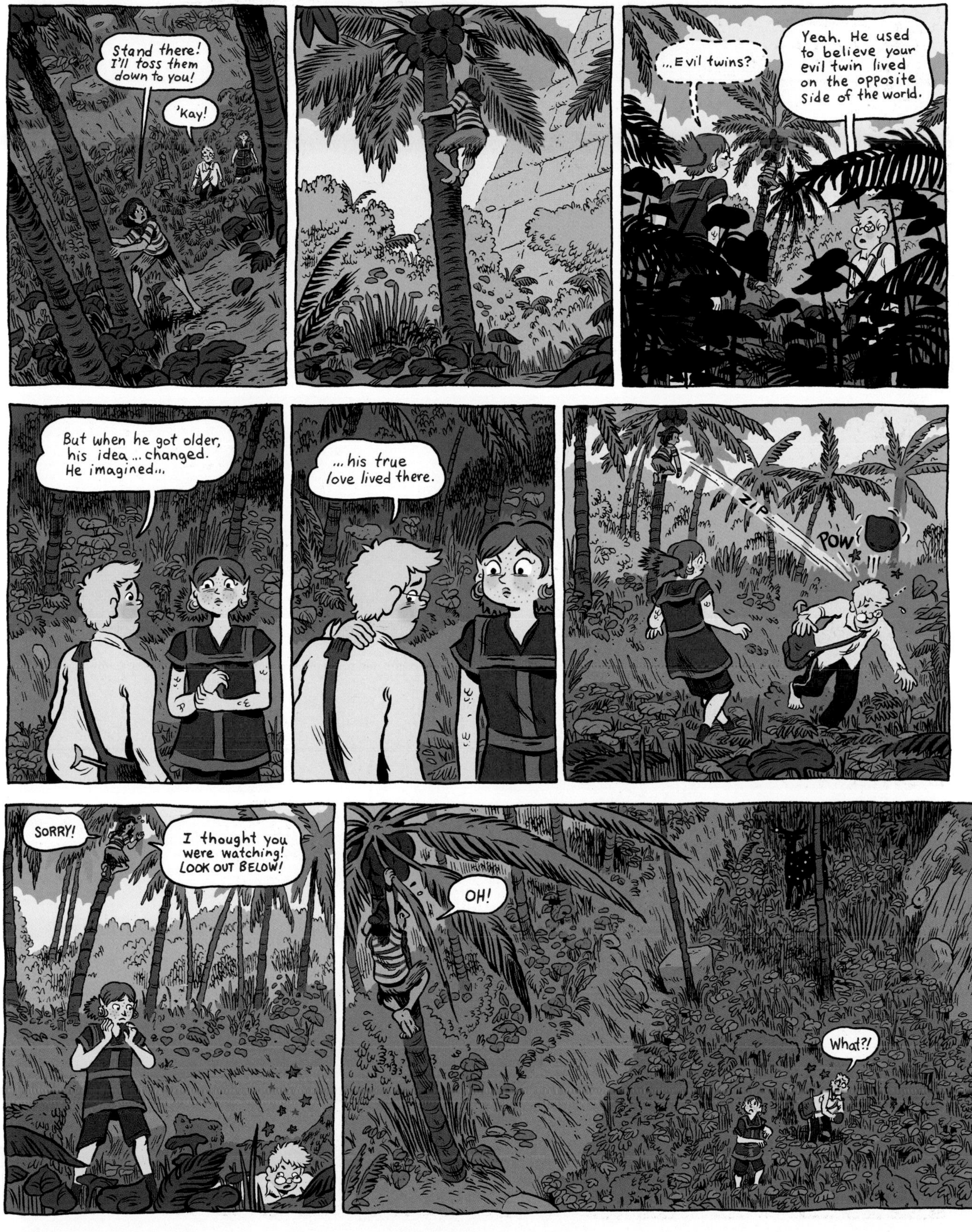
Stand there! I'll toss them down to you!
'Kay!
...Evil twins?
Yeah. He used to believe your evil twin lived on the opposite side of the world.
But when he got older, his idea... changed. He imagined...
...his true love lived there.
ZIP
POW
SORRY!
I thought you were watching! LOOK OUT BELOW!
OH!
What?!

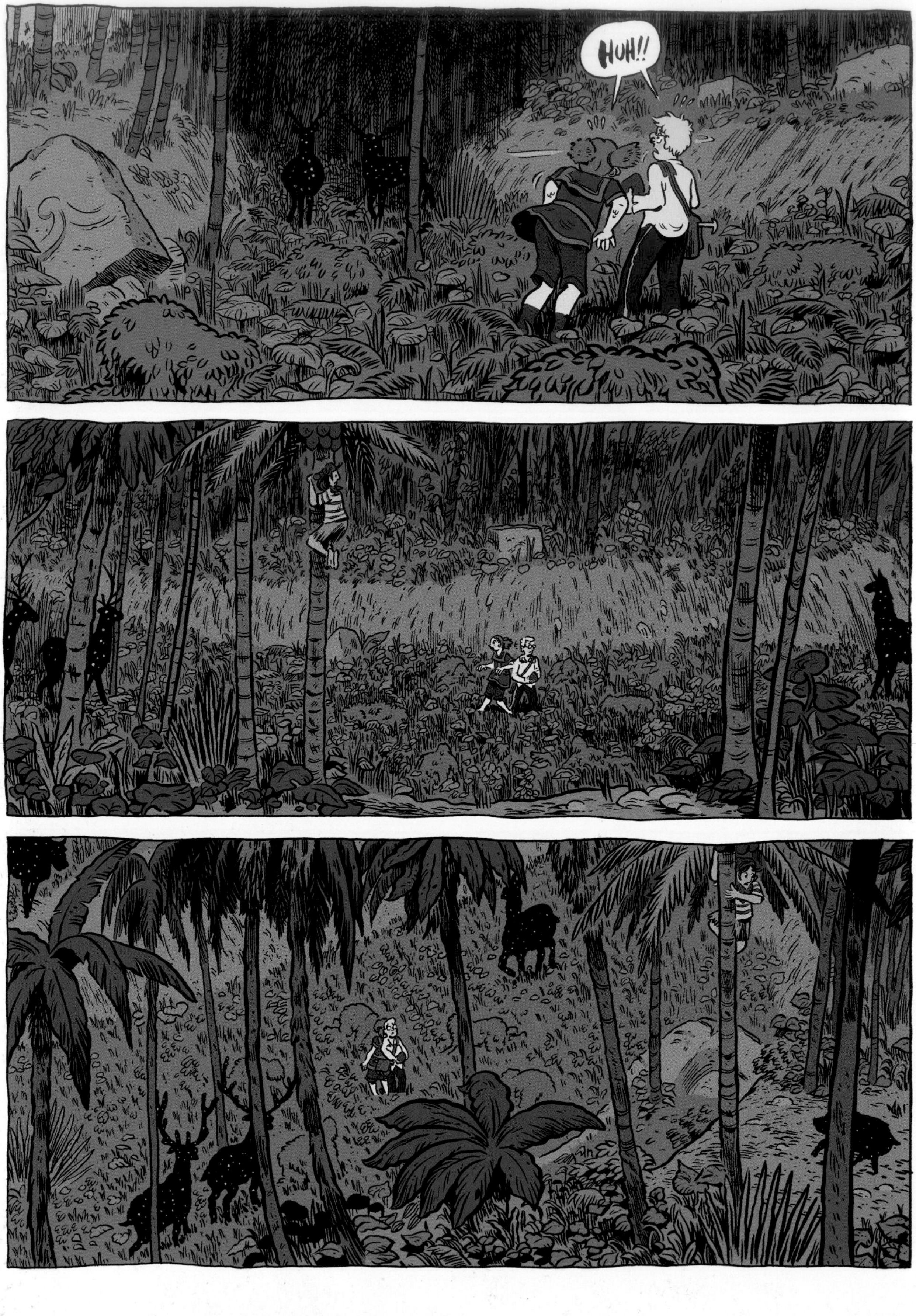
HUH!!

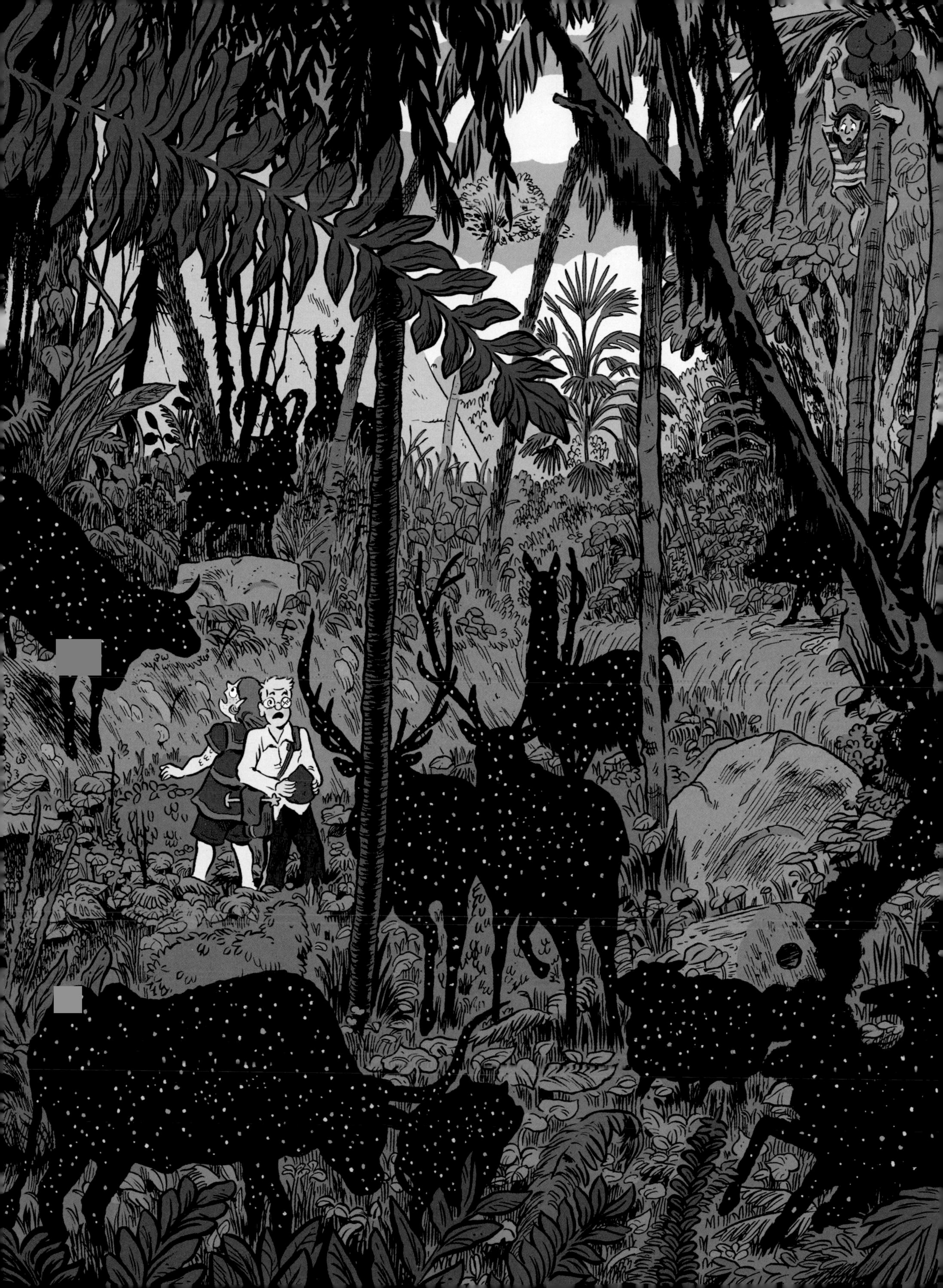

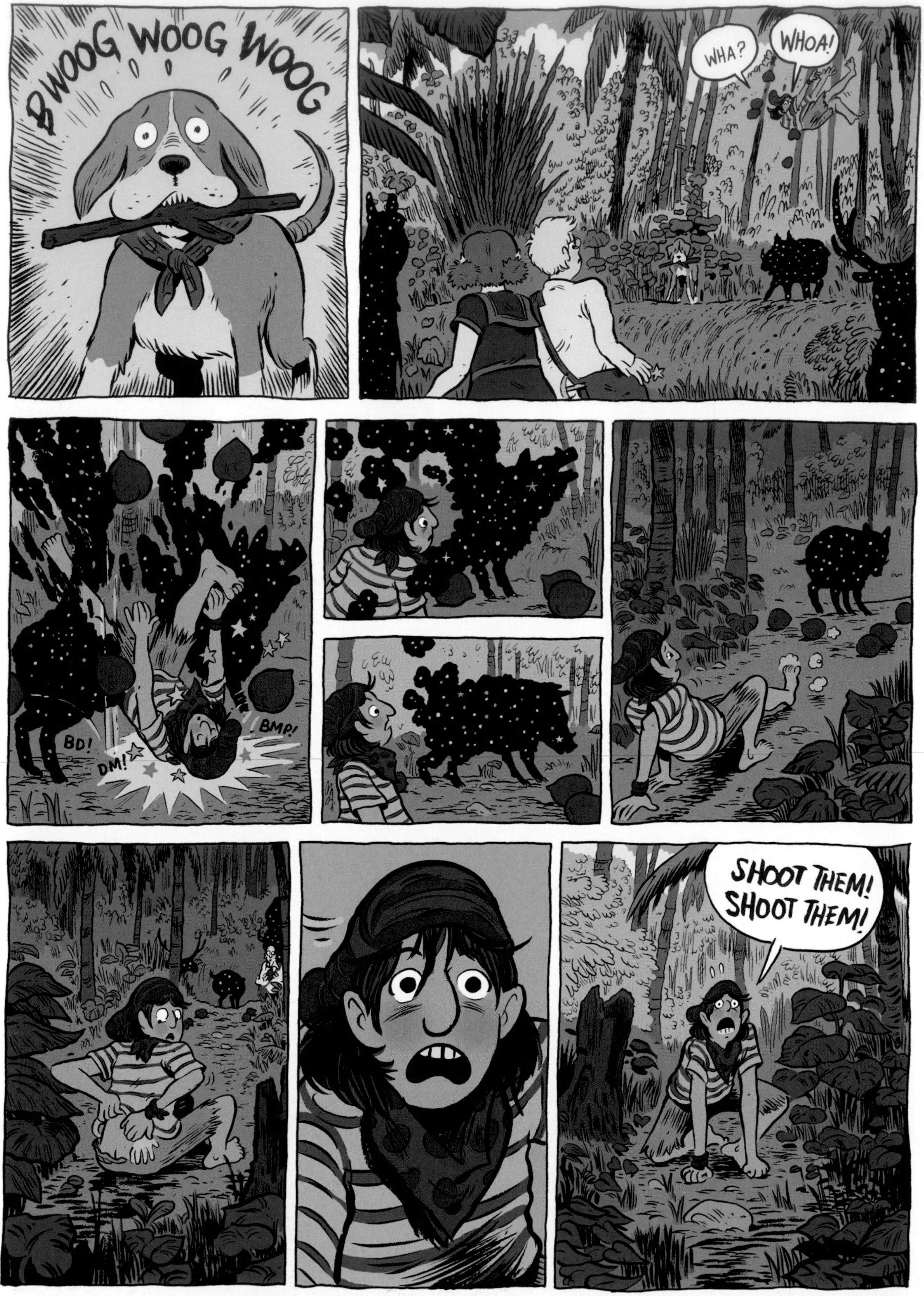
BWOOG WOOG WOOG
WHA?
WHOA!
BD!
DM!
BMP!
SHOOT THEM! SHOOT THEM!

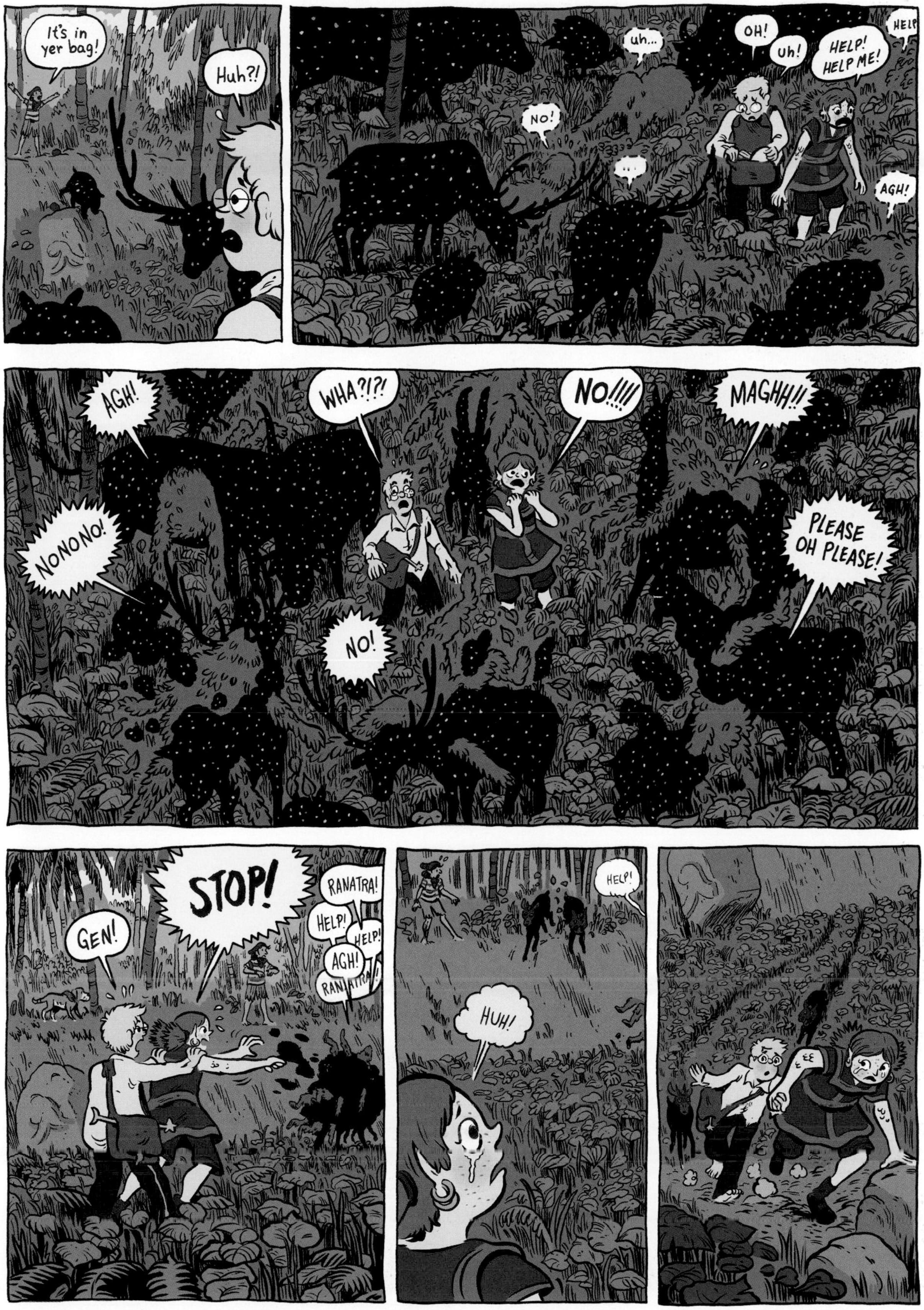
It's in yer bag!
Huh?!
uh...
OH!
Uh!
HELP! HELP ME!
HELP
NO!
...
AGH!
AGH!
WHA?!?!
NO!!!!
MAGHH!!
NONONO!
PLEASE OH PLEASE!
NO!
GEN!
STOP!
RANATRA!
HELP!
HELP!
AGH!
RANATRA!
HELP!
HUH!

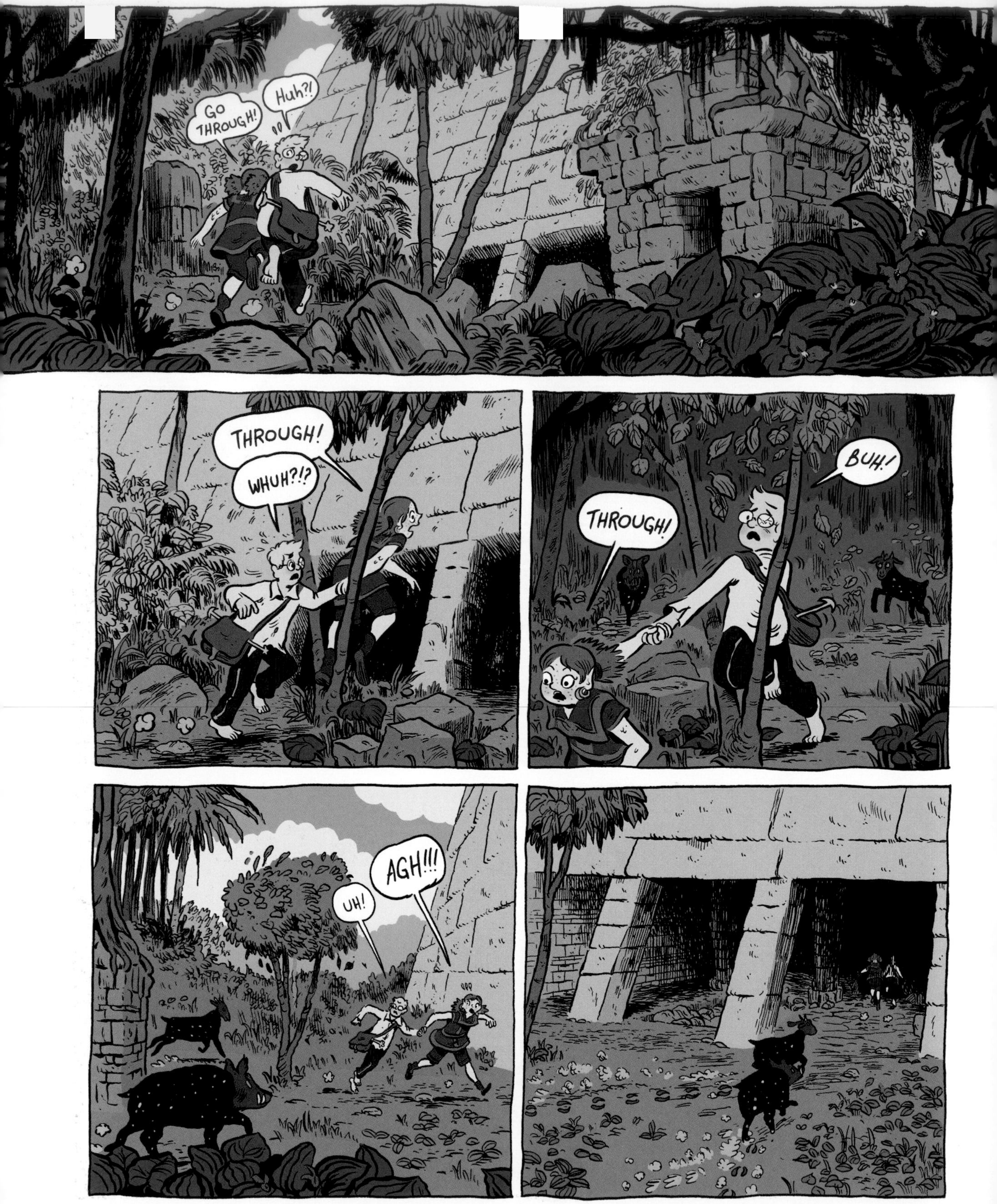
GO THROUGH!
Huh?!
THROUGH!
WHUH?!?
THROUGH!
BUH!
UH!
AGH!!!

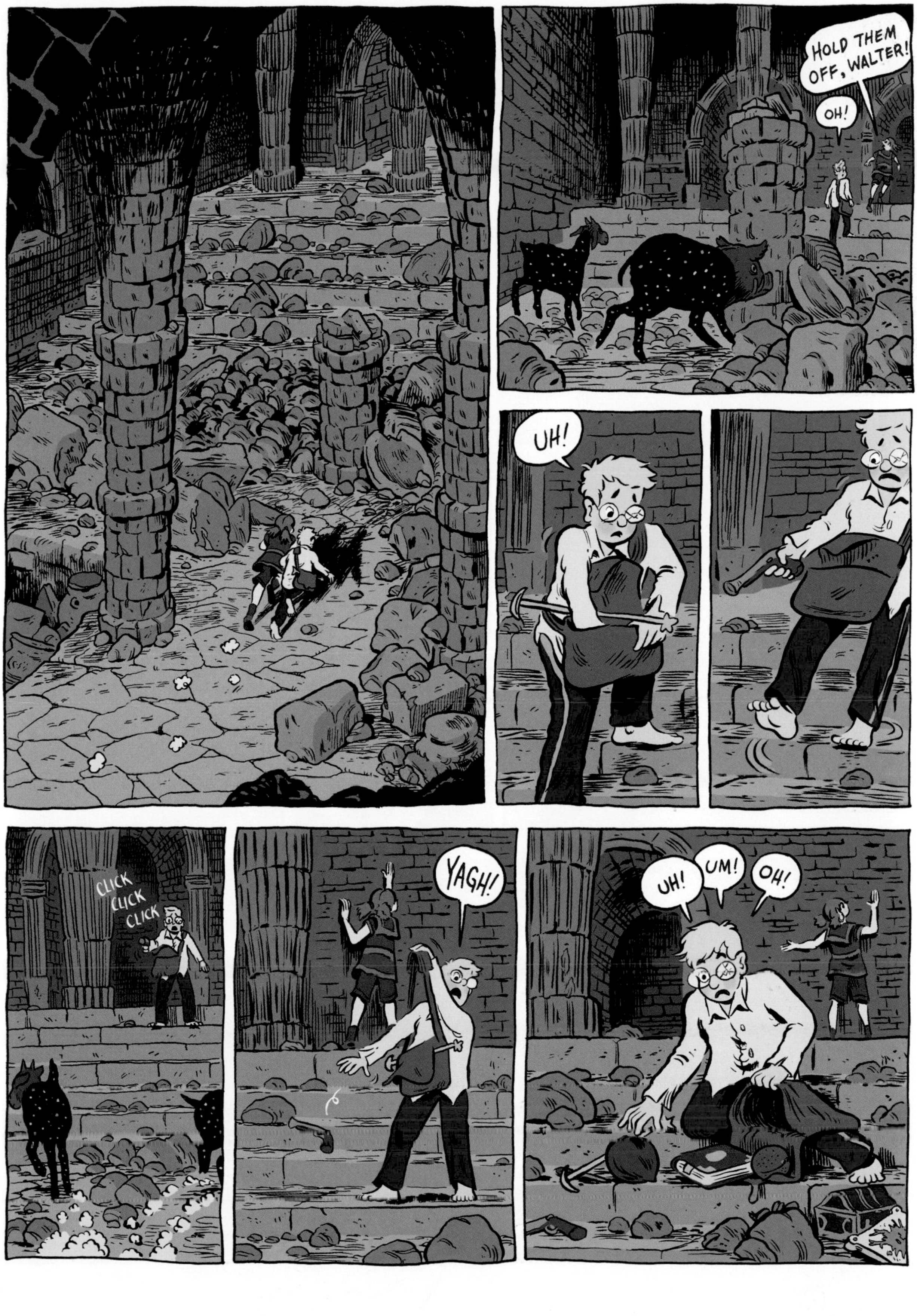
HOLD THEM OFF, WALTER!
OH!
UH!
CLICK
CLICK
CLICK
YAGH!
UH!
UM!
OH!

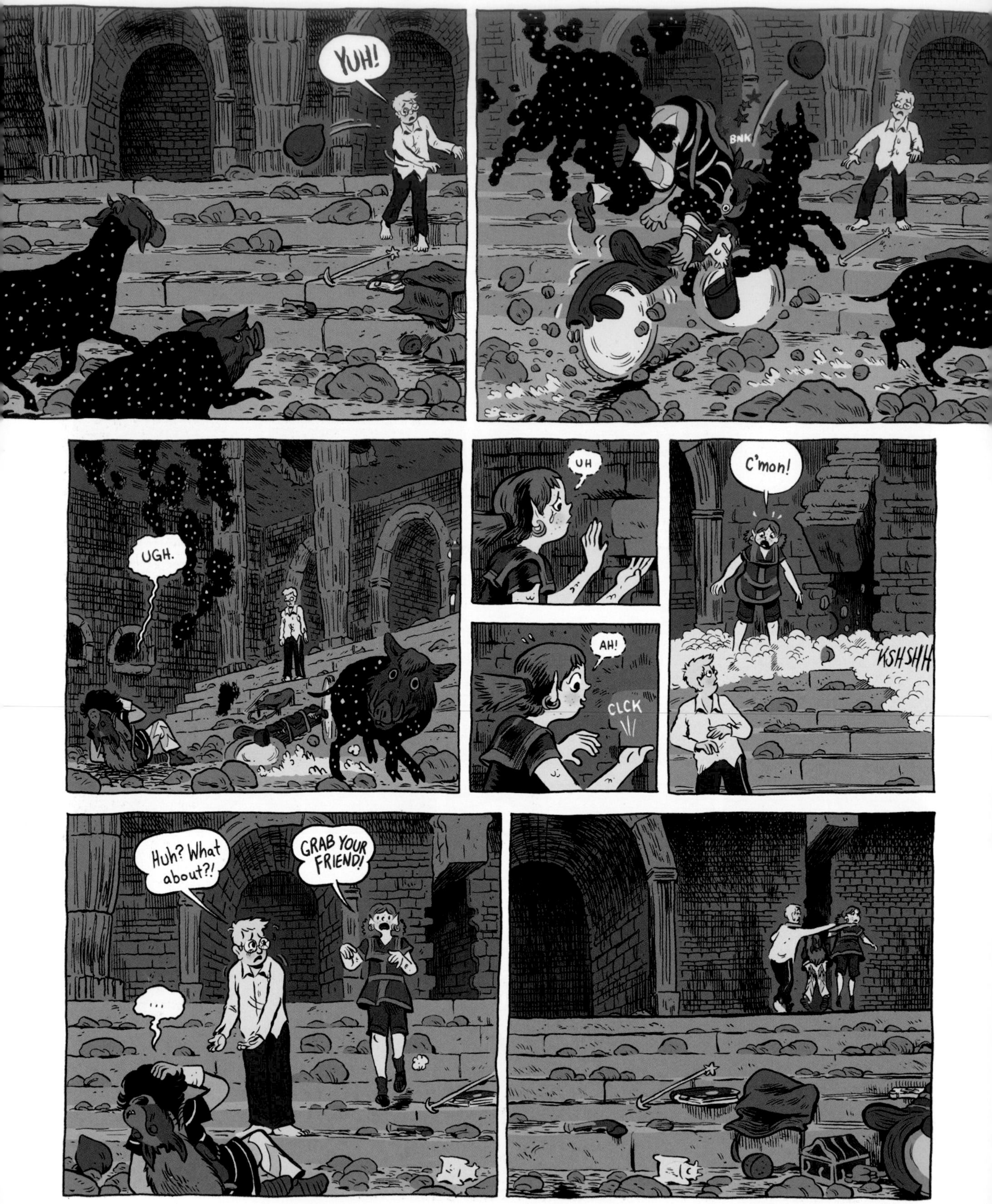
YUH!
BNK
UGH.
UH
AH!
CLCK
C'mon!
KSHSHH
Huh? What about?!
GRAB YOUR FRIEND!
...

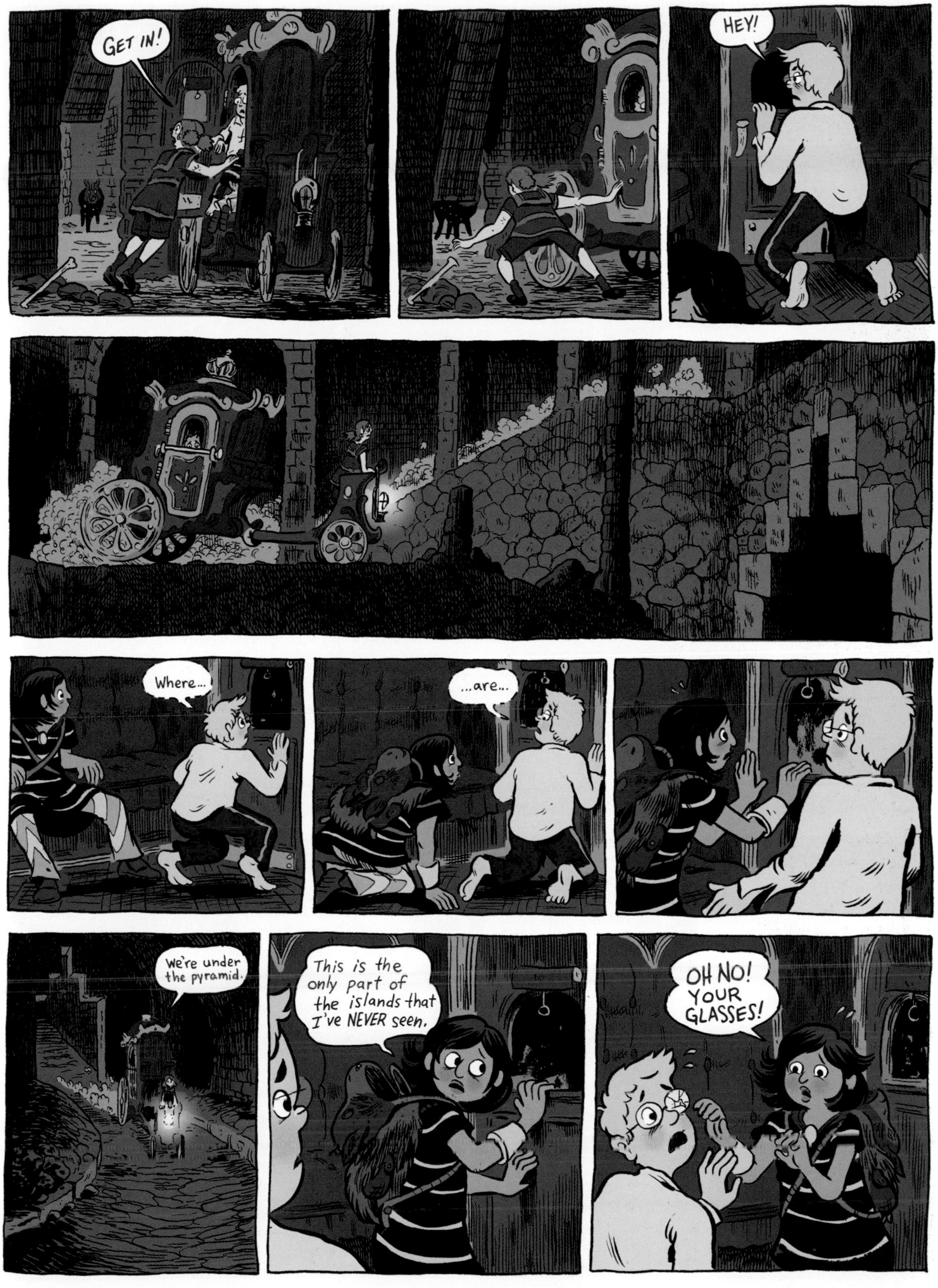
GET IN!
HEY!
Where...
...are...
We're under the pyramid.
This is the only part of the islands that I've NEVER seen.
OH NO! YOUR GLASSES!

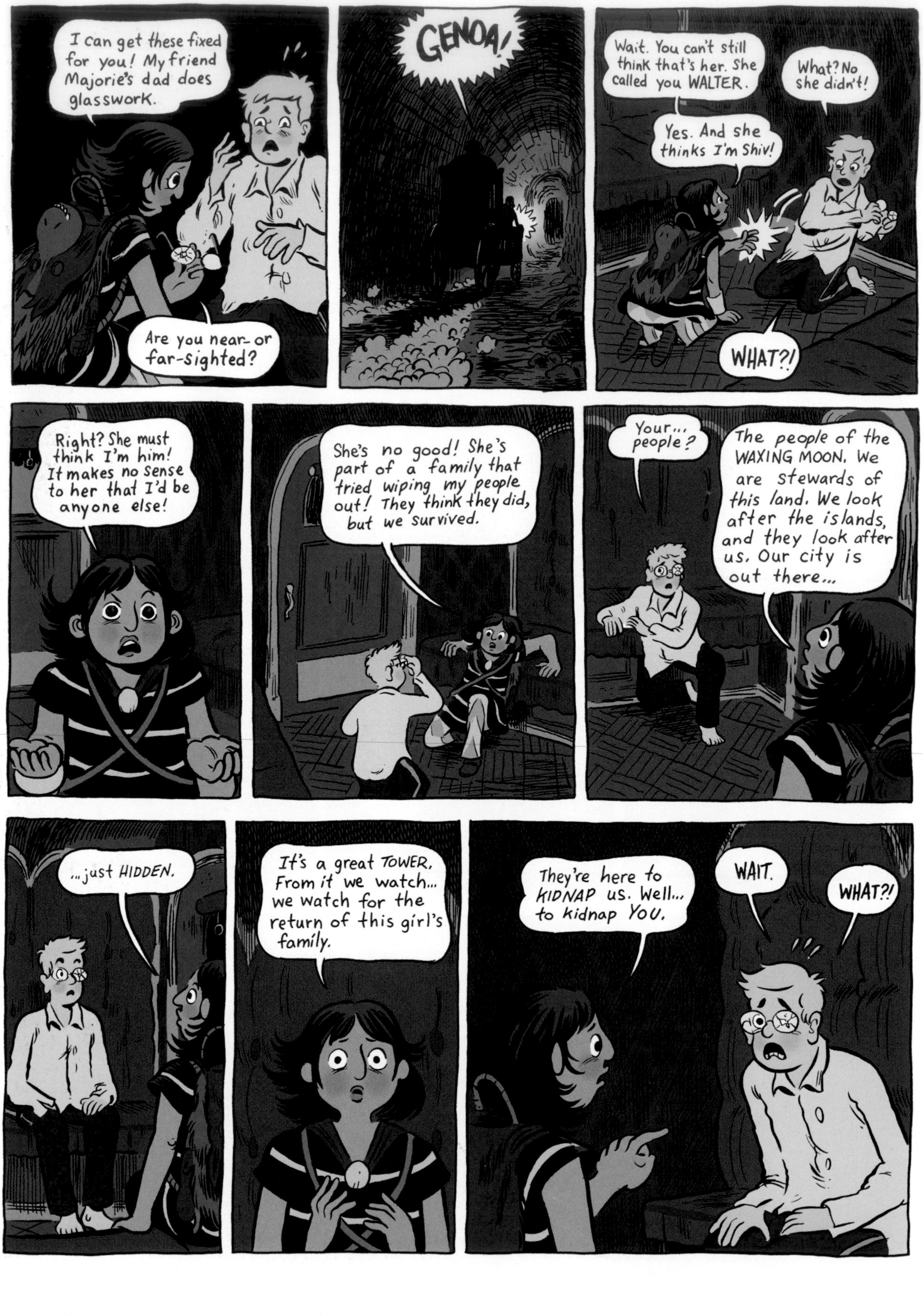

I can get these fixed for you! My friend Majorie's dad does glasswork.
Are you near- or far-sighted?
GENOA!
Wait. You can't still think that's her. She called you WALTER.
What? No she didn't!
Yes. And she thinks I'm Shiv!
WHAT?!
Right? She must think I'm him! It makes no sense to her that I'd be anyone else!
She's no good! She's part of a family that tried wiping my people out! They think they did, but we survived.
Your... people?
The people of the WAXING MOON. We are stewards of this land. We look after the islands, and they look after us. Our city is out there...
...just HIDDEN.
It's a great TOWER. From it we watch... we watch for the return of this girl's family.
They're here to KIDNAP us. Well... to kidnap YOU.
WAIT.
WHAT?!

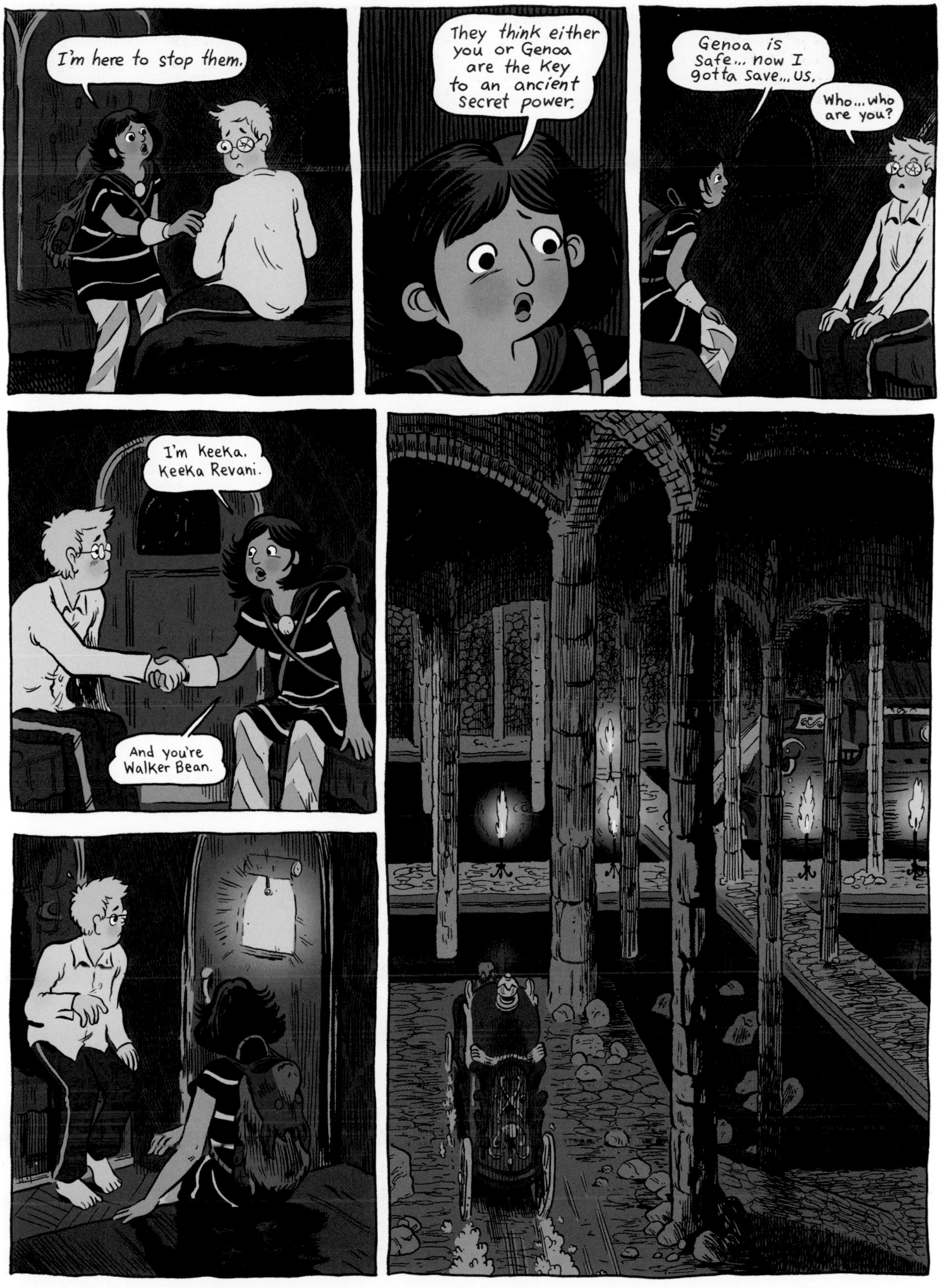
I'm here to stop them.
They think either you or Genoa are the key to an ancient secret power.
Genoa is safe... now I gotta save... us.
Who... who are you?
I'm Keeka. Keeka Revani.
And you're Walker Bean.

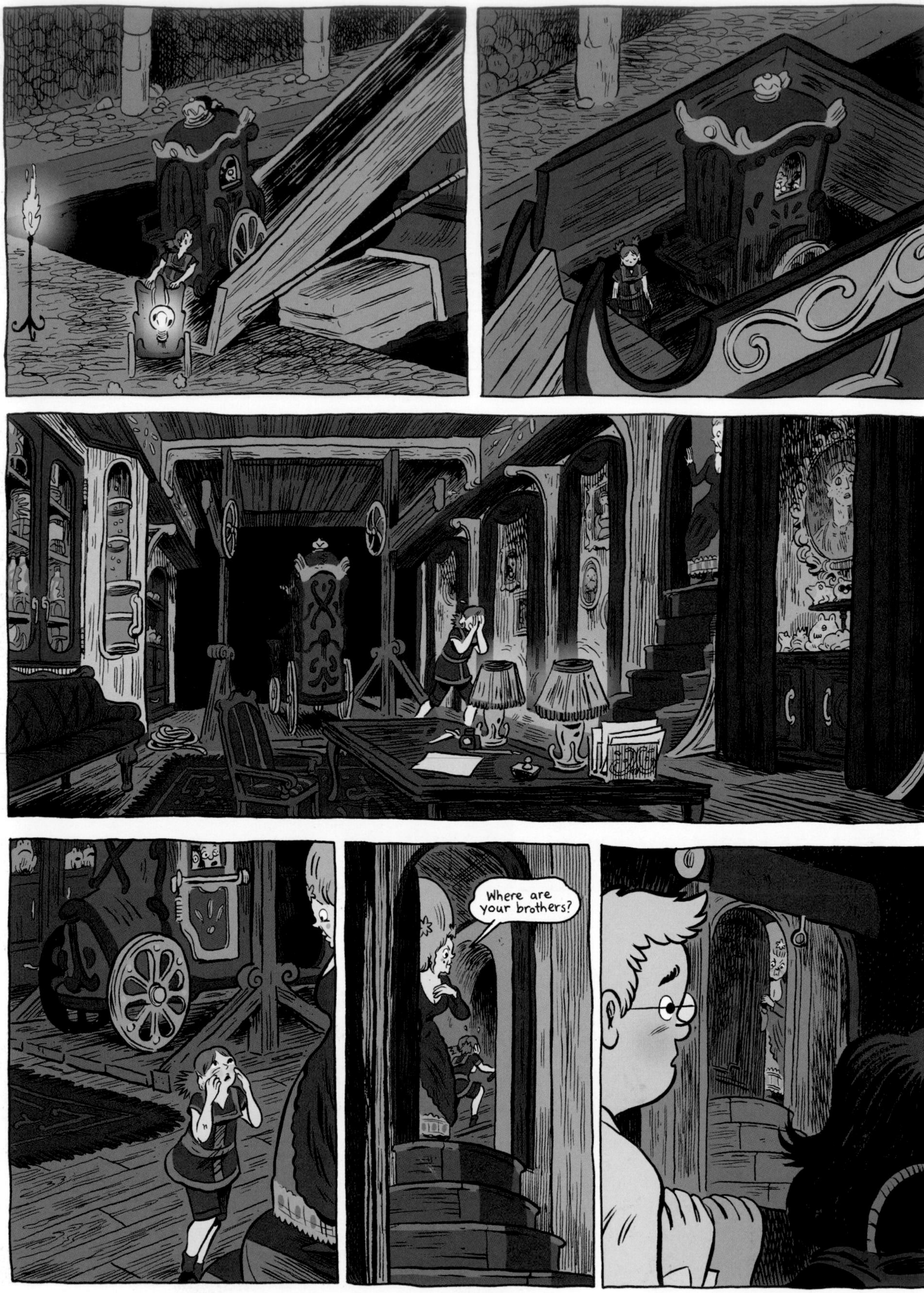
Where are your brothers?

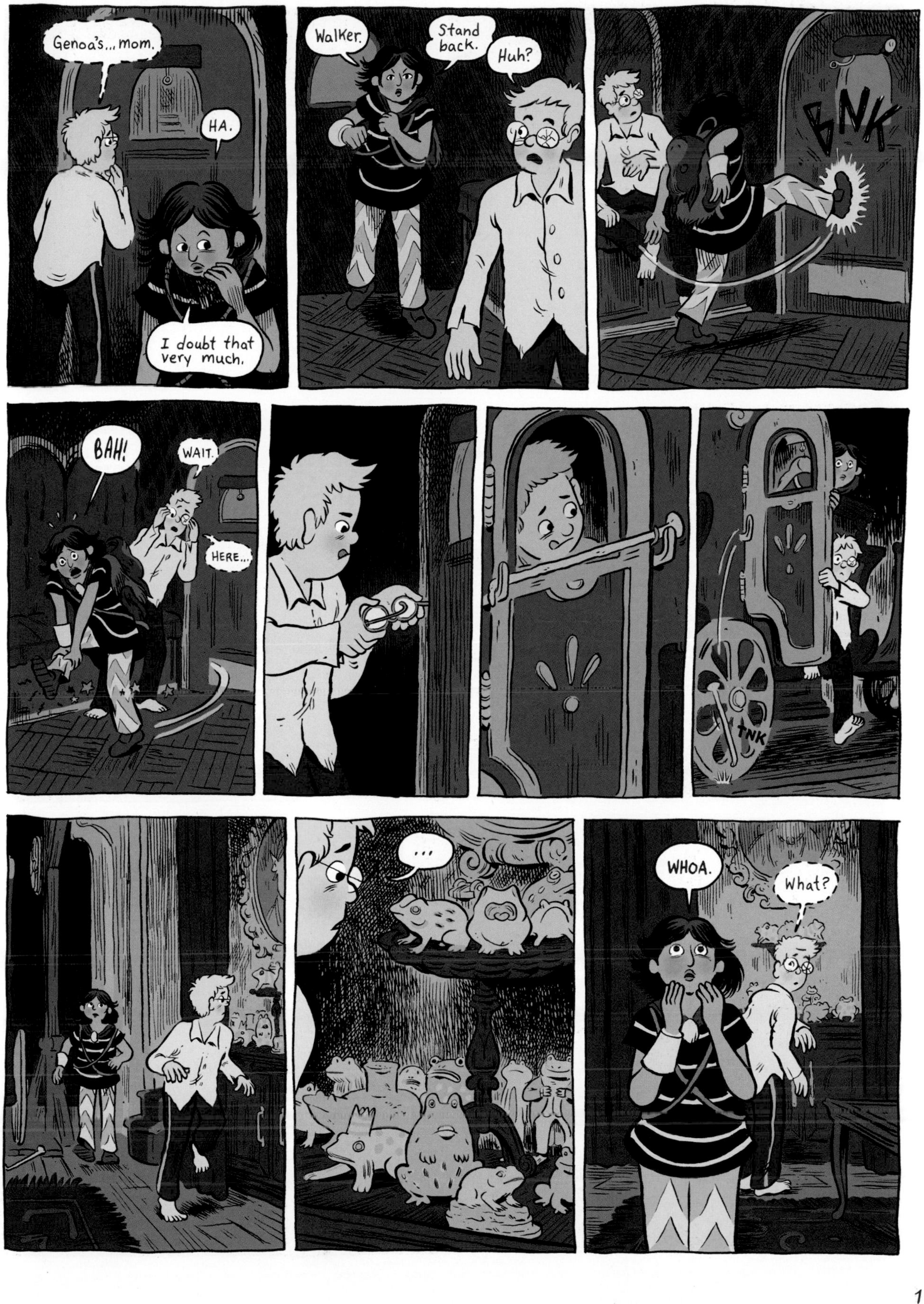
Genoa's... mom.
HA.
I doubt that very much.
Walker.
Stand back.
Huh?
BNK
BAH!
WAIT.
HERE...
TNK
...
WHOA.
What?

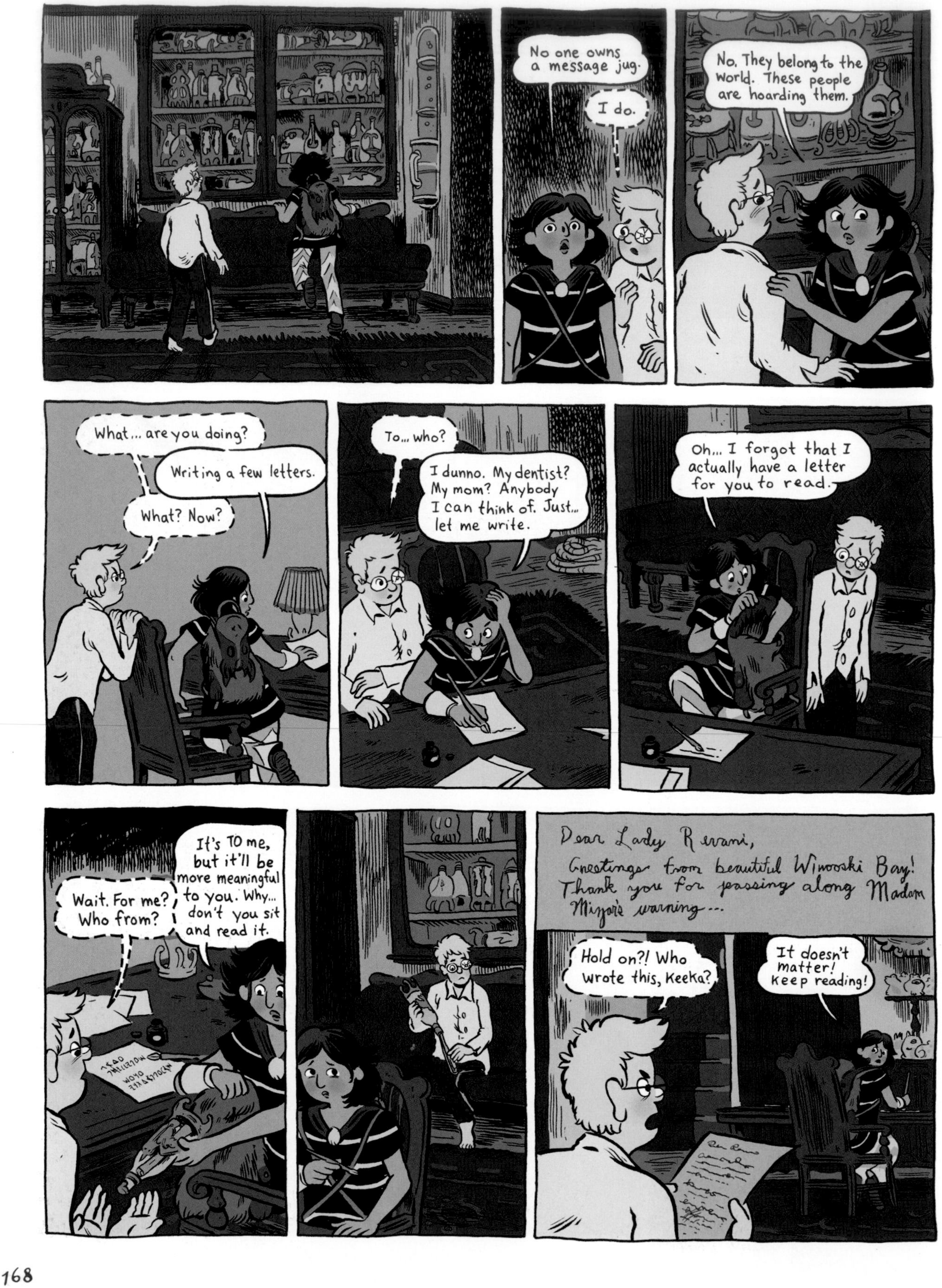
No one owns a message jug.
I do.
No. They belong to the world. These people are hoarding them.
What... are you doing?
Writing a few letters.
What? Now?
To... who?
I dunno. My dentist? My mom? Anybody I can think of. Just... let me write.
Oh... I forgot that I actually have a letter for you to read.
Wait. For me? Who from?
It's TO me, but it'll be more meaningful to you. Why... don't you sit and read it.
Dear Lady Revani,
Greetings from beautiful Winooski Bay! Thank you for passing along Madam Miyar's warning...
Hold on?! Who wrote this, Keeka?
It doesn't matter! Keep reading!

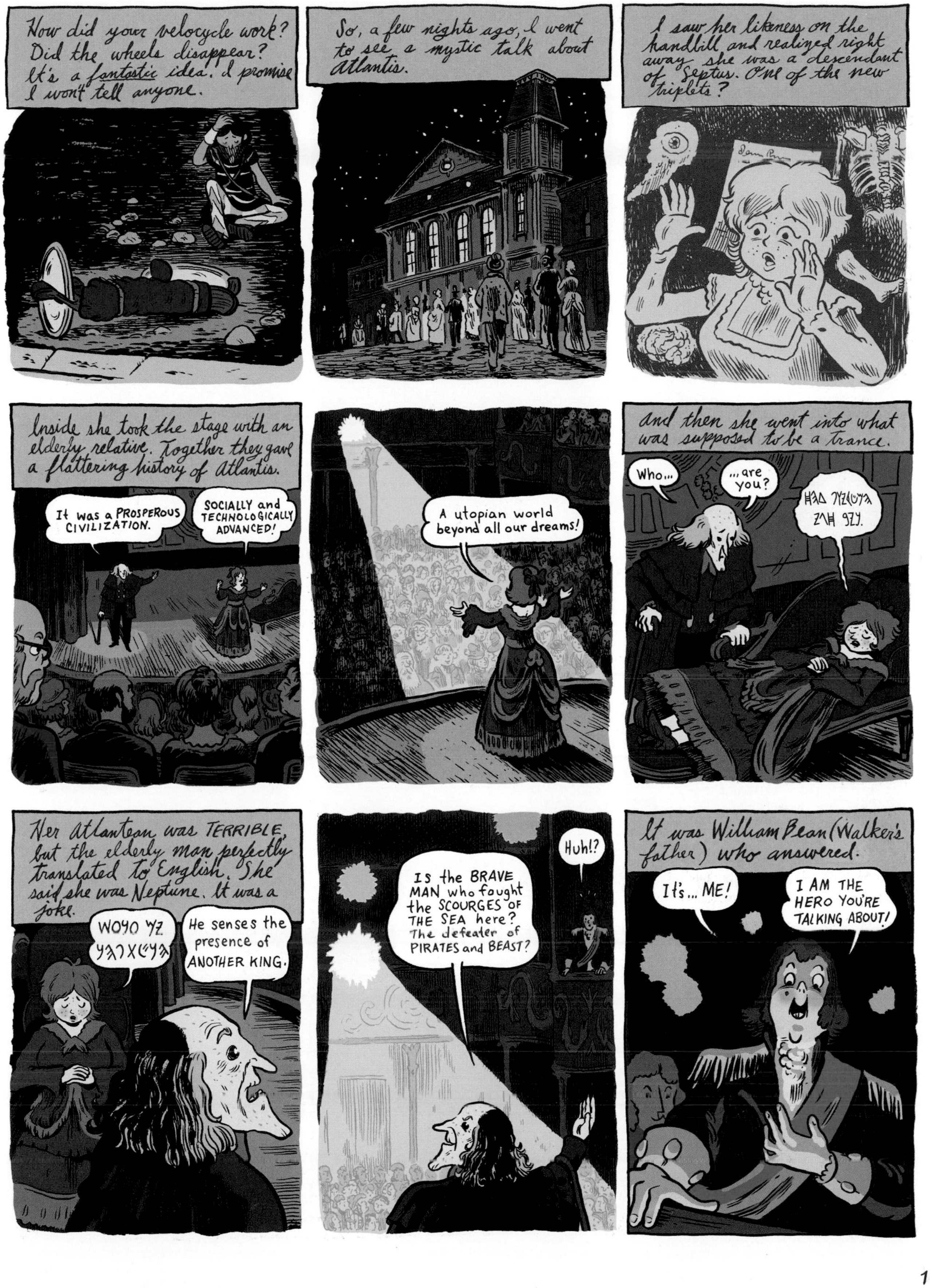
How did your velocycle work? Did the wheels disappear? It's a fantastic idea. I promise I won't tell anyone.
So, a few nights ago, I went to see a mystic talk about Atlantis.
I saw her likeness on the handbill and realized right away she was a descendant of Septus. One of the new triplets?
Inside she took the stage with an elderly relative. Together they gave a flattering history of Atlantis.
It was a PROSPEROUS CIVILIZATION.
SOCIALLY and TECHNOLOGICALLY ADVANCED!
A utopian world beyond all our dreams!
And then she went into what was supposed to be a trance.
Who...
...are you?
Her Atlantean was TERRIBLE, but the elderly man perfectly translated to English. She said she was Neptune. It was a joke.
He senses the presence of ANOTHER KING.
Huh!?
IS the BRAVE MAN who fought the SCOURGES OF THE SEA here? The defeater of PIRATES and BEAST?
It was William Bean (Walker's father) who answered.
It's... ME!
I AM THE HERO YOU'RE TALKING ABOUT!

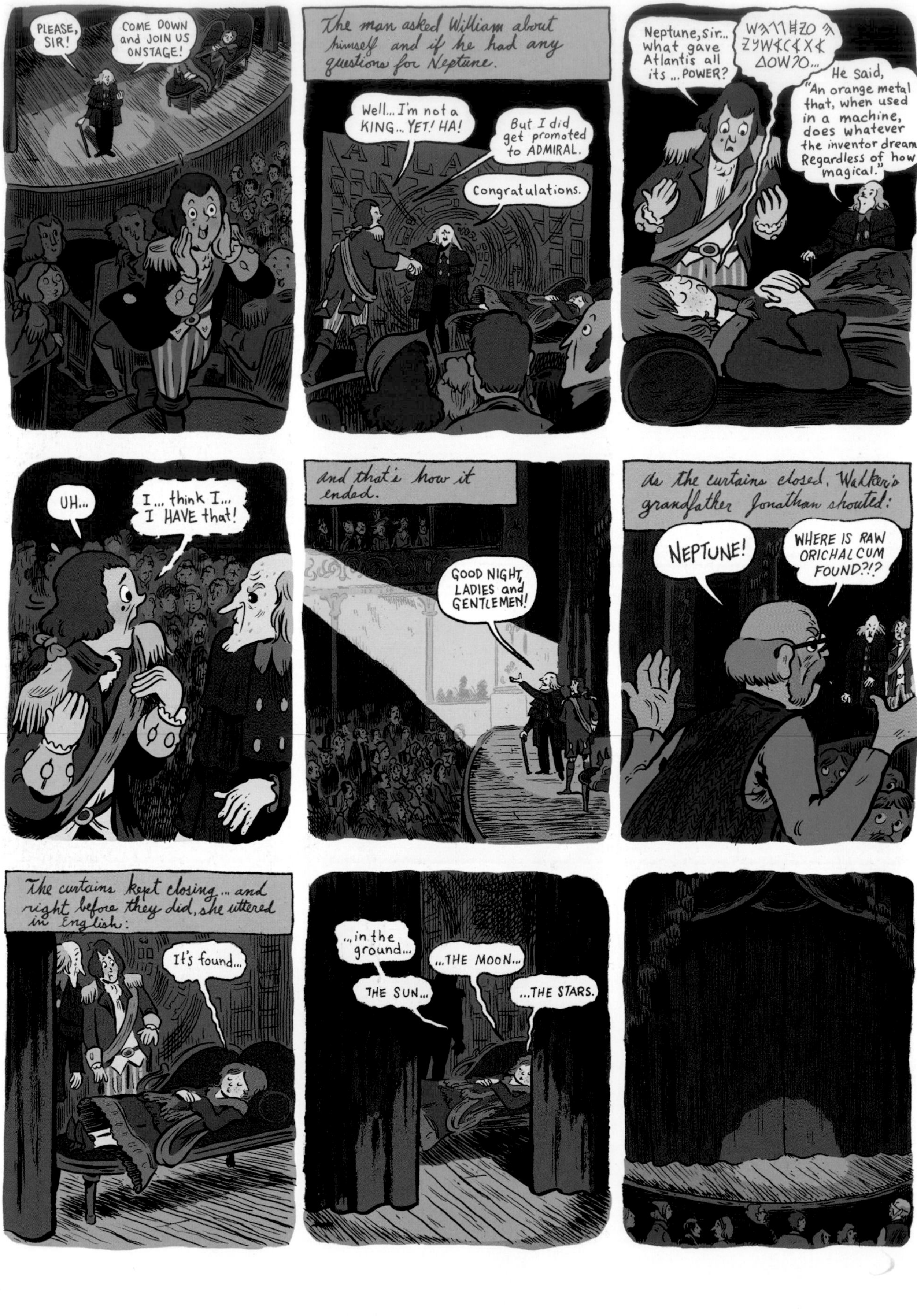
PLEASE, SIR!
COME DOWN and JOIN US ONSTAGE!
The man asked William about himself and if he had any questions for Neptune.
Well... I'm not a KING... YET! HA!
But I did get promoted to ADMIRAL.
Congratulations.
Neptune, sir... what gave Atlantis all its ... POWER?
He said, "An orange metal that, when used in a machine, does whatever the inventor dreams. Regardless of how magical."
UH...
I... think I... I HAVE that!
and that's how it ended.
GOOD NIGHT, LADIES and GENTLEMEN!
As the curtains closed, Walker's grandfather Jonathan shouted:
NEPTUNE!
WHERE IS RAW ORICHALCUM FOUND?!?
The curtains kept closing... and right before they did, she uttered in English:
It's found...
...in the ground...
THE SUN...
...THE MOON...
...THE STARS.

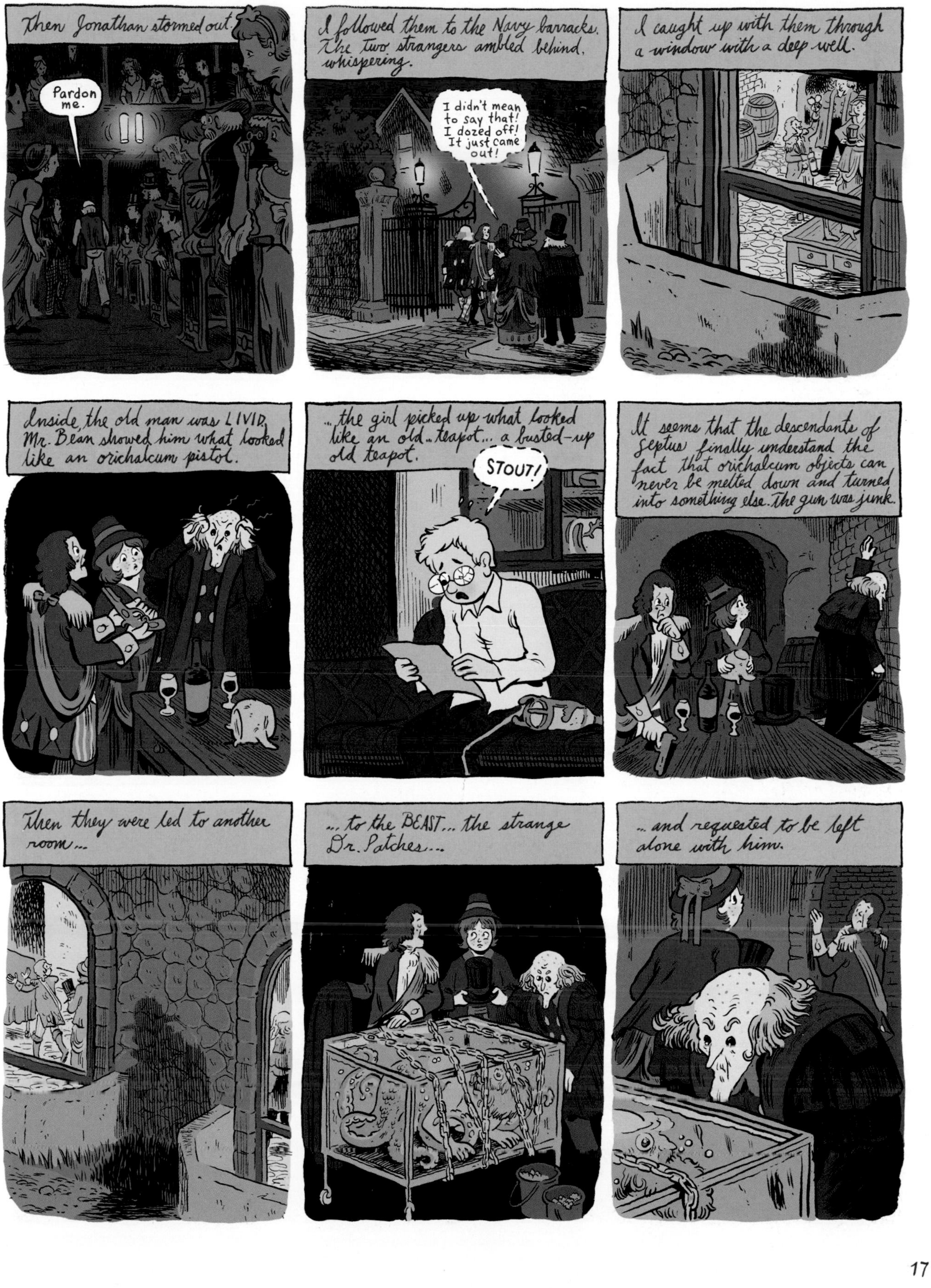

Then Jonathan stormed out.
Pardon me.
I followed them to the Navy barracks. The two strangers ambled behind, whispering.
I didn't mean to say that! I dozed off! It just came out!
I caught up with them through a window with a deep well.
Inside, the old man was LIVID. Mr. Bean showed him what looked like an orichalcum pistol.
...the girl picked up what looked like an old... teapot... a busted-up old teapot.
STOUT!
It seems that the descendants of Septus finally understand the fact that orichalcum objects can never be melted down and turned into something else. The gun was junk.
Then they were led to another room...
...to the BEAST... the strange Dr. Patches...
...and requested to be left alone with him.

The old man spoke to the monster for a long time. The two KNEW each other!

They were interrupted by a commotion in the hall.

Outside, a man, most certainly Jonathan Bean, was running off. The NAVY followed.

STOP HIM!!

I looked for Jonathan at his home for the past few days. He seems to have vanished. I'm worried.

OKAY! STOP READING!

Wha? What?

I need your help!

What?! What have you done?

STUFF THOSE LETTERS IN THE BOTTLES!

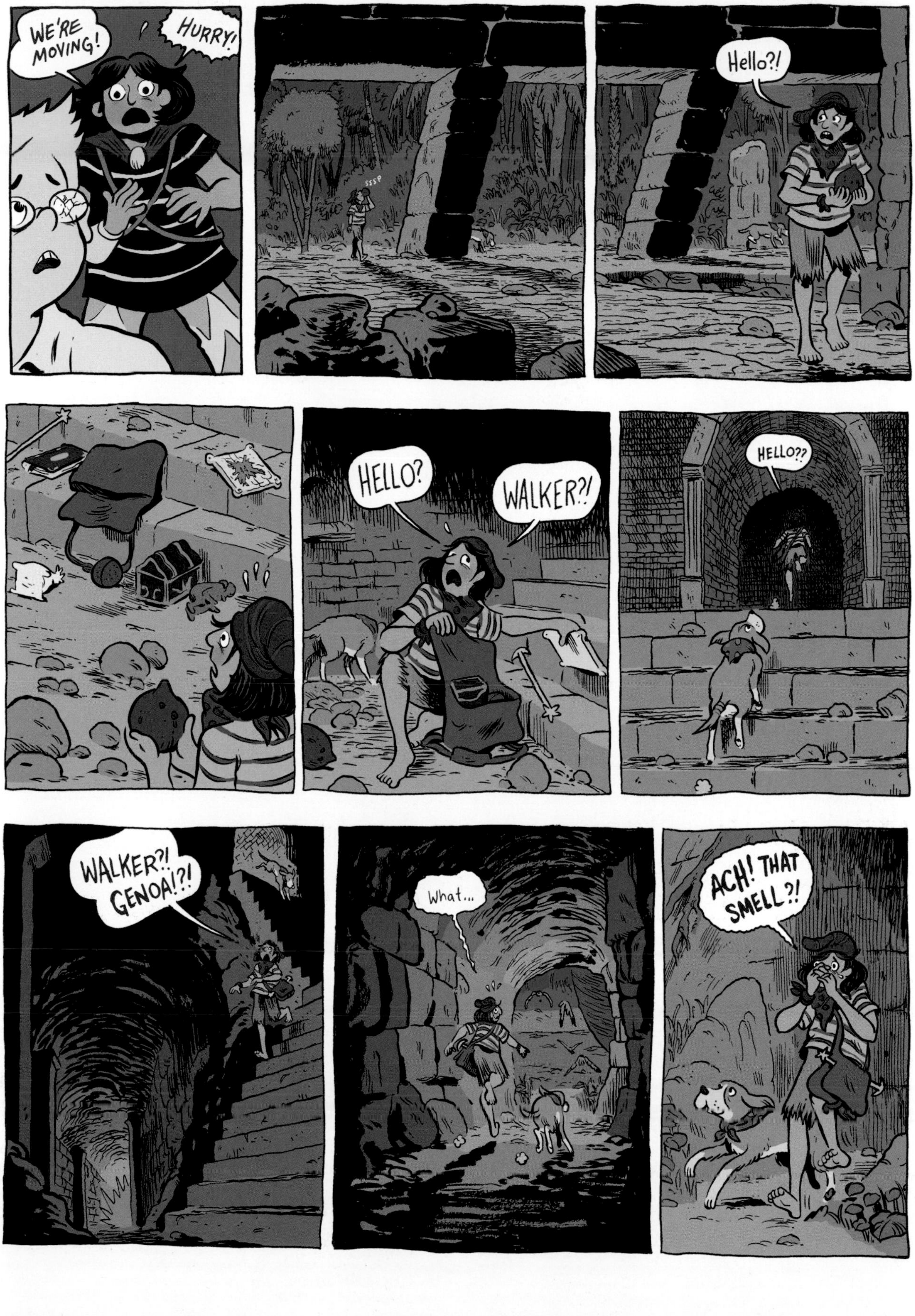
WE'RE MOVING!
HURRY!
SSSP
Hello?!
HELLO?
WALKER?!
HELLO??
WALKER?! GENOA!?!
What...
ACH! THAT SMELL?!

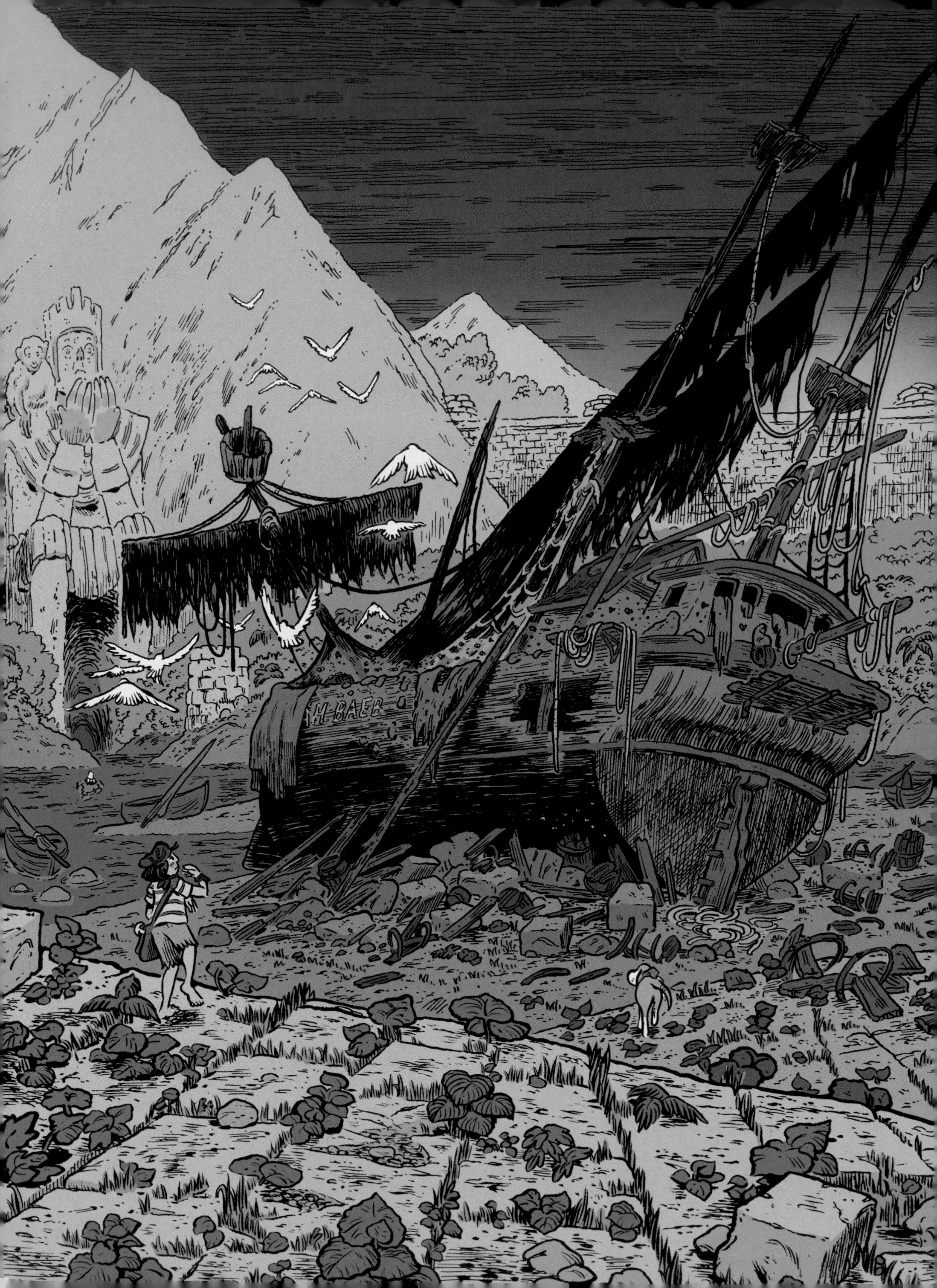
H BAEB

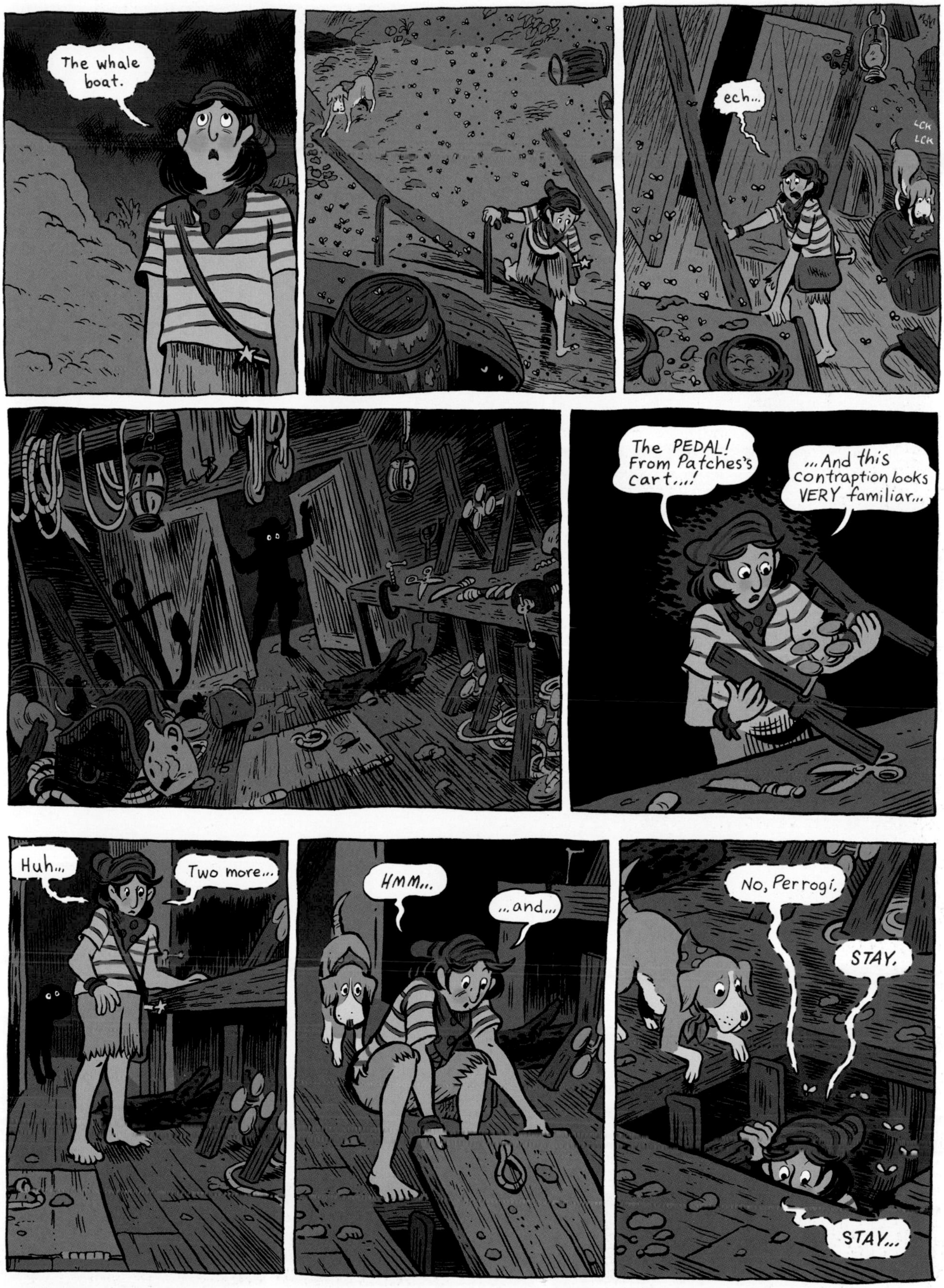
The whale boat.
ech...
LCK LCK
The PEDAL! From Patches's cart...!
...And this contraption looks VERY familiar...
Huh...
Two more...
HMM...
...and...
No, Perrogi,
STAY.
STAY...

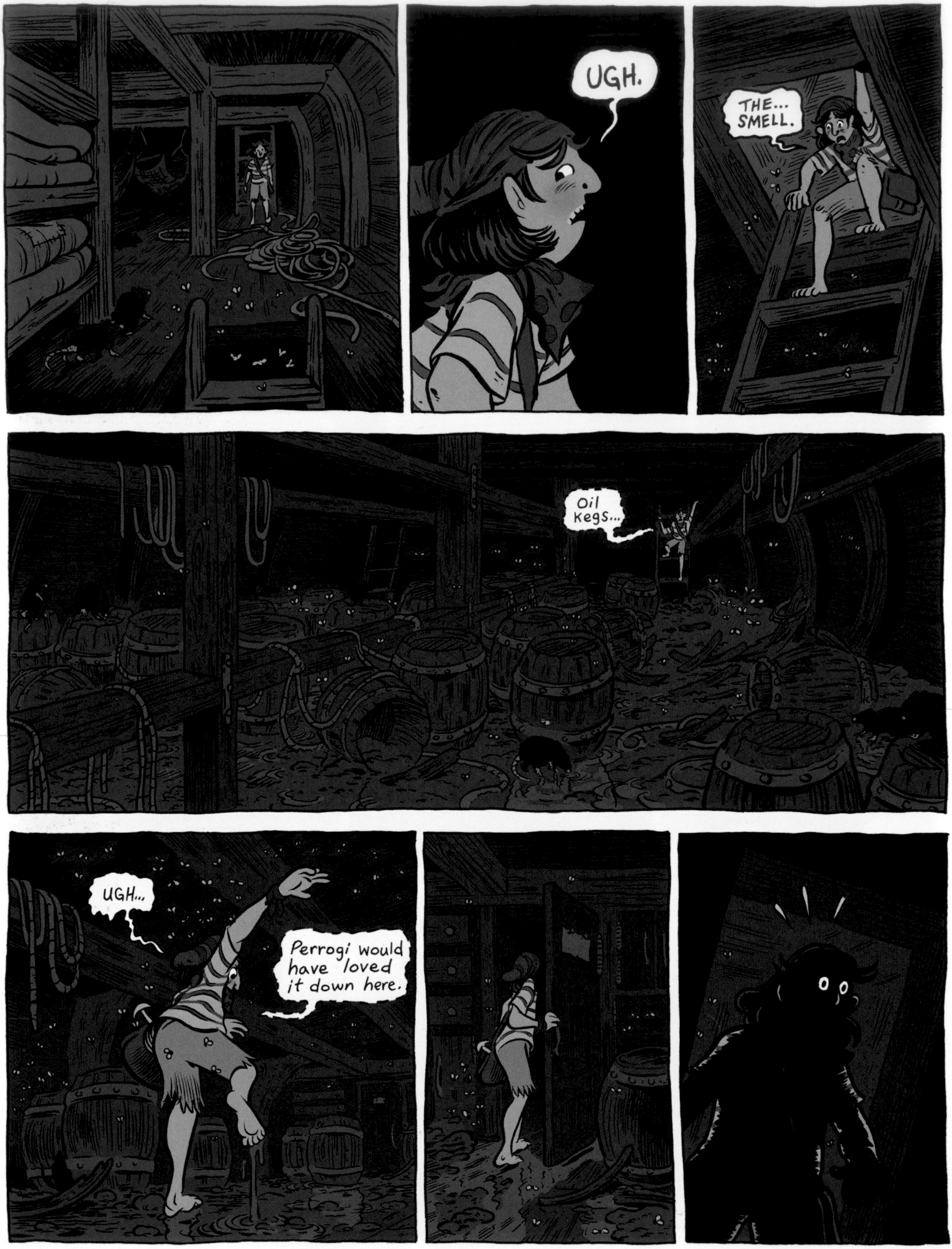
UGH.
THE... SMELL.
Oil kegs...
UGH...
Perrogi would have loved it down here.

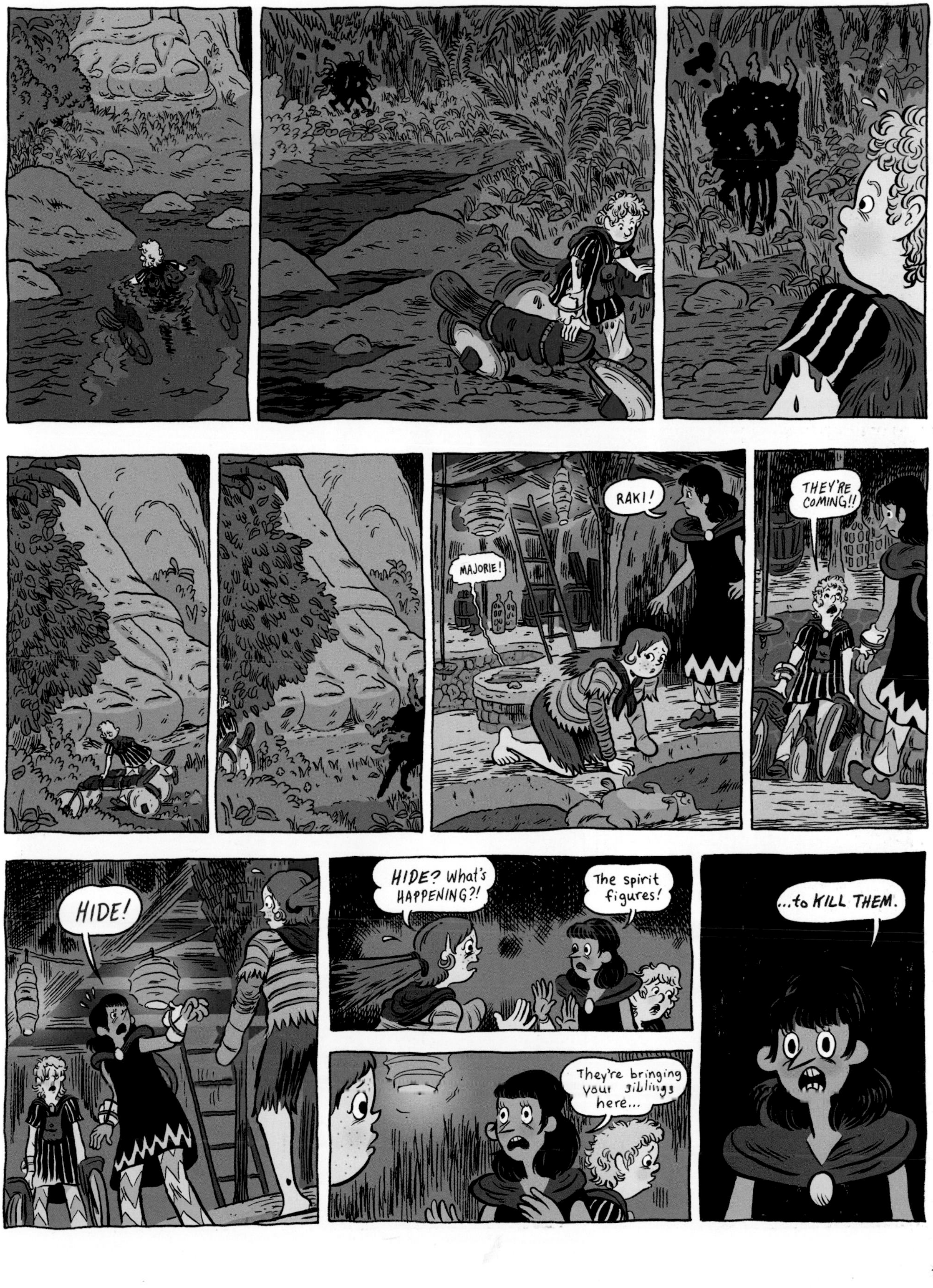
RAKI!
MAJORIE!
THEY'RE COMING!!
HIDE!
HIDE? What's HAPPENING?!
The spirit figures!
They're bringing your siblings here...
...to KILL THEM.

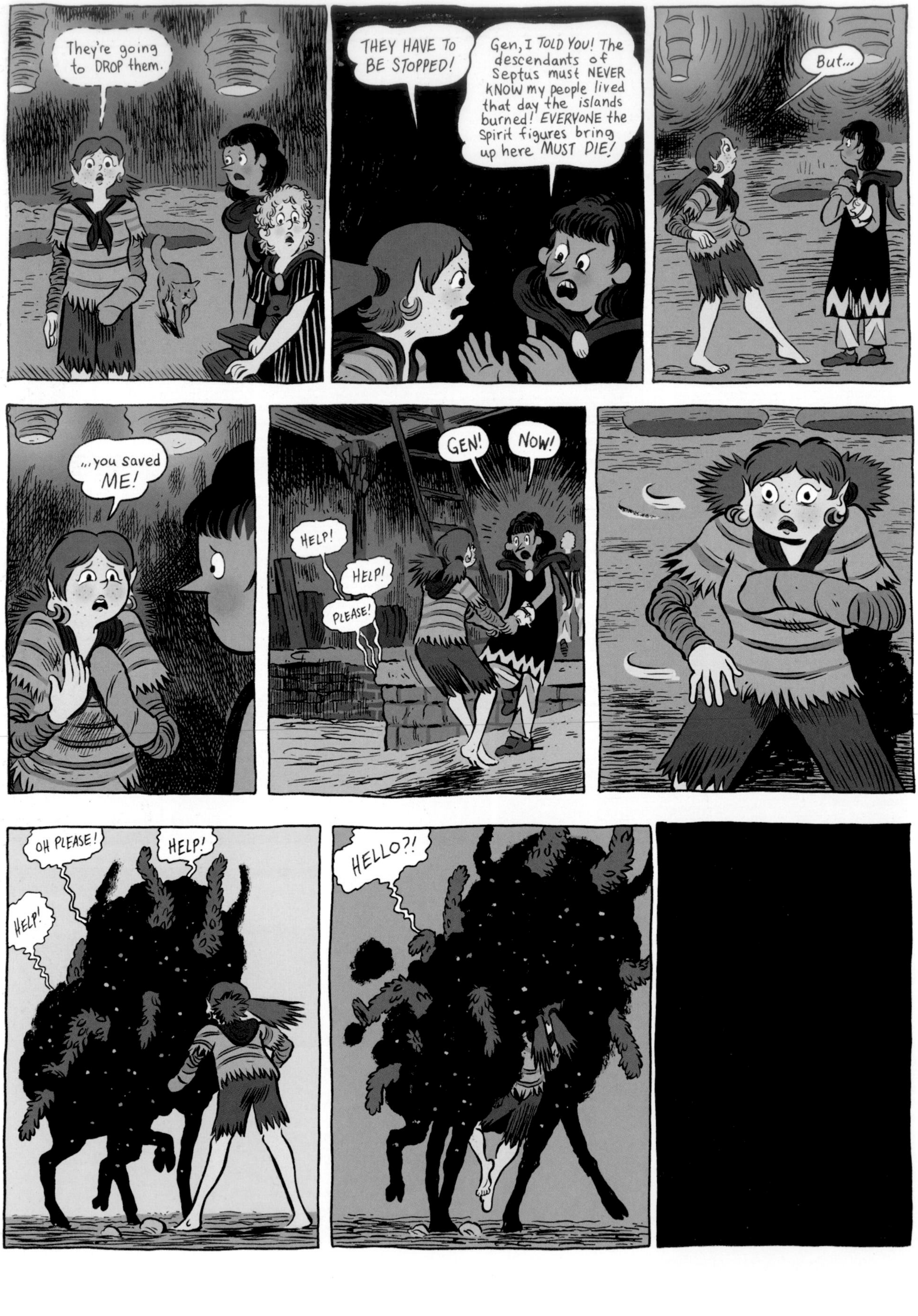

They're going to DROP them.
THEY HAVE TO BE STOPPED!
Gen, I TOLD YOU! The descendants of Septus must NEVER KNOW my people lived that day the islands burned! EVERYONE the spirit figures bring up here MUST DIE!
But...
...you saved ME!
GEN!
NOW!
HELP!
HELP!
PLEASE!
OH PLEASE!
HELP!
HELP!
HELLO?!

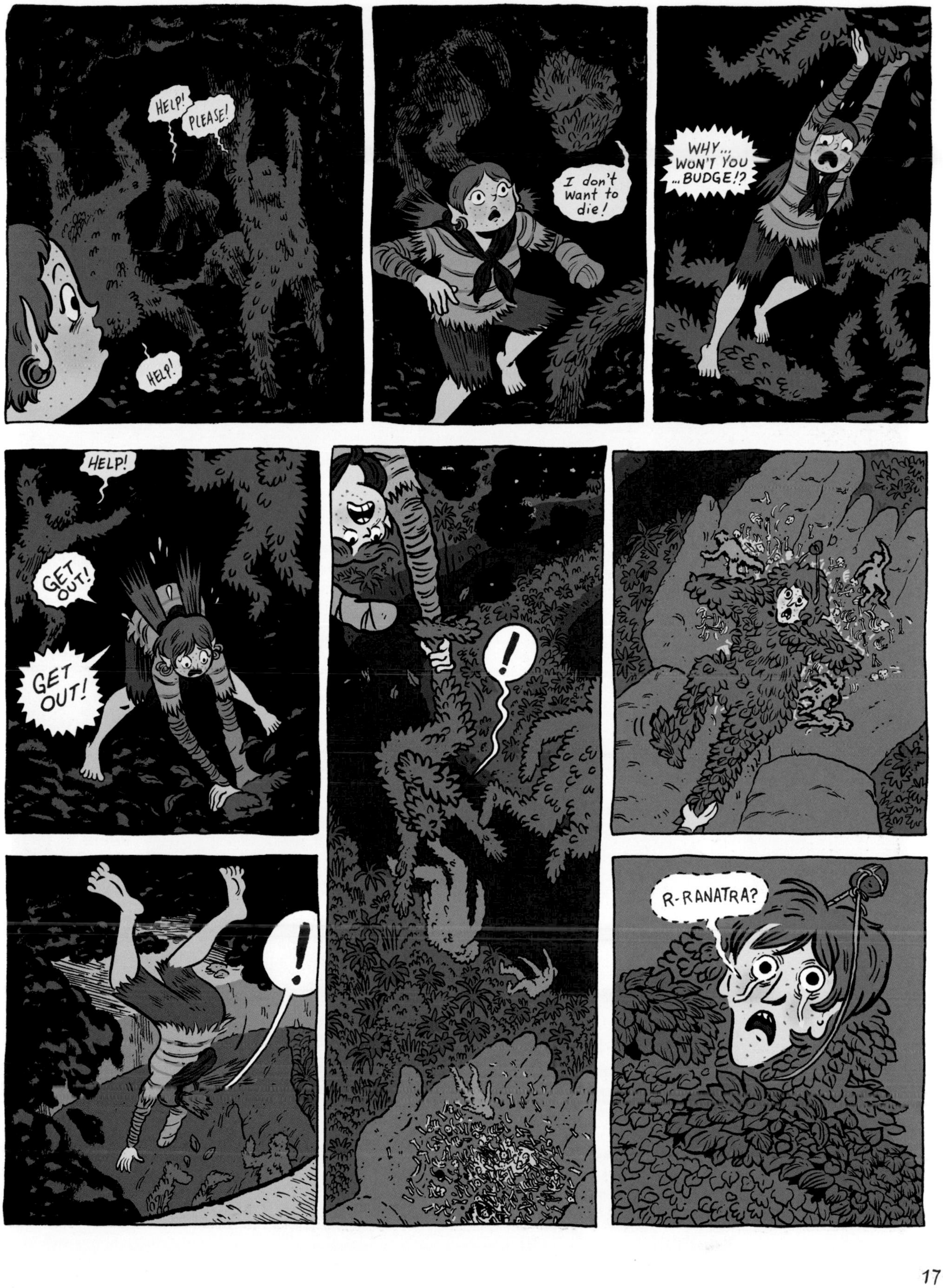
HELP!
PLEASE!
HELP!
I don't want to die!
WHY... WON'T YOU ...BUDGE!?
HELP!
GET OUT!
GET OUT!
!
!
R-RANATRA?

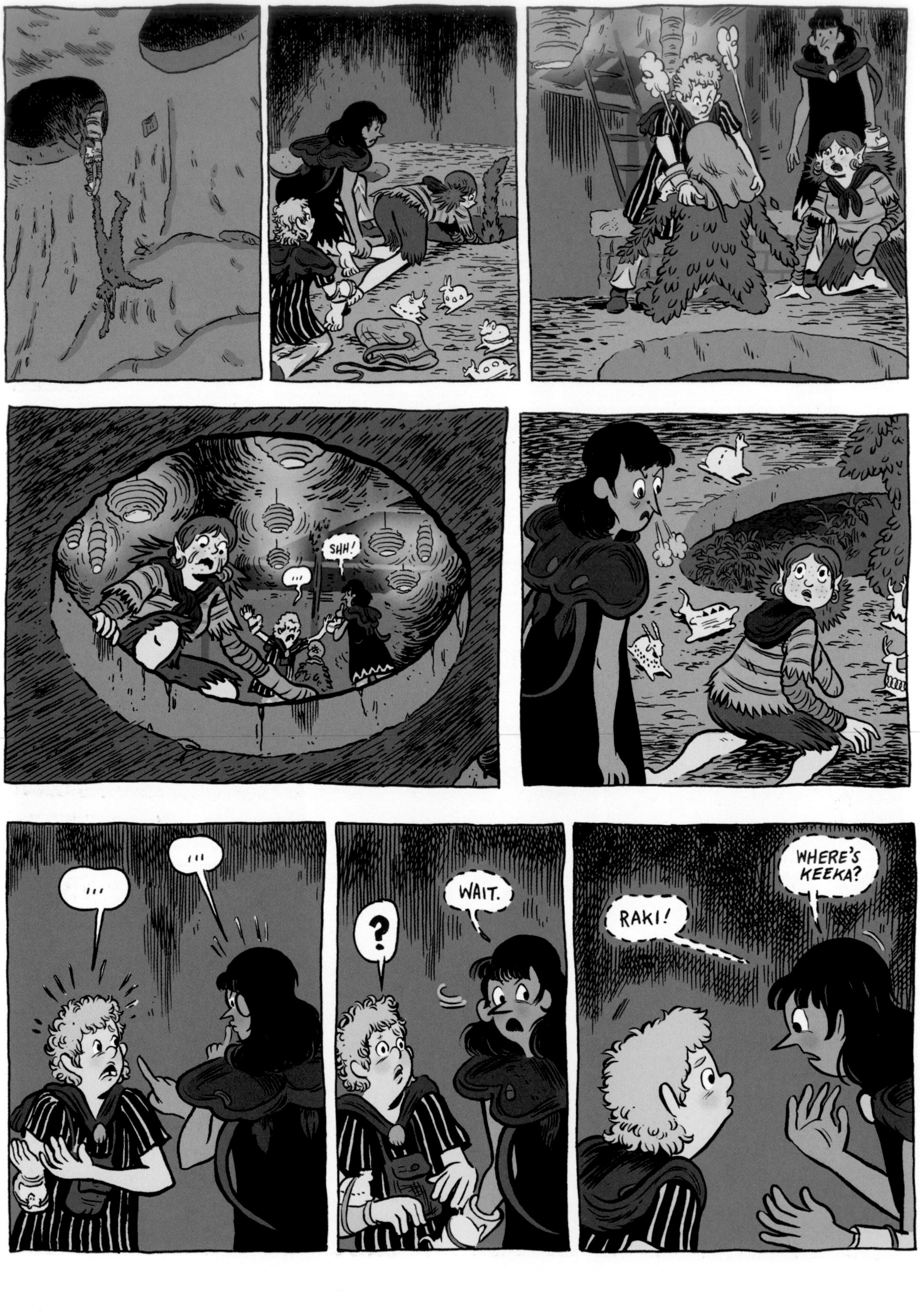
SHH!
...
...
...
?
WAIT.
RAKI!
WHERE'S KEEKA?

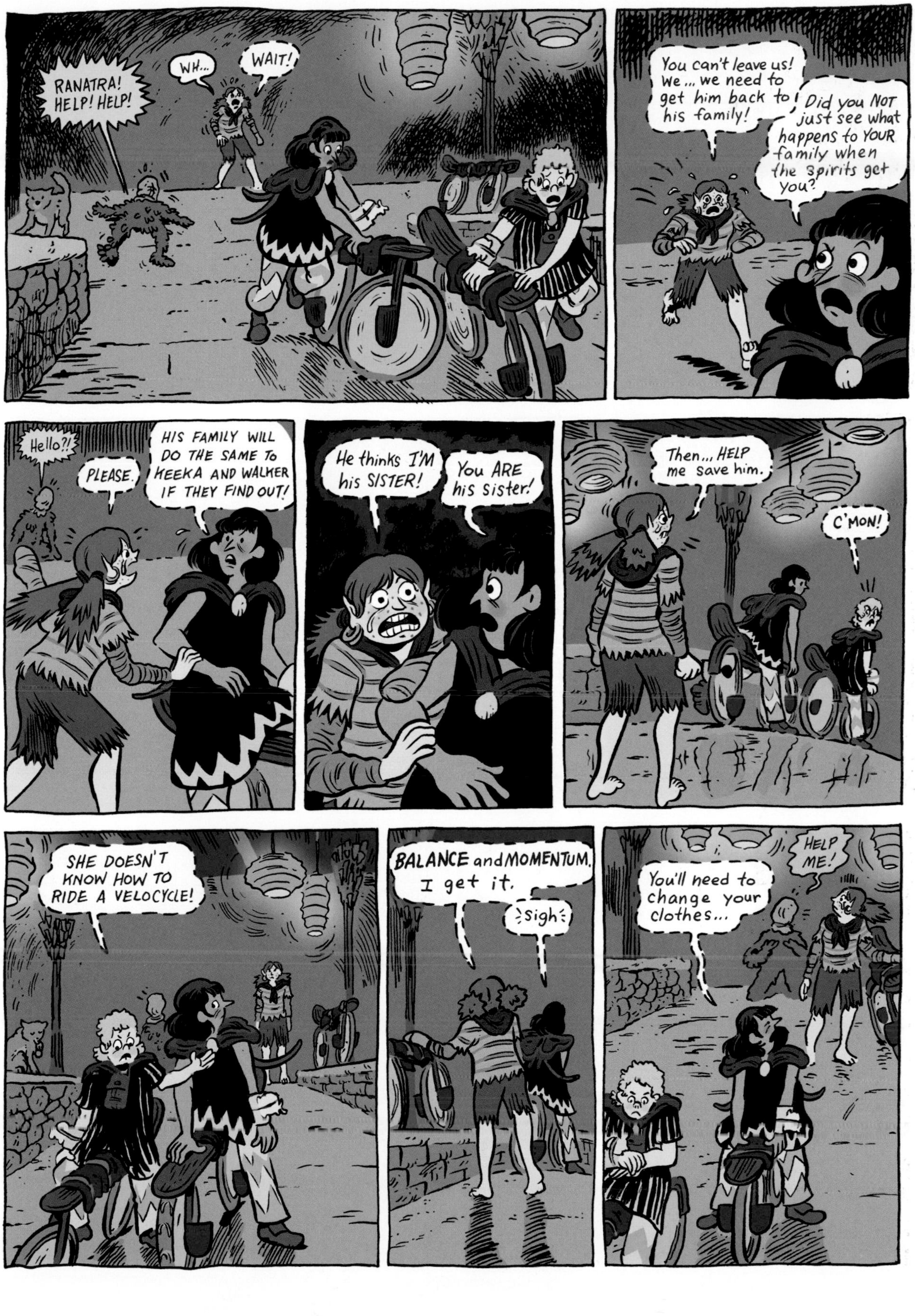
RANATRA! HELP! HELP!
WH...
WAIT!
You can't leave us! We... we need to get him back to his family!
Did you NOT just see what happens to YOUR family when the spirits get you?
Hello?!
PLEASE.
HIS FAMILY WILL DO THE SAME TO KEEKA AND WALKER IF THEY FIND OUT!
He thinks I'M his SISTER!
You ARE his sister!
Then... HELP me save him.
C'MON!
SHE DOESN'T KNOW HOW TO RIDE A VELOCYCLE!
BALANCE and MOMENTUM. I get it.
sigh
HELP ME!
You'll need to change your clothes...

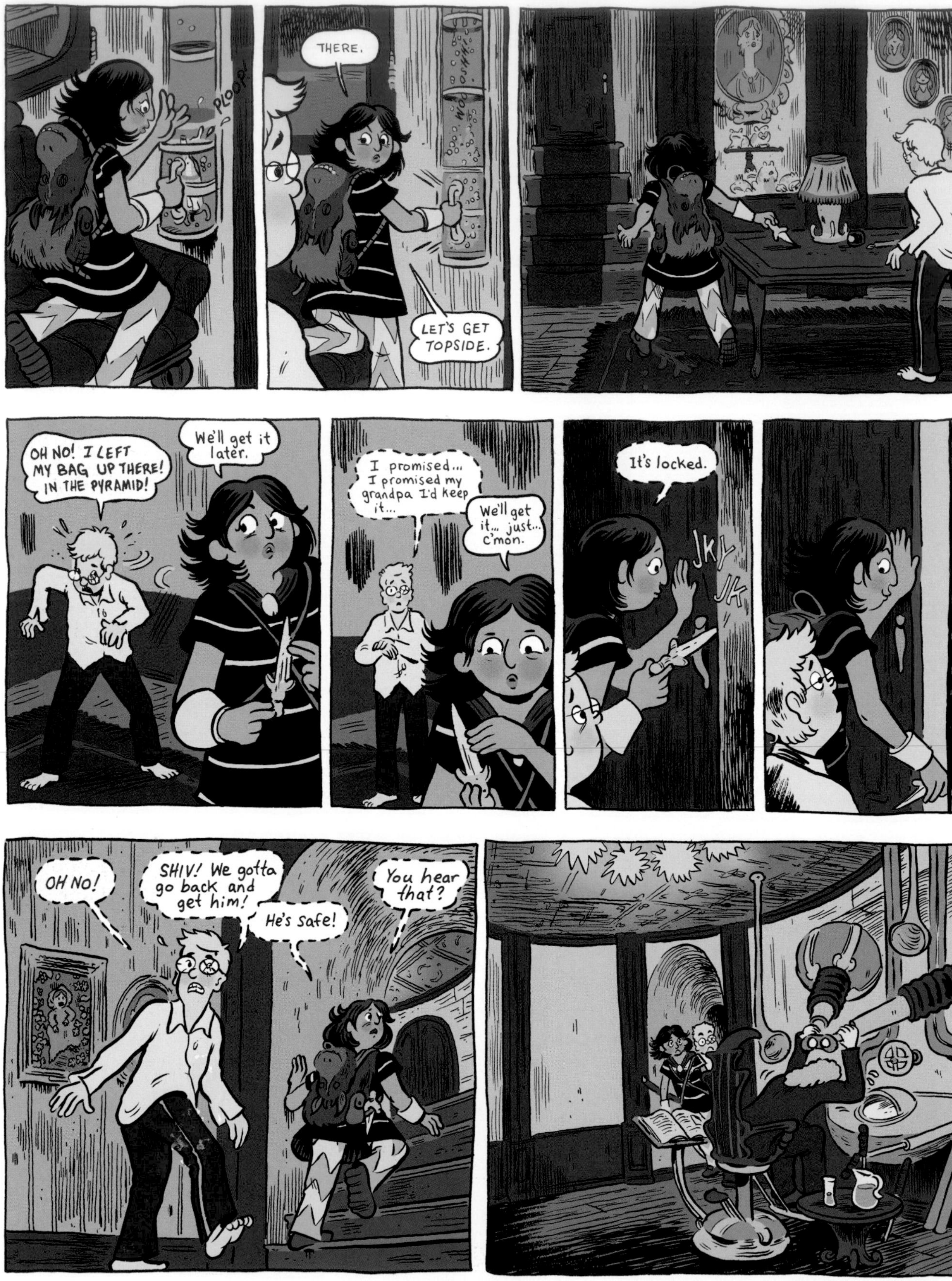

PLOOP!
THERE.
LET'S GET TOPSIDE.
OH NO! I LEFT MY BAG UP THERE! IN THE PYRAMID!
We'll get it later.
I promised... I promised my grandpa I'd keep it...
We'll get it... just... c'mon.
It's locked.
JKY JK
OH NO!
SHIV! We gotta go back and get him!
He's safe!
You hear that?

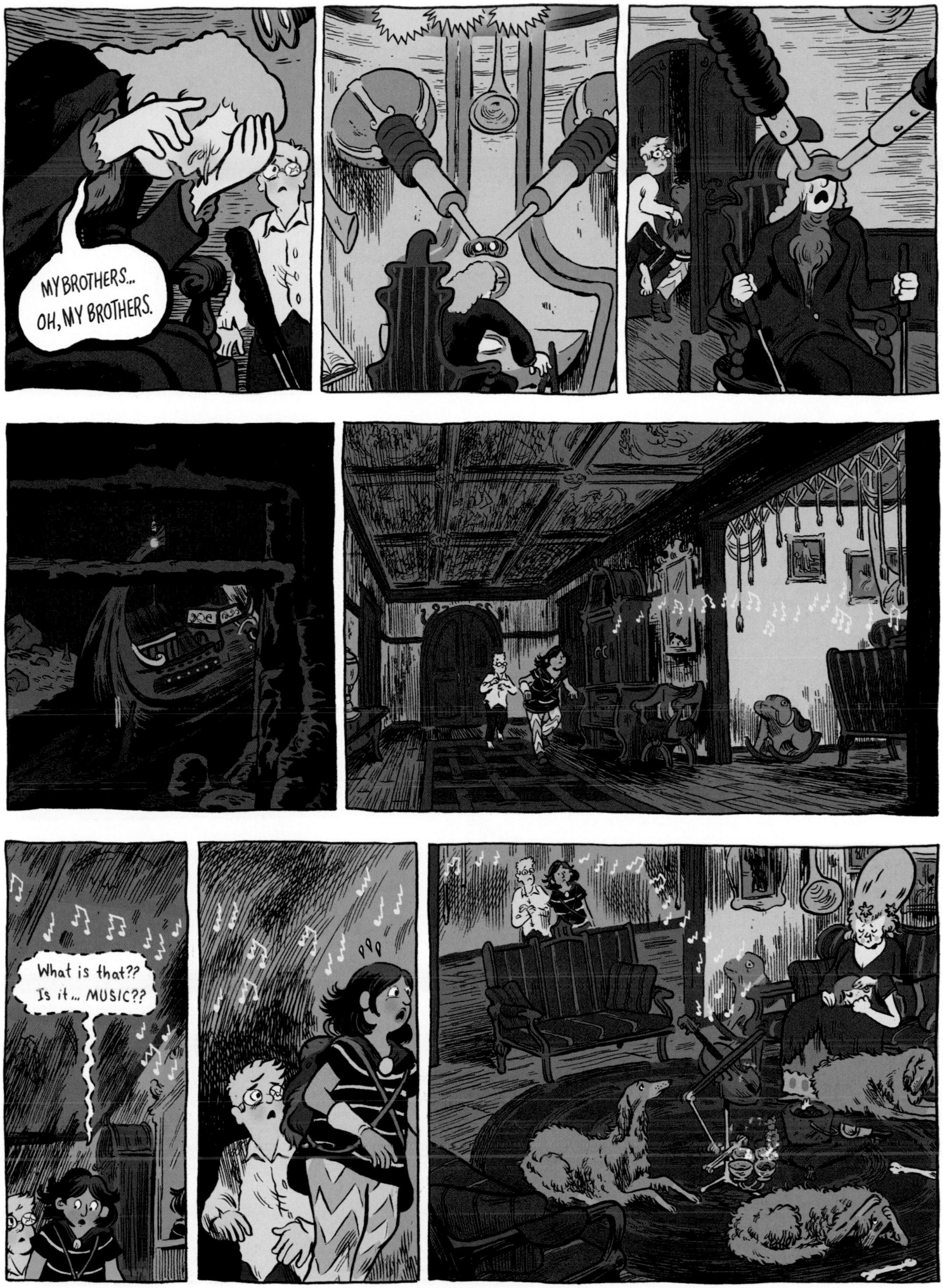

MY BROTHERS...
OH, MY BROTHERS.
What is that??
Is it... MUSIC??

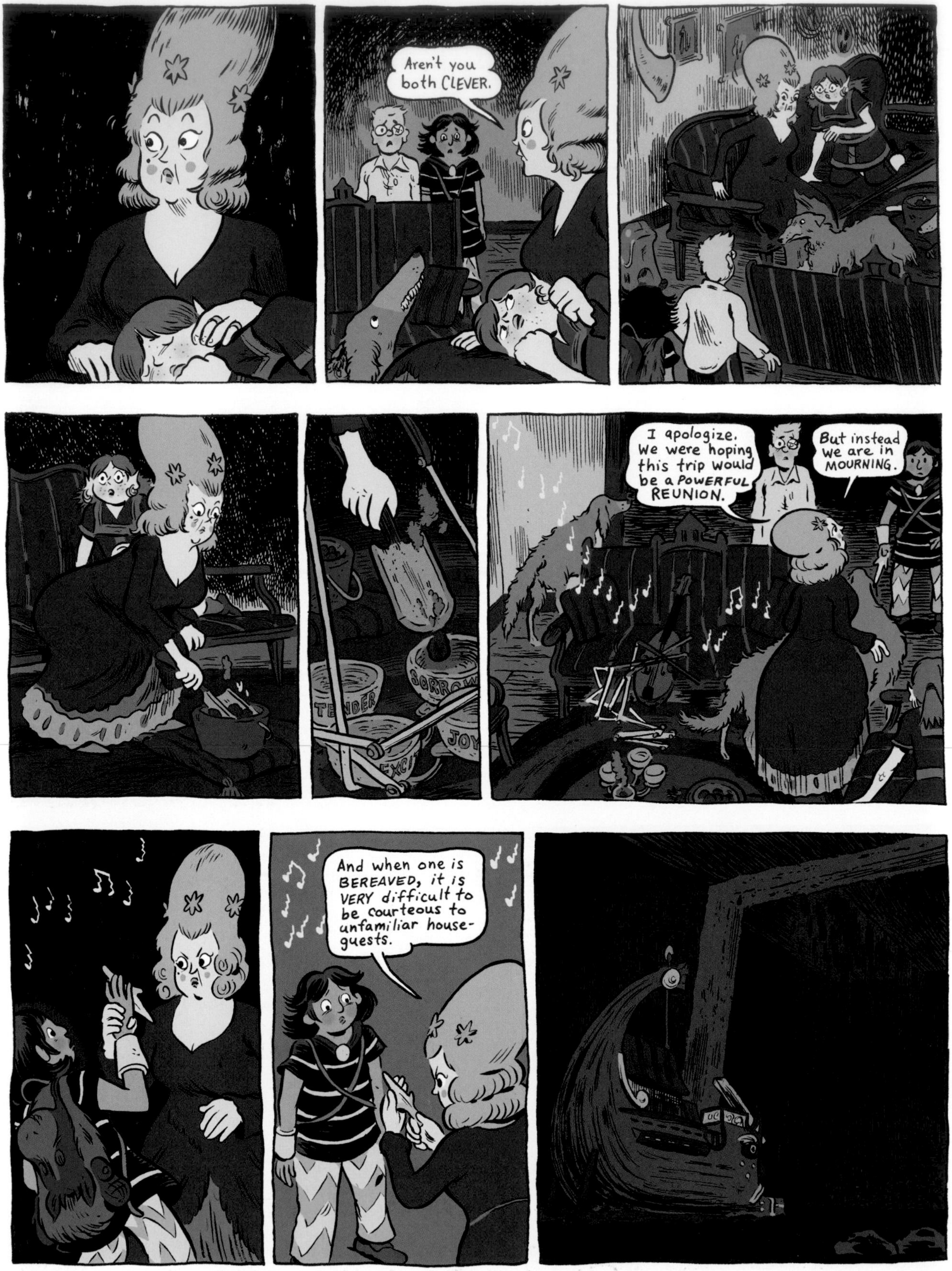

Aren't you both CLEVER.
I apologize. We were hoping this trip would be a POWERFUL REUNION.
But instead we are in MOURNING.
TENDER
SORROW
JOY
EXCIT
And when one is BEREAVED, it is VERY difficult to be courteous to unfamiliar house-guests.

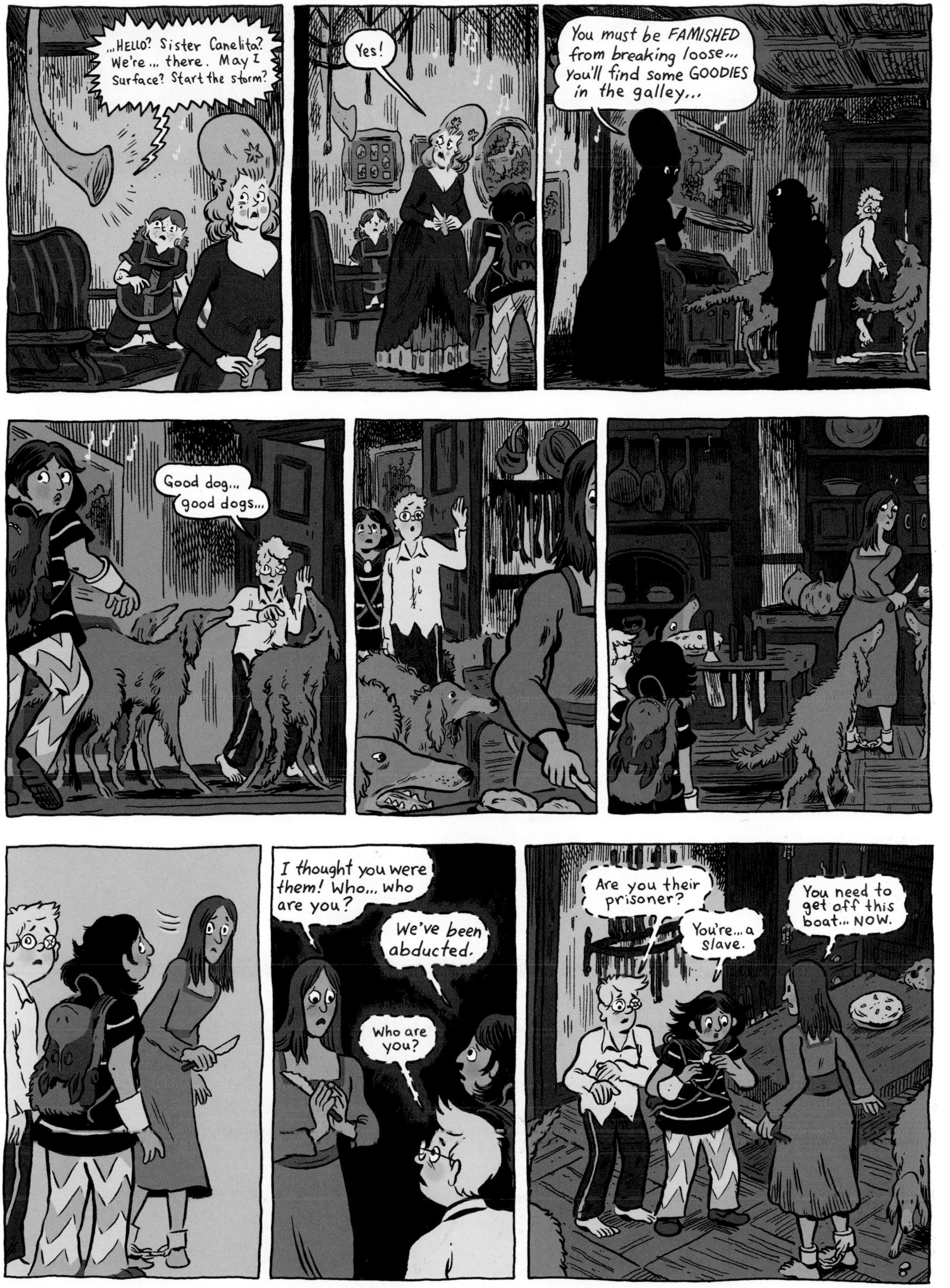
...HELLO? Sister Canelita? We're ... there. May I surface? Start the storm?
Yes!
You must be FAMISHED from breaking loose... You'll find some GOODIES in the galley...
Good dog... good dogs...
I thought you were them! Who... who are you?
We've been abducted.
Who are you?
Are you their prisoner?
You're... a slave.
You need to get off this boat... NOW.

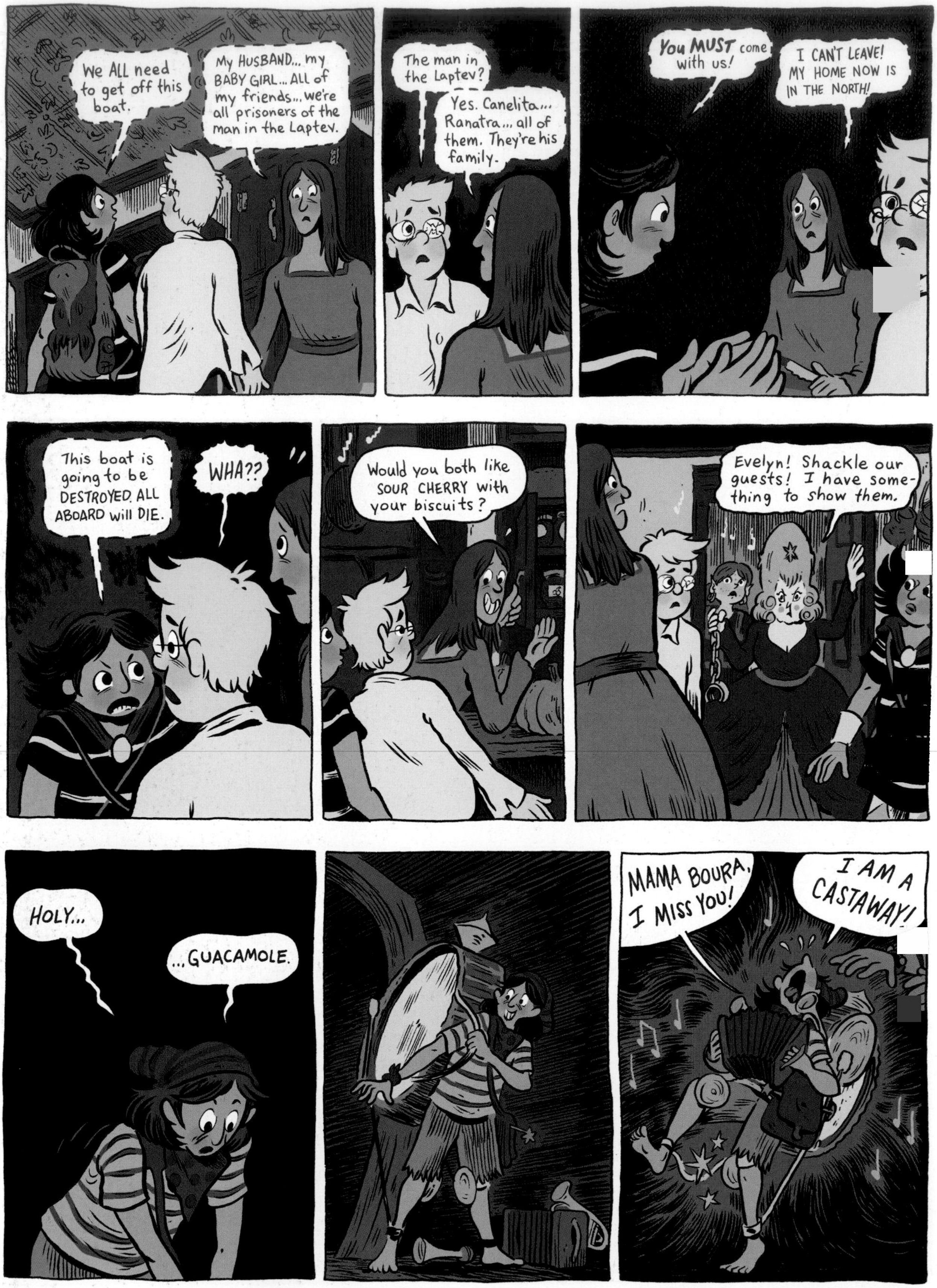

We ALL need to get off this boat.
My HUSBAND... my BABY GIRL... All of my friends... we're all prisoners of the man in the Laptev.
The man in the Laptev?
Yes. Canelita... Ranatra... all of them. They're his family.
You MUST come with us!
I CAN'T LEAVE! MY HOME NOW IS IN THE NORTH!
This boat is going to be DESTROYED. ALL ABOARD will DIE.
WHA??
Would you both like SOUR CHERRY with your biscuits?
Evelyn! Shackle our guests! I have something to show them.
HOLY...
...GUACAMOLE.
MAMA BOURA, I MISS YOU!
I AM A CASTAWAY!

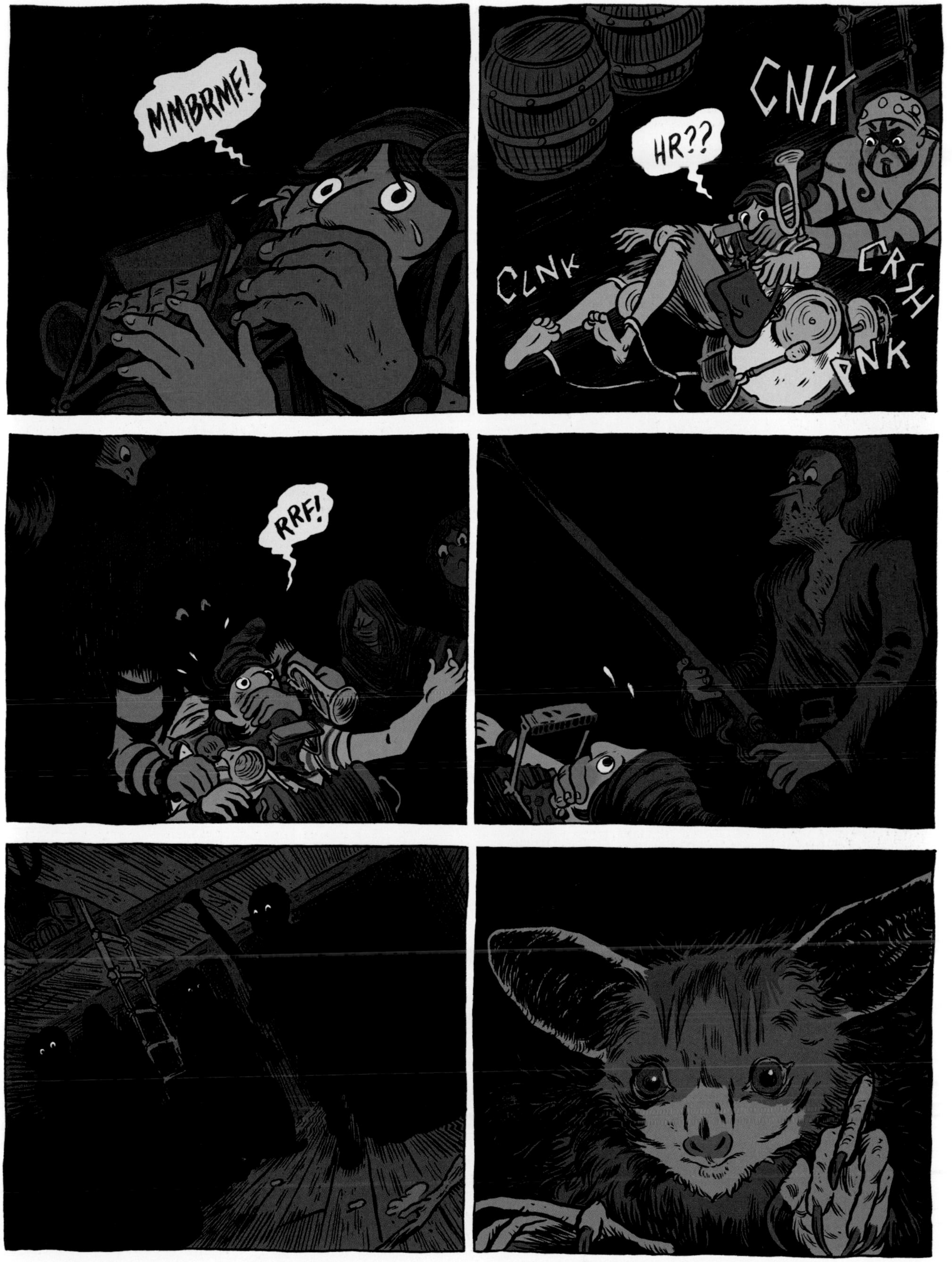
MMBRMF!
CNK
HR??
CLNK
CRSH
PNK
RRF!

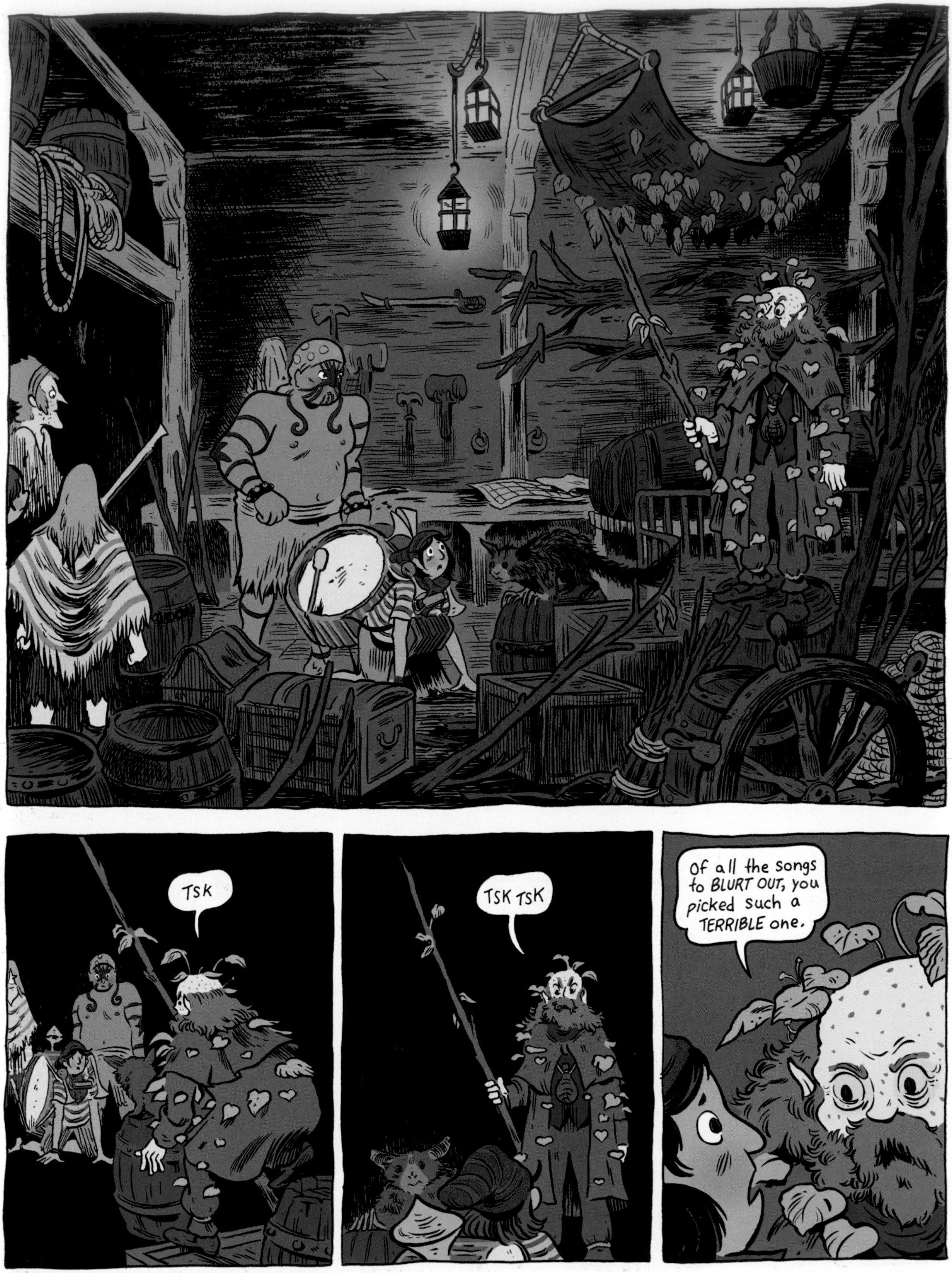
TSK
TSK TSK
Of all the songs to BLURT OUT, you picked such a TERRIBLE one.

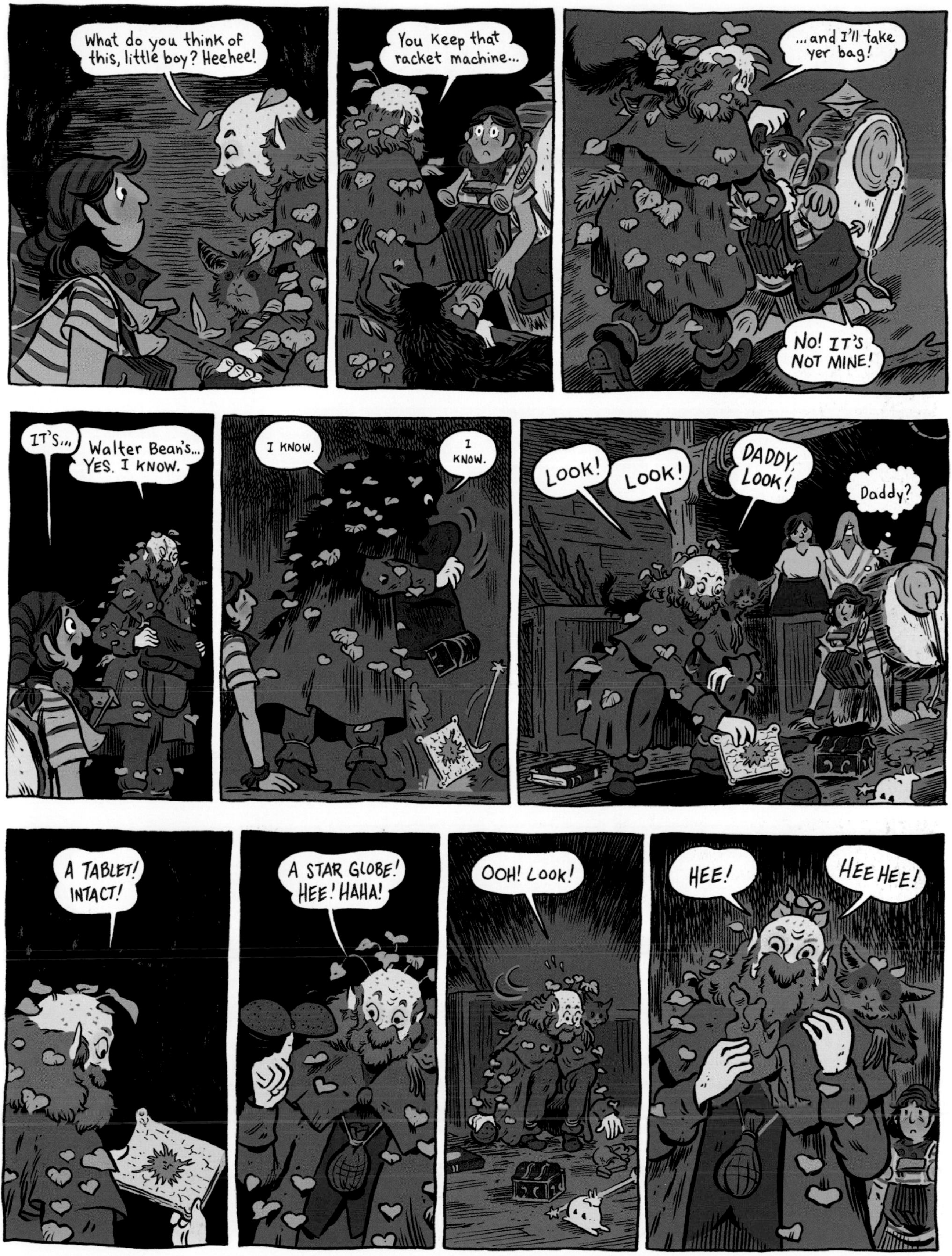
What do you think of this, little boy? Heehee!
You keep that racket machine...
...and I'll take yer bag!
No! IT'S NOT MINE!
IT'S...
Walter Bean's... YES. I KNOW.
I KNOW.
I KNOW.
LOOK!
LOOK!
DADDY, LOOK!
Daddy?
A TABLET! INTACT!
A STAR GLOBE! HEE! HAHA!
OOH! LOOK!
HEE!
HEE HEE!

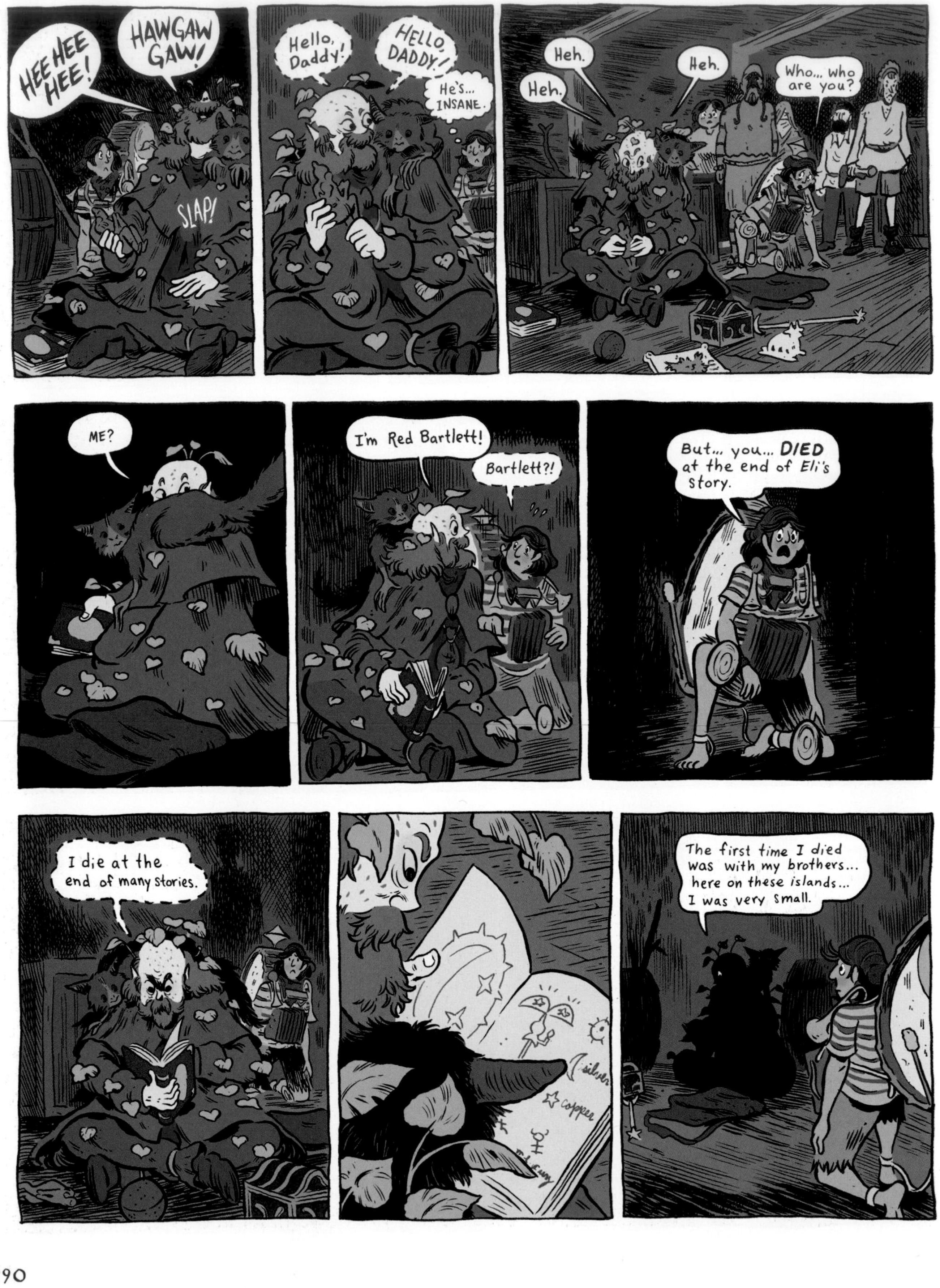

HEE HEE HEE!
HAWGAW GAW!
SLAP!
Hello, Daddy!
HELLO, DADDY!
He's... INSANE.
Heh.
Heh.
Heh.
Who... who are you?
ME?
I'm Red Bartlett!
Bartlett?!
But... you... DIED at the end of Eli's story.
I die at the end of many stories.
silver
copper
The first time I died was with my brothers... here on these islands... I was very small.

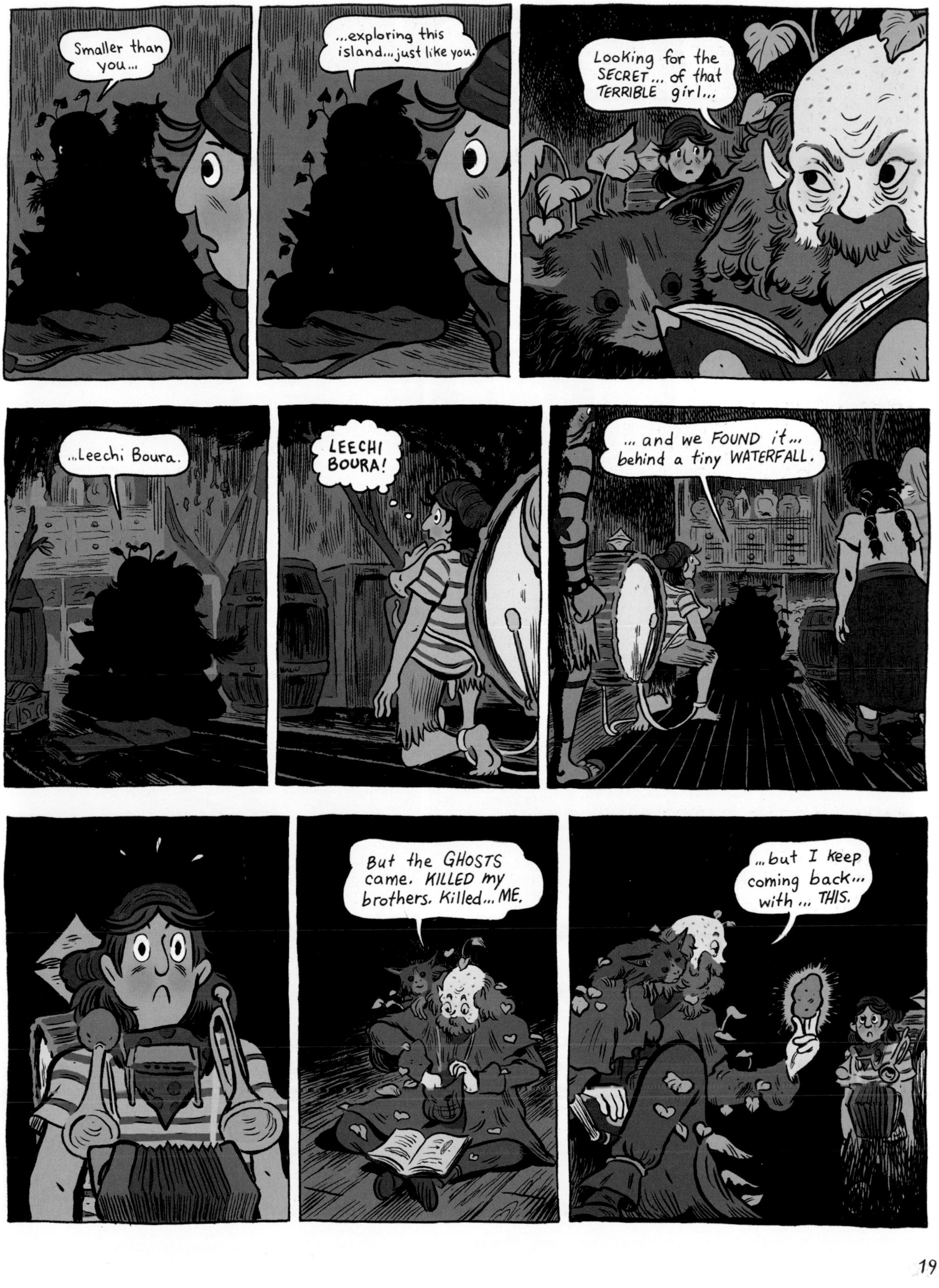
Smaller than you...
...exploring this island..., just like you.
Looking for the SECRET... of that TERRIBLE girl...
...Leechi Boura.
LEECHI BOURA!
... and we FOUND it... behind a tiny WATERFALL.
But the GHOSTS came. KILLED my brothers. Killed... ME.
...but I keep coming back... with ... THIS.

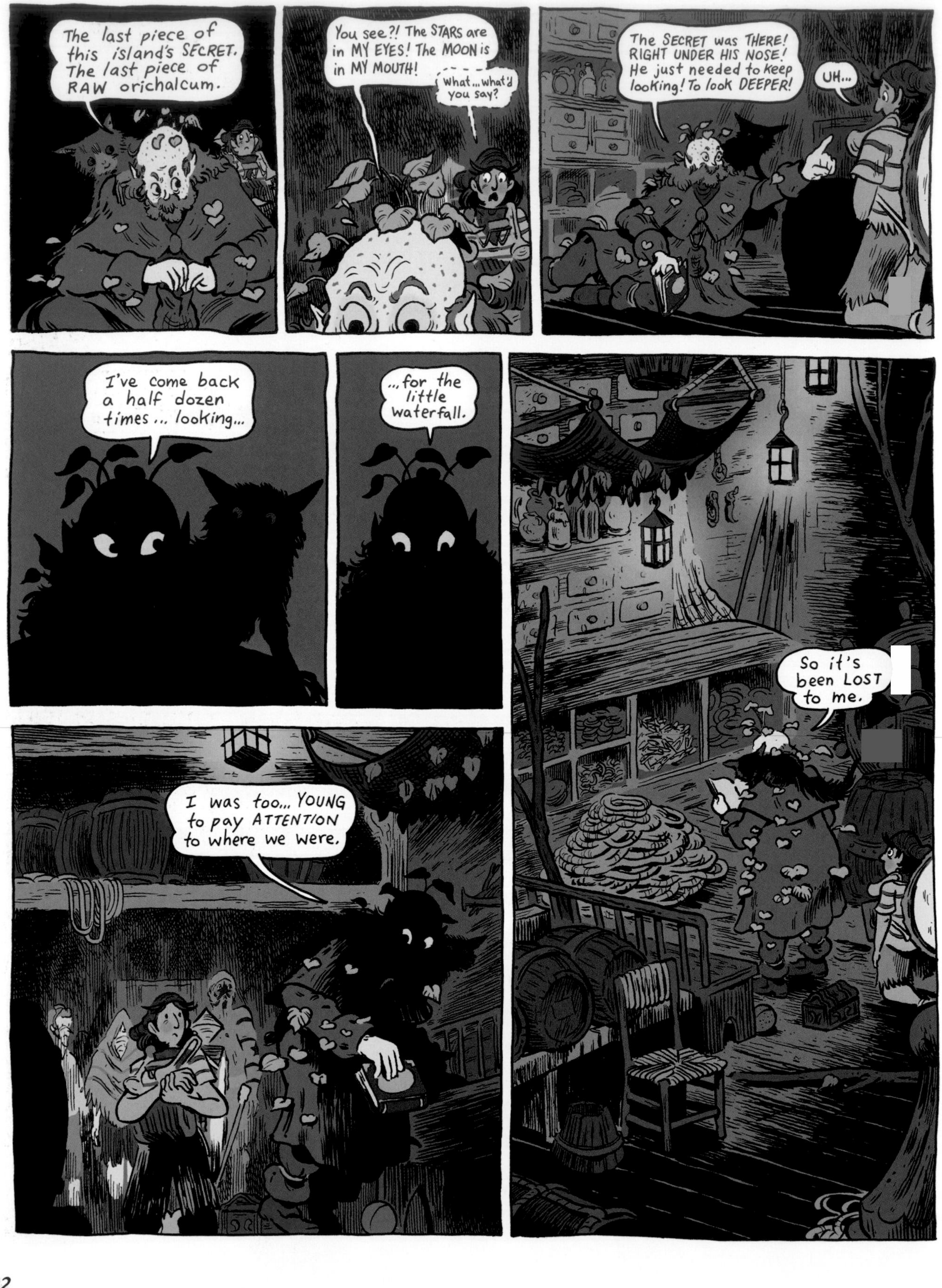
The last piece of this island's SECRET. The last piece of RAW orichalcum.
You see?! The STARS are in MY EYES! The MOON is in MY MOUTH!
What... what'd you say?
The SECRET was THERE! RIGHT UNDER HIS NOSE! He just needed to keep looking! To look DEEPER!
UH...
I've come back a half dozen times... looking...
...for the little waterfall.
So it's been LOST to me.
I was too... YOUNG to pay ATTENTION to where we were.

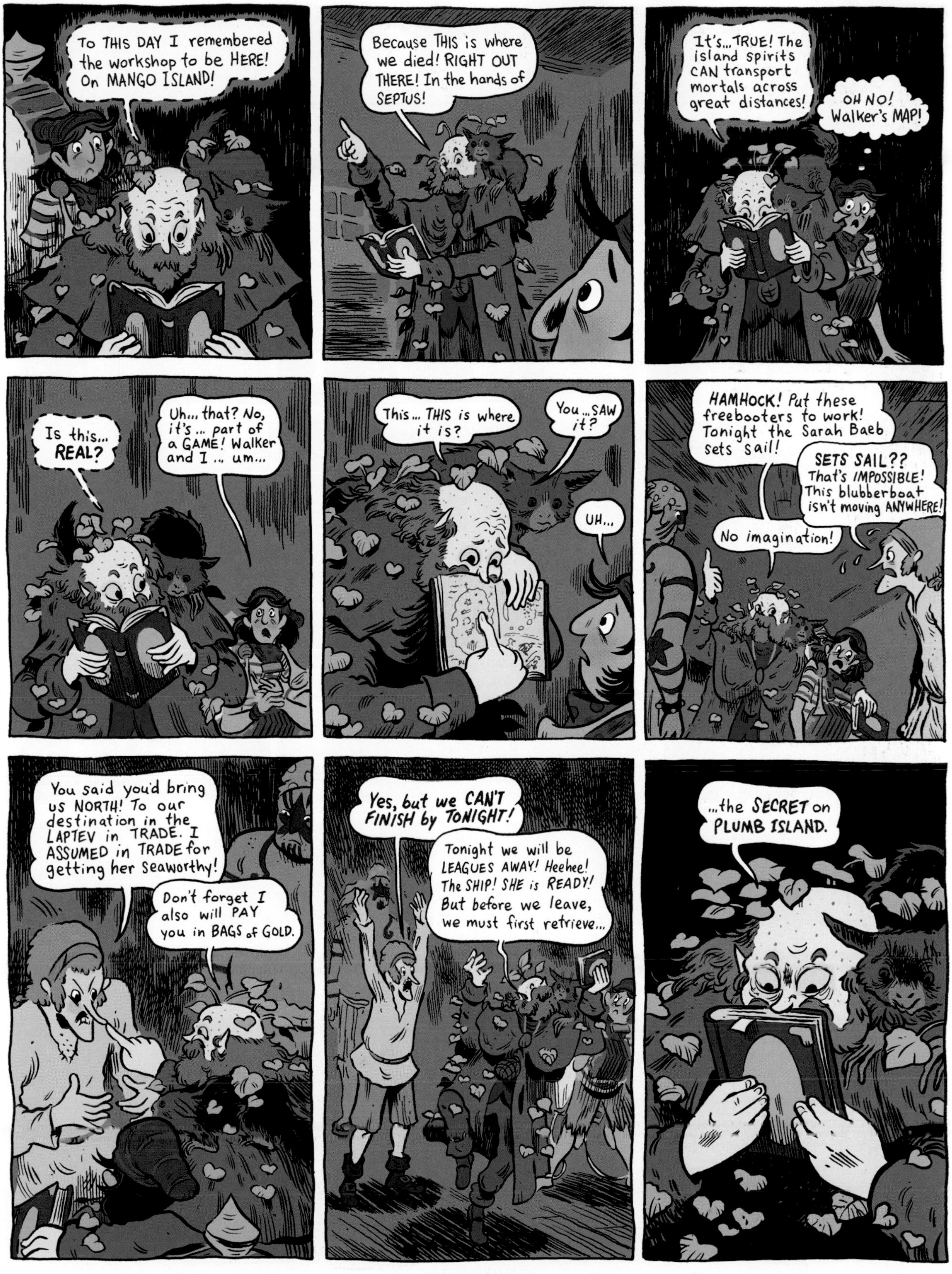
To THIS DAY I remembered the workshop to be HERE! On MANGO ISLAND!
Because THIS is where we died! RIGHT OUT THERE! In the hands of SEPTUS!
It's... TRUE! The island spirits CAN transport mortals across great distances!
OH NO! Walker's MAP!
Is this... REAL?
Uh... that? No, it's... part of a GAME! Walker and I... um...
This... THIS is where it is?
You... SAW it?
UH...
HAMHOCK! Put these freebooters to work! Tonight the Sarah Baeb sets sail!
SETS SAIL?? That's IMPOSSIBLE! This blubberboat isn't moving ANYWHERE!
No imagination!
You said you'd bring us NORTH! To our destination in the LAPTEV in TRADE. I ASSUMED in TRADE for getting her seaworthy!
Don't forget I also will PAY you in BAGS of GOLD.
Yes, but we CAN'T FINISH by TONIGHT!
Tonight we will be LEAGUES AWAY! Heehee! The SHIP! SHE is READY! But before we leave, we must first retrieve...
...the SECRET on PLUMB ISLAND.

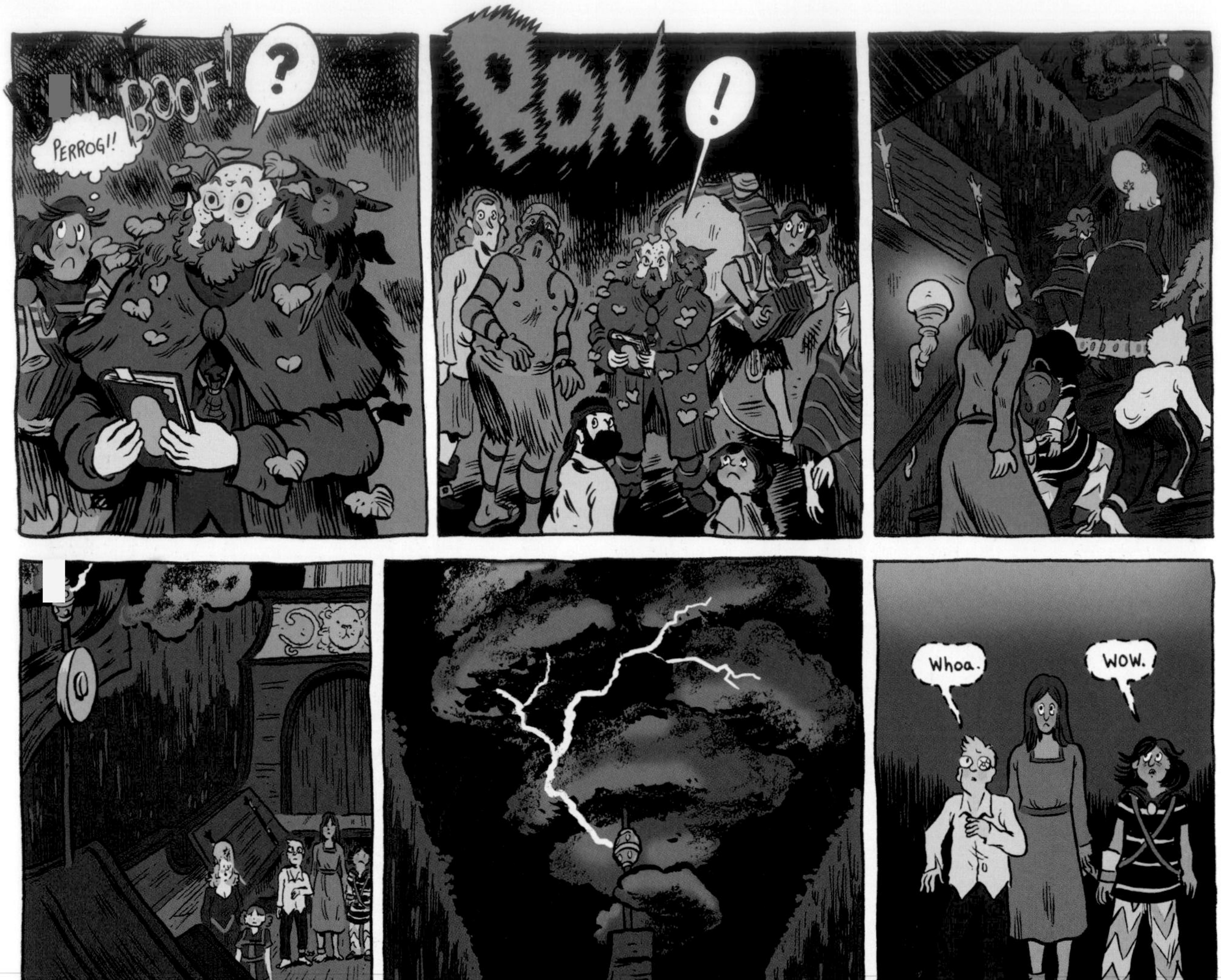
BOOF!
?
PERROG!!
BOM
!
Whoa.
WOW.
BOM!

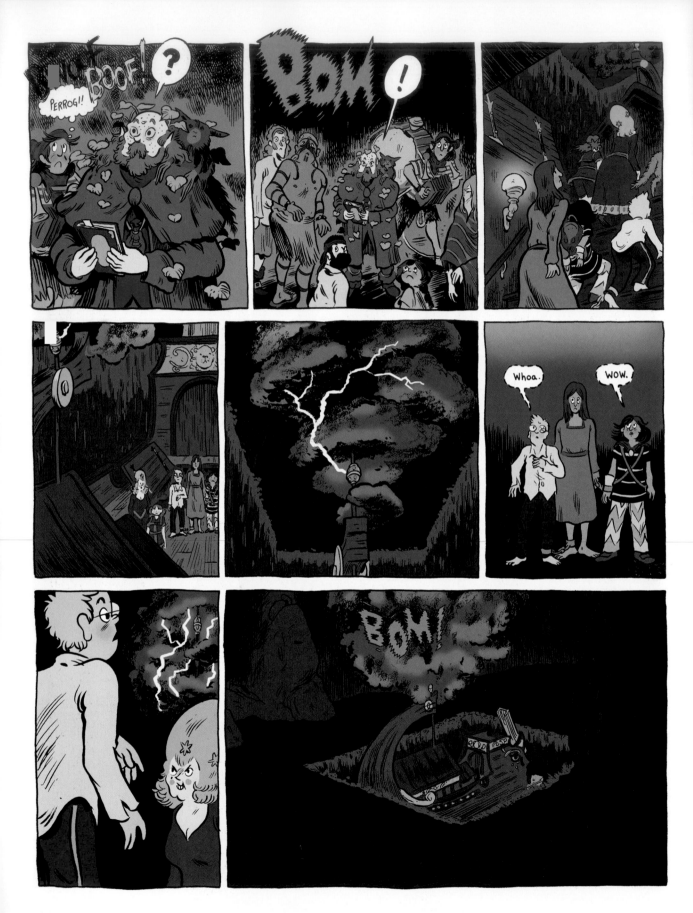

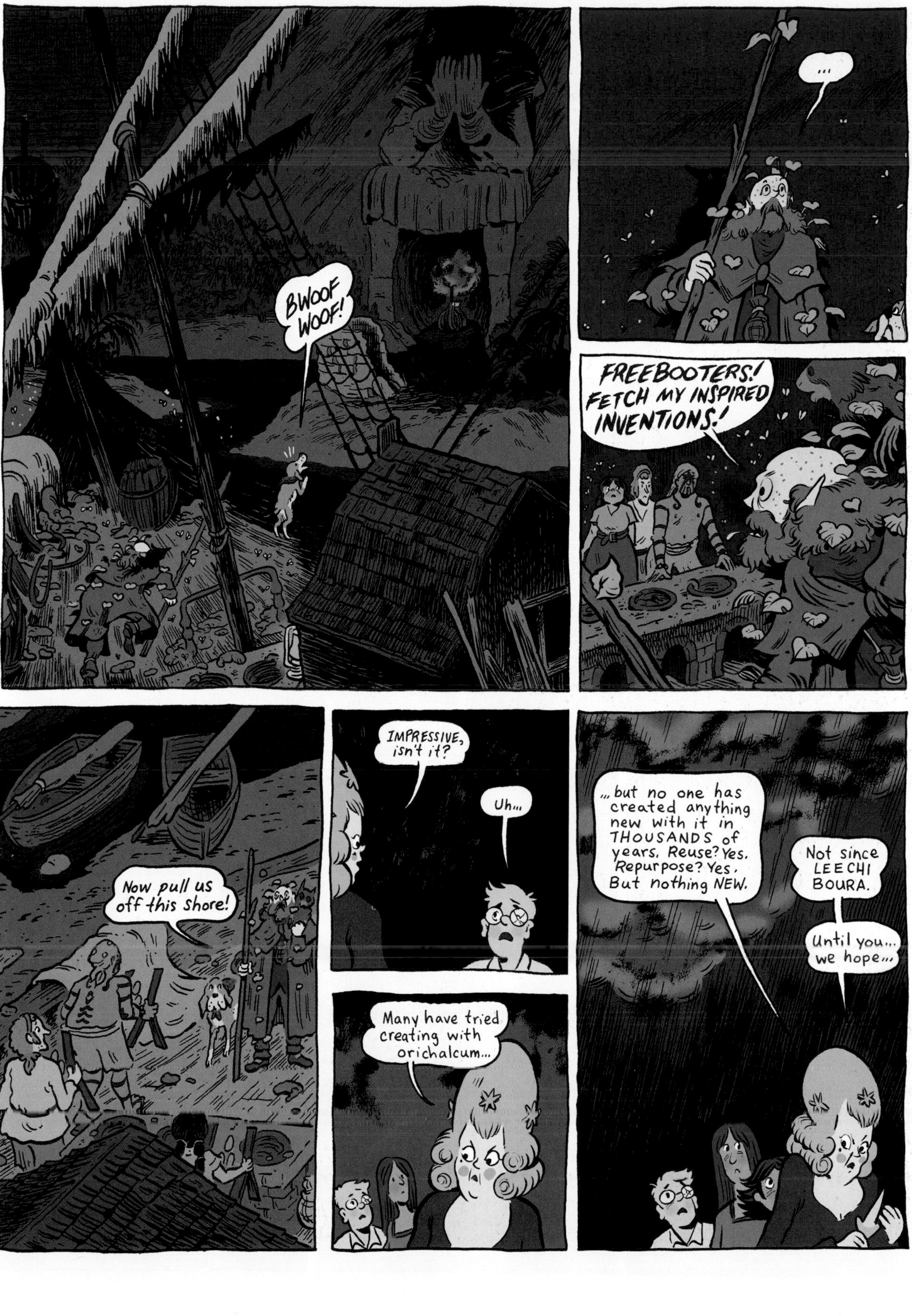
BWOOF WOOF!
...
FREEBOOTERS! FETCH MY INSPIRED INVENTIONS!
Now pull us off this shore!
IMPRESSIVE, isn't it?
Uh...
Many have tried creating with orichalcum...
... but no one has created anything new with it in THOUSANDS of years. Reuse? Yes. Repurpose? Yes. But nothing NEW.
Not since LEECHI BOURA.
Until you... we hope...

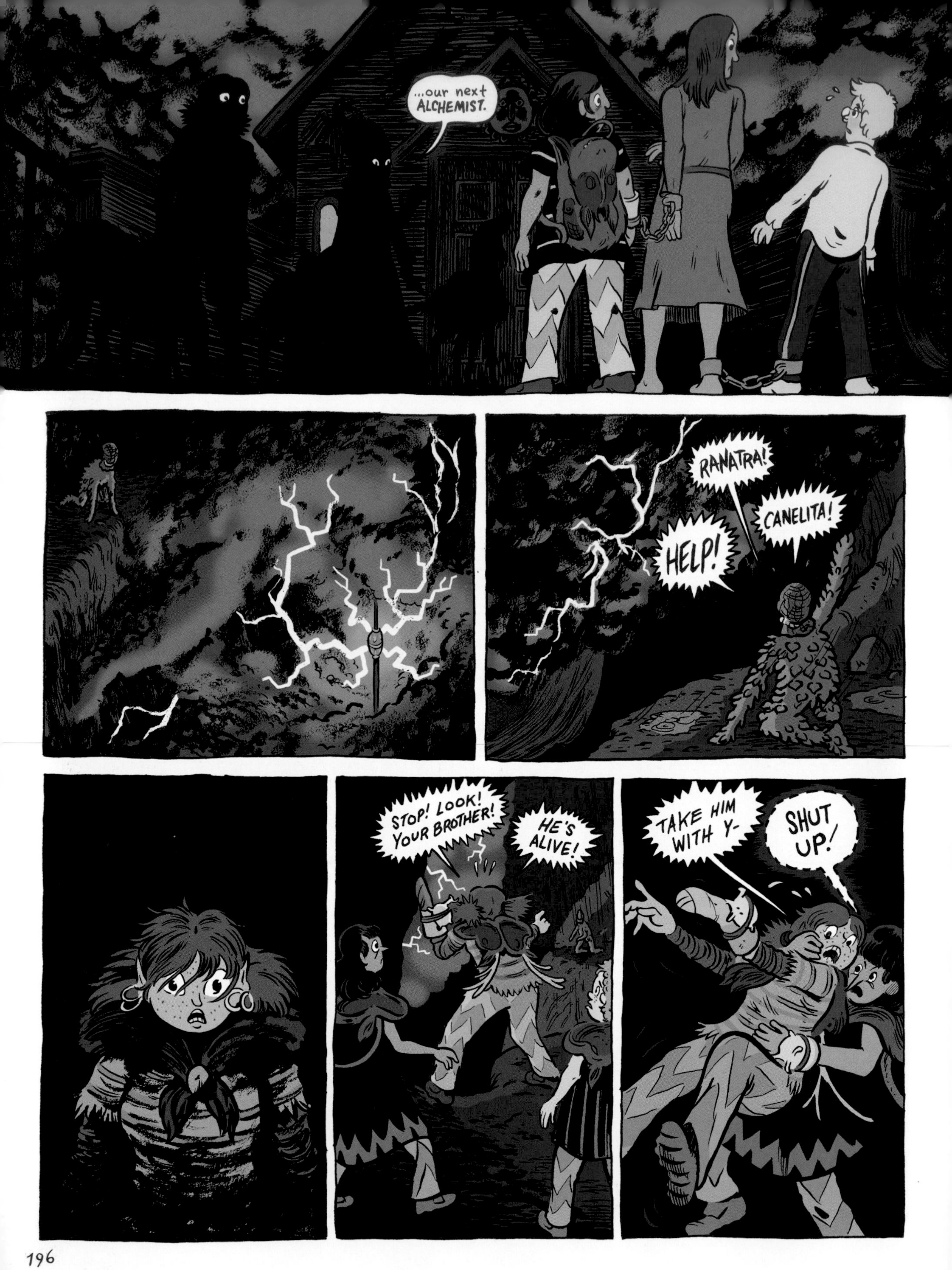
...our next ALCHEMIST.
RANATRA!
CANELITA!
HELP!
STOP! LOOK! YOUR BROTHER!
HE'S ALIVE!
TAKE HIM WITH Y-
SHUT UP!

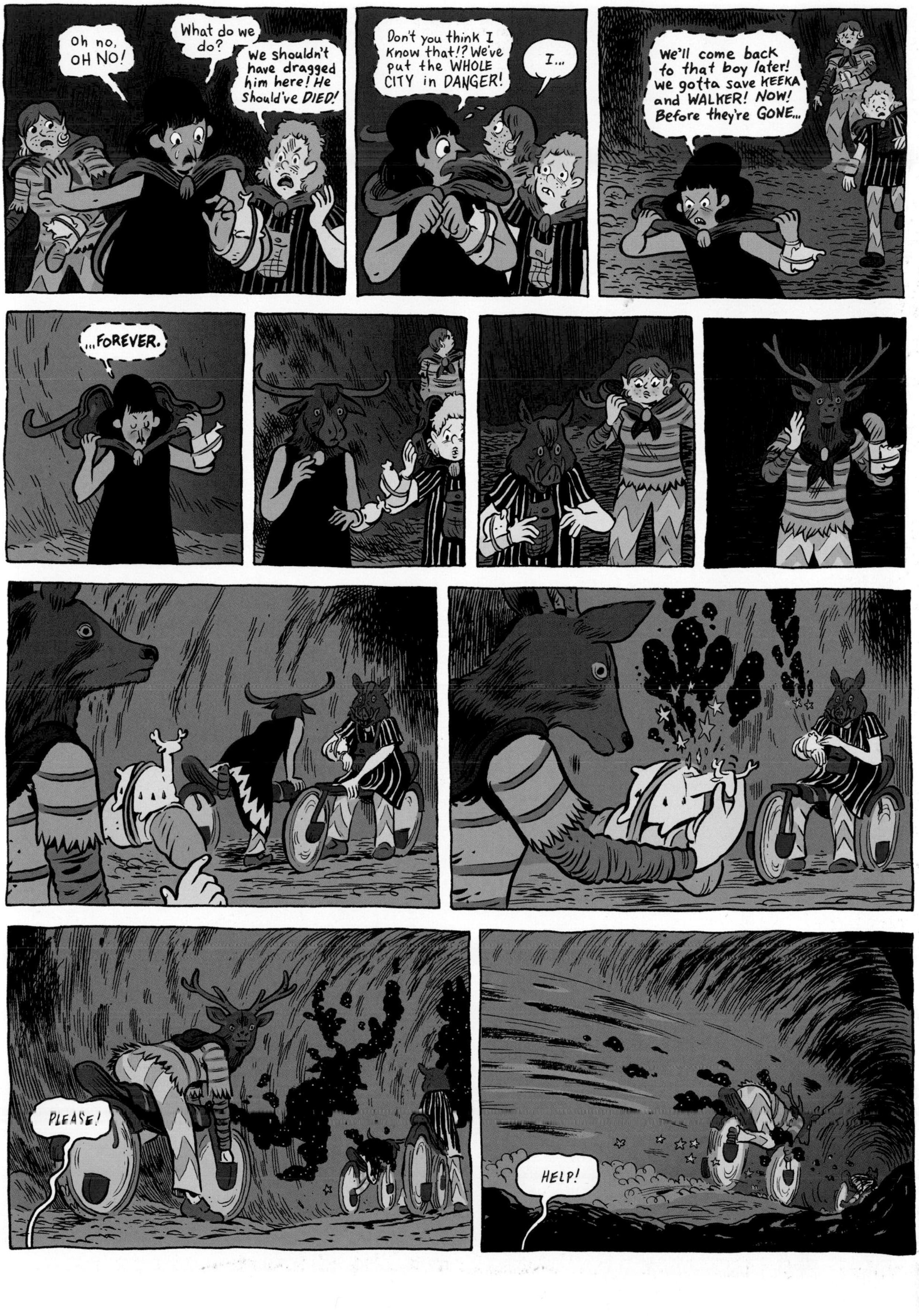

Oh no, OH NO!
What do we do?
We shouldn't have dragged him here! He should've DIED!
Don't you think I know that!? We've put the WHOLE CITY in DANGER!
I...
We'll come back to that boy later! We gotta save KEEKA and WALKER! NOW! Before they're GONE...
...FOREVER.
PLEASE!
HELP!

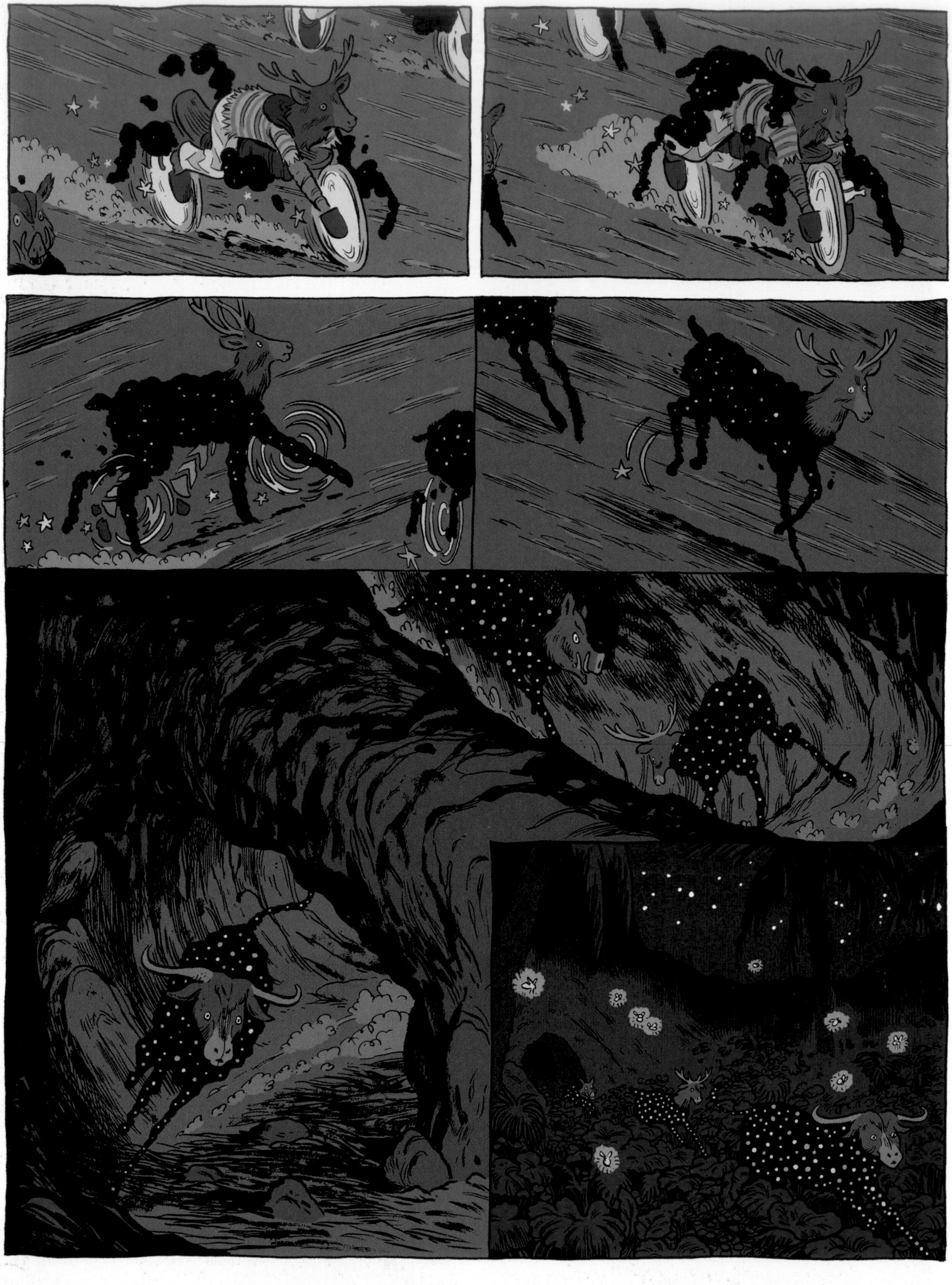

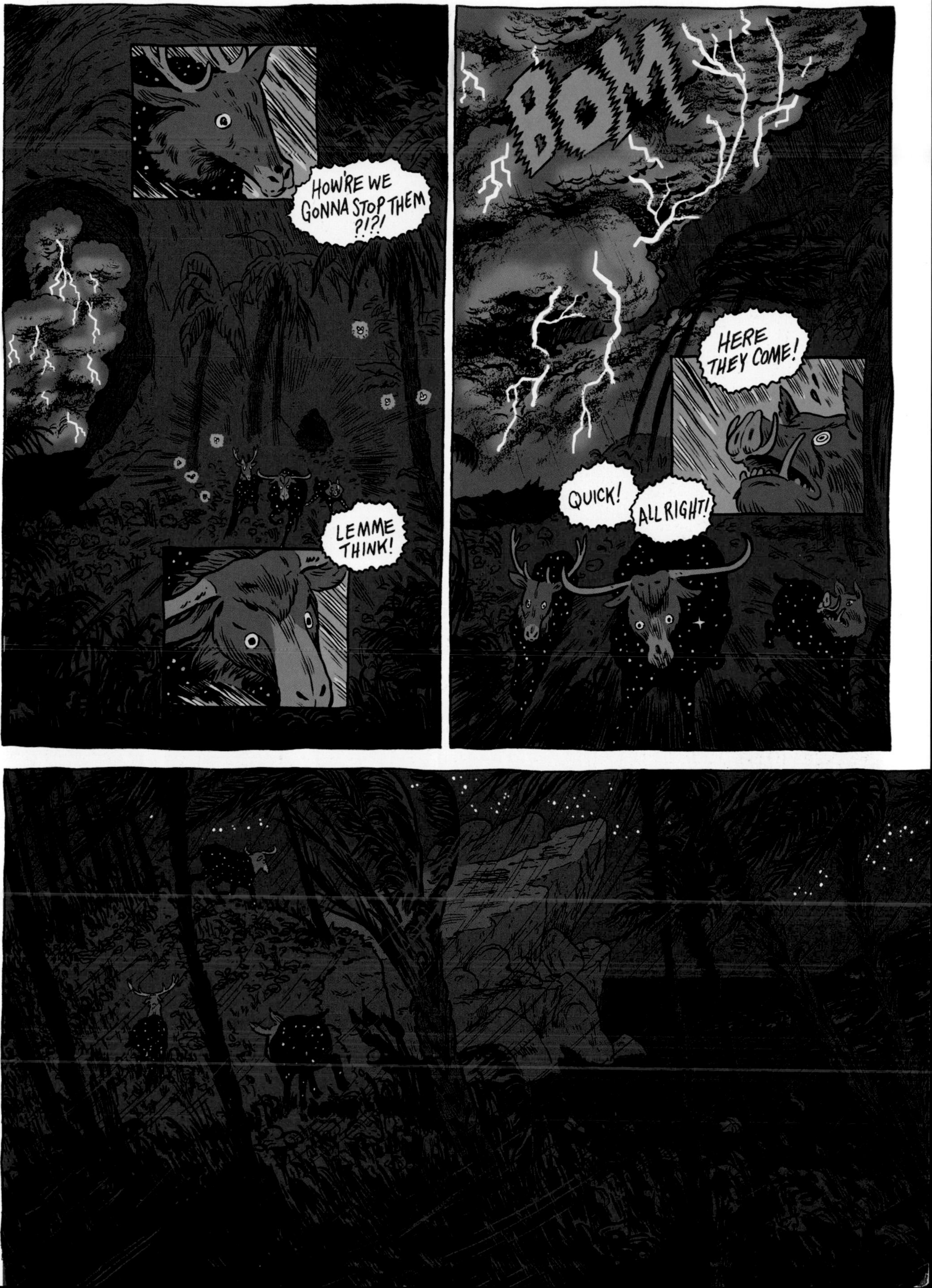
HOW'RE WE GONNA STOP THEM ?!?!
LEMME THINK!
BOOM
HERE THEY COME!
QUICK!
ALL RIGHT!

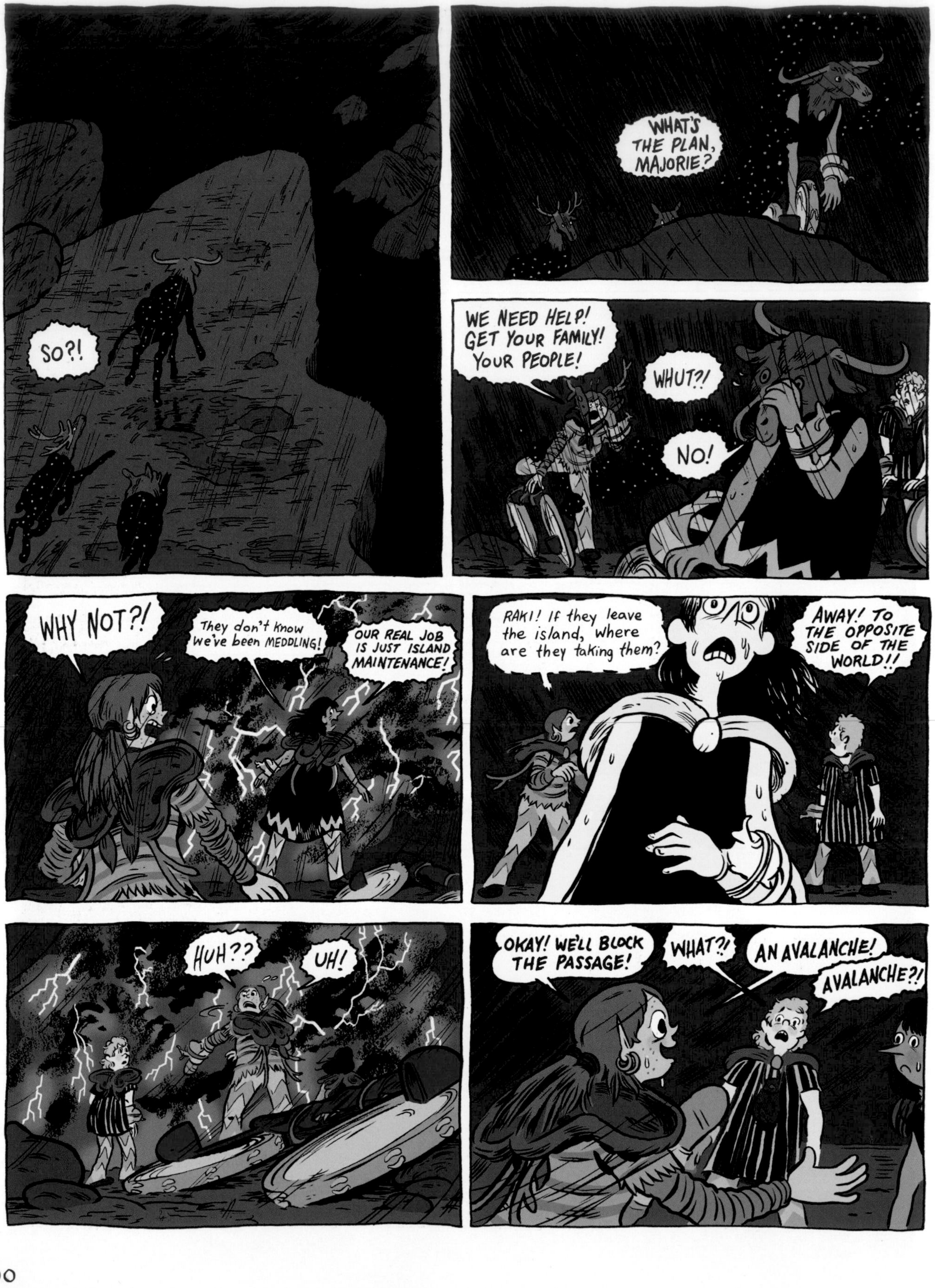
SO?!
WHAT'S THE PLAN, MAJORIE?
WE NEED HELP! GET YOUR FAMILY! YOUR PEOPLE!
WHUT?!
NO!
WHY NOT?!
They don't know we've been MEDDLING!
OUR REAL JOB IS JUST ISLAND MAINTENANCE!
RAKI! If they leave the island, where are they taking them?
AWAY! TO THE OPPOSITE SIDE OF THE WORLD!!
HUH??
UH!
OKAY! WE'LL BLOCK THE PASSAGE!
WHAT?!
AN AVALANCHE!
AVALANCHE?!

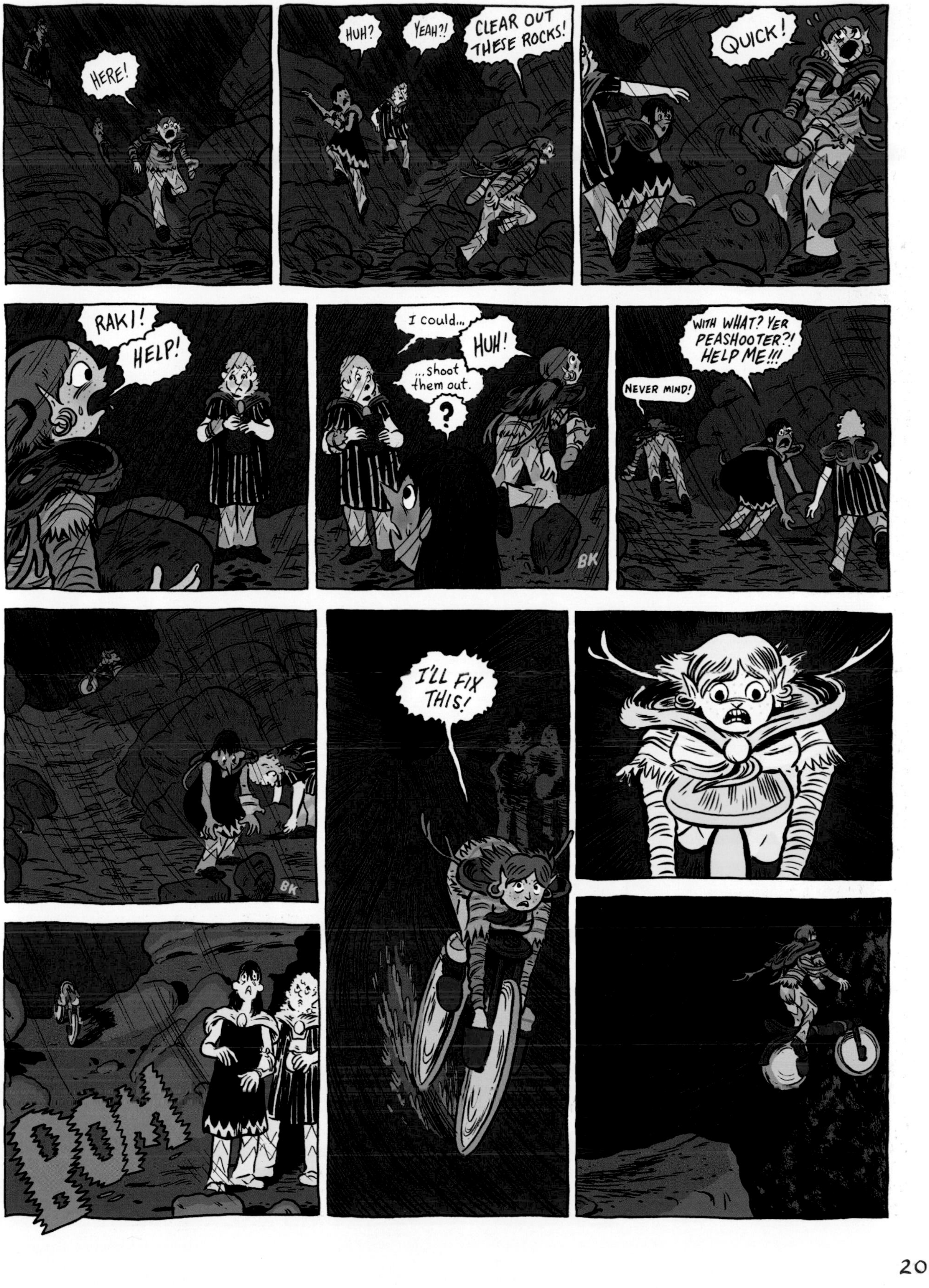
HERE!
HUH?
YEAH?!
CLEAR OUT THESE ROCKS!
QUICK!
RAKI!
HELP!
I could...
HUH!
...shoot them out.
?
WITH WHAT? YER PEASHOOTER?! HELP ME!!!
NEVER MIND!
BK
I'LL FIX THIS!
BOOM

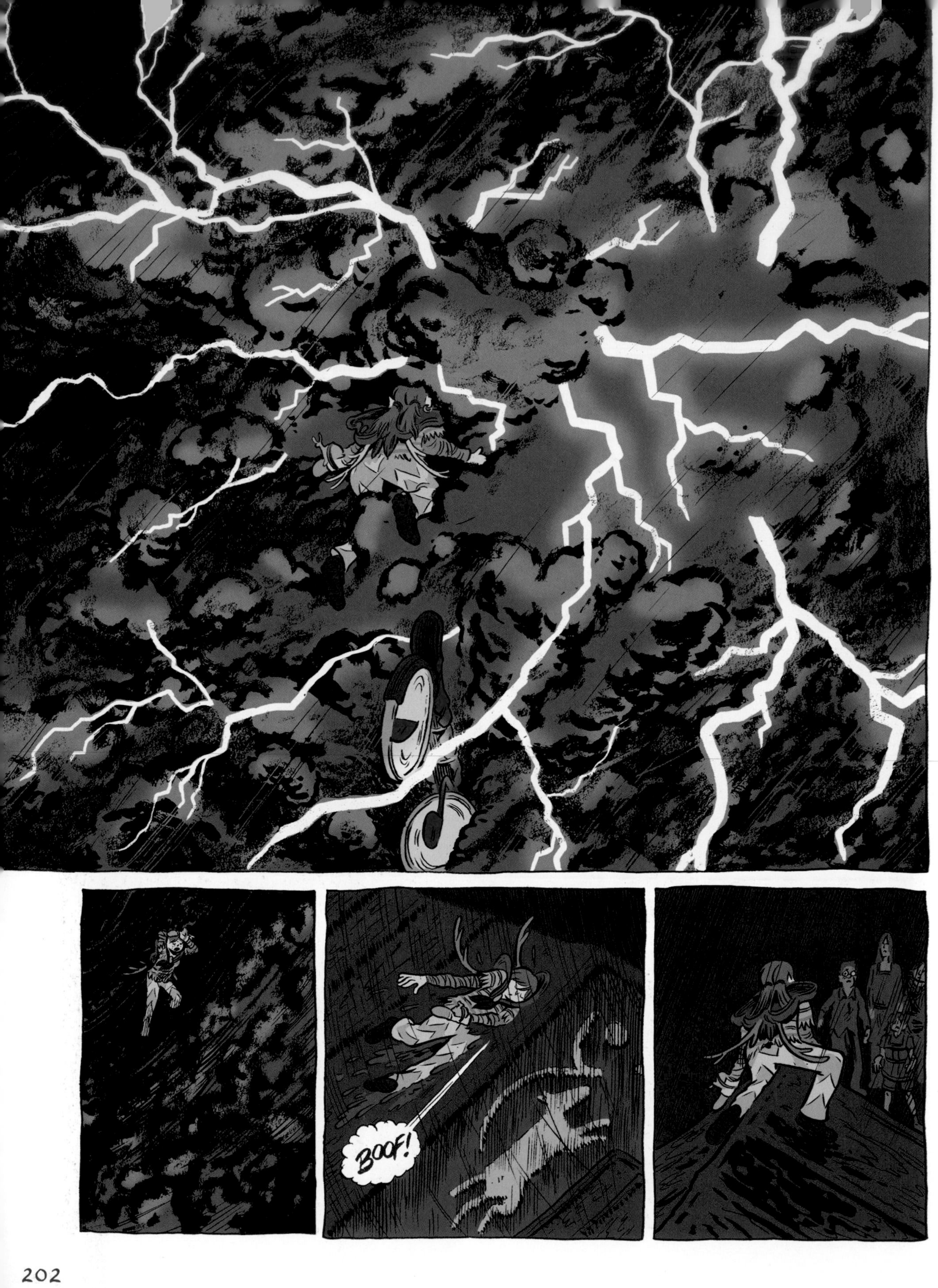
BOOF!

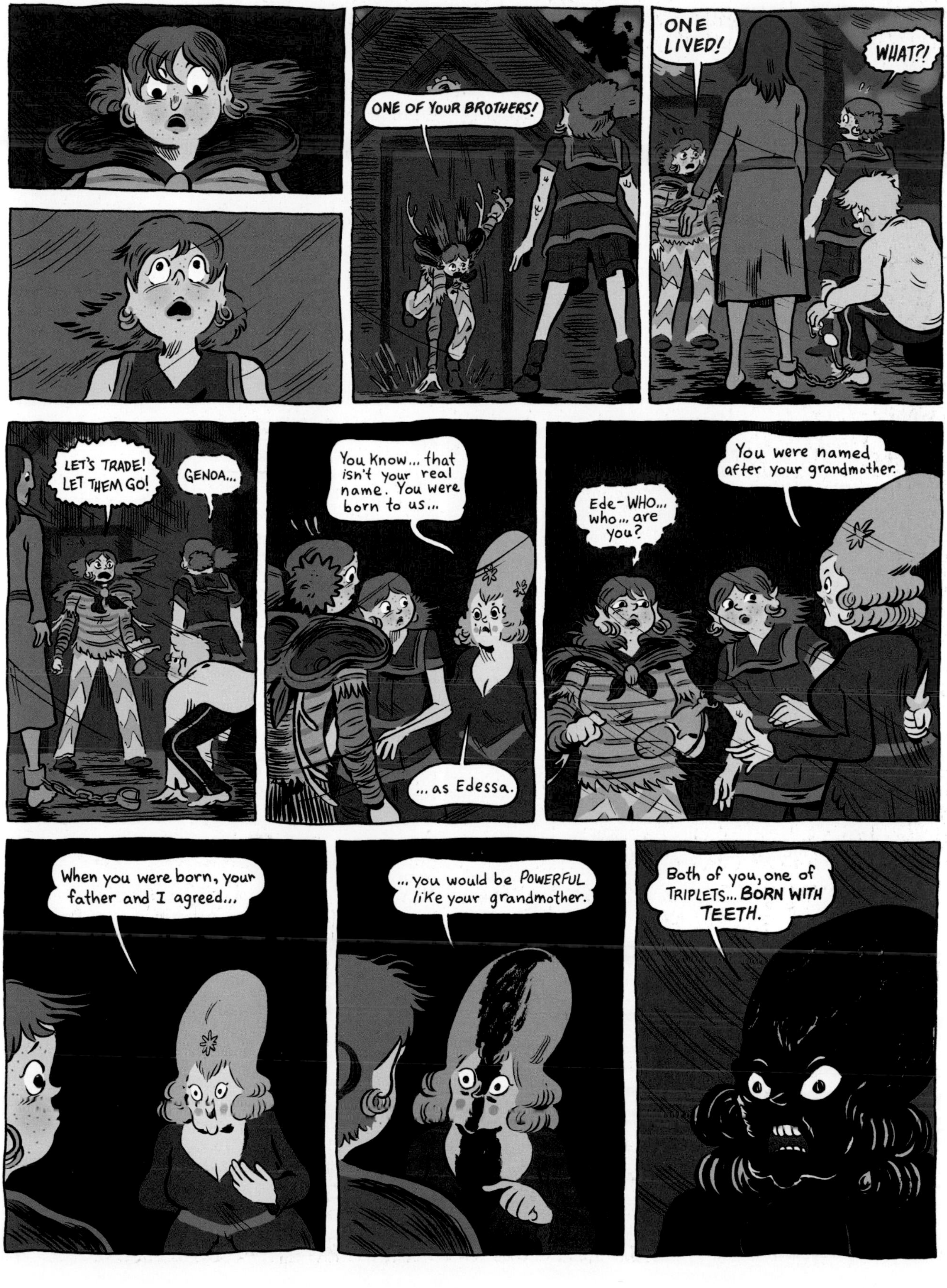

ONE OF YOUR BROTHERS!
ONE LIVED!
WHAT?!
LET'S TRADE! LET THEM GO!
GENOA...
You know... that isn't your real name. You were born to us...
...as Edessa.
Ede-WHO... who... are you?
You were named after your grandmother.
When you were born, your father and I agreed...
...you would be POWERFUL like your grandmother.
Both of you, one of TRIPLETS... BORN WITH TEETH.

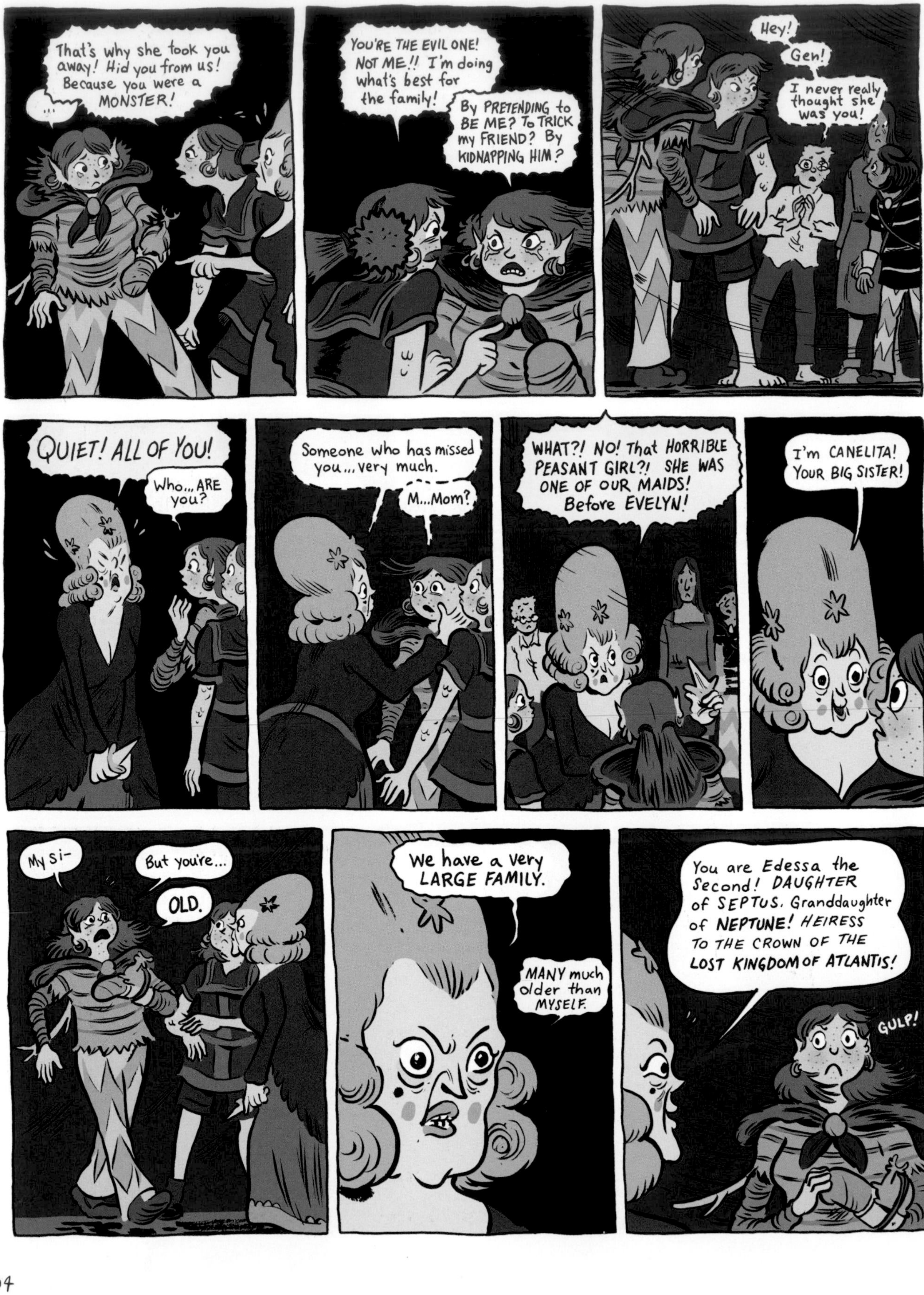
That's why she took you away! Hid you from us! Because you were a MONSTER!
...
YOU'RE THE EVIL ONE! NOT ME!! I'm doing what's best for the family!
By PRETENDING to BE ME? To TRICK my FRIEND? By KIDNAPPING HIM?
Hey!
Gen!
I never really thought she was you!
QUIET! ALL OF YOU!
Who... ARE you?
Someone who has missed you... very much.
M...Mom?
WHAT?! NO! That HORRIBLE PEASANT GIRL?! SHE WAS ONE OF OUR MAIDS! Before EVELYN!
I'm CANELITA! YOUR BIG SISTER!
My si-
But you're...
OLD.
We have a very LARGE FAMILY.
MANY much older than MYSELF.
You are Edessa the Second! DAUGHTER of SEPTUS, Granddaughter of NEPTUNE! HEIRESS TO THE CROWN OF THE LOST KINGDOM OF ATLANTIS!
GULP!

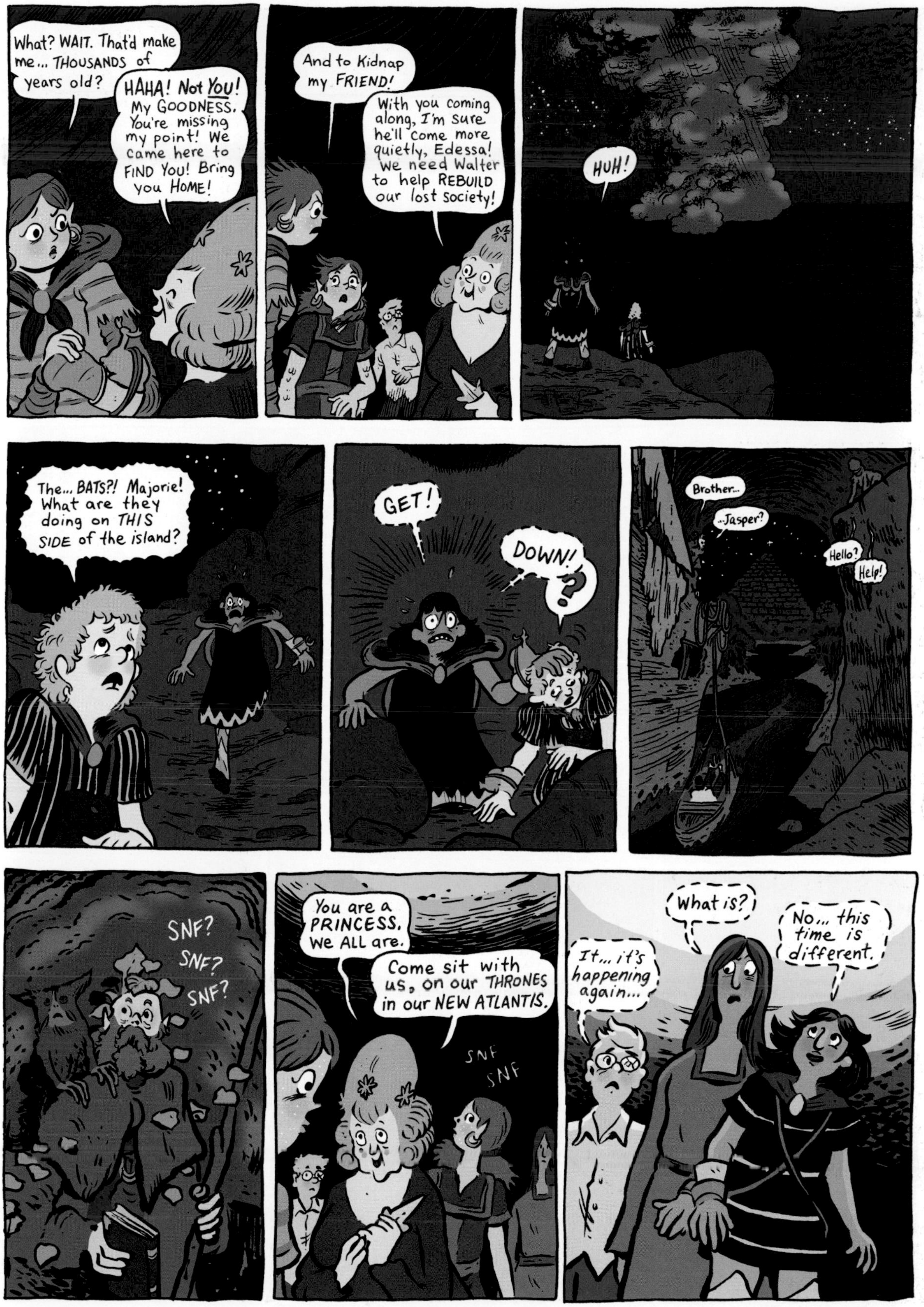

What? WAIT. That'd make me... THOUSANDS of years old?
HAHA! Not YOU! My GOODNESS. You're missing my point! We came here to FIND YOU! Bring you HOME!
And to Kidnap my FRIEND!
With you coming along, I'm sure he'll come more quietly, Edessa! We need Walter to help REBUILD our lost society!
HUH!
The... BATS?! Majorie! What are they doing on THIS SIDE of the island?
GET!
DOWN!
?
Brother...
...Jasper?
Hello?
Help!
SNF?
SNF?
SNF?
You are a PRINCESS. We ALL are.
Come sit with us, on our THRONES in our NEW ATLANTIS.
SNF
SNF
It... it's happening again...
What is?
No... this time is different.

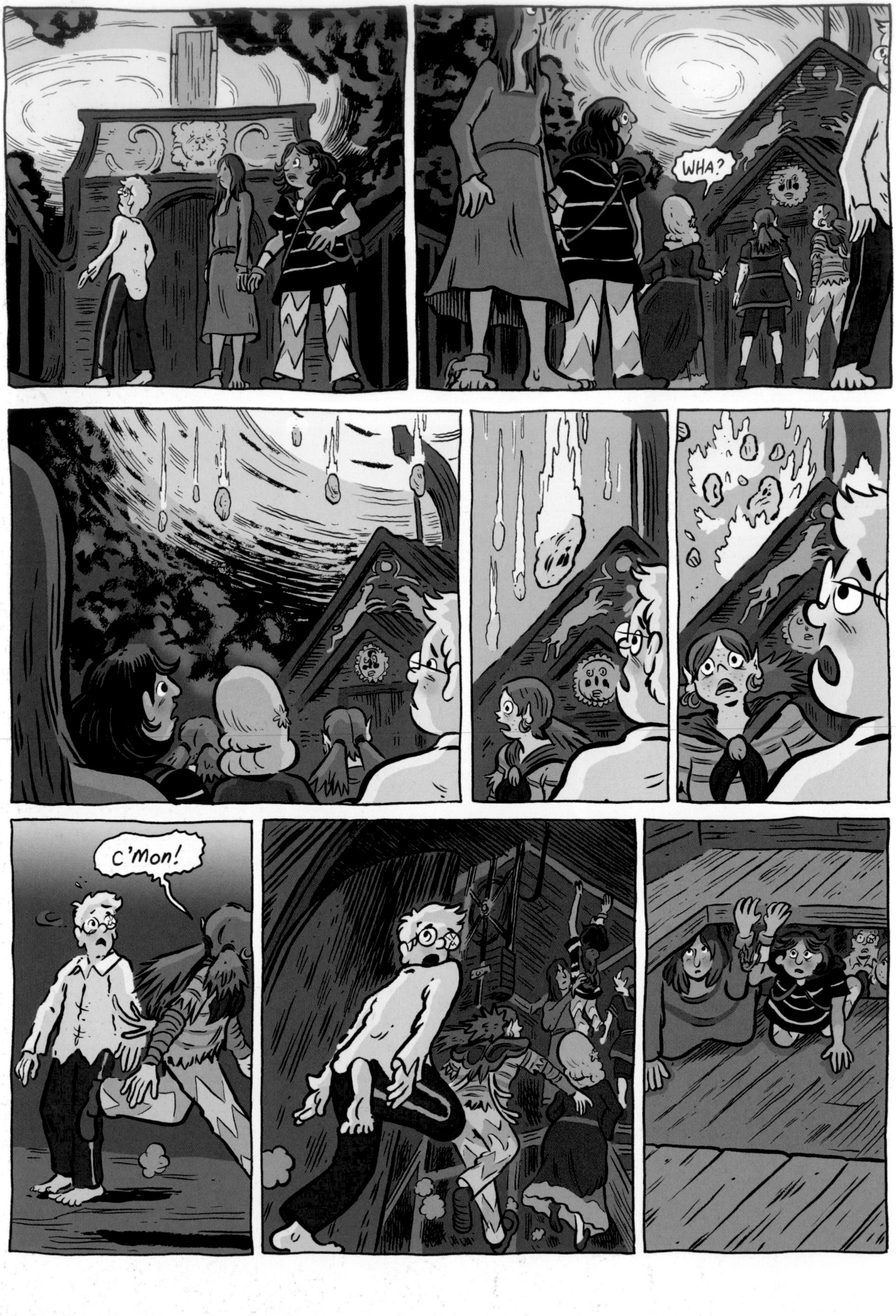
WHA?
C'Mon!

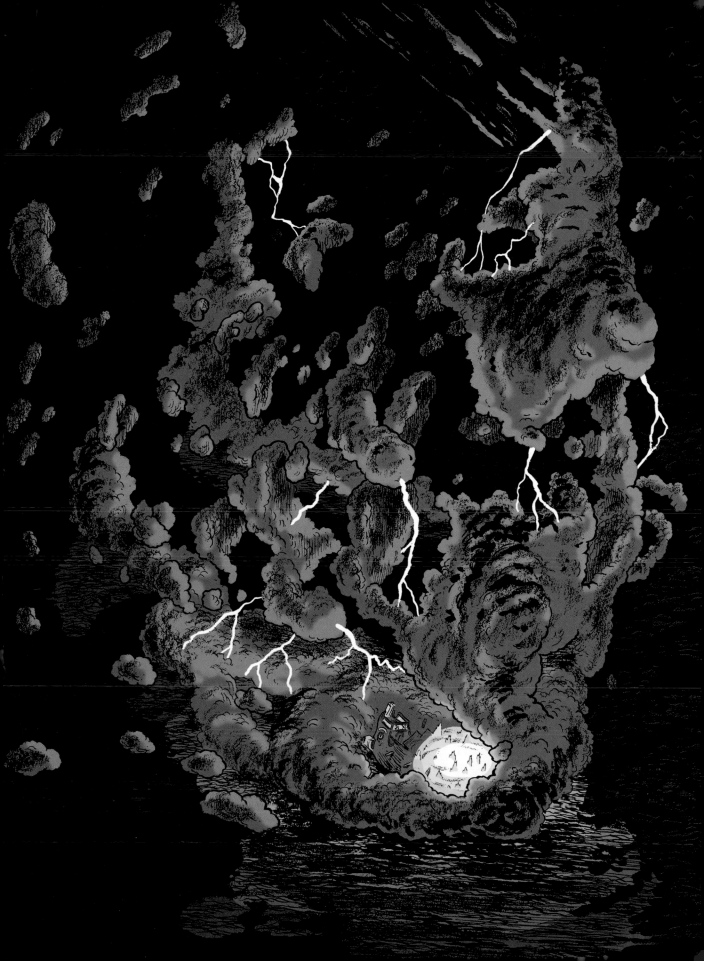

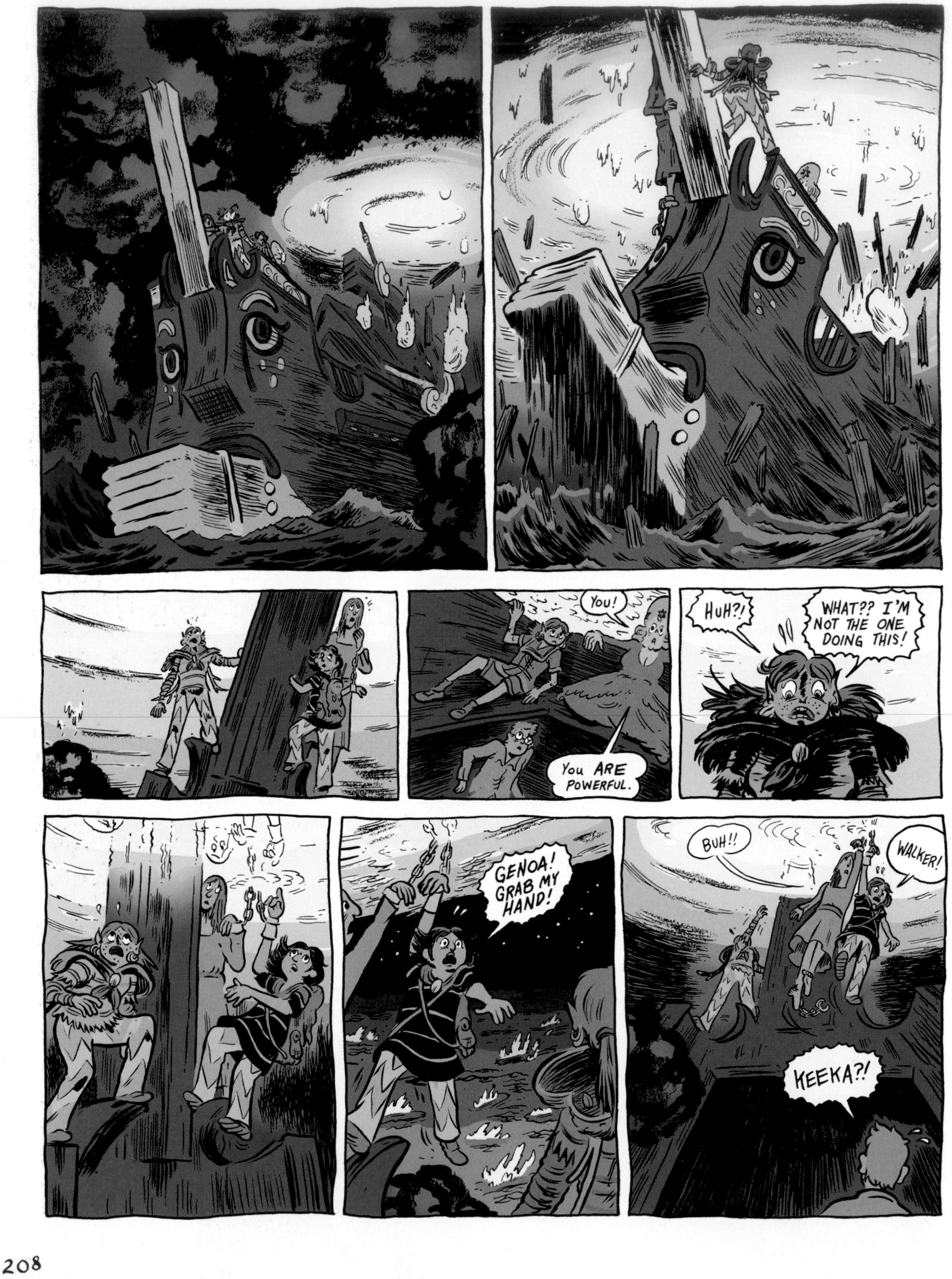
You!
You ARE POWERFUL.
HUH?!
WHAT?? I'M NOT THE ONE DOING THIS!
GENOA! GRAB MY HAND!
BUH!!
WALKER!
KEEKA?!

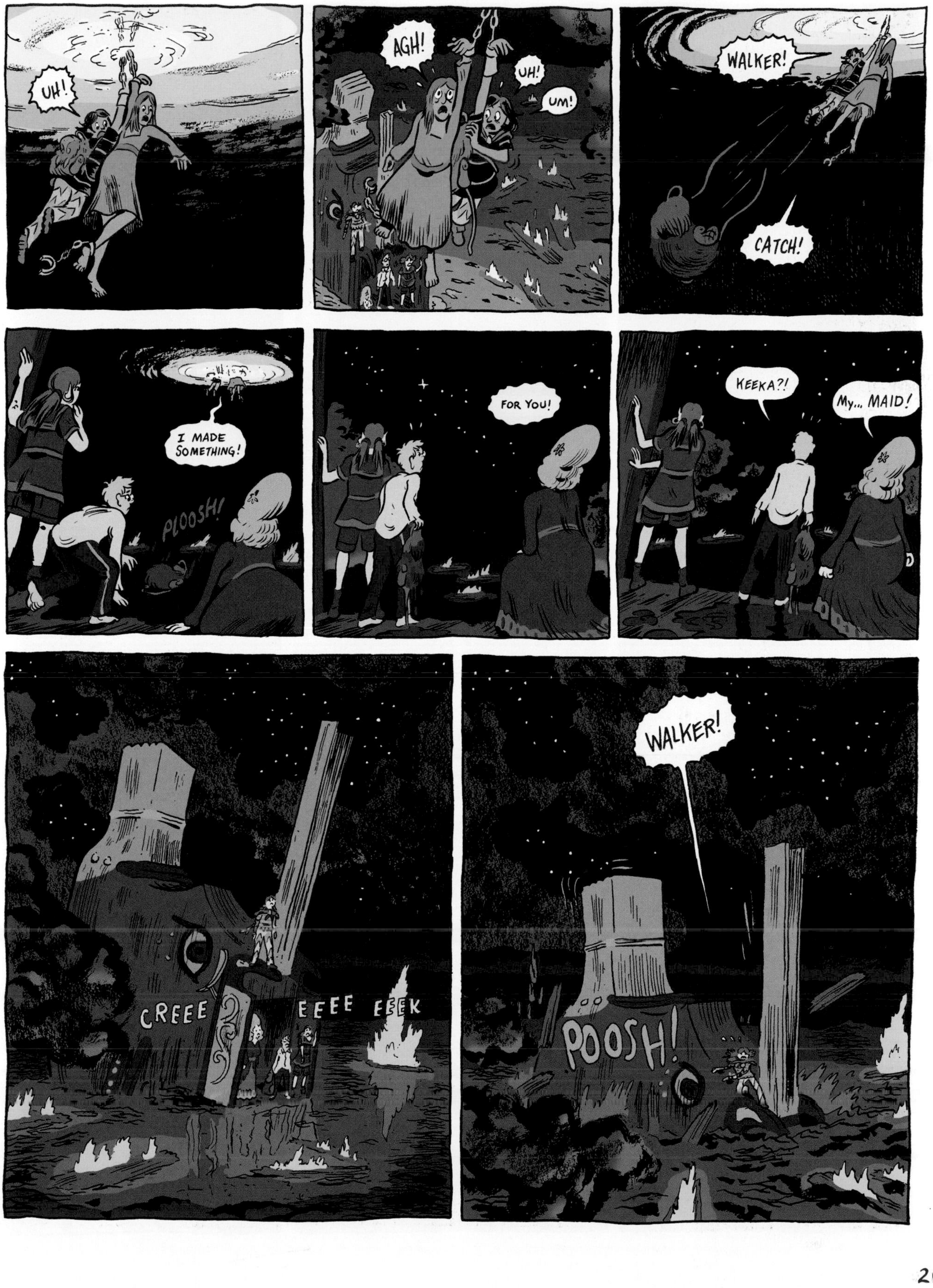
UH!
AGH!
UH!
UM!
WALKER!
CATCH!
I MADE SOMETHING!
PLOOSH!
FOR YOU!
KEEKA?!
MY... MAID!
CREEE
EEEE EEEK
WALKER!
POOSH!

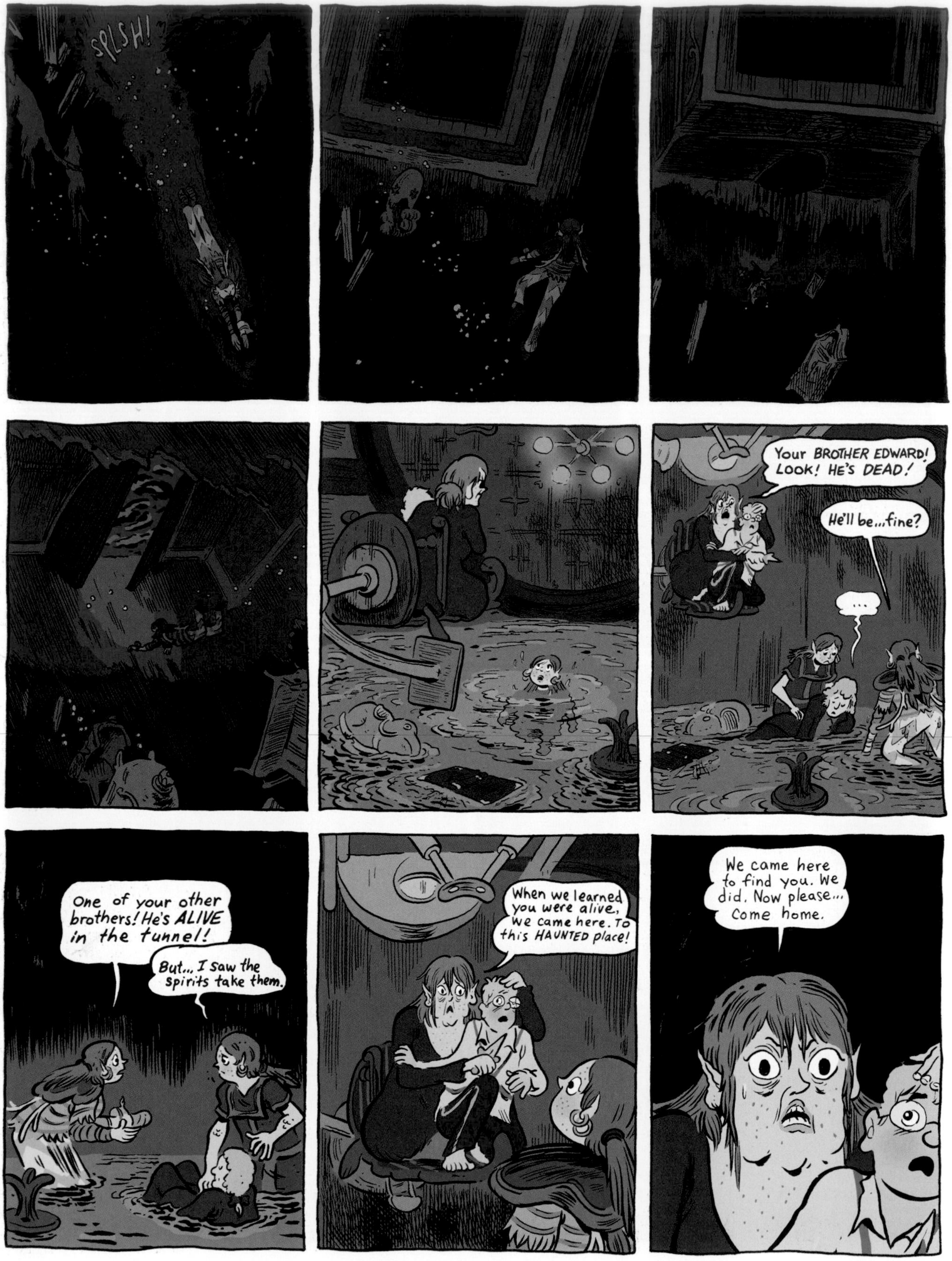
SPLSH!
Your BROTHER EDWARD! LOOK! HE'S DEAD!
He'll be...fine?
...
One of your other brothers! He's ALIVE in the tunnel!
But... I saw the spirits take them.
When we learned you were alive, we came here. To this HAUNTED place!
We came here to find you. We did. Now please... Come home.

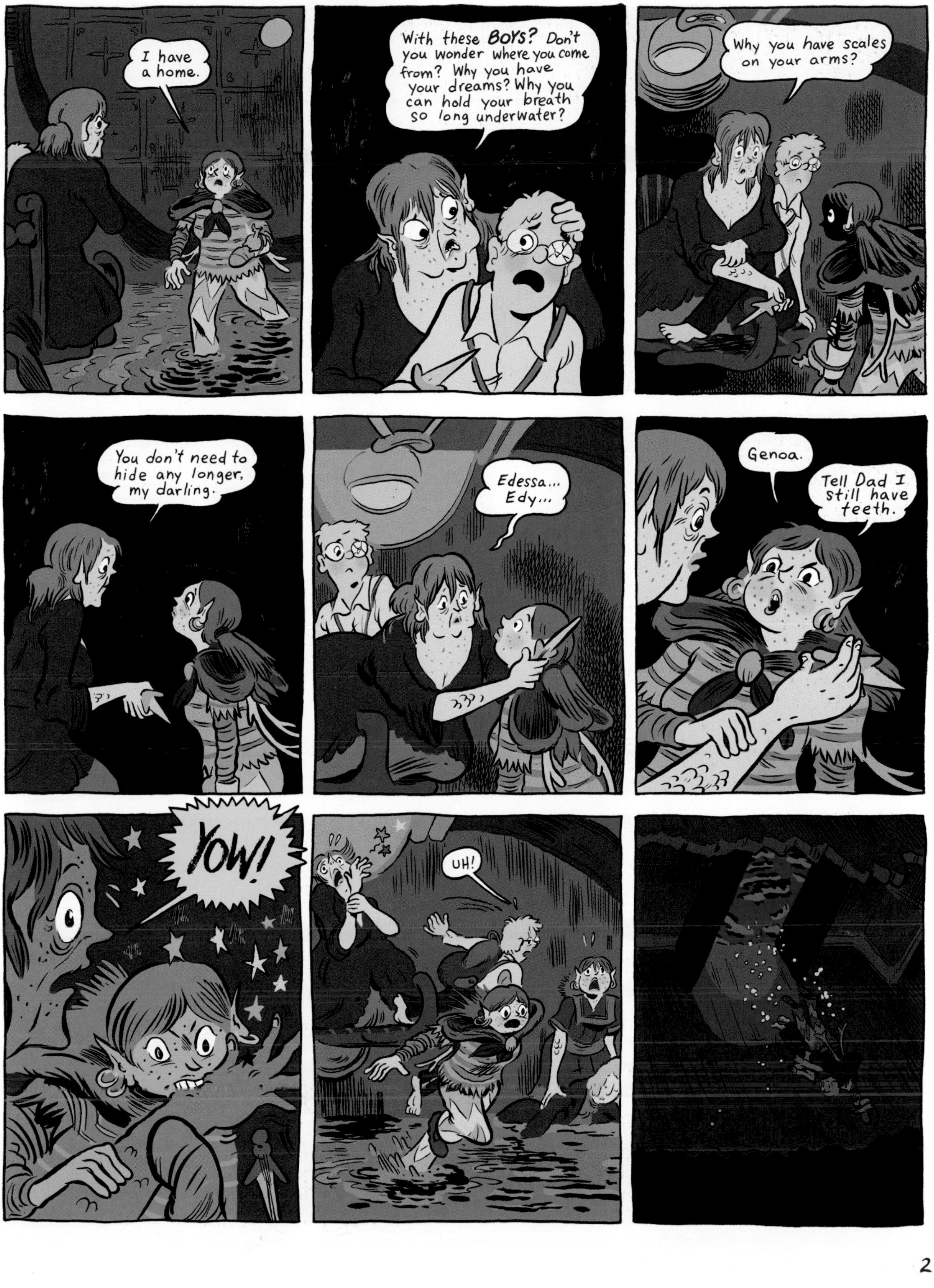
I have a home.
With these BOYS? Don't you wonder where you come from? Why you have your dreams? Why you can hold your breath so long underwater?
Why you have scales on your arms?
You don't need to hide any longer, my darling.
Edessa... Edy...
Genoa.
Tell Dad I still have teeth.
YOW!
UH!

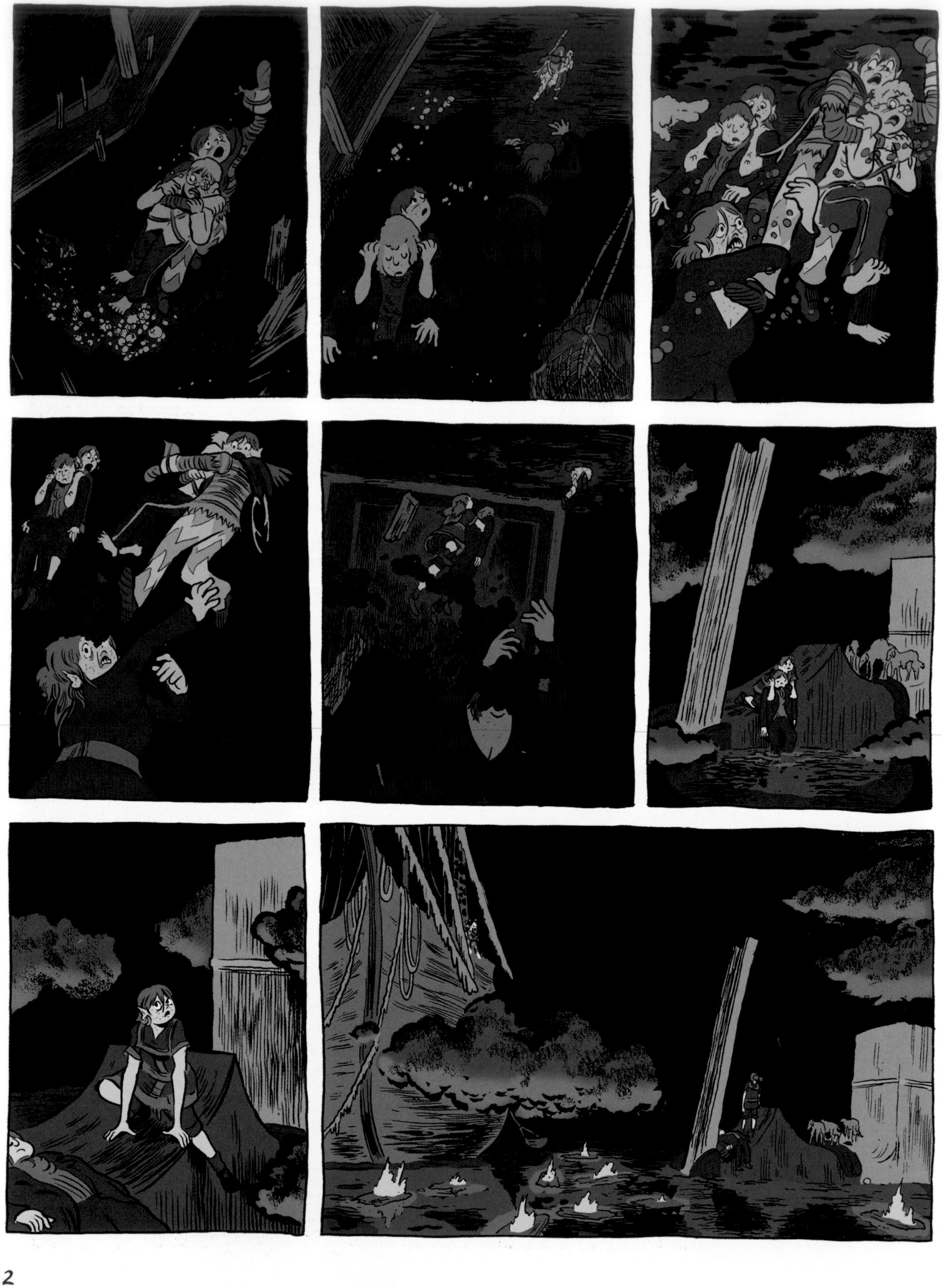

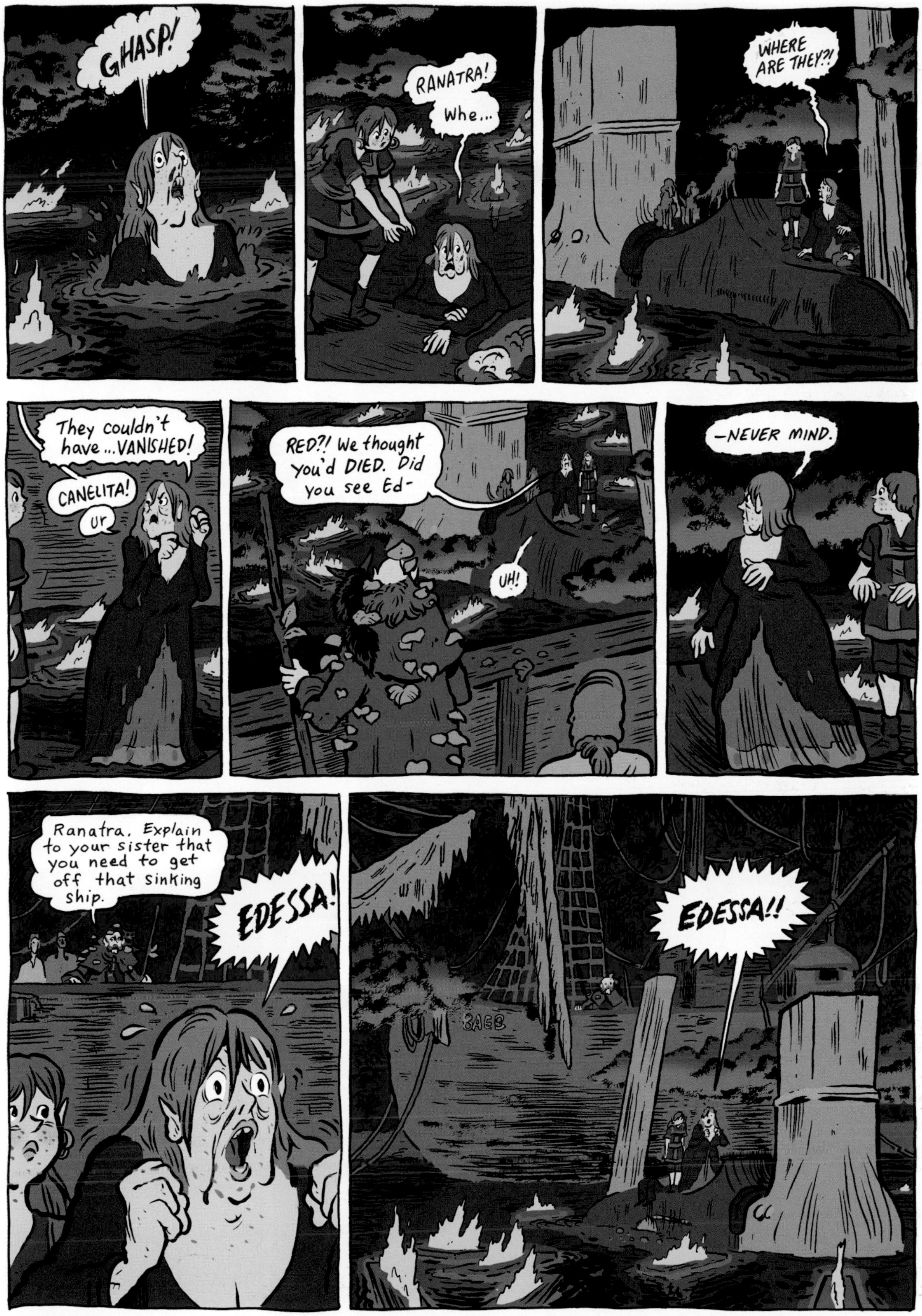
GHASP!
RANATRA!
Whe...
WHERE ARE THEY?!
They couldn't have... VANISHED!
CANELITA!
Ur
RED?! We thought you'd DIED. Did you see Ed-
UH!
—NEVER MIND.
Ranatra. Explain to your sister that you need to get off that sinking ship.
EDESSA!
EDESSA!!
BAEB

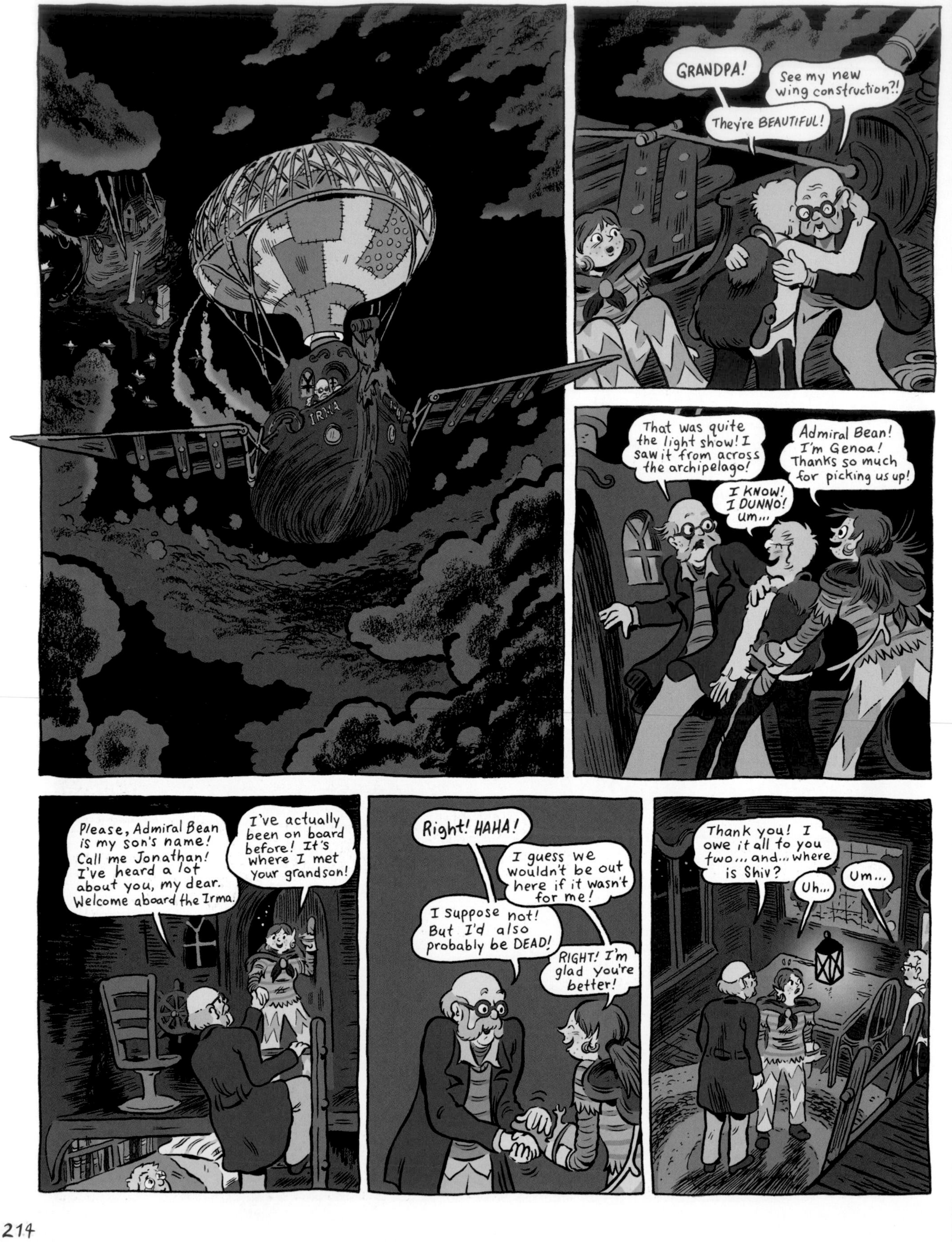
GRANDPA!
See my new wing construction?!
They're BEAUTIFUL!
That was quite the light show! I saw it from across the archipelago!
Admiral Bean! I'm Genoa! Thanks so much for picking us up!
I KNOW! I DUNNO! Um...
Please, Admiral Bean is my son's name! Call me Jonathan! I've heard a lot about you, my dear. Welcome aboard the Irma.
I've actually been on board before! It's where I met your grandson!
Right! HAHA!
I guess we wouldn't be out here if it wasn't for me!
I suppose not! But I'd also probably be DEAD!
RIGHT! I'm glad you're better!
Thank you! I owe it all to you two... and... where is Shiv?
Uh...
Um...

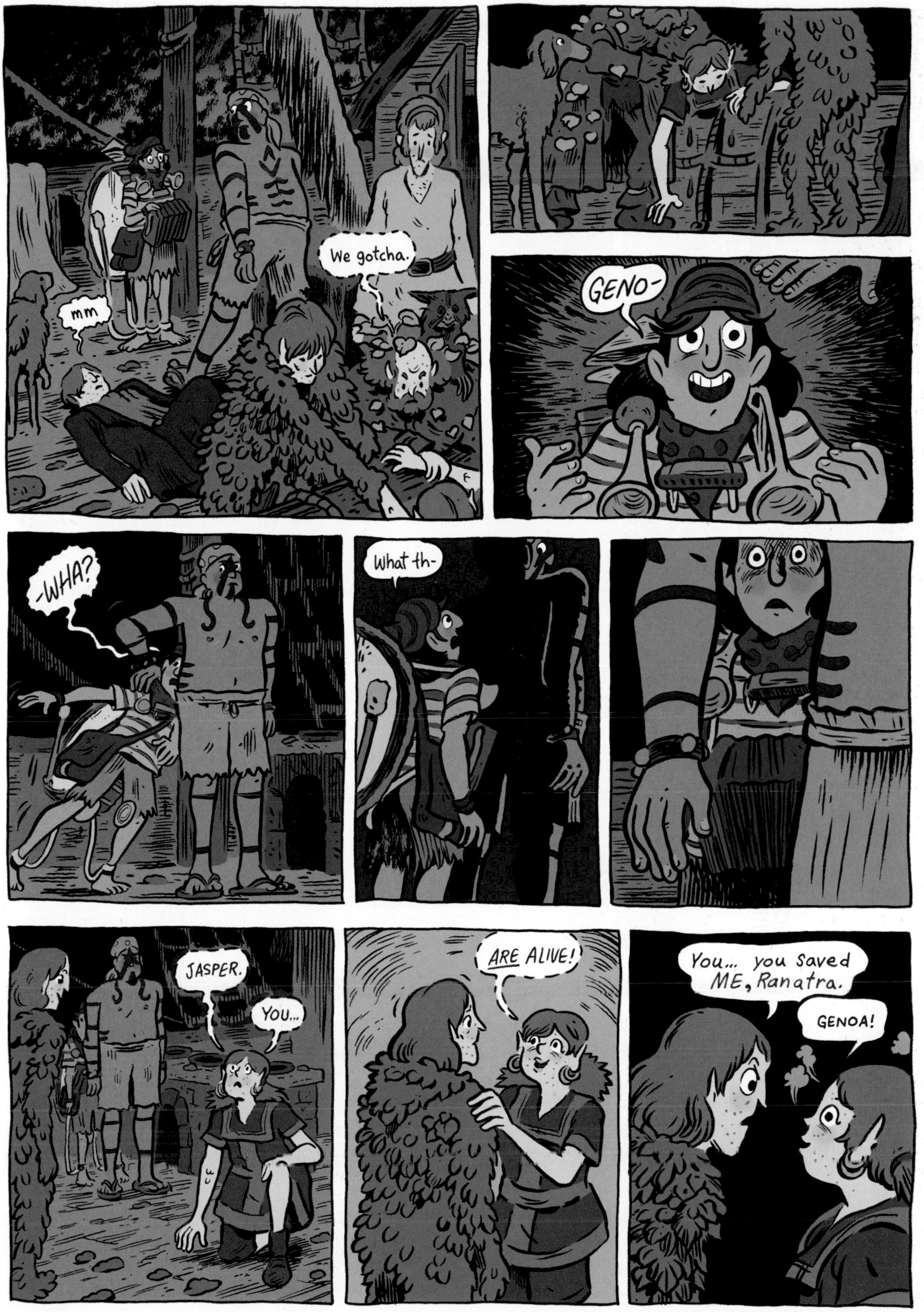
We gotcha.
mm
GENO-
-WHA?
What th-
JASPER.
YOU...
ARE ALIVE!
You... you saved ME, Ranatra.
GENOA!

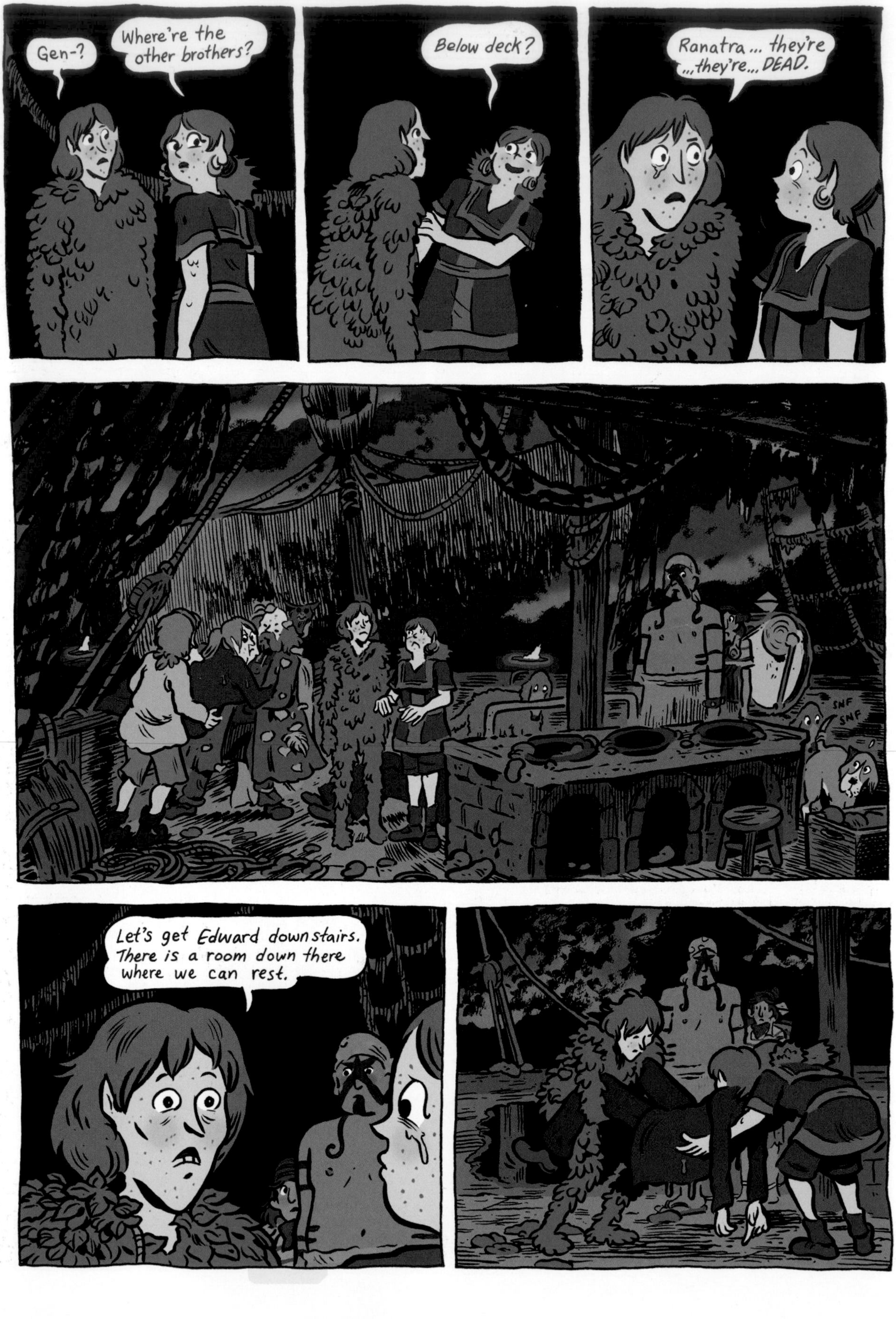
Gen-?
Where're the other brothers?
Below deck?
Ranatra... they're ...they're... DEAD.
SNF SNF
Let's get Edward downstairs. There is a room down there where we can rest.

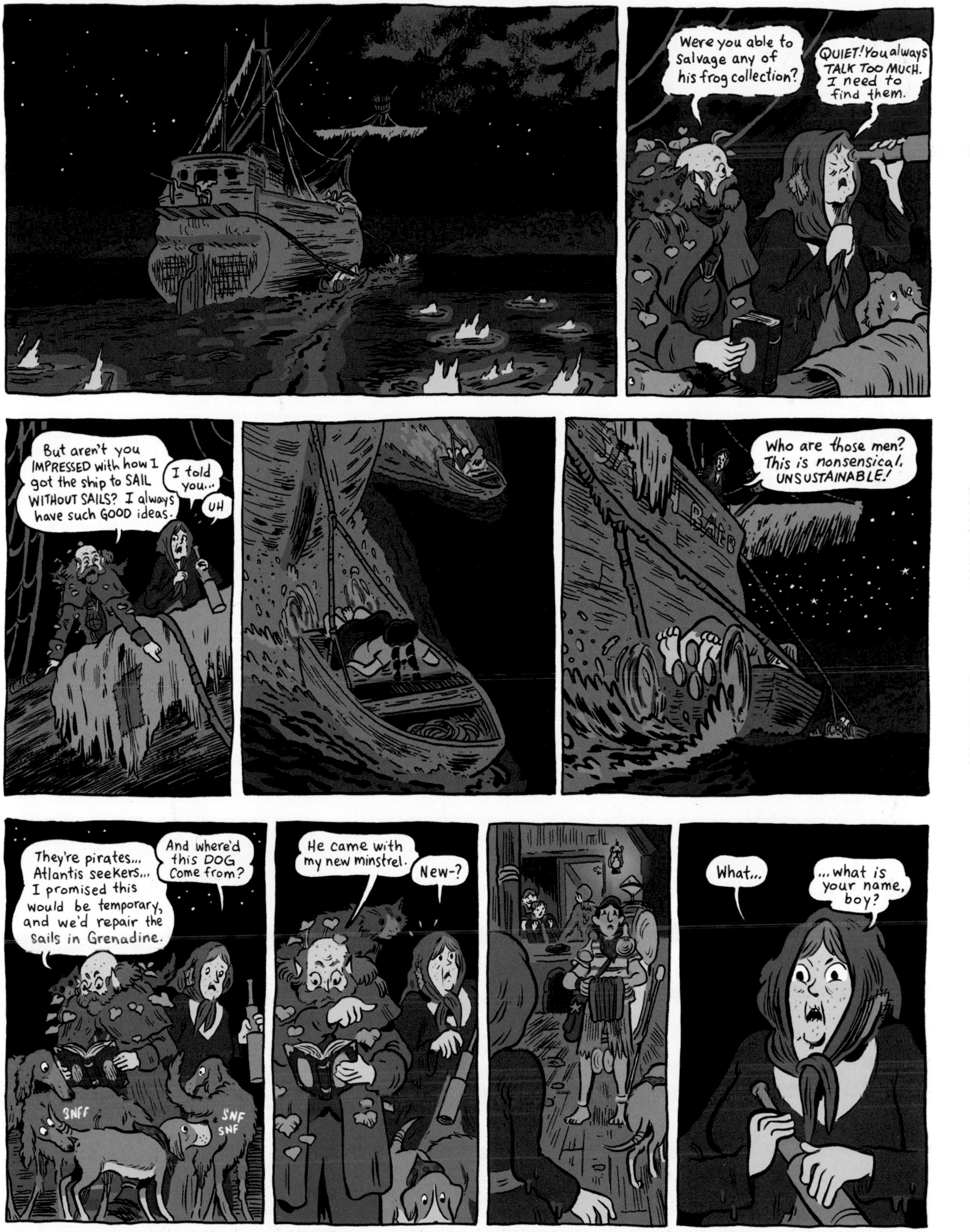
Were you able to salvage any of his frog collection?
QUIET! You always TALK TOO MUCH. I need to find them.
But aren't you IMPRESSED with how I got the ship to SAIL WITHOUT SAILS? I always have such GOOD ideas.
I told you...
UH
Who are those men? This is nonsensical. UNSUSTAINABLE!
They're pirates... Atlantis seekers... I promised this would be temporary, and we'd repair the sails in Grenadine.
And where'd this DOG come from?
SNFF
SNF SNF
He came with my new minstrel.
New-?
What...
...what is your name, boy?

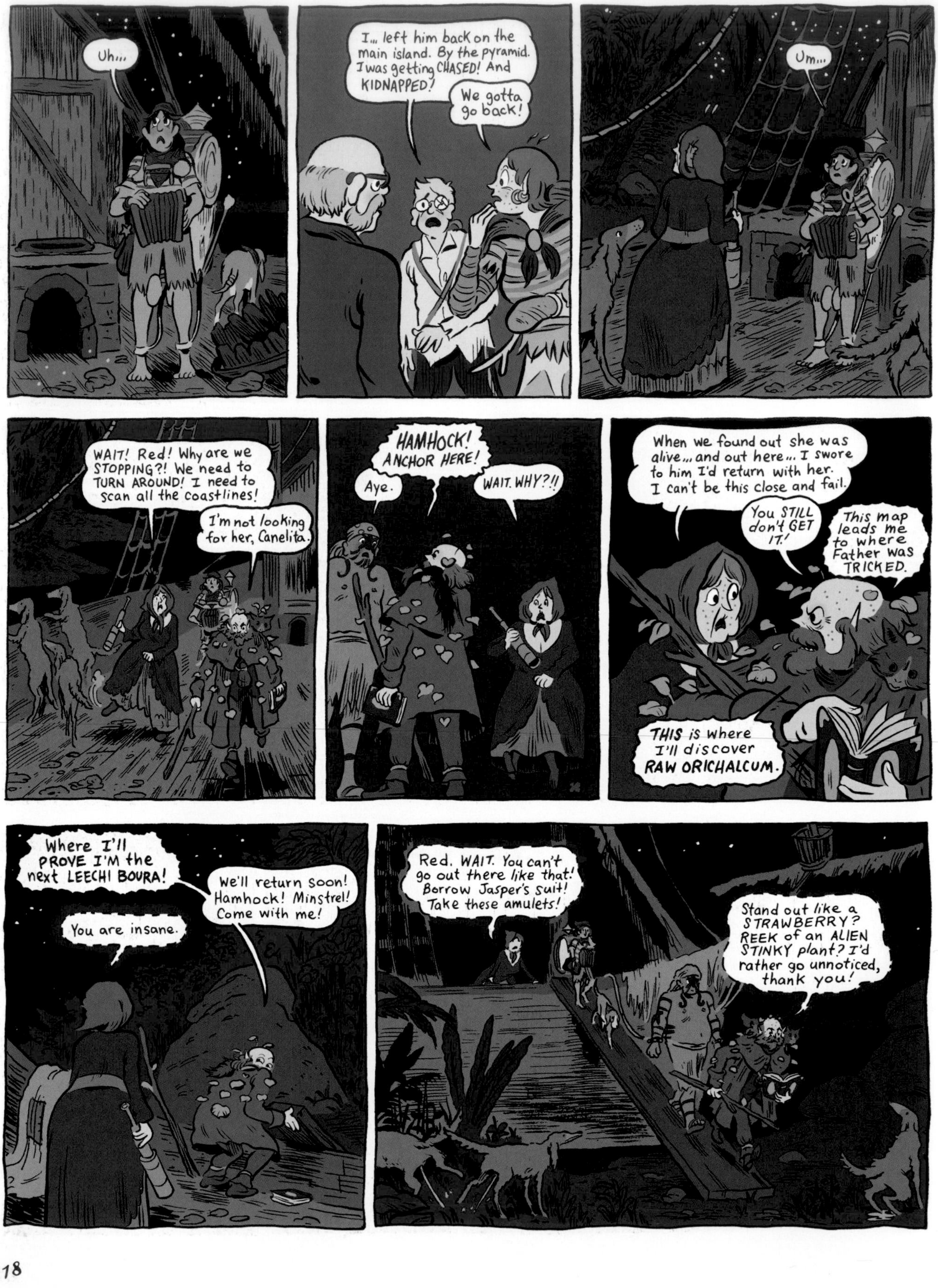
Uh...
I... left him back on the main island. By the pyramid. I was getting CHASED! And KIDNAPPED!
We gotta go back!
Um...
WAIT! Red! Why are we STOPPING?! We need to TURN AROUND! I need to scan all the coastlines!
I'm not looking for her, Canelita.
HAMHOCK! ANCHOR HERE!
Aye.
WAIT. WHY?!!
When we found out she was alive... and out here... I swore to him I'd return with her. I can't be this close and fail.
You STILL don't GET IT!
This map leads me to where Father was TRICKED.
THIS is where I'll discover RAW ORICHALCUM.
Where I'll PROVE I'M the next LEECHI BOURA!
We'll return soon! Hamhock! Minstrel! Come with me!
You are insane.
Red. WAIT. You can't go out there like that! Borrow Jasper's suit! Take these amulets!
Stand out like a STRAWBERRY? REEK of an ALIEN STINKY plant? I'd rather go unnoticed, thank you!

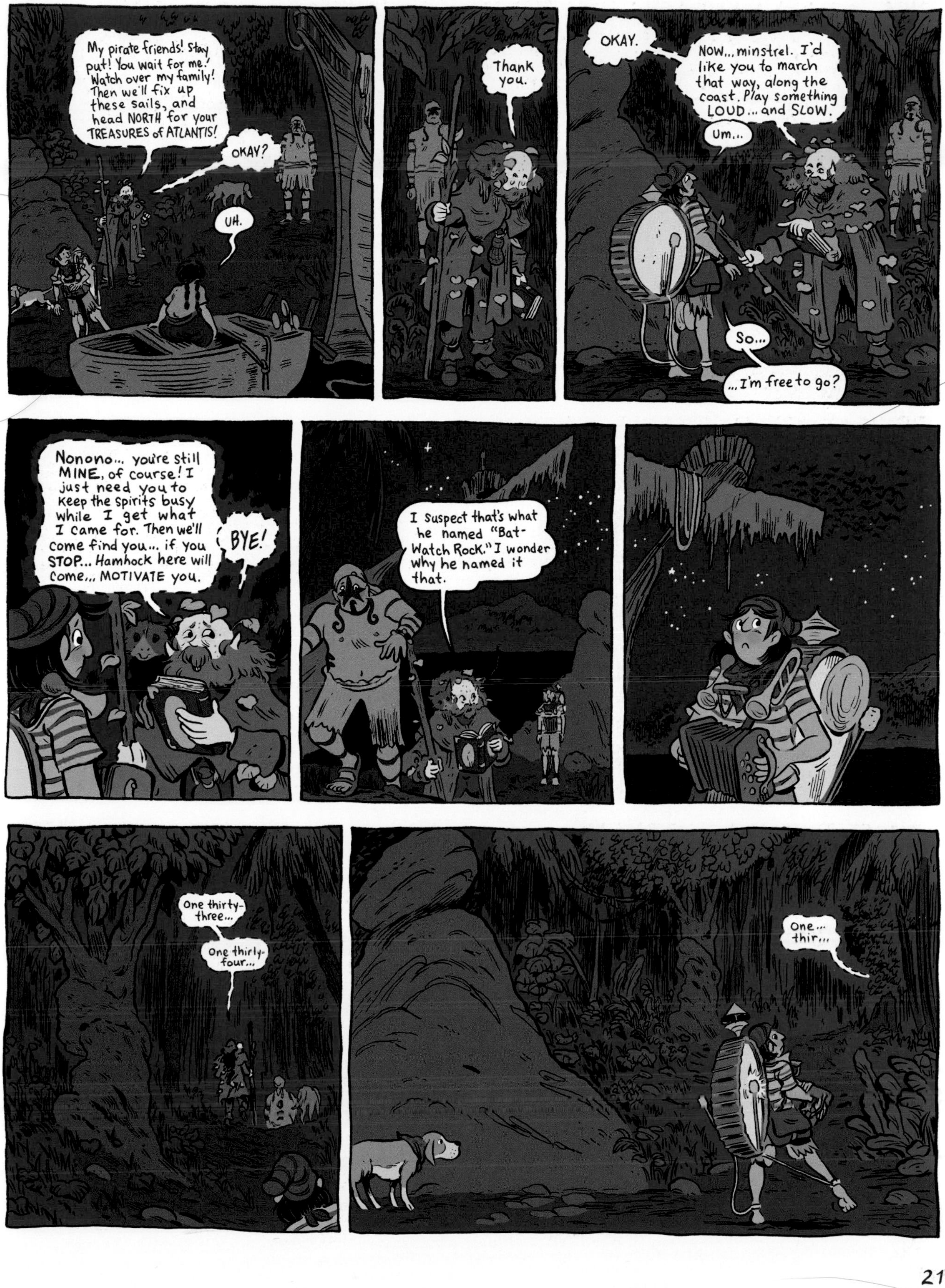
My pirate friends! Stay put! You wait for me! Watch over my family! Then we'll fix up these sails, and head NORTH for your TREASURES of ATLANTIS!
OKAY?
UH.
Thank you.
OKAY.
NOW... minstrel. I'd like you to march that way, along the coast. Play something LOUD... and SLOW.
Um...
So...
...I'm free to go?
Nonono... you're still MINE, of course! I just need you to keep the spirits busy while I get what I came for. Then we'll come find you... if you STOP... Hamhock here will come... MOTIVATE you.
BYE!
I suspect that's what he named "Bat-Watch Rock." I wonder why he named it that.
One thirty-three...
One thirty-four...
One... thir...

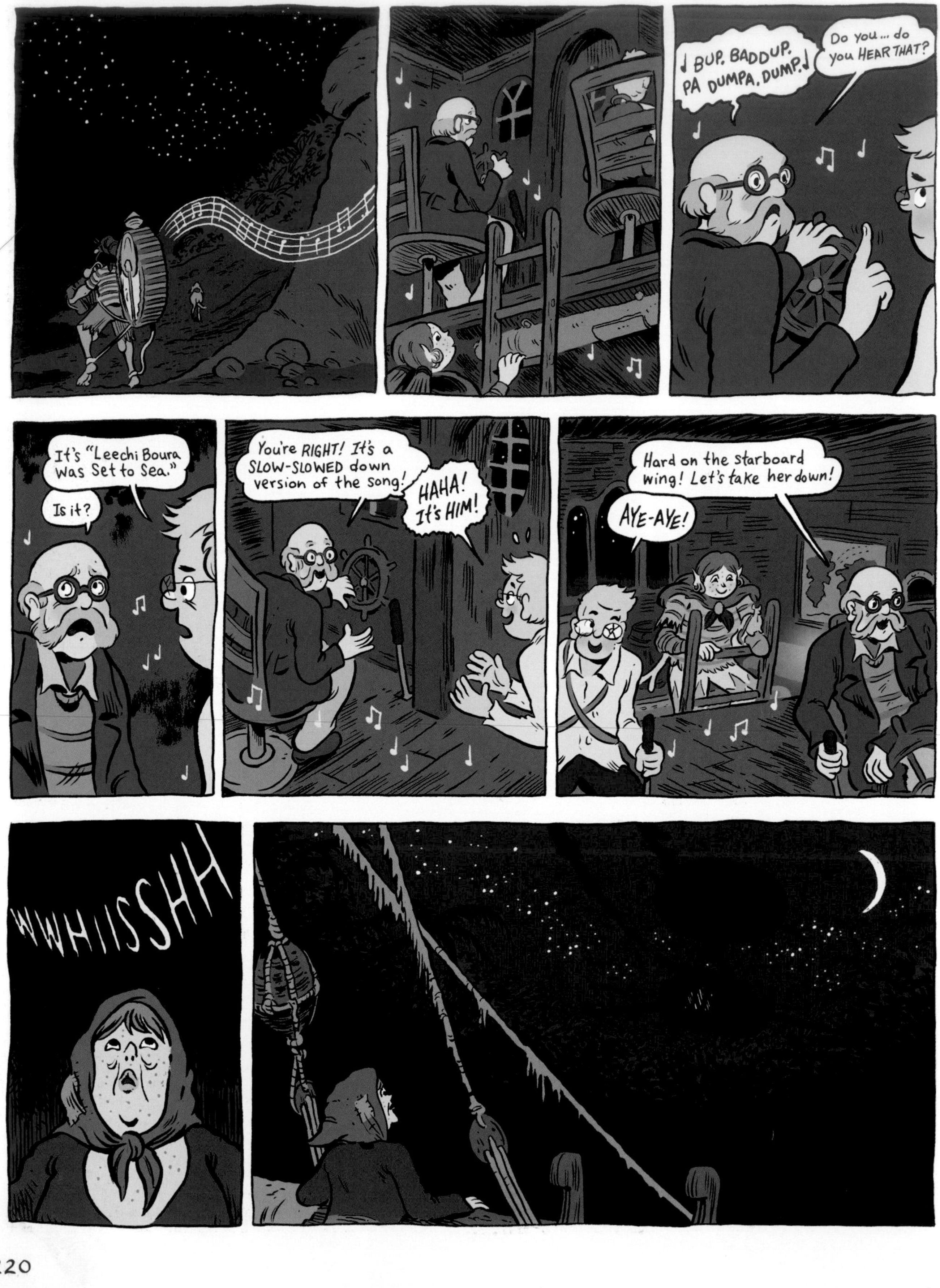
BUP. BADDUP. PA DUMPA. DUMP.
Do you... do you HEAR THAT?
It's "Leechi Boura Was Set to Sea."
Is it?
You're RIGHT! It's a SLOW-SLOWED down version of the song!
HAHA! It's HIM!
Hard on the starboard wing! Let's take her down!
AYE-AYE!
WWHIISSHH

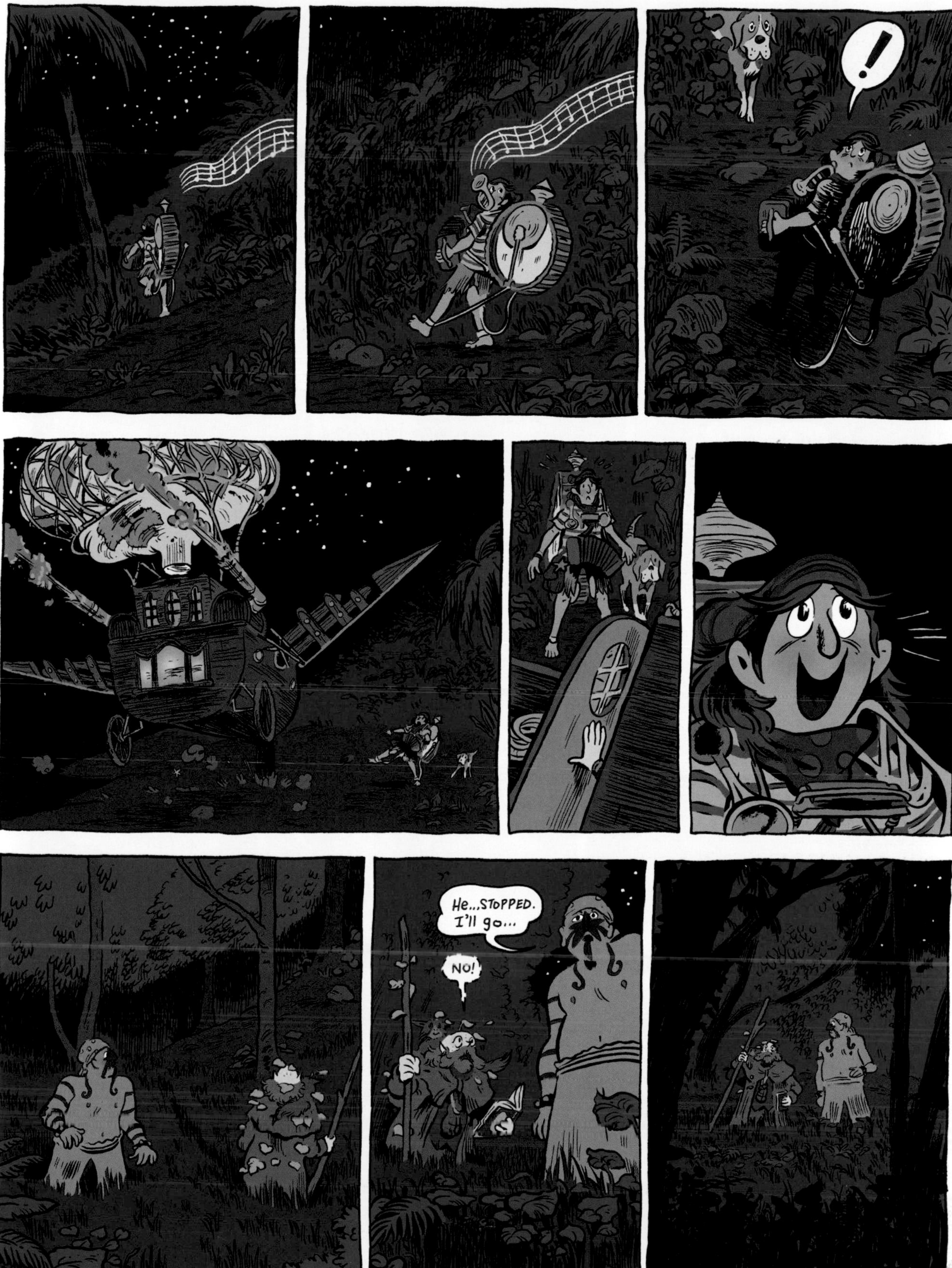
!
He...STOPPED. I'll go...
NO!

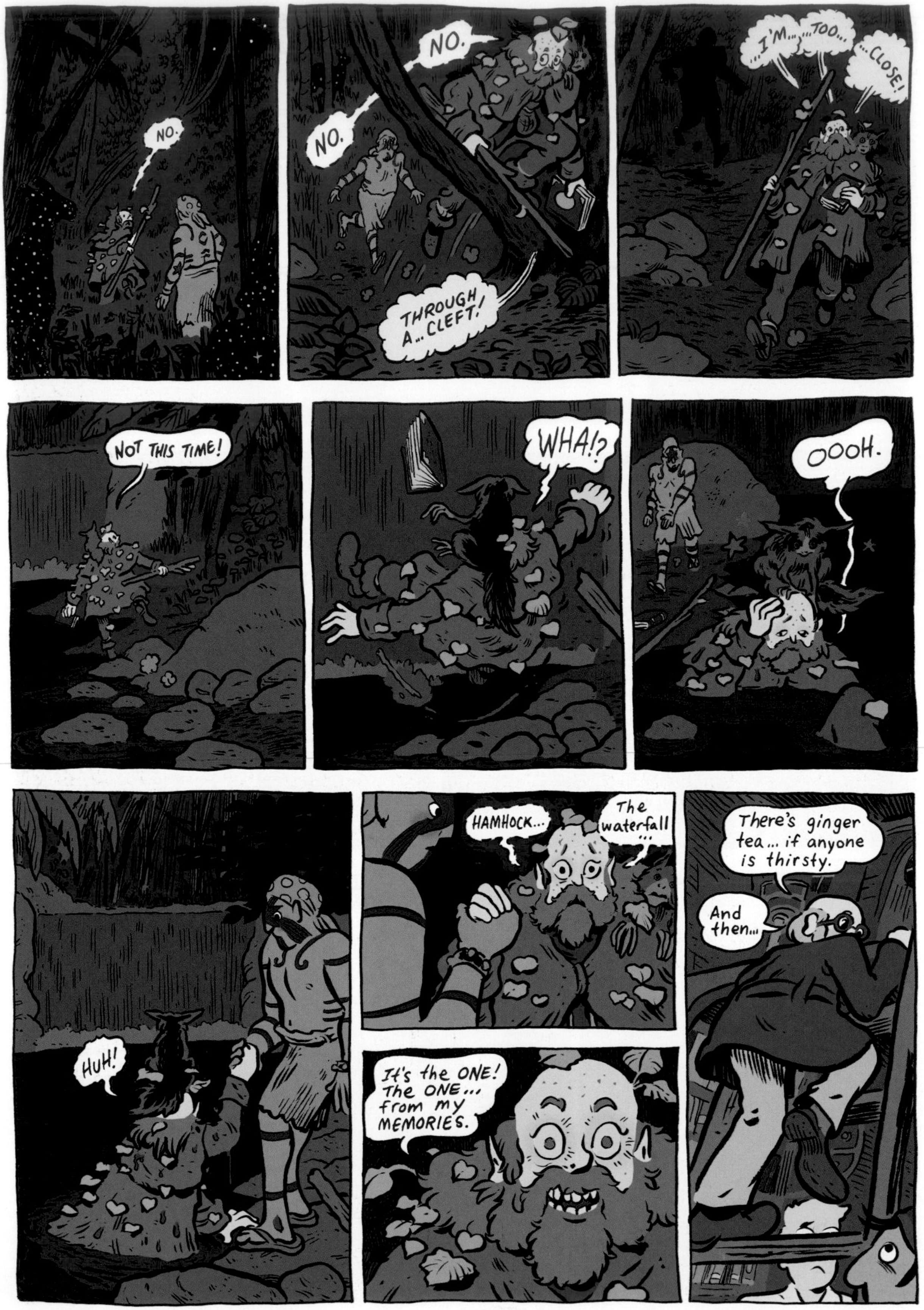

NO.
NO.
NO.
THROUGH A... CLEFT!
I'M... ...TOO... ...CLOSE!
NOT THIS TIME!
WHA!?
OOOH.
HUH!
HAMHOCK...
The waterfall...
It's the ONE! The ONE... from my MEMORIES.
There's ginger tea... if anyone is thirsty.
And then...

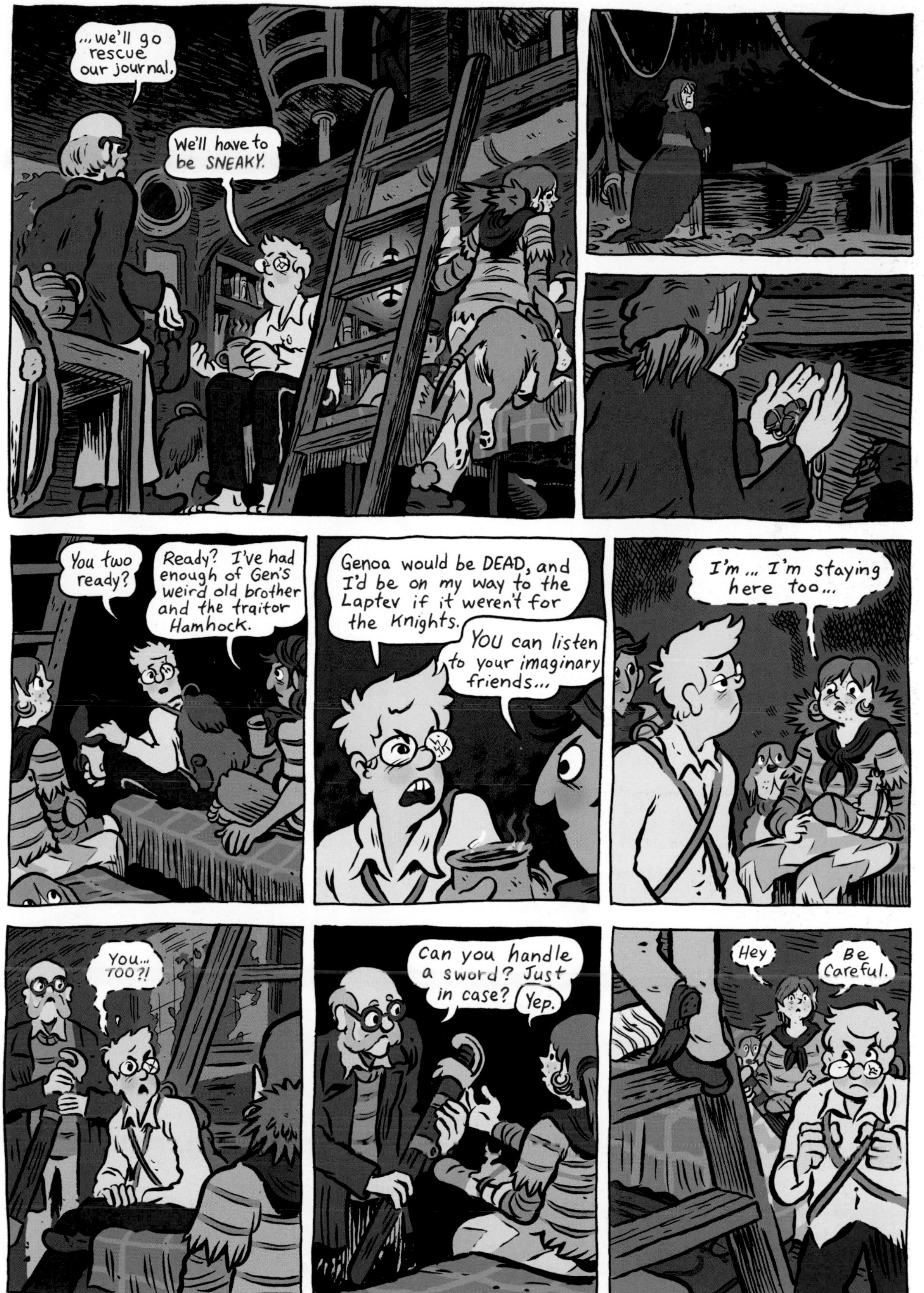

...we'll go rescue our journal.
We'll have to be SNEAKY.
You two ready?
Ready? I've had enough of Gen's weird old brother and the traitor Hamhock.
Genoa would be DEAD, and I'd be on my way to the Laptev if it weren't for the Knights.
YOU can listen to your imaginary friends...
I'm... I'm staying here too...
You... TOO?!
Can you handle a sword? Just in case?
Yep.
Hey
Be Careful.

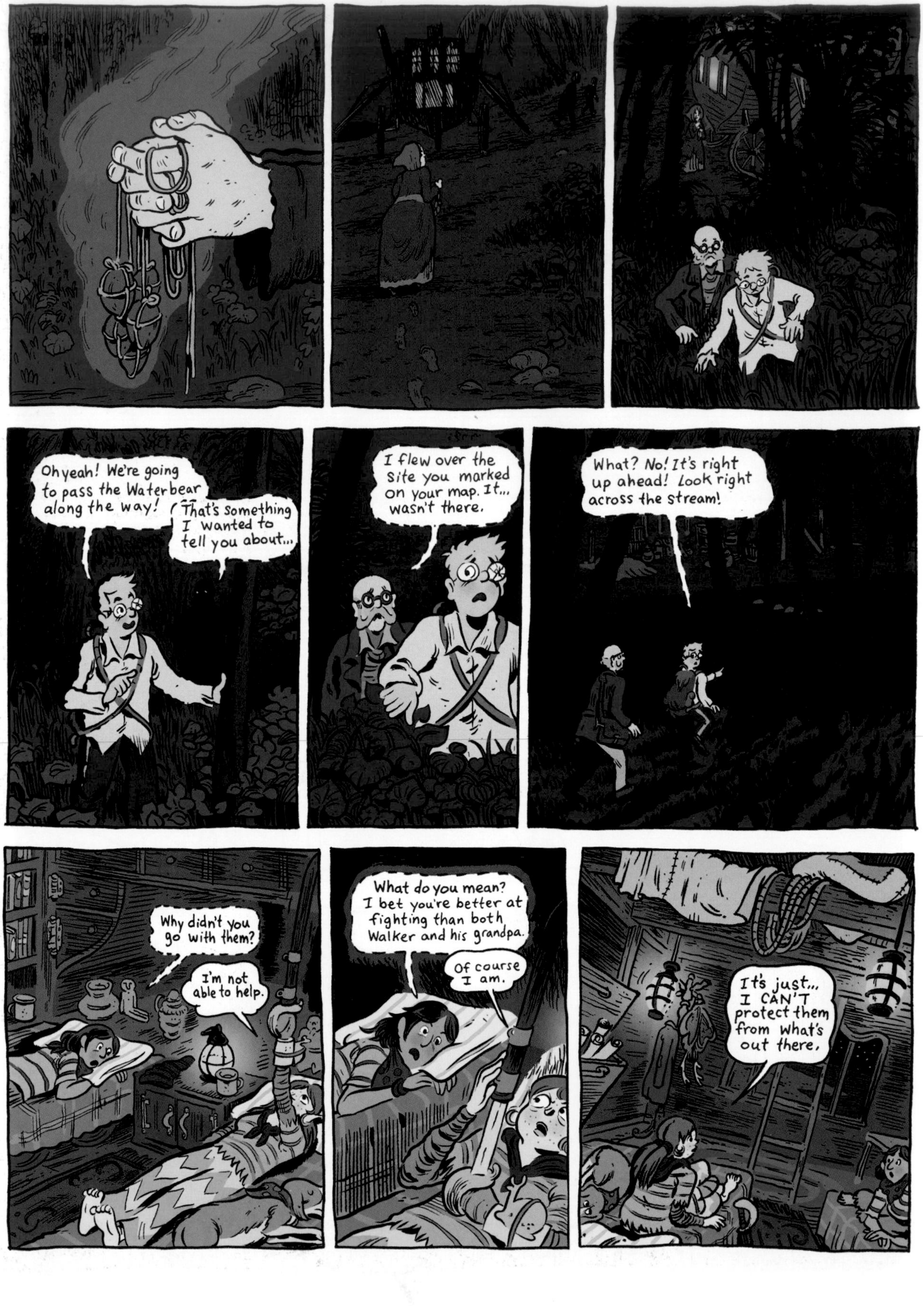
Oh yeah! We're going to pass the Waterbear along the way!
That's something I wanted to tell you about...
I flew over the site you marked on your map. It... wasn't there.
What? No! It's right up ahead! Look right across the stream!
Why didn't you go with them?
I'm not able to help.
What do you mean? I bet you're better at fighting than both Walker and his grandpa.
Of course I am.
It's just... I CAN'T protect them from what's out there.

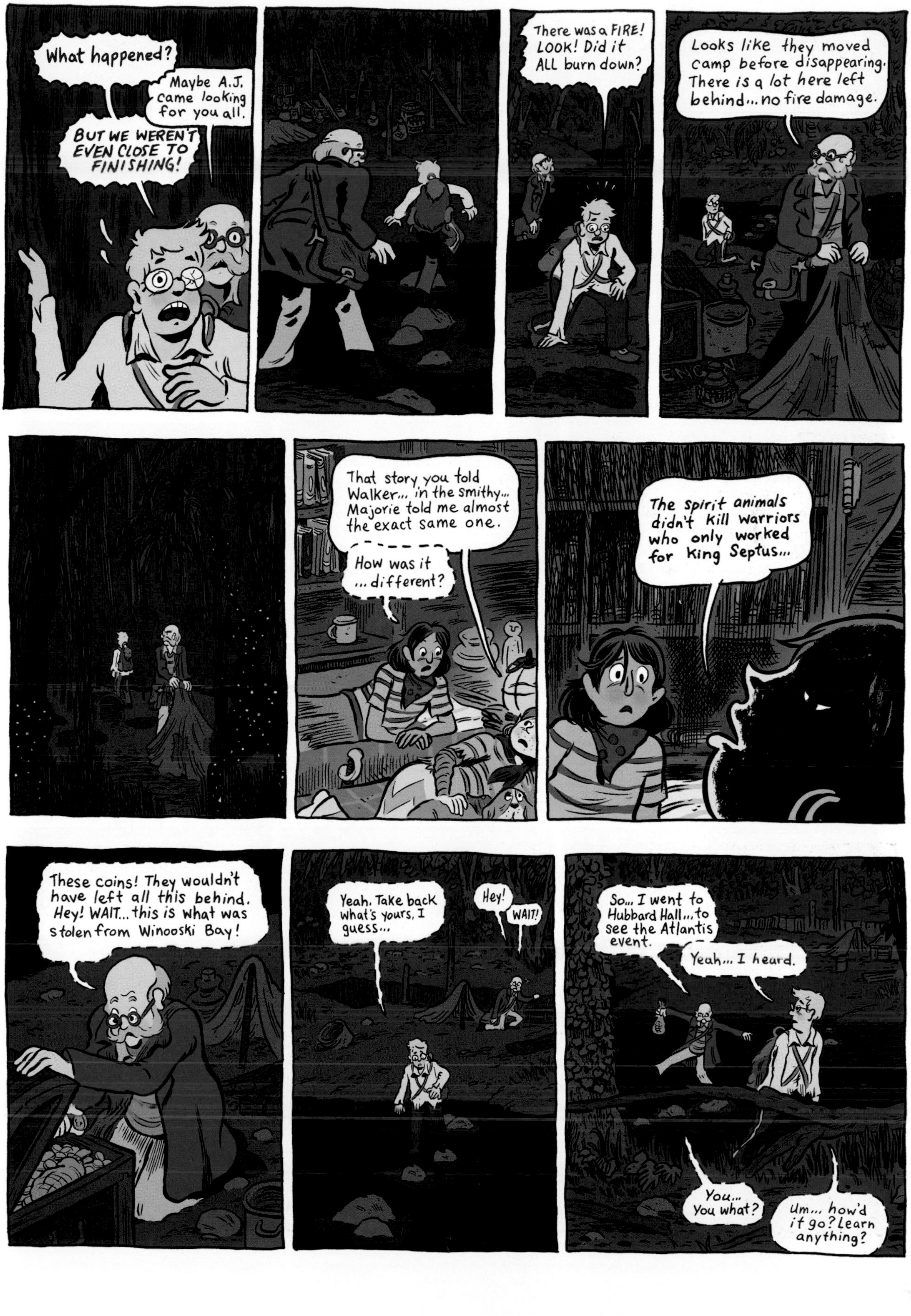
What happened?
Maybe A.J. came looking for you all.
BUT WE WEREN'T EVEN CLOSE TO FINISHING!
There was a FIRE! LOOK! Did it ALL burn down?
Looks like they moved camp before disappearing. There is a lot here left behind... no fire damage.
That story you told Walker... in the smithy... Majorie told me almost the exact same one.
How was it ...different?
The spirit animals didn't kill warriors who only worked for King Septus...
These coins! They wouldn't have left all this behind. Hey! WAIT... this is what was stolen from Winooski Bay!
Yeah. Take back what's yours, I guess...
Hey!
WAIT!
So... I went to Hubbard Hall... to see the Atlantis event.
Yeah... I heard.
You... You what?
Um... how'd it go? Learn anything?

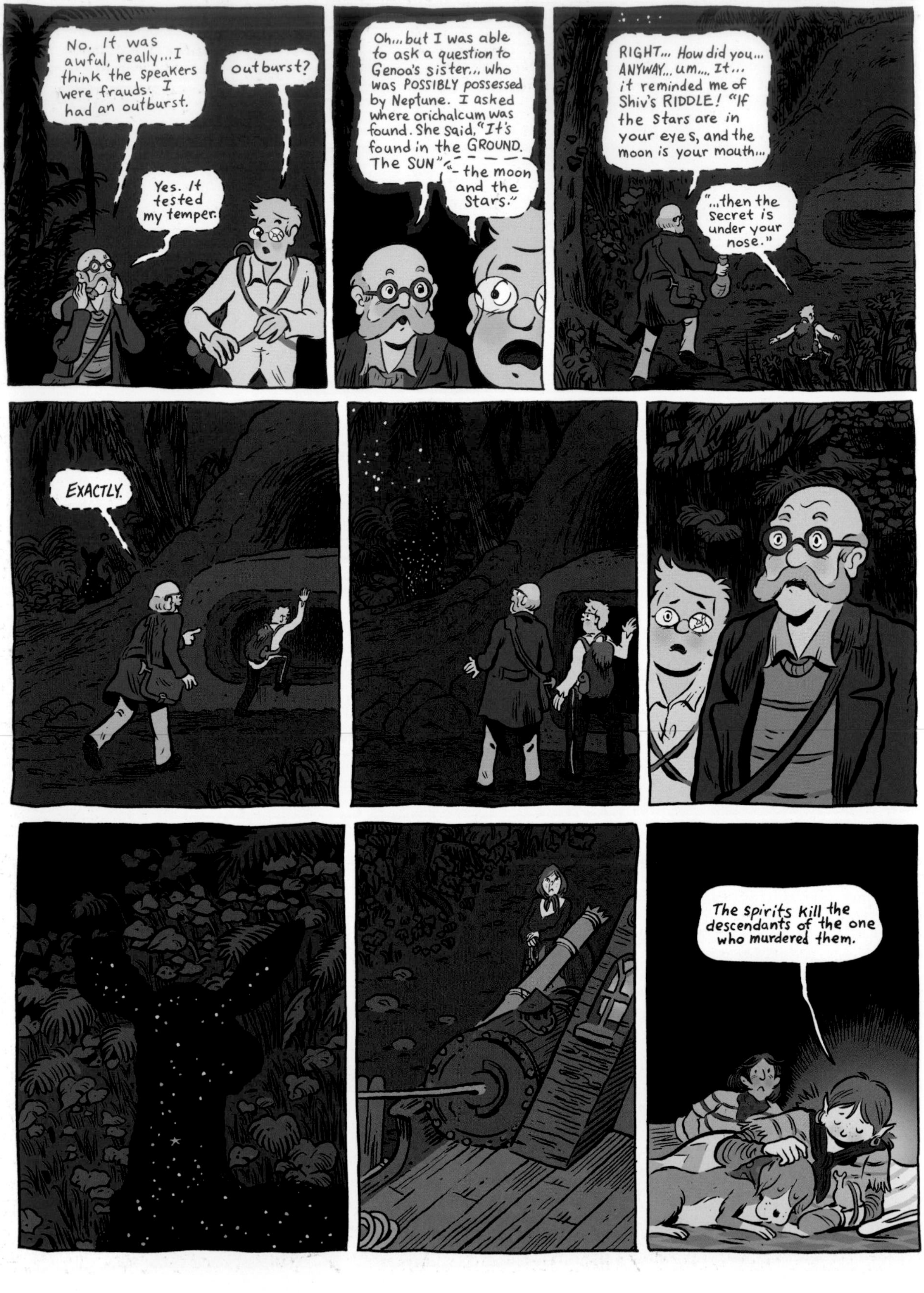
No. It was awful, really... I think the speakers were frauds. I had an outburst.
outburst?
Yes. It tested my temper.
Oh... but I was able to ask a question to Genoa's sister... who was POSSIBLY possessed by Neptune. I asked where orichalcum was found. She said, "It's found in the GROUND. The SUN"
"- the moon and the Stars."
RIGHT... How did you... ANYWAY... um... It... it reminded me of Shiv's RIDDLE! "If the stars are in your eyes, and the moon is your mouth...
"...then the secret is under your nose."
EXACTLY.
The spirits kill the descendants of the one who murdered them.

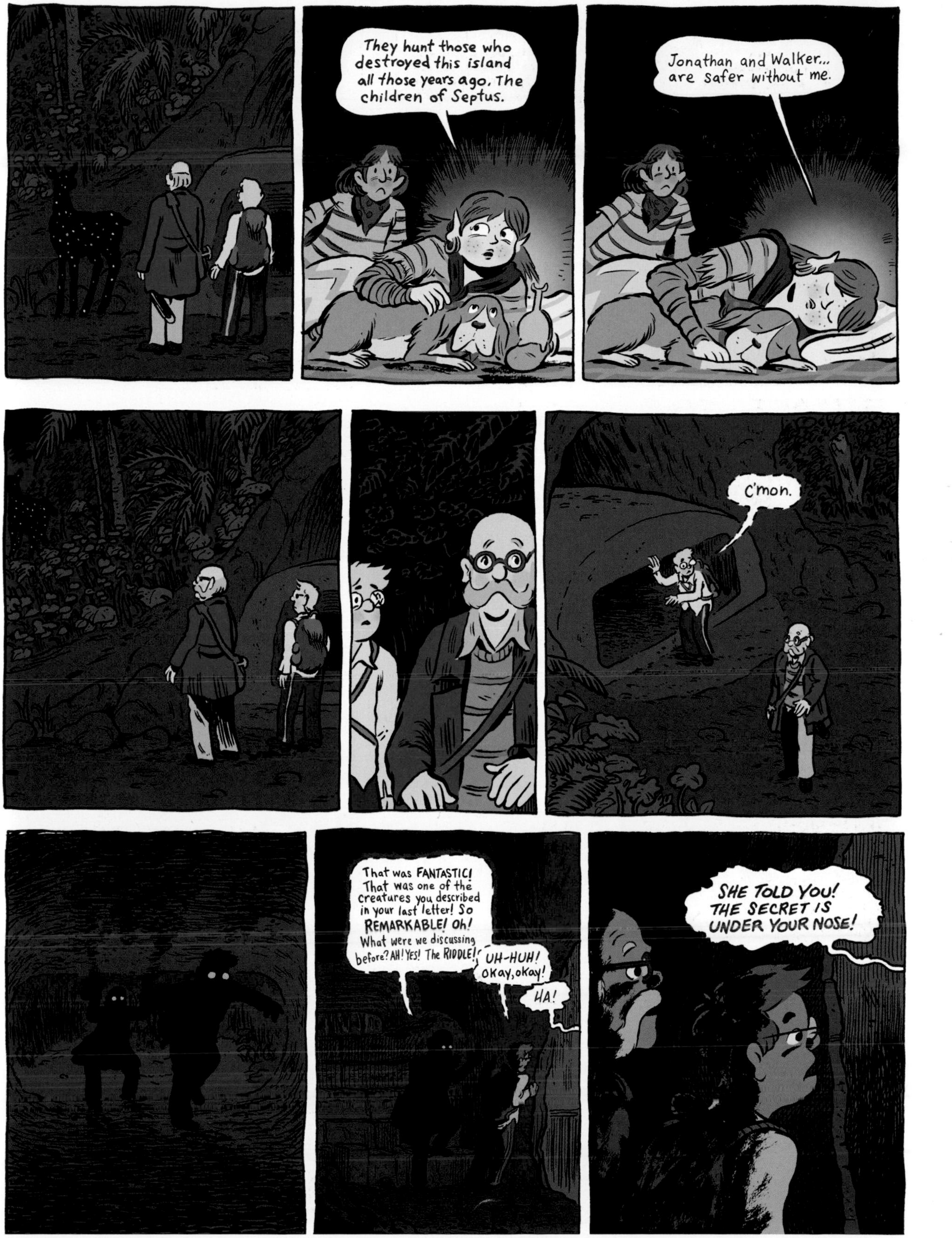
They hunt those who destroyed this island all those years ago. The children of Septus.
Jonathan and Walker... are safer without me.
C'mon.
That was FANTASTIC! That was one of the creatures you described in your last letter! So REMARKABLE! Oh! What were we discussing before? AH! YES! The RIDDLE!
UH-HUH! OKAY, OKAY!
HA!
SHE TOLD YOU! THE SECRET IS UNDER YOUR NOSE!

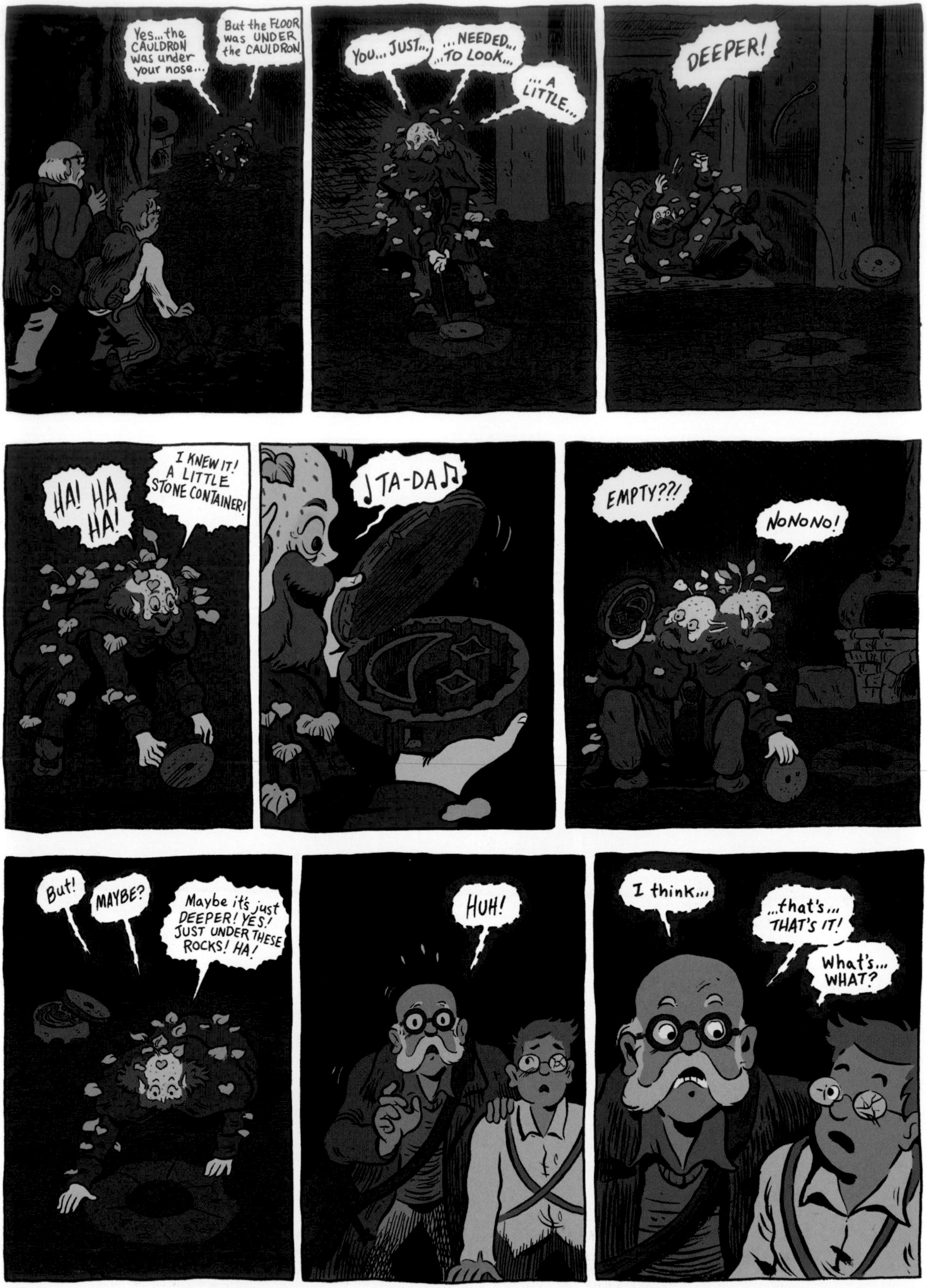
Yes... the CAULDRON was under your nose...
But the FLOOR was UNDER the CAULDRON.
YOU... JUST...
...NEEDED... ...TO LOOK...
...A LITTLE...
DEEPER!
HA! HA HA!
I KNEW IT! A LITTLE STONE CONTAINER!
♩TA-DA♫
EMPTY??!
NONONO!
But!
MAYBE?
Maybe it's just DEEPER! YES! JUST UNDER THESE ROCKS! HA!
HUH!
I think...
...that's... THAT'S IT!
What's... WHAT?

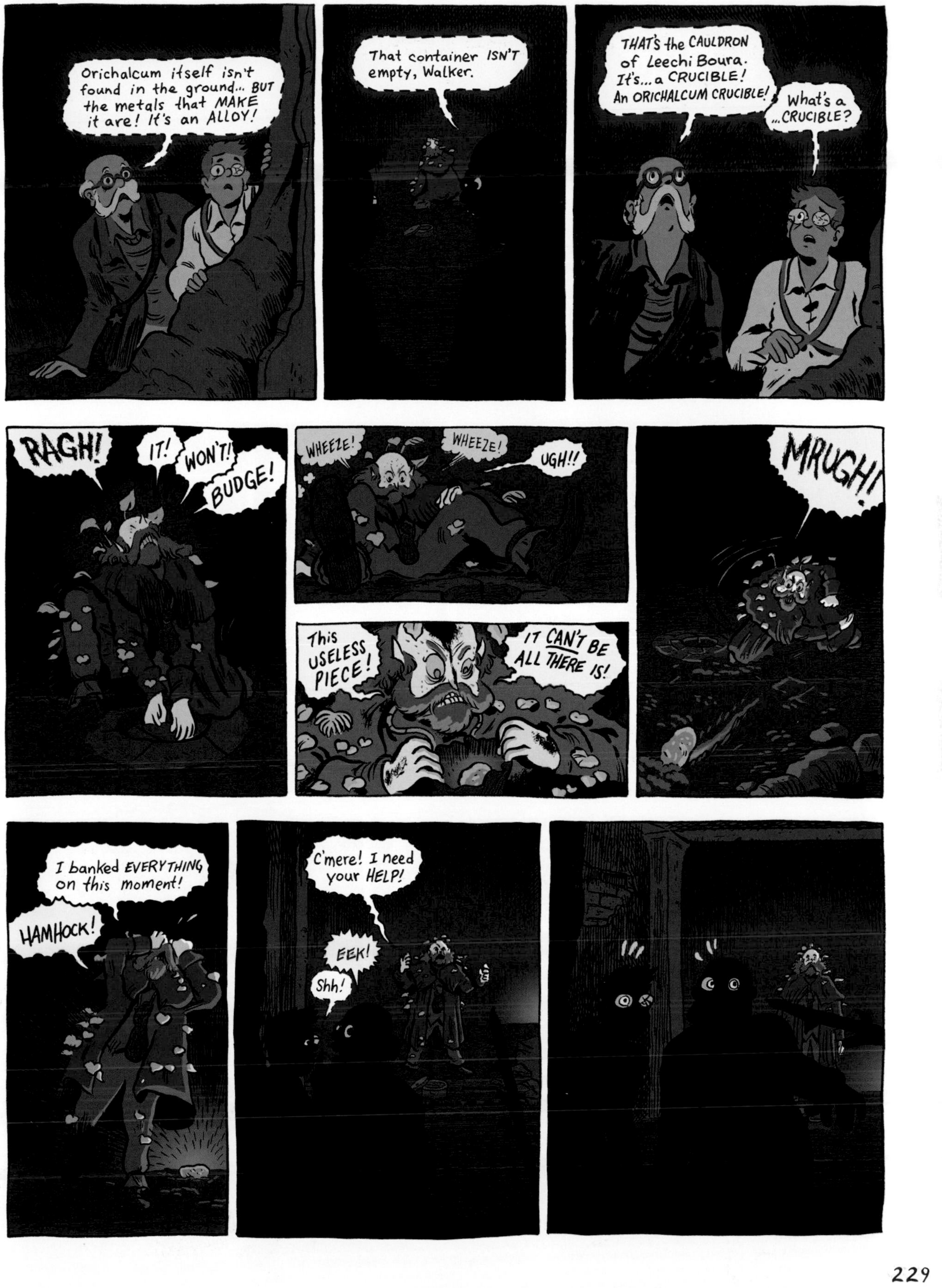
Orichalcum itself isn't found in the ground... BUT the metals that MAKE it are! It's an ALLOY!
That container ISN'T empty, Walker.
THAT'S the CAULDRON of Leechi Boura. It's... a CRUCIBLE! An ORICHALCUM CRUCIBLE!
What's a ...CRUCIBLE?
RAGH!
IT!
WON'T!
BUDGE!
WHEEZE!
WHEEZE!
UGH!!
This USELESS PIECE!
IT CAN'T BE ALL THERE IS!
MRUGH!
I banked EVERYTHING on this moment!
HAMHOCK!
C'mere! I need your HELP!
EEK!
Shh!

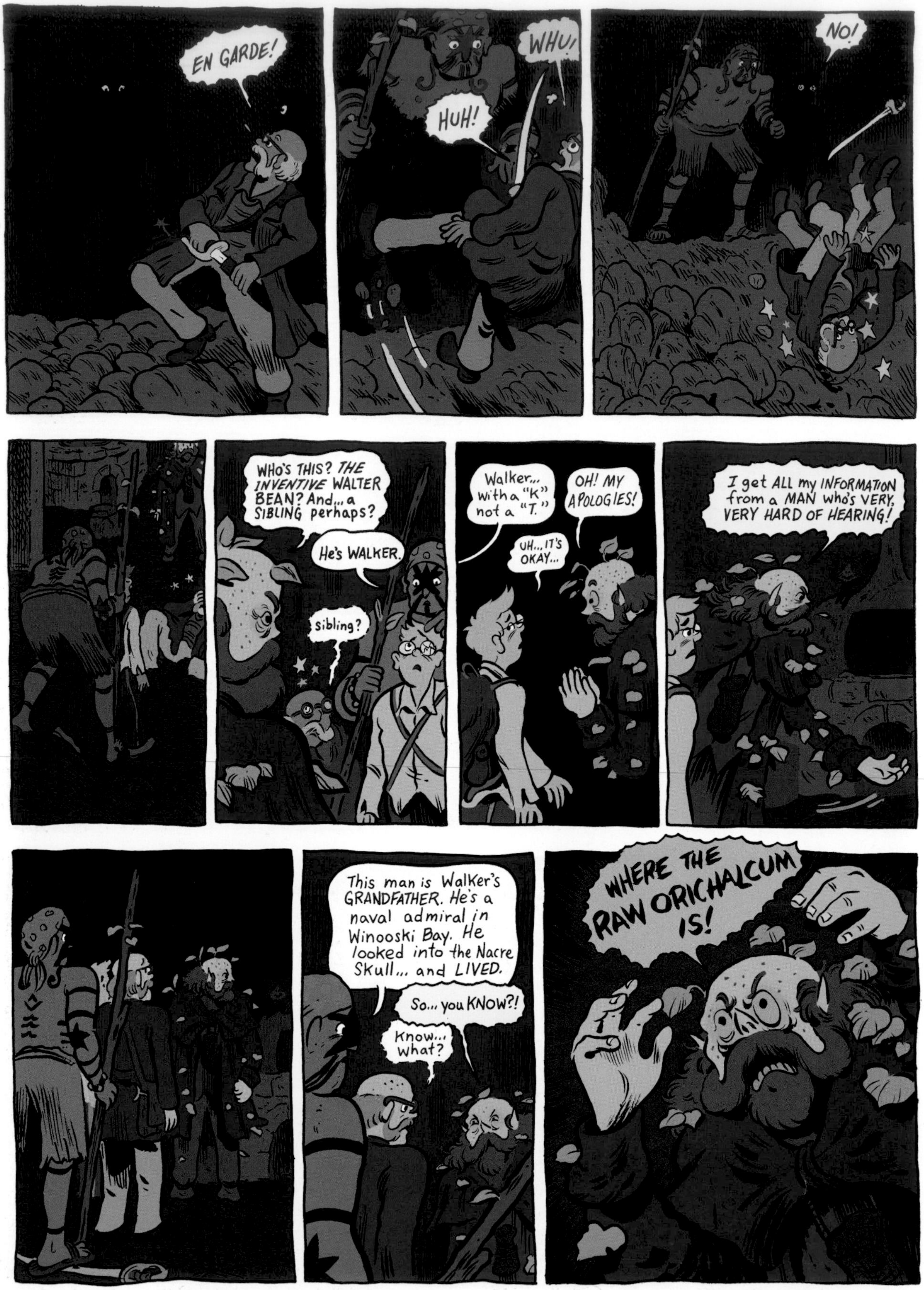
EN GARDE!
WHU!
HUH!
NO!
WHO'S THIS? THE INVENTIVE WALTER BEAN? And... a SIBLING perhaps?
He's WALKER.
sibling?
Walker... with a "K" not a "T."
OH! MY APOLOGIES!
UH... IT'S OKAY...
I get ALL my INFORMATION from a MAN who's VERY, VERY HARD OF HEARING!
This man is Walker's GRANDFATHER. He's a naval admiral in Winooski Bay. He looked into the Nacre Skull... and LIVED.
So... you KNOW?!
Know... what?
WHERE THE RAW ORICHALCUM IS!

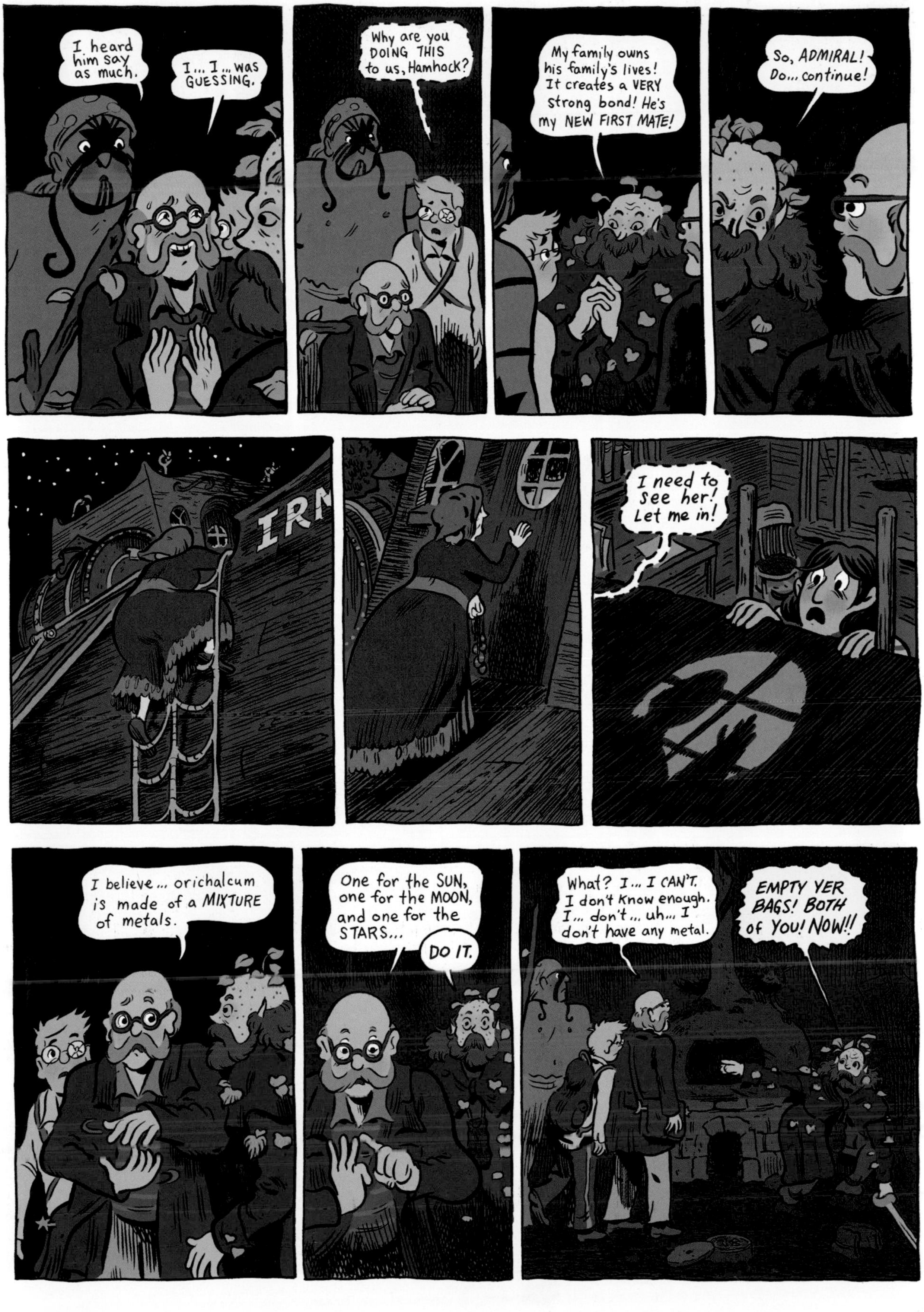
I heard him say as much.
I... I... was GUESSING.
Why are you DOING THIS to us, Hamhock?
My family owns his family's lives! It creates a VERY strong bond! He's my NEW FIRST MATE!
So, ADMIRAL! Do... continue!
IRM
I need to see her! Let me in!
I believe... orichalcum is made of a MIXTURE of metals.
One for the SUN, one for the MOON, and one for the STARS...
DO IT.
What? I... I CAN'T. I don't know enough. I... don't... uh... I don't have any metal.
EMPTY YER BAGS! BOTH OF YOU! NOW!!

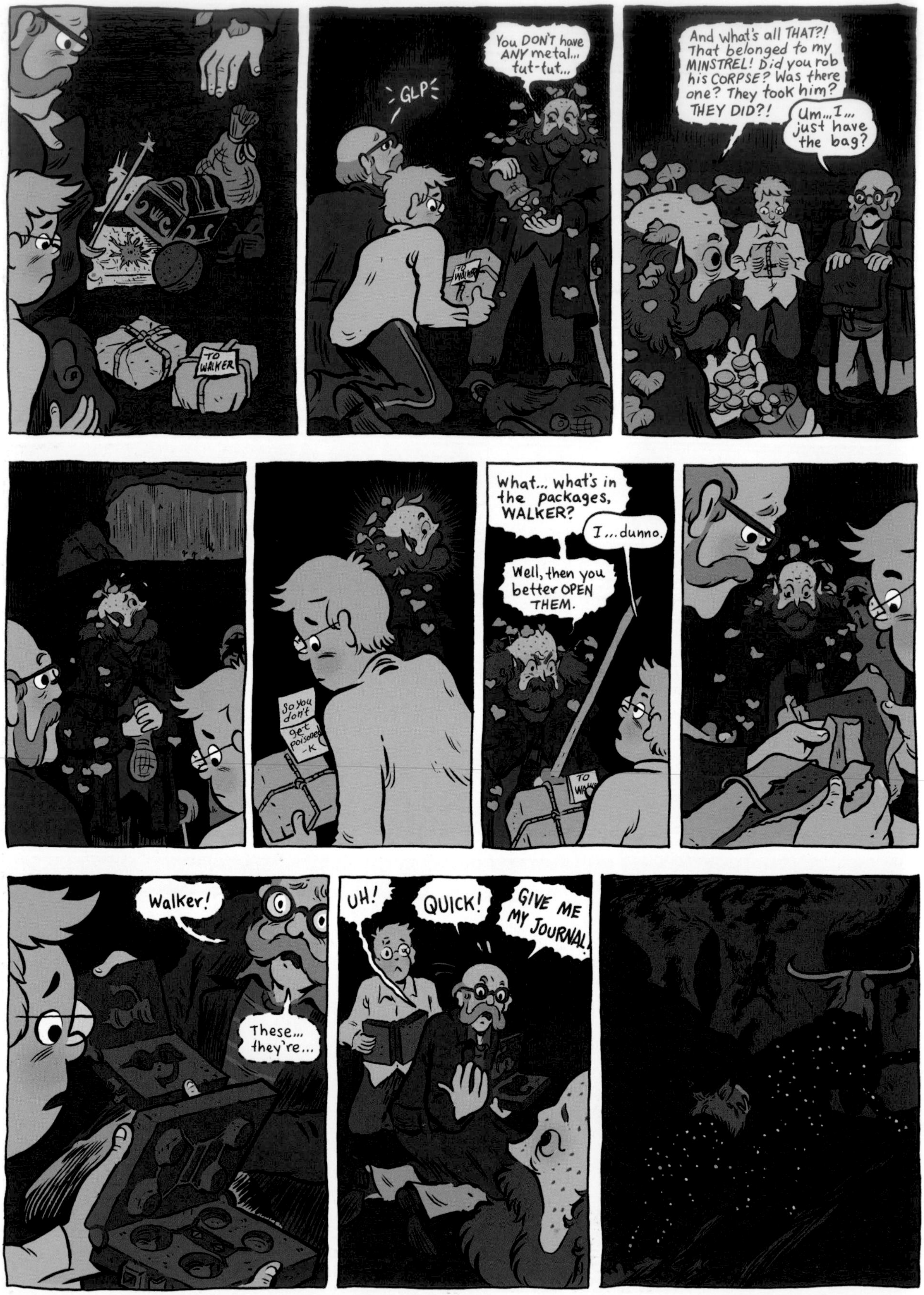

TO WALKER
GLP
You DON'T have ANY metal... tut-tut...
TO WALKER
And what's all THAT?! That belonged to my MINSTREL! Did you rob his CORPSE? Was there one? They took him? THEY DID?!
Um... I... just have the bag?
So you don't get poisoned -K
What... what's in the packages, WALKER?
I... dunno.
Well, then you better OPEN THEM.
Walker!
These... they're...
UH!
QUICK!
GIVE ME MY JOURNAL!

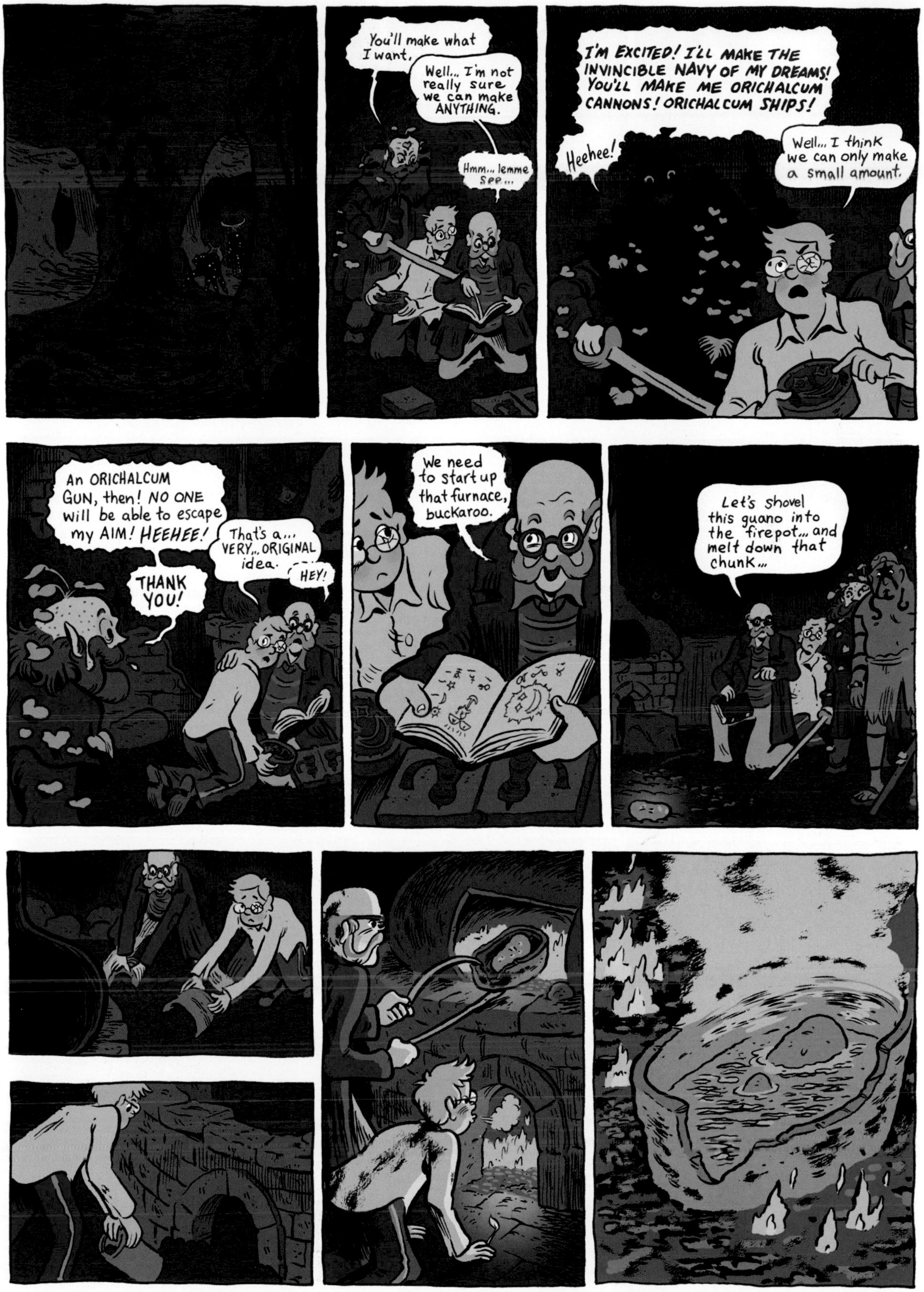

You'll make what I want.
Well... I'm not really sure we can make ANYTHING.
Hmm... lemme see...
I'M EXCITED! I'LL MAKE THE INVINCIBLE NAVY OF MY DREAMS! YOU'LL MAKE ME ORICHALCUM CANNONS! ORICHALCUM SHIPS!
Heehee!
Well... I think we can only make a small amount.
An ORICHALCUM GUN, then! NO ONE will be able to escape my AIM! HEEHEE!
That's a... VERY... ORIGINAL idea.
THANK YOU!
HEY!
We need to start up that furnace, buckaroo.
Let's shovel this guano into the firepot... and melt down that chunk...

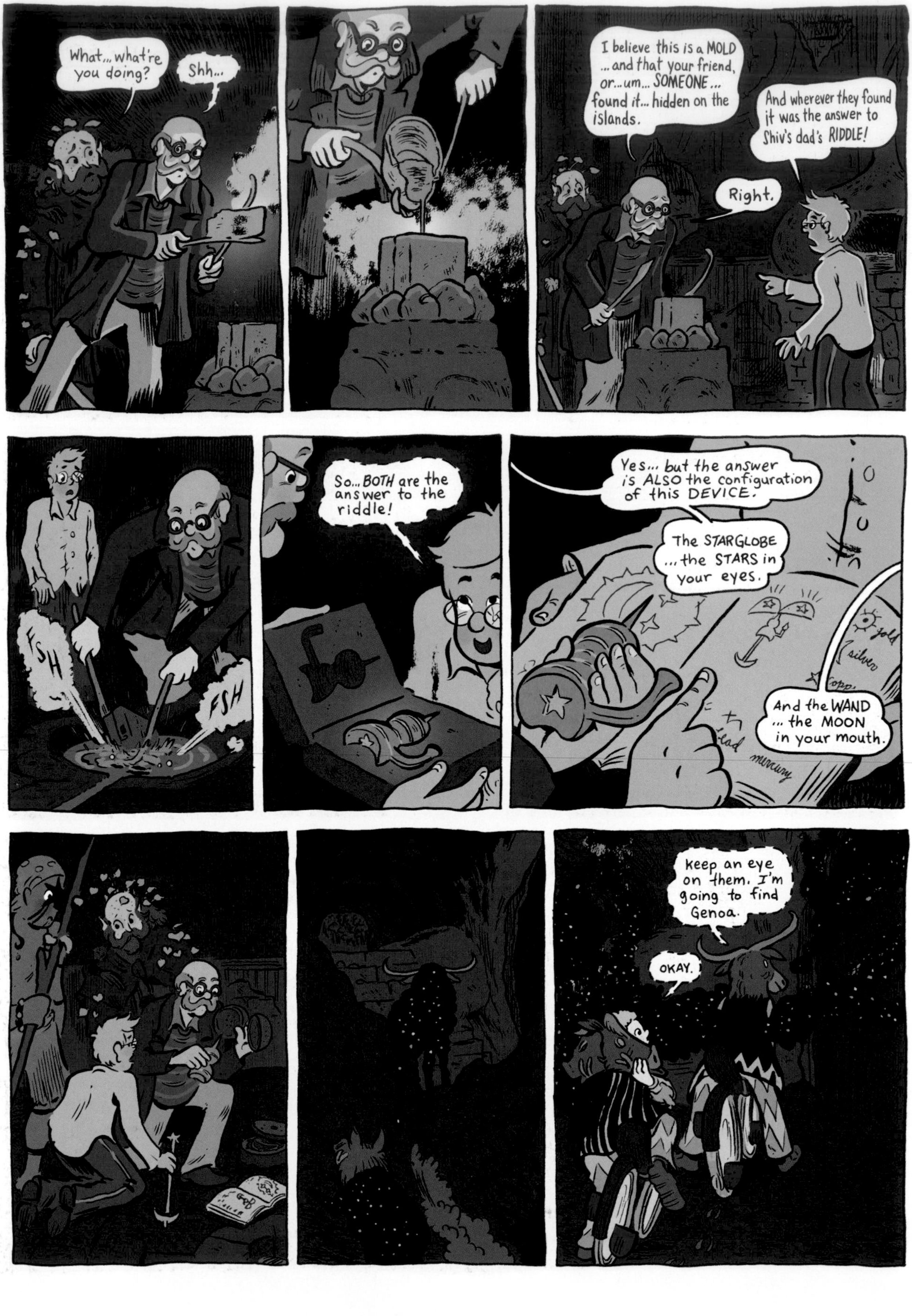

What... what're you doing?
Shh...
I believe this is a MOLD ...and that your friend, or...um... SOMEONE... found it... hidden on the islands.
And wherever they found it was the answer to Shiv's dad's RIDDLE!
Right.
FSH
FSH
So... BOTH are the answer to the riddle!
Yes... but the answer is ALSO the configuration of this DEVICE.
The STARGLOBE ...the STARS in your eyes.
And the WAND ...the MOON in your mouth.
gold
silver
mercury
Keep an eye on them. I'm going to find Genoa.
OKAY.

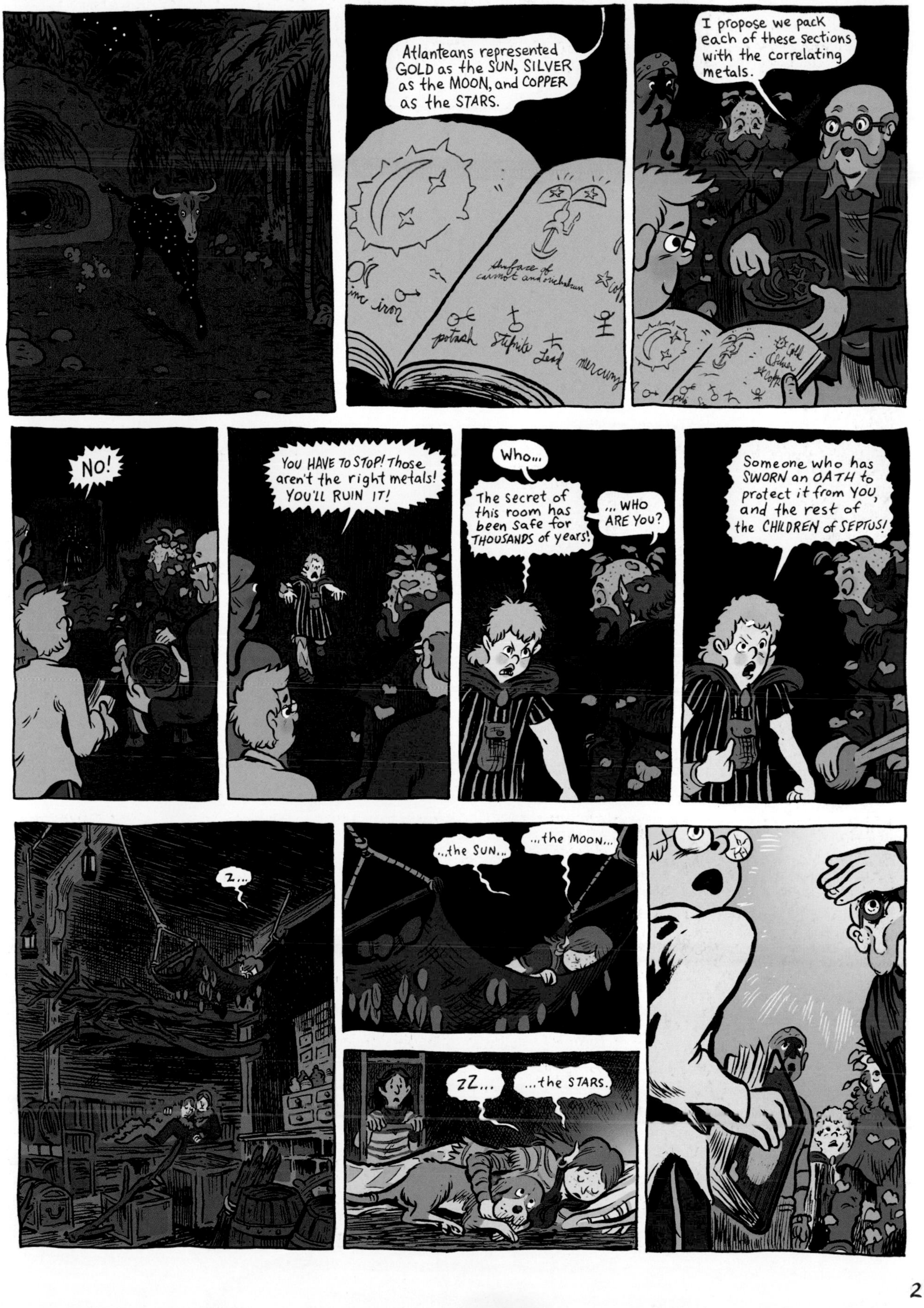
Atlanteans represented GOLD as the SUN, SILVER as the MOON, and COPPER as the STARS.
I propose we pack each of these sections with the correlating metals.
NO!
YOU HAVE TO STOP! Those aren't the right metals! YOU'LL RUIN IT!
Who...
The secret of this room has been safe for THOUSANDS of years!
... WHO ARE YOU?
Someone who has SWORN an OATH to protect it from YOU, and the rest of the CHILDREN of SEPTUS!
Z...
...the SUN...
...the MOON...
ZZ...
...the STARS.

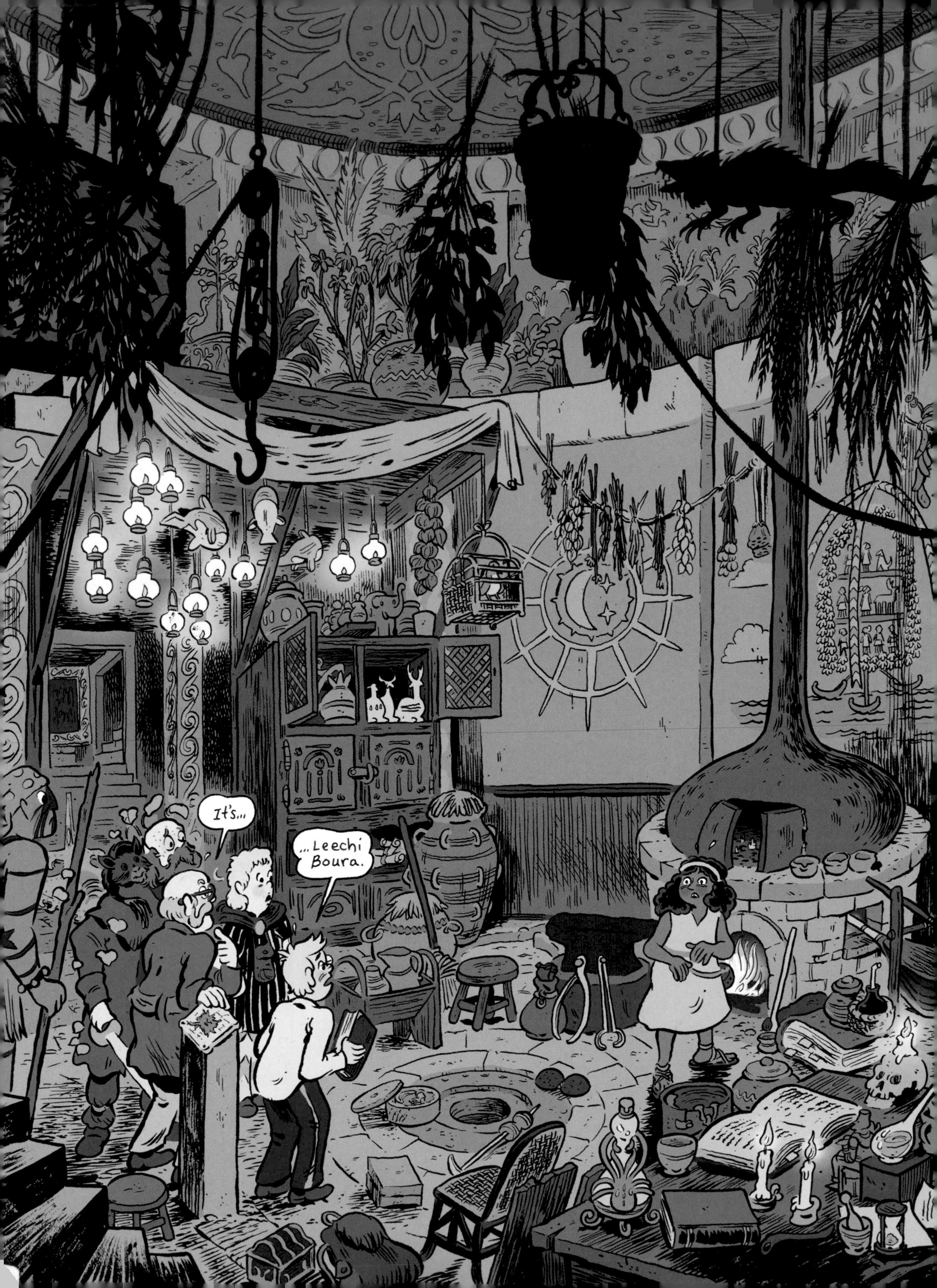
It's...
...Leechi Boura.

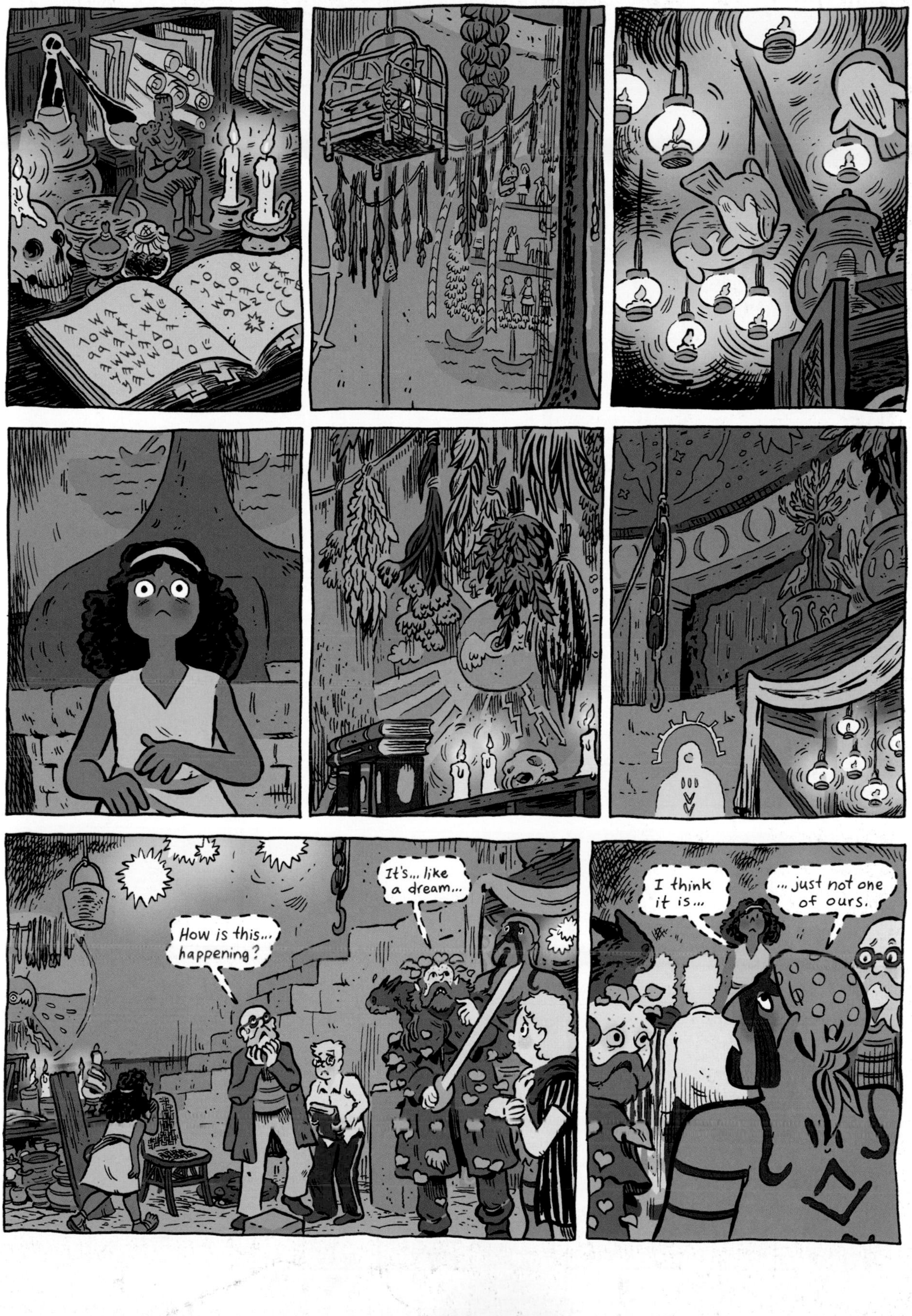

How is this... happening?
It's... like a dream...
I think it is...
... just not one of ours.

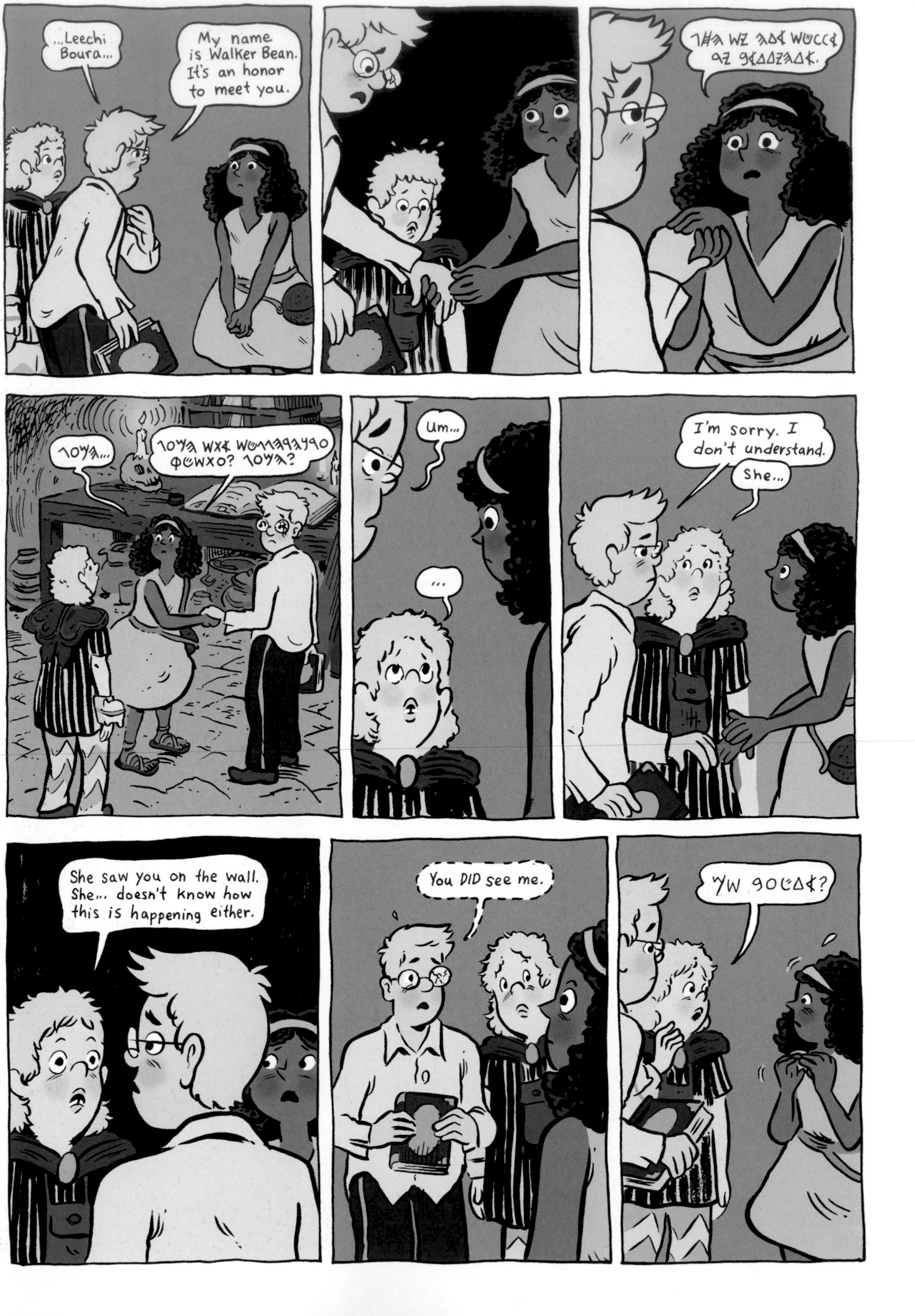

...Leechi Boura...
My name is Walker Bean. It's an honor to meet you.
Um...
...
I'm sorry. I don't understand.
She...
She saw you on the wall. She... doesn't know how this is happening either.
You DID see me.

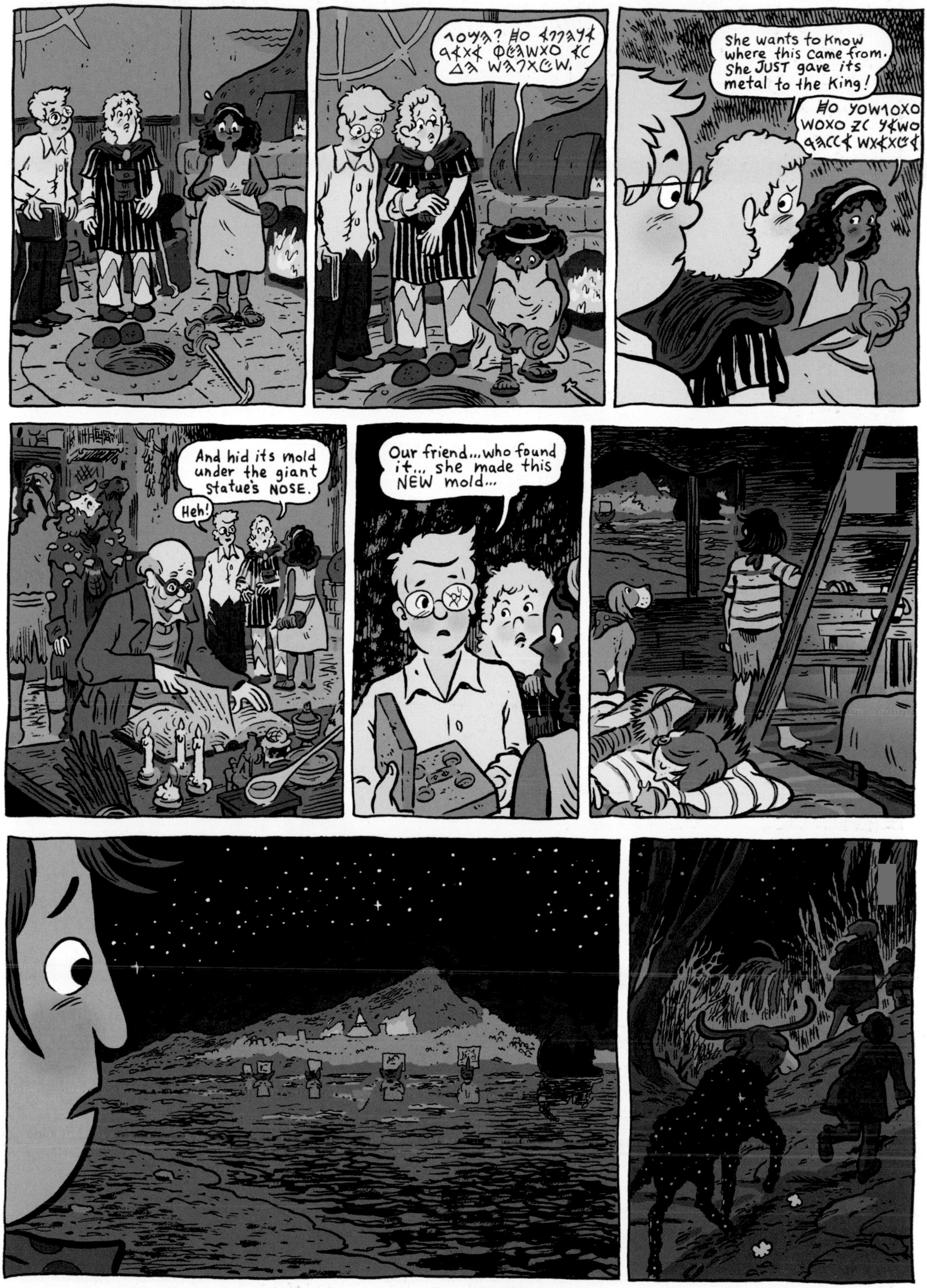
She wants to know where this came from. She JUST gave its metal to the King!
And hid its mold under the giant statue's NOSE.
Heh!
Our friend... who found it... she made this NEW mold...

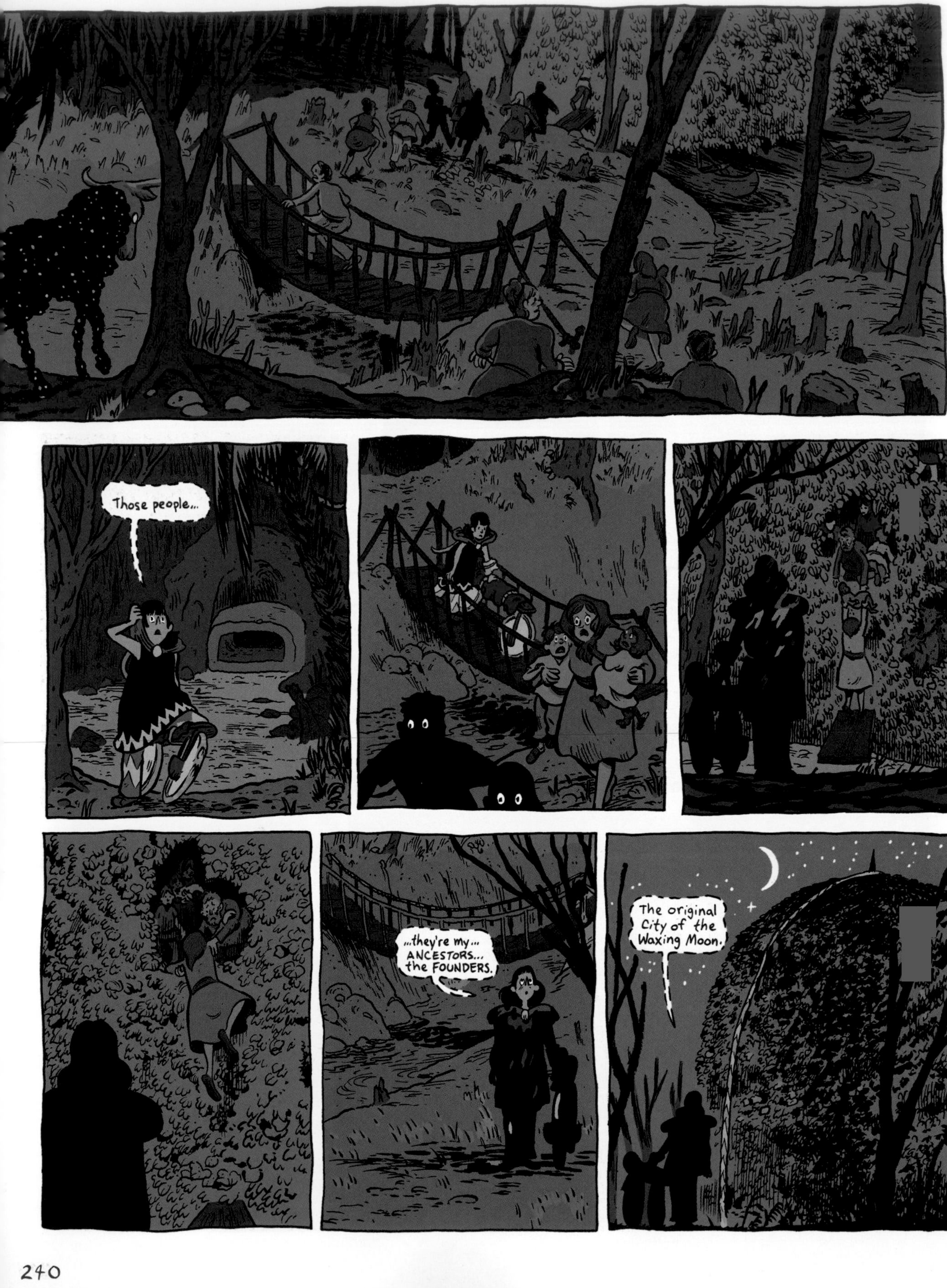
Those people...
...they're my... ANCESTORS... the FOUNDERS.
The original City of the Waxing Moon.

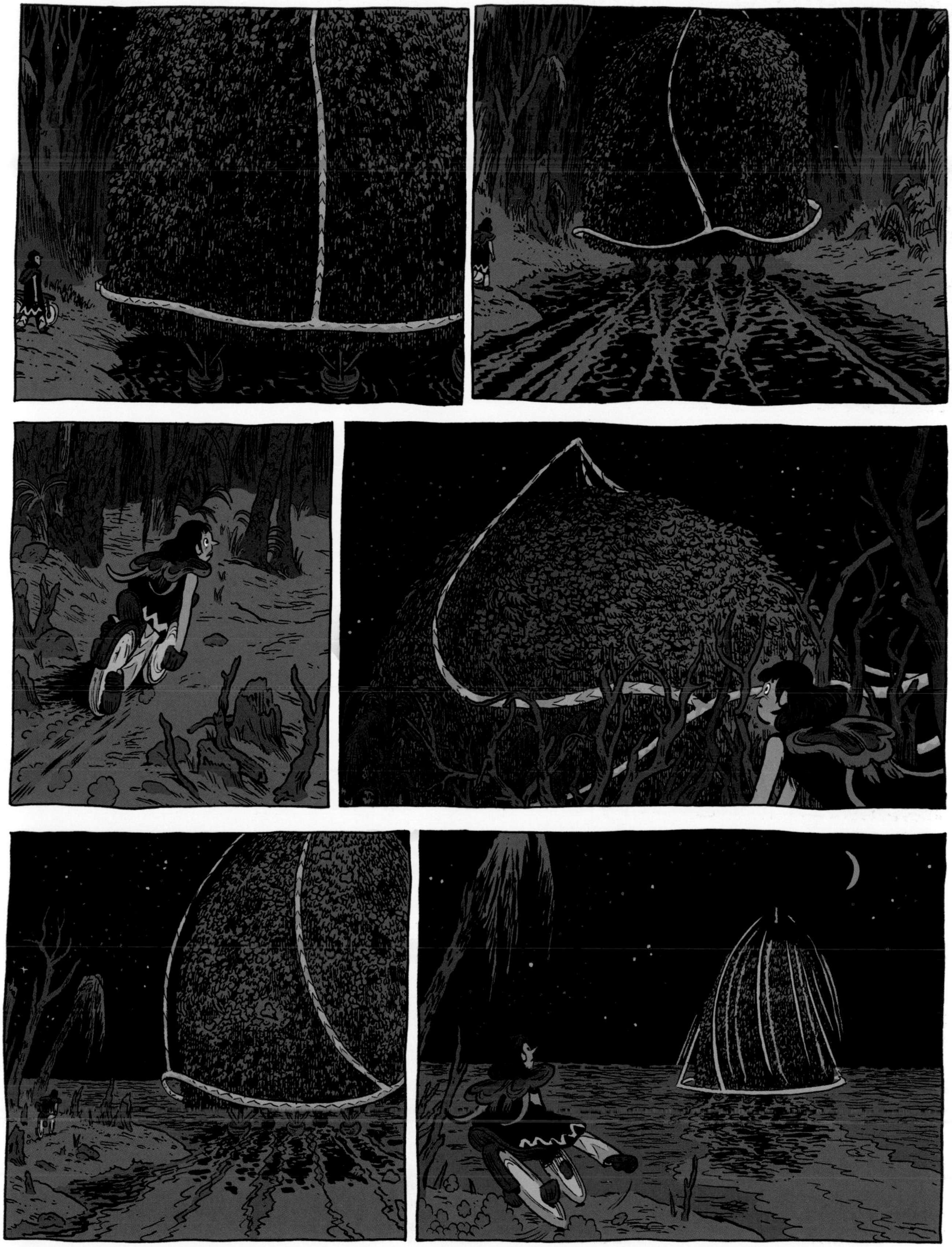

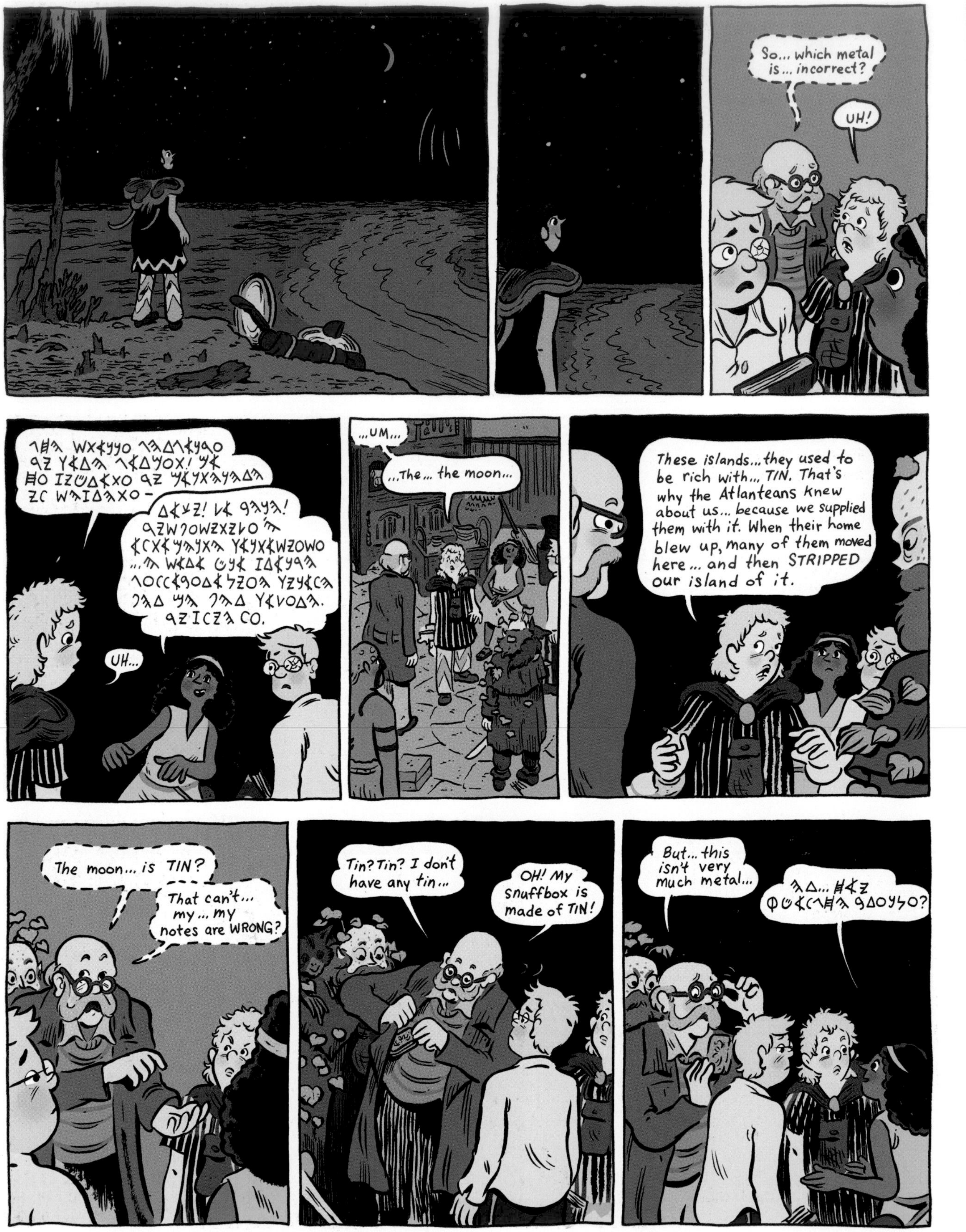
So... which metal is... incorrect?
UH!
UH...
...UM...
...The... the moon...
These islands... they used to be rich with... TIN. That's why the Atlanteans knew about us... because we supplied them with it. When their home blew up, many of them moved here... and then STRIPPED our island of it.
The moon... is TIN?
That can't... my... my notes are WRONG?
Tin? Tin? I don't have any tin...
OH! My snuffbox is made of TIN!
But... this isn't very much metal...

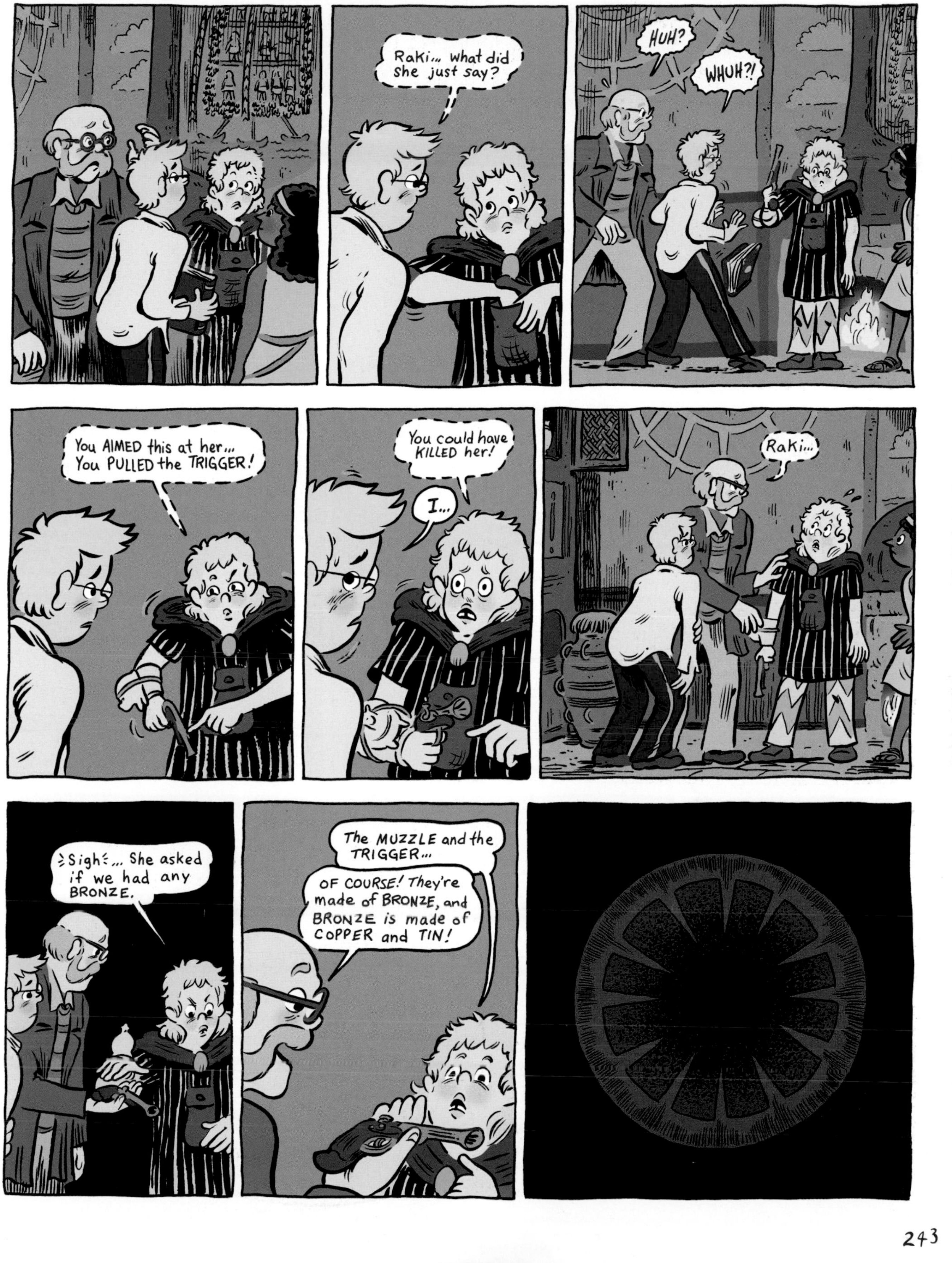
Raki... what did she just say?
HUH?
WHUH?!
You AIMED this at her... You PULLED the TRIGGER!
You could have KILLED her!
I...
Raki...
≷Sigh≷... She asked if we had any BRONZE.
The MUZZLE and the TRIGGER...
OF COURSE! They're made of BRONZE, and BRONZE is made of COPPER and TIN!

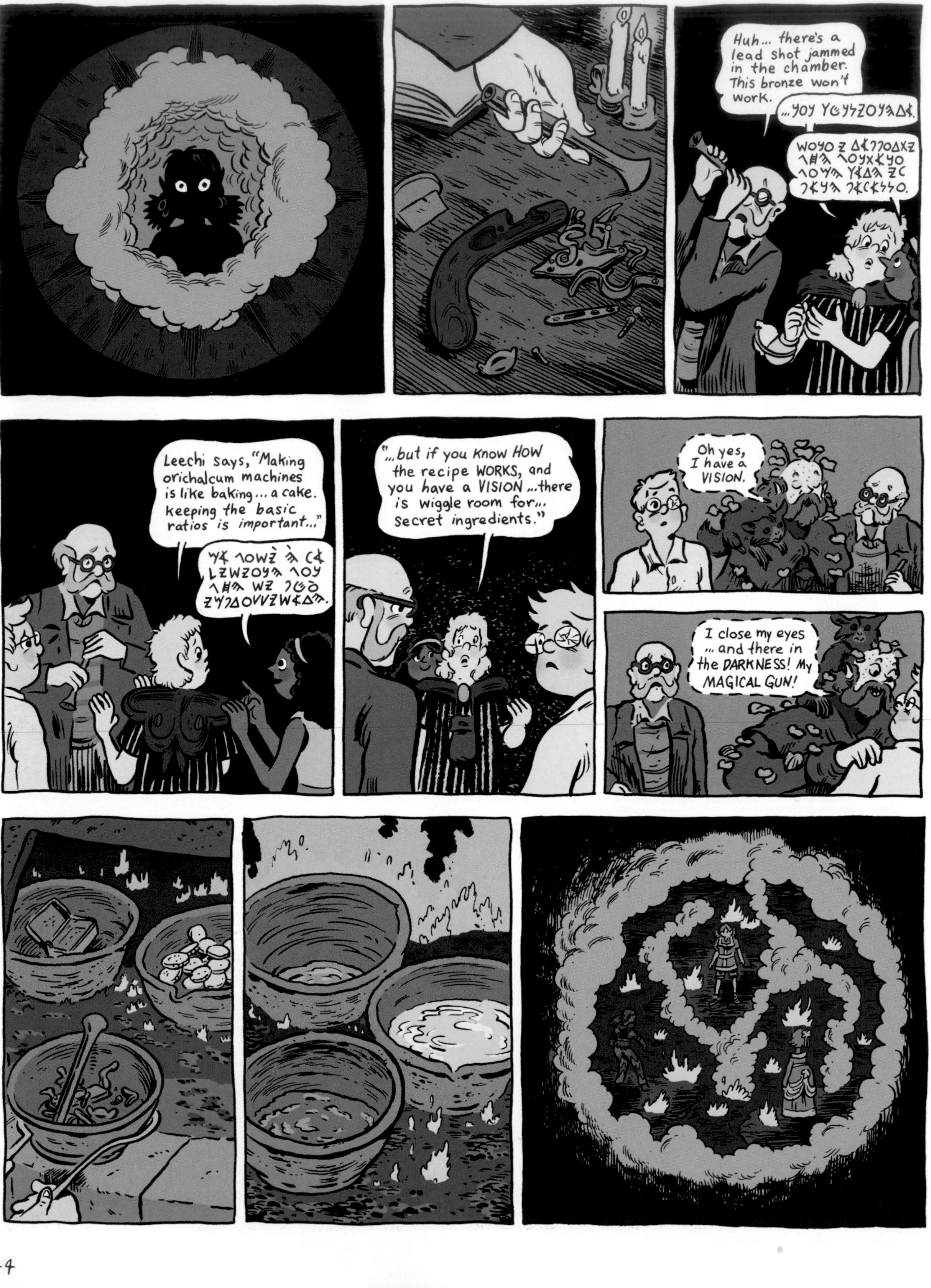

Huh... there's a lead shot jammed in the chamber. This bronze won't work.
Leechi says, "Making orichalcum machines is like baking... a cake. Keeping the basic ratios is important..."
"...but if you know HOW the recipe WORKS, and you have a VISION ...there is wiggle room for... secret ingredients."
Oh yes, I have a VISION.
I close my eyes ... and there in the DARKNESS! My MAGICAL GUN!

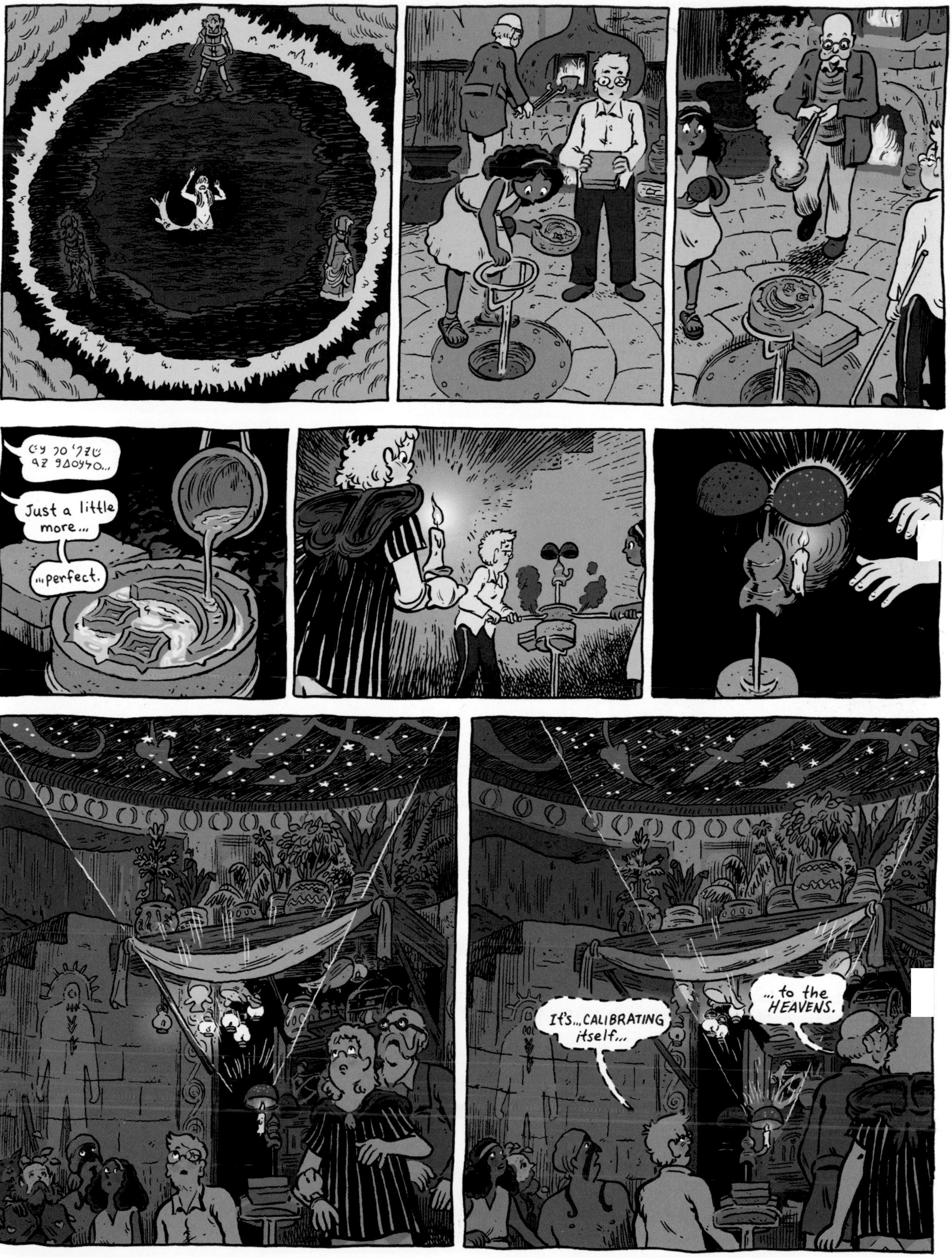
Just a little more...
...perfect.
It's... CALIBRATING itself...
... to the HEAVENS.

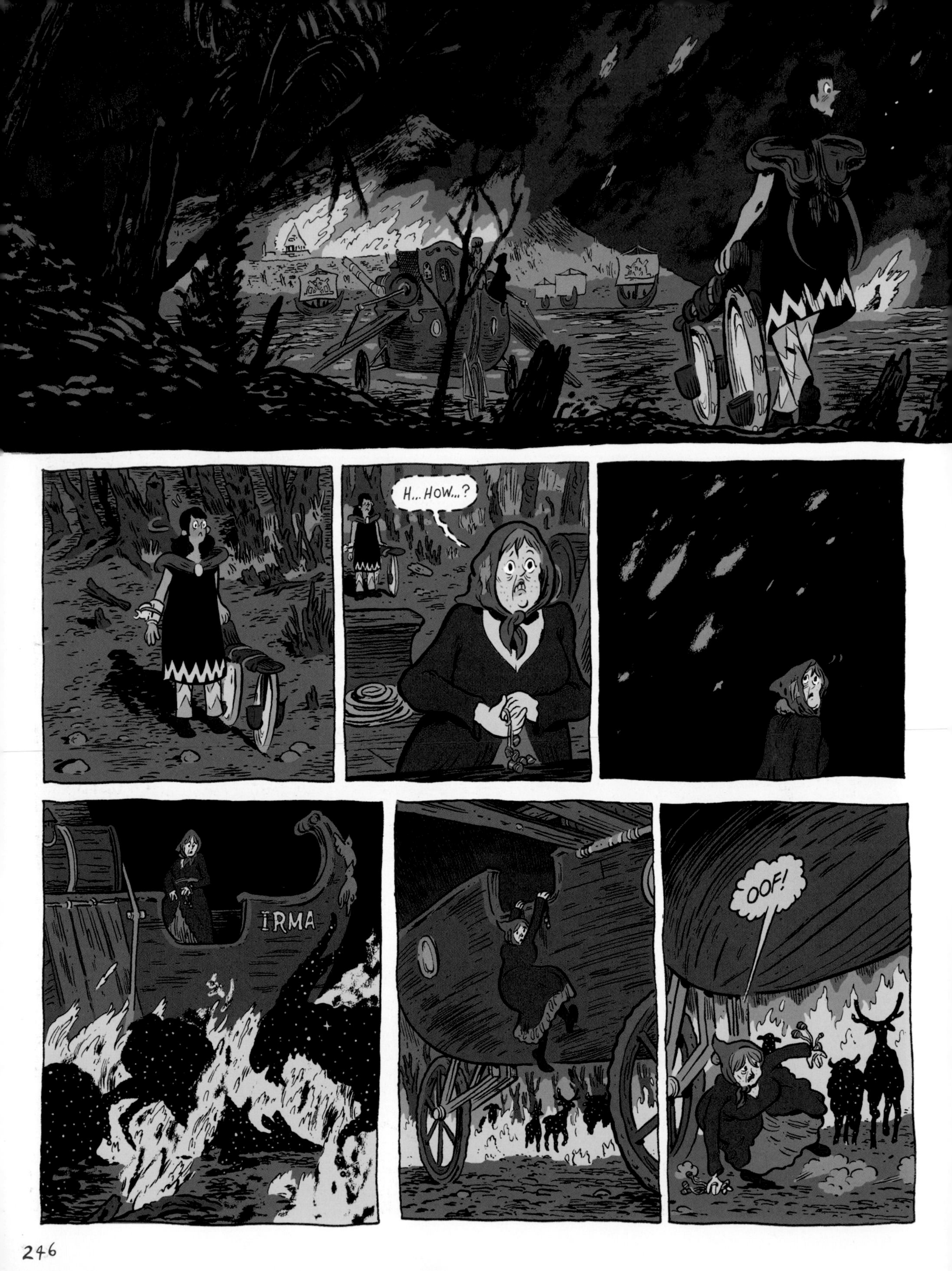
H... HOW...?
IRMA
OOF!

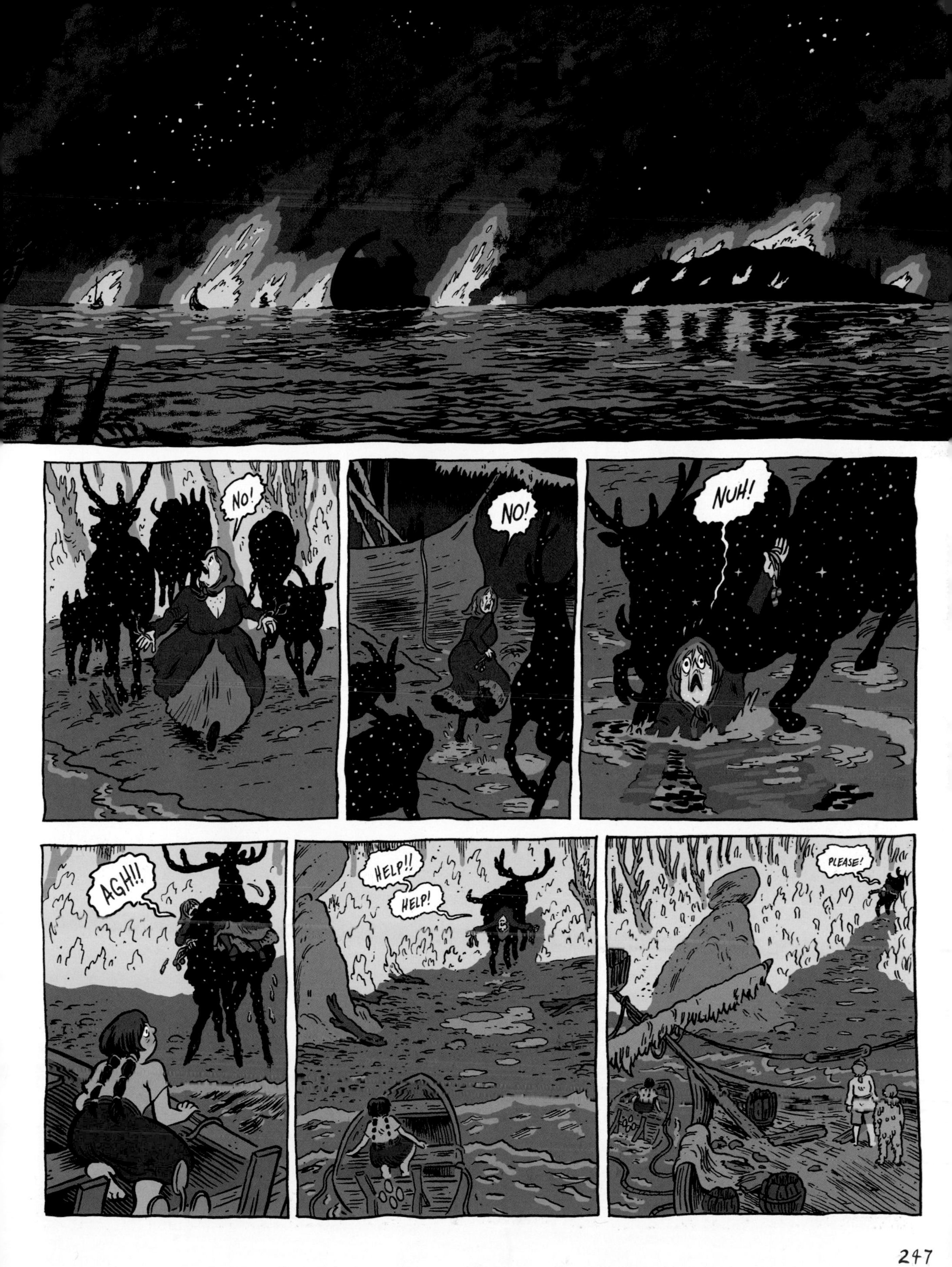
NO!
NO!
NUH!
AGH!!
HELP!!
HELP!
PLEASE!

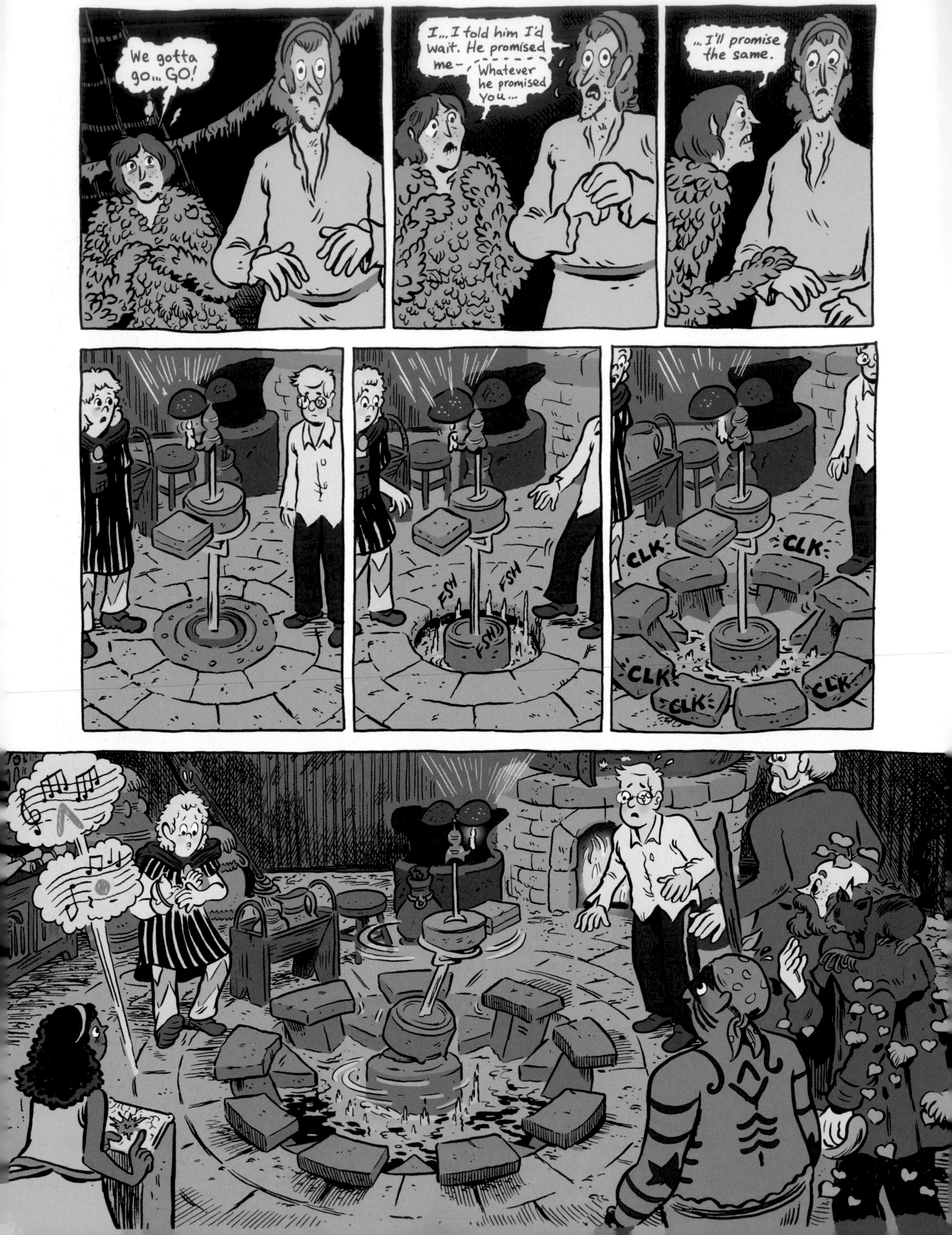
We gotta go... GO!
I... I told him I'd wait. He promised me–
Whatever he promised you...
...I'll promise the same.
FSH
FSH
FSH
CLK
CLK
CLK
CLK
CLK

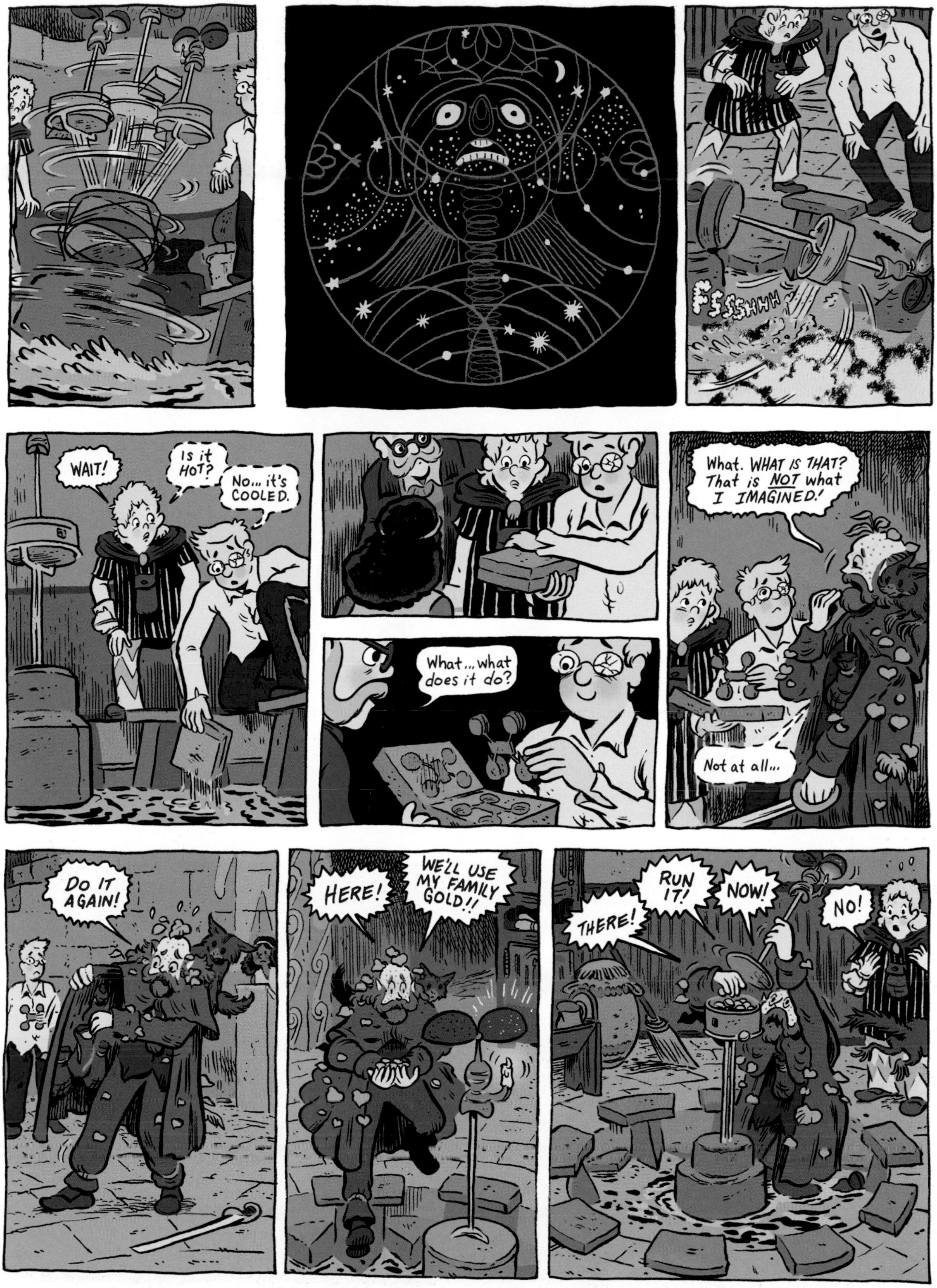
FSSSHWH
WAIT!
Is it HOT?
No... it's COOLED.
What. WHAT IS THAT? That is NOT what I IMAGINED!
What... what does it do?
Not at all...
DO IT AGAIN!
HERE!
WE'LL USE MY FAMILY GOLD!!
THERE!
RUN IT!
NOW!
NO!

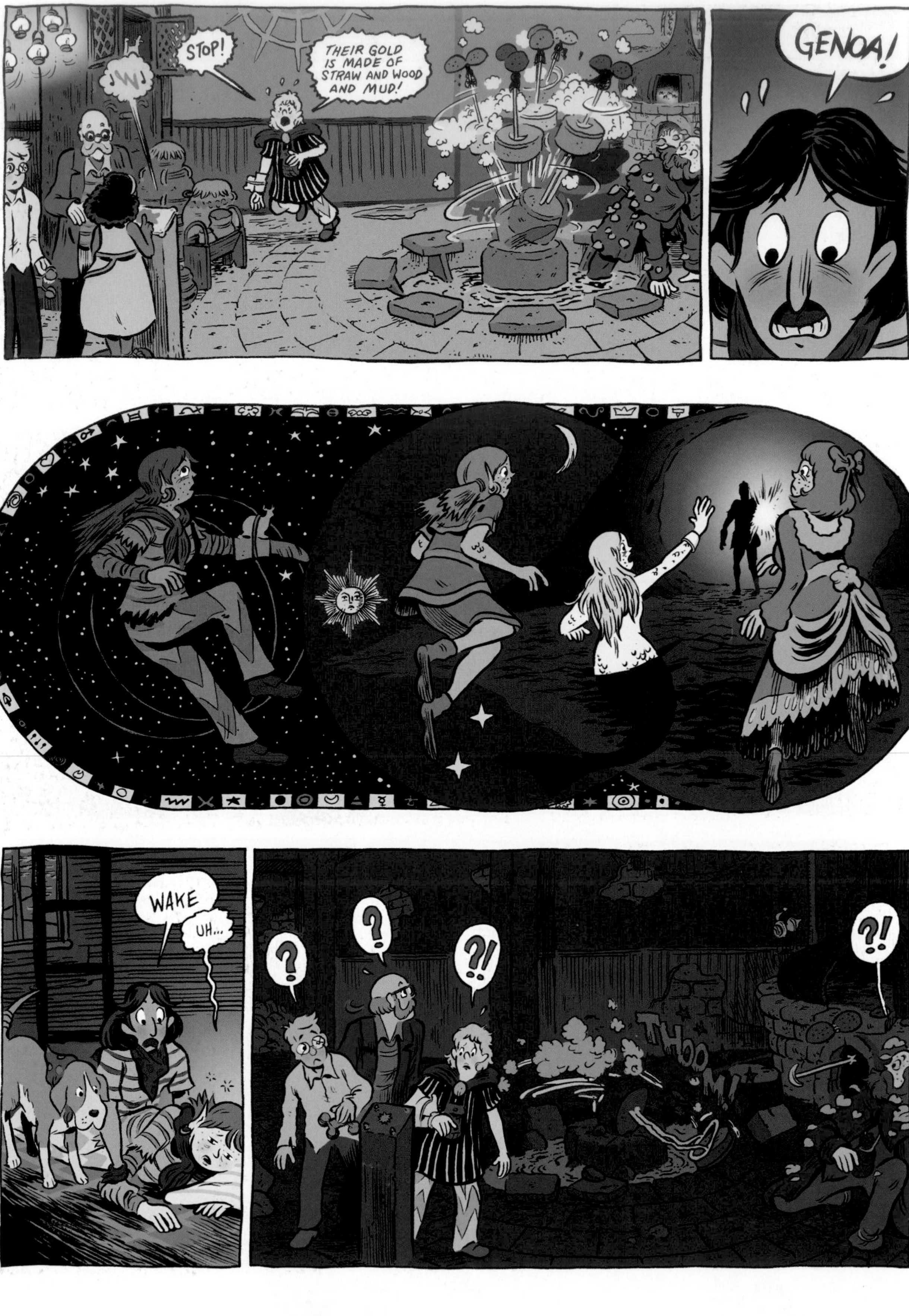
STOP!
THEIR GOLD IS MADE OF STRAW AND WOOD AND MUD!
GENOA!
WAKE
UH...
?
?
?!
THOOM!
?!

NO.
YES.
GUH!
HUH
AAGHH

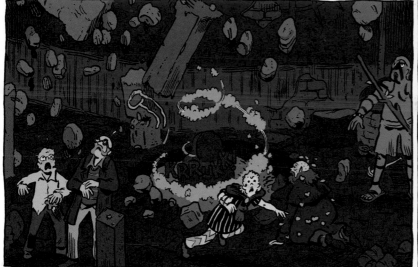

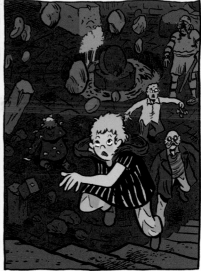

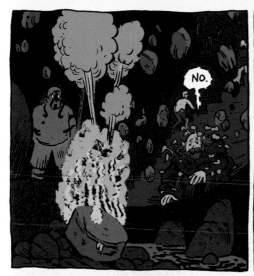

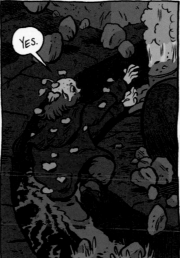

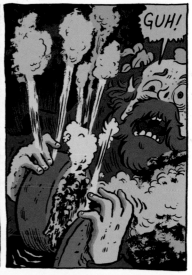

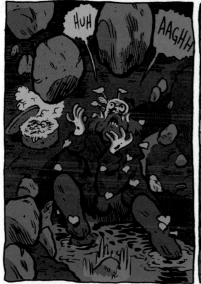

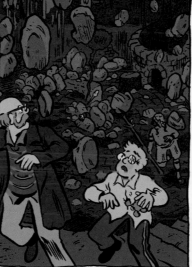

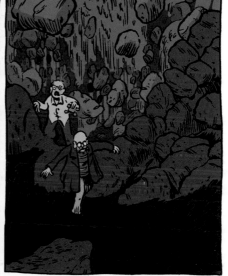

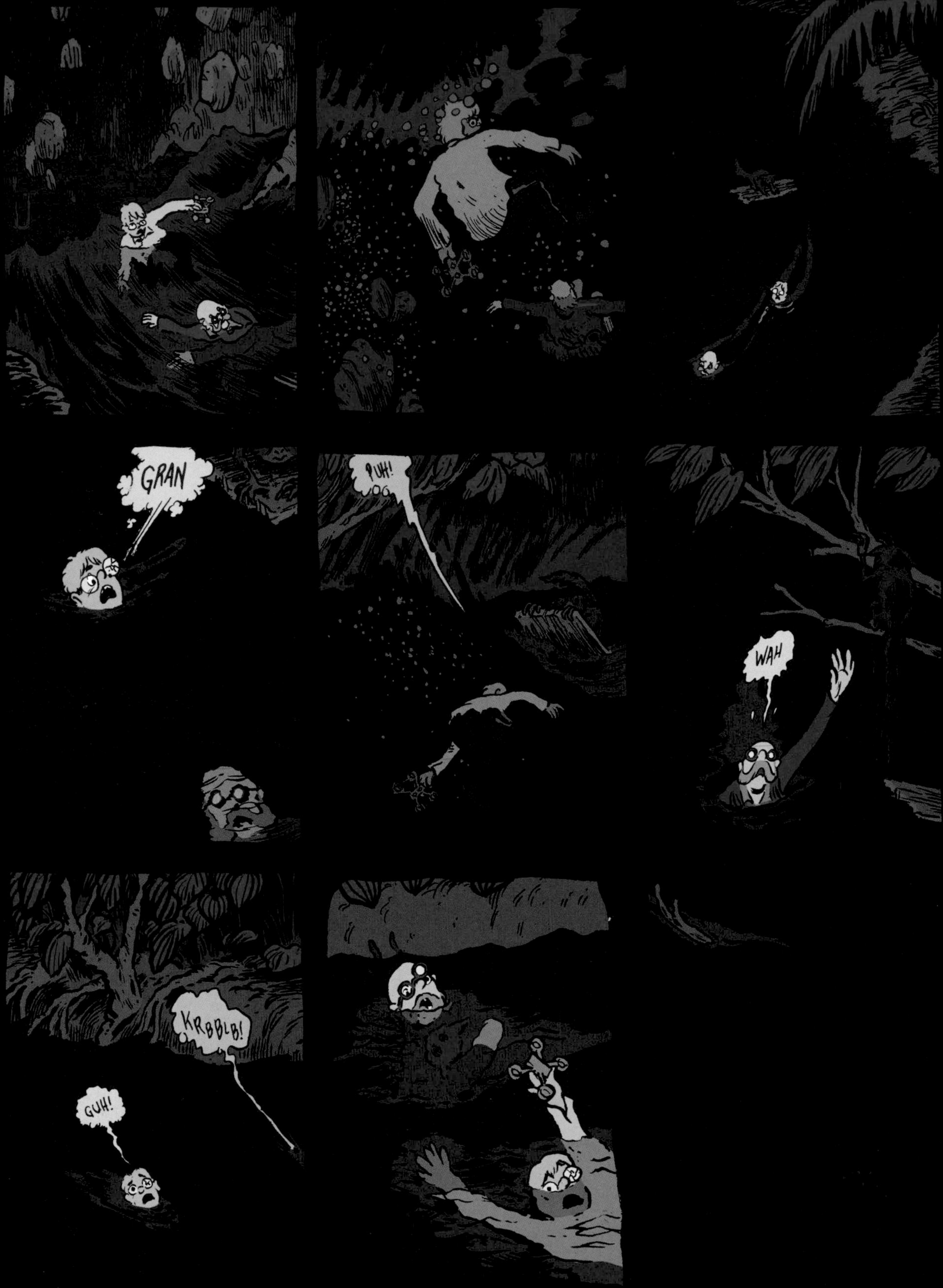
GRAN
PUH!
WAH
KRBBLB!
GUH!

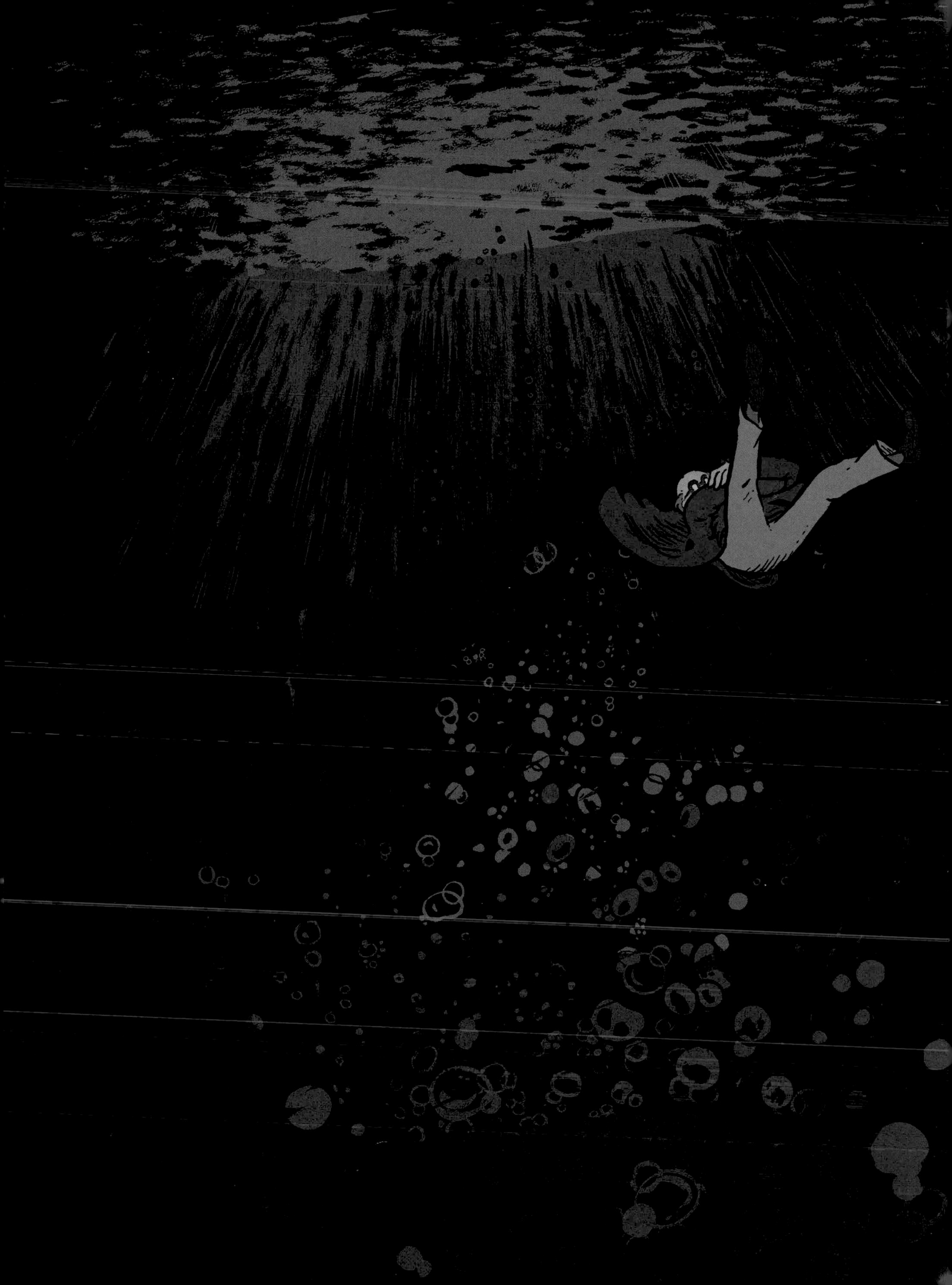

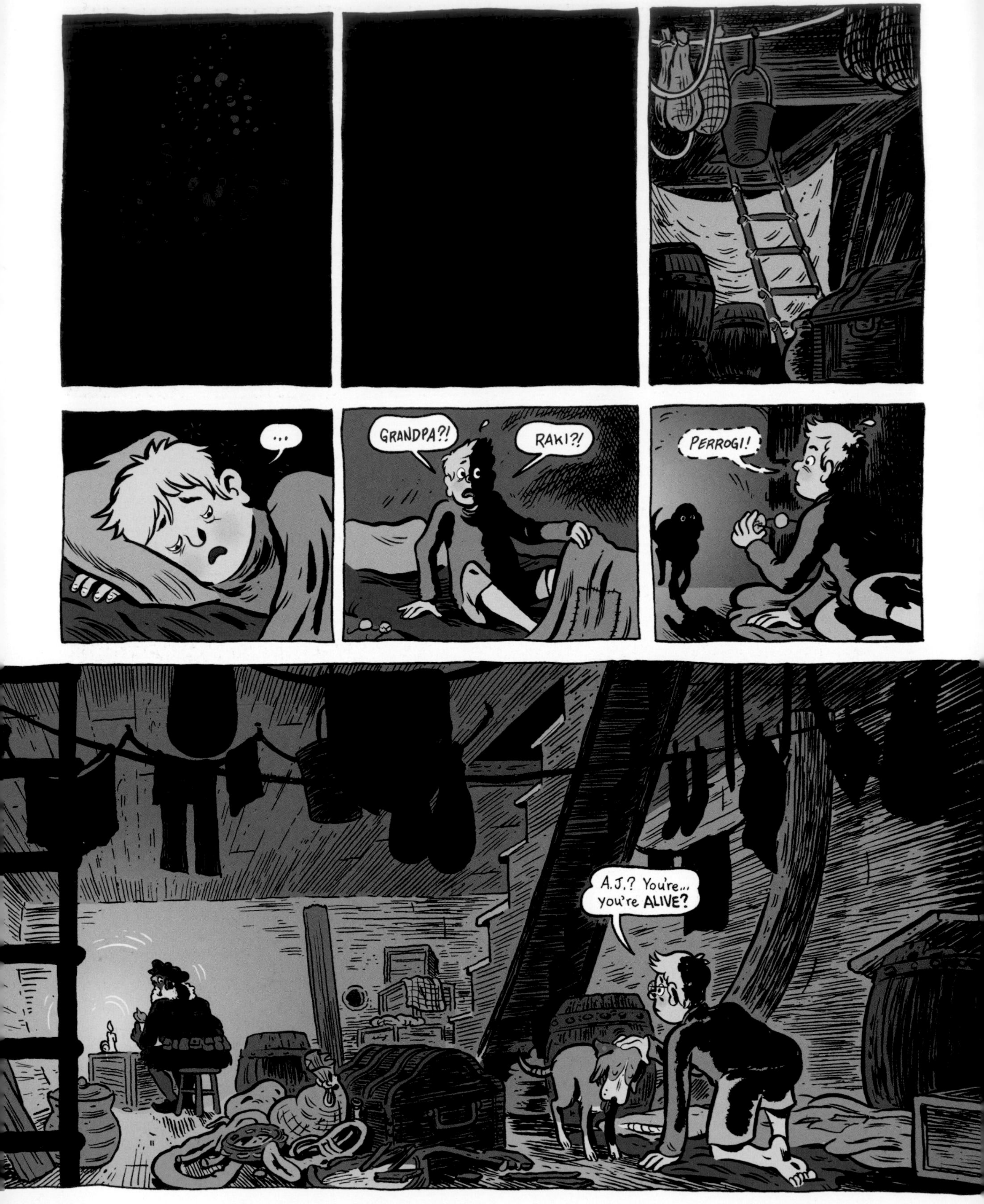
...
GRANDPA?!
RAKI?!
PERROGI!
A.J.? You're...
you're ALIVE?

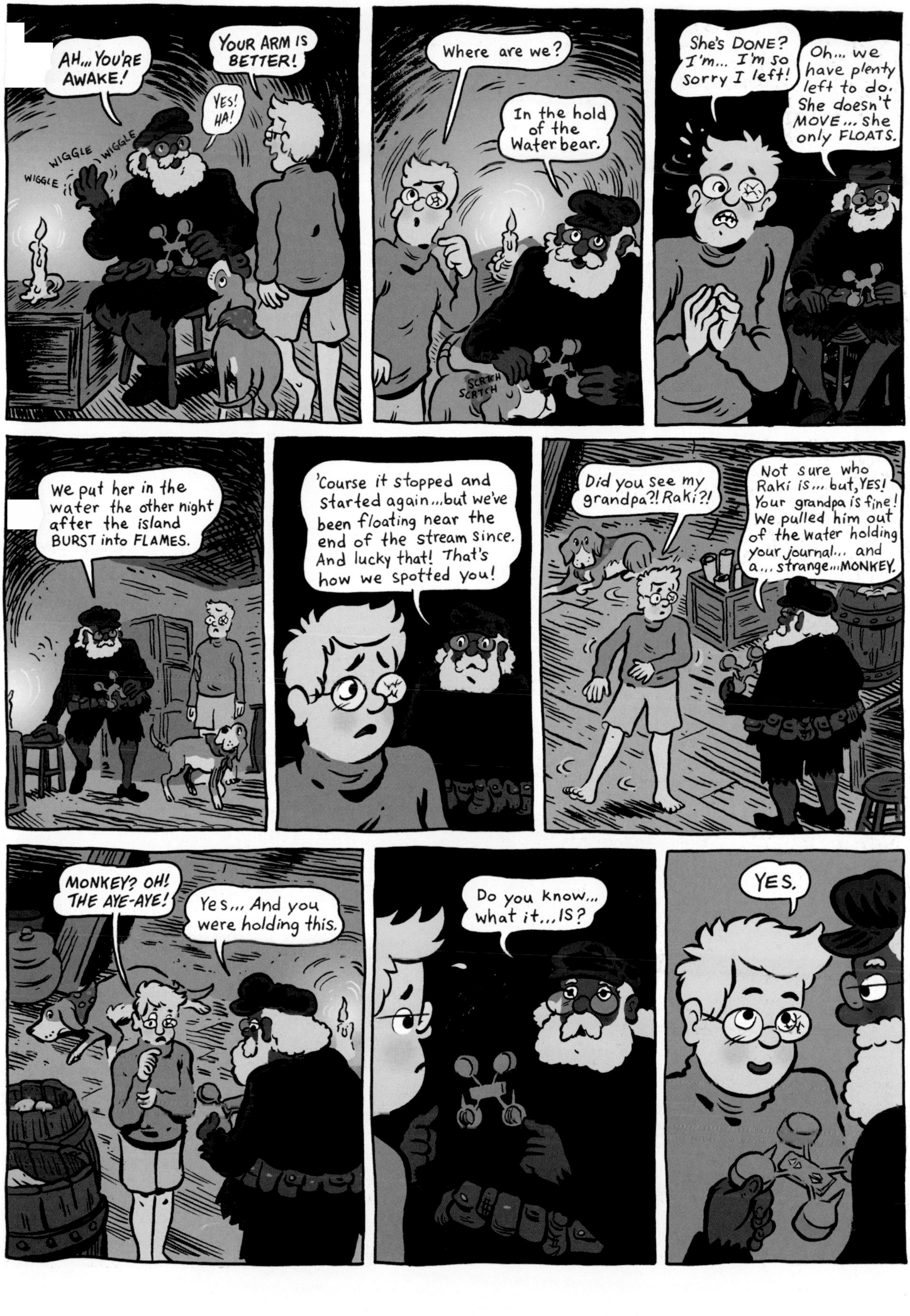
AH... YOU'RE AWAKE!
YOUR ARM IS BETTER!
YES! HA!
WIGGLE WIGGLE WIGGLE
Where are we?
In the hold of the Waterbear.
SCRTCH SCRTCH
She's DONE? I'm... I'm so sorry I left!
Oh... we have plenty left to do. She doesn't MOVE... she only FLOATS.
We put her in the water the other night after the island BURST into FLAMES.
'Course it stopped and started again...but we've been floating near the end of the stream since. And lucky that! That's how we spotted you!
Did you see my grandpa?! Raki?!
Not sure who Raki is... but, YES! Your grandpa is fine! We pulled him out of the water holding your journal... and a... strange... MONKEY.
MONKEY? OH! THE AYE-AYE!
Yes... And you were holding this.
Do you know... what it... IS?
YES.

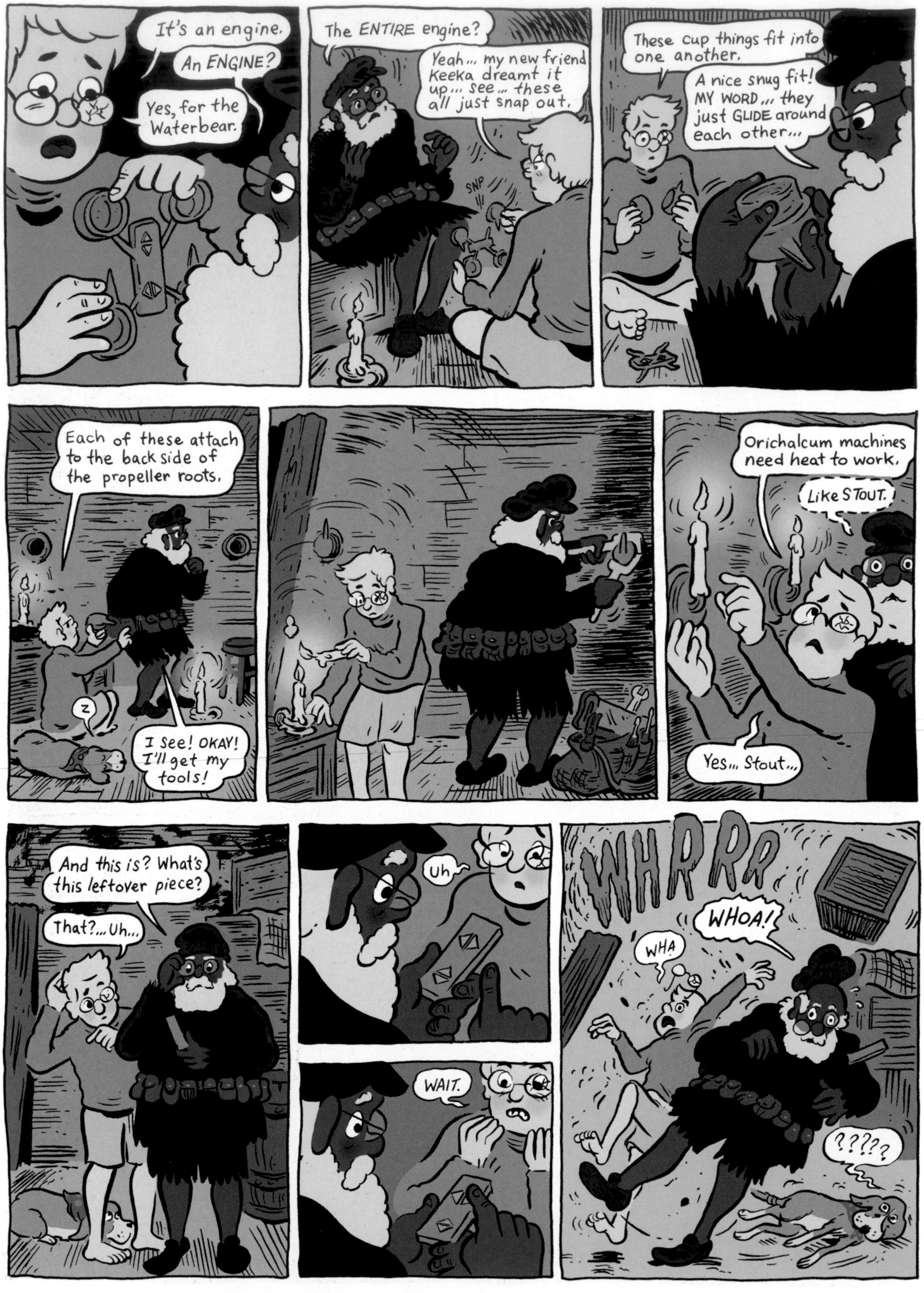
It's an engine.
An ENGINE?
Yes, for the Waterbear.
The ENTIRE engine?
Yeah... my new friend Keeka dreamt it up... see... these all just snap out.
SNP
These cup things fit into one another.
A nice snug fit! MY WORD... they just GLIDE around each other...
Each of these attach to the back side of the propeller roots.
Z
I see! OKAY! I'll get my tools!
Orichalcum machines need heat to work.
Like STOUT.
Yes... Stout...
And this is? What's this leftover piece?
That?... Uh...
Uh
WAIT.
WHRRR
WHOA!
WHA
????

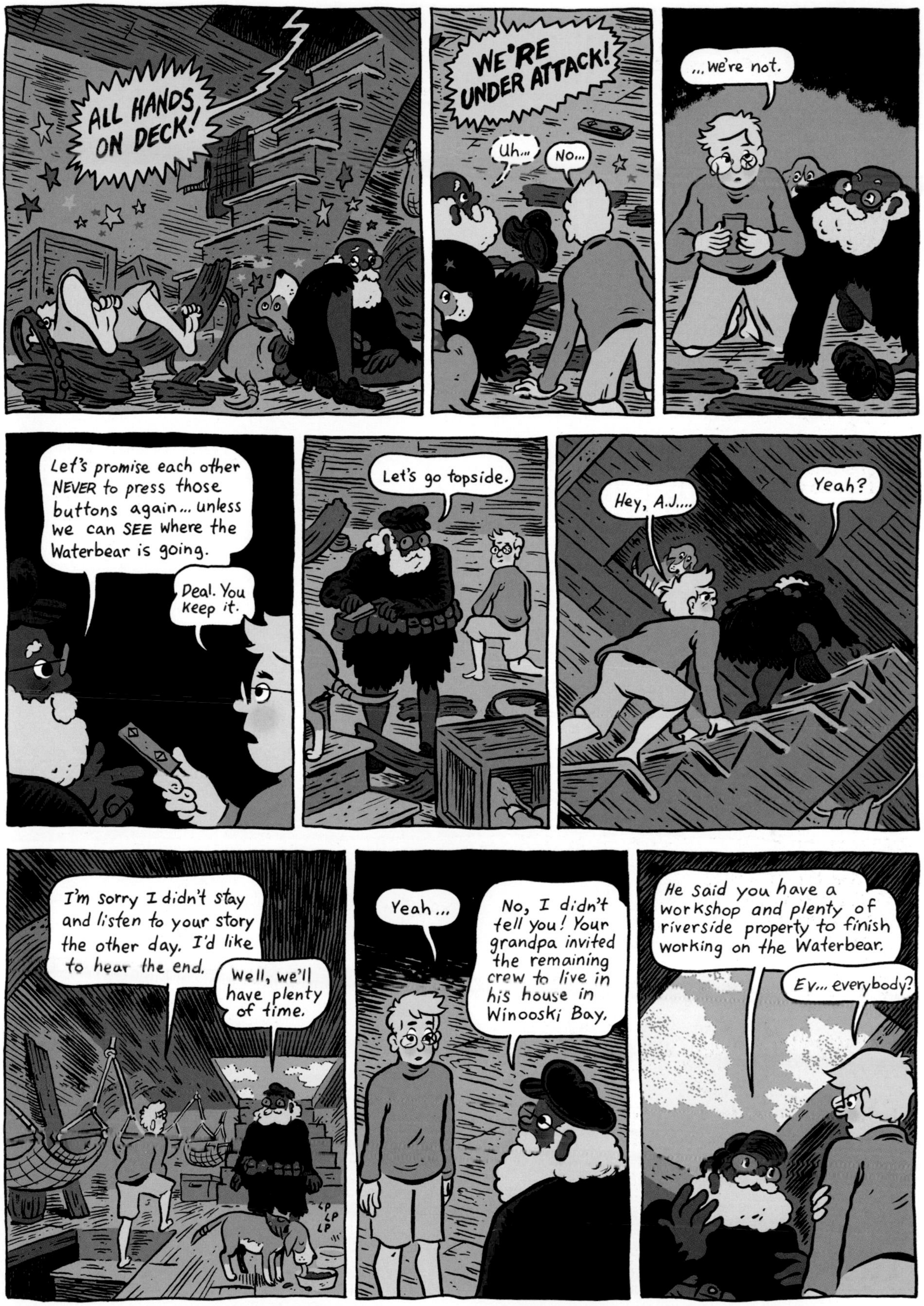
ALL HANDS, ON DECK!
WE'RE UNDER ATTACK!
Uh...
No...
...we're not.
Let's promise each other NEVER to press those buttons again... unless we can SEE where the Waterbear is going.
Deal. You keep it.
Let's go topside.
Hey, A.J....
Yeah?
I'm sorry I didn't stay and listen to your story the other day. I'd like to hear the end.
Well, we'll have plenty of time.
LP LP LP
Yeah...
No, I didn't tell you! Your grandpa invited the remaining crew to live in his house in Winooski Bay.
He said you have a workshop and plenty of riverside property to finish working on the Waterbear.
Ev... everybody?

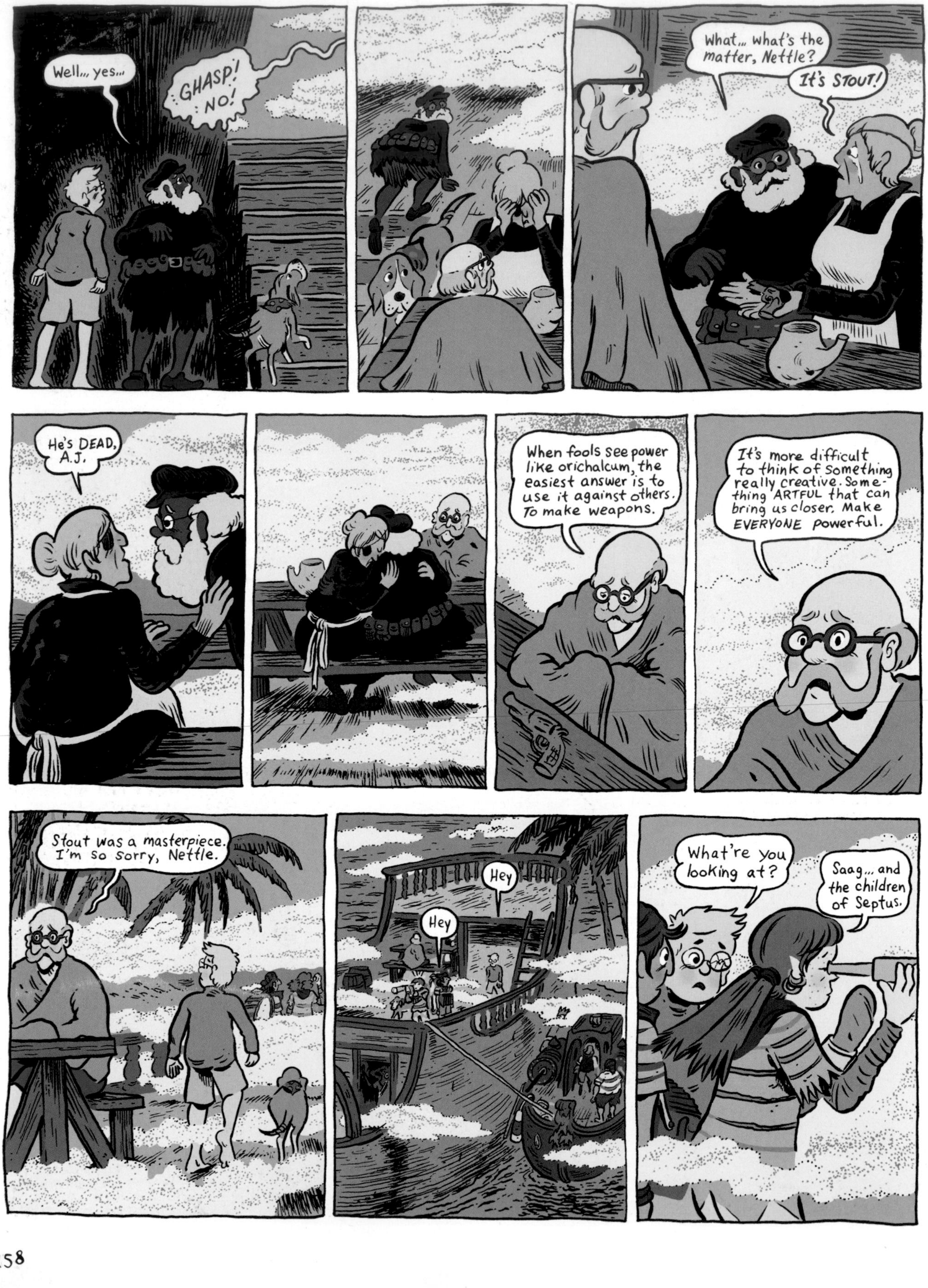
Well... yes...
GHASP! NO!
What... what's the matter, Nettle?
It's STOUT!
He's DEAD, A.J.
When fools see power like orichalcum, the easiest answer is to use it against others. To make weapons.
It's more difficult to think of something really creative. Something ARTFUL that can bring us closer. Make EVERYONE powerful.
Stout was a masterpiece. I'm so sorry, Nettle.
Hey
Hey
What're you looking at?
Saag... and the children of Septus.

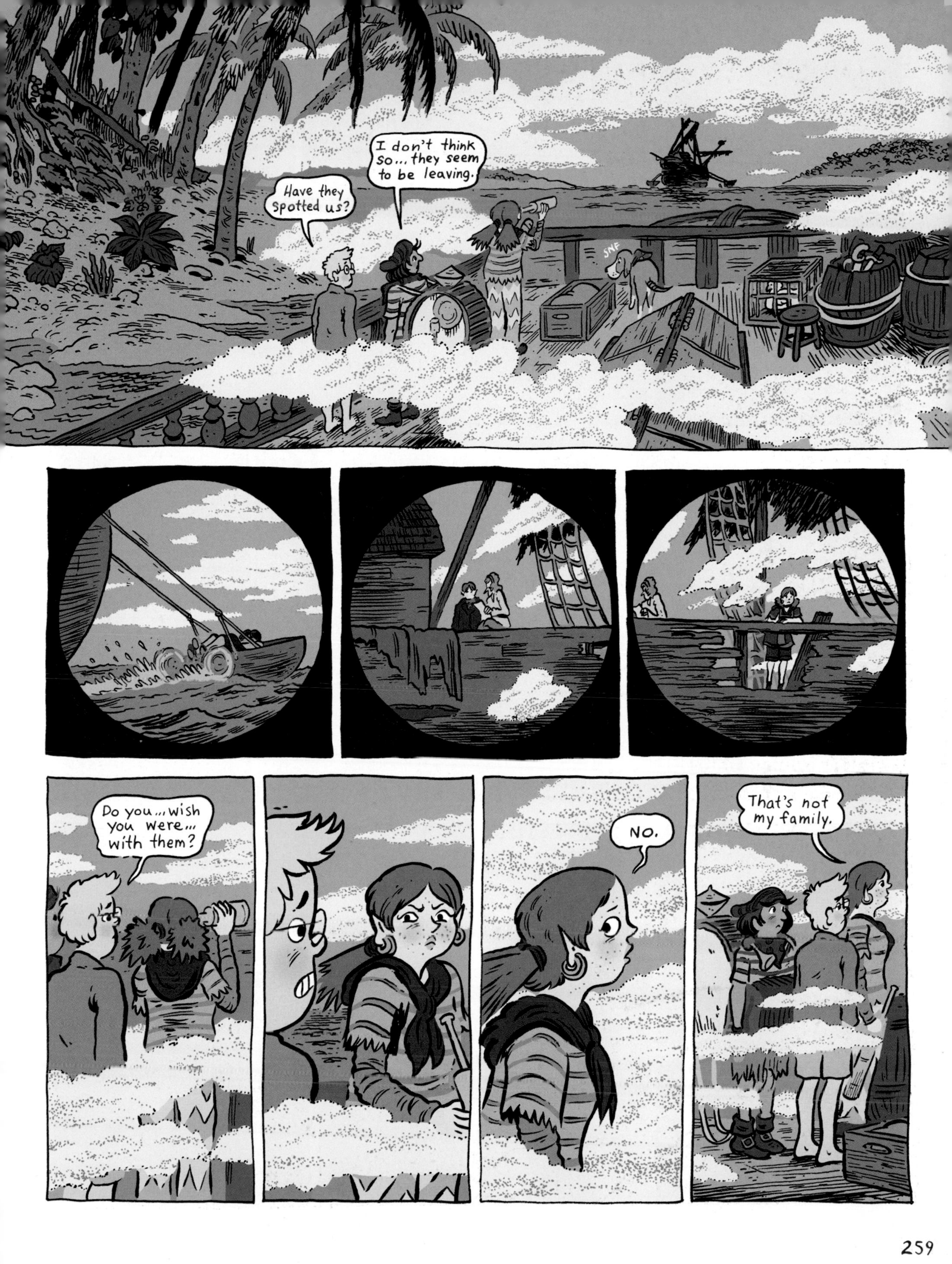
Have they spotted us?
I don't think so... they seem to be leaving.
SNF
Do you... wish you were... with them?
NO.
That's not my family.

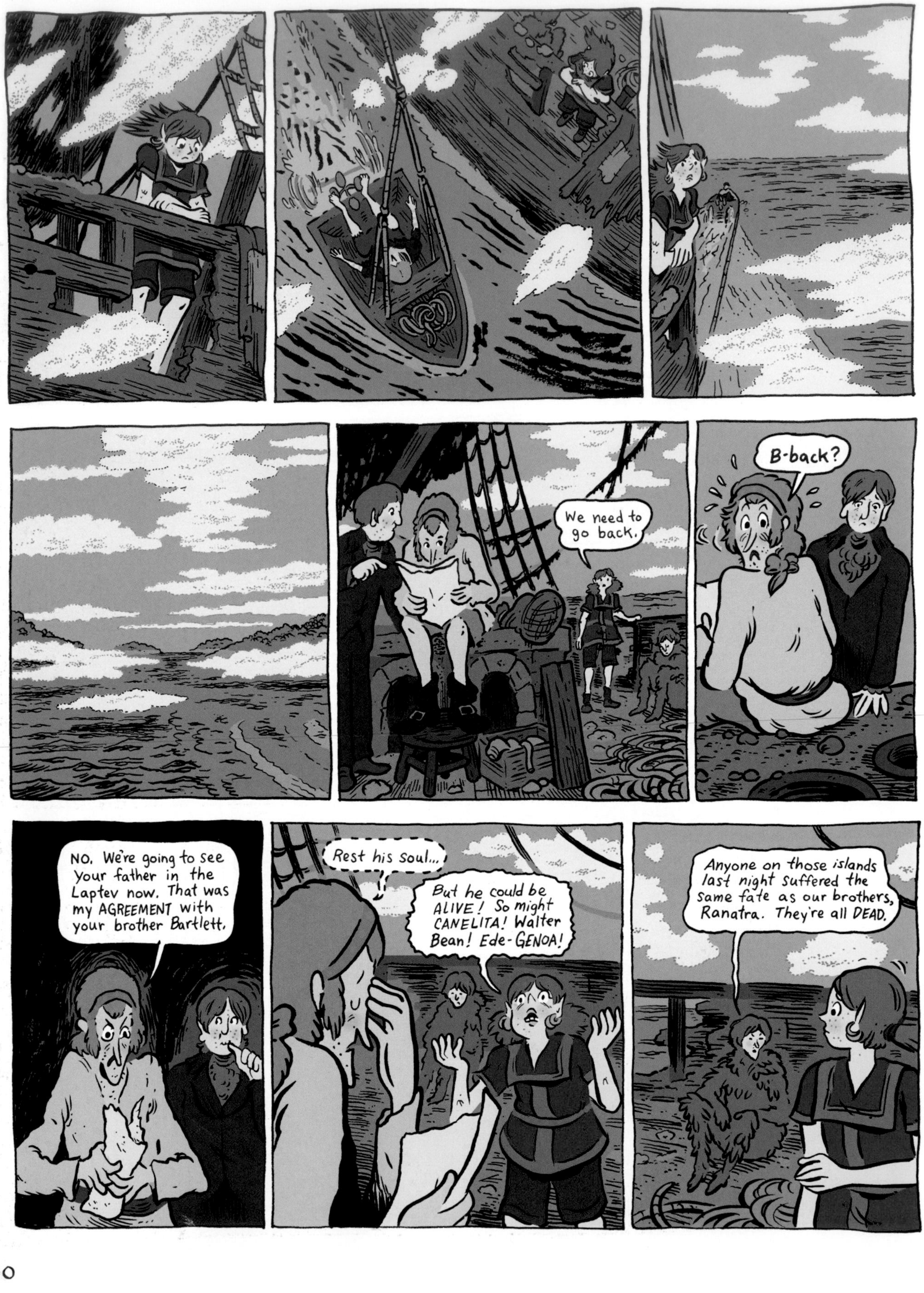
We need to go back.
B-back?
NO. We're going to see your father in the Laptev now. That was my AGREEMENT with your brother Bartlett.
Rest his soul...
But he could be ALIVE! So might CANELITA! Walter Bean! Ede-GENOA!
Anyone on those islands last night suffered the same fate as our brothers, Ranatra. They're all DEAD.

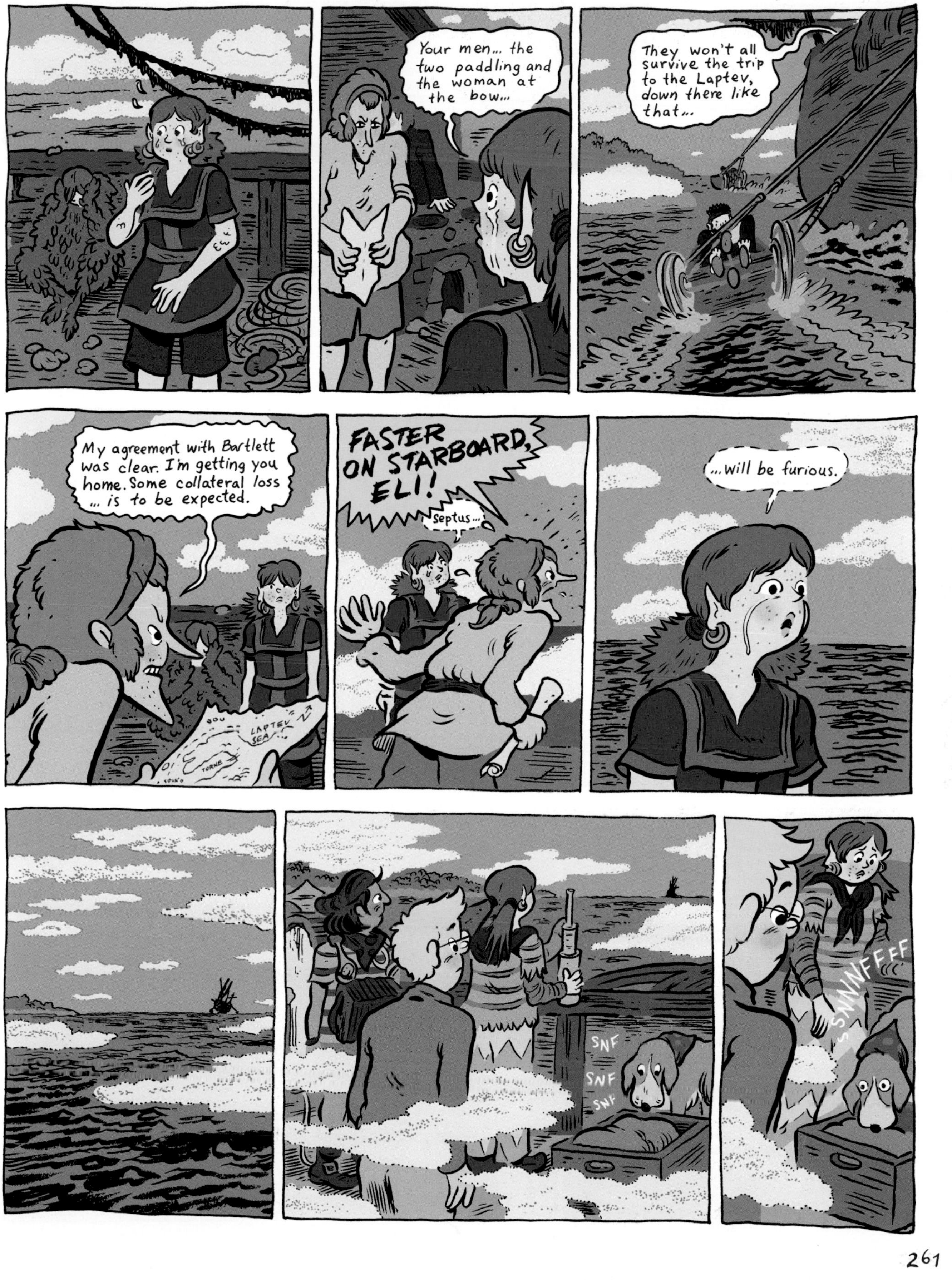
Your men... the two paddling and the woman at the bow...
They won't all survive the trip to the Laptev, down there like that...
My agreement with Bartlett was clear. I'm getting you home. Some collateral loss ... is to be expected.
LAPTEV SEA
FASTER ON STARBOARD, ELI!
Septus...
...will be furious.
SNF
SNF
SNF
SNNNFFFF

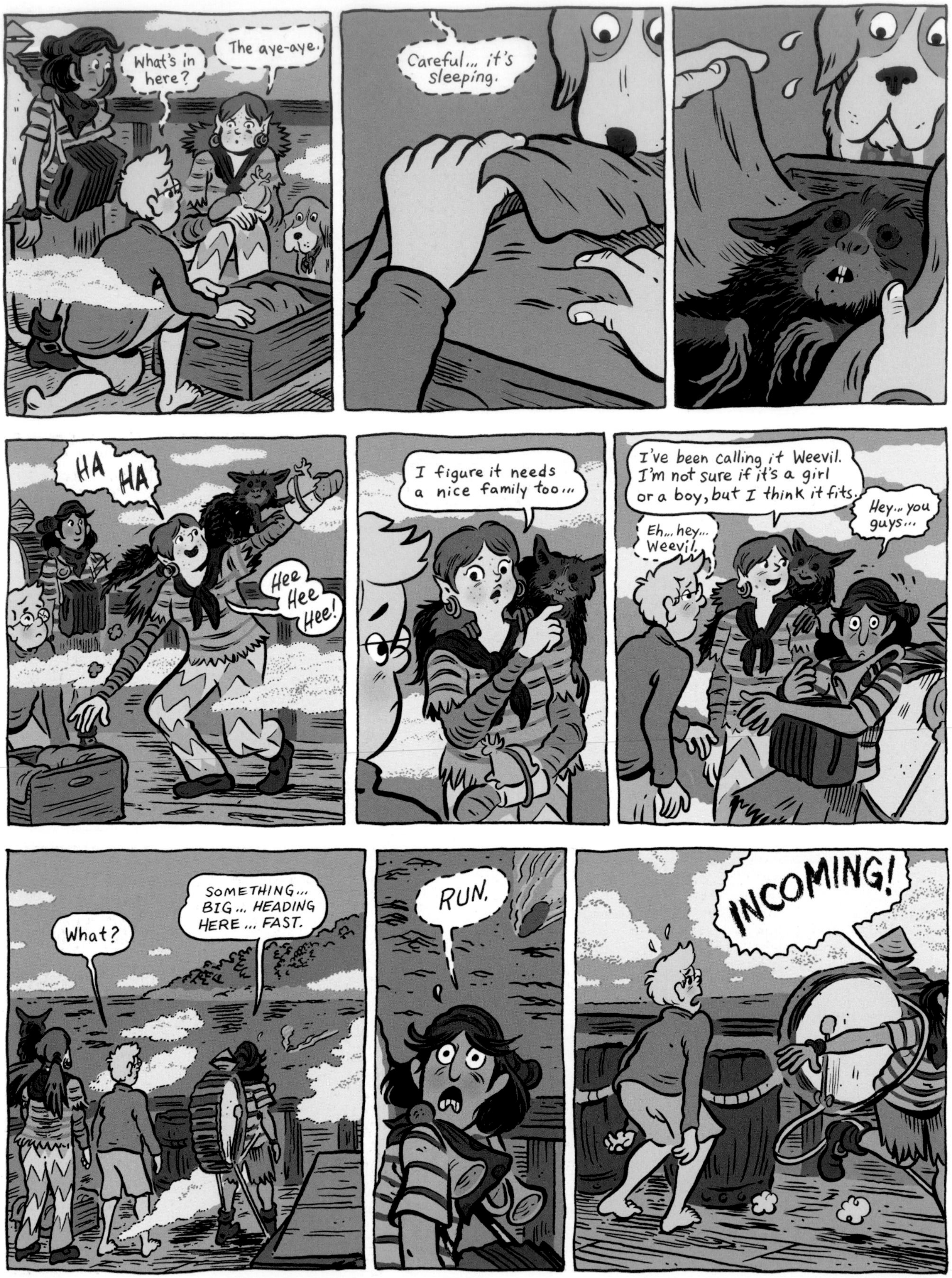
What's in here?
The aye-aye.
Careful... it's sleeping.
HA HA
Hee Hee Hee!
I figure it needs a nice family too...
I've been calling it Weevil. I'm not sure if it's a girl or a boy, but I think it fits.
Eh... hey... Weevil.
Hey... you guys...
What?
SOMETHING... BIG... HEADING HERE... FAST.
RUN.
INCOMING!

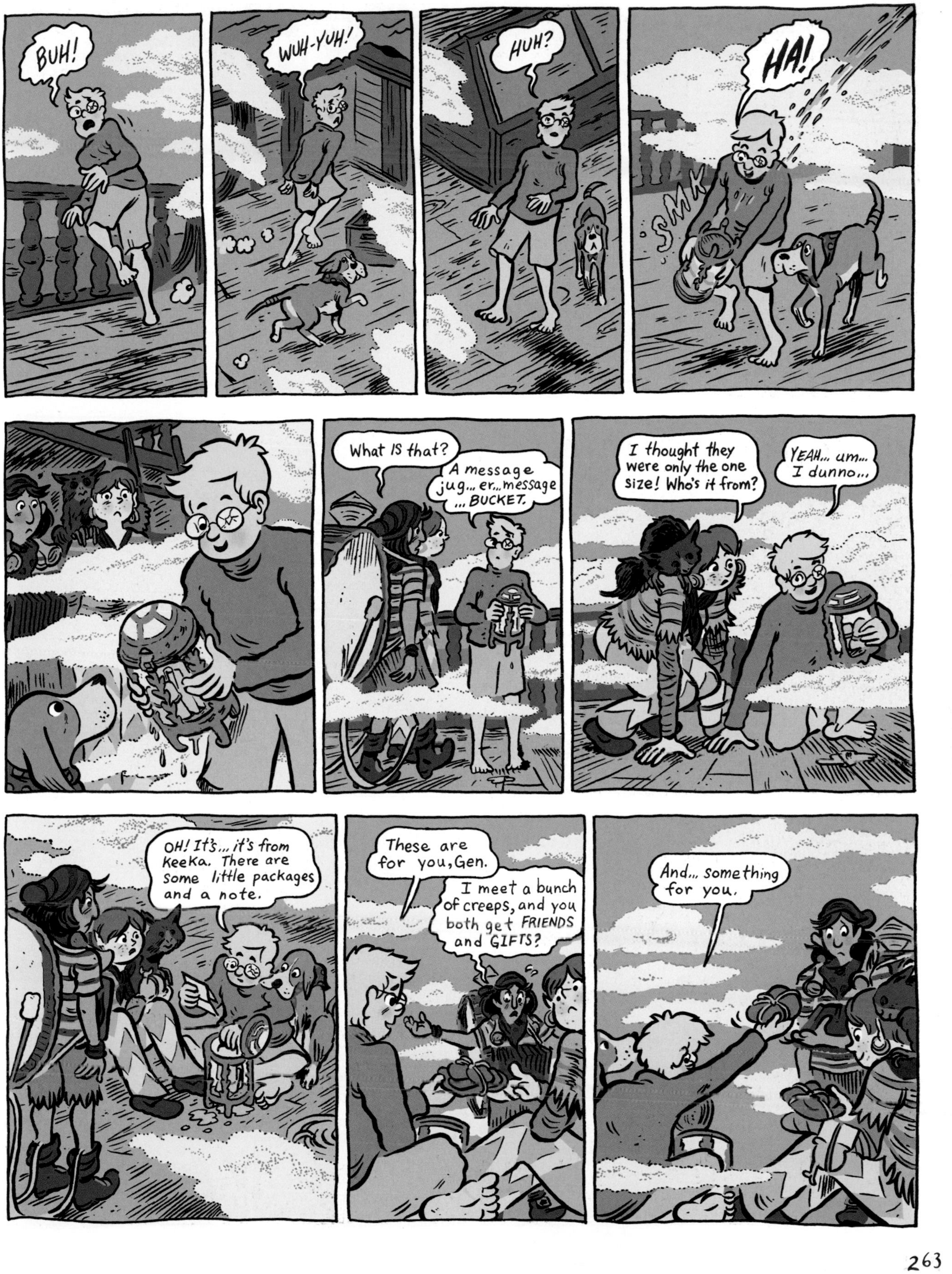
BUH!
WUH-YUH!
HUH?
HA!
SMK
What IS that?
A message jug... er... message ... BUCKET.
I thought they were only the one size! Who's it from?
YEAH... um... I dunno...
OH! It's... it's from Keeka. There are some little packages and a note.
These are for you, Gen.
I meet a bunch of creeps, and you both get FRIENDS and GIFTS?
And... something for you.

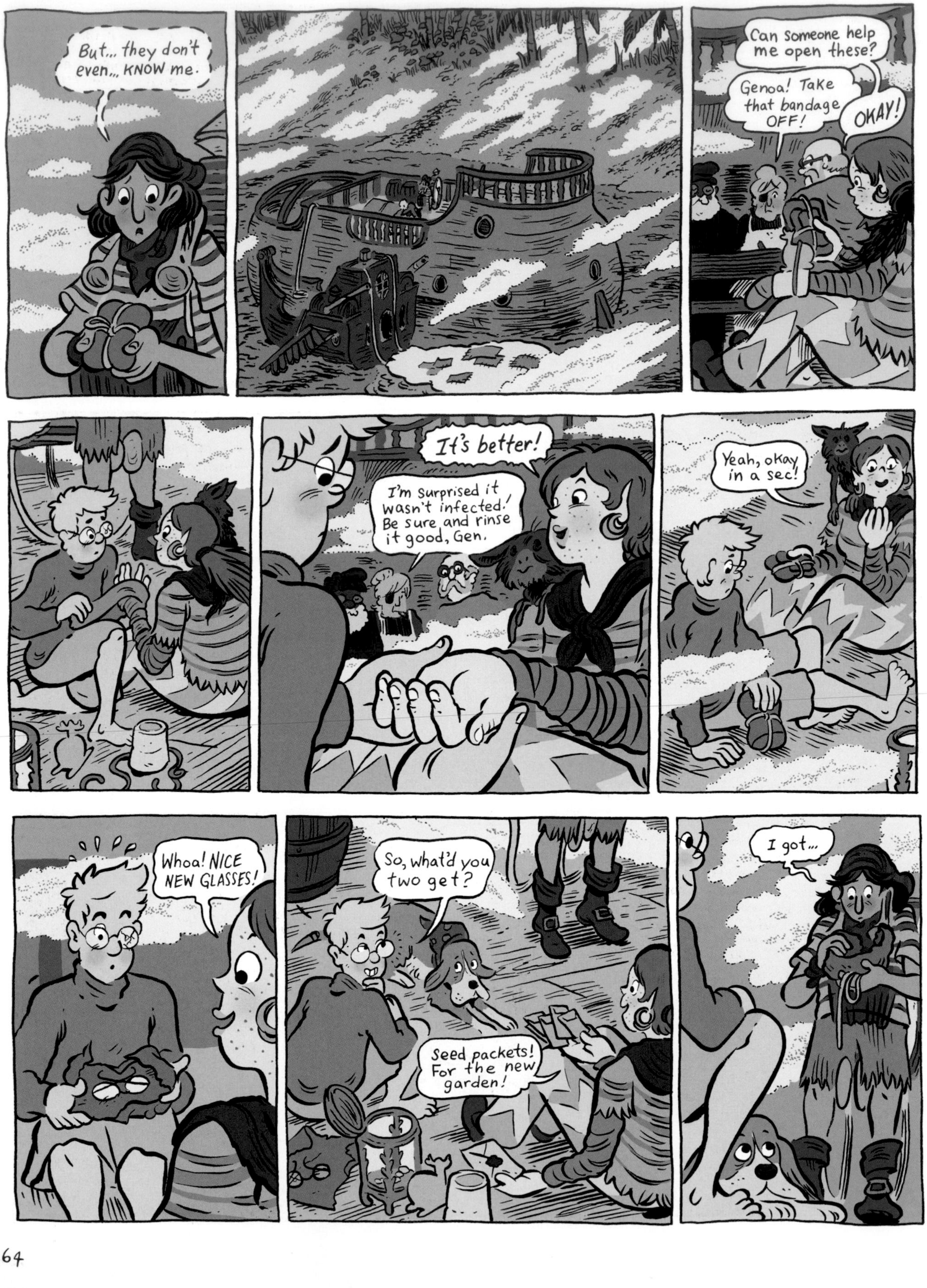
But... they don't even... KNOW me.
Can someone help me open these?
Genoa! Take that bandage OFF!
OKAY!
It's better!
I'm surprised it wasn't infected! Be sure and rinse it good, Gen.
Yeah, okay, in a sec!
Whoa! NICE NEW GLASSES!
So, what'd you two get?
Seed packets! For the new garden!
I got...

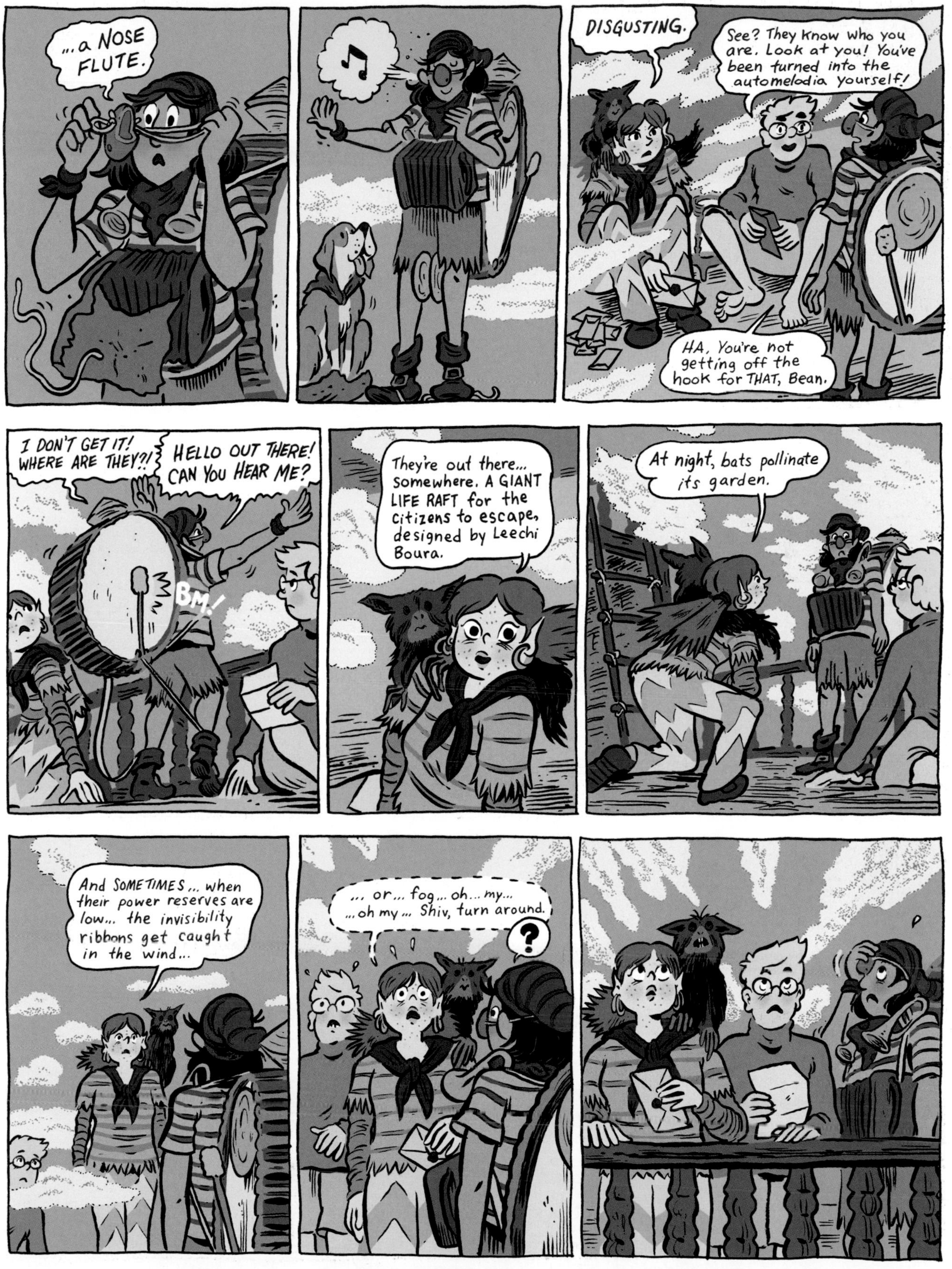
...a NOSE FLUTE.
DISGUSTING.
See? They know who you are. Look at you! You've been turned into the automelodia yourself!
HA. You're not getting off the hook for THAT, Bean.
I DON'T GET IT! WHERE ARE THEY?!
HELLO OUT THERE! CAN YOU HEAR ME?
BM!
They're out there... somewhere. A GIANT LIFE RAFT for the citizens to escape, designed by Leechi Boura.
At night, bats pollinate its garden.
And SOMETIMES... when their power reserves are low... the invisibility ribbons get caught in the wind...
... or... fog... oh... my... ...oh my... Shiv, turn around.
?

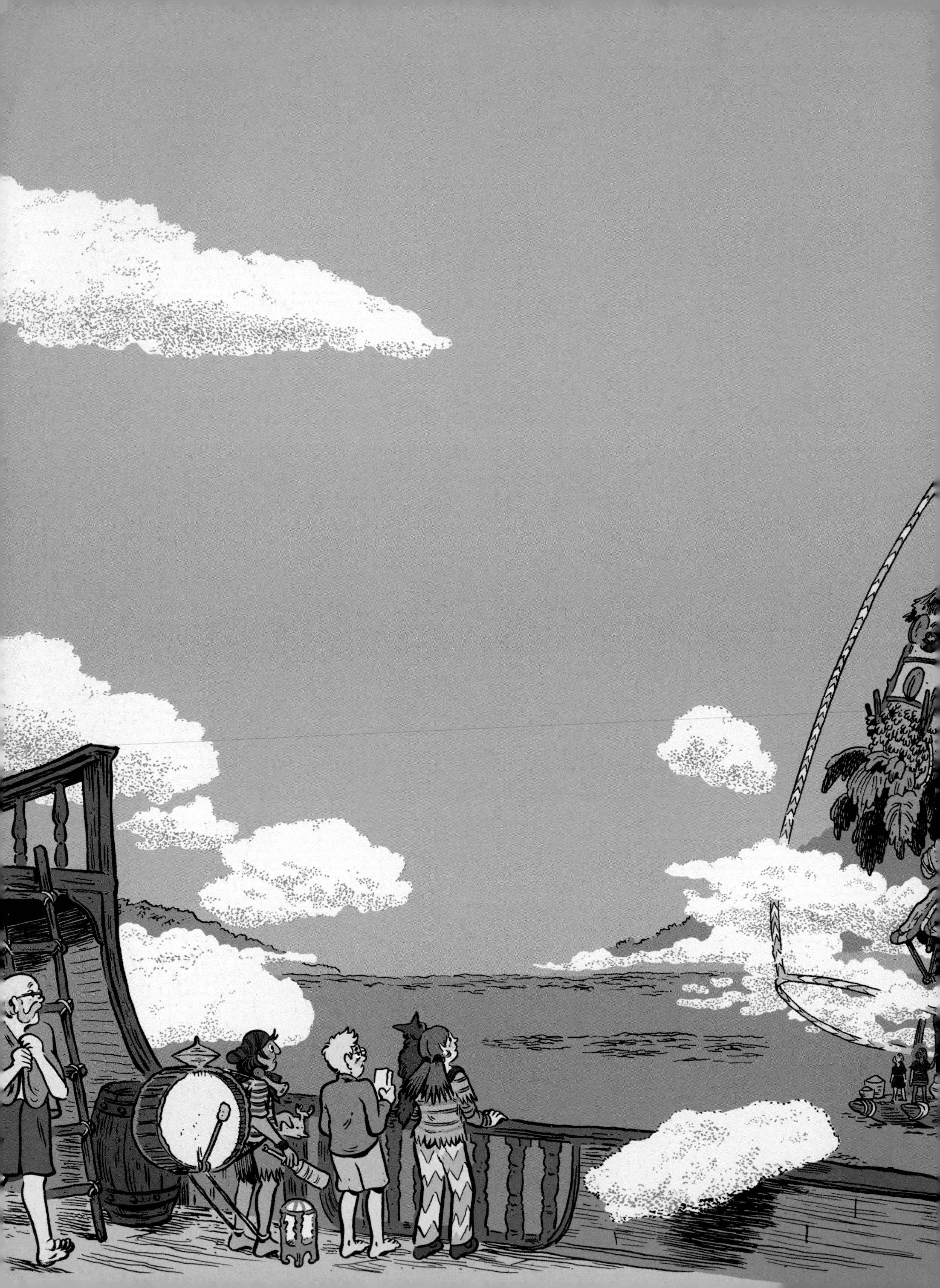

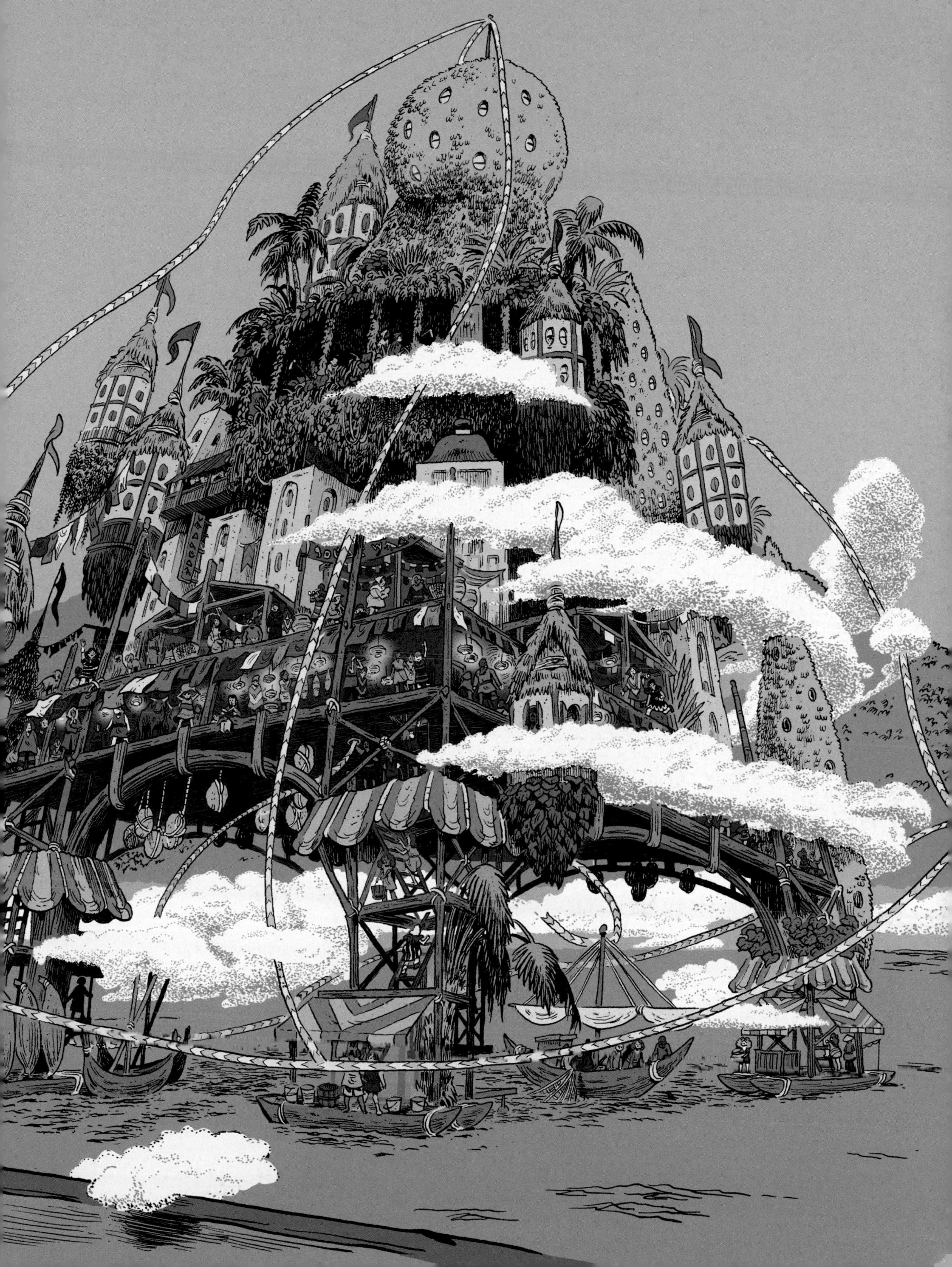

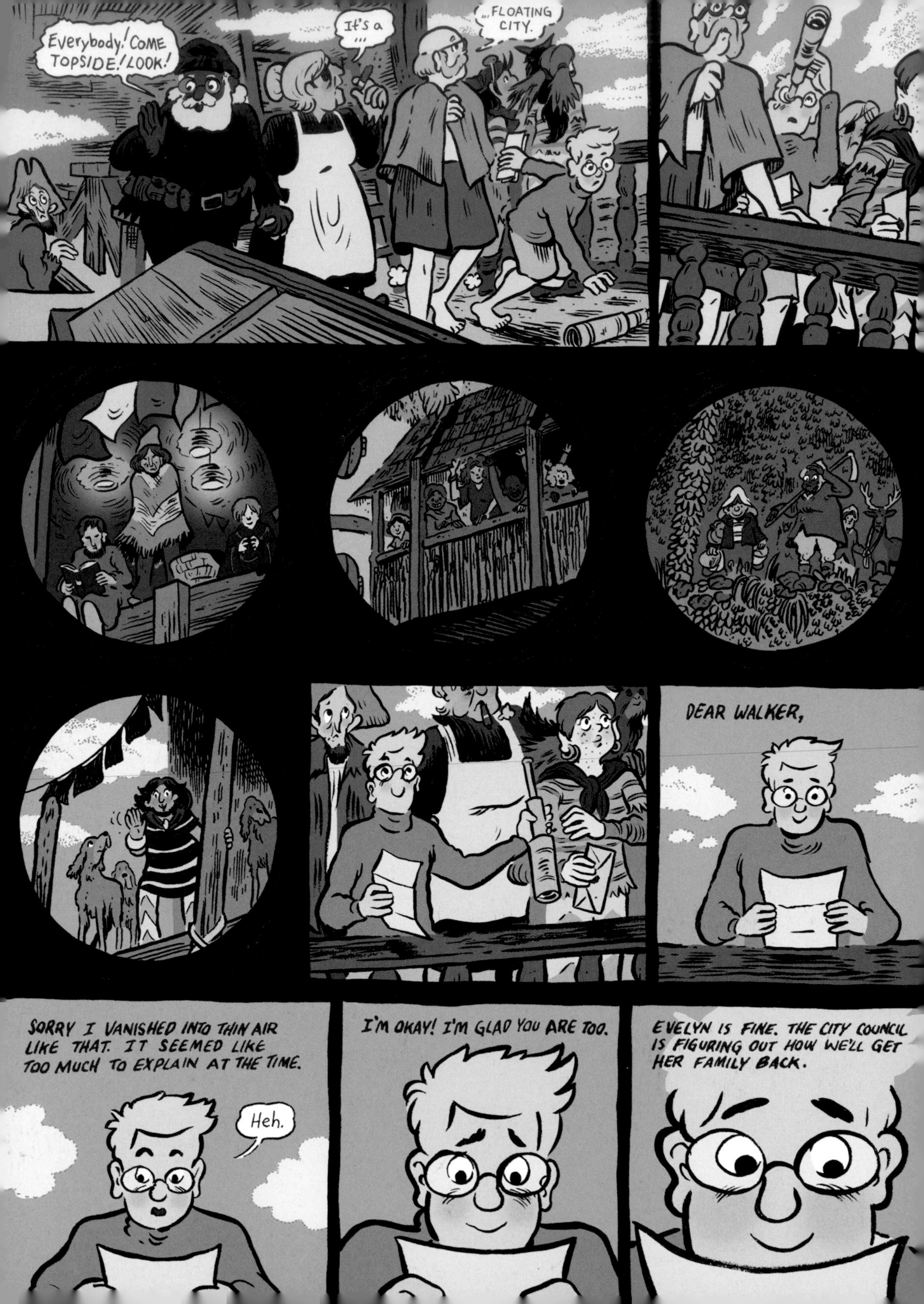
Everybody! COME TOPSIDE! LOOK!
It's a ...
... FLOATING CITY.
DEAR WALKER,
SORRY I VANISHED INTO THIN AIR LIKE THAT. IT SEEMED LIKE TOO MUCH TO EXPLAIN AT THE TIME.
Heh.
I'M OKAY! I'M GLAD YOU ARE TOO.
EVELYN IS FINE. THE CITY COUNCIL IS FIGURING OUT HOW WE'LL GET HER FAMILY BACK.

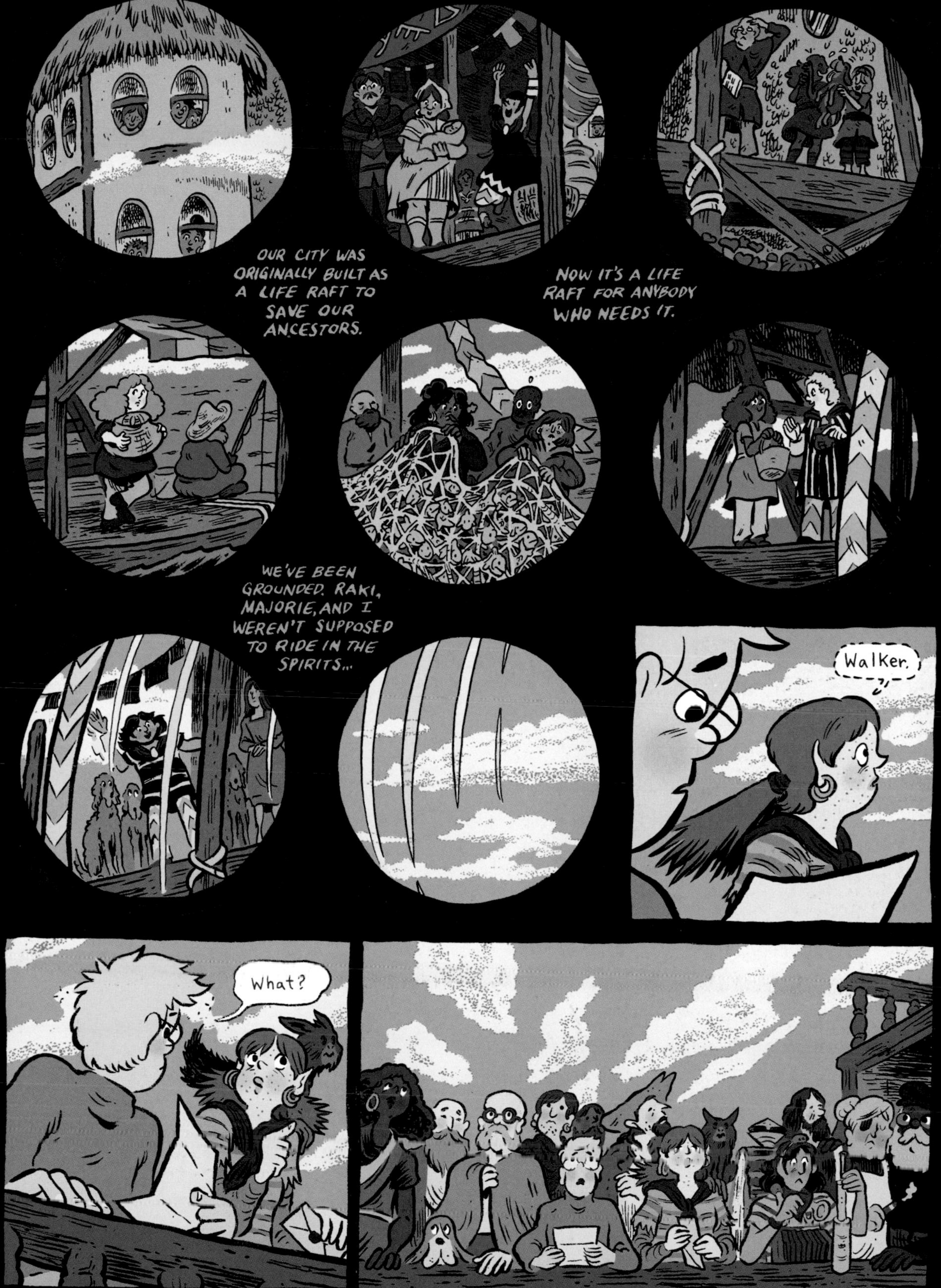
OUR CITY WAS ORIGINALLY BUILT AS A LIFE RAFT TO SAVE OUR ANCESTORS.
NOW IT'S A LIFE RAFT FOR ANYBODY WHO NEEDS IT.
WE'VE BEEN GROUNDED. RAKI, MAJORIE, AND I WEREN'T SUPPOSED TO RIDE IN THE SPIRITS...
Walker.
What?

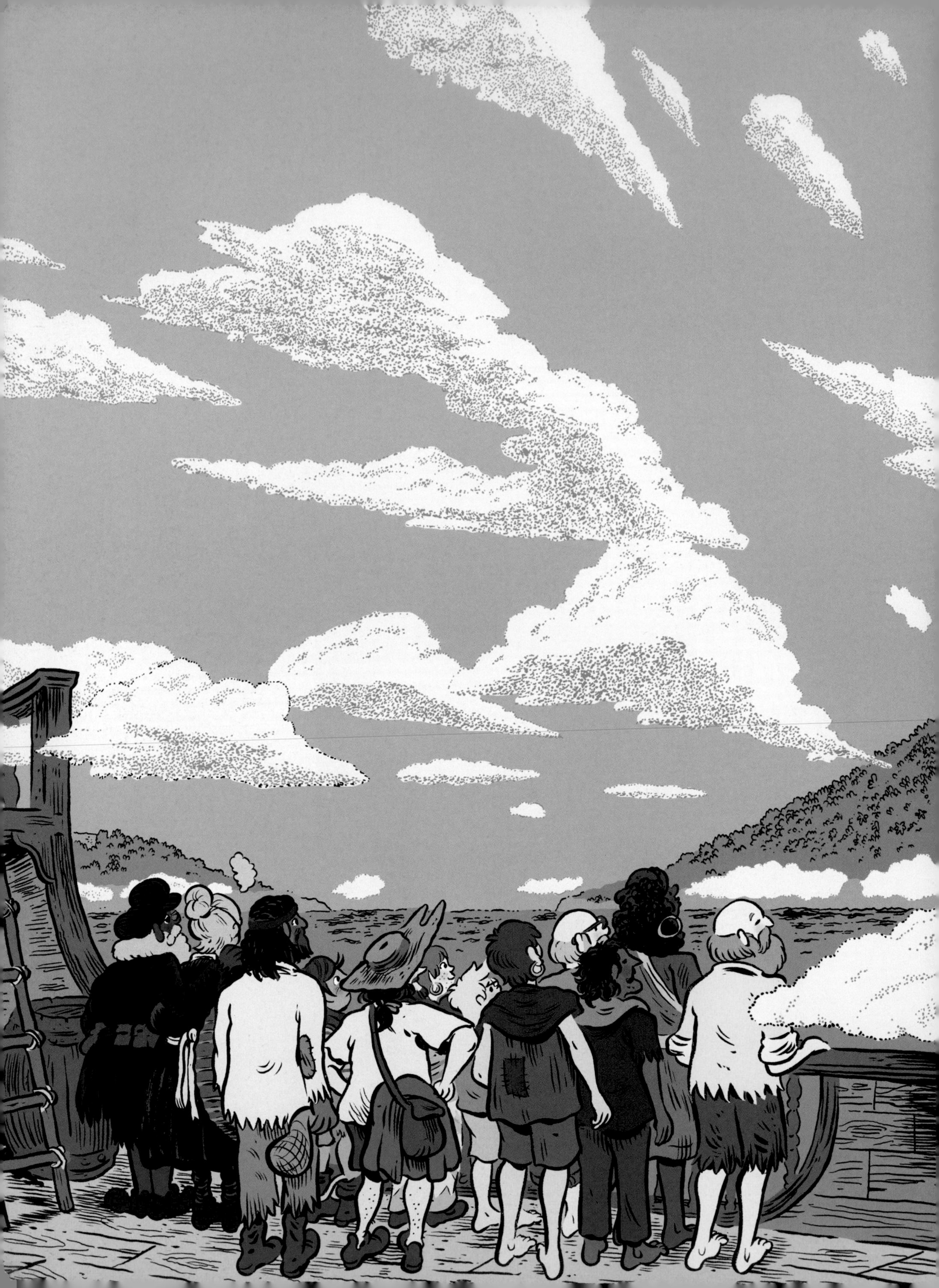

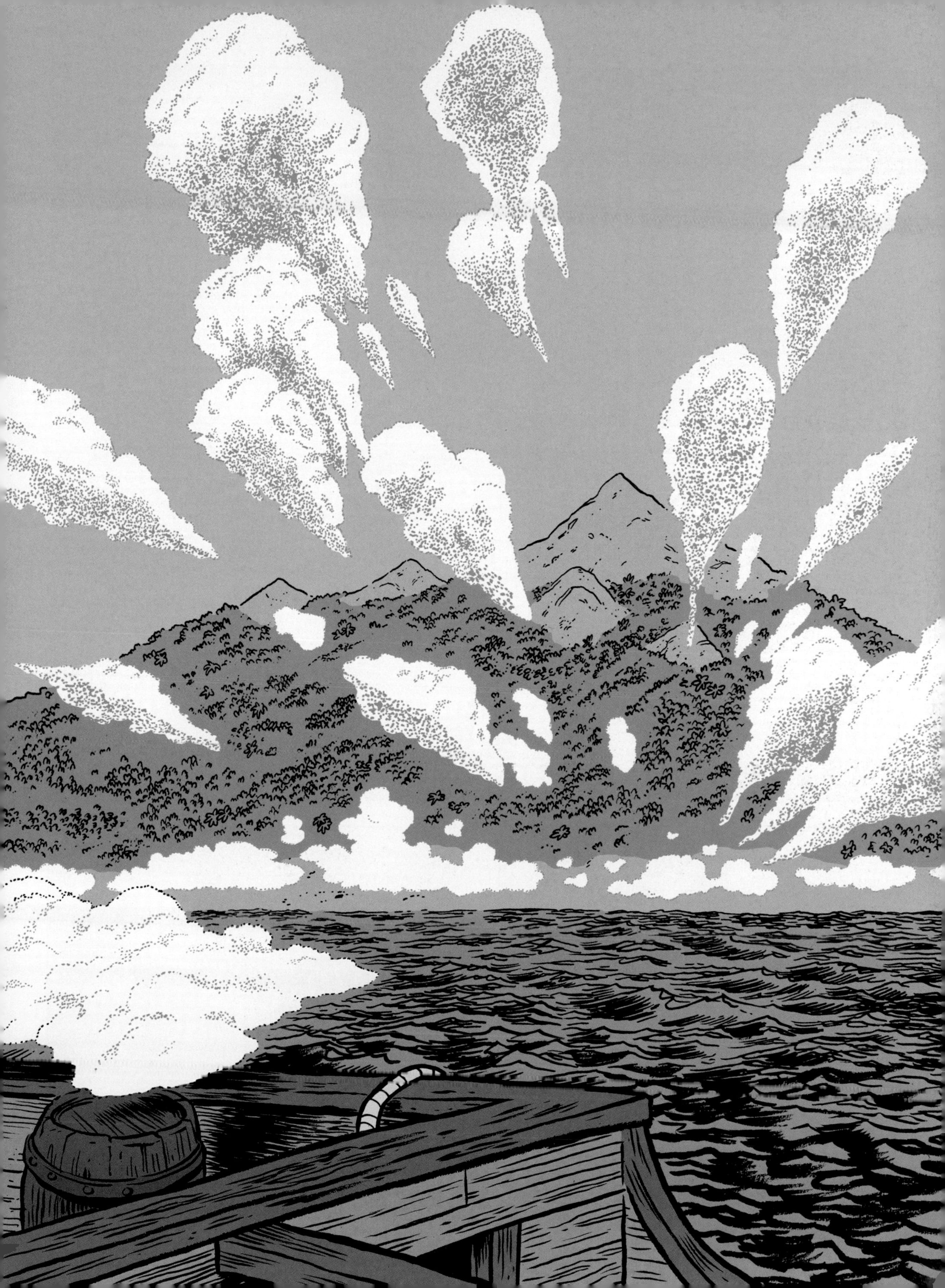

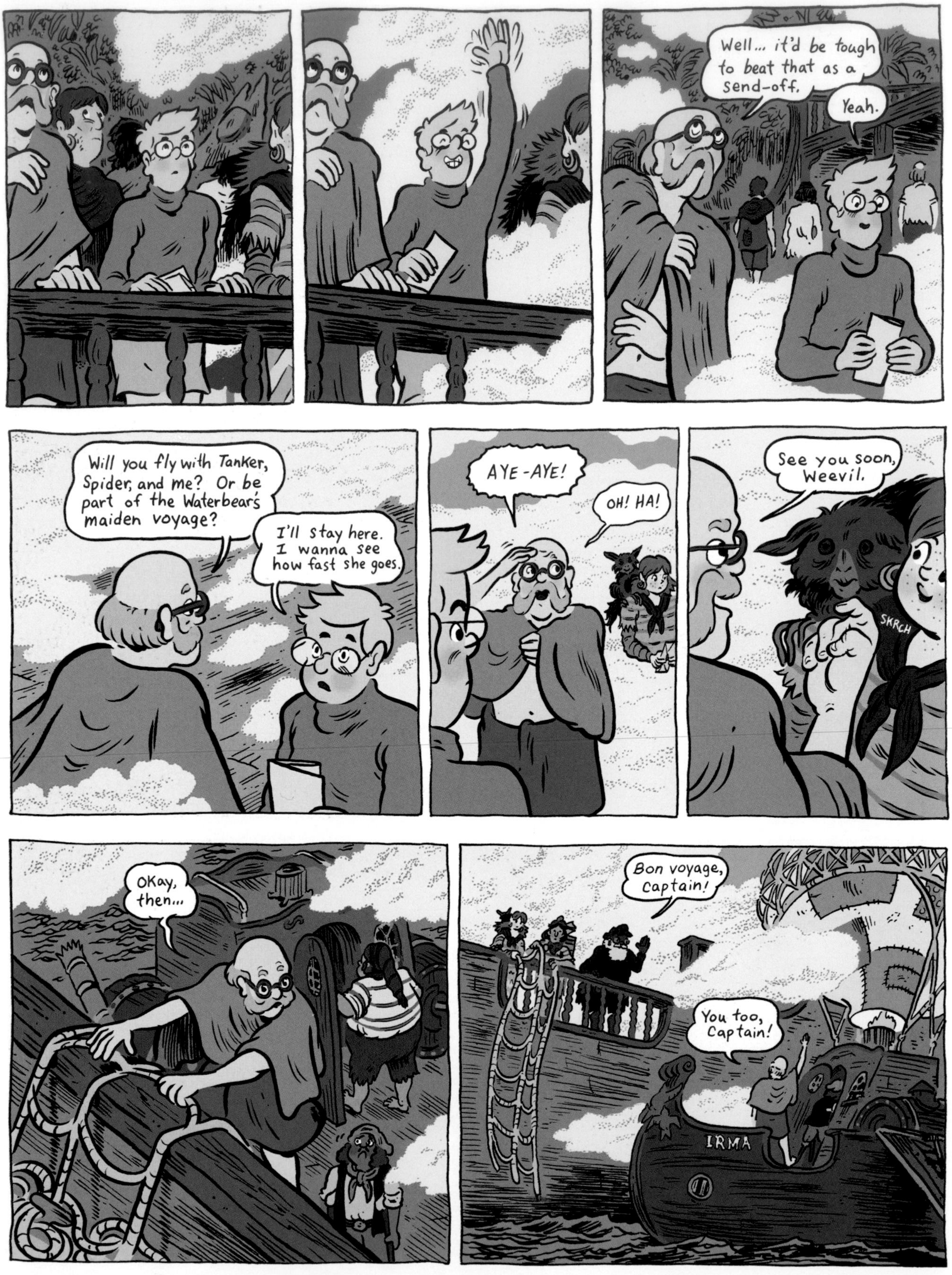
Well... it'd be tough to beat that as a send-off.
Yeah.
Will you fly with Tanker, Spider, and me? Or be part of the Waterbear's maiden voyage?
I'll stay here. I wanna see how fast she goes.
AYE-AYE!
OH! HA!
See you soon, Weevil.
SKRCH
OKay, then...
Bon voyage, Captain!
You too, Captain!
IRMA

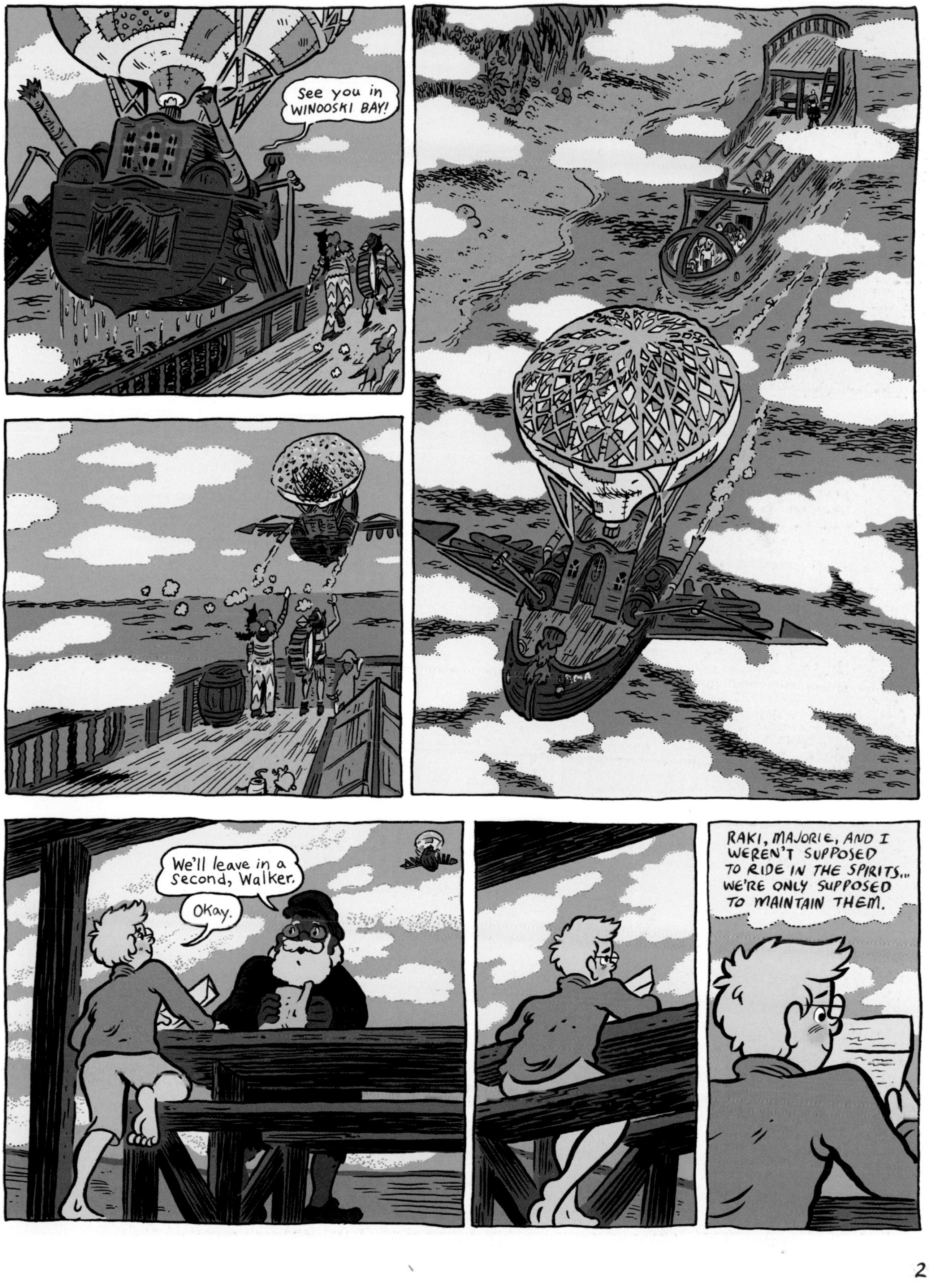
See you in WINOOSKI BAY!
We'll leave in a second, Walker.
Okay.
RAKI, MAJORIE, AND I WEREN'T SUPPOSED TO RIDE IN THE SPIRITS... WE'RE ONLY SUPPOSED TO MAINTAIN THEM.

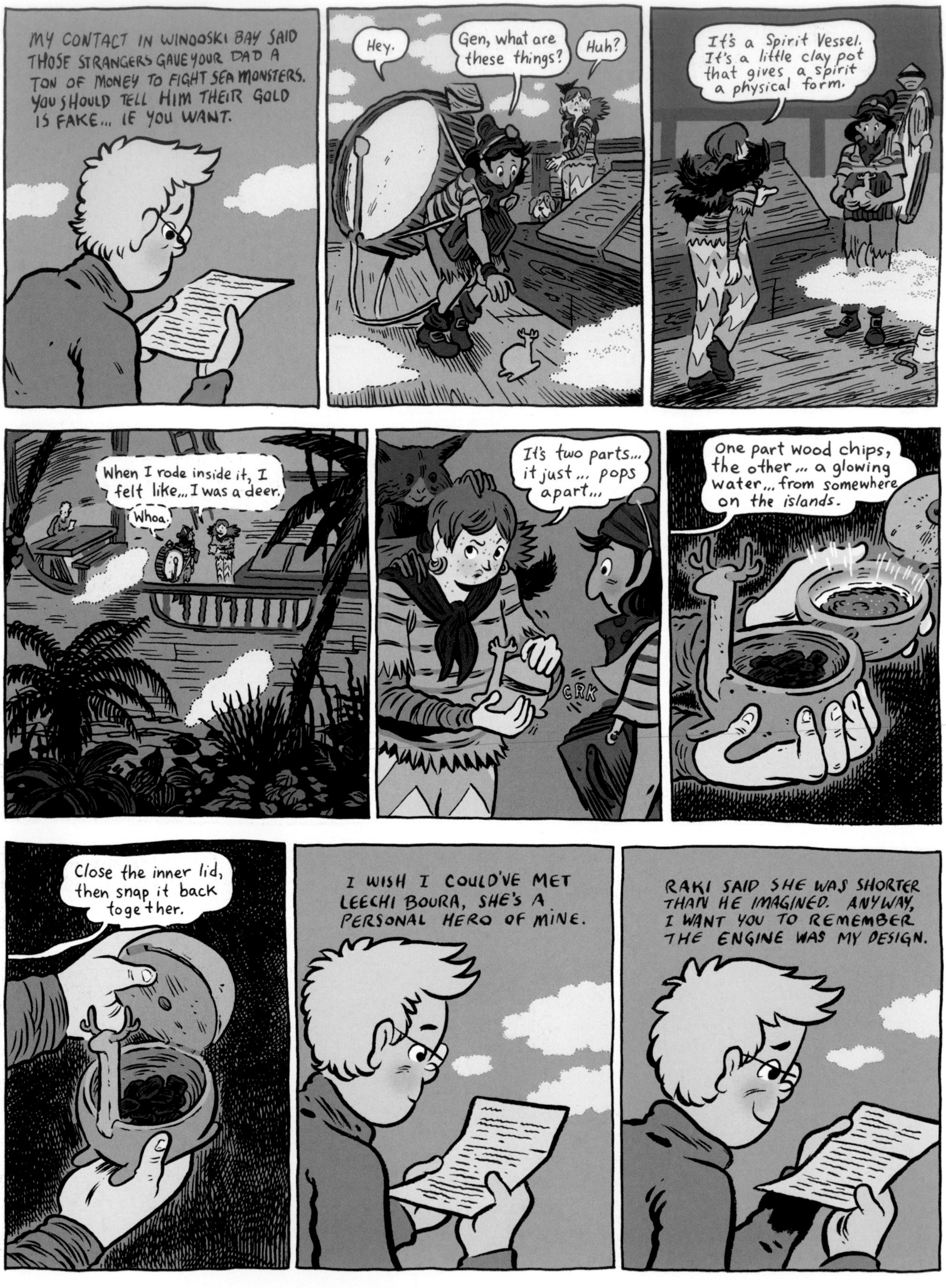
MY CONTACT IN WINDOSKI BAY SAID THOSE STRANGERS GAVE YOUR DAD A TON OF MONEY TO FIGHT SEA MONSTERS. YOU SHOULD TELL HIM THEIR GOLD IS FAKE... IF YOU WANT.
Hey.
Gen, what are these things?
Huh?
It's a Spirit Vessel. It's a little clay pot that gives a spirit a physical form.
When I rode inside it, I felt like... I was a deer.
Whoa.
It's two parts... it just... pops apart...
CRK
One part wood chips, the other... a glowing water... from somewhere on the islands.
Close the inner lid, then snap it back together.
I WISH I COULD'VE MET LEECHI BOURA, SHE'S A PERSONAL HERO OF MINE.
RAKI SAID SHE WAS SHORTER THAN HE IMAGINED. ANYWAY, I WANT YOU TO REMEMBER THE ENGINE WAS MY DESIGN.

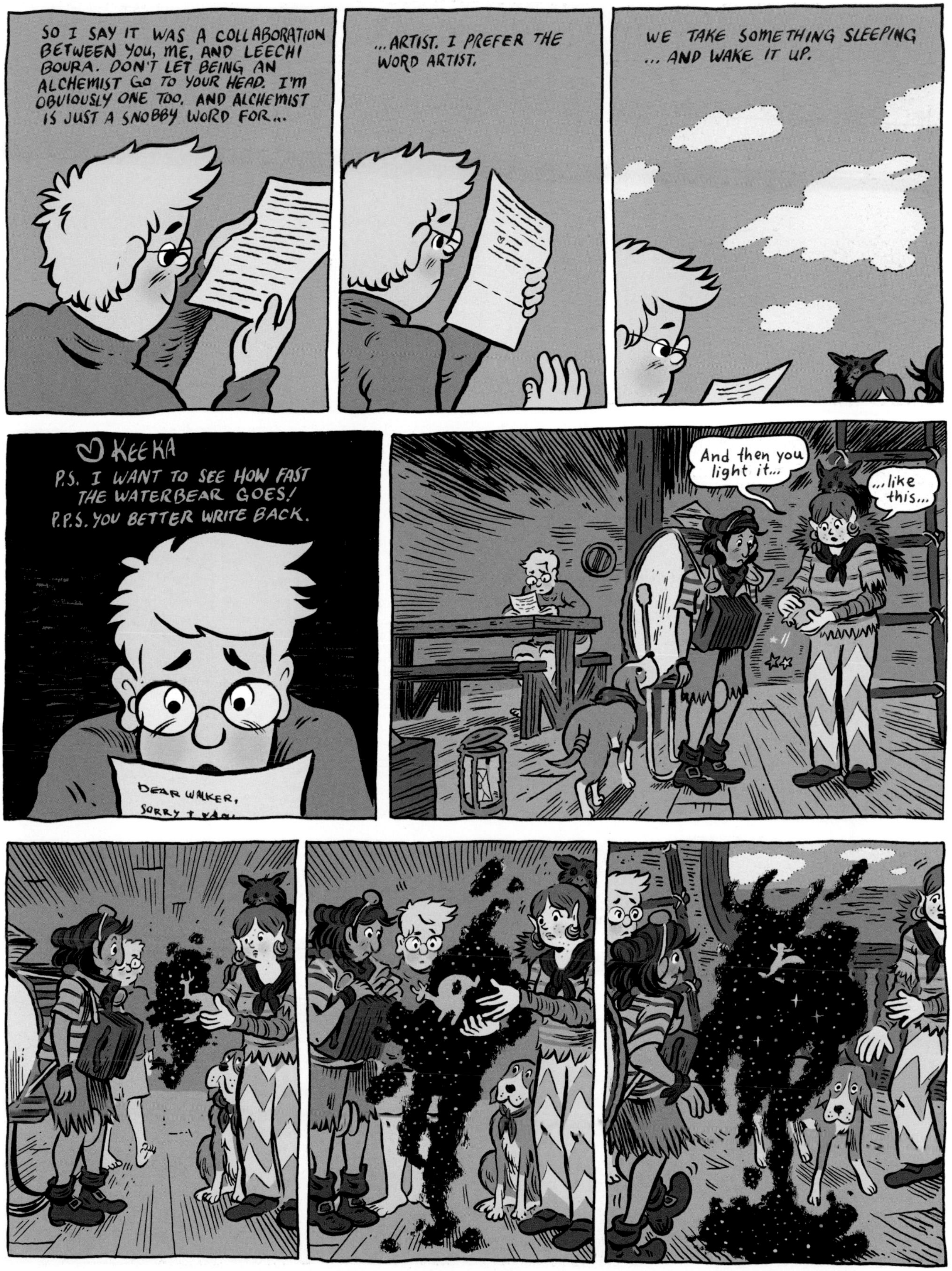
SO I SAY IT WAS A COLLABORATION BETWEEN YOU, ME, AND LEECHI BOURA. DON'T LET BEING AN ALCHEMIST GO TO YOUR HEAD. I'M OBVIOUSLY ONE TOO, AND ALCHEMIST IS JUST A SNOBBY WORD FOR...
...ARTIST. I PREFER THE WORD ARTIST.
WE TAKE SOMETHING SLEEPING ... AND WAKE IT UP.
KEEKA
P.S. I WANT TO SEE HOW FAST THE WATERBEAR GOES!
P.P.S. YOU BETTER WRITE BACK.
DEAR WALKER,
And then you light it...
...like this...

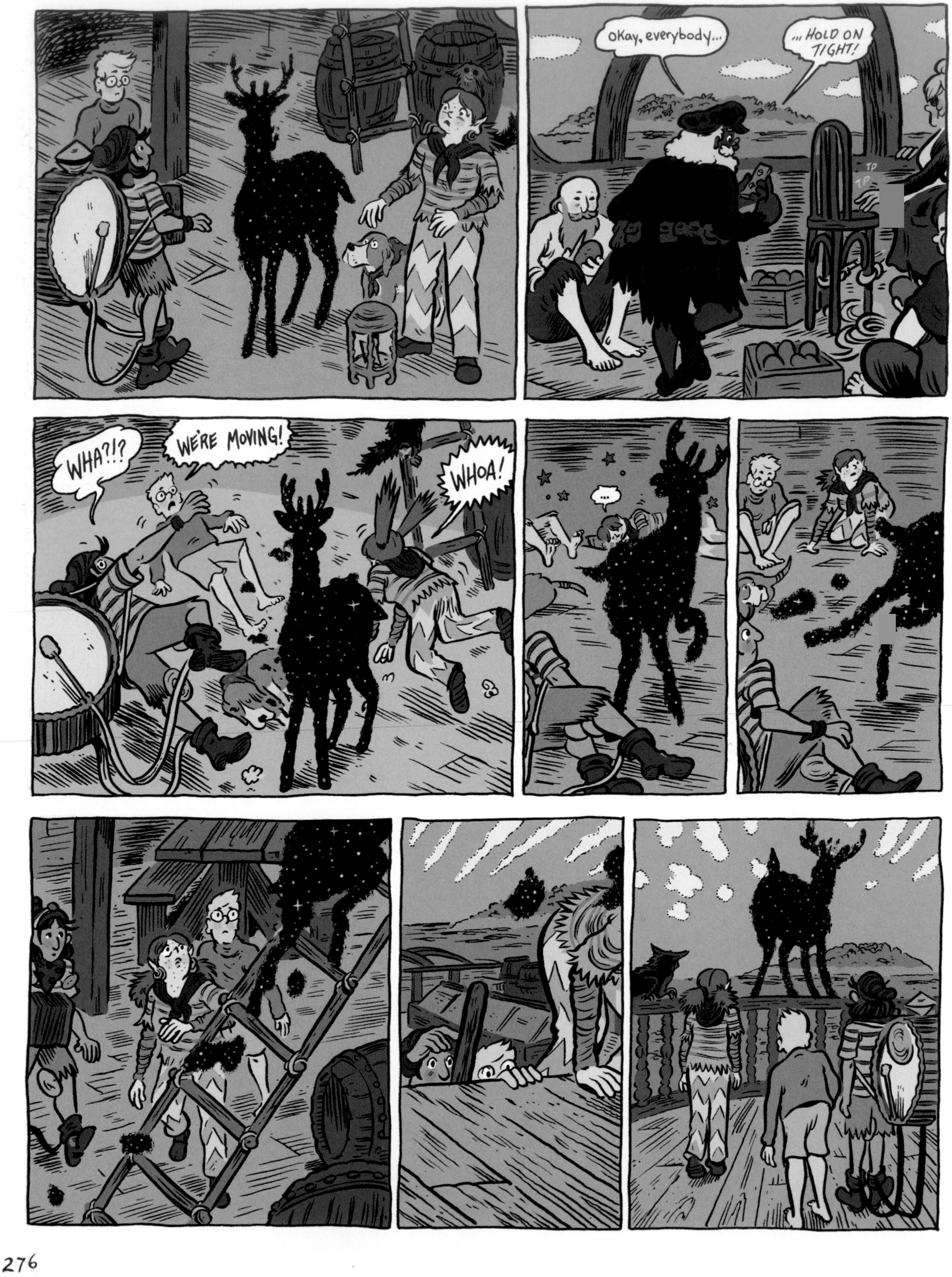
OKay, everybody...
... HOLD ON TIGHT!
TP
TP
WHA?!?
WE'RE MOVING!
WHOA!
...

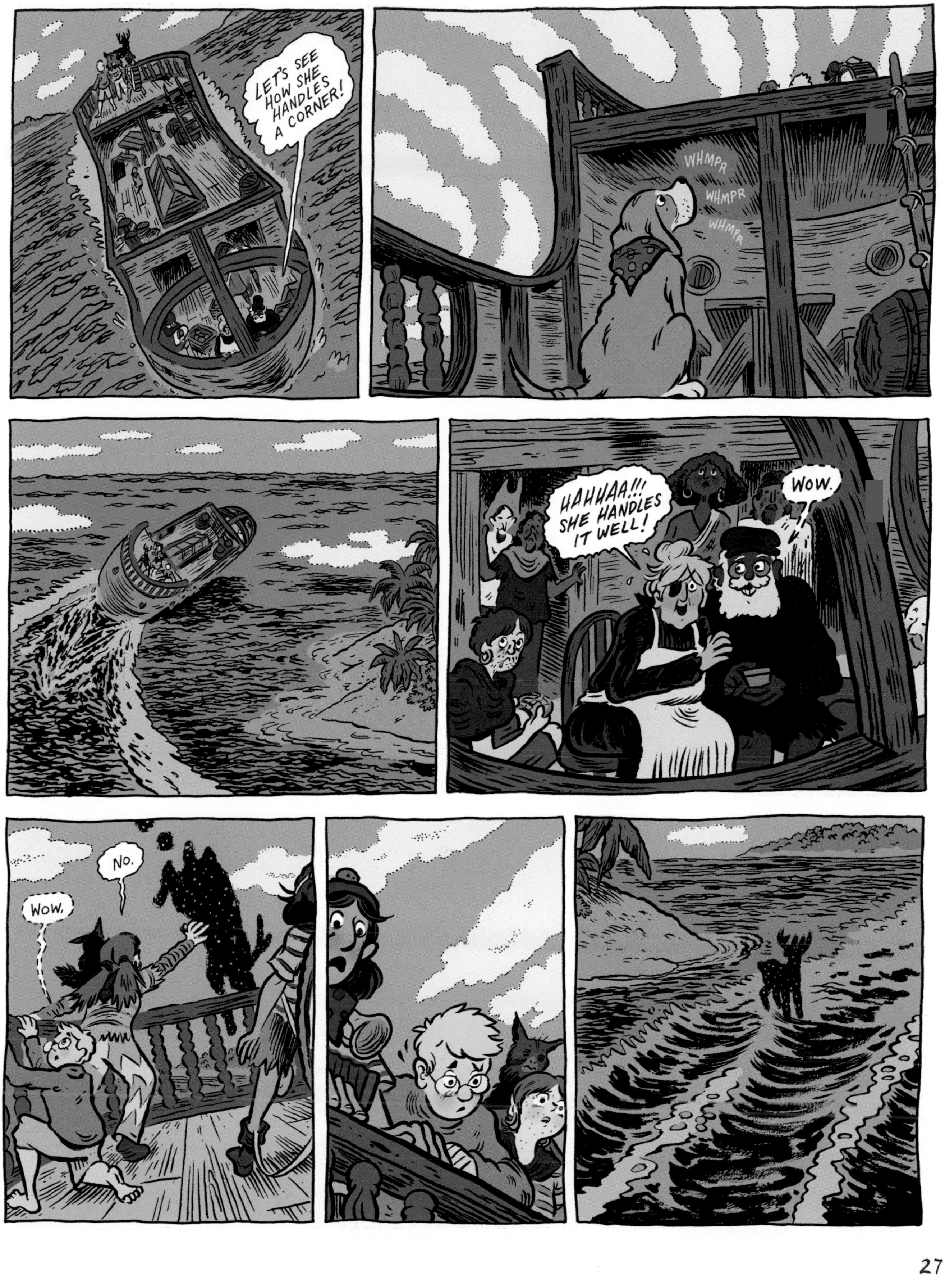
LET'S SEE HOW SHE HANDLES A CORNER!
WHMPR
WHMPR
WHMPR
HAHHAA!!! SHE HANDLES IT WELL!
WOW.
NO.
WOW.

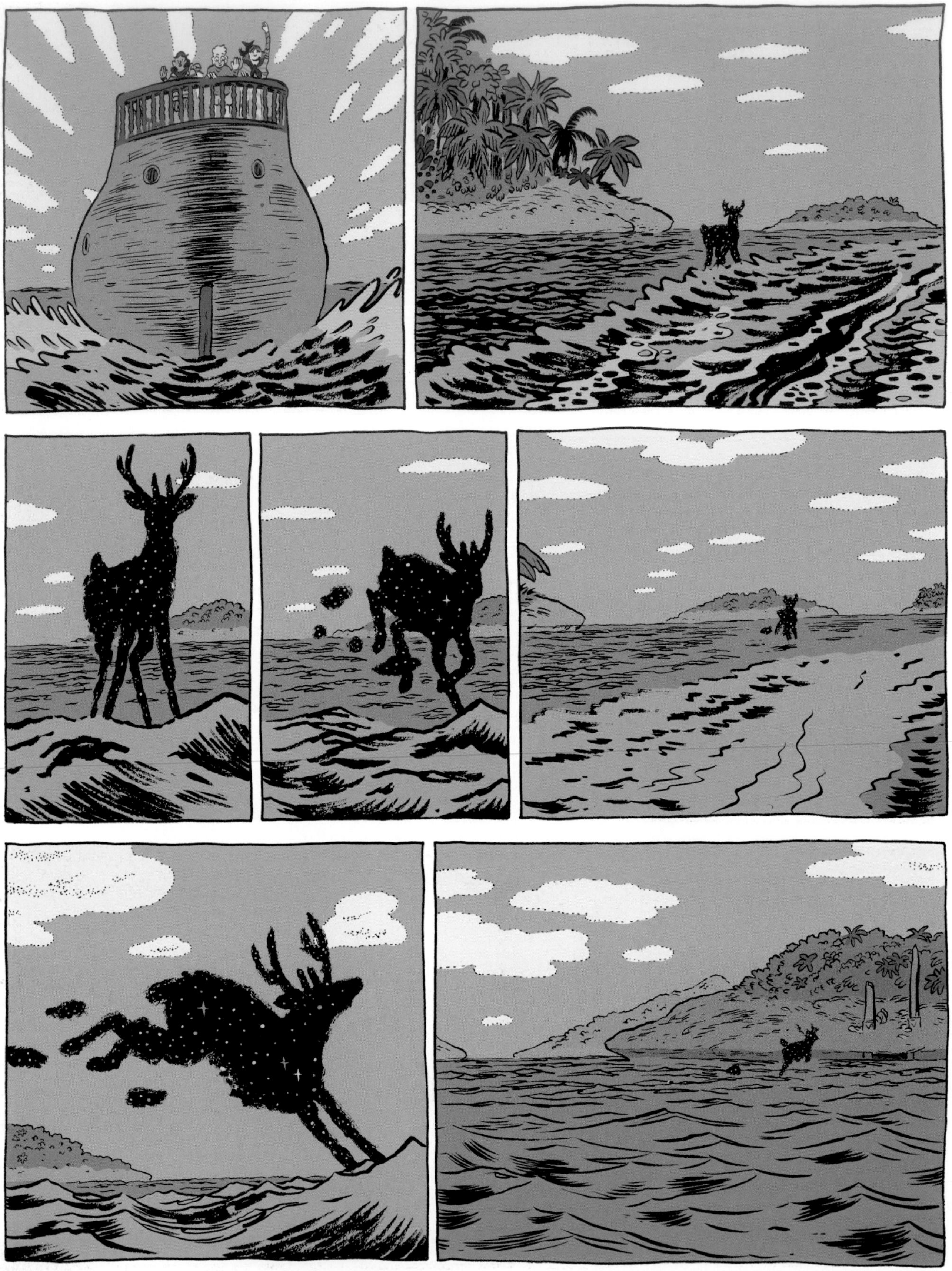

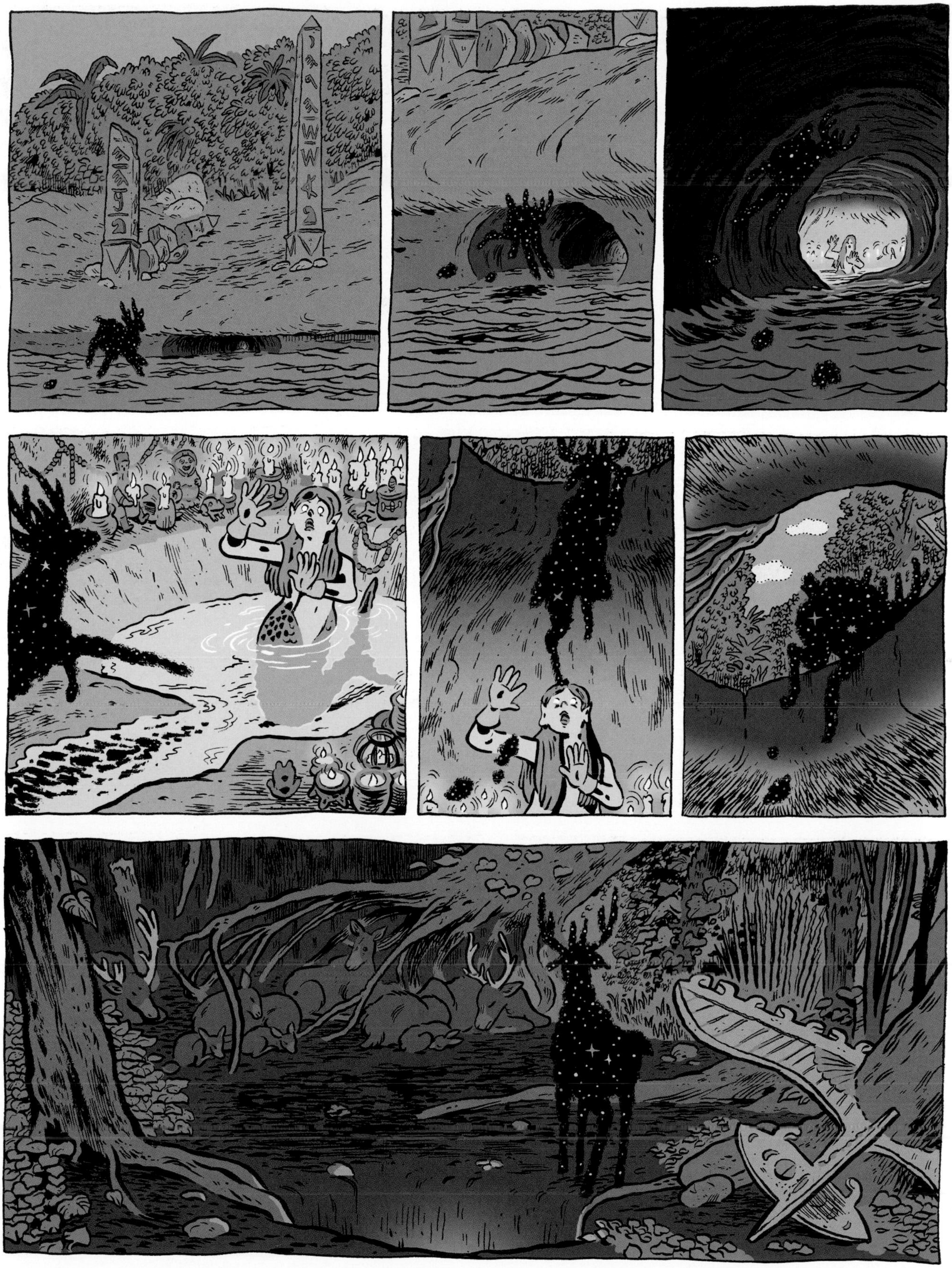

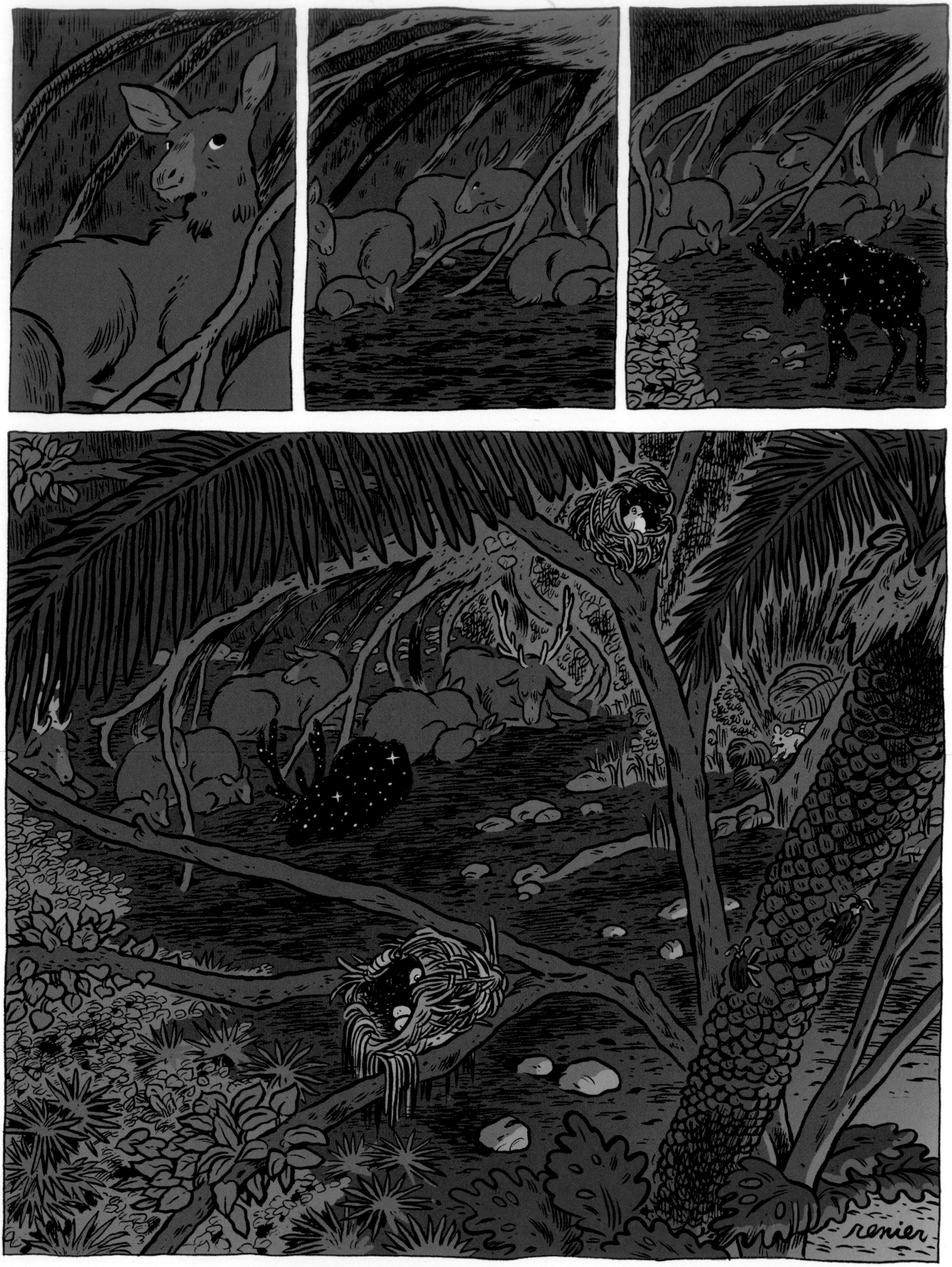
renier